THE DEEP WOODS
THE TWILIGHT WOODS
THE EDGELANDS
The Edge.

THE EDGE CHRONICLES

THE TWIG TRILOGY

PAUL STEWART & CHRIS RIDDELL

DOUBLEDAY

For Joseph, William, Anna, Katy and Jack

THE TWIG TRILOGY
A DOUBLEDAY BOOK 978 0 385 61345 3

Published in Great Britain by Doubleday,
an imprint of Random House Children's Books
A Random House Group Company

This collected edition published 2007

Beyond the Deepwoods
First published by Doubleday in 1998

Stormchaser
First published by Doubleday in 1999

Midnight Over Sanctaphrax
First published by Doubleday in 2000

1 3 5 7 9 10 8 6 4 2

RANDOM HOUSE CHILDREN'S BOOKS
61–63 Uxbridge Road, London W5 5SA

www.**kidsatrandomhouse**.co.uk
www.rbooks.co.uk

Addresses for companies within The Random House Group Limited can be found at: www.randomhouse.co.uk/offices.htm

THE RANDOM HOUSE GROUP Limited Reg. No. 954009

A CIP catalogue record for this book is available from the British Library.

Printed and bound in Great Britain by Clays Ltd, St Ives plc

·Introduction·

Far far away, jutting out into the emptiness beyond, like the figurehead of a mighty stone ship, is the Edge. A torrent of water pours endlessly over the lip of rock at its overhanging point. This is the Edgewater river.

Its source, Riverrise, lies far back inland, high up in the dark and forbidding Deepwoods. Dark and deeply mysterious, the Deepwoods is a harsh and perilous place for those who call it home; the countless tribes and strange groupings who scratch a living in the dappled sunlight and moonglow beneath its lofty canopy.

Where the clouds descend, there lie the Edgelands, a barren wasteland of swirling mists, spirits and nightmares. On its borders lie the Twilight Woods. Bathed in their never-ending golden half-light, the Twilight Woods are enchanting - but also treacherous. On occasions, the twilight is disturbed by violent storms which blow in from beyond the Edge. The lightning bolts they release create stormphrax, a substance so valuable that many have risked their lives to possess it.

At its lower reaches, the Twilight Woods give way to the Mire. It is a stinking, polluted place, rank with the slurry from the factories and foundries of Undertown. Dirty, over-crowded and often violent, Undertown is also the centre of all economic activity. It buzzes, it bustles, it vibrates with energy.

At the centre of Undertown is a great iron ring, to which a long and heavy chain extends up into the sky. At its end is a great floating rock formed long ago in the Stone Gardens. Upon it, the magnificent city of Sanctaphrax has been constructed.

With its tall thin towers connected by viaducts and walkways, Sanctaphrax is a seat of learning. The subjects studied there are as obscure as they are jealously guarded and, despite the apparent air of fusty, bookish benevolence, Sanctaphrax is a seething cauldron of rivalries, plot and counter-plot, and bitter faction-fighting.

The Deepwoods, the Edgelands, the Twilight Woods, the Mire and the Stone Gardens. Undertown and Sanctaphrax. The River Edgewater. Names on a map.

Yet behind each name lie a thousand tales - tales that have been recorded in ancient scrolls, tales that have been passed down the generations by word of mouth - tales which even now are being told.

What follows are three of those tales.

BEYOND THE DEEPWOODS

.CHAPTER ONE.

The Snatchwood Cabin

Twig sat on the floor between his mother's knees, and curled his toes in the thick fleece of the tilder rug. It was cold and draughty in the cabin. Twig leaned forwards and opened the door of the stove.

'I want to tell you the story of how you got your name,' his mother said.

'But I know that story, Mother-Mine,' Twig protested.

Spelda sighed. Twig felt her warm breath on the back of his neck, and smelled the pickled tripweed she had eaten for lunch. He wrinkled his nose. Like so much of the food which the woodtrolls relished, Twig found trip-weed disgusting, particularly pickled. It was slimy and smelled of rotten eggs.

'This time it will be a little different,' he heard his mother saying. 'This time I will finish the tale.'

Twig frowned. 'I thought I'd already heard the ending.'

Spelda tousled her son's thick black hair. He's grown so fast, she thought, and wiped a tear from the end of her rubbery button-nose. 'A tale can have many endings,' she said sadly, and watched the purple light from the fire gleaming on Twig's high cheekbones and sharp chin. 'From the moment you were born,' she began, as she always began, 'you were different . . .'

Twig nodded. It had been painful, so painful, being *different* when he was growing up. Yet it amused him now to think of his parents' surprise when he had appeared: dark, green-eyed, smooth-skinned, and already with unusually long legs for a woodtroll. He stared into the fire.

The lufwood was burning very well. Purple flames blazed all round the stubby logs as they bumped and tumbled around inside the stove.

The woodtrolls had many types of wood to choose from and each had its own special properties. Scentwood, for instance, burned with a fragrance that sent those who breathed it drifting into a dream-filled sleep, while wood from the silvery-turquoise lullabee tree sang as the flames lapped at its bark – strange mournful songs, they were, and not at all to everyone's taste. And then there was the bloodoak, complete with its parasitic sidekick, a barbed creeper known as tarry vine.

Obtaining bloodoak wood was hazardous. Any woodtroll who did not know his woodlore was liable to end up satisfying the tree's love of flesh – for the bloodoak and the tarry vine were two of the greatest dangers in the dark and perilous Deepwoods.

Certainly the wood of the bloodoak gave off a lot of heat, and it neither smelled nor sang, but the way it wailed and screamed as it burned put off all but a few. No, among the woodtrolls, lufwood was by far the most popular. It burned well and they found its purple glow restful.

Twig yawned as Spelda continued her story. Her voice was high-pitched but guttural; it seemed to gurgle in the back of her throat.

'At four months you were already walking upright,' she was saying, and Twig heard the pride in his mother's words. Most woodtroll children remained down on their knuckles until they were at least eighteen months old.

'But . . .' Twig whispered softly. Drawn back inside the story despite himself, he was already anticipating the next part. It was time for the 'but'. Every time it arrived Twig would shudder and hold his breath.

'But,' she said, 'although you were so ahead of the others physically, you would not speak. Three years old you were, and not a single word!' She shifted round in her chair. 'And I don't have to tell you how serious *that* can be!'

Once again his mother sighed. Once again Twig screwed up his face in disgust. Something Taghair had once said came back to him: 'Your nose knows where you belong.' Twig had taken it to mean that he would always recognize the unique smell of his own home. But what if he was wrong? What if the wise old oakelf had been saying – in his usual roundabout way – that because his nose didn't like what it smelled, this was *not* his home?

Twig swallowed guiltily. This was something he had wished so often as he'd lain in his bunk after yet another day of being teased and taunted and bullied.

Through the window, the sun was sinking lower in the dappled sky. The zigzag silhouettes of the Deepwood pines were glinting like frozen bolts of lightning. Twig knew there would be snow before his father returned that night.

He thought of Tuntum, out there in the Deepwoods far beyond the anchor tree. Perhaps at that very moment he was sinking his axe into the trunk of a bloodoak. Twig shuddered. His father's felling tales had filled him with deep horror on many a howling night. Although he was a master carver, Tuntum Snatchwood earned most of his money from the illicit repair of the sky pirates' ships. This meant using buoyant wood – and the most buoyant wood of all was bloodoak.

Twig was uncertain of his father's feelings towards him. Whenever Twig returned to the cabin with a bloodied nose or blacked eyes or clothes covered in slung mud, he wanted his father to wrap him up in his arms and soothe the pain away. Instead, Tuntum would give him advice and make demands.

'Bloody *their* noses,' he said once. 'Black *their* eyes. And throw not mud but *dung*! Show them what you're made of.'

Later, when his mother was smoothing hyleberry salve onto his bruises, she would explain that Tuntum was only concerned to prepare him for the harshness of the world outside. But Twig was unconvinced. It was not concern he had seen in Tuntum's eyes but contempt.

Twig absent-mindedly wound a strand of his long, dark hair round and round his finger as Spelda went on with her story.

'Names,' she was saying. 'Where would we woodtrolls be without them? They tame the wild things of the Deepwoods, and give us our own identity. Ne'er sip of a nameless soup, as the saying goes. Oh, Twig, how I fretted when, at three years old, you were still without a name.'

Twig shivered. He knew that any woodtroll who died without a name would be doomed to an eternity in open sky. The trouble was that until an infant had uttered its first word the naming ritual could not take place.

'Was I really so silent, Mother-Mine?' said Twig.

Spelda looked away. 'Not a single word passed your lips. I thought perhaps you were like your great-grandfather Weezil. He never spoke either.' She sighed. 'So on your third birthday, I decided to perform the ritual anyway. I . . .'

'Did great-grandfather Weezil look like me?' Twig interrupted.

'No, Twig,' said Spelda. 'There has never been a Snatchwood – nor any other woodtroll – who has ever looked like you.'

Twig tugged at the twist of hair. 'Am I ugly?' he said.

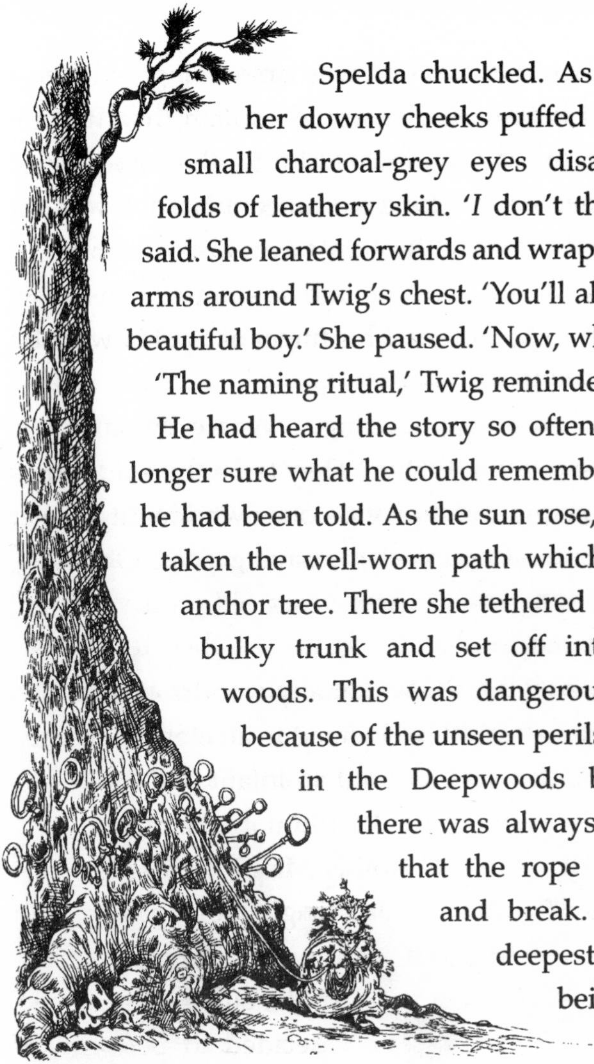

Spelda chuckled. As she did so, her downy cheeks puffed out and her small charcoal-grey eyes disappeared in folds of leathery skin. '*I* don't think so,' she said. She leaned forwards and wrapped her long arms around Twig's chest. 'You'll always be my beautiful boy.' She paused. 'Now, where was I?'

'The naming ritual,' Twig reminded her.

He had heard the story so often, he was no longer sure what he could remember and what he had been told. As the sun rose, Spelda had taken the well-worn path which led to the anchor tree. There she tethered herself to its bulky trunk and set off into the dark woods. This was dangerous, not only because of the unseen perils that lurked in the Deepwoods but because there was always the chance that the rope would snag and break. Woodtrolls' deepest terror was being lost.

Those who did stray from the path and lose their way were vulnerable to attacks from the gloamglozer – the wildest of all the wild creatures in the Deepwoods. Every woodtroll lived in constant terror of an encounter with the fearsome beast. Spelda herself had often frightened her older children with tales of the forest bogeyman: 'If you don't stop being such a naughty woodtroll,' she would say, 'the gloamglozer will get you!'

Deeper and deeper into the Deepwoods, Spelda went. All round her the forest echoed with howls and shrieks of concealed beasts. She fingered the amulets and lucky charms around her neck, and prayed for a swift and safe return.

Finally getting to the end of her tether, Spelda pulled a knife – a *naming* knife – from her belt. The knife was important. It had been made especially for her son, as knives were made for all the woodtroll children. They were essential for the naming ritual and, when the youngsters came of age, each one was given his or her individual naming knife to keep.

Spelda gripped the handle tightly, reached forwards and, as the procedure demanded, hacked off a piece of wood from the nearest tree. It was this little bit of Deepwood which would reveal her child's name.

Spelda worked quickly. She knew only too well that the sound of chopping would attract inquisitive, possibly deadly, attention. When she was done she tucked the wood under her arm, trotted back through the woods, untied herself from the anchor tree, and returned to the cabin. There she kissed the piece of wood twice and threw it into the fire.

'With your brothers and sisters, the names came at once,' Spelda explained. 'Snodpill, Henchweed, Pooh-sniff; as clear as you like. But with you the wood did nothing but crackle and hiss. The Deepwoods had refused to name you.'

'And yet I have a name,' said Twig.

'Indeed you have,' said Spelda. 'Thanks to Taghair.'

Twig nodded. He remembered the occasion so well. Taghair had just returned to the village after a long spell away. Twig remembered how overjoyed the woodtrolls had all been to have the oakelf back among them. For Taghair, who was well versed in the finer points of woodlore, was their adviser, their counsellor, their oracle. It was to him that the woodtrolls came with their worries.

'There was already quite a gathering beneath his ancient lullabee tree when we arrived,' Spelda was saying. 'Taghair was sitting in his empty caterbird cocoon, holding forth about where he had been and what he had seen on his travels. The moment he saw me, however, his eyes opened wide and his ears rotated. "Whatever's up?" he asked.

'And I told him. I told him everything. "Oh, for goodness sake, pull yourself together," he said. Then he pointed to you. "Tell me," he said. "What is that round the little one's neck?"

'"That's his comfort cloth," I said. "He won't let anyone touch it. And he won't be parted from it neither. His father tried once – said the boy was too old for such childish things. But he just curled up into a ball and cried and cried till we gave it back to him."'

Twig knew what was coming next. He had heard it so many times before.

'Then Taghair said, "Give it to me," and stared into your eyes with those big black eyes of his – all oakelves have eyes like that. They can see those parts of the world that remain hidden to others.'

'And I gave him my comfort cloth,' whispered Twig. Even now he didn't like anyone touching it, and kept it tightly knotted around his neck.

'That you did,' continued Spelda. 'And I can scarce believe it to this day. But that wasn't all, oh, no.'

'Oh, no,' echoed Twig.

'He took your cloth and he sort of stroked it, all gentle like, as if it was a living thing, and then he traced the pattern on it with his fingertip, ever so lightly. 'A lullabee tree,' he said at last, and I saw that he was right. I'd always thought it was just a pretty pattern – all those squiggles and little stitches – but no, it was a lullabee tree all right, plain as the nose on your face.'

Twig laughed.

'And the strange thing was, you didn't mind old

Taghair touching your cloth. You just sat there, all serious and silent. Then he gave you that stare of his again and said in a soft voice, "You're part of the Deepwoods, silent one. The naming ritual has not worked, but you are a part of the Deepwoods . . . A part of the Deepwoods," he repeated, his eyes glazing over. Then he raised his head and spread wide his arms. "His name shall be . . ."'

'. . . Twig!' Twig exclaimed, unable to keep silent a moment longer.

'That's right,' said Spelda, laughing. 'Out you came with it, just like that. Twig! The first word you ever spoke. And then Taghair said, "You must look after him well, for the boy is special."'

Not *different,* but *special*! It was the one fact that had kept him going when the other woodtroll children had picked on him so mercilessly. Not a single day had passed without some incident or other. But the worst time of all was when he'd been set upon during the fateful trockbladder match.

Before then, Twig had loved the game. Not that he was very good at it, but he had always enjoyed the excitement of the chase – for trockbladder was a game that involved a great deal of running about.

It was played on a large square of land between the back of the village and the forest. The pitch was criss-crossed with well-worn paths beaten out by generations of young woodtrolls. Between these bare tracks, the grass grew thick and tall.

The rules of the game were simple. There were two teams, with as many woodtrolls on each side as wanted to play. The aim was to catch the trockbladder – the bladder of a hammelhorn stuffed with dried trockbeans – and run twelve paces, calling out the numbers as you went. If you managed that, you were allowed a shot at the central basket, which could double your score. However, since the ground was often slippery, the trockbladder always squidgy, and the entire opposing team was trying to wrest the ball away, this was not as easy as it sounded. In his eight years of playing the game, Twig had never once managed to score a trockbladder.

On this particular morning, no-one was having much luck. Heavy rain had left the pitch waterlogged and the game kept stopping and starting as, time after time, woodtroll after woodtroll came sliding off the muddy paths.

It wasn't until the third quarter that the trockbladder landed near enough to Twig for him to seize it and start running. 'ONE, TWO, THREE . . .' he yelled out as, with the trockbladder wedged beneath the elbow of his left arm, he belted along the paths which led to the centre of the pitch. The nearer to the basket you were when you reached twelve, the easier it was to score.

'FOUR, FIVE . . .' In front of him half-a-dozen members of the opposing team were converging on him. He

darted down a path to the left. His opponents chased after him.

'SIX, SEVEN . . .'

'To me! Twig, to me!' various members of his own team called out. 'Pass it!'

But Twig didn't pass it. He wanted to score. He wanted to hear his team-mates' cheers, to feel their hands slapping him on the back. For once, he wanted to be the hero.

'EIGHT, NINE . . .'

He was completely surrounded.

'PASS IT TO ME!' he heard. It was Hoddergruff, calling from the far side of the pitch. Twig knew that if he chucked the ball to him now his friend would have a good chance of scoring for the team. But that was no good. You remembered who scored, not who set the goal up. Twig wanted everyone to remember that *he* had scored.

He paused. Half of the opposing team were almost upon him. He couldn't go forwards. He couldn't go back. He looked round at the basket. So near and yet so far, and he wanted that goal. He wanted it more than anything.

All at once, a little voice in his head seemed to say, 'But what's the problem? The rules say nothing about sticking to the path.' Twig looked back towards the basket, and swallowed nervously. The next instant he did what no woodtroll before had ever done: *he left the path.* The long grass whipped at his bare legs as he loped towards the basket.

'TEN, ELEVEN . . . TWELVE!' he screamed, and dunked the bladder down through the basket. 'A trockbladder!' he cried, and looked round happily. 'A twenty-four pointer. I've scored a tro . . .' He stopped. The woodtrolls on both teams were glaring at him. There were no cheers. No slaps on the back.

'You stepped from the path!' one of them shouted.

'*No-one* steps from the path,' cried another.

'But . . . but . . .' Twig stammered. 'There's nothing in the rules that says . . .'

But the other woodtrolls were not listening. They knew, of course, that the rules didn't mention keeping to the paths – but then why should they? In trockbladder, as in their lives, the woodtrolls never *ever* strayed from the paths. It was a given. It was taken as read. It would have made as much sense to have a rule telling them not to stop breathing!

All at once, as if by some pre-arranged signal, the woodtrolls fell on Twig. 'You lanky weirdo,' they cried as they kicked him and punched him. 'You hideous gangly freak!'

A sudden fiery pain tore through Twig's arm. It felt as if it had been branded. He looked up to see a wodge of his smooth flesh being viciously twisted by a handful of hard spatula-fingers.

'Hoddergruff,' Twig whispered.

The Snatchwoods and the Gropeknots were neighbours. He and Hoddergruff had been born within a week of each other, and grew up together. Twig had thought they were friends. Hoddergruff sneered, and twisted the skin round still further. Twig bit into his lower lip and fought back the tears. Not because of the pain in his arm – that he could bear – but because Hoddergruff had now also turned against him.

As Twig had stumbled home, battered, bruised and bleeding, it was the fact that he'd lost his only friend that hurt most. Now, because he was different, he was also alone.

*

'*Special!*' said Twig, and snorted.

'Yes,' said Spelda. 'Even the sky pirates recognized that fact when they saw you,' she added softly. 'That is why your father . . .' Her voice faltered. 'Why we . . . That is why you must leave home.'

Twig froze. Leave home? What did she mean? He spun round and stared at his mother. She was weeping.

'I don't understand,' he said. 'Do you want me to go?'

'Of course I don't, Twig,' she sobbed. 'But you'll be thirteen in less than a week. An adult. What will you do then? You cannot fell wood like your father. You . . . you're not built for it. And where will you live? The cabin is already too small for you. And now that the sky pirates know about you . . .'

Twig twisted the knot of hair round and round his finger. Three weeks earlier he had gone with his father far into the Deepwoods, where woodtrolls felled and fashioned the wood that they sold to the sky pirates.

Whereas his father could walk upright beneath the lowest branches, Twig had had to stoop. And even that wasn't enough. Time and again he knocked his head, until his scalp had become a mass of angry red grazes. In the end Twig had had no option but to crawl on his hands and knees to the clearing.

'Our latest felling recruit,' Tuntum had said to the sky pirate in charge of delivery that morning.

The pirate glanced over his clipboard and looked Twig up and down. 'Looks too tall,' he said, and went back to his paperwork.

Twig stared at the sky pirate. Tall and upright, he looked magnificent with his tricorn hat and tooled leather breastplate, his parawings and waxed side-whiskers. His coat was patched in places but was, with its ruffs, tassles, golden buttons and braid, none the less splendid for that. Each of the numerous objects that hung from special hooks seemed to shout of adventure.

Twig found himself wondering who the sky pirate had fought with that cutlass, with its ornately jewelled hilt – and what had caused the nick in its long curved blade. He wondered what marvels the sky pirate had seen through his telescope, what walls he had scaled with the grappling irons, what distant places his compass had led him to.

Suddenly, the sky pirate looked up again. He caught Twig staring at him and raised a quizzical brow. Twig stared at his feet. 'Tell you what,' the sky pirate said to Tuntum. 'There's always a place for a tall young man on a sky ship.'

'No,' said Tuntum sharply. 'Thank you very much for the offer,' he added politely. 'But, no.'

Tuntum knew his son wouldn't last ten minutes on board ship. The sky pirates were shiftless, shameless rogues. They would slit your throat as soon as look at you. It was only because they paid so well for the buoyant Deepwood timber that the woodtrolls had anything to do with them at all.

The sky pirate shrugged. 'Just a thought,' he said, and turned away. 'Pity, though,' he muttered.

As Twig crawled back through the Deepwoods behind his father, he thought of the ships he had watched flying overhead, sails full, soaring off, up and away. 'Skyriding,' he whispered, and his heart quickened. Surely, he thought, there are worse things to do.

Back in the woodtroll cabin, Spelda thought otherwise. 'Oh those sky pirates!' she grumbled. 'Tuntum should never have taken you to meet them in the first place. Now they'll be back for you, as sure as my name's Spelda Snatchwood.'

'But the sky pirate I saw didn't seem bothered whether I joined the crew, or not,' said Twig.

'That's what they pretend,' said Spelda. 'But look what happened to Hobblebark and Hogwort. Seized from their beds they were, and never seen again. Oh, Twig, I couldn't bear it if that happened to you. It would break my heart.'

Outside, the wind howled through the dense Deepwoods. As darkness fell, the air was filled with the sounds of the wakening night creatures. Fromps coughed and spat, quarms squealed, while the great banderbear beat its monstrous hairy chest and yodelled to its mate. Far away in the distance Twig could just make out the familiar rhythmical pounding of the slaughterers, still hard at work.

'What am I to do, then?' Twig asked softly.

Spelda sniffed. 'In the short term, you're to go and

stay with Cousin Snetterbark,' she said. 'We've already sent message, and he's expecting you. Just until things blow over,' she added. 'Sky willing, you'll be safe there.'

'And *after*,' said Twig. 'I can come home again then, can I?'

'Yes,' said Spelda slowly. Twig knew at once that there was more to come.

'But?' he said.

Spelda trembled and hugged the boy's head to her chest. 'Oh, Twig, my beautiful boy,' she sobbed. 'There is something else I must tell you.'

Twig pulled away and looked up at her troubled face. There were tears rolling down his own cheeks now. 'What is it, Mother-Mine?' he asked nervously.

'Oh, Gloamglozer!' Spelda cursed. 'This isn't easy.' She looked at the boy tearfully. 'Although I have loved you as my own since the day you arrived, you are not my son, Twig. Nor is Tuntum your father.'

Twig stared in silent disbelief. 'Then, who am I?' he said.

Spelda shrugged. 'We found you,' she said. 'A little bundle, all wrapped up in a shawl, at the foot of our tree.'

'*Found* me,' Twig whispered.

Spelda nodded, leaned forwards and touched the cloth knotted at Twig's neck. Twig flinched.

'My comfort cloth?' he said. 'The shawl?'

Spelda sighed. 'The very same,' she said. 'The shawl we found you wrapped in. The shawl you won't be parted from, even now.'

Twig stroked the fabric with trembling fingers. He heard Spelda sniff.

'Oh, Twig,' she said. 'Although we are not your parents, Tuntum and I have loved you like our very own. Tuntum asked me to say ... goodbye for him. He said ...' She stopped, overwhelmed with sadness. 'He said to tell you that ... that, whatever happens, you must never forget ... he loves you.'

Now that the words were said, Spelda abandoned herself to her grief completely. She wailed with misery, and uncontrolled sobbing racked her entire body.

Twig knelt across and wrapped his arms right round his mother's back. 'So I am to leave at once,' he said.

'It's for the best,' Spelda said. 'But you will return, Twig. Won't you?' she added uncertainly. 'Believe me, my beautiful boy, I didn't ever want to have to tell you the end of the tale, but ...'

'Don't cry,' said Twig. 'This *isn't* the end of the tale.'

Spelda looked up and sniffed. 'You're right,' she said, and smiled bravely. 'It's more of a beginning, isn't it? Yes, that's what it is, Twig. A new start.'

.CHAPTER TWO.

The Hover Worm

The sounds of the Deepwoods echoed loudly all round as Twig walked along the path through the trees. He shivered, tightened his scarf and pulled up the collar of his leather jacket.

He hadn't wanted to leave that evening at all. It was dark and cold. But Spelda had been insistent. 'There's no time like the present,' she'd said several times as she got together the bits and pieces that Twig would need for his journey: a leather bottle, a rope, a small bag of food and – most precious of all – his naming knife. Twig had finally come of age.

'Anyway, you know what they say,' she added, as she reached up and tied two wooden charms around her son's neck. 'Depart by night, arrive by day.'

Twig knew Spelda had been putting on a brave face. 'But be careful,' she insisted. 'It's dark out there and I know what you're like, forever dreaming and dawdling and wondering what's round the next corner.'

'Yes, mother,' said Twig.

'And don't "yes, mother" me,' said Spelda. 'This is important. Remember, stick to the path if you want to steer clear of the fearsome gloamglozer. We woodtrolls *always* stick to the path.'

'But I'm not a woodtroll,' mumbled Twig, tears stinging his eyes.

'You're my little boy,' said Spelda, hugging him tightly. 'Stick to the path. Woodtrolls know best. Now, be off with you, and give my love to Cousin Snetterbark. You'll be back before you know it. Everything will be back to normal. You'll see . . .'

Spelda couldn't finish. The tears were coming thick and fast. Twig turned and set off down the shadowy path into the gloom.

Normal! he thought. *Normal!* I don't want things to be normal. Normal is trockbladder games. Normal is felling trees. Normal is always being left out, never belonging. And why should it be any different at Cousin Snetterbark's?

Being pressganged into crewing a sky ship suddenly seemed more appealing than ever. The sky pirates roamed the skies above the Deepwoods. Surely their airborne adventures must be better than anything down here on the forest floor.

A desperate howl of pain echoed through the trees. For a second, the Deepwoods were still. The next second the night sounds returned, louder than before, as if each and every creature was rejoicing that *it* was not the one who had fallen prey to some hungry predator.

As he walked on, Twig began putting names to the creatures he could hear out there in the treacherous Deepwoods, away from the path. It helped to calm his pounding heart. There were squealing quarms and coughing fromps in the trees above his head. Neither of them could harm a woodtroll – at least, not fatally. Away to his right, he heard the chattering screech of a razorflit, about to dive. The next instant, the air was filled with the scream of its victim: a woodrat, perhaps, or a leafgobbler.

Some way further on, with the dark path still stretching out in front of him, the forest opened up. Twig stopped and stared at the silver moonlight that snaked along the trunks and branches, and gleamed on the waxy leaves. This was the first time he had been out in the forest after dark, and it was beautiful – more beautiful than he had ever imagined.

With his eyes gazing up at the silvery leaves, Twig took a step forward, away from the shadowy path. The moonlight bathed him in its cold glow and made his skin shine like metal. His billowing breath gleamed, snow-bright.

'In-*cred*-ible,' said Twig, and took a couple of steps more.

Below his feet, the glittering frost cracked and crunched. Icicles hung down from a weeping-willoak, and the beads of liquid on a dewdrop tree had frosted and frozen, and glistened now like pearls. A wispy sapling with fronds like hair swayed in the icy breeze.

'A-*maz*-ing,' said Twig, as he wandered on. Now left. Now right. Now round a corner. Now over a slope. It was all so mysterious, all so new.

He stopped by a bank of quivering plants with tall spiky leaves and budded stems, all glinting in the moonlight. All at once, the buds began to pop open. One by one. Until the bank was covered with massive round flowers – with petals like shavings of ice – that turned their heads to the moon, and glowed with its brilliance.

Twig smiled to himself and turned away. 'Just a *weeny* bit further . . .' he said.

A tumblebush tumbled past him and disappeared into the shadows. Moonbells and tinkleberries jingled and jangled in the gathering wind.

Then Twig heard another noise. He spun round. A small, sleek, furry brown creature with a corkscrew tail scurried across the forest floor, squeaking with terror.

The screech of a woodowl sliced through the air.

Twig's heart began to race. He looked round him wildly. There were eyes in the shadows. Yellow eyes. Green eyes. Red eyes. And all of them staring at him. 'Oh, no,' he moaned. 'What have I *done*?'

Twig knew what he had done. 'Never stray from the path,' Spelda had said. Yet that was *precisely* what he had done. Entranced by the silvery beauty of the Deepwoods, he had strayed from the safety of the path.

Twig groaned. 'I can't do anything right! Stupid! Stupid! Stupid!' he shouted at himself, as he stumbled this way and that, desperately trying to find his way back to the path. 'STU—'

All at once he heard something; a sound which silenced his voice and froze him to the spot. It was the wheezing pant of a halitoad – a huge and dangerous reptile, with breath so foul it could stun its victim at twenty paces. At ten paces the stench was lethal. A single evil-smelling belch had been enough to kill Hoddergruff's uncle.

What could he do? Where could he go? Twig had never been away from the Deepwoods paths on his own before. He started this way, stopped, ran the other way, and stopped again. The sound of the wheezing halitoad seemed to be all round him. He darted into the shadows of some dark undergrowth and crouched down behind the trunk of a tall and lumpy tree.

The halitoad came closer. Its rasping breath grew louder. Twig's palms were wet and his mouth was dry; he couldn't swallow. The fromps and the quarms fell silent, and in the awful stillness Twig's heart beat like a drum. Surely the halitoad must be able to hear it. Perhaps it had gone. Twig peered cautiously round the trunk of the tree.

MISTAKE! his brain screamed, as he found himself staring into two yellow slit-eyes glinting back at him from the darkness. A long coiled tongue flicked in and out, tasting the air. Suddenly, the halitoad inflated like a bullfrog. It was about to blast its jet of venomous breath. Twig closed his eyes, held his nose and clamped his mouth shut. He heard a fizzing hiss.

The next moment, there was a muffled thud from behind him as something fell to the ground. Twig nervously opened one eye and inspected. A fromp was lying on the forest floor. Its furry, prehensile tail was twitching. Twig remained perfectly still as the halitoad shot out its sticky tongue, grasped the hapless fromp and scuttled off with it into the undergrowth.

'That was close!' Twig said, and sighed with relief. He wiped the sweat from his brow. '*Too* close!'

The moon had turned milky, and the shadows had deepened. As Twig wandered miserably on, the gloom clung to him like a damp blanket. The halitoad might be gone but that was the least of his worries. The fact remained that he had strayed from the path. Now, he was lost.

Often Twig stumbled, sometimes he fell. His hair became wet with sweat, though his bones were chilled to the marrow. He didn't know where he was going, he didn't know where he'd been; he hoped he wasn't simply going round in circles. He was also tired, yet each time he paused to rest a growl or snarl or a ferocious roar would set him trotting off again.

At last, unable to go any farther, Twig stopped. He sank to his knees and lifted his head to the sky.

'Oh, Gloamglozer!' he cursed. 'Gloamglozer! Gloamglozer!' His voice rang out in the frosty night air. 'Please. Please. Please,' he cried. 'Let me find the path again. If only I hadn't left the path! Help me! Help me! Help . . .'

'HELP!'

The cry of distress cut through the air like a knife. Twig jumped to his feet and looked round.

'HELP ME!' It wasn't an echo.

The voice was coming from Twig's left. Instinctively, he ran to see what he could do. The next moment he stopped again. What if it was a trap? He remembered Tuntum's bloodcurdling tales of woodtrolls who had been lured to their death by the false calls of the daggerslash, a monstrous creature with forty razor-sharp claws. It looked like a fallen log – until you stepped on it. Then its paws would snap shut, and so they would remain until the body of the victim had started to decay. For the daggerslash ate only carrion.

'For pity's sake, help me, someone,' came the voice again, but weaker now.

Twig could not ignore the desperate plea a moment longer. He drew his knife – just in case – and set off towards the voice. He hadn't gone more than twenty paces when he tripped over something sticking out from the bottom of a humming combbush.

'Ouch!' cried the voice.

Twig spun round. He'd tripped on a pair of legs. Their owner sat up and glared at him angrily.

'You oaf!' he exclaimed.

'I'm sorry, I . . .' Twig began.

'And don't stare,' he interrupted. 'It's very rude.'

'I'm sorry, I . . .' Twig said again. It was true; he *was* staring. A shaft of moonlight was shining down through the forest onto a boy, and the sight of his red-raw face, crimson hair waxed into flame-like points, and necklaces of animal teeth, had startled Twig. 'You're a slaughterer, aren't you?' he said.

With their bloodied appearance, the slaughterers looked – and sounded – ferocious. It was said that the generations of spilt blood had seeped through their pores and down into the follicles of their hair. Yet, although their business was indeed the butchery of the tilder they hunted and the hammelhorns they reared, the slaughterers were a peaceable folk.

Nevertheless, Twig could not hide his revulsion. Apart from the occasional Deepwood traveller, the slaughterers were the woodtrolls' nearest neighbours. They traded together – carved wooden items and basketware, for meat and leather goods. However, the woodtrolls, like everyone else in the Deepwoods, despised the slaughterers. They were, as Spelda put it, the bottom of the pot. No-one wanted to associate with the folk who had blood, not only on their hands, but all over their bodies.

'Well?' said Twig. 'Are you a slaughterer?'

'What if I am?' said the boy defensively.

'Nothing, I . . .' Lost in the Deepwoods, you couldn't afford to be too choosy about your companions. 'I'm Twig,' he said.

The boy touched his forehead lightly and nodded. 'My name's Gristle,' he said. 'Please take me back to my village. I can't walk. Look,' he said, and pointed to his right foot.

Twig saw the six or seven angry purple marks at the back of his heel. Already the whole foot had swollen to twice its normal size. Even as Twig watched, the swelling spread up his leg.

'What's happening?' gasped Twig.

'It's . . . it's . . .'

Twig realized the boy was staring at something behind him. He heard something hiss, and spun round. And there, hovering just above the ground, was the vilest creature Twig had ever seen.

It was long and lumpy, with luminous slime-green skin that glistened moistly in the milky moonlight. Along the length of its body were bulging yellow spots that oozed a clear liquid. Wriggling and squirming, the creature fixed Twig with its huge cold eyes.

'What is it?' he whispered to Gristle.

'A hover worm,' came the reply. 'Whatever you do, don't let it get you.'

'No chance,' said Twig bravely, and reached for his knife. It wasn't there. 'My knife,' he cried. 'My naming knife. I . . .' And then Twig remembered. He had been carrying it when he tripped over Gristle's legs. It must be on the ground somewhere.

Twig stared ahead, too terrified to take his eyes off the hover worm for so much as a second. The creature continued to writhe. The hissing sound was coming not from its mouth, but from rows of ducts along its underbelly. These expelled the air which kept the worm hovering aloft.

It moved nearer, and Twig found himself staring at the creature's mouth. It had rubbery lips and floppy feelers, and gulped constantly at the air. Suddenly the lips parted.

Twig gasped. The hover worm's mouth was full of tentacles, each one with a dripping sucker at the end. As the jaws widened, the tentacles sprang out and wriggled like maggots.

'The knife,' Twig muttered to Gristle. 'Find my knife.'

He heard Gristle rummaging through the dry leaves. 'I'm trying,' he said. 'I can't . . . Yes,' he cried. 'I've got it!'

'Quick!' said Twig desperately. The hover worm was quivering, ready to attack. He reached behind his back for the knife. 'Hurry UP!'

'Here!' said Gristle, and Twig felt the familiar bone handle in his palm. He closed his hand around it, and gritted his teeth.

The hover worm swayed in the air, backwards and forwards, and trembling all the while. Twig waited. Then suddenly, and with no warning, the hover worm struck. It flew at Twig's neck, mouth agape and tentacles taut. It stank of rancid grease.

Terrified, Twig leapt back. The hover worm abruptly switched direction in mid-air and came at him from the other side. Twig ducked.

The creature shot over his head, hissed to a halt, coiled itself round, and attacked again.

This time it came from the front – just as Twig had hoped. As the creature's tentacles were about to suction themselves onto his exposed neck, Twig twisted round and lunged forwards. The knife plunged into the soft underbelly of the worm, and ripped along the row of air ducts.

The effect was instant. Like a balloon that has been inflated and released, the creature spun wildly through the air with a loud *thpthpthpthppppp*. Then it exploded, and a mass of small, slimy scraps of yellow and green skin fluttered down to the ground.

'YEAH!' Twig roared and punched the air. 'I've actually been and gone and done it! The hover worm is dead.'

As he spoke, dragon's smoke billowed from his mouth. The night had become bitter with an icy north wind. Yet Twig was not cold. Far from it. A glow of pride and excitement warmed his whole body.

'Hel' me,' came a voice from behind him. It sounded strange – as though Gristle was talking while eating.

'It's OK,' said Twig as he pulled himself to his feet. I . . . GRISTLE!' he screamed.

The slaughterer was all but unrecognizable. Before

Twig's battle with the hover worm, Gristle's leg had been swollen. Now his entire body had swelled up. He looked like a huge dark red ball.

'Ta' me home,' he mumbled unhappily.

'But I don't know where your home is,' said Twig.

'I'll ta' you,' said Gristle. 'Lif' me u'. I'll give you birectio's.'

Twig bent down and gathered the slaughterer up in his arms. He was surprisingly light.

Twig started walking. 'Le',' said Gristle a while later, followed by, 'Le' agai'. Ri'. Strai' o'.' As Gristle continued to swell, even the simplest words became impossible. In the end, he had to press his podgy hands against Twig's shoulders to indicate which way to go.

If Twig had been going in circles before, he certainly wasn't now. He was being steered towards somewhere new.

'WOBBLOB!' Gristle shouted. 'BLOBBERWOBBER!'

'What?' said Twig sharply. But, even as he spoke, he realized what was happening. Gristle's body, which had been light when he'd picked it up, was now *less* than weightless. The massive, bulging mass was on the point of floating up and away.

He tried his best to hold on round Gristle's waist – at least, the place where his waist had once been – but it was impossible. It was like holding a sackful of water; the difference being that this particular sack was trying to fall *upwards*. If he let go, Gristle would disappear into the sky.

Twig wiped the sweat from his brow. Then he wedged the inflated boy between two branches, taking care to choose a tree without thorns. He didn't want Gristle to burst. He pulled the rope Spelda had given him from his shoulder, tied one end to Gristle's leg, and the other round his own waist – and set off once more.

It wasn't long before Twig was in difficulty again. With each step, the upward pull grew stronger. It became more and more difficult to remain on the ground. He clutched hold of the branches of bushes he passed, to keep himself anchored. But it was no good. The slaughterer was simply too buoyant.

All at once, Twig's legs were dragged off the ground,

his hands lost their grip on the branches, and he and Gristle floated up into the air.

Up and up, they went, into the icy night and towards open sky. Twig tore in vain at the knotted rope around his waist. It wouldn't budge. He stared down at the fast receding ground and, as he did so, something occurred to him – something awful.

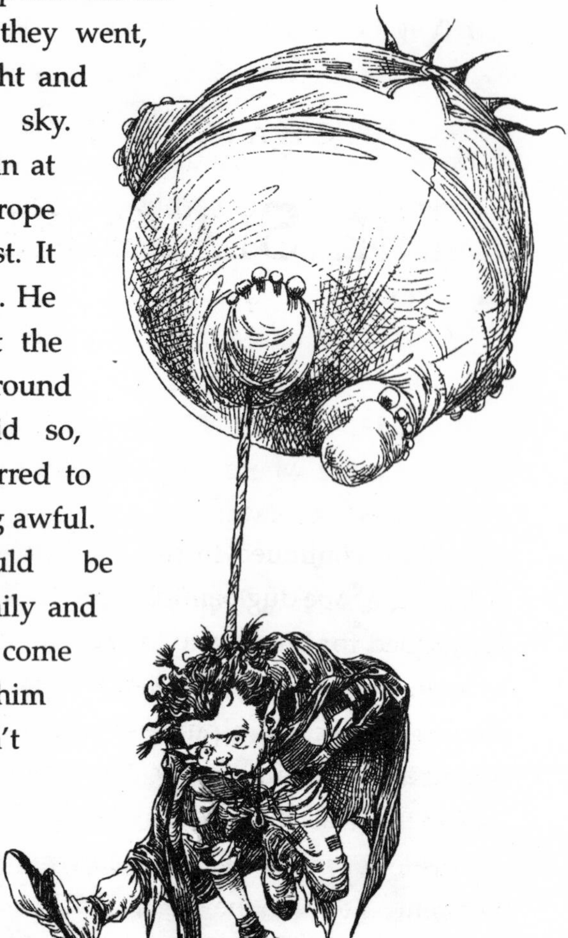

Gristle would be missed. His family and friends would come looking for him when he didn't return. Twig, on the other hand, had done what woodtrolls never did. He had strayed from the path. No-one would come looking for him.

.CHAPTER THREE.

THE SLAUGHTERERS

As Twig continued to rise up through the cold, dark air, the rope dug painfully into the bottom of his ribs. He gasped for breath and, as he did so, a curious whiff of acrid smoke filled his head. It was a mixture of wood smoke, leather and a pungent smell that Twig couldn't identify. Above him, Gristle grunted urgently.

'Are we near your village?' Twig asked.

Gristle grunted again, more insistently this time. Suddenly, between the leaves, Twig caught sight of flickering flames and blood-red smoke. There was a fire, not twenty paces away.

'Help!' Twig bellowed. 'HELP US!'

Almost at once, the ground below him was swarming with the blood-red slaughterers, each carrying a flaming torch.

'UP HERE!' Twig shrieked.

The slaughterers raised their heads. One of them pointed. Then, without a word being spoken, they slipped into action. Calm and methodical, they removed ropes which had been hanging round their shoulders, and made slipknots at one end. Then, with the same unhurried sense of purpose, they began tossing the makeshift lassos up into the air.

Twig moaned as the ropes tumbled back through the air beneath him. He spread his legs wide and held his feet out, hooked and rigid. The slaughterers tried again, but with Gristle pulling him still higher, their task was getting more difficult by the second.

'Come on,' Twig muttered impatiently, as the slaughterers tried again and again to lasso one of his feet. Above him, he heard muffled cries as Gristle's inflated body crashed through the uppermost branches. The next instant, Twig's own head plunged into the dense green canopy. The bruised leaves gave off a lush earthy smell.

What will it look like? Twig found himself wondering. *Above* the Deepwoods. In the realm of the sky pirates.

Before he had a chance to find out, he felt something land on his hooked foot and tighten around his ankle. One of the slaughterers' ropes had found its target at last. There was a strong tug on his leg, then another and another. The leaves slapped back into his face, and the earthy smell grew stronger.

All at once, he saw the ground way down below him – and his foot with the loop of rope around his ankle. Twenty or so of the slaughterers had a hold of the other end. Slowly, jerkily, they were pulling the rope in.

When Twig's feet finally touched the ground, the slaughterers immediately turned their attention to Gristle. Working in utter silence, they slipped their ropes around his arms and legs, and took the strain. Then, one of them pulled out his knife and sliced through the rope which was still tied round Twig's chest. And Twig was free. He bent double and breathed in deeply, gratefully.

'Thank you,' he wheezed. 'I don't think I could have lasted much longer. I . . .' He looked up. With the immense bulk of Gristle tethered above them, the whole group of slaughterers was trotting back to the village. Twig had been left on his own. What was more, it was beginning to snow.

'Thanks a lot,' he snorted.

'They're worried, is all,' came a voice from behind him. Twig looked round. A slaughterer girl was standing there, her face lit up by the flickering light of her flaming torch. She touched her forehead, and smiled. Twig smiled back.

'I'm Sinew,' she said. 'Gristle's my brother. He's been missing for three nights.'

'Do you think he'll be all right?' asked Twig.

'As long as they get an antidote inside him before he explodes,' she said.

'Explodes!' cried Twig, trying not to imagine what would have happened if they *had* soared up into the sky.

Sinew nodded. 'The venom turns to hot air. And there's only so much hot air a person can take,' she added grimly. Behind her, came the sound of a gong being banged. 'Come,' she said. 'You look hungry. Lunch is about to be served.'

'Lunch?' said Twig. 'But it's the middle of the night.'

'Of course,' said Sinew, puzzled. 'I suppose you eat lunch in the middle of the *day*,' she said, and laughed.

'Well, yes,' said Twig. 'Actually, we do.'

Sinew shook her head. 'You're strange!' she said.

'No,' Twig chuckled as he followed her through the trees. 'I'm Twig!'

As the village opened up in front of him, Twig stopped and stared. It was all so very different from his own village. The slaughterers lived in squat huts, rather than tree cabins. And whereas the woodtroll cabins were all tiled with lufwood for buoyancy, the slaughterers had constructed their huts with dense leadwood which anchored them firmly to the ground. There were no doors to their dwellings, only thick hammelhornskin curtains, designed to keep out draughts, not neighbours.

Sinew led Twig towards the fire he had first glimpsed through the overhead branches. It was huge and hot, burning on a raised circular stone platform in the very centre of the village. Twig looked behind him in amazement. Although, beyond the village, the snow was falling thicker than ever, none fell inside. The dome of warmth from the blazing fire was so intense that it melted the snow away to nothing before it could ever land.

Four long trestle tables, set for lunch, formed a square around the fire. 'Sit anywhere,' said Sinew, as she plonked herself down.

Twig sat beside her and stared ahead at the roaring flames. Although the fire was burning fiercely, each and every log remained on the ground.

'What are you thinking?' he heard Sinew say.

Twig sighed. 'Where I come from,' he said, 'we burn buoyant wood – lufwood, lullabee, you know. It's all right, but you have to use a stove. I've . . . I've never seen a fire outside like this.'

Sinew looked concerned. 'Would you rather go in?'

'No!' said Twig. 'That's not what I meant. This is nice. At home – well, where I was brought up – everyone disappears inside their cabins when it's cold. It can be very lonely when the weather's bad.' Twig didn't add that it was pretty lonely for him the rest of the time, too.

By now all the benches were full and, at the far end, the first course was already being served. As a delicious fragrance wafted across, Twig realized just how hungry he was.

'I recognize that smell,' he said. 'What is it?'

'Tilder sausage soup, I think,' said Sinew.

Twig smiled to himself. Of course. The soup was a delicacy the grown-up woodtrolls got to eat on Wodgiss Night. Every year he'd wondered what it tasted like. Now he was about to find out.

'Move your elbow, love,' came a voice from behind him. Twig looked round. An old woman was standing there with a ladle in her right hand, and a round pot in her left. When she saw Twig, she drew back sharply, her smile disappeared and she gave a little shriek. 'A ghost!' she gasped.

'It's all right, Gram-Tatum,' said Sinew, leaning over. 'This is Twig. He's from Outside. It's him we have to thank for saving Gristle's life.'

The old woman stared at Twig. 'It was *you* who brought Gristle back to us?' she said.

Twig nodded. The old woman touched her forehead and bowed. 'Welcome,' she said. Then she lifted both her arms high in the air and beat the soup-pot loudly with the ladle. 'Hush up!' she cried. She climbed onto the bench and looked at the square of expectant faces. 'We have in our midst a brave young man by the name of Twig. He rescued our Gristle and brought him back to us. I want you all to raise your glasses and bid him welcome.'

All round the table, the slaughterers – young and old – stood up, touched their foreheads, raised their glasses and cried out, 'Welcome, Twig!'

Twig looked down shyly. 'It was nothing,' he mumbled.

'And now,' said Gram-Tatum, climbing back down. 'I dare say you're feeling hungry. Tuck in, love,' she said, as she ladled the soup into his bowl. 'And let's see if we can't get some colour into those cheeks of yours,' she added.

The tilder sausage soup tasted as delicious as it had smelled. Simmered until the sausages were soft, in stock seasoned with nibblick and orangegrass, the soup was rich and spicy. It was also just the start. Juicy hammelhorn steaks, rolled in seasoned knotroot flour and deep-fried in tilder oil came next, accompanied by earth-apples and a tangy blue salad. And this was followed by honey trifle and dellberry blancmange and small wafer biscuits drenched in treacle. Twig had never eaten so well – nor drunk so much. A large jug full of woodapple cider stood in the centre of each of the four tables, and Twig's mug was never allowed to empty.

As the meal went on, the atmosphere grew increasingly rowdy. The slaughterers forgot about their guest, and the air – already warmed by the blazing fire – became warmer still, with laughter and joking, with the telling of tales and sudden bursts of song. And when Gristle himself appeared, apparently none the worse for his ordeal, everyone went mad!

They cheered, they clapped, they whooped and whistled, their crimson faces aglow in the bright firelight. Three men jumped up and hoisted Gristle onto their shoulders, and while they paraded him round and round, the rest of the slaughterers beat their mugs on the table and sang a simple song in their deep and syrupy voices.

'Welcome back lost slaughterer
Welcome like a stranger
Welcome back from the deep deep woods
Welcome back from danger.'

Over and over they repeated the verse – not all together, but as a round, with each table of slaughterers waiting their turn to start singing. The air was filled with swirling harmonies, more beautiful than Twig had ever heard. Unable to resist, he joined in. He banged the table to the beat with his own mug, and was soon singing the words with the rest.

After the third circuit of the tables, the men approached Twig himself. They stopped directly behind him, and placed Gristle down on the ground. Twig stood up and looked at the slaughterer boy. Everyone fell silent. Then, without saying a word, Gristle touched his forehead, stepped solemnly forwards and touched Twig on *his* forehead. His face broke into a smile. 'We are brothers now.'

Brothers! Twig thought. If only. 'Thank you, Gristle, but . . . Whoooah!' he cried, as he himself was hoisted up onto the men's shoulders.

Swaying precariously from side to side, Twig smiled, then grinned, and then laughed with delight as the men carried him once, twice, three and four times round the table, faster and faster. He looked down dizzily at the red blur of happy faces beaming back at him, and knew that he had never felt as welcome as he did now, here in the bubble of warmth and friendliness that was the slaughterers' Deepwoods home. It would be nice, he thought, if I could stay here.

At that moment, the air resounded with the sound of the gong clanging for a second time. The three slaughterers stopped running abruptly, and Twig felt the earth once again beneath his feet.

'Lunch is over,' Sinew explained as the slaughterers all jumped up from their benches and, still laughing and singing, returned to work. 'Would you like to look round?' she asked.

Twig stifled a yawn and smiled sheepishly. 'I'm not used to being up at this time,' he said.

'But it's the middle of the night,' said Gristle. 'You can't be sleepy!'

Twig smiled. 'I was up all day,' he said.

Sinew turned to her brother. 'If Twig wants to go to bed . . .'

'No, no,' said Twig firmly. 'I'd like to look round.'

They took him first to the hammelhorn pens. Twig stood on the bottom rail and looked at the shaggy beasts with their curling horns and sad eyes. They were chewing drowsily. Twig leaned over and patted one of the animals on the neck. Irritated, the hammelhorn knocked his hand away with a toss of its horned head. Twig drew back nervously.

'They may look docile,' said Sinew, 'but hammelhorns are unpredictable animals by nature. You can't turn your back on them for a minute. Those horns can hurt!'

'*And* they're clumsy,' Gristle added. 'That's why we all have to wear thick boots.'

'We've a saying,' said Sinew. '"The smile of the hammelhorn is like the wind" – you never know when it's going to change.'

'But they do taste good!' said Gristle.

At the smoke house, Twig saw row upon row of tilder carcasses hanging on hooks. A large kiln, fuelled with redoak chips, produced a deep crimson smoke which gave the tilder ham its distinctive flavour. It was this smoke, rather than blood, which had stained the slaughterers' skin.

Not a single part of the tilder was wasted. The bones were dried and used like wood; the fat was used for cooking, for oil-lamps and candles, and for greasing the cogs of the tarp rollers; the coarse fur was spun into rope, and the antlers were carved into all kinds of objects – from cutlery to cupboard handles. It was the leather, however, which was the most valuable part of the animal.

'This is where the hide is rilked,' said Gristle.

Twig watched the red-faced men and women pummelling the hides with large round stones. 'I've heard this sound before,' he said. 'When the wind is from the north-west.'

'It softens the leather,' Sinew explained. 'Makes it easier to mould.'

'And these,' said Gristle, moving on, 'are the tanning vats. We use only the finest leadwood bark,' he added proudly.

Twig sniffed at the steaming vats. It was the smell he'd noticed when he was floating above the village.

'That's why our leather's so popular,' said Sinew.

'The best in the Deepwoods,' said Gristle. 'Even the sky pirates use it.'

Twig spun round. 'You deal with the sky pirates?' he said.

'Our best customers,' said Gristle. 'They don't come often, but when they do visit they take whatever we've got.'

Twig nodded, but his mind was elsewhere. Once again, he saw himself standing at the prow of a pirate ship, with the moon above and the wind in his hair, sailing across the sky.

'Will they be back soon?' he asked at last.

'The sky pirates?' said Gristle, and shook his head. 'It's not long since they were last here. They won't be back for a while now.'

Twig sighed. He suddenly felt immensely weary. Sinew noticed his eye-lids growing heavy. She took him by the arm.

'Come,' she said. 'You must rest. Ma-Tatum will know where you're to sleep.'

This time, Twig did not argue. Almost dead on his feet, he followed Sinew and Gristle to their hut. Inside, a woman was mixing something red in a bowl. She looked up. 'Twig!' she said, and wiped her hands on her apron. 'I've been wanting to see you.' She bustled her way towards him and enfolded him in her stubby arms. The top of her head pressed against Twig's chin.

'Thank you, Pale One,' she sobbed. 'Thank you so much.' Then she pulled herself away and dabbed at her eyes with the corner of her apron. 'Take no notice,' she sniffed. 'I'm just a silly old woman . . .'

'Ma-Tatum,' said Sinew. 'Twig needs to sleep.'

'I can see that,' she said. 'I've already put some extra bedding in the hammock. But before that, there are one or two important things I . . .' She began rummaging furiously through a chest of drawers, and the air was soon filled with the things she was *not* looking for. 'Ah, here we are!' she exclaimed at last, and handed Twig a large furry waistcoat. 'Try it on,' she said.

Twig slipped the waistcoat over his leather jacket. It fitted perfectly. 'It's so warm,' he said.

'It's a hammelhornskin waistcoat,' she told him, as she did up the toggles at the front. 'Our speciality,' she added, 'and not for sale.' She cleared her throat. 'Twig,' she said. 'I would like you to accept it as a token of my gratitude for bringing Gristle back to me, safe and sound.'

Twig was overwhelmed. 'Thank you,' he said. 'I . . .'

'Stroke it,' said Gristle.

'What?' said Twig.

'Stroke it,' he repeated, and giggled excitedly.

Twig ran his palm down over the fleecy fur. It was soft and thick. 'Very nice,' he said.

'Now the other way,' Gristle persisted.

Twig did as he was told. This time the fur bristled and stiffened. 'YOW!' he cried, and Gristle and Sinew burst out laughing. Even Ma-Tatum was smiling. 'It's like needles,' said Twig, sucking at his hand.

'Dead or alive, you should never rub a hammelhorn up the wrong way,' Ma-Tatum chuckled. 'I'm glad you like my gift,' she added. 'May it serve you well.'

'It's very kind of you . . .' Twig began. But Ma-Tatum was not yet done.

'And this will protect you from the unseen dangers,' she said, and slipped a tooled leather charm around his neck.

Twig smirked. Mothers, it seemed, were superstitious, wherever they lived.

'You would do well not to mock,' said Ma-Tatum sharply. 'I see from your eyes that you have far to go. There is much out there that would do you harm. And though there is an antidote for every poison,' she added, and smiled at Gristle, 'once you fall into the clutches of the gloamglozer, then you're done for.'

'The gloamglozer?' said Twig. 'I know about the gloamglozer.'

'The most evil creature of all,' said Ma-Tatum, her voice cracked and low. 'It lurks in shadows. It stalks us slaughterers, sizing up its victim all the while, planning its death. Then it pounces.'

Twig chewed nervously at the end of his scarf. It was the same gloamglozer who was feared by woodtrolls – that monstrous beast which lured woodtrolls who strayed from the path to certain death. But that was just in stories, wasn't it? Even so, as Ma-Tatum continued talking, Twig shuddered.

'The gloamglozer consumes its victim while its heart is still beating,' Ma-Tatum whispered, her voice trailing away to nothing. 'RIGHT!' she announced loudly, and clapped her hands together.

Twig, Sinew and Gristle all jumped.

'Ma-aa!' Sinew complained.

'Well!' said Ma-Tatum sternly. 'You young people. Always scoffing and mocking.'

'I didn't mean . . .' Twig began, but Ma-Tatum silenced him with a wave of her blood-red hand.

'*Never* take the Deepwoods lightly,' she warned him. 'You won't last five minutes if you do.' Then she leaned forwards and seized his hand warmly. 'Now go and rest,' she said.

Twig didn't need telling twice. He followed Gristle and Sinew out of the hut, and went with them across the village square to the communal hammocks. Strung between the trunks of a triangle of dead trees, the hammocks swung gently to and fro, all the way up. Twig was, by now, so tired he could scarcely keep his eyes open. He followed Gristle up a ladder which was lashed to the side of one of the trees.

'This is ours,' said the slaughterer when they reached the uppermost hammock. 'And there's your bedding.'

Twig nodded. 'Thanks,' he said. The quilt Ma-Tatum had left for him was near the far end. Twig wobbled across the hammock on his hands and knees, and wrapped it around him. The next moment he was fast asleep.

Twig was not disturbed by the rising sun, nor by the sound of the stone slab being dragged across the ground until the fire was directly beneath the hammocks. And when it was time for Gristle and Sinew and the others of the Tatum family to go to bed, Twig didn't notice a thing as they climbed into the massive hammock and settled down all round him.

Twig slipped into a red dream. He was dancing with red people in a huge red hall. The food was red, the drink was red – even the sun streaming in through the far windows was red. It was a happy dream. A warm dream. Until the whispering began, that is.

'Very cosy, very nice,' it hissed. 'But this is not where you belong, is it?'

In his dream, Twig looked round. A gaunt, cloaked figure was slinking off behind a pillar. As it did so, it scratched a long sharp fingernail over the red surface. Twig stepped tentatively forwards. He stared at the scratch in the wood: it was weeping like an open wound. Suddenly the whispering returned directly in his ear.

'I'm still here,' it said. 'I'm *always* here.'

Twig spun round. He saw no-one.

'You silly little fool,' came the voice again. 'If you want to discover your destiny, you must follow *me*.'

Twig stared in horror as a bony hand with yellow talons emerged from the folds of the cloak, reached up and clasped the hood. It was about to reveal its face. Twig tried to turn away, but he couldn't move.

All at once, the creature cackled with hideous laughter and let its hand drop down by its side. 'You shall know me soon enough,' it hissed, and leaned towards him conspiratorially.

Twig's heart pounded furiously. He felt the warmth of the creature's breath against his ear, and smelt a sulphurous mustiness which seeped from its hooded cloak.

'WAKE UP!'

The sudden cry exploded inside Twig's head. He shouted out in fear, opened his eyes and looked around him in confusion. It was light and he was high up, lying on something soft. Beside him were red-skinned individuals, all snoring softly. He looked at Gristle's face, calm in sleep and everything came back to him.

'Wakey WAKEY, up there,' he heard.

Twig clambered to his knees and looked over the edge of the hammock. Far below him was a slaughterer – the only one still up. He was stoking the fire.

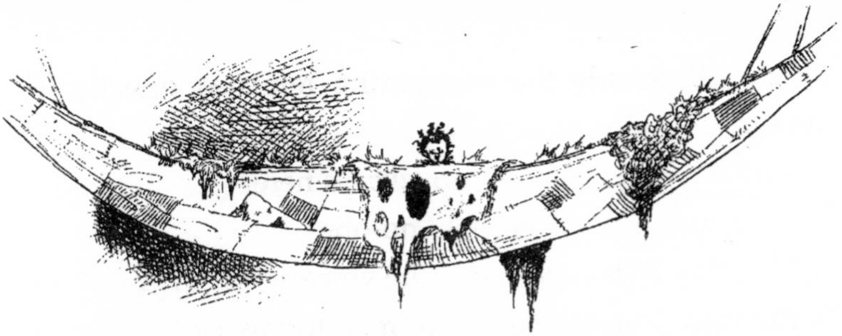

'Was that you?' Twig called down.

The slaughterer touched his forehead lightly and nodded. 'Ma-Tatum told me not to let you sleep through the day, Master Twig,' he called back. 'Not with your being a creature of the sun.'

Twig looked up at the sky. The sun was almost at its highest. He made his way to the end of the hammock, taking care not to wake any of the slumbering family, and climbed down the ladder.

'That's it, Master Twig,' said the slaughterer, and helped him down from the bottom rung. 'You've a long journey in front of you.'

Twig frowned. 'But I thought I might stay awhile,' he said. 'I like it here and I won't be missed by Cousin Snetterbark – at least, not for the time being . . .'

'Stay here?' said the slaughterer in a sneering voice. 'Stay here? Oh, you wouldn't fit in here at all. Why, Ma-Tatum said only this daybreak what a gawky, ugly little fellow you are, with no feeling for leather . . .'

'Ma-Tatum said that?' Twig swallowed the lump rising in his throat. 'But she gave me this coat,' he said, touching it lightly. The fur bristled and stood on end. 'Ouch!' he yelped.

'Oh, that,' wheedled the slaughterer. 'You don't want to take no notice of that. It's just an old coat. Can't give them away normally,' he added, and laughed spitefully. 'No. You want to go back to your own kind, and the path you want lies just over that way.'

The slaughterer pointed into the forest. As he did so a flock of grey birds billowed noisily up into the sky.

'I will!' said Twig. His eyes were smarting but he wouldn't cry – not in front of this little man with his red face and fiery hair.

'And watch out for the gloamglozer!' the slaughterer called out, his voice nasal and mocking, as Twig reached the trees.

'I'll watch out for the gloamglozer, all right,' muttered Twig. 'And for stuck-up slaughterers who treat you like a hero one minute and a barkslug the next!'

He turned to say as much, but the slaughterer was already gone. Twig was on his own once more.

.CHAPTER FOUR.

THE SKULLPELT

As the forest, green, shadowy and forbidding, closed in around him once more Twig nervously fingered the talismans and amulets round his neck, one by one. If there was some powerful evil at the heart of the Deepwoods, then could these small pieces of wood and leather truly be enough to keep it at bay?

'I hope I'll never have to find out,' he muttered.

On and on Twig walked. The trees became unfamiliar. Some had spikes, some had suckers, some had eyes. All of them looked dangerous to Twig. Sometimes they grew so close together that, despite his misgivings, Twig had no choice but to squeeze between their gnarled trunks.

Time and again, Twig cursed his shape and size. Unlike the woodtrolls and slaughterers, who were short, or the banderbear, which was strong, he was not designed for a life in the Deepwoods.

And yet, when the trees abruptly thinned out, Twig grew still more anxious. There was no sign of the promised path. He glanced over his shoulder for any creature that might mean him harm as he scurried across the wide dappled clearing as quickly as he could, and back into the trees. Apart from a small furry creature with scaly ears which spat at him as he passed, none of the Deepwoods inhabitants seemed interested in the gangly youth hurrying through their domain.

'Surely if I keep going, I'll reach the path,' he said. 'Surely!' he repeated, and was shocked by how small and uncertain his voice sounded.

Behind him an unfamiliar high-pitched squeal echoed round the air. It was answered by a second squeal to his left, and a third to his right.

I don't know what *they* are, thought Twig. But I don't like the sound of them.

He kept walking straight ahead, but quicker now. Beads of sweat broke out across his forehead. He bit into his lower lip and started to run. 'Go away,' he whispered. 'Leave me alone.'

As if in response, the squeals echoed louder and closer than before. Head lowered and arms raised, Twig ran faster. He crashed through the undergrowth. Creepers lashed his body. Thorns scratched his face and hands. Branches swung across his path, as if trying to trip him up or knock him senseless. And all the while the forest was growing deeper and denser and – as the canopy of leaves closed above his head – dismally dark.

Suddenly, Twig found himself staring at a turquoise

light which sparkled like a jewel far away in front of him. For a moment he wondered whether the unusual colour might signal danger. But only for a moment. Already, the strains of soft hypnotic music were washing over him.

As he got closer, the light spilled out onto the leafy forest floor. Twig looked down at his feet, awash with turquoise-green. The music – a swirl of voices and strings – grew louder.

Twig paused. What should he do? He was too frightened to go on. But he couldn't go back. He *had* to go on.

Chewing on the edge of his scarf, Twig took a step forwards. Then another. And another . . . The turquoise light washed all over him, so dazzling he had to shield his eyes. The music, loud and sad, filled his ears. Slowly, he lowered his hands and looked around.

Twig was standing in a clearing. Although the turquoise light was bright, it was also misty. Nothing was clear. Shadowy shapes floated before his eyes, crossed one another, and disappeared. The music grew louder still. All at once, a figure stepped out of the mist and stood before him.

It was a woman, short and stocky, with beaded tufts of hair. Twig couldn't see her face.

'Who are you?' he asked. And yet, as the music rose to a slushy crescendo, Twig knew the answer to his question. The short stumpy legs, the powerful shoulders and, when she moved her head to one side, the profile of that rubbery nose. Apart from the strange clothes she was wearing, there was no doubt.

'Mother-Mine,' said Twig softly.

But Spelda turned away, and began to walk off into the turquoise mist. The unfamiliar blue fur gown she was wearing trailed along the ground behind her.

'DON'T GO!' Twig bellowed after her. 'MOTHER! SPELDA!'

The music grew increasingly frantic. The singing voices became discordant.

'COME BACK!' Twig cried, and he sprinted off after her. 'DON'T LEAVE ME!'

He ran and ran through the dazzling mist. Sometimes he knocked into branches and stumps he hadn't seen, sometimes he tripped and fell sprawling to the ground. Each time, he picked himself up, brushed himself down and set off once more.

Spelda had come looking for him; that much was clear. She must have known I was in trouble, he thought; that I strayed from the path. She's come to take me home after all. I can't lose her now!

Then Twig saw her again. She was standing some way ahead, with her back to him. The music had become soft and gentle, and the voices sang a soothing lullaby. Twig approached the figure, his whole body tingling with expectation. He ran up to her, calling out her name. But Spelda didn't move.

'Mother,' Twig cried. 'It's me.'

Spelda nodded and turned slowly. Twig was shaking from head to toe. Why was she acting so strangely?

The music was low. Spelda was standing in front of Twig, head bowed, and with the hood of the fur gown hanging down over her face. Slowly, she opened her arms to him, to wrap him up in her warm embrace. Twig stepped forwards.

At that moment, Spelda let out a terrible scream and staggered back, flapping wildly at her head. The music became loud again. It beat, urgent and rhythmical, like a pounding heart. She screamed a second time – a savage cry that chilled Twig to the bone – and struck out frantically at the air around her.

'Mother-Mine!' Twig cried. 'What's happening?'

He saw blood trickling down from a gash on her scalp. Another cut appeared on her shoulder, and yet another on her back. The blue gown turned to violet as the blood spread. And still she writhed and screamed and lashed out at her unseen assailant.

Twig stared aghast. He would have helped if he could. But there was nothing – absolutely nothing at all – that he could do. He had never felt so useless in his life.

Suddenly, he saw Spelda clutching at her neck. Blood gushed out between her fingers. She whimpered softly, collapsed, and lay on the ground twitching horribly.

Then she fell still.

'NOOOOO!' Twig wailed. He dropped to his knees and shook the body by the shoulders. There was no sign of life. 'She's dead,' he sobbed. 'And it's all my fault. Why?' he howled. 'Why? Why? Why?'

Burning tears ran down his face and splashed onto the bloodstained gown as Twig hugged his mother's lifeless body.

'That's it,' came a voice from above his head. 'Let it all out. Wash the lies away.'

Twig looked up. 'Who's there?' he said, and wiped his eyes. He saw nothing, no-one. The tears continued to come.

'It's me, and I'm here,' said the voice.

Twig stared up at the place the voice was coming from, but still couldn't see anything. He jumped to his feet. 'Come on, then!' he screamed, and pulled the knife from his belt. 'Try having a go at me!' He stabbed at the air wildly. 'COME ON!' he roared. 'SHOW YOURSELF, YOU COWARD!'

But it was no good. The invisible assassin remained invisible. Revenge would have to wait. Tears of sorrow, of frustration, of rage streamed down Twig's cheeks. He couldn't stop.

Then something strange began to happen. At first Twig thought he was imagining it. But no. Everything around him was slowly changing. The mist thinned, the turquoise light began to dim – even the music faded away. Twig discovered he was still in the forest after all. More alarmingly, as he looked round, he saw what it was that had spoken to him.

'You!' Twig gasped. He recognized the creature from the tales that Taghair had told him. It was a caterbird, or rather *the* caterbird, for each of their number considered themselves to be one and the same. The pain of loss rose in his throat. 'Why did you do it?' he blurted out. 'Why did you kill Spelda? My own mother!'

The great caterbird cocked its head to one side. A shaft of sunlight glinted off the massive horned bill, and a purple eye swivelled round to inspect the boy.

'It wasn't your mother, Twig,' it said.

'But I saw her,' said Twig. 'I heard her voice. She *said* she was my mother. Why would she . . .'

'Take a look,' it said.

'I . . .'

'Look at her fingers. Look at her toes. Pull back her hair and look at her face,' the caterbird insisted. 'Then tell me it's your mother.'

Twig returned to the body and crouched down. Already, it looked different. The coat now looked less like an item of clothing, more like real fur. He ran his gaze along the outstretched arm, and realized that no sleeve could ever be so tight fitting. He moved around the body, and suddenly caught sight of a hand: three scaly fingers tipped with orange claws. And the feet were the same. Twig gasped and looked back at the caterbird. 'But . . .'

'The face,' the bird said firmly. 'Look at the face, and see what I saved you from.'

With trembling fingers, Twig reached forwards and pulled back the crumpled fur. He yelped with horror. Nothing could have prepared him for what he saw.

Taut scaly skin, like brown oilpaper wrapped around a skull; bulging yellow eyes, glaring blindly back at him; and the mouth with its rows of hooked teeth, contorted by rage and pain.

'What is it?' he asked quietly. 'The gloamglozer?'

'Oh, no, not the gloamglozer,' replied the bird. 'There are some who call it a skullpelt,' it said. 'A hunter of dreamers who lose their way in the lullabee groves.'

Twig looked up. There were lullabee trees all around, humming softly in the dappled light. He touched the scarf round his neck.

'When among the lullabee trees,' the bird went on, 'you see only what the trees want you to see – until it is too late. It was lucky for you that I hatched when I did.'

Above the caterbird a giant cocoon dangled like a discarded sock.

'You hatched from that?' said Twig.

'Naturally,' said the caterbird. 'Where else? Aah, little one, you have so much to learn. Taghair was right.'

'You know Taghair?' Twig gasped. 'But I don't understand.'

The caterbird tutted impatiently. 'Taghair sleeps in our cocoons and dreams our dreams,' it explained. 'Yes, I know Taghair, as I know all other caterbirds. We share the same dreams.'

'I wish Taghair was here now,' said Twig sadly. 'He'd know what I ought to do.' His head was throbbing from the hum of the trees. 'I'm useless,' he sighed. 'A miserable excuse for a woodtroll. I strayed from the path. I'm lost for ever and I've nobody to blame but myself. I wish that . . . that the skullpelt had torn me limb from limb. At least that would have been an end to it!'

'Now, now,' said the caterbird gently, and hopped down beside him. 'You know what Taghair would say, don't you?'

'I don't know *anything*,' Twig wailed. 'I'm a failure.'

'He would say,' the caterbird went on, 'if you stray from the well-trodden path, then tread your own path for others to follow. Your destiny lies beyond the Deepwoods.'

'*Beyond* the Deepwoods?' Twig looked up into the caterbird's purple eyes. 'But there is no beyond to the Deepwoods. The Deepwoods go on for ever and ever. There is up and there is down. The sky is up and the woods are down, and that is that. Every woodtroll knows that this is so.'

'Every woodtroll sticks to the path,' said the caterbird softly. 'Maybe there is no *beyond* for a woodtroll. But there is for you.'

Suddenly, with a loud clap of its jet-black wings, the caterbird leaped from the branch and soared up into the air.

'STOP!' Twig yelled. But it was already too late. The great caterbird was flapping away over the trees. Twig stared miserably ahead of him. He wanted to shout, he wanted to scream, but the fear of attracting the attention of one of the fiercer Deepwoods' creatures kept his mouth clamped firmly shut.

'You were at my hatching and I shall watch over you always,' came the caterbird's distant call. 'When you truly need me, I shall be there.'

'I truly need you now,' Twig muttered sulkily.

He kicked the dead skullpelt. It gave a long, low groan. Or was it just the sound of the lullabee trees? Twig didn't wait to find out. He left the lullabee grove and ran headlong off into the endless, pathless depths of the dark and sombre Deepwoods.

The forest was dark with night once more when Twig stopped running. He stood, hands on hips and head bowed, gasping for breath. 'I ca . . . can't go another st . . . step,' he panted. 'I just can't.'

There was nothing else for it. Twig would have to find a safe place to spend the night. The tree nearest to him had a massive trunk and a thick covering of broad green leaves which would protect him if the weather worsened. More importantly, it looked harmless. Twig collected together a pile of dry fallen leaves and pushed them into a dip between the roots of the tree. Then he crawled onto his makeshift mattress in his makeshift cot, curled himself into a ball and closed his eyes.

All around him the night sounds whined, wailed and screamed. Twig folded his arm over his head to cut out the unnerving din. 'You'll be all right,' he said to himself. 'The caterbird promised to watch over you.'

And with that he drifted off to sleep, unaware that at that moment, the caterbird was otherwise engaged with a family of bushnymphs, many many miles away.

.CHAPTER FIVE.

THE BLOODOAK

At first it was just a tickle, which Twig swatted away in his sleep. He smacked his lips drowsily and rolled over onto his side. Nestling in his cot of leaves beneath the ancient spreading tree, Twig looked so young and small and vulnerable.

A long, thin squirmy creature it was doing the tickling. As Twig's breathing grew more regular once again, it wriggled around in mid-air directly in front of his face. It flexed and writhed in the warm air each time Twig breathed out. All at once, it darted forwards and began probing the skin around the boy's mouth.

Twig grumbled sleepily, and his hand brushed at his lips. The squirmy creature dodged the slender fingers, and scurried up into the dark tunnel of warmth above.

Twig sat bolt upright, instantly wide awake. His heart pounded. There was something up his left nostril!

He grabbed his nose and squeezed it till his eyes watered. Abruptly, the whatever-it-was scraped down over the soft membrane inside his nose, and was out. Twig winced, and his eyes screwed shut with pain. His heart pounded all the more furiously. What was there? What could it possibly be? Fear and hunger wrestled with one another in the pit of Twig's stomach.

Scarcely daring to look, Twig peered out through the crack in one eye. Catching sight of a flash of emerald-green, Twig feared the worst, and scuttled back on his hands and feet. The next moment, he slipped, his legs shot out in front of him and he came crashing down on his elbows. He stared back into the gloomy half-light of the new morning. The wriggly green creature had not moved.

'I'm being silly,' Twig muttered. 'It's just a caterpillar.'

Leaning back, he squinted up into the dark canopy. Behind black leaves, the sky had turned from brown to red. The air was warm, but the backs of his legs were damp with the early morning moisture of the Deepwoods. It was time to make a move.

Twig climbed to his feet and was brushing the twigs and leaves out of the hammelhornskin waistcoat when – *WHOOOOSH* – the air hissed with a sound like a lashing whip. Twig gasped, and stared in frozen horror as the emerald green caterpillar lunged at him and flew round his outstretched wrist once, twice, three times.

'Aaaargh!' he screamed as sharp thorns dug into his skin – and he cursed himself for letting his guard slip.

For the wriggly green creature wasn't a caterpillar at all. It was a creeper, a tendril, the emerald tip of a long and viciously barbed vine that writhed and swayed through the shadowy forest like a serpent, seeking out warm-blooded prey. Twig had been lassoed by the terrible tarry vine.

'Let me go!' he cried, tugging frantically at the stout vine. 'LET ME GO!'

As he pulled, so the claw-like thorns punctured his skin and sank deep into the softness of his inner arm. Twig yelped with pain and watched, terrified, as tiny crimson beads of blood grew and burst and trickled down over his hand.

A thick, sickly wind stirred his hair and ruffled the fur of his hammelhornskin waistcoat. It carried the scent of his blood into the shadows. From out of the darkness came the soft clattering noise of a thousand razor-sharp teeth gnashing impatiently. Then the wind changed, and Twig gagged on the metallic stench of death.

He scratched and scraped at the vine. He bit into it, only to spit out the vile bitterness a moment later. He pulled, he prised, he tugged and tore at the vine, but it was too tough. He couldn't break its ferocious grip. He could not get free.

Suddenly the vine gave a tremendous yank, and Twig was wrenched forwards.

'Mfffllbluchh!' he spluttered as he landed with a thud on the forest floor, and his mouth was filled with the rich brown loamy soil. It tasted of . . . of tildermeat sausages. But rancid, sour. He retched emptily and spat again. 'Stop!' Twig screamed.

But the tarry vine paid him no heed. Over rocks and tree stumps, it dragged its victim; through wood-nettles and tripweed. Bumping, banging, crashing.

Twig knew, however, that no matter how badly he was knocked and battered and stung, the worst was still to come. Passing a combbush, he clutched desperately at a branch and clung on for dear life. Where was the caterbird now that he needed him?

For a moment the vine snagged on some roots. A squeal of sudden fury echoed from the shadows, and the tarry vine sent a wave

of whiplash rippling along its length. Twig gripped as tightly as he could onto the branches, but the vine was too strong. The bush sprang out of the ground, roots and all, and Twig found himself being bumped over the forest floor faster than ever.

Below him now were hard, white, knobbly objects which dug into him as the tarry vine dragged him on. The further he went, the more there were. Twig gasped with sudden terror. They were bones: thigh bones, backbones, ribs and empty grinning skulls.

'No, NO, **NO**!' Twig screamed. But the air was dead, and his cries were snuffed out by the blood-red light.

Jerking his head round, Twig peered into the shadows in front of him. He saw a tree trunk, thick and rubbery, that grew out of the white mound where the bones lay thickest.

It pulsed and squealed; it glistened with sticky saliva which oozed from countless gaping suckers. From high above him, where the branches divided, Twig heard the gnashing of a thousand mandible-like teeth, as each one opened and shut noisily, greedily – louder, and *louder* and LOUDER! It was the sound of the terrible flesh-eating bloodoak.

'My knife,' thought Twig feverishly as the clattering grew faster, the stench fouler, the squealing increasingly agitated.

He fumbled around on his belt feverishly and gripped the smooth handle of his naming knife. Then, with one swift movement, he pulled it from its sheath, swung his arm over his head and brought the blade down with all his strength.

There was a sound of soggy splintering, and a spurt of glistening green slime squirted into his face. Yet, as his arm suddenly jerked back, Twig knew he'd done it. He wiped the slime from his eyes.

Yes! There it was, the vine, swaying hypnotically to and fro above him. Back and forwards it went, back and forwards, to and fro. Twig was rooted to the spot. He watched, transfixed, as the severed end stopped dripping and the liquid congealed to form a knobbly green blob at the end of the vine, the size of his fist.

Abruptly, the rubbery skin split, the blob burst open and, with a rasping slurp, a long tentacle tipped with emerald-green sprang out. It sensed the air and quivered.

Then a second tentacle appeared, and a third. Twig stared, unable to move. Where one vine had been, now there were three. They reared up, ready to strike and – *S-S-S-SWOOOOOSH* – all three of them lunged.

Twig screamed with pain and terror as the tentacles lashed themselves tightly round his ankles. Then, before he could do anything about it, the tarry vine tugged his feet out from under him and hoisted him, upside down, high up into the air.

The whole forest blurred before Twig's eyes as the blood rushed to his head. It was all he could do to keep hold of the knife. Wriggling and squirming and grunting with effort, he heaved himself up, clung hold of the vine, and began jabbing and stabbing.

'FOR SKY'S SAKE, LET ME GO!' he cried.

Green slime immediately began bubbling to the surface. It oozed round the knife and over his hand, oily and slippery. Twig lost his grasp and tumbled back through the air.

Dangling helplessly by his feet, he twisted his neck back and looked down. He was above the top of the main tree-trunk. Directly beneath him were the thousand razor-sharp teeth he had heard clattering so greedily. Arranged in a wide circle, they glinted in the red light.

All at once, they sprang open. Twig found himself staring down into the crimson gorge of the bloodthirsty tree. It slobbered and slavered noisily. The stench was atrocious. Twig gagged emptily.

Now he would never ride the sky pirates' ships. Nor reach his destiny. Nor even leave the Deepwoods.

With his last bit of strength, Twig struggled frantically to pull himself upwards again. The hammelhornskin waistcoat slipped down over his eyes. He felt the fur stiffen as he rubbed it the wrong way. Again and again, he reached up and – finally – he managed to clutch hold of the vine. As he did so, it released his feet.

Twig cried out with fear as he swung loose, and dug in with his fingernails. Now, instead of trying to cut himself free, he was desperate to hold on – desperate not to be dropped down into the gaping mouth of the bloodoak. Hand over hand, he tried to climb the vine but, slippery with the slime, it slid back between his fingers. For every inch he went up, he slithered back half a dozen.

'Help,' he whimpered softly. 'Help me.'

The vine gave a violent jerk. Twig lost his grip and the tarry vine flicked him away.

Feet first, arms flailing, he dropped through the air. He landed with a sickening squelch deep down inside the cavernous mouth of the flesh-eating bloodoak. The teeth snapped shut above his head.

It was pitch black in the tree, and loud with the sound of hideous gurgling. 'I can't move,' he gasped. All round him, the monstrous throat constricted, and rings of hard woody muscle squeezed him tightly. 'Can't bre . . . e . . . eathe!'

One thought went round and round his head, too awful to take in. *I'm being eaten alive!* Deeper and deeper down he went. *Eaten alive . . .'*

Suddenly the bloodoak juddered. A rumbling, grumbling burp burbled up from the inner depths of the tree, and a blast of foul air rushed up past Twig. For an instant, the muscles released their grip.

Twig gasped and slipped down a little further. The thick hair on the hammelhornskin waistcoat bristled as it was brushed up the wrong way. The bloodoak juddered again.

The gurgling grew louder as the bloodoak continued to cough, until the whole spongy tube shook with a deafening roar. Beneath him, Twig felt something strange pressing against the bottom of his feet, pushing him upwards.

All at once, the retching tree released its grip on Twig's body for a second time. It had to get rid of the spiky object which had become lodged in its throat. It burped, and the pressure of air which had built up below suddenly exploded with such violence that it shot Twig back up the hollow trunk.

He burst into the air with a loud *POP* and soared off in a shower of spittle and slime. And for a moment, Twig felt he was actually flying. Up and away he went, as free as a bird.

And then down again, crashing through branches, as he hurtled back to the ground. He landed with a heavy thud that jarred every bone in his body. For a moment he lay there, scarcely daring to believe what had happened.

'You saved my life,' he said, smoothing the fur of the hammelhornskin waistcoat. 'Thank you for your gift, Ma-Tatum.'

Hurt, but not that badly, it occurred to Twig that something must have broken his fall. He reached below him tentatively.

'Oy!' a voice protested.

Startled, Twig rolled over and looked up. Not some*thing*, but some*body*! He tightened his grip on the knife, still in his hand.

.CHAPTER SIX.

The Gyle Goblin Colony

Twig climbed shakily to his feet, and looked at the character lying on the ground. He had a flat head, a bulbous nose and heavy-lidded eyes; he was dressed in filthy rags and covered in dirt from head to toe. He stared at Twig suspiciously.

'You did drop down on us from a great height,' he said.

'I know, I'm sorry about that,' said Twig, and shuddered. 'You wouldn't believe what I've just been through. I . . .'

'You did hurt us,' the goblin interrupted. His nasal voice buzzed round inside Twig's head. 'Are you the gloamglozer?' it said.

'The gloamglozer?' said Twig. 'Of course not!'

'The most terrifying creature in all the Deepwoods, it be,' the goblin said, its ears twitching. 'It does lurk in the dark corners of the sky and drop down upon the unsuspecting.' The goblin's eyes became two thin slits. 'But then perhaps you do know that already.'

'I'm no gloamglozer,' Twig said. He returned his knife to its sheath, reached forwards and helped the goblin to his feet. The bony hand felt hot and sticky to the touch. 'I'll tell you what, though,' Twig added. 'I was almost *eaten* just now – by a bloodo . . .'

But the goblin was no longer listening. 'He does say he is not the gloamglozer,' he called into the shadows.

Two more of the squat, angular goblins appeared. Apart from the differing patterns of streaked dirt on their faces, the three of them were identical. Twig's nose wrinkled up at the sickly sweet odour they gave off.

'In that case,' said the first, 'we do best return to the colony. Our Grossmother will wonder where we are.'

The others nodded, picked up their bundles of weeds and swung them up onto their flat heads.

'Wait!' Twig cried. 'You can't just go. You've got to help me. COME BACK!' he yelled, and sped off after them.

The forest was dense and overgrown. Through cracks in the canopy, Twig saw that the sky had turned to pinky-blue. Little light penetrated the gloom beneath.

'Why won't you listen to me?' said Twig miserably.

'Why should we?' came the reply.

Twig trembled with loneliness. 'I'm tired and hungry,' he said.

'So what!' they jeered.

Twig bit into his lower lip. 'And I'm lost!' he shouted angrily. 'Can't I go with you?'

The goblin directly in front of him turned and shrugged. 'It be all the same to us what you do.'

Twig sighed. It was the nearest to an invitation he was likely to get. At least they hadn't said he *couldn't* go with them. The goblins were unpleasant but, as Twig had already learned, you couldn't afford to be too fussy in the Deepwoods. And so, picking out the tarry vine's thorny splinters from his wrist as he went, Twig did go with them.

'Do you have names?' he called out, some while later.

'We are gyle goblins,' they all replied as one.

A little farther after that, they were suddenly joined by three more goblins, and then another three – and then half a dozen more. They all looked the same. It was only the objects balanced on their flat heads that singled them out. One was carrying a wicker tray of berries, one, a basket of knotted roots, another, a huge bulbous gourd of purple and yellow.

All at once, the thronging crowd emerged from the forest and Twig was swept along with them into a sunlit clearing. In front of him stood a magnificent construction made of a pink, waxen material, with sagging windows and drooping towers. It was as tall as the tallest trees and stretched back farther than Twig could see.

The goblins began chattering excitedly. 'We are back,' they cried, as they surged forwards. 'We are home. Our

Grossmother will be pleased with us. Our Grossmother will feed us.'

Squeezed on all sides by the crush of bodies, Twig could hardly breathe. Suddenly, his feet left the ground and he found himself being carried on against his will. A great gateway loomed up in front of him. The next moment he was sucked beneath the towering arch in the flood of gyle goblins, and on into the colony itself.

Once inside, the goblins hurried off in all directions. Twig tumbled to the floor with a thud. More and more of the goblins continued to pour in. They stepped on his hands, they tripped over his legs. With one arm raised protectively, Twig struggled to his feet and tried in vain to get back to the door.

Jostled and bounced, he was driven across the hall and down one of the many tunnels. The air became closer, clammier. The walls were sticky and warm and glowed with a deep pink light.

'You've got to help me,' Twig pleaded as the goblins shoved past him. 'I'm hungry!' he cried, and grabbed a long woodsap from one of the passing baskets.

The goblin, whose fruit it was, turned on him angrily. 'That does not be for you,' he snapped, and snatched the woodsap back.

'But I *need* it,' said Twig weakly.

The goblin turned his back, and was gone. Twig felt anger bubbling up inside him. He was hungry. The goblins had food – yet they wouldn't let him have any. All at once his anger exploded.

The goblin with the woodsaps hadn't got far. Barging

past the others, Twig steadied himself, threw himself at the goblin's ankles – and missed.

He sat up, dazed. He was lying next to a narrow alcove set back in the wall. It was into this opening that the goblin had darted. Twig smiled grimly as he climbed to his feet. He had the goblin cornered.

'You!' he yelled. 'I want some of that fruit and I want it now.'

The red woodsaps gleamed in the pink light. Twig could already taste their syrupy flesh on his tongue.

'I did tell you once,' said the goblin as he swung the basket down off his head. 'They do not be for you.' And with that, he tipped the entire load of woodsaps down a hole in the floor. Twig heard them bouncing down a long chute and landing far below – with a muffled *plattsh*.

Twig stared at the goblin open-mouthed. 'Why did you do *that*?' he said.

But the goblin left without saying a word.

Twig slumped to the floor. 'Horrible little beast,' he muttered. Others came with their loads of roots, fruits, berries and leaves. None of them noticed Twig. None of them heard him pleading for something to eat. Eventually, Twig fell silent and stared down at the sticky floor. The stream of goblins dwindled.

It was only when a latecomer arrived, grumbling to himself about the time, that Twig looked up again. The goblin looked flustered. His hands shook as he tipped his load of succulent yellow tubroots down the hole.

'At last,' he sighed. 'Now for some food.'

Food. *Food*! The wonderful word echoed round Twig's

head. He leapt up and followed the goblin.

Two right turns and a left fork later, Twig found himself in a vast, cavernous chamber. It was round and high and domed, with glistening walls and thick pillars like dripping candles. The air was cloying with the familiar sickly sweet smell, and sticky on the skin.

Although packed, the chamber was quite still. The gyle goblins were all staring upwards, open-mouthed and wide-eyed, at a point in the very centre of the domed ceiling. Twig followed their gaze and saw a wide tube slowly descending. Clouds of pink steam billowed out from its end, making the stuffy air more stifling still.

The tube came to a halt inches above a trough. The goblins held their breath as one. There was a click and a gurgle, a final puff of steam, and all at once a torrent of thick, pink honey poured out of the bottom of the tube and into the trough.

At the sight of the honey, the goblins went wild. Voices were raised, fists flew. Those at the back surged forwards, while those at the front fought with each other. They scratched, they scraped, they tore at one another's clothes in a frenzied effort to be first at the steaming pink honey.

Twig drew back, away from the rioting goblins. He felt behind him for the wall and worked his way around the outside of the chamber. And when he came to a flight of stairs, he climbed it. Halfway to the top, he stopped, sat, and looked down on the goblins.

The pink honey was splashing and splattering everywhere as the goblins struggled to get as much of the gooey mixture as they could. Some were slurping from their cupped hands. Some had plunged their heads into the sticky mess and were gulping it down in greedy mouthfuls. One had jumped into the trough and was lying directly under the tube with his mouth open. A look of mindless contentment spread over his spattered features.

Twig shook his head in disgust.

All at once, there was a loud CLONK and the stream of pink honey stopped. Feeding time was over. A half-hearted groan went up and several of the goblins clambered into the trough to lick it clean. The rest began to file away; calmly, peacefully. Along with their hunger, the frantic atmosphere had also disappeared.

The chamber was all but empty when Twig climbed to his feet. He paused. There was another noise. PUFF-PANT, it went. SQUELCH, CLATTER. And again. PUFF-PANT, SQUELCH, CLATTER.

Heart pounding, Twig spun round and peered up into the darkness above him. He fingered his amulets nervously.

PUFF-PANT, SQUELCH, CLATTER.

Twig gasped with terror. Something was approaching. Something he didn't like the sound of one tiny little bit.

PUFF-PANT, SQUELCH, CLATTER, G-R-O-A-N!

All at once, the doorway at the top of the stairs was filled with the BIGGEST, the FATTEST, the MOST MONSTROUSLY OBESE creature Twig had ever *ever* EVER seen. She – for it was female – moved her head and surveyed the scene below her. Beady eyes peered over her fat cheeks, and the rolls of blubber around her neck wobbled.

'No peace for the wicked,' she muttered. Her voice sounded like bubbling mud. Plob plob plob plob plob. 'Still,' she added softly, shifting the mop and bucket in her hands. 'Grossmother's boys be worth it.'

She squished and squeezed herself through the doorway, wodge by wobbling wodge. Twig leaped to his feet, flew down the stairs and hid in the only place there was to hide – beneath the trough. The noise continued – PUFF-PANT, SQUELCH, CLATTER. THUD! Twig peeked nervously out.

The Grossmother was moving quickly for one so immense. Closer she came, closer and closer. Twig shivered with dread, 'She must have seen me,' he groaned, and shrank back as far into the shadows as he could.

The bucket clattered to the floor, the mop plunged into the water and the Grossmother began cleaning the mess her 'boys' had left. In the trough and around it she slopped, humming wheezily as she worked. Finally, she seized the bucket and threw the remaining water *underneath* the trough.

Twig yelped with surprise. The water was icy cold.

'What was that?' the Grossmother shrieked, and began prodding and jabbing beneath the trough with her mop. Time and again, Twig dodged out of the way. But then his luck ran out. The mop slammed into his chest and sent him skidding backwards, out into the open. The Grossmother was upon him at once.

'Ugh!' she exclaimed. 'Vile . . . disgusting . . . revolting VERMIN! Contaminating my beautiful colony.'

She seized Twig by the ear, swung him up off the ground and plonked him into the bucket. Then she rammed the mop down on top of him, picked the whole lot up and hauled herself back to the top of the stairs.

Twig lay still. His chest ached, his ear throbbed – the bucket swayed. He heard the Grossmother squeeze herself back through the door, and then through another. The sweet, sickly smell grew stronger than ever. Suddenly the swaying stopped. Twig waited a moment, then pushed the mop aside and peered over the edge.

The bucket was hanging from a hook, high up above a vast steamy kitchen. Twig gasped. There was no way down.

He watched the Grossmother wobble across the room to where two massive pots were bubbling away on a stove. She seized a wooden paddle and plunged it into the simmering pink honey. 'Stir, stir, stir,' she sang. 'Got to keep it stirring.'

Then she dipped a podgy finger into the pot, and sucked it thoughtfully. Her face broke into a smile. 'Perfect,' she said. 'Though perhaps we could do with just a little more.'

She laid the paddle down and heaved her massive bulk over to a shadowy recess at the back of the kitchen. There, looking out of place next to the cupboards and table, Twig saw a well. The Grossmother seized the wooden handle and began turning. When the end of the rope suddenly popped up into view, she looked perplexed.

'Where's the blooming bucket got to?' she muttered.

Then she remembered.

'Unnh!' she grunted with surprise a moment later, as she unhooked the bucket and glanced inside. 'I did forget to put the rubbish out.'

Twig stared out of the bucket nervously as the Grossmother lumbered back to the sink. What exactly did 'putting the rubbish out' involve? He discovered all too soon as a powerful jet of water – so cold it took his breath away – thundered down onto him. He felt himself spinning round and round as the Grossmother swilled the bucket.

'Whooaaah!' he cried out dizzily.

The next moment, the Grossmother tipped the bucket up and sloshed the whole lot – Twig and all – down the disposal chute.

'Aaaarrgh!' he screamed as he tumbled, over and over, helter-skelter all the way down to the bottom of the long chute, out and – *PLATTSH* – onto a warm, soft, soggy mound.

Twig sat up and looked round. The long, flexible tube he'd fallen down was only one of many. All of them were swaying gently this way and that, illuminated by the roof of waxy pink which glowed far, far above his head. He would never be able to climb back up that high. What was he to do now?

'First things first,' Twig thought, his eye catching sight of a woodsap, still intact, lying on the rotting pile to his right. He picked it up and wiped it on his hammelhorn-skin waistcoat till the red skin gleamed. He bit into the fruit hungrily. Red juice dribbled down his chin.

Twig smiled happily. 'Scrumptious!' he slurped.

.CHAPTER SEVEN.

SPINDLEBUGS AND MILCHGRUBS

Twig finished the woodsap and tossed the core away. The painful gnawing in his stomach had gone. He climbed to his feet, wiped his hands on his jacket and looked round. He was standing at the centre of a huge compost heap in an underground cavern as colossal as the colony above it.

Gritting his teeth and trying hard not to breathe in, Twig squelched across to the far side of the rotting vegetation and climbed up onto the enclosing bank. He stared up at the ceiling far above his head. 'If there's a way in,' he muttered grimly, 'there *must* be a way out.'

'Not necessarily,' came a voice.

Twig started. Who had spoken? It was only when the creature moved towards him, and the light glinted on its translucent body and wedge-shaped head, that Twig realized how close it was.

Tall and angular, it looked like some kind of giant glass insect. Twig had never seen anything like it before. He knew nothing of the underground swarms of spindlebugs, nor of the lumbering milchgrubs they tended.

Suddenly, the insect lunged forwards and seized Twig's collar in its claws. Twig cried out as he found himself face to face with the twitching head, all waving feelers and huge multi-faceted eyes, which gleamed green and orange in the dim light.

'I got another one over here,' the creature called. There was the sound of approaching scurrying, and the spindlebug was joined by three others.

'I don't know what's the matter with her upstairs,' said the first.

'Downright sloppy, I call it,' said the second.

'She'd be the first one to complain if the honey was off,' said the third. 'We'll *have* to have a word with her.'

'Fat lot of good that'll do,' said the first. 'If I've told her once, I've told her a thousand times . . .'

'VEGETABLE, NOT ANIMAL!' they all cried together, and trilled with irritation.

The insect holding Twig stared at him closely. 'Not like the usual pests we get,' it observed. 'This one's got hair.' Then, without any warning, it lurched to one side and bit savagely into Twig's arm.

'YOUCH!' Twig screamed.

'Eeeeyuk!' squealed the spindlebug. 'It's *sour*!'

'What did you do that for?' Twig demanded.

'*And* it can talk!' said another in surprise. 'You'd best get it into the incinerator before it can cause any trouble.'

Twig gasped. The *incinerator*? He wrenched himself free of the insect's pincer-grip, and dashed off along the criss-cross of raised walkways. A shrill buzz of alarm immediately went up as the four furious insects gave chase.

As Twig ran, so the underground landscape began to change. He passed field after field being hoed and raked by more of the gardening insects. Further on, and the soil was dotted with the pink spots of something beginning to sprout. Further still, and the fields were full of glistening pink fungus that grew up like spongy antlers.

'Now we've got you,' came a voice.

Twig skidded to a halt. Two of the spindlebugs were in front of him. He turned. The other two were advancing from behind. There was nothing else for it. Twig leapt

down from the walkway and raced across the field, crushing a swathe through the pink fungus as he ran.

'HE'S IN THE FUNGUS BEDS,' the insects screeched. 'HE MUST BE STOPPED!'

Twig's heart sank when he realized he was not the only one amongst the pink toadstools. The whole field was full of huge, lumbering creatures, as transparent as the insects, and all busy grazing on the fungus.

Twig saw the chewed food coursing through tubes inside the bodies, down into the stomach, and along the tail to a huge, bulbous sac filled with a pink liquid. One of the beasts glanced up and let out a low growl. Others joined in. Before long the air was throbbing with the sound of roaring.

'DETAIN THE PEST!' came the shrill cry of the gardener

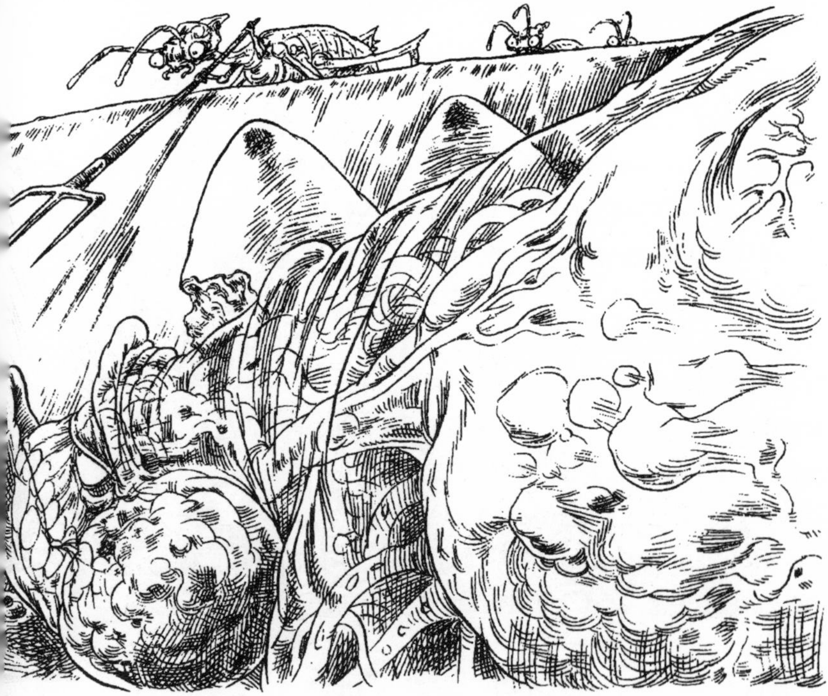

insects. The milchgrubs began to advance.

Twig darted this way, that way, dodging between the massive animals as they blundered towards him. Slipping and sliding on the crushed fungus, he made it to the far side only just in time. Even as he was scrambling up the bank, he felt the warm breath of one of the milchgrubs, as the beast snapped at his ankles.

Twig looked around him anxiously. To his left and right was the walkway, but both directions were blocked. Behind him were the milchgrubs, trundling ever closer. In front was a grooved slope which disappeared down into the shadows.

'Now what?' he panted. There was no choice. He *had* to go down the slope. He spun round and hurtled headlong into the shadowy darkness.

'NOW HE'S HEADING FOR THE HONEY PIT!' the spindlebugs screeched. 'CUT HIM OFF. *NOW*!'

But with their massive honey sacs which they dragged carefully behind them, the milchgrubs were slow. Twig soon left them far behind as he raced down the slope. *If I can just . . .* Twig thought. Suddenly the ground opened up before him. Twig cried out. He was running too fast to stop.

'NO!' His legs pedalled desperately in mid-air. 'AAAARGH!' he screamed, and plummeted down.

PLOP!

He landed in the middle of a deep pool and sank. A moment later, he resurfaced, coughing and spluttering, and splashed about frantically.

The clear pink liquid was warm and sweet. It filled Twig's ears and eyes, his mouth; some of it slipped down his throat.

He stared up at the sheer sides of the pit and groaned. Things had gone from bad to worse. He'd *never* be able to climb out.

Far above him the spindlebugs and milchgrubs were coming to the same conclusion. 'Nothing to be done,' Twig heard them saying. '*She'll* have to sort it out. *We've* got work to do.'

And with that – as Twig struggled to tread water in the sticky liquid – the spindlebugs crouched down and began tugging at teats on the milchgrubs' honey sacs. Pink jets squirted down into the pit.

'They're milking them,' Twig gasped in amazement. The sticky pink honey landed all round him. 'GET ME OUT!' he roared. 'You *can't* leave me here . . . blobber blobber blob blob . . .'

Twig had begun to sink. The hammelhornskin waistcoat which before had saved his life, now threatened to take it. Its thick fleece had soaked up the sticky liquid and become heavy. Down, down, down Twig was dragged, eyes open, down into the viscous pinkness. He tried to swim back to the surface, but his arms and legs had turned to wood. He was at the end of his strength.

Drowndead in rosy honey, he thought miserably.

And as if *that* wasn't bad enough, he realized that he wasn't alone. Something was disturbing the calmness of the pool. It was a long snake-like creature with a massive head which was thrashing through the pink liquid. Twig's heart pounded in his ears. Drowndead or devoured. What a choice! He squirmed round and kicked out wildly.

But the beast was too quick for him. Its body snaked round behind him, and the wide gaping jaws came up from underneath – and swallowed him whole.

Up, up, up, he rose, through the rosy syrup and . . . out. Twig gasped and coughed and gulped down huge lungfuls of air. He wiped his eyes clean and, for the first time, saw the long body and massive head for what they really were. A rope and a bucket.

Past the steep walls he went; past the group of angular spindlebugs, still busy squeezing the last drops of pink honey from the now deflated sacs of their milchgrubs, and on into the upper reaches of the great cavern. The bucket swung perilously. Twig clung onto the rope, scarcely daring, though unable *not*, to look down.

Far below was the patchwork of pink and brown fields. Above him, a black hole in the glowing roof was coming nearer and nearer and . . .

All at once his head popped out, and Twig found himself back in the steamy heat of the kitchen. The fat and flabby face of the Grossmother was directly in front of him.

'Oh, no,' Twig groaned.

Sweat rolled down over the Grossmother's bulging brow and cheeks as she secured the end of the rope. Her body wobbled with every movement, sloshing and slewing like a sackful of oil. Twig ducked down as she unhooked the bucket, and prayed she wouldn't notice the crown of his head above the surface of the honey.

Humming tunelessly, the Grossmother slopped the full bucket over to the stove, hefted it up onto her trembling shoulder and sloshed the contents into a pot. Twig fell into the bubbling goo with a squelchy *ploff*.

'Ugh!' Twig exclaimed, his disgust drowned out by the Grossmother's puffing and panting as she returned to the well for more. 'What's going on?'

The honey was hot – hot enough to turn the clear bucketful instantly opaque. It gurgled and plopped all round him, splashing into his face. Twig knew he had to get out before he was boiled alive. He heaved himself up out of the thickening steamy mixture onto the rim of the pot and splatted down onto the top of the stove.

Now what? he wondered. The floor was too far down to risk jumping, and the Grossmother was already returning with yet another bucket of honey from the well. He scuttled off behind the pot, crouched down and hoped she wouldn't see him.

With his heart beating fit to burst, Twig listened to the Grossmother hum and stir and sip the pink honey as it came to the boil. 'Hmmm,' she mumbled, and smacked her lips noisily. 'Tastes a bit funny,' she said thoughtfully. 'Sort of sour . . .' She sipped again, and hiccuped. 'Oh, I'm sure it's fine.'

She plodded off and snatched a couple of tea towels from the table. Twig looked round him desperately. The honey was now ready. It was time it was poured into the feeding tube. Surely she'll see me! he thought.

But Twig was in luck. As the Grossmother wrapped the cloths around the first scalding pot, and heaved it from the stove, Twig ducked round behind the second. And when she plonked it back into place and went to empty the second pot, he darted behind the first. The Grossmother, intent on getting the honey for her boys ready in time, never noticed a thing.

Twig remained hidden as the Grossmother struggled to empty the second huge pot into the feeding tube. After a considerable amount of grunting and groaning, he heard a ratchet clicking round. He peeked out.

The Grossmother was pulling a lever up and down. As she did so, the long tube, now full of the heated pink honey, sank down through the floor and into the chamber below. She pulled a second lever, and he heard the click and gurgle of the honey being released into the trough. A roar of gluttonous joy echoed up from the hall below.

'There you are,' the Grossmother whispered, and a satisfied smile spread over her gargantuan features. 'Sup well, my boys. Enjoy your meal.'

Twig scraped the sticky honey off his jacket and licked his fingers.

'Yeuch!' he said and spat out. Boiled up, the honey tasted vile. He wiped his mouth on the back of his hand. It was time for him to make his getaway. If he waited for the Grossmother to do the washing-up, he'd be caught for sure. And the last thing he wanted was to be dropped back down the disposal chute. But where *was* the Grossmother?

Twig squeezed himself between the two empty pots and peered round. He couldn't see her anywhere.

Meanwhile, the tumultuous racket from the chamber below showed no sign of easing up. If anything it was getting louder and – to Twig's ears – more agitated.

The Grossmother, too, must have sensed that something was wrong. 'What is it, my treasures?' Twig heard her saying.

He twisted round in alarm, and squinted into the shadows. And there she was, her monstrous bulk sprawled out in an armchair in the far corner of the kitchen. Her head was back and she was dabbing at her brow with a damp cloth. She looked worried.

'What *is* it?' she said a second time.

Twig didn't care what was wrong. This was his chance

to escape. If he knotted the tea towels together, he should be able to shin down to the floor. He squeezed back between the pots but too quickly. In his haste, he knocked against one of the pots and could only stare in horror as it toppled over, away from him. For an instant it hovered in mid-air, before crashing to the floor with a resounding CLANG!

'Oh, me!' the Grossmother squeaked and leaped to her feet with remarkable speed. She saw the fallen pot. She saw Twig. 'Aaaaah!' she screamed, her beady eyes blazing. 'More vermin! And at my cooking pots!'

She grabbed her mop, raised it in front of her and advanced purposefully towards the stove. Twig quaked where he stood. The Grossmother brought the mop up above her head and . . . froze. The expression on her face turned from one of fury to one of utter terror.

'You . . . you haven't been *in* the honey, have you?' she said. 'Tell me you haven't. Contaminating it, adulterating it . . . you vile and disgusting little creature. Anything can happen if the honey is soured. *Anything*. It turns my boys wild, it does. You don't know . . .'

At that moment the door behind her burst open and a furious cry of 'THERE SHE BE!' went up.

The Grossmother swung round. 'Boys, boys,' she said sweetly. 'You *know* the kitchens are out of bounds.'

'Get her!' the goblins screamed. 'She did try to poison us.'

'Of course I didn't,' the Grossmother whimpered as she backed away from the advancing torrent of goblins.

She turned, raised a flabby arm and pointed a fat finger at Twig. 'It was . . . *that*!' she squealed. 'It got into the honey pot.'

The gyle goblins were having none of it. 'Let's do her!' they raged. The next instant they were all over her. Scores of them. Screaming and shouting, they pulled her to the ground and began rolling her over and over across the sticky kitchen floor to the disposal chute.

'It was just a bad . . . *ooof* . . . a bad batch,' she grumbled. 'I'll . . . *unnh* . . . My stomach . . . ! I'll make a new lot.'

Deaf to her excuses and promises, the goblins rammed her head down the chute. Her increasingly desperate cries became muffled. The goblins leaped to their feet and jumped up and down on her massive bulk, trying to push her down through the narrow opening. They squished her. They squeezed her. They pummelled and pounded her until all at once, with a squelchy *plopff*, the immense wobbling body of fat disappeared.

Meanwhile, Twig had finally got down from the stove and made an immediate dash for it. Just as he reached the door, he heard a colossal SPLODGE! echoing up through the hole. He knew that the Grossmother had landed on one of the compost heaps in the great cavern below.

The goblins whooped and cheered with malicious delight. Their poisoner had been dealt with. But they weren't satisfied yet. They turned their anger on the kitchen itself. They smashed the sink. They trashed the stove. They snapped off the levers and broke the tube.

They sent the pots and stirring paddles tumbling down the chute, and roared with laughter when a cry of 'Ouch, my head!' came echoing up from the cavern below.

And *still* they weren't done! With a howl of fury they turned on the well, hitting it, kicking it, breaking it into a thousand little bits, till all that was left was a hole in the floor.

'Get the cupboards! Get the shelves! Get her arm-chair!' they yelled, and they pushed and shoved everything they could lay their hands on down through the hole they had made. Finally, all that was left in the kitchen was Twig himself. A bloodcurdling cry went up, like the roar of a wounded animal raging with pain. 'Get *him*!' the goblins screamed.

Twig spun round, raced through the door and dashed off down the dimly lit tunnel. The gyle goblins pounded after him.

To the left and to the right, Twig ran.

This way and that.

On and on through the endless maze of the honeycombed colony.

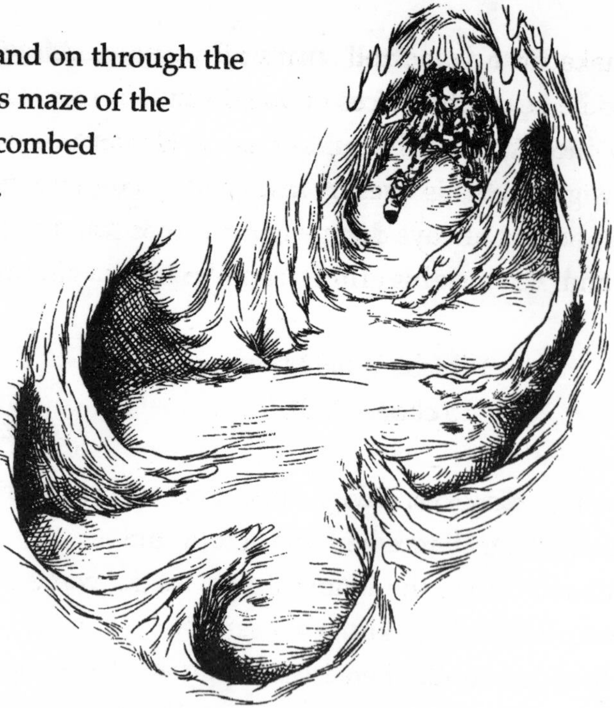

The sound of the raging goblins gradually faded away to nothing.

'I've lost them,' said Twig with a sigh of relief. He looked round at the tunnel, stretching away in front and behind. He swallowed nervously. 'I've also lost *myself*,' he muttered miserably.

Some minutes later, Twig came to a crossroads. He stopped. His stomach churned. There were twelve tunnels leading off it, like the spokes of a wheel.

'Which way *now*?' he said, and groaned. Everything had gone wrong. Everything! Not only had he strayed from the path, now he'd even managed to stray from the *forest*!' And *you* wanted to ride a sky ship,' he said to himself bitterly. 'Some chance! A stupid, gangly little mistake for a woodtroll, that's all you are.' And in his head he heard the voices of Spelda and Tuntum chiding him once again. 'He wouldn't listen. He never learns.'

Twig closed his eyes. A lost child once more, he did what he had always done when a choice proved too big for him: he stuck his arm out and began to spin round.

'Which? What? Where? Who?
I do choose YOU!'

Opening his eyes, Twig stood and stared down the tunnel which chance had selected for him.

'Chance is for the ignorant and weak,' came a voice that turned Twig's skin to gooseflesh.

He spun round. There in the shadows stood one of the goblins. His eyes glinted like fire. What was this new twist to the gyle goblin's behaviour? Twig wondered.

'If you do truly want to get out of the colony, Master Twig,' the goblin said, more softly now, 'you must follow me.' So saying, he turned on his heel and marched off.

Twig swallowed nervously. Of course he wanted to get out, but what if this was just a trick? What if he was being led into an ambush?

It was hot in the tunnel, so stiflingly hot he felt dizzy and sick. The low waxy ceiling oozed sticky drops which plashed on his head and slid down his neck. His stomach ached for something to eat.

'I've got no choice,' he whispered.

The goblin's cloak flapped round a corner and disappeared from sight. Twig followed.

The pair of them walked along tunnels, up and down flights of stairs and through long empty chambers. The air was rank with the smell of staleness and decay; it was hard to breathe and Twig's head spun. His skin was clammy; his tongue was dry.

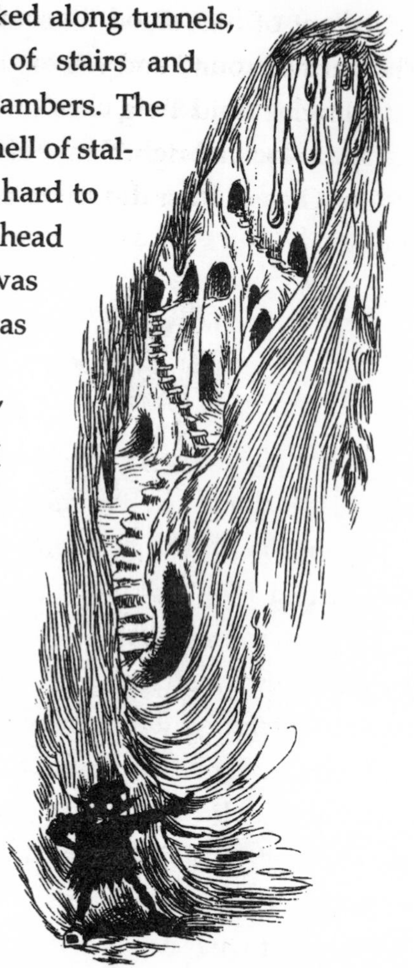

'Where are we going?' he called out weakly. 'I reckon you're as lost as I am.'

'Trust me, Master Twig,' came the wheedling reply and, even as he spoke, Twig felt a cool draught hit his face.

He shut his eyes and breathed in the fresh air. When he opened them again, the goblin was out of sight. The next moment, as he rounded a corner, Twig saw light. Sunlight! Streaming in through the towering arched doorway.

Twig broke into a run. Faster and faster he sprinted, scarcely able to believe that he'd made it. Down the final tunnel . . . across the hall . . . and OUT!

'YES!' he shouted.

In front of him stood a group of three gyle goblins. They turned round and stared at him dully.

'All right?' said Twig cheerfully.

'Do we look all right?' said one.

'Our Grossmother did try to poison us,' said another.

'So we did punish her,' said the third.

The first one looked down at his dirty bare feet miserably. 'But we did act too hastily,' he said.

The others nodded. 'Who will feed us now? Who will protect us from the gloamglozer?' they said.

Suddenly, all three of them burst into tears. 'We *need* her,' they wailed in unison.

Twig stared back at the dirty gyle goblins in their filthy rags and snorted. 'You *need* to think for yourselves,' he said.

'But we're tired and hungry,' the goblins whined.

Twig stared back at them angrily. 'So . . .' He paused. He was about to say 'so what?', as the three unhelpful goblins had said to him before. But he was not a gyle goblin. 'So am I,' he said simply. 'So am I.'

And with that he turned away from the gyle goblin colony, crossed the courtyard and marched back into the surrounding Deepwoods.

.CHAPTER EIGHT.

THE BANDERBEAR

Twig undid the toggles of his fleecy jacket as he walked on. The wind had changed direction and there was an autumnal feel to the air. The weather was as unpredictable as everything else in the treacherous Deepwoods.

All round him, the forest was dripping as a recent fall of snow rapidly melted from the canopy above. Still hot, Twig stopped, closed his eyes and turned his face upwards. The icy water splashed onto his face. It was cool and refreshing.

Suddenly, something large and heavy struck Twig's head – BOOF – so hard that he was knocked to the ground. He lay still, not daring to look. What had hit him? The gloamglozer? Could the fearsome creature *really* exist? If it did, it was no use cowering. Twig opened his eyes, jumped to his feet and drew his knife.

'Where are you?' he screamed. 'Show yourself!'

Nothing appeared. Nothing at all. And the only sound to be heard was the steady 'drip drip drip' from the trees. Then came the second BOOF. Twig spun round. A huge pillow of snow, which must have slipped from the branches overhead, had completely flattened a combbush.

Twig put his hand up. There was snow in his hair. There was snow all around him. He started to laugh. 'Snow,' he said. 'That's all it is. Just snow.'

The dripping increased as Twig continued on his way. Like heavy rain it was, pouring down below. Twig was soon wet through and, as he trudged deeper into the Deepwoods, the ground became more and more boggy. Every step became an effort – an effort made all the worse by hunger.

'With the slaughterers,' he muttered. 'That was the last time I had a proper meal. And Sky knows how long ago that was.'

Twig looked up. The sun was bright and even down on the diamond-dappled forest floor he could feel its ripening warmth. Fragile twists of mist were coiling up from the soggy soil. And as the hammelhornskin dried out, Twig himself began to steam.

His hunger was impossible to ignore. It squirmed and gnawed inside his stomach. It growled impatiently. 'I know, I know,' said Twig. 'And as soon as I find something, you can have it. The trouble is, what?'

When he came to a tree heavy with a deep, dark purple harvest, he stopped. Some of the round, plump pieces of fruit were so ripe they had split their skins and were dripping golden juice. Twig licked his lips. The fruit looked so juicily sweet, so succulently delicious. He reached up and clasped one.

It was soft to the touch and came away from its stalk with a slurp. Twig turned it over in his hand. He polished it on his furry waistcoat. Slowly, he brought it to his mouth and . . .

'No!' he said. 'I dare not.' And he hurled the fruit away. His stomach gurgled angrily. 'You'll have to wait,' Twig snapped, and marched grimly on, muttering under his breath about how stupid he'd been even to *consider* eating something unknown. For although many of the fruits and berries in the Deepwoods were sweet and nourishing, many more were deadly.

A single drop of juice from the rosy heartapple, for instance, was enough to kill you on the spot. And death was far from the only danger. There was fruit which could blind you, fruit which could explode inside you, fruit which could leave you paralysed. There was one, the scrapewort berry, which brought you out in a warty blue rash that never disappeared. And there was another, the pipsap, which shrank those who ate it – the more you ate, the smaller you became. Those unfortunates who had too many disappeared altogether.

'*Much* too dangerous,' Twig said to himself. 'I'll just have to hang on till I come to a tree I do recognize.'

Yet, as Twig continued through the Deepwoods, of all the countless different types of tree he saw, there wasn't a single one that looked familiar.

'This is what comes of growing up with woodtrolls,' he sighed wearily.

Since they never strayed from the path, the woodtrolls relied on others to provide them with fruit from the Deepwoods. They were barterers, not foragers. Now, more than ever before, Twig wished this were not the case.

Trying hard to ignore his stomach's protests, Twig tramped on. His body felt heavy but his head was oddly light. Mouth-watering fragrances wafted towards him from the fruit trees, while the fruits themselves seemed to glow enticingly. For hunger is a curious creature. It dulls the brain, but heightens the senses. And when a twig cracked, far away in front of him, Twig heard it as though it had broken right beside him.

He stopped dead and peered ahead. Someone or something was there. Twig advanced, taking care not to tread on any of the brittle twigs himself. Closer he went, darting from tree to tree. He heard something moan close by and crouched down out of sight. Then, heart chugging, he edged slowly forwards, peered nervously round – and found himself face to face with a huge and hairy mountain of a beast.

It was rubbing the side of its furry face gently with one massive clawed paw. When their eyes met, the creature threw back its head, bared its teeth and howled at the sky.

'Aaaargh!' Twig screamed, and scrambled back behind the tree. Shaking with fear, he heard the splinter and crack of snapping branches as the beast lumbered off, crashing its way through the undergrowth. All at once the noise stopped, and the air filled with a plaintive yodel. The next instant, from far away, a second voice yodelled in reply.

'Banderbears!' said Twig.

He'd heard them often enough before, but this was the first Twig had seen. It was even bigger than he'd imagined.

Although prodigiously large and strong, the banderbear is a timid creature. Its large doleful eyes are said to see the world larger than it really is.

Twig peeked round the tree again. The banderbear had gone. A trail of crushed vegetation led back into the forest. 'That's one path I *won't* be taking,' he said. 'I . . .'

He froze to the spot. The banderbear had *not* gone. It was standing there, not ten paces away. With its pale green fur, it was almost perfectly camouflaged. 'Wuh!' it groaned softly and raised a giant paw to its cheek. 'Wuu-uh?'

The creature was truly massive, at least twice as tall as Twig himself, and built like a vast pyramid. It had tree-trunk legs, and arms so long its knuckles grazed the ground. The four claws at the end of each limb were all as long as Twig's forearms, as were the two tusks that curved up from its jutting lower jaw. Only its ears – delicate winglike objects, constantly on the flutter – did not look as though they had been hewn from rock.

The banderbear fixed Twig with its sad eyes. 'Wuu-uh?' it groaned again.

It was in pain, that much was clear. Despite its size, it looked oddly vulnerable. Twig knew it must need his help. He took a step forwards. The banderbear did the same. Twig smiled. 'What's the matter?' he said.

The banderbear opened its mouth wide and prodded around clumsily inside with a single claw. 'Uh-uuh.'

Twig swallowed nervously. 'Let me see,' he said.

The banderbear came closer. It moved by placing both forepaws on the ground and swinging its hind legs forwards. As it approached, Twig was surprised to see grey-green moss growing in its fur. It was this that made the banderbear appear green.

'Wuh,' it grunted as it stopped in front of the boy. It opened its mouth and Twig was struck by a blast of putrid warm air. He winced and turned his face away. 'WUH!' the banderbear grunted impatiently.

Twig looked up. 'I . . . I can't reach that high,' he explained. 'Even on tiptoes. You'll have to lie down,' he said and pointed at the ground.

The banderbear nodded its enormous head and lay at Twig's feet. And, as Twig looked down into its huge and sorrowful eyes, he saw something unexpected quivering there in the dark green depths. It was fear.

'Open wide,' Twig said softly, and he opened his own mouth to show what he meant. The banderbear followed suit. Twig found himself staring into the creature's cavernous mouth, over the rows of savage teeth and down the gaping tunnel of its throat. Then he saw it, at the back of the mouth on the left; a tooth so rotten it had turned from yellow to black.

'Sky above!' Twig exclaimed. 'No wonder you're in pain.'

'Wuh wuh, wh-uuuh!' the banderbear groaned and tugged his hand repeatedly away from its mouth.

'You want me to pull it out?' said Twig.

The banderbear nodded, and a large tear rolled down from the corner of each eye.

'Be brave,' Twig whispered. 'I'll try not to hurt.'

He knelt down, rolled up his sleeves and took a closer look at the inside of the banderbear's mouth. The tooth, though dwarfed by the two huge tusks, was still the size of a small mustard pot. It was nestling in gum so red and swollen, it looked ready to burst. Twig reached gingerly in and clasped the rotten tooth.

The banderbear immediately flinched and turned sharply away. One razor-sharp tusk scraped across Twig's arm, drawing blood. 'Yow! Don't do that!' he shouted. 'If you want me to help you, you must keep perfectly still. Got that?'

'Wuh-wuh!' the banderbear mumbled.

Twig tried again. This time, although its huge eyes narrowed with pain, the banderbear did not move as Twig grasped the tooth.

'Tug and twist,' he instructed himself as he tightened his grip on the pitted tooth. He braced himself ready. 'Three. Two. One. NOW!' he yelled.

Twig tugged and twisted. He tugged so hard he toppled backwards, wrenching the tooth round as he did so. It juddered and rasped as the roots were torn from the gum. Blood and pus spurted out. Twig crashed down to the ground. In his hands was the tooth.

The banderbear leaped up, eyes flashing furiously. It bared its teeth, it beat its chest, it shattered the silence of the Deepwoods with a deafening roar. Then, overcome with a terrible rage, it began tearing wildly at the surrounding forest. Bushes were uprooted, trees knocked down.

Twig stared in horror. The pain must have driven the creature crazy. He struggled to his feet and tried to slip away before the beast could turn its fury on him . . .

But he was already too late. The banderbear had caught sight of him out of the corner of its eye. It swung round. It tossed aside an uprooted sapling. 'WUH!' it bellowed and bounded towards him, all wild eyes and glinting teeth.

'No,' Twig whispered, terrified that he was about to be torn limb from limb.

The next instant the banderbear was upon him. He felt its massive arms wrapping themselves around his body and smelled the musty odour of mossy fur as he was crushed against the creature's belly.

And there the two of them remained. Boy and banderbear, hugging each other gratefully in the dappled light of the Deepwoods afternoon.

'Wuh-wuh,' said the banderbear at last, and loosed its arms. It pointed inside its mouth and scratched its head questioningly.

'Your tooth?' said Twig. 'I've got it here,' and he held it out to the banderbear on the palm of his hand.

Delicately for one so immense, the banderbear took the tooth and wiped it on its fur. Then it held it up to the light so that Twig could see the hole which had been eaten right the way through. 'Wuh,' it said, and touched the amulets around Twig's neck. It handed the tooth back.

'You want me to wear it round my neck?' said Twig.

'Wuh,' said the banderbear. 'Wuh-wuh.'

'For good luck,' said Twig.

The banderbear nodded. And when Twig had slipped it onto the thong with Spelda's lucky charms it nodded again, satisfied.

Twig smiled. 'Feel better now?' he said.

The banderbear nodded solemnly. Then it touched its chest and extended its arm towards Twig.

'Is there something you can do for me in return?' said Twig. 'Not half! I'm starving,' he said. 'Food, food,' he added, and patted his stomach.

The banderbear looked puzzled. 'Wuh!' it grunted, and swung its arm round in a wide arc.

'But I don't know what's safe to eat,' Twig explained. 'Good? Bad?' he said, pointing to different fruits.

The banderbear beckoned, and led him across to a tall bell-shaped tree with pale green leaves and bright red fruit, so ripe it was dripping. Twig licked his lips greedily. The banderbear reached up, plucked a single piece of fruit in its claws and held it out for Twig.

'Wuh,' it grunted insistently, and patted its own stomach. The fruit was good; Twig should eat.

Twig took the fruit and bit into it. It was more than good. It was delicious! Sweet, succulent and with a hint of woodginger. When it was gone, he turned to the banderbear and patted his stomach again. 'More,' he said.

'Wuh,' grinned the banderbear.

*

They made an odd couple – the furry mountain and the stick boy – and occasionally Twig would ask himself why the banderbear stuck round. After all, it was so big and strong, and knew so much about the secrets of the Deepwoods that it didn't need Twig.

Maybe it, too, had felt lonely. Maybe it was grateful to him for pulling out the aching tooth. Or maybe it was simply that the banderbear liked him. Twig hoped so. Certainly *he* liked the banderbear – he liked him more than anyone he had ever known. More than Taghair. More than Gristle. More even than Hoddergruff, when the two had still been friends. How far away and long ago his life with the woodtrolls seemed.

Twig realized that by now cousin Snetterbark must have sent word that he hadn't arrived. What must they be thinking? He knew what Tuntum's gruff response would be. 'Strayed from the path,' he could hear his father saying. 'Always knew he would. He was never a woodtroll. His mother was too soft on him.'

Twig sighed. Poor Spelda. He could see her face, wet with tears. 'I told him,' she would weep. 'I told him to stay on the path. We loved him like one of our own.'

But Twig wasn't truly one of theirs. He didn't belong – not with the woodtrolls, nor with the slaughterers and certainly not in the sticky honeycombs of the gyle goblin colony.

Perhaps this is where he belonged, with the lonely old banderbear in the endless Deepwoods, wandering from meal to meal, sleeping in the soft, safe, secret places that only banderbears know. Always on the move, never staying in one place for long, and never following a path.

Sometimes, when the moon rose above the ironwood pines, the banderbear would stop and sniff the air, its small ears fluttering and its eyes half closed. Then it would take a deep breath and let out a forlorn yodelling call into the night air.

From far, far away, there would come a reply: another solitary banderbear calling back across the vastness of the Deepwoods. Perhaps one day they would stumble across each other. Perhaps not. That was the sorrow in their song. It was a sorrow Twig understood.

'Banderbear?' he said, one sweltering afternoon.

'Wuh?' the banderbear replied, and Twig felt a giant paw on his shoulder, powerful yet gentle.

'Why do we never meet the banderbears you call to at night?' he asked.

The banderbear shrugged. That was simply the way it was. It reached up and picked a green star-shaped fruit from a tree. It prodded it, sniffed it – and growled.

'No good?' said Twig.

The banderbear shook its head, split the fruit open with a claw and let it drop to the ground. Twig looked round.

'What about them?' he said, pointing up to a small round yellow fruit dangling far above his head.

The banderbear stretched up and pulled off a bunch. Sniffing all the while, it turned the fruit over and over in its massive paws. Then it gently removed an individual fruit from the bunch, nicked the skin with its claw and sniffed again. Finally, it touched the bead of syrup against the tip of its long black tongue and smacked its lips. 'Wuh-wuh,' it said at last, and handed the whole bunch over.

'Wonderful,' Twig slurped. How lucky he was to have the banderbear to show him what he could and couldn't eat. He pointed to himself, then to the banderbear. 'Friends,' he said.

The banderbear pointed to himself, and then to Twig. 'Wuh,' he said.

Twig smiled. High above him but low in the sky, the sun sank, and the light in the forest turned from lemon yellow to a rich golden glow, that poured through the leaves like warm syrup. He yawned. 'I'm tired,' he said.

'Wuh?' said the banderbear.

Twig pressed his hands together and rested the side of his head against them. 'Sleep,' he said.

The banderbear nodded. 'Wuh. Wuh-wuh,' it said.

As they set off, Twig smiled to himself. When they had first met, the banderbear's snoring had kept him awake. Now, he would have found it hard to fall asleep without the comforting rumble beside him.

They continued walking, with Twig following the path that the banderbear made through the dense undergrowth. Passing a spiky blue-green bush, Twig reached out absentmindedly and picked a couple of the pearly white berries that grew in clusters at the base of each spike. He popped one of them into his mouth.

'Are we nearly there?' he asked.

The banderbear turned. 'Wuh?' it said. Suddenly its wide eyes grew narrow and its wispy ears began to flap.

'WUUUH!' it roared, and made a lunge at the boy.

What was the matter now? Had the banderbear gone crazy again?

Twig turned on his heels and leaped out of the way of the massive beast as it hurtled towards him. It could crush him without even meaning to. The banderbear crashed to the ground, flattening the vegetation. 'WUH!' it roared again, and swung at him savagely.

The blow caught Twig on the arm. It sent him spinning round. His hand opened and the pearly berry flew off into the undergrowth. Twig landed on the ground with a bump. He looked up. The banderbear was towering above him menacingly. Twig went to scream. As he did so, the other berry – the one in his mouth – slid back and lodged itself in the back of his throat. And there it remained.

Twig coughed and spluttered, but the berry would not shift. His face went from pink to red to purple as he gasped for air. He staggered to his feet and stared up at the banderbear. Everything was beginning to swim in front of his eyes. 'Can' bre'!' he groaned, and clutched at his throat.

'Wuh!' the banderbear cried out. It grabbed Twig by the ankles.

Twig felt himself being hoisted upside down into the air. The banderbear's heavy paw began pummelling his back. Again and again it thumped down but *still* the berry would not budge. Again and again and . . .

POP!

The berry shot out of Twig's mouth and bounced across the ground.

Twig gasped and gulped at the air. Panting uncontrollably, he squirmed and wriggled upside down in the banderbear's grasp. 'Down,' he rasped. The banderbear scooped Twig up with its free arm and lay him gently on a pile of dry leaves. It crouched low and pushed its face up close.

'Wuh-wuh?' it said.

Twig looked into the concerned face of the banderbear. Its eyes were open wider than ever. It frowned questioningly. Twig smiled and wrapped his arms around the banderbear's neck.

'Wuh!' it said.

The banderbear pulled away and looked Twig in the eye. Then it turned and pointed at the berry that had so nearly choked him. 'Wuh-wuh,' it said angrily, clutched at its stomach and rolled on its back in mock agony.

Twig nodded solemnly. The berry was also poisonous. 'Not good,' he said.

'Wuh,' said the banderbear, leaping to its feet. 'Wuh-wuh-wuh!' it cried, and jumped up and down, up and down. And, as it continued to pummel and pound the offending berry, the trampled vegetation all round was shredded and the ground beneath flew up in clouds of dust. Tears of laughter streamed down Twig's face.

'It's OK,' he said. 'I promise.'

The banderbear came over and patted Twig gently on the head. 'Wu . . . wu . . . Fr . . . wuh. Fr-uh-nz,' it said.

'That's right,' Twig smiled. 'Friends.' He pointed to himself again. 'Twig,' he said. 'Say it. Twig.'

'T-wuh-g,' said the banderbear and beamed proudly. 'T-wuh-g! T-wuh-g! T-wuh-g!' it said, over and over, and it stooped down, seized the boy and swung him up onto its shoulders. Together, they lurched off into the darkening woods.

It wasn't long before Twig was foraging for himself. He wasn't as skilful as the banderbear with its giant claws and sensitive nose, but he learned quickly and the Deepwoods gradually became a less frightening place. All the same, in the dark black night, it was a comfort to feel the great heaving bulk of the banderbear beside him, its gruff snores soothing him back to sleep.

Twig thought about his woodtroll family less and less. He hadn't forgotten them exactly, it was just that there didn't seem any need to think much about anything. Eat, sleep, eat some more . . .

Every now and then, though, Twig was jolted out of the Deepwoods dream, once when he saw a sky ship in the distance, and a few times when he thought he saw the caterbird in the dappled branches of lullabee trees.

But life went on. They ate and slept and yodelled at the moon. And then it happened.

It was a crisp autumnal evening, and Twig was once again up on the banderbear's shoulders. They were searching out a sleeping place for the night when suddenly, out of the corner of his eye, Twig saw a flash of orange. He glanced round. Some way behind them was a small furry creature, like a ball of orange fluff.

A little further on and Twig looked round for a second time. Now there were four of the fluffy little creatures, all frisking about like hammelhorn lambs.

'Sweet,' he said.

'Wuh?' said the banderbear.

'Behind us,' Twig said, tapping the banderbear on the shoulder and pointing back.

The pair of them turned. By now there were a dozen of the curious animals, all bouncing along after them. When it caught sight of the creatures, the banderbear's ears began swivelling round and round, and from its mouth came a soft but high-pitched squeal.

'What is it?' said Twig and chuckled. 'You're not going to tell me you're frightened of *them*!'

The banderbear only squealed all the louder, and trembled from the ends of its ears to the tips of its toes. It was all Twig could do to hold on.

'Wig-wig!' the banderbear bellowed.

As Twig watched, the number of fluffy orange

creatures doubled, then doubled again. They scampered about in the twilight glow, this way and that, but never getting any nearer. The banderbear grew more and more agitated. It shuffled about nervously from foot to foot, squealing all the while.

Suddenly, it had had enough. 'Wuh-wuh!' it cried.

Twig gripped the banderbear's long hair and held on tightly as it lurched forwards. It trundled blindly through the forest. *Bump, bump, bump.* It was all Twig could do not to fall off. He glanced behind him. There was no doubt about what was happening: the orange balls of fluff were giving chase.

Twig's own heart was racing now. On their own the little creatures had looked sweet, but as a group there was something curiously menacing about them.

Faster and faster, the banderbear ran. It crashed through the woods, flattening everything before it. Time and again, Twig had to duck down behind its huge head as branches and bushes came hurtling towards him. The wig-wigs simply followed the path the great beast was carving – and it wasn't long before the ones at the front were catching up.

Twig looked down anxiously. Four or five of the creatures were now leaping at the banderbear's feet every time they touched the ground. Suddenly one of them clung on.

'Sky above!' Twig gasped as the fluffy ball split in half and two rows of savage teeth like the jags on a bear trap sprang into view. The next instant the teeth slammed shut on the banderbear's leg.

'Wuh-ooooo!' it screeched.

With Twig still clinging on for grim death, the banderbear leaned over, tore the wig-wig off, and tossed it away. The ferocious little beast rolled back over the ground, only to be replaced by four more.

'Squash them! Crush them!' Twig screamed.

But it was hopeless. No matter how many of the wig-wigs the banderbear sent flying through the air, there were always a dozen or more to take their place. They clung to its legs, to its arms; they crawled up its back towards the banderbear's neck, up towards Twig!

'Help me!' he screamed.

The banderbear jerked abruptly upright and stumbled over to a tall tree. Twig felt its huge paws round his waist as it pulled him from its shoulders and placed him high up into the branches of the tree, far out of reach of the bloodthirsty wig-wigs.

'T-wuh-g,' it said. 'Fr-uh-nz.'

'You climb up too,' said Twig. But as he looked back into the banderbear's sad eyes, he knew that would never be possible.

The wig-wigs bit into the banderbear's legs again and again until finally with a low moan, the huge beast toppled down to the ground. Its body was immediately covered with the vicious creatures.

Twig's eyes filled with tears. He turned away, unable to look. He clamped his hands over his ears but couldn't shut out the cries of the banderbear as it battled on.

Then the Deepwoods fell silent. Twig knew it was all over.

'Oh, banderbear,' he sobbed. 'Why? Why? Why?'

He wanted to jump down, knife unsheathed, and kill every single one of the wig-wigs. He wanted to avenge the death of his friend. Yet he knew all too well that there was not a thing he could do.

Twig wiped his eyes and looked down. The wig-wigs had gone. And of the banderbear, there wasn't a trace to be seen, not a bone, not a tooth or claw, not a single scrap of mossy fur. From far away there came the forlorn yodelling call of a distant banderbear. Time after time its heartrending cry echoed through the trees.

Twig held the tooth around his neck tightly in his hand. He sniffed. 'It can't answer you now,' he whispered tearfully. 'Or ever again.'

.CHAPTER NINE.

THE ROTSUCKER

Twig stared down into the twilight shadows beneath him. He couldn't see any of the wig-wigs. They had co-ordinated their deadly attack in silence, neither squeaking nor squealing throughout the entire operation. The only sound to be heard had been the crunching of bones and slurping of blood. Now the vicious little beasts had slipped away silently and were gone.

At least, Twig *hoped* they were gone. He sniffed again, and wiped his nose on his sleeve. He couldn't afford to be wrong.

Above his head the sky turned from brown to black. The moon rose, low and luminous. The stillness of dusk had already been broken by the first stirrings of the night creatures and now as Twig continued to sit and stare, unable to move, those sounds of night-time grew. They

whooped and wailed, they shuffled and screeched: invisible but no less perceptible for that. In the darkness you see with your ears.

Below Twig's swinging legs the forest floor steamed. A fine coiling mist wove itself round and around the trunks of the trees. It was as if the Deepwoods were simmering; with peril, with evil.

'I'll stay up here,' Twig whispered to himself as he pulled himself to his feet. 'Till morning.'

With his arms outstretched for balance, Twig made his way along the branch to the trunk of the tree. There he began to climb. Higher and higher he went, looking for some configuration of branches that would both support his weight and offer some comfort in the long night ahead.

As the leaves around him grew denser, Twig's eyes began to sting and water. He plucked a leaf and looked at it carefully. It was angular and glowed a pale turquoise. 'Oh, banderbear,' he sighed. 'Of all the trees you could have chosen, why did you have to place me in a lullabee tree?'

There was no point climbing any further. The upper branches of the lullabees were notoriously brittle. What was more, it was cold so high up. The biting wind was turning his exposed arms and legs to gooseflesh. Twig shifted round to the far side of the trunk and started back down again.

Abruptly, the moon disappeared. Twig paused. The moon remained hidden and the wind plucked at his fingers. Slowly, slowly, guided by the touch of the rough bark on his feet, Twig climbed carefully down. Wig-wigs or no wig-wigs, one slip and he'd crash down to certain death below.

With both hands gripping tightly to the branch by his head, and his left foot, leg bent at the knee, resting in a knothole in the trunk, Twig eased himself down. Droplets of cold sweat beaded his brow as his right foot probed the darkness for somewhere to stand.

Lower and lower he stretched. His arms ached. His

left leg felt as though it was about to be torn from its socket. Twig was on the point of giving up when, all at once, the very tip of his big toe found what it had been looking for: the next branch down.

'At last,' Twig whispered.

He relaxed his elbows, released his toegrip in the knothole and swung down till both feet landed on the branch. His toes sank deep into something soft and fluffy.

'No!' he yelped, and recoiled in horror.

There was something on the branch. An animal of some kind. Perhaps the wig-wigs were able to climb trees after all.

Kicking out blindly, Twig tried his best to pull himself back up to the safety of the branch above his head. But it was no use. He was tired. He heaved himself up, only to find his arms were too weak to take him quite far enough. His hands were beginning to lose their grip.

Suddenly, the moon burst brightly through the forest canopy. It sent flickering silver darts shooting down between the windblown leaves. Kite-shaped patterns of light played on the tree trunk, on the suspended body of Twig, and on the forest floor, far, far below him.

Twig felt his sharp chin pressing hard against his chest as he strained to see directly beneath him. His eyes confirmed what his toes had told him. There was something – *two somethings* – on the rough bark. They were clinging to the branch like the furry paws of some great beast which was climbing up to get him.

Tentatively, Twig lowered his legs and prodded them

with his toes. They were cold. They did not move.

Twig eased himself lower onto the broad branch and crouched quickly down. Close up, the two objects were not furry at all. They looked more like two balls of gossamer thread that had been wound round and round the branch. Twig inspected beneath the branch. His body quivered with excitement.

There, suspended from a silken rope, was a cocoon. Now Twig had seen cocoons before. Taghair slept in one, and he had been present in the lullabee grove when the caterbird had hatched. He had never, however, been so near to one. The long pendulous object was larger, and far more beautiful, than he had ever imagined.

'Amazing,' he whispered.

Woven from the finest filaments of thread, the cocoon looked as if it had been spun from sugar. It was broad and bulbous, and shaped like a giant woodpear which, as it swayed to and fro in the wind, glistened in the moonlight.

Twig reached down under the branch and grasped the silken rope. Then, taking care not to slip in his eagerness, he slid over the edge and lowered himself, hand over hand, until he was sitting astride the cocoon itself.

It felt like nothing Twig had ever felt before: soft to the touch – impossibly soft – but firm enough to hold its shape. And as Twig plunged his fingers into the thick silky wadding, a sweet and spicy fragrance rose up all around him.

A sudden gust of wind sent the cocoon twisting round. Above him, the brittle branches whistled and

cracked. Twig gasped and clutched hold of the rope. He looked down giddily at the dappled forest floor far below him. Something was there, scratching about noisily in the dead leaves. He could neither go up, nor down.

'But then I don't need to,' Twig said to himself. 'I can spend the night in the caterbird cocoon.' And as he spoke the words, his entire body tingled. He remembered the caterbird's words: *Taghair sleeps in our cocoons and dreams our dreams*. 'Perhaps,' Twig whispered excitedly, 'I, too, might dream their dreams.'

Mind made up, Twig twisted himself round until he was facing the cocoon. His nose pressed against the springy down. The sweet, spicy smell grew more intense and, as he lowered himself still further, the silken cocoon caressed his cheek. Finally, his feet came to rest on the matted rim, where the emerging caterbird had rolled back the fabric of the cocoon.

'Ready, steady . . . go!' said Twig.

He let go of the rope and dropped inside. The cocoon swung wildly for an instant. Twig closed his eyes, petrified that the rope would not hold. The swaying stopped. He opened his eyes again.

It was warm inside the cocoon – warm and dark and reassuring. Twig's heart ceased its frantic pounding. He breathed deeply of the aromatic perfume and was overwhelmed by a feeling of well-being. Nothing could hurt him now.

Twig curled himself up into a ball, knees bent and one arm folded beneath his head, and sank down into the padded softness. It was like being immersed in warm, scented oil. He felt snug, he felt safe and secure, he felt sleepy. His tired limbs grew heavy. His eyelids slowly closed.

'Oh, banderbear,' he whispered drowsily. 'Of all the trees you could have chosen, thank Sky you placed me in a lullabee tree.'

And, as the wind rocked the wonderful cocoon gently to and fro, to and fro, to and fro, Twig drifted off to sleep.

*

By the middle of the night, the clouds had all disappeared, carried away on winds, which had themselves now dropped. The moon was once again low in the sky. Far away in the distance, a sky ship, sails all hoisted to catch the sluggish air, sailed across the moonlit night.

The leafy surface of the Deepwoods canopy sparkled like water under the moon's glow. All at once a shadow passed across it: the shadow of a flying creature which glided low over the top of the forest.

It had broad and powerful black leathery wings, scalloped at the back and tipped with vicious claws. The very air seemed to tremble as the wings flapped, ponderous yet purposeful, across the indigo sky. The creature's head was small, scaly and where the mouth should have been a long tubular snout stuck out. It slurped and snuffled, and a foul-smelling vapour puffed into the air with every wing-beat.

Little light from the sinking moon penetrated the forest now, but the creature was not deterred. Raised brassy-yellow eyes cast two wide beams of light which scoured the shadowy depths. Round and around it flew, back and forth. It would not give up until it found what it had come for.

Suddenly its luminous eyes locked on to something hanging from the branch of a tall turquoise lullabee: something large and rounded and glistening. The creature let out a piercing squawk, folded its wings and crashed down through the forest canopy. Then, with its strong stubby legs extended, it landed heavily on the branch of the tree and hunkered down. It cocked its head to one side and listened.

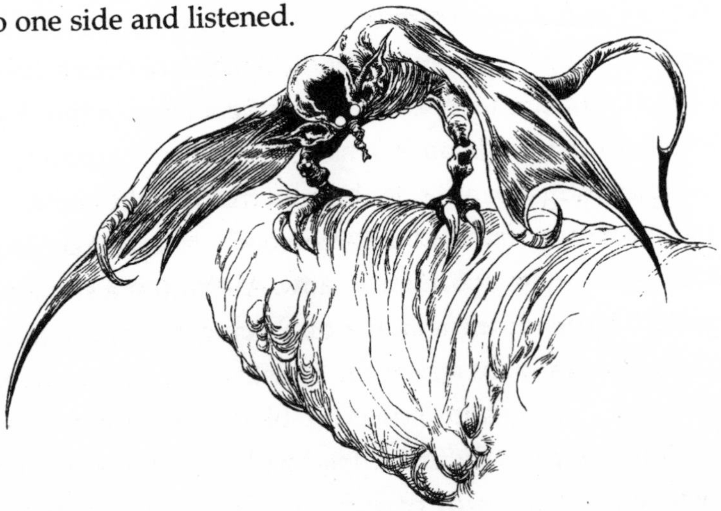

The sound of gentle breathing floated up towards it. It sniffed at the air and its whole body trembled with anticipation. It took a step forward. Then another. And another.

Designed for flight, the creature walked slowly, clumsily, gripping hold with one clawed foot before releasing the next. It walked right round the massive branch until it was hanging upside down.

With its talons digging into the rough bark above it, the creature's head was level with the opening to the cocoon. It poked inside it and prodded around with the bony tip of its long, hollow snout. It trembled again, more violently than before, and from deep down inside its body came a gurgling sound. Its stomach convulsed and a stream of bilious liquid spurted out of the end of its snout. Then it withdrew.

The yellow-green liquid fizzed where it landed and gave off twists of vapour. Twig screwed up his nose, but did not wake. In his dreams he was lying in a meadow beside a babbling, crystal-clear brook. Crimson poppies swayed back and forwards, filling the air with a smell so sweet it left him breathless.

Talons still firmly gripping the branch, the creature turned its attention to the cocoon itself. Filament by filament, it teased apart the matted clumps of wadding around the opening with the claws on its wings. It drew them silently across the hole. Quickly, the opening was closed.

Twig's eyelids fluttered. He was in a cavernous hallway now, lined with diamonds and emeralds which sparkled like a million eyes.

The creature flapped its wings and seized the branch in its wing-claws. It let go with its feet and then, suspended in mid-air, manoeuvred itself along the branch until its body was directly over the top of the cocoon. It splayed its legs and began sucking in air noisily. As it did so, its stomach inflated and the scales at the base of its abdomen stood up on end. Beneath each one was a rubbery pink duct which, as the creature continued to gulp at the air, slowly opened up.

All at once it grunted, and a sharp spasm juddered through its body. From the ducts, powerful jets of a sticky black substance squirted down onto the cocoon.

'Mffll-bnn,' Twig mumbled in his sleep. 'Mmmsh . . .'

The glutinous tar-like liquid soaked in and slid down over the cocoon in all directions, soon covering it completely. When it set, the cocoon became an impenetrable prison.

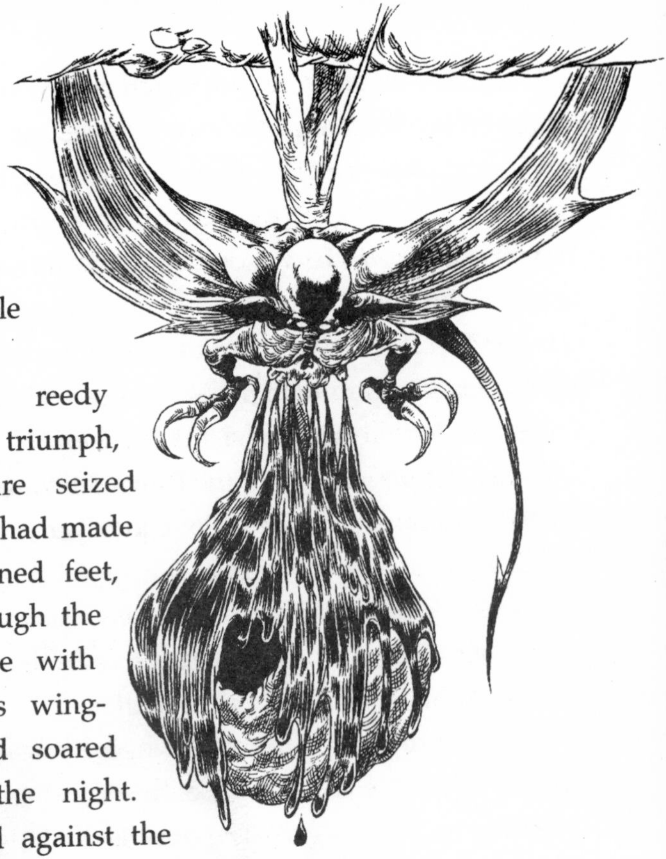

With a reedy squawk of triumph, the creature seized the pod it had made in its taloned feet, sliced through the silken rope with one of its wing-claws, and soared off into the night. Silhouetted against the violet sky, the creature's huge wings beat up and down; below it the deadly pod swayed back and forwards, back and forwards.

Twig was floating on a raft in the middle of a sapphire sea. The sun, warm and yellow, beat down on his face as he bobbed along over the waves. All of a sudden, a ridge of black clouds cut out the light. The sea grew rougher, and rougher still.

Twig snapped his eyes open. He stared round him wildly. It was black. Pitch black. He lay there, motionless, unable to make sense of what was happening. His eyes refused to grow accustomed to the dancing darkness. There was no light. Not a glimmer. A bolt of terror zinged in his head and shot down his spine.

'What's going on?' he screamed. 'Where's the opening?'

Struggling round to a crouching position, Twig felt about the surrounding casing with trembling fingers. It was hard to the touch. It echoed when knocked – *boom, boom, boom* – impervious to his pounding fists.

'Let me out,' he screamed. 'LET ME OUT!'

The rotsucker screeched and lurched to one side as the sudden movement inside the pod knocked it off balance. It beat its wings powerfully and gripped the matt black ridges all the more firmly in its talons. It was used to its quarry struggling to escape. The frantic jerks and jolts would soon subside. They always did.

Twig was beginning to pant. Stinging sweat ran down into his eyes. The acrid smell of bile clung to him like a second skin. He gagged. The darkness seemed to spin. He opened his mouth and a loose vomit gushed forth. It was fruity, sour, full of pips and seeds. A picture came to him of the banderbear handing him something delicious; the banderbear that had been devoured by the horrible wig-wigs. Twig opened his mouth again and his whole body convulsed. *Whooaarrsh!* The vomit splashed against the curved walls of Twig's prison and slopped around his feet.

The rotsucker shifted the juddering pod round in its talons again. The feathery lightness of dawn was already fanning out across the far horizon. Soon be back. Soon be home, little one. Then you can take your place with the others in my treetop store.

Choking. Heaving. Eyes streaming in the acrid blackness. Head pounding with the lack of air. Twig pulled his naming knife from his belt and gripped it tightly. Leaning forward on his knees, he began stabbing in a frenzy at the casing in front of him. The knife slipped round. Twig paused and wiped his sweaty palm down his trousers.

The knife had served him well already – against the hover worm, against the tarry vine – but would the steel blade be strong enough to shatter the shell? He slammed the point hard against the casing. It had to be. Again. And again. It just *had* to be.

Ignoring the jolts and judders which came from inside the pod, the rotsucker kept on towards its lofty store. It could already see the other pods silhouetted against the light, high up in the skeletal trees. Struggle away, my supper-lugs. The greater the struggle, the sweeter the soup, and the sound of the rotsucker's wheezy chortle echoed through the darkness. Soon you will fall as still as all the rest.

And when that happened, the evil-smelling bile the rotsucker had squirted into the cocoon would get to work. It would digest the body, turning the flesh and bones to slimy liquid. After a week, five days if the weather was warm, the rotsucker would drill a hole in the top of the pod with the serrated circle of hard bone at the end of its snout, insert the long tube and suck up the rich fetid stew.

'Break, break, break,' Twig muttered through gritted

teeth as he slammed his naming knife against the casing over and over and over again. Then, just as he was about to give up, the pod resounded with a loud crack as the casing finally gave. A chunk of shell the size of a plate fell away into the darkness.

'YES!' Twig screamed.

Air, fresh air, streamed in through the hole. Gasping with exhaustion, Twig leaned forwards, placed his face to the hole and gulped deeply. In out, in out. His head began to clear.

The air tasted good.

It tasted of life.

Twig peered ahead. Far away in front of him, a row of jagged dead pines stood black against the pink sky. At the top of one of the trees a clutch of egg-shaped objects lined a branch: they were sealed caterbird cocoons.

'Got to make the hole bigger,' Twig told himself as he raised the knife high above his head. 'And quickly.' He brought it down hard against the casing. It landed with an unfamiliar thud. 'What the . . . ?' He looked down and groaned.

The blow which had broken through the rock-hard shell had also shattered the blade of the knife. All he was holding was the handle. 'My naming knife,' said Twig, choking back the tears. 'Broken.'

Tossing the useless piece of bone aside, Twig leant against the back of the pod and began kicking viciously at the casing.

'Break, Sky damn you!' he roared. 'BREAK!'

The rotsucker wobbled in mid-flight. What's going on now, eh? My, my, what a determined supper-lugs you are. Let me just shift you round a little. There. That's better. Wouldn't want to drop you, would we?'

Twig kicked harder than ever. The pod echoed with the sounds of splintering shell and falling fragments. Suddenly, two wide cracks zigzagged across the casing, the warm glow of morning fuzzing their edges.

'Aaaii!' he shrieked. 'I'm falling.'

The rotsucker screeched with fury as the pod lurched. It found itself tumbling down through the air. Keep still, curse you! Beating its tired wings fiercely it pulled itself out of the plummeting spiral. But something was wrong. It knew that now. What are you playing at, my naughty little supper-lugs? You should be dead by now. But be sure I shan't let you go.

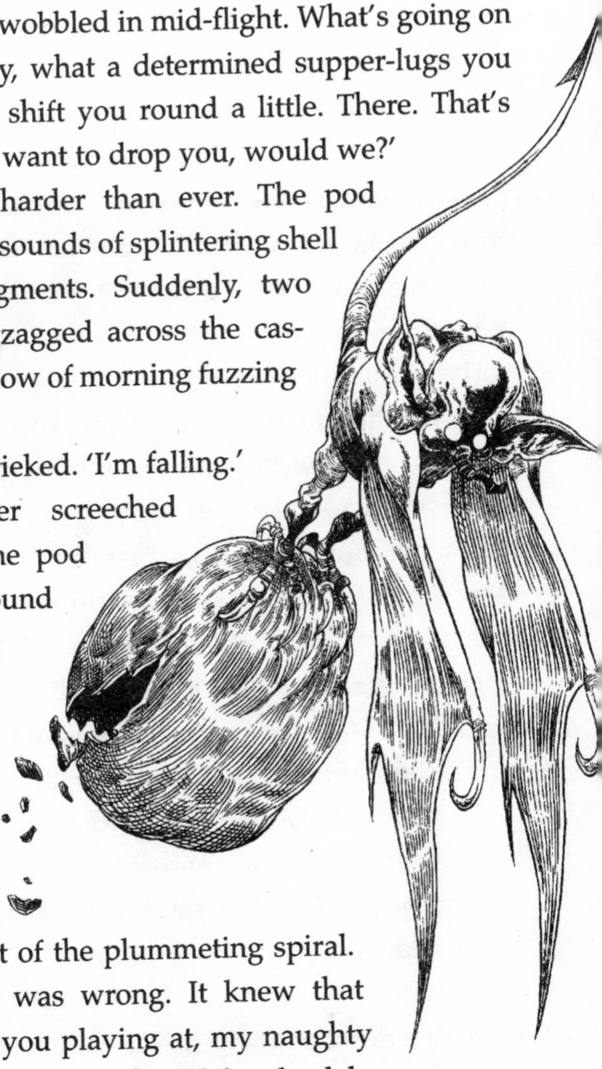

Twig kicked again, and the crack ripped over his head and round behind his back. Again, and it continued below him. He glanced down. There was a jagged line of light between his legs. The vomit and bile drained away.

Whatever happened now, the rotsucker was bound to go hungry. The pod was disintegrating. Its quarry would never putrefy.

Twig stared in horror at the crack below him, as the smear of green grew wider. He stopped kicking. Falling from this height would be too dangerous. More than ever before, he needed help. 'Caterbird,' he shrieked. 'Where are you?'

The rotsucker wheezed. Bad supper-lugs! Bad! It was almost at the end of its strength, sinking lower in the sky. Its brassy-yellow eyes swivelled round to look at its tree-top store. So near and yet so far.

Beneath him, the smudge turned from green to brown. Twig looked more closely. The forest had thinned out and, in parts, died. Long bleached skeletons of trees littered the glittering ground. Some were still standing, their dead branches reaching upwards, grasping at the air like bony fingers.

All at once there was a tremendous crash. The pod had hit the top of one of those dead branches. Twig was thrown back. His head smashed against the shell. The crack widened, and the pod, with Twig still in it, was falling.

Down, down, down. Twig's stomach churned. His heart was in his mouth. He closed his eyes, took a deep breath and braced himself for impact.

SQUELLLP!

He had landed in something soft, something which, even now, was oozing in between the cracks in the shell like grainy liquid chocolate. He dipped his finger in the brown substance and put it tentatively to his nose. It was mud. Thick peaty mud. He was in the middle of a boggy swamp.

Wobbling awkwardly, Twig reached up, slipped his fingers between the largest of the cracks, and tugged. The mud was already up to his ankles. At first nothing happened. Even now, the tar soaked fibres of the cocoon were formidably strong. The mud reached Twig's knees.

'Come *on*!' he said.

With his elbows locked, he prised the crack a little further apart. The veins stood out on his temples, his muscles knotted. Abruptly, light came streaming down on him. The shell had finally split in two.

'Oh, no,' he cried, as the larger piece of the broken pod immediately turned up on its end and slipped down into the mud. 'Now what?'

His only hope lay with the smaller piece, still floating on the surface. If he could just climb up, maybe he could use it as a makeshift boat.

In the sky above him he heard a shrill shriek of fury. He looked up. There, circling above his head, was a hideous and repulsive creature. It was watching him through gleaming blank yellow eyes. Broad black leathery wings, glistening with sweat, flapped noisily into the air. Suddenly, it turned and dived, and the next instant Twig felt sharp talons grazing his head and pulling out tufts of hair by the roots.

The creature wheeled round and dived again. Rubbery threads of green saliva were streaming down from the end of its long snout. This time, Twig ducked. As it swooped in close, it screeched again and sprayed him with a shower of the evil-smelling bile.

Gagging emptily, Twig heard the fading clap-clap of wings. The vile creature was flapping away. When he looked up again it was perched at the top of a distant dead tree, black against the curdled morning sky. Beneath it, hung the cluster of pods, each one full of rotting matter. Twig sighed with relief. The creature had given up. He would not be joining the others in that line of death.

A moment later, his relief turned to panic. 'I'm sinking!' he cried out.

Clutching the piece of shell, Twig tried desperately to heave himself up out of the bog. But each time he pulled down, the shell tipped over, taking on still more of the mud. At his third attempt, it sank completely.

The mud was round his stomach now, and rising. He flailed his arms about and kicked out with his legs, but the thick ooze only sucked him deeper down.

'Oh, Gloamglozer!' Twig wailed. 'What do I do?'

'Don't panic, that's the important thing,' came a voice.

Twig gasped. There was someone there, watching him struggle. 'Help!' he screamed. 'HELP ME!'

He twisted himself round as best he could, a movement which lost him another couple of inches. Past his chest now, the mud was creeping up to the base of his neck. A short bony goblin with a flat head and yellow skin was leaning up against a dead tree, chewing a piece of straw.

'You want *me* to help *you*?' it said, its voice sing-song and nasal.

'Yes. Yes, I do. You've got to help me,' he said, and spluttered as the mud trickled into his mouth and down his throat.

The goblin smirked and tossed the straw aside. 'Then I shall, Master Twig,' it said. 'So long as you're sure.'

It reached up, snapped a dead branch from the tree and held it out across the treacherous swamp. Twig spat the foul mud from his mouth and made a lunge for it. He grasped hold of the bleached wood and clung on for dear life.

The goblin pulled. Twig was dragged through the thick sucking mud, closer and closer to the bank. He spat. He spluttered. He prayed the branch would not break. All at once he felt solid ground beneath his knees, then his elbows. The goblin let the branch drop and Twig crawled out of the swamp.

Free at last, Twig collapsed. And there he lay, exhausted, face down in the dusty earth. He owed his life to the goblin. Yet when he finally lifted his head to thank his rescuer, he found himself once more alone. The flat-head was nowhere to be seen.

'Hey,' Twig called weakly. 'Where are you?'

There was no answer. He pulled himself to his feet and looked about him. The goblin had gone. All that remained was the piece of straw, chewed at one end, which lay on the ground. Twig crouched down beside it. 'Why did you run off?' he murmured.

He sat down in the dust and hung his head. All at once he was struck by another question. How had the flat-head goblin known his name?

.CHAPTER TEN.

THE TERMAGANT TROGS

It was still. The sun beat down, hot and bright. All the vomiting in the sealed pod had left Twig's throat feeling as if it had been sandpapered. He needed a drink.

He picked himself up and looked back at his shadow which stretched far out across the treacherous swamp. At the end of it lay still water. It sparkled tantalizingly. If only there was some way of getting to it without being sucked down into the mud. Twig spat and turned away again.

'It's probably stagnant anyway,' he muttered.

He stomped off across the spongy wasteland. The swamp had once extended this far. Now, apart from the occasional patch of pale-green algae, nothing grew. Yet there was life there. With every step Twig took, clouds of vicious woodmidges flew up and buzzed round him. They landed on his face, his arms, his legs –

and where they landed, so they bit.

'Get off! Get away!' Twig cried as he slapped at the voracious insects. 'If it's not one thing, it's . . . YOUCH!' Slap. '. . . another!' Slap. Slap. Slap.

Twig started to run. The woodmidges flew with him, like satin sheets flapping in the wind. Faster. Faster. Past the bony skeletons of dead trees. Headlong over the bouncy peat. Stumbling, slipping, but never stopping. Out of the desolate home of the evil rotsucker, and back to the Deepwoods.

Twig smelled them before he reached them. The loamy soil, the luxuriant foliage, the succulent fruit – familiar scents that set his mouth watering and his heart clopping faster than ever. The woodmidges were less impressed. As the rich and fertile smells grew stronger, so their numbers dropped. They abandoned their quarry and returned to the wasteland, where the air was pungent and sour.

Twig trudged onwards and upwards. The Deepwoods wrapped themselves around him like a vast green quilt. There were no tracks, no paths; he had to carve his own way through the lush undergrowth. Through woodfern and bullbracken he went, up slopes and down dips. When he came to a sallowdrop tree, he stopped.

The sallowdrop, with its long waving fronds of pearly leaves, only grew near water. The banderbear had taught him that. Twig pushed aside the beaded curtains of the hanging branches, and there, babbling along over a bed of pebbles, was a stream of crystal clear water.

'Thank Sky,' Twig rasped and fell to his knees. He cupped his hands and dipped them in the ice-cold water. He took a sip, swallowed, and felt the cold liquid coursing down inside his body. It tasted good; earthy and sweet. He drank more, and more. He drank until his stomach was full and his thirst was quenched. Then, with a grateful sigh, Twig dropped down into the stream with a splash.

And there he lay. The water ran over him, soothing the woodmidge bites, cleaning his clothes and hair. He remained there until every trace of mud and vomit and stinking bile had been washed away.

'Clean again,' he said, and pulled himself back onto his knees.

All at once, a flash of orange darted across the water. Twig froze. Wig-wigs were orange! Head still bowed, Twig raised his eyes and peered nervously through his lank and dripping hair.

Crouched down behind a rock on the far side of the stream was not a wig-wig but a girl. A girl with pale, almost translucent skin and a shock of orange hair. Company.

'Hey!' Twig called out. 'I . . .' But the girl darted out of sight. Twig leapt to his feet. 'OY!' he yelled as he splashed across the stream. Why wouldn't she wait? He leaped up the bank and onto the rock. Some way ahead, he noticed the girl dodging behind a tree. 'I won't hurt you,' he panted to himself. 'I'm nice. Honest!'

By the time he reached the tree, however, the girl was gone again. He saw her glance back before slipping into a glade of swaying greatgrass. Twig dashed in after her. He wanted her to stop, to come back, to talk to him. On and on he ran. Around trees, across clearings – always close, but never quite close enough.

As she raced behind a broad and ivy-clad trunk, the girl looked back for a third time. Twig felt the hairs at the nape of his neck stand on end; his hammelhornskin waistcoat bristled. What if the girl wasn't checking to see whether she had given him the slip? What if she was making sure that he was still following?

He kept on, but more cautiously now. Round the tree he went. The girl was nowhere to be seen. Twig looked up into the branches. His heart was hammering, his scalp tingled. There could be anything hiding up in the dense foliage waiting to pounce – anything at all.

He fingered his amulets. He took another step forwards. Where *was* the girl? Was it all just another horrible trap . . . ?

'Waaaaiii!' Twig screamed.

The ground had opened up and Twig was falling. Into the earth he tumbled, and down a long curving tunnel. Bump, bump, roll, bumpety, roll, crash, bang and *plaff*, down onto a thick bed of soft straw.

Twig looked up, dazed. Everything was spinning. Yellow lights, twisted roots – and four faces staring down at him.

'Where you bin?' two of them were saying. 'You know I don't like you going upground. It's too dangerous. You'll get carried off by the gloamglozer one day, my girl, and that's a fact.'

'I can look after myself,' the other two replied sulkily.

Twig shook his head. The four faces became two. The larger one loomed closer, all bloodshot eyes and corrugated lips.

'And what's this?' it complained. 'Oh, Mag, what have you brought back *now*?'

The pale-skinned girl stroked Twig's hair. 'It followed me home, Mumsie,' she said. 'Can I keep it?'

The older woman pulled her head away and folded her arms, breathing in, and swelling up, as she did so. She stared at Twig suspiciously. 'I trust he's not a *talker,*' she said. 'I've told you before, I draw the line at pets that can talk.'

Twig swallowed anxiously.

Mag shook her head. 'I don't think so, Mumsie. The occasional noise, but no words.'

Mumsie grunted. 'You'd better be telling me the truth. Talkers means trouble.'

Mumsie was enormous, with rippling forearms and a neck as broad as her head. What was more, unlike the girl, whose pale skin made her almost invisible in the subterranean gloom, Mumsie was all too visible. With the exception of her face, almost every bit of exposed skin was covered with iridescent tattoos.

There were trees, weapons, symbols, animals, faces, dragons, skulls; you name it. Even her bald head had been tattooed. What Twig had first taken for curls of hair plastered to her scalp, were in fact coiled snakes.

She reached up and scratched thoughtfully under her broad nose, inadvertently flexing her biceps as she did so. The sleeve of her patterned dress rode up with a rustle – and Twig found himself staring at a picture of a young girl with fiery orange hair. Beneath it, in indigo letters, was a tattooed message: MUMSIE LOVES MAG.

'Well?' said Mag.

Her mother sniffed. 'Mag,' she said, 'you can be such a trying trog at times. But . . . I suppose so,' she said. 'HOWEVER,' she added, interrupting Mag's whoops of delight, '*you're* responsible for it. Do you understand? *You* feed it, *you* exercise it, and if it makes a mess in the cavern, *you* clean it up. Do I make myself clear?'

'Crystal clear, Mumsie,' said Mag.

'And if I hear so much as a single word,' she went on, 'I'll wring its scrawny little neck. Right?'

Mag nodded. She reached forwards and grabbed Twig by the hair. 'Come on,' she said.

'Yow!' Twig helped, and slapped her hand away.

'It hit me,' Mag howled at once. 'Mumsie, my pet hit me – it *hurt* me!'

Twig suddenly felt himself being whisked up off the floor and swung round. He stared petrified into the trog-woman's ferocious bloodshot eyes. 'If you ever, EVER push, slap, scratch or bite my little moonbeam, I'll—'

'Or in any other way hurt my body,' Mag butted in.

'Or in any other way hurt her body, I'll—'

'*Or* my feelings.'

'— hurt her body or her feelings, I'll—'

'Or try to run away . . .'

'Or try to run away,' Mumsie repeated. 'You're dead!' Her paper dress rustled as she shook him. 'Obedient and dumb, that's the rule. OK?'

Twig didn't know whether to nod or not. If he wasn't allowed to speak, was he expected to understand? With Mumsie's massive fist gripping his coat so tightly, he could scarcely move anyway. She sniffed, and dropped him onto the floor.

Twig looked up warily. Mag was standing behind her mother, her hands held primly at her front. Her face bore an expression of impossible smugness. She leant forwards and tugged his hair for a second time. Wincing with pain, Twig climbed passively to his feet.

'That's more like it,' Mumsie growled. 'What are you going to call it?' she said.

Mag shrugged and turned to her new pet. 'Have you got a name?' she said.

'Twig,' he replied automatically – and immediately wished he hadn't.

'What's that?' roared Mumsie. 'Was that a word?' She prodded Twig hard in the chest. 'Are you a talker after all?'

'Twigtwigtwigtwig,' he said, desperately trying to make it sound as unwordlike as possible. 'Twigtwigtwig!'

Mag put her arm around Twig's shoulders and smiled

up at her mother. 'I think I'll call him Twig.'

Mumsie glared at Twig through narrowed eyes. 'One word, that's all,' she snarled. 'And I'll rip your head off.'

'Twig's going to be just fine,' Mag reassured her. 'Come along, boy,' she said to him. 'Let's go and play.'

Mumsie stood, hands on hips, watching as Mag dragged him away. Twig kept his head down. 'I'll be keeping my eye on that one,' he heard her say. 'You see if I don't.'

As they continued along the tunnel, Mumsie's threats faded away. There were stairs and ramps and long narrow slopes that took them lower, always lower, deep down into the ground. Twig felt uneasy at the thought of the weight of all that earth and rock above him. What was to stop it falling down? What was to stop it swallowing him up?

All at once, the oppressive walkway came to an end. Twig stared round him, trembling with amazement. The pair of them were standing in an immense underground cavern.

Mag let go of his hair. 'You'll like it down here with us termagant trogs, Twig,' she was saying. 'It's never too hot, it's never too cold. There's no rain, no snow, no wind. There are no dangerous plants and no wild beasts . . .'

Twig's fingers moved automatically to the tooth around his neck, and a tear trickled down his cheek.

No dangerous plants and no wild beasts, he thought. But no sky, no moon . . . The girl prodded him roughly in the back, and Twig walked on. And no freedom.

Like the tunnels, the cavern glowed with a pale light. Below his feet, the ground had been trampled flat under generations of trogfeet. Above, the lofty ceiling towered far over his head. Spanning the two, like knobbly pillars, were long thick gnarled roots.

It's like a mirror-image of the Deepwoods themselves, he thought. But the Deepwoods of winter, when the trees are stripped and bare.

Bathed in the cavern's glow, the roots were gaunt and twisted and . . . Twig gasped. He'd been wrong. The light wasn't shining *on* the tree roots, but *from* them.

'Twig!' barked Mag sternly, as he ran for a closer look.

White, yellow, mushroom-brown; at least half of the long thick roots were giving out a softly pulsing glow. Twig placed his hand against one. It was warm, and throbbed faintly.

'TWIG!' Mag screeched. 'HEEL!'

Twig looked round. Mag was glaring menacingly. Obedient and dumb, Twig remembered. He trotted over and stood by her side.

Mag patted him on the head. 'Interested in the roots, are you?' she said. 'They provide us with all we need.'

Twig nodded, but remained silent.

'Light, of course,' said Mag, pointing to the roots that glowed. 'Food,' and she broke off two nodules from some fibrous roots. One she popped into her mouth. The other she handed to Twig, who stared at it unenthusiastically. 'Eat!' said Mag insistently. 'Go on!' And when Twig still refused to put it in his mouth, she added sweetly, 'I'll tell Mumsie.'

The nodule was crunchy and juicy. It tasted of toasted nuts. 'Mmm-mmm,' Twig mumbled and licked his lips theatrically.

Mag smiled and moved on. 'These we dry and grind for flour,' she explained. 'These we pulp and turn into paper. These burn well. And this . . .' she began, stopping next to a bulbous flesh-coloured root. 'Strange,' she said, and frowned. 'I didn't know these grew wild.' She turned to Twig and looked him up and down. 'Twig,' she said sternly. 'You must never, *ever* eat this type of root.'

A little further on, they came to a place where most of the vertical roots had been cut, to form a clearing around a deep lake of dark water. Those roots which remained fanned out near the ground, domed and serpentine. In amongst them, was a collection of huge capsules, each one separate from, but connected to, its neighbour. Rounded, buff-coloured and with small dark circular entrances, the capsules formed a mound up to five storeys high in places.

'The trogcombs are where we live,' said Mag. 'Follow me.'

Twig smiled to himself. Mag hadn't grabbed him by the hair. She was beginning to trust him.

The capsules, Twig discovered, were made of a thick papery substance, like Mumsie's dress, only thicker. It cracked under his feet as Twig stumbled up the interconnecting walkways, and echoed hollowly when he tapped on the round walls.

'Don't do that!' said Mag sharply. 'It annoys the neighbours.'

Mag's capsule was situated to the top left of the mound and was considerably larger inside than it looked from the outside. The light from the roots glowed creamily through the walls. Twig sniffed. There was a hint of cinnamon in the air.

'You must be tired,' Mag announced. 'Your place is over there,' she said, pointing to a basket. 'Mumsie doesn't like pets sleeping on my bed.' She grinned mischievously. 'But I do! Come on, up you jump,' she said, patting the end of the bed. 'I won't tell her if you don't,' she said and burst out laughing.

Twig did as he was told. Forbidden it might have been, but the thick papery mattress was soft and warm. Twig fell instantly into a deep and dreamless sleep.

Some hours later – day and night had no meaning in the constant glow of the trog dwellings – Twig woke to the feel of someone patting his head. He opened his eyes.

'Sleep well?' said Mag brightly.

Twig grunted.

'Good,' she said, jumping out of bed, 'coz we've got loads to do. We'll do a spot of nodule collecting and root-milk tapping for breakfast. Then, after we've cleaned up, Mumsie wants us to help with some paper making. So many of us girls have been turning termagant recently, they're running out of dress material.

'And then if you're good,' Mag continued without taking a breath, 'we'll go walkies. But first of all,' she said, fiddling with his hair and running her fingers gently over his cheek. 'First of all, Twig darling, I'm going to make you look beautiful.'

Twig groaned, and watched miserably as Mag busied herself in a small cupboard. A moment later she was back, carrying a trayful of bits and pieces. 'There,' she said, placing it on the floor. 'Now come and sit in front of me.'

Reluctantly, Twig did as he was told.

Mag took a soft grey lump of spongy rootfibre and washed him with water she'd fetched from the lake earlier, and perfumed with roseroot. Next, she patted him dry and drenched him in a dark, spicy powder. When Twig sneezed, Mag wiped his running nose for him with a handkerchief.

It's the indignity of it all! Twig thought, as he turned his head angrily away.

'Now, now!' Mag chided him. 'We wouldn't want Mumsie to hear that you've been a naughty pet, would we?'

Twig fell still, and remained so as Mag picked up a wooden comb, and began to tease the tangles from his matted hair.

'You've got nice hair, Twig,' she said. 'Thick and black . . .' She tugged vigorously at a stubborn knot. 'But *very* tangled! Why under Earth did you let it get into this state?' She tugged again.

Twig winced. His eyes watered, and he bit into his lower lip until the blood came. But he didn't make a sound.

'*I* brush my hair twice a day,' said Mag, throwing back her bright orange mane with a toss of her head. She got closer to Twig. 'Soon,' she whispered, 'it will fall out. Every single hair. And then I, too, will turn termagant. Just like Mumsie.'

Twig nodded sympathetically.

'I can't wait!' Mag exclaimed, to his surprise. 'A termagant. Can you imagine, my little Twig, darling?' She lay the comb down. 'No,' she said, 'of course you can't. But then that's because you're a male. And males—'

She stopped to uncork a small bottle, and poured some thick yellow liquid into the palm of her hand. It was sweet, yet pungent, and as she rubbed it into Twig's hair his scalp tingled and his eyes began to smart.

'— can't be termagants.' She paused again. Then, selecting a small bunch of hair from the rest, she split it into three thin locks, and began to plait it. 'Mumsie says it's all because of the root. The Mother Bloodoak,' she said reverently.

Twig shuddered at the very mention of the bloodthirsty, flesh-hungry, tree, which had so nearly taken his own life. He stroked his hammelhornskin waistcoat gratefully.

'It's that pinky root we saw on our way here, Twig,' she went on as she threaded beads onto the finished braid. 'Do you remember? The one I told you never to eat. It's poisonous for males, you see? Deadly poisonous,' she said in a hushed whisper. 'Though not for us females,' she added.

Twig heard her chuckle as she separated a second bunch of hair.

'It's the rootsap that makes Mumsie and all the others so big and strong. "When the Mother Bloodoak courses red, the termagants shall all be fed." That's how the saying goes.'

Twig flinched. 'When the Mother Bloodoak courses red . . .' That was something he knew all about. His stomach churned queasily as Mag continued to braid and bead his hair.

'Ooh, you are beginning to look pretty, Twig,' said Mag. Twig grimaced. 'Of course,' she went on thoughtfully, 'the trog males aren't happy with the situation. Horrible, scrawny, sneaky, weedy, weasely individuals that they are,' she said, screwing up her nose in disgust. She sighed. 'Still, they have their uses. After all, *someone* has to cook and clean!'

Thank Sky I'm just a pet, thought Twig.

'They tried to sabotage everything once,' she went on. 'Before I was born. Apparently, all the males got together and tried to burn the Mother Bloodoak down. The termagants were furious. Beat them black and blue, they did. They haven't tried anything since!' she added, and laughed unpleasantly. 'Useless bunch of wasters!'

Twig felt three more beads being knotted into place.

'Anyway,' said Mag more quietly, 'these days the main roots are well guarded . . .' Her voice trailed away. 'There!' she announced. 'Turn round and let me look at you.'

Twig did so.

'Perfect!' she said. 'Come on, Twig, darling. Let's go and see about that breakfast.'

Time passed, as time does, though in the unchanging trog cavern it was difficult to tell how much. Certainly Mag seemed to be forever clipping the nails on his fingers and toes. And the last time she had groomed his hair she commented more than once on how long it had grown.

Pampered and petted by Mag and the other trog females, Twig's life with the termagants was pleasant enough. Yet he found the subterranean world oppressive. He missed fresh air and the bite of the wind. He missed sunrise and sunset. He missed the smell of rain, the sound of birdsong, the colour of the sky. Most of all, he missed the banderbear.

The curious thing about living underground – *beneath* the Deepwoods, with its terrors and dangers – was that it gave Twig time to think. With the banderbear, there had been no need to think at all. There was always food to be foraged; there were always sleeping places to be found. Now, with everything on hand, Twig had nothing to do *but* think.

When he had first arrived, Mag seldom let Twig out of her sight. Lately, however, the novelty of having a new pet seemed to have worn off. Mag had fitted him with a collar and taken to tethering him to her bed whenever she went out without him.

The rope was long enough for Twig to go anywhere he wanted within the papery capsule, and even allowed him to get half-way down the stairs outside. But each time he reached the end of the rope, and the collar tightened around his neck, Twig was reminded that he was a prisoner, and his heart longed to return to the Deepwoods above.

Perhaps he would finally find the path and return home to his family. Spelda would be overjoyed at her son returning from the Deepwoods. Even Tuntum might smile, clap him on the back and invite him on a tree-felling trip. Everything would be different. He'd fit in this time, try harder, he'd do what woodtrolls do, think woodtroll thoughts, and he'd never, *never*, stray from the path again.

The collar chafed his neck. Then again, he thought, wouldn't he be just as much a prisoner if he did go back? Forever trying to be like a woodtroll but never quite belonging.

He thought of the caterbird. What *had* become of it? 'So much for watching over me,' he muttered bitterly. *Your destiny lies beyond the Deepwoods*, it had told him. Twig snorted. 'Beyond!' he said. 'Beneath more like, with my destiny to remain the pampered pet of a spoilt child. Oh, Gloamglozer!' he cursed.

There was a rustling outside the trogcomb. Twig froze. I must stop talking to myself, he thought. One of these days, I'll be found out.

The next moment, Mag came bursting into the capsule. She had a folded length of brown paper over one arm. 'I've been told to prepare myself,' she announced excitedly.

She lay the paper out on the floor and began drawing. Twig nodded towards it and looked puzzled.

Mag smiled. 'Soon, Twig, darling,' she said. 'I will have this tattooed on my back.' Twig looked down at the picture with more interest. It was of a massive muscular termagant; legs apart, hands on hips, and with a ferocious expression on the face. 'We all do,' she explained.

Twig smiled weakly. He pointed to the picture, then at Mag herself and back at the picture.

'Yes,' said Mag. 'It's me. Or will be.'

Twig pointed to himself and cocked his head to one side.

'Oh, Twig,' she whispered gently. 'I'll *always* love you.'

Twig sat back, reassured. At that moment, however, there came from outside the sound of heavy footfalls. Twig's feeling of well-being dissolved and he began chewing the corner of his scarf. It was Mumsie.

'Mag?' she screeched. 'MAG!'

Mag looked up. 'I'm in here,' she called back, and the entrance was filled with the towering figure of Mumsie herself.

'You're to come with me,' she said to Mag. 'Now.'

'Is it time?' Mag asked eagerly.

'It's time,' came the gruff reply.

Mag leaped off the bed. 'Did you hear that, Twig? It's time! Come on.'

'You'll not need no pet where you're going,' said Mumsie.

'Oh, Mumsie, plee-ease!' Mag wheedled.

'I'm telling you, you won't want it there. Not after.'

'I will!' said Mag defiantly.

Twig looked from one to the other. Mumsie was scowling. Mag was smiling.

'You *would* like to come, wouldn't you?' she said.

Twig smiled back. Anything was better than more time spent tethered to the bed. He nodded his head vigorously up and down.

'You see,' said Mag triumphantly. 'I told you.'

Mumsie snorted. 'You credit that animal with far too much sense . . .'

'Please, Mumsie. Please!' Mag pleaded.

'Oh, if you must,' said Mumsie wearily, as she gathered up the painted paper. 'But you're to keep it on its lead.' She rounded on Twig and fixed him with her bloodshot glare. 'And woe betide you if you do anything – ANYTHING AT ALL – to spoil my Mag's big day!'

There was an air of expectation outside. The paths leading round the lake were thick with female trogs all heading in the same direction. Some were neighbours who Twig recognized. Some were strangers to him. 'See how far they've come,' said Mag delightedly.

On the far side of the lake, they came to a high fence which formed a vast circular enclosure. Clusters of the thin listless males hung round the guarded entrance. They cringed and whimpered as Mumsie cut a swathe through them.

'Stay close, Twig,' Mag snapped, and yanked at the lead.

Together, the three of them entered the enclosure. As they appeared, a roar of approval went up from the crowd assembled inside. Mag hung her head and smiled shyly.

Twig was greeted by a sight that he could scarcely believe was real. Extending down from far above his head was an enormous set of roots which fanned out near the ground to form an immense and lofty dome. Hand in hand around it stood the termagants, their tattooed skin bathed in the root's fleshy pink light.

Mumsie took hold of Mag's hand. 'Come,' she said.

''Ere!' said one of the guards. 'That creature can't enter the Inner Sanctuary.'

Mumsie noticed the lead still wound around Mag's other hand. 'Course it can't,' she said. She snatched the lead away and tied one end firmly to a twist of root. 'You can get it later,' she said, and chuckled throatily.

This time Mag made no move to stop her. As if in a trance, she stepped through the break in the circle of hands and on into the dome of roots itself. She didn't look back.

Twig peered through the gaps in the roots. At the very centre was the taproot. Thick and knobbly, it glowed brighter than all the rest. Mag – his little Mag – was standing with her back to it. Her eyes were closed. Suddenly the termagants began to chant.

'Oh! Ma-Ma Mother Bloodoak!
Oh! Ma-Ma Mother Bloodoak!'

Over and over, louder and louder, they cried, until the entire cavern quaked with the deafening noise. Twig clamped his hands over his ears. In front of the taproot Mag had begun to squirm and writhe.

All at once, the cacophony came to an end. The silence trembled uncertainly. Twig watched as Mag turned to face the root. She raised her arms. She looked upwards.

'BLEED FOR ME!' she cried.

Before her voice had faded away, a sudden change came over the dome. The termagants gasped. Twig jumped away fearfully as the root he was tethered to abruptly changed colour. He looked round. The whole vast network of roots was glowing a deep and bloody crimson.

'Yes!' cried Mumsie, 'the time is indeed upon our daughter, Mag.'

She pulled a small object from the folds of her paper dress. Twig squinted to see. It looked like the tap from a barrel. She placed it against the pulsing red central root and hammered it home with her fist. Then, smiling at Mag, she pointed to the floor.

Mag knelt before the spout, raised her head and opened wide her mouth. Mumsie turned the spigot and a stream of frothing red liquid immediately gushed out. It splashed over her head and streamed down her back, her arms, her legs. Twig saw Mag's shoulders rising and falling in the crimson light.

'She's drinking it!' he shuddered.

Mag drank and drank and drank; she drank so much that Twig thought she must burst. Finally, she sighed a deep sigh and let her head fall forward. Mumsie switched off the flow of liquid. Mag climbed unsteadily to her feet. Twig gasped. The thin pale-skinned girl was beginning to expand.

Upwards, outwards, her whole body was growing larger. The flimsy dress she had been wearing split and fell to the ground – and still she grew. Massive shoulders, bulging biceps, tree-trunk legs . . . And her head! It was already immense when, suddenly, the hair – that wild shock of orange – cascaded down to the ground. The transformation was complete.

'Welcome!' said Mumsie, wrapping the freshly painted dress around the newest termagant in the trog-cavern.

'Welcome!' cried the circle of her termagant sisters.

Mag turned slowly round in acknowledgement. Twig recoiled with fear. Where was the pale thin girl who had loved him and looked after him? Gone. In her place was a fearsome and terrible termagant trog. Once tattooed, she would look exactly like her mother, Mumsie.

Mag continued to look around. Their eyes met. She smiled. Twig smiled back. Perhaps she hadn't changed – inside, at least. A thick slobbering tongue, like a slab of liver, emerged from Mag's mouth and slurped over her corrugated lips. Her bloodshot eyes glinted.

'YOU LITTLE PIECE OF VERMIN!' she bellowed.

Twig looked over his shoulders in horror. Surely she couldn't be addressing him. Not her pet. Not her 'Twig, darling'. 'Mag!' he cried out. 'Mag, it's me!'

'Aaaargh!' screamed Mumsie. 'I *knew* he was a talker.'

'Yes,' said Mag coldly. 'But not for much longer.'

Twig felt the earth shaking as she pounded towards him. With trembling fingers he tugged at the knot. In vain. Mumsie had tied it far too tight. Twig gripped hold of the rope, placed both feet up against the root and

pressed back as hard as he possibly could. Nothing happened.

'Don't even think of escaping!' Mag roared.

Twig shifted his grip and tried again. There was a crack, and he flew back through the air. The rope had held – but not the root. A frothing red substance oozed from where it had severed.

'Whoooooaaahhh!' Mag raged.

Twig turned on his heels and ran. He darted between two of the guards and sprinted down towards the lake. The trog males stood around gawping.

'Move!' Twig yelled as he elbowed them out of the way.

He could hear Mag behind him, followed closely by the rest of the termagants. 'Rip out his gizzards!' they were screeching. 'Tear off his legs! Smash him to smithereens!'

Twig reached the lake. He sped away to the left. A group of half a dozen trog males were standing in front of him.

'STOP HIM!' Mag ordered loudly. 'CATCH THE LITTLE BEAST!'

Then, louder still, when they simply stepped aside as Twig thundered past: 'YOU PATHETIC LITTLE MORONS!'

Twig glanced back over his shoulder. Mag was gaining on him. There was a look of terrible determination in her bloodshot eyes. Oh, Mag, he thought. What have you become?

Mag drew level with the trog males. They were watching her askance; all, that is, apart from one. As Mag lumbered past him, he stuck out his leg. It caught Mag's foot. She stumbled. She lurched. She lost her balance and

came crashing to the ground.

Twig gasped with surprise. It had been no accident.

Mag sprawled round and made a grab for the trog male, but he was too agile for her. He leaped to his feet, limped out of reach and looked up. Cupping his hands to his mouth, he called to Twig.

'What are you waiting for? Head for the roots where they shine brightest. Over in that direction.' There was a wheedling, mocking tone to his voice.

Twig looked round.

'Well?' the trog male gave a twisted smile. 'Do you want to be skinned alive by your little mistress? Follow the wind, pampered pet – and don't look back.'

.CHAPTER ELEVEN.

GARBLE, GABTROLL AND HEARTCHARMING

Twig did exactly as instructed. He ran headlong across the trog-cavern towards a distant point where the lights from the roots glowed brightest and not once did he look back. He could hear the furious termagants behind him, panting, pounding; sometimes catching up, sometimes falling behind.

As he neared the patch of brightness, it revealed itself to be a densely packed cluster of gleaming white roots. Which way now? His scalp tingled, his heart throbbed. There were half a dozen tunnels in front of him. Which one – if any – would lead him outside?

'He's lost!' he heard one of the termagants bellowing.

'Head him off,' instructed another.

'Then, off with his head!' roared yet another, and they all screeched with hideous laughter.

Twig was desperate. He would have to escape down

one of the tunnels but what if the one he chose was a dead end? And all the while he was trying to decide which one to take, the termagants were trundling closer. Any second they would bear down upon him. Then it would be too late.

Twig shuddered with fear and exhaustion. As he hurried past the entrance to one tunnel, a cold draught of air turned his sweating skin to gooseflesh. Of course! *Follow the wind*: the trog male's words. Without a second thought, Twig dashed down into the airy tunnel.

Wide at first, the opening soon grew both narrower and lower. Twig didn't mind. The more he had to stoop, the less likely it was that the huge termagants would be able to follow. He heard them, grunting and groaning and cursing their misfortune. All at once the tunnel turned a corner and came to an abrupt halt.

'Oh, what?' Twig groaned. It was a *real* dead end. He stared in horror at a pile of bleached bones which lay half covered by sand and shale. There was a skull, and the beaded remnants of plaited hair; a twist of rope was looped around the crumbling neck. It was a pet that had not managed to escape.

Just ahead of him, a single root extended down into the tunnel. Twig reached out his hand. It felt as dead as everything else; cold, stiff, and not shining. So where was the light coming from? He looked up, and there, far far above his head, was a small circle of silvery brilliance.

'He's found one of the air shafts,' came the furious voice of one of the termagants.

Twig pulled himself up into the branch-like growths of the root. 'Indeed I have,' he muttered.

Hand over foot over foot over hand he went, climbing towards the light. Arms aching and fingers trembling, he looked up again. The light seemed no nearer. A wave of alarm coursed through his body. What if the hole at the top wasn't large enough for him to climb through?

Foot over hand over hand over foot, higher and higher he continued, his breathing loud and rhythmical. Ooh. Aah. Ooh! Aah! At last, the circle of light did start to look bigger. Hurrying up the last few feet of root as quickly as he dared – it was a long way back down to the bones at the bottom of the shaft – Twig stretched his arm out into the warm sunlight.

'Thank Sky it's daytime,' he sighed. He heaved himself out onto the grass and rolled over. 'Otherwise I'd have never found my way ou . . .' Twig fell silent. He was not alone. The air was alive with panting, with snarling, with the juicy odour of decay. Slowly, he lifted his head.

Lolling tongues and flared black nostrils. Ice-pick teeth, bared, glinting, slavering. Yellow eyes, staring impassive – sizing him up.

'W . . . w . . . woodwolves,' he stammered.

The ruff of snow-white fur around their necks bristled at the sound of his voice. Twig swallowed. They were *whitecollar* woodwolves: the worst kind – and here was a whole pack of them. Twig inched back towards the air shaft. Too late. The woodwolves, noticing the movement, let out a low bloodcurdling growl. With open jaws and dripping fangs, the one nearest him leaped up from the ground and launched itself at his throat.

'Aaaargh!' Twig screamed. The outstretched paws of the beast thumped into his chest. The pair of them toppled backwards and landed heavily on the ground.

Twig kept his eyes shut tight. He could smell the warm rotten breath on his face as the wood-wolf sniffed and tasted. He felt a row of pinpricks along the side of his neck. The woodwolf had him in its jaws. One movement – from either of them – and that would be that.

Just then, above the deafening pounding of his heart, Twig heard a voice. 'What's going on here, then?' it said. 'What have you found, eh, lads? Something for the pot?'

The woodwolves snarled greedily, and Twig felt the teeth pressing down sharply into his skin.

'Drop it!' the voice commanded. 'Stealth! Drop it, I say!'

The teeth withdrew. The stench receded. Twig opened his eyes. A short elf-like creature clutching a heavy whip, was standing there and glaring at him. 'Friend or food?' he demanded.

'F . . . f . . . friend,' Twig stuttered.

'Get up, friend,' he said. The woodwolves twitched as Twig climbed to his feet. 'They won't hurt you,' he said, seeing Twig's discomfort. 'So long as I don't tell them to,' he smirked.

'You wouldn't do that,' said Twig. 'W . . . would you?'

'All depends,' came the reply. The woodwolves began pacing to and fro, licking their lips and yelping excitedly. 'We small people have to stay on our guard. Stranger equals danger, that's my motto. You can't be too careful in the Deepwoods.' He looked Twig up and down. 'Mind you,' he said, '*you* don't look too much of a threat.' He wiped his hand vigorously on his trousers and thrust it forward. 'The name's Garble,' he said. 'Garble the Hunter, and this here is my pack.' One of the woodwolves snarled. Garble gave it a vicious kick.

Twig reached out and shook the hand being offered him. All round them, the woodwolves were whipping themselves up into a slavering frenzy. Garble stopped in mid-shake, pulled his hand away and inspected it.

'Blood,' he said. 'No wonder the lads found you. The smell of it drives them proper crazy, it does.' He crouched down and carefully wiped his hand on the grass until all trace of the blood had disappeared. He looked up. 'So what exactly are you?' he said.

'I'm . . .' Twig began, and then stopped. He wasn't a woodtroll. But then, what was he? 'I'm Twig,' he said simply.

'A twig? Never heard of 'em. You look a bit like a lop-ear or even a blunderhead. Even *I* find it difficult to tell them apart. Fetch a good price though, they do. The sky pirates are always after goblins from the wilder tribes. They make good fighters even if they are a bit difficult to control . . . Are the twigs good fighters?'

Twig shifted uneasily from foot to foot. 'Not really,' he said.

Garble sniffed. 'Wouldn't get much for you, anyway,' he said. 'Scrawny little specimen that you are. Still, you might make a ship's cook. Can you cook?'

'Not really,' Twig said again. He was inspecting his hand. There was a cut on his little finger, but it didn't look too bad.

'Just my luck,' said Garble. 'I was on the trail of a big lumpskull – would have made me a pretty penny, I can tell you – and what happens? He goes running straight into the jaws of a bloodoak and that's the end of him. Terrible mess. And then the boys pick up your scent. Hardly worth the bother,' he added, and spat on the ground.

It was then that Twig noticed what Garble the Hunter was wearing. The dark fur was unmistakeable. How many times had he stroked fur exactly like it: sleek, smooth and tinged with green.

'Banderbear,' Twig breathed, his blood beginning to boil. This obnoxious little elf was wearing the pelt of a banderbear.

Garble was shorter than Twig, considerably shorter. In a straight fight, Twig was sure he could overpower him easily. But, as the circle of yellow eyes stared at him unblinking, Twig had to swallow his indignation.

'Can't stand around all day, chatting,' Garble went on. 'I've got some serious hunting to be getting on with. Don't have time to waste on wolf-bait like you. I'd get that hand seen to, if I was you. Might not be so lucky next time. Come on, boys.'

And, with the yelping pack all round him, Garble

turned and disappeared into the trees.

Twig sank to his knees. He was back in the Deepwoods, but this time there was no banderbear to protect him. No sweet, lonely banderbear, just wolves and hunters and lumpskulls and blunderheads and . . .

'Why?' he wailed. 'Why all this? WHY?'

'Because,' came a voice – a voice that sounded gentle and kind.

Twig looked up and started with horror. The creature that had spoken looked neither gentle nor kind. In fact, she was monstrous.

'So what brings you . . . SLURP . . . to this part of the . . . SLURP . . . Deepwoods?' she said.

Twig kept his head down. 'I'm lost,' he said.

'Lost? Nonsense . . . SLURP . . . You're here!' she laughed.

Twig swallowed nervously. He raised his head.

'That's better . . . SLURP . . . Now why don't you tell me all about it, m'dear. Gabtrolls is very good . . . SLURP . . . listeners,' and she flapped her huge bat-like ears.

The yellow light of late afternoon glowed through the pink membrane of her ears, picking out the delicate network of blood vessels. It glistened on her greasy face and glinted on the eye-stalks. It was these – long, thick, rubbery, swaying; now contracting, now elongating, and both topped off with bulbous green spheres – which had so startled Twig. His stomach still felt queasy, yet he couldn't look away.

'Well?' the gabtroll said.

'I . . .' Twig began.

'SLURP!'

Twig shuddered. Each time the long yellow tongue flipped out to lick and moisten one or other of the unblinking green eyes, he forgot what he was going to say. The eye-stalks extended towards him. The eyeballs stared at both sides of his face at the same time. 'What you need, m'dear,' said the gabtroll finally, 'is a nice cup of . . . SLURP . . . oakapple tea. While we're waiting.'

As they walked side by side in the fading orange light, the gabtroll talked. And talked and talked and talked. And as she went on, in her soft lilting voice, Twig no longer noticed her ears or her eyes or even that long slurping tongue. 'I ain't never fitted in, you understand,' she was explaining.

Twig understood only too well.

'Course, gabtrolls have been purveyors of fruit and vegetables for generations,' she went on. 'Growing produce and selling it at the various market-clearings. Yet I knew . . .' She paused. 'I said to myself, Gabba, I said, you just b'ain't cut out for a life of hoeing and haggling. And that's a fact.'

They emerged in a glade bathed in the deep red glow of the setting sun. The light gleamed on something round and metallic. Twig squinted into the shadows. A small covered wagon was standing beneath the hanging fronds of a sallowdrop tree. The gabtroll waddled towards it. Twig watched as she unhooked a lantern and set it swinging from a branch.

'Throw a little light on the matter,' she chuckled, and proceeded to pull the wagon out from its hiding place.

Twig looked it over. For a moment, it seemed to disappear. He shook his head. It returned again.

'Clever, eh?' said the gabtroll. 'I spent ages mixing the paints.'

Twig nodded. From the wheels beneath the wooden frame to the animal skin which had been stretched over hoops to make a waterproof covering, every inch of the wagon had been daubed with various shades of green and brown. It was perfectly camouflaged for the forest. Twig's eyes focused on some writing on the side: curious curling letters that looked like twisted leaves.

'Yes, that's me,' said the gabtroll, with a lick of her eyeballs. '"Gabmora Gabtroll. Apothecaress and Wise One". Now let's see about that tea, shall we?'

She bustled up the wooden steps and disappeared inside the wagon. Twig watched her from the outside as she placed a kettle on the stove, and spooned some orange flakes into a pot.

'I'd ask you in . . .' she said, looking up. 'But, well . . .' She flapped her hand round at the chaos within the wagon.

There were stoppered jars and bottles swilling with amber liquid and the innards of small beasts, there were boxes and crates full of seeds and leaves, and sackfuls of nuts spilling onto the floor. There were tweezers and scalpels, and chunks of crystal, and a pair of scales, and sheaves of paper, and rolls of bark. Herbs and dried flowers hung in bunches from hooks, alongside strings of desiccated slugs, and a selection of dead animals: woodrats, oakvoles, weezits, all swaying gently as the gabtroll busied herself with the tea.

Twig waited patiently. The moon rose, and promptly vanished behind a bank of black cloud. The lamplight glowed brighter than ever. Beside a stubby log Twig noticed a heart shape had been scratched into the dirt. A stick lay across it.

'Here we are, m'dear,' said the gabtroll as she emerged, a steaming mug in each hand and a tin under her arm. She set everything down on the log. 'Help yourself to a seedrusk,' she said. 'I'll just get us something to park our behinds on.'

She unhooked two more of the logs from the underside of the wagon. Like everything else, they were so well camouflaged that Twig hadn't noticed them. She plonked herself down.

'But enough of me,' she said. 'I could go on for ever about my life in the Deepwoods, travelling from here to there, constantly on the move, mixing my potions and poultices and helping out wherever I can . . . How's the tea?'

Twig sipped and prepared to wince. 'It's . . . lovely,' he said, surprised.

'Oakapple peel,' she said. 'Good for the nails, good for the heart, and excellent for . . .' She coughed, and her eyes went in and out on their stalks. 'For keeping you *regular,* if you take my meaning. And taken with honey – as this is – it's an unbeatable cure for vertigo.' She leaned towards Twig and lowered her voice. 'Far be it for me to boast,' she said, 'but I know much more than most about the things which live and grow in the forest.'

Twig said nothing. He was thinking about the banderbear.

'I understand their *properties,*' she added, and sighed. 'For my pains.' She sipped her tea. Her eye-stalks looked round. One of them focused in on the stick lying across the heart shape. Take this for instance. What do you think it is?'

'A stick?'

'It's a heartcharmer,' she said. 'It shows me the path I have to follow.' She peered round into the forest. 'We still have time . . . Let me give you a little demonstration.'

She stood the stick in the centre of the heart with one finger holding it upright. She closed her eyes, whispered 'Heart lead me where you will', and lifted her finger. The stick dropped.

'But it's landed in exactly the same position as before,' said Twig.

'Naturally,' said the gabtroll. 'For that is the way my destiny leads.'

Twig jumped to his feet. He seized the stick. 'Can I have a go?' he said excitedly.

The gabtroll shook her head, and her eyes swung dole-

fully to and fro. 'You must find your own stick . . .'

Twig darted off towards the trees. The first one he came to was too high; the second too tough. The third was perfect. He climbed up and broke off a small branch, stripped the leaves and bark until it looked just right, and jumped down again.

'Aaaargh!' he screamed, as something – some ferocious, slavering black beast – seized him, slammed him to the ground and pinned him down. The silhouette of its massive shoulders flickered in the lamp-light. Its yellow eyes glinted. Its jaws opened and . . .

It yowled with pain.

'Karg!' the gabtroll screamed, as she brought the stick down on the beast's nose for a second time. 'How many times have I got to tell you? Only carrion! Now take your food and get to the wagon this instant. And hurry up about it. You're late!'

Reluctantly, the beast released Twig's shoulders. It turned, sunk its teeth into the corpse of a tilder lying next to the tree, and dragged it obediently back towards the glade.

The gabtroll helped Twig to his feet. 'Nothing damaged,' she said, looking him over. She nodded towards his attacker. 'A much underrated beast, the prowlgrin. Loyal – generally. Intelligent – very. And stronger than any ox. What's more, as its owner, you don't have to worry about food. It takes care of itself. If I could just get it to stick to animals that have already died.' Her eyes bounced about as she laughed. 'Can't have it eating my customers. Bad for business!'

Back at the clearing, the prowlgrin was crouched down between the shafts of the wagon, tearing into the remains of the dead tilder. The gabtroll slipped a harness over its head, tied a girth around its middle and fastened the straps.

Twig stood to one side, watching, stick in hand. 'You're not going, are you?' he said, as she slung the logs and tea things into the back of the wagon. 'I thought . . .'

'I was just waiting for Karg to get himself fed and watered,' she explained, climbing up into the front seat. She took up the reins. 'Now, I'm afraid . . . Places to go, people to heal . . .'

'But what about me?' said Twig.

'I *always* travel alone,' said the gabtroll firmly. She tugged on the reins and set off.

Twig watched the lamp swaying back and forth as the wagon clattered away. Before he was plunged once again into darkness, he stood his stick in the centre of the heart. His fingers trembled as he held it in place. He closed his eyes and whispered softly, 'Heart lead me where you will.' He lifted his finger. Opened his eyes. The stick was still standing.

He tried again. Finger on. 'Heart lead me . . .' Finger off. Still the stick did not fall.

'Hey!' Twig cried out. 'The stick's just standing there.' The gabtroll peered round the side of the wagon, her eye-stalks gleaming in the lamplight. 'Why won't it fall down?'

'Haven't a clue, m'dear,' she replied, and with that she was gone.

'Some wise one!' Twig muttered angrily, and kicked the stick far away into the undergrowth.

The flickering lamplight disappeared. Twig turned and stumbled off into the darkness in the opposite direction, cursing his luck. No-one stays. No-one cares. And it's all my fault. I should never, *ever* have strayed from the path.

.CHAPTER TWELVE.

THE SKY PIRATES

Far above Twig's head, the clouds thinned. They swirled and squirmed around the moon like a bucketful of maggots.

Twig stared upwards, spellbound, horrified: so much skybound activity while, down on the forest floor, it was all so still. Not a leaf stirred. The heavy air felt charged.

All at once, a flash of blue-white light splashed across the far reaches of the sky. Twig counted. When he got to eleven, a booming roll of thunder rumbled. Again the sky lit up, brighter than before; again the thunder sounded. This time Twig only counted to eight. The storm was getting closer.

He began to run. Slipping, stumbling, sometimes falling, he hurried across the treacherous forest floor – now bright as day, now black as pitch. A wind had got up, dry, electric. It tousled his hair and set the fleece of his hammelhornskin waistcoat bristling.

With his eyes full of the pinky after-dazzle of each lightning bolt, the darkness that followed was all the darker. Twig staggered on blindly. The wind gusted at his back. There was a crackle in the sky directly above his head and a jagged fork of absolute brilliance tore the sky apart. The thunder struck at once with a CR-R-R-R-R-R-R-ASH! The air trembled. The earth shook. Twig fell to the ground and wrapped his arms around his head. 'It's f . . . falling,' he stammered. 'The open sky is falling.'

A second eye-blinding ear-splitting mix of thunder and lightning battered the forest. Then a third. And a fourth. Yet all the time, that space between the two was growing. Twig climbed shakily to his feet. The forest, one moment brightly lit like a tribe of dancing skeletons, the next plunged into darkness, was still around him; the sky still above.

He climbed one of the trees, a tall and ancient lufwood to watch the storm receding. Up and up, he went. The swirling wind plucked at his hands and feet. At the top, he rested in a swaying fork, panting for breath. The air smelled of rain, but no rain fell. The lightning stabbed, the sky glowed, the thunder rumbled. Abruptly, the wind dropped.

Twig wiped his eyes and, with his fingers, combed away the last remaining beads and bows. He watched them bounce and flutter out of sight below him. He looked up, and there, just for a second, silhouetted against the lightning sky . . .

Twig's heart missed a beat. 'A sky ship,' he whispered.

The lightning faded. The ship disappeared. Another flash, and the sky lit up again.

'But now it's facing the other way,' Twig said. More lightning, and the sky grew brighter still. 'It's spinning,' he gasped. 'It's caught in a whirlwind.'

Round and round the sky ship went, faster and faster; so fast that even Twig felt dizzy. The mainsail flapped wildly; the rigging lashed the air. Powerless, out of control, the sky ship was being dragged towards the swirling vortex at the centre of the storm.

Suddenly, a single solitary finger of lightning zigzagged down out of the cloud. It hurtled towards the spinning sky ship – and struck. The ship rolled to one side. Something small and round and twinkling like a star fell away from the side, and tumbled down towards the forest below. The sky ship spiralled down after it.

Twig gasped. The sky ship was dropping out of the sky like a stone.

It went dark again. Twig chewed his hair, his scarf, his nails. It remained dark. 'One more flash,' Twig pleaded. 'Just so I can see what's . . .'

The flash came, illuminating a long stretch across the distant horizon. In the dim light, Twig saw three bat-like creatures hovering above the falling ship. And, as he watched, two . . . three more joined them, each one leaping from the decks and fluttering away on the ebbing

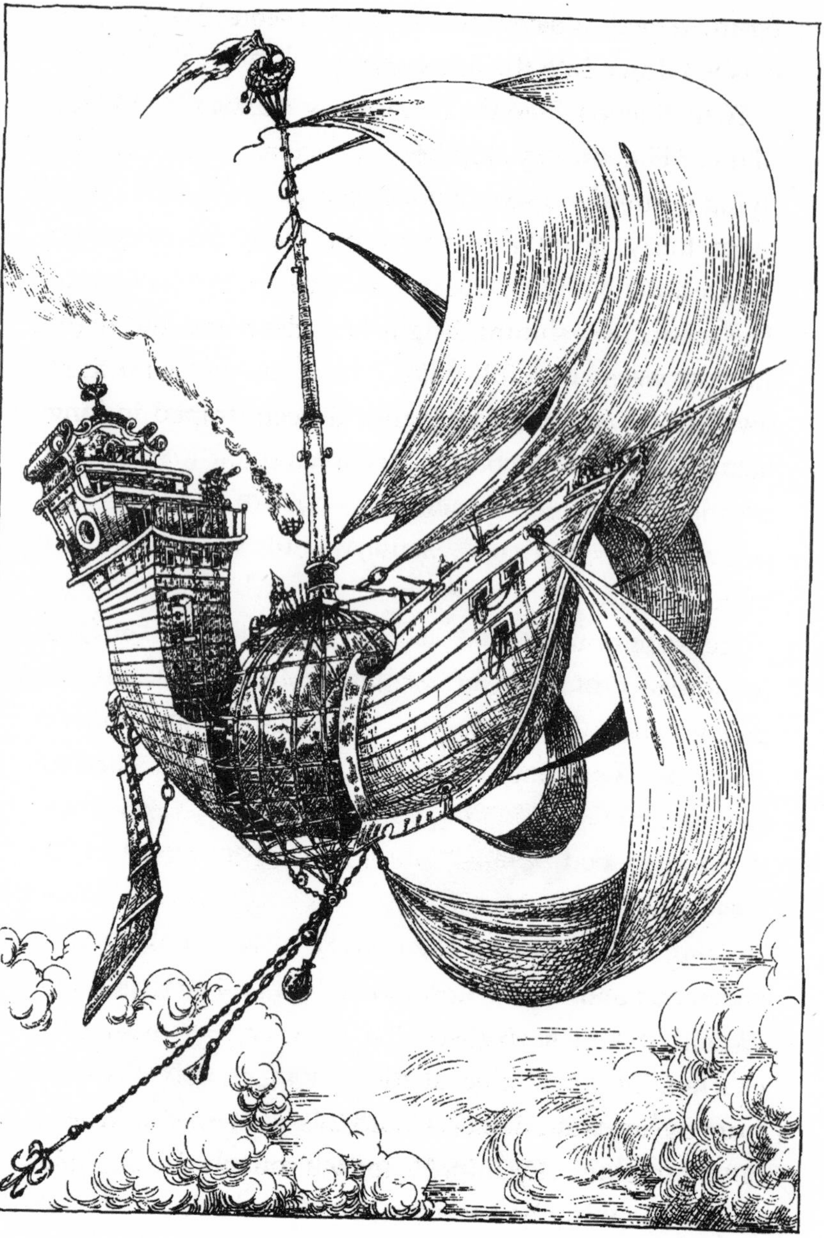

wind. The sky pirates were abandoning ship. An eighth figure leaped to safety just seconds before the sky ship crashed down into the forest canopy.

Twig flinched. Had the whole crew managed to escape in time? Had the sky ship been smashed to bits? Had the flying figures he'd seen landed safely?

He fairly flew back down the tree and raced off through the woods as fast as his legs would carry him. The moon was shining bright and clear, and the night animals were all in full voice. The trees, shot with their own shadows, looked as if they'd been draped in long nets. Apart from the occasional fallen branch, and whiff of smouldering greenwood, there was no sign that the storm had passed that way. Twig ran till he could run no more.

He stood doubled over, a stitch in his side, and gulped for breath. Moonbirds twittered loudly from their perches above his head. Then Twig heard another noise. A hissing. A spitting. He walked forwards. It seemed to be coming from a combbush just up ahead. He pushed the branches aside, and was immediately struck by a blast of intense heat.

Lying half-buried in the ground was a rock. It was enormous and round, and glowed white-hot. The grass around it had shrivelled, the overhanging bush was charred. Twig squinted at the rock, sheltering his eyes from the heat and dazzle. Could this be the *star* he'd seen falling from the sky ship. He looked round. The ship and its crew couldn't be far away.

The moonbirds were squawking irritably over something or other. Twig clapped his hands, and they flew off. Out of the silence that followed, Twig heard the low murmur of voices.

He crept forwards. The voices grew louder. He caught sight of a tall, heavy-set red-faced man with a thick knotted beard, and ducked down behind a fallen branch. It was a sky pirate.

'We'd best find the others,' he was saying, his voice deep and chewy. He chuckled. 'The look on Slyvo's face when he jumped. White as codflesh he was, and green at the gills.'

'He was up to something,' a reedy voice replied matter-of-factly. 'Up to no good.'

Twig stretched up to see who was speaking.

'You're not wrong there, Spiker,' said the bearded pirate gruffly. 'He's not been happy since that business with the ironwood. That 'lectric storm was a blessing in disguise, or my name's not Tem Barkwater.' He paused. 'I just hope the cap'n's all right.'

'Sky willing,' came the reply.

Twig stretched up again, but could still see only the one pirate. He stepped up onto the branch for a better look and – CRACK – the wood gave under his foot.

'What was that?' bellowed Tem Barkwater. He spun round and scoured the silvery shadows.

'Probably just an animal,' the second sky pirate said.

'I'm not so sure,' said Tem Barkwater slowly.

Twig cowered down. The whispering sound of tip-toe footsteps approached. Twig looked up. He found himself staring into the delicate yet broad face of someone little older than himself – an oakelf by the look of him. It must be Spiker.

The oakelf stared at Twig, a puzzled frown playing over his features. Finally, 'Do I know you?' he said.

'You find anything?' Tem Barkwater called.

Spiker continued to stare. His tufted ears twitched. 'Yes,' he said quietly.

'What's that?'

'I said *yes*!' he shouted back, and seized Twig by the shoulder. The hammelhornskin fleece turned at once to needles, and stabbed the oakelf's hand. He yelped, pulled away and sucked his fingers tenderly, all the while staring suspiciously at Twig. 'Follow me,' he instructed.

'What have we here, then?' said Tem Barkwater, as Spiker and Twig emerged before him. 'Lanky little so'n'so, ain't he?' he said, and squeezed Twig's upper arm with a bulging finger and thumb. 'Who are you, lad?'

'Twig, sir,' said Twig.

'Extra hand on board, eh?' he said, and winked at Spiker.

Twig felt a thrill of excitement shudder through his body.

'If there's still an "on board" left,' the oakelf commented.

'Course there is!' said Tem Barkwater. He laughed throatily. 'Just a matter of finding out where it's got to.'

Twig cleared his throat. 'I think it's over there,' he said, pointing to his right.

Tem Barkwater turned and stooped and pressed his large, red hairy face into Twig's. 'And how would you know that?'

'I . . . I saw it crash,' he said uncertainly.

'You *saw* it,' he bellowed.

'I was up a tree. Watching the storm. I saw the sky ship get trapped in the whirlwind.'

'You saw it,' Tem Barkwater repeated, more softly now. He clapped his hands together. 'Then you'd better lead us there, Twig, me-old-mucker.'

It was a mixture of luck and guesswork that got him there, but get there he did. They hadn't gone more than a hundred steps before Tem Barkwater spied the hull ahead of them, glinting in the moonlight high up in the branches. 'There she is,' he murmured. 'The *Stormchaser*, herself. Well done, lad,' he said to Twig, and slapped him heartily on the shoulder.

'Sssh!' hissed Spiker. 'We're not the first ones back.'

Tem cocked his head to one side. 'It's that rogue of a quartermaster, Slyvo Spleethe,' he muttered.

Spiker raised a finger to his lips, and the three of them stood stock-still, straining to hear the murmured conversation.

'It would seem, my dear Mugbutt, that our captain has over-reached himself,' Slyvo was saying. His voice was nasal and precise, with every *d* and *t* being spat out like something distasteful.

'Over-reached himself!' came a low gruff echo.

Tem Barkwater shifted about restlessly. His face grew thunderously dark. He craned his neck. 'The Stone Pilot's with them, too,' he whispered.

Twig stole a glance through a gap in the leaves. There were three pirates there. Mugbutt was a flat-head goblin. With his broad flat skull and wide ears, he was typical of his kind, yet fiercer by far than the flat-head who had helped Twig out of the swamp. Behind him stood a squat creature dressed in a heavy overcoat and heavier boots.

His head was hidden beneath a large pointed hood which extended down over his chest. Two round glass panels allowed him to see out. He did not speak. The third pirate was Slyvo Spleethe himself; a tall yet stooped figure, all angles and points. His nose was long, his chin sharp, and behind his steel-rimmed spectacles his shifty eyes were constantly on the move.

'I mean, far be it from me to say I told you so,' he continued, 'but . . . well . . . If we *had* left the ironwood, *as* I suggested . . . The price of the stuff is plummeting anyway at the moment.' There was a pause, and a sigh. 'If we *had* left it, we wouldn't have been anywhere near the storm.'

'Near the storm,' growled Mugbutt.

'Still. Who am *I* to argue with fate? If the command of the ship was destined to fall upon my shoulders, I must accept my responsibility with . . .' He searched for the right word.

Mugbutt filled the silence. 'Responsibility with . . .'

'Oh, do stop interrupting me!' Slyvo snapped. 'You are brave in battle, Mugbutt, don't get me wrong; a credit to your tribe. But you lack any sense of occasion.'

'Occasion,' Mugbutt repeated.

Slyvo grunted impatiently. 'Come,' he said. 'Let's break the glad tidings to the others.'

Tem could remain still no longer. 'Treacherous dog,' he growled as he burst through the undergrowth and into the clearing. The Stone Pilot, Mugbutt and Slyvo Spleethe all spun round.

'My *dear* Tem,' said Slyvo, his disappointment turning

instantly to a tight-lipped smile. 'And Spiker. You two made it too.'

Twig held back; watching, listening.

'*He* ought to be chained up,' said Tem, pointing at the flat-head goblin. 'Cap'n's orders.'

Slyvo lowered his head coyly and fiddled with one of the knots in his moustache. 'The thing is,' he whimpered, looking up over his glasses. 'As I was just saying to Mugbutt here, our illustrious captain, Quintinius Verginix, is . . .' He looked round theatrically. '*Not* here.' He smirked. 'And Mugbutt does *so* enjoy his freedom.'

Tem grunted. For the time being, at least, there was nothing he could do. 'What state is the ship in?' he asked.

Slyvo looked up. 'How's it going, Stope?' he called.

'OK,' came a voice, which squeaked as it spoke. 'Superficial damage, mainly. The rudder's taken a hammering. But nothing I can't fix.'

'Will she soon be sky-worthy?' said Slyvo impatiently.

A head poked out from the overhead foliage. A hard bullet-head it was, with a close-fitting metal frame over the skull which held a bolted jaw in place. 'She won't be sky-worthy till we get the flight-rock back in place,' he said.

Slyvo grimaced and stamped his feet sulkily. 'Can't you improvise? Lufwood, bloodoak – they rise. Just burn more . . .'

Stope Boltjaw tutted and shook his head. 'Can't do it,' he said. 'You could never contain a fire the size it would have to be to achieve the required lift, and besides . . .'

'There must be *something* you can do!' Slyvo screamed. 'I still don't understand why the blasted rock fell in the first place.'

'Coz it was struck by lightning,' said Stope Boltjaw.

'I know *that*, you idiot!' snapped Slyvo. 'But . . .'

'Cold rock rises, hot rock sinks,' Stope continued patiently. 'Scientific fact. And I'll tell you another scientific fact. What heats up, cools down. If you lot don't find that flight-rock before much longer, it'll have floated off for ever. And now, if you'll excuse me, I've got the cradle-moorings to repair – just in case you should find it.' His head disappeared back behind the leafy branches.

Slyvo bit into his lips. The blood drained from his face. 'You heard him,' he snarled. 'FIND THE FLIGHT-ROCK!'

Spiker and Mugbutt turned and hurried off. The Stone Pilot plodded after them. Tem Barkwater held his ground.

'Well?' Slyvo demanded.

'I might be able to tell you where the rock is. On one condition. When it's back in place, we wait for the cap'n.'

'Oh, but of *course*,' said Slyvo. 'I give you my *word*.' He reached out and shook Tem by the hand.

From his place in the undergrowth, Twig saw the

quartermaster's other arm swing round behind his back. The hand was missing two fingers, and the raw scars looked recent. The two remaining fingers were stiffly crossed.

Tem nodded. 'I aim to ensure that you keep your word,' he said. He turned away. 'Twig,' he called out. 'Are you there, lad? Come out where I can see you.'

Twig stood up and stepped forwards.

'A spy!' hissed Slyvo.

'A witness,' said Tem. 'To what you promised.' He turned to Twig. 'Do you know where the flight-rock landed?' he asked. Twig hesitated. He glanced up at Slyvo Spleethe. 'It's all right,' Tem assured him.

Twig nodded. 'I know, all right,' he admitted. 'I saw it. Like a shooting star it looked – well, a *dropping* star. A *falling* star . . .'

'Get on with it!' said Slyvo sharply.

Twig blushed. He was talking too much. But he couldn't help it. The whiff of adventure about the rough and rugged sky pirates quickened his heart and loosened his tongue. He turned away from Slyvo's intense gaze and started walking. 'It's this way,' he said.

'Hey, you lot,' Slyvo Spleethe called out to Spiker, Mugbutt and the Stone Pilot. 'Follow us.'

Twig led the ragtag rabble of pirates back through the forest. The way looked familiar in the swaying lamp-light. He first heard, and then saw the humming combbush. He marched up to it and parted the branches. The stone was still there, embedded in the ground. It glowed a deep buttery yellow.

'It was white before,' said Twig.

'It's cooling down,' said Tem. 'The trick will be to get it back to the sky ship while it's light enough to carry, but heavy enough not to fly away.'

Slyvo turned to the Stone Pilot. '*You* are responsible for transporting it,' he said.

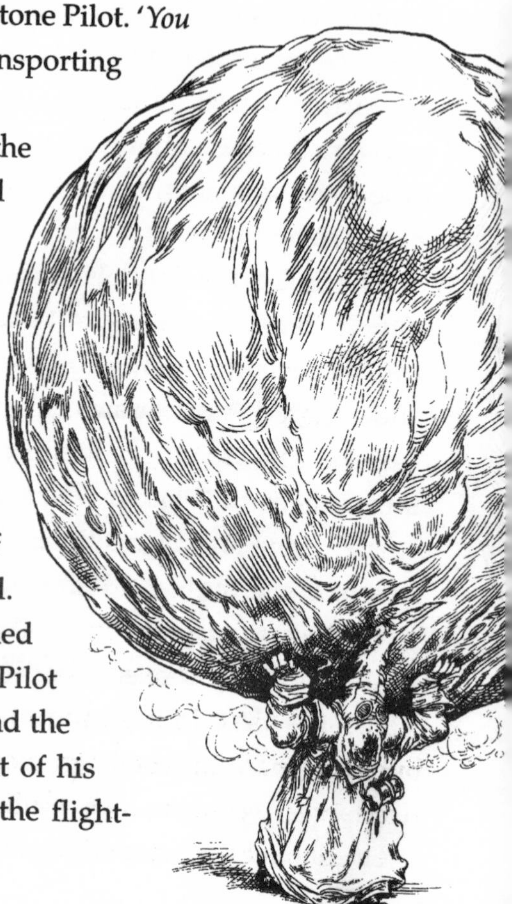

From deep within the Stone Pilot's pointed hood came a grunt of acknowledgement. He lumbered forwards, crouched down and embraced the rock in his broad arms. The sleeves and front of his fireproof coat hissed. Twig sniffed. The air smelt of scorched mud. The Stone Pilot heaved and strained, and the glass panels at the front of his hood misted over. But the flight-rock did not budge.

'Empty your water flasks onto it,' said Tem.

'Yes,' Slyvo said, remembering his new responsibilities. 'Empty your water flasks onto it.' He and the others began pouring water onto the glowing stone. Where it landed, the water hissed and turned the rock a shade of orange. 'More!' Slyvo commanded.

The sky pirates trotted off, returning soon after with their flasks refilled. Little by little, the rock turned a rich deep red. It began to wobble in its earthy setting. The Stone Pilot tried again. This time the rock came out of the ground with a soft *ssss-quap*.

Staggering under the weight and wheezing, the Stone Pilot trudged back to the clearing. The others tramped after him. Because of the intense heat radiating from the rock, there was nothing they could do to help, nothing but hope and pray.

The hull of the sky ship came into view. 'We've got it, Stope,' Tem called ahead. 'We've got the flight-rock.'

'I'll be ready directly,' Stope Boltjaw shouted back, and Twig again noticed the squeaking sound as he spoke. 'I'm just making sure the grappling hooks and anchor are secure,' he said. 'Wouldn't want her leaving without us.'

The Stone Pilot grumbled. The cooling rock was threatening to slip out of his grasp at any moment.

'Have you rigged up the cradle?' Slyvo called up.

'What do you take me for?' came the irritated reply. 'Of course I have! I used some of the ironwood. It's less buoyant than lufwood or bloodoak, but more fire-resistant – in case the rock's still too hot.'

The Stone Pilot grunted urgently.

'It's rising!' Spiker yelled.

Stope Boltjaw's head appeared out of the tree. 'Can you climb with it?' he asked.

The Stone Pilot shook his head and groaned. It was all he could do to keep the increasingly buoyant rock in his grasp.

'In that case,' Stope called down. 'We'll go for plan B. But it'll need pinpoint accuracy if it's going to work. The Stone Pilot will have to get the rock *directly* beneath the cradle before releasing it. So, left a couple of paces . . .'

The Stone Pilot shuffled awkwardly to the left.

'Stop. Forwards a tad. STOP! Back a bit. Left. Back a bit more.' Stope paused. 'That should do it,' he whispered. 'When I say *now*, let the rock go – but be careful not to nudge it when you do.'

Twig peered up into the tree. He saw Stope Boltjaw open the door of a cage-like contraption attached to the centre of the hull. He held it open with his foot and raised a long harpoon ready.

'Now!' he called.

The Stone Pilot gently released his load. For a moment, the rock hovered in the air. It rotated. Then it began to rise, slowly at first, but soon gathering speed. Twig saw Stope Boltjaw bracing himself against a branch. The rock came closer. It was going to miss the cradle! Stope leaned forwards and gently prodded the rock with his harpoon. It shifted slightly to the left, and continued rising.

'Come on, come on,' Slyvo urged the flying rock. He turned to Mugbutt. 'If he does it, I want everyone on board at once,' he hissed. Twig listened closely. 'And if Tem Barkwater objects,' he went on, 'deal with him, Mugbutt. OK?'

KER-DONK! The stone landed in the cradle. SLAM-CLICK. Stope Boltjaw kicked the door shut with his foot. He bent down and secured the catch. 'Done it!' he roared triumphantly.

Twig's heart fluttered. The wonderful pirate ship was sky-worthy once more, and he whooped and cheered with the rest.

'This shall not go unremembered, Stope Boltjaw,' Slyvo announced. 'Well done!'

'Yes!' came a second voice, deep and sonorous. 'Well done!'

Everyone spun round.

'Cap'n!' Tem Barkwater grinned. 'You made it!'

'Indeed I did, Tem,' came the solemn reply.

Twig gazed at the captain. He looked magnificent. He was tall and, unlike the stooping Slyvo Spleethe, stood upright, proud and elegant. His side whiskers were waxed, and a black leather patch stretched across one eye. From his long pirate's coat hung a multitude of objects: from goggles and telescope to grappling irons and daggers. By his side was a long curved cutlass, which glinted in the silver moonlight. Twig started. Hadn't he seen such a cutlass before, with its jewelled handle and nick in the blade?

Just then, an eighth figure emerged from the undergrowth. Twig stared. It was a banderbear, though quite different from his old friend, for this one was white with red eyes – an albino. It pulled the dead body of a hammelhorn from its shoulder and let it fall to the ground. Then it took its place behind the captain.

'Ah, Hubble,' the captain said. 'Just who I wanted to see. Take the flat-head and chain him up.'

The banderbear pointed up to the sky ship. 'Wuh?' it said.

'No,' said the captain. 'To a tree. But a strong one, mind.'

Mugbutt snarled and raised a fist in defiance. The banderbear swatted it away and seized the chain round the goblin's neck, almost lifting him off his feet.

'Easy, Hubble,' ordered the captain.

The banderbear lowered its arm and jerked the chain. Mugbutt was led away.

'Do you think that is altogether *wise*, sire?' came the whining voice of Slyvo Spleethe. 'Here we are in the Deepwoods. *Anything* might be out there . . . Mugbutt could be useful in case of a surprise attack.'

The captain turned and fixed Slyvo with his good eye. 'Do you think I cannot read your mutinous heart, Spleethe?' he said. 'Your friends in the Undertown League of Free Merchants are no use to you out here in the Deepwoods. We're an independent crew, and *I* give the orders. One more word and I'll have you sky-fired. Do I make myself clear?'

'What's sky-fired?' Twig whispered to Spiker.

'Tied to a branch of burning bloodoak,' the oakelf whispered back. 'You go up like a rocket, screaming all the way.'

Twig shuddered.

'We'll stay here the night and depart at first light,' the captain was saying. He turned to Tem. 'Right then, ship's cook,' he said, kicking at the dead hammelhorn. 'Get cooking!'

'Aye-aye, cap'n,' said Tem keenly.

'Spiker, plot us a route back to Undertown. I don't want to be stuck in these accursèd woods any longer than necessary.' He looked up. 'How much longer will you need to effect repairs, Boltjaw?'

'A couple of hours, cap'n,' came the reply. 'I've just got to chamfer the new bidgits and realign the rudder pins . . .'

'And the Stone Pilot?'

'He's down in the engine room re-boring the flange ducts.'

'Excellent work,' said the captain. He turned and looked down at Twig.

And it was at that moment that Twig knew for sure that he had met the captain before. It was the eye-patch which had stopped him recognizing him at once. He was the one Tuntum and he had met all that time ago in the forest when his woodtroll father had been trying to set him up with a job. The tall elegant sky pirate with his jewelled sword – with the nick in the blade. How could he have forgotten?

'Why are you just standing there gawping?' the captain barked. 'Help the others with the fire.'

Twig set to work at once. He dashed into the forest to collect kindling. When he returned, however, the fire was already ablaze, roaring and crackling. With every log that Spiker and Tem Barkwater tossed onto the fire, a mighty shower of orange sparks filled the air. The fire sang and groaned and hissed with the different woods. Occasionally a piece of blazing lufwood floated up from the flames and soared off into the sky like an emergency flare.

Twig shuddered. Growing up with the woodtrolls, he had been taught to respect fire – the most treacherous necessity of all to a forest-dweller. That was why they burnt buoyant woods in stoves. The sky pirates' carelessness appalled him.

He was busy kicking burning branches back into the main blaze when Hubble returned from chaining Mugbutt securely to the tree. It was looking for the captain, yet as it passed Twig, it paused.

'Wuh!' it bellowed, and pointed at the tooth around Twig's neck.

'I wouldn't go too near Hubble if I was you,' Tem Barkwater called. 'It's an unpredictable beast at the best of times.'

But Twig took no notice. Despite the white banderbear's ferocious appearance, there was a familiar sadness in its eyes. It stretched out a claw and gently touched the tooth.

'T-wuh-g,' it growled.

Twig stared back in amazement. Hubble knew who he was. He remembered the times his old friend had yodelled to the moonlit sky. He remembered the yodelled replies. Could it have been Hubble's desolate cry that Twig had heard the night the banderbear had died?

Hubble touched its chest and then pointed to Twig. 'Fr-uh-nz,' it said.

Twig smiled. 'Friends,' he said.

At that moment, there came the sound of the captain's angry voice. He wanted Hubble, and he wanted him now. Hubble swung round and plodded off obediently. Twig looked up to see Tem Barkwater staring at him in disbelief.

'I swear I have never seen the like in all my born days,'

he said. 'Friends with a banderbear! Whatever next?' He shook his head. 'Come on, young'un,' he said. 'Help me over here.'

Tem was standing by the fire. Having expertly skinned the hammelhorn, he had skewered it on a length of ironwood and placed it above the flames. The air was now thick with the smell of roasting meat. Twig joined him, and the pair of them turned the spit round and round, round and round.

By the time that Stope Boltjaw announced he had finished his repairs and came down from the tree, the hammelhorn was cooked. Tem banged a gong.

'Grub's up!' he called.

Twig sat down between Tem Barkwater and Spiker. The captain and Hubble were opposite them, with Slyvo Spleethe sitting back a little, in the shadows. The Stone Pilot hadn't appeared, and Mugbutt the flat-head goblin, still chained to a tree, had to make do with the scraps he was thrown.

As the sky pirates filled their empty stomachs with black bread and steaming chunks of hammelhorn meat, washed down with mugfuls of woodale, their spirits lifted.

'Of course,' laughed Tem Barkwater, 'we've been in worse scrapes than this, ain't we, cap'n?'

The captain grunted. He didn't seem to feel like talking.

'Why, that time we raided the league ships over Sanctaphrax itself. Never thought we'd get away with it. Cornered we were, nowhere to run, and a boarding party of wild flat-head goblins with murder on their minds popping up out of the cargo holds of those big, fat league ships. Never seen Spleethe shake so much – nor run so fast, neither. Kept saying, "There should have been liverbirch in the holds!" . . .'

'And so there should,' muttered Slyvo. 'Would have made us all a packet, too . . .'

'But the captain wasn't running, oh no, not him – not Cloud Wolf,' Tem chuckled. 'He just pulled out that great sword of his and set about the lot of them, Hubble following on behind. It was murder all right, but not the kind those goblins had in mind. That's where we got Mugbutt. Only one left standing. Mighty good fighter, but needs watching . . . It's also where the captain lost 'is eye. Fair exchange, he calls it.'

'Enough, Tem,' sighed the captain.

'It weren't no fair exchange when I lost my jaw,' broke in Stope Boltjaw, his ironwood replacement squeaking as he spoke. 'Had my back turned attending to the grappling socket. Ulbus Pentephraxis creeps up behind me with a hunting axe. I never stood a chance.' He spat into the fire. '*He's* now a league captain living the life of luxury in Undertown. Leaguesmen!' He hawked and spat again.

'Oh, they're not so bad,' wheedled Slyvo Spleethe, shifting closer to the fire. 'Now when *I* was starting out in Undertown as . . .'

'Spiker,' the captain interrupted. 'Have you plotted that course?' The oakelf nodded. 'Good lad,' he said, and looked slowly round the circle of pirates, suddenly sombre. 'The three rules of sky sailing. Never set sail before you've plotted your course, never fly higher than your longest grappling rope, and on no account dock in uncharted areas.'

The pirates nodded earnestly. Each and every one of them knew the perils of getting lost in the vast green leafy ocean. The fire was low. Twig watched the flickering flames reflected in the captain's thoughtful eye.

'I did that once,' he went on. 'Landed where I should not have landed.' He sighed. 'But then I had no choice.'

The pirates looked at one another in surprise. It was unlike the captain to speak of himself. They topped up their mugs and drew closer. The darkness wrapped itself around them.

'A wet and stormy night, it was,' Captain Quintinius Verginix – Cloud Wolf – began. Twig's body tingled with excitement. 'A cold night,' he said. 'A night of expectation and of sorrow.'

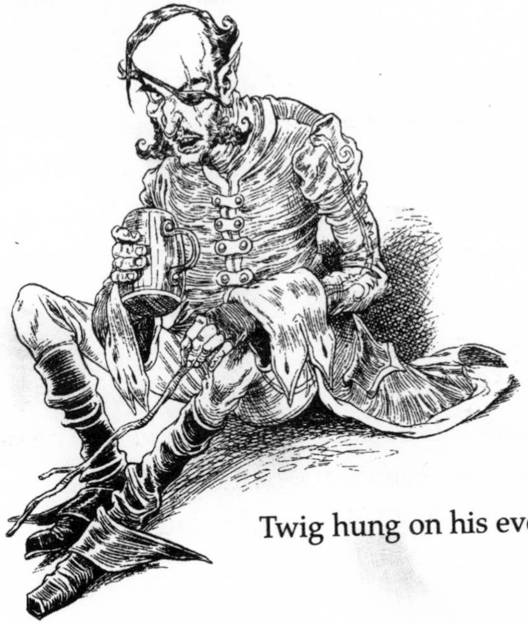

Twig hung on his every word.

'At that time I was a crew member on board a league ship.' He looked round at the circle of faces, bathed in the dying fire-glow, mouths open, eyes wide, and smiled. 'You load of ruffians,' he chuckled. 'If you think I'm a hard taskmaster, you should have served under Multinius Gobtrax. Ruthless, demanding, punctilious – the worst sort of league captain you'll ever meet.'

Twig watched the fireflies playing roly-poly in the air and darting in and out of the leaves. The wind had dropped completely and his hair and skin felt damp. He chewed on the corner of his scarf.

'Picture it,' the captain said. Twig closed his eyes. 'There were but five of us on board the ship, and only four who were in any state to sail her: Gobtrax and his bodyguard, the Stone Pilot and me. Maris was already nine months with child. The storm had caught us unawares and dragged us way off course. Worse than that, the up-currents were terrible strong. Before we could weigh anchor or secure the grappling irons, we'd been sucked up, far above the forest and towards . . . open sky.'

Twig's head spun. Straying from the path was bad enough, but being lost in open sky . . .

'We lowered the sails, but still we continued to rise. I crouched down next to Maris. "Everything's going to be all right," I said, though I scarce believed it myself. We would never get back to Undertown before she went into labour, and even if we did – the birth of the child was little cause for celebration.'

Twig opened his eyes and looked at the captain. He was staring into the glowing embers of the fire, playing idly with the waxed points of his side-whiskers. His single eye shone moistly.

'Was there something wrong with it?' asked Twig.

The captain stirred. 'No,' he said. 'Only the fact that it was a child at all . . .' He paused, and his eye glazed over. 'Maris and I had big decisions to make,' he said. 'I was ambitious. I intended one day to command my own sky ship – I couldn't be doing with a child weighing me down. A captain or a father, that was the choice I had. It was no choice at all. I told Maris that we could travel together, but *she* would have to choose between the baby and me. She chose me.' He breathed deeply in, and out. 'Mother Horsefeather agreed to take the child off our hands.'

Complete silence fell around the camp-fire. The pirates looked down at the ground awkwardly. They felt uneasy listening to their Cloud Wolf opening up in this way. Tem Barkwater busied himself with stoking up the fire.

The captain sighed. 'At least, that was the plan. Yet

there we were, miles from Undertown, and being drawn ever upwards.' He nodded up to the sky ship. 'It was the Stone Pilot who saved us then, as he saved us this evening. He doused the buoyant-wood burners, released the balance-weights, and when that was not enough, he climbed over the side and began chipping away at the flight-rock. Bit by bit, as slivers and shards broke off, our ascent slowed. Then we stopped. Then we started to go down. By the time the hull of the ship touched down on the forest, there were six on board. Maris had given birth.'

The captain stood up and began pacing agitatedly back and forth. 'What to do?' he said. 'We were grounded now in the Deepwoods, and the baby wouldn't survive the journey on foot back to Undertown. Gobtrax ordered us to get rid of the brat. He said he wouldn't wait. Maris was hysterical, but Gobtrax's bodyguard – a hulking great cloddertrog – made it clear that he'd snap my neck if I objected ... What *could* I do?'

The pirates shook their heads earnestly, solemnly. Tem poked at the fire.

'We left the sky ship and set off into the forest. I remember how loud the creatures of the night were, and how still the tiny bundle in Maris's arms. Then we came across a small village of woodtrolls ...'

Twig started. The hairs at the back of his neck stood on end. Icy shivers strummed his spine.

'Odd creatures,' the captain mused. 'Stocky, dark, not that bright. They live in tree cabins ... I had to tear the child away from Maris. The look in her eyes at that moment! It was as if all the life drained out of her. She never spoke a word again . . .' The captain sniffed.

Twig's heart beat faster and faster.

'I wrapped the baby up in a shawl,' he went on, his voice little more than a whisper. 'The birthing-shawl that Maris had made for it. Stitched it all herself, she did. With a lullabee tree for luck, she said. I left the bundle at the foot of a cabin tree, and the pair of us left. We didn't once look back.'

The captain paused and stared ahead into the shadows of the forest, hands clasped behind his back. Despite the roaring flames, Twig was cold. He had to clamp his jaws firmly shut to still his chattering teeth.

'You made the right decision, cap'n,' said Tem Barkwater quietly.

The captain turned. 'I made the *only* decision, Tem,' he replied. 'It's in the blood. My father was a sky pirate captain, as was his father, and his father before him. Perhaps . . .'

Twig's head was whirling, buzzing; thought after thought collided with one another. The abandoned baby. The woodtrolls. The scarf – his comfort cloth, still tightly tied around his neck. *My* scarf, he thought. He stared at the majestic sky pirate captain. Could you really be my father? he wondered. Does your blood flow through my veins? Will I also command a sky ship one day?

Maybe. Maybe not. There was something Twig had to know. 'Th . . . the baby,' he said nervously.

The captain spun round and looked at him, actually seeing him it seemed for the first time. The eyebrow above the patch raised questioningly.

'This is Twig, cap'n,' said Tem Barkwater. 'He found the flight-rock and . . .'

'I believe the lad can speak for himself,' said the captain. 'What did you want to say?'

Twig climbed to his feet and looked down at the ground. His breath came short and jerky; he could barely speak. 'Sire,' he said. 'Was the baby a g . . . girl . . . – or a boy?'

Quintinius Verginix stared back at Twig, his brow deeply furrowed. Perhaps he could not remember. Perhaps he remembered only too well. He stroked his chin. 'It was a boy,' he said finally. The sound of chains jangled behind him as Mugbutt rolled over in his sleep. The captain drained his mug and wiped his mouth. 'Early start tomorrow,' he said. 'We could all do with some shut-eye.'

Twig thought he would never sleep again. His heart was a-flutter, his imagination was working overtime.

'Hubble, you're on first watch,' the captain said. 'Wake me at four.'

'Wuh,' the banderbear grunted.

'And be careful of our treacherous friend here.'

Twig started with alarm, until he realized the captain was referring to Slyvo Spleethe.

'Here,' said Spiker, as he handed Twig a blanket. 'Take this. I'll be warm enough tonight in my caternest.' And with that, the oakelf climbed the tree, boarded the sky ship and made his way up to the cocoon at the top of the mast.

Twig wrapped the blanket around him and lay down on a bed of quilted leaf-fall. The fire was burning bright and hot. Glittering sparks and glowing embers rose skywards. Twig stared into the dancing flames.

But for the sky pirate – this captain Cloud Wolf, the one who had caused Spelda and Tuntum to send Twig away for fear he would be forced to join his crew – but for him, Twig would never have left the woodtroll village in the first place. He would never have strayed from the path. He would never have been lost.

But now he understood. He had *always* been lost, not just when he left the path but from the very beginning, when this sky pirate had left him wrapped in the birthing-shawl beneath the Snatchwood cabin. Now he'd been found again. Three short sentences kept going round and round his head.

I've found my path. I've found my destiny. I've found my father!

Twig closed his eyes. The image of the heartcharming stick pointing upwards sprang into his mind. That was where his future lay: in the sky, with his father.

.CHAPTER THIRTEEN.

THE GLOAMGLOZER

There was stillness. Then there was movement. Then there was stillness again.

The first stillness was that point of deepest, darkest silence shortly before the dawn. Twig rolled over, pulling Spiker's blanket tightly round him. His dreams were full of sky ships sailing across the indigo depths. Twig was standing at the helm. He raised his collar against the wind. 'Gallantly sailing,' he murmured, and smiled in his sleep.

The movement was brief and purposeful: a flurry of activity. Twig was still at the helm holding a straight course, while all around him the crew busied themselves with the nets as they flew towards an incoming flock of migrating snowbirds. It would be baked snowbird for supper.

The ropes clacked and jingled against the mast. 'Hard

to starboard,' came a voice. Twig sighed, and rolled over onto his other side.

The second stillness was orange – a desert of flickering emptiness. There were no more voices, not even his own. His back was cold, his face was hot. His eyes snapped open.

At first, what he saw made no sense. A fire in front of him. Charred bones and patches of grease in the dust. The dense canopy above, with stripes of bright early morning sunlight lancing the air.

Twig sat bolt upright. Suddenly, the events of the previous night came back to him. The storm. The sky ship. Stumbling across the flight-rock. Eating with the sky pirates. Finding his father . . . So where were they all now?

They had gone without him. Twig howled with pain and loss and desolation. Tears streamed down his face, turning the stripy sunlight to star-shaped rainbows. They had left him behind! His choking sobs filled the air. 'Why, my father, why?' he cried out. 'Why have you abandoned me? Again!'

His words faded away, and with them his hopes of ever finding his way beyond the Deepwoods. He hung his head. The forest seemed quieter than usual. No coughing fromps, no squealing quarms, no screeching razorflits. Not only had the sky pirates gone, but it was as if they had taken all the woodland creatures with them.

Yet the air was not completely silent. There was a low roaring sound, a hissing sound, a crackling sound

which, even as Twig sat there with his head in his hands, grew in volume. The heat at his back became more intense. The hammelhornskin waistcoat began to prickle ominously. Twig spun round.

'Yaaaiii!' he screamed. It wasn't sunlight he had seen. It was fire. The Deepwoods were ablaze.

A piece of burning oakwood which had floated away from the sky pirates' slapdash fire had become lodged in the branches of a lullabee tree. The lullabee had smouldered and smoked; hours later it burst into flames. Fanned on by the stiff breeze, the fire had rapidly spread. Now, from the forest floor to the tips of the canopy leaves, a solid wall of red and orange flames was advancing across the forest.

The heat was overwhelming. Twig swooned as he stumbled to his feet. A blazing branch crashed down beside him, the sparks exploding like droplets of gold. Twig took to his heels and ran.

And he ran and he ran – with the wind at his side – trying desperately to reach the end of the fiery wall before the flames consumed him. He ran as he had never run before, yet not fast enough. At both ends, the wall of fire was curling round. Soon, he would be surrounded.

The burning air scorched the fur on his jacket, sweat poured over his face and streamed down his back, his head throbbed with the relentless blast of molten air. The curving ends of the wall closed in further.

'Faster,' Twig said, urging himself on. 'FASTER!'

He sped past a halitoad, whose short stubby front legs had slowed its escape, fatally. A hover worm, bewildered by the heat and smoke, flew round and round in circles before disappearing into the flames in an explosion of fetid steam. To his right, Twig caught sight of the writhing green of a tarry-vine trying in vain to dodge the advancing fire: the bloodoak it was attached to screamed and squalled as the first of the orange tongues lapped at the base of its trunk.

On and on Twig ran. The two ends of the wall of fire had almost come together now. He was all but encircled. His only hope of escape lay in the narrow gap remaining between the towering flames. Like two curtains hooked to the sky, they were being drawn across. Twig made a dash for the opening. His lungs burned with heat and acrid smoke; his head swam. As if in a dream, he watched the shimmering curtains of fire close.

Twig stopped and looked about him. He was slapbang in the middle of the burning circle. He was done for.

All round him, bushes and branches were smoking. Flames broke out, guttered and burst into life once again. Giant woodsucculents hissed and steamed as the water within their fat angular limbs began to boil. Fatter and fatter they grew, until – BANG, BANG, BA-BA-BA-BANG – they exploded. Like corks from bottles of woodfizz, their seeds shot through the air in a jet of frothing liquid.

The water doused the flames. But only for a second. Twig backed away from the advancing fire. He looked over his shoulder. It was getting closer there, too. To his left, to his right, the fire was closing in. Twig looked up

into the sky. 'Oh, Gloamglozer,' he whispered. 'Help.'

All at once, a tremendous noise cut through the roar of the fire. Twig spun round. The purple flames of a burning lufwood tree were dancing not twenty yards away. The creaking, cracking noise came again. Twig saw the whole tree tremble. It was about to fall on top of him. He glanced this way, that way. There was nowhere to run, nowhere to hide, and nothing to protect himself with. Again the noise echoed round about him – rasping, jarring, like the rotten tooth Twig had pulled from the banderbear's swollen jaw.

'NO!' Twig screamed as the tree wobbled and shook. For a second it remained suspended in the air. Twig fell to the ground and rolled into a ball. A blast of blistering air battered his body. He clamped his eyes shut and waited, petrified, for the tree to come crashing down on him.

Nothing happened. He waited some more. Still nothing. But how? Why? Twig lifted his head, opened his eyes – and gasped in amazement.

The massive lufwood tree – now a blazing purple inferno – was hovering above the ground. The wood, so buoyant when alight, had dragged the very roots from the earth and was rising slowly up towards the sky. On either side were two more lufwoods whose anchoring roots were, even now, being torn out of the ground. The melancholy voice of a lullabee filled the air as it, too, rose up above the blazing forest. The sky itself seemed to be on fire.

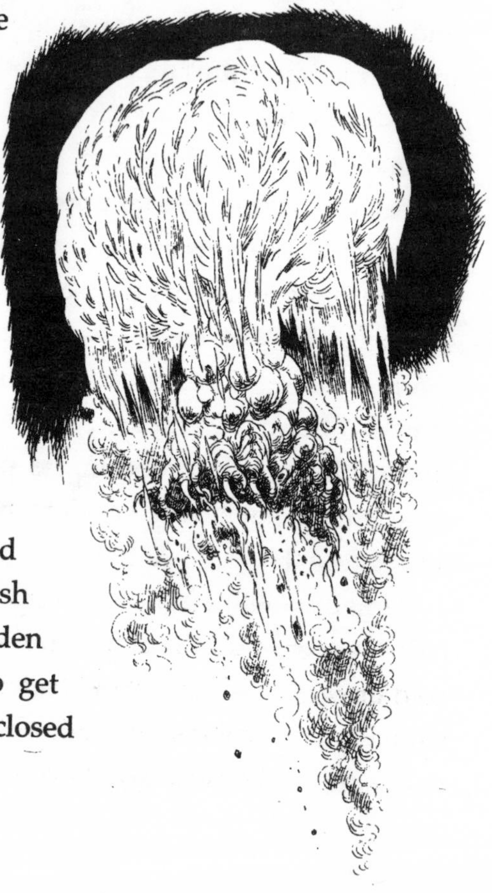

Where the burning trees had been, now there was darkness. It looked like a gappy smile. Twig seized his chance and made a headlong dash towards the sudden opening. He had to get there before it closed again.

'Near-ly . . . near-ly . . .' he panted.

The fire was on both sides of him. He ducked his head and lifted the collar of his jacket against the shimmering heat as he ran the gauntlet of flames. Just a few steps more . . . Just a little bit further . . .

He raised his arm to shield his eyes, and sprinted through the enclosing flames. His throat stung, his skin prickled, his nostrils caught the whiff of his own scorched hair.

All at once, the heat grew less intense. Twig was outside the circle of fire. He ran on a little more. The wind had dropped; the smoke was thickening. He stopped and turned and watched for a moment, as the great balls of purple and turquoise rose, ablaze and airborne, majestically into the darkening sky.

He'd done it. He'd escaped the forest fire!

Yet there was no time for congratulating himself. Not yet, at least. The coils of smoke were winding themselves around him; filling his eyes and mouth. Blinding him. Choking him.

On and on, Twig stumbled, breathing through his scarf which he held tightly against his face. Further and further. His head throbbed, his lungs ached, his eyes smarted and streamed. 'I can't go on,' Twig spluttered. 'I *must* go on.'

He kept walking till the roaring of the forest fire was just a memory, till the acrid smoke was replaced with a cold grey mist which – though as blindingly thick as the smoke – was wonderfully refreshing; he kept on to the very edge of the Deepwoods. And still he did not stop.

The mist thickened and thinned.

There were no more trees. No bushes, no shrubs, no plants or flowers. Beneath Twig's feet, the ground became hard, as the spongy earth of the Deepwoods gave way to a pavement of pitted rock, slippery from the thick greasy mist. He picked his way carefully over the treacherous slabs. One slip, and his foot would become wedged in the deep fissures between.

The mist thinned and thickened, as it always did. For these were the Edgelands, that narrow stretch of barren rock which separated the Deepwoods from the Edge itself. Beyond lay the unknown, the uncharted, the un-

explored; a place of seething craters and swirling fogs – a place into which even the sky pirates never ventured intentionally.

The gathering breeze blew in from over the Edge. It brought with it the whiff of sulphur as broad tongues of fog lolled over the top of the cliff and lapped at the rock. The air was filled with the moans and groans of an eternity of mournful lost souls. Or was it only the rising wind softly howling?

Twig trembled. Was this the place the caterbird had meant when he told him his destiny lay beyond the Deepwoods? He wiped the beads of water away from his face and leaped over a wide crack in the rock. As he landed, his ankle buckled under him. He yelped, collapsed and rubbed at the throbbing joint tenderly. Gradually, the pain grew less acute. He hobbled to his feet and tentatively placed his weight down.

'I think it's all right,' he muttered with relief.

Out of the sulphurous mist came a reply. 'I am glad to hear it, Master Twig,' it said.

Twig gasped. This was definitely not the wind playing tricks. It was a voice. A real voice. More than that, it was a *familiar* voice.

'You have travelled far since you strayed from the woodtroll path,' it continued, lilting, slightly mocking. 'So very, very far. And I have tracked you every step of the way.'

'Wh . . . who are you?' stammered Twig, peering into the grey swirling mists. 'Why can't I see you?'

'Oh, but you have seen me often enough, Master Twig,' the wheedling voice continued. 'In the sleepy morning of the slaughterers' camp, in the sticky corridors of the gyle goblin colony, in the underground cavern of the termagant trogs . . . I was there. I was always with you.'

Twig went weak at the knees. He was confused, frightened. He racked his brains, trying to make sense of the words he was hearing. He *had* heard the soft insistent voice before, that much was certain. And yet . . .

'Can you really have forgotten, *Master* Twig,' came the voice again, and the air hissed with a nasal snigger.

Twig fell to his knees. The rock was cold and clammy to the touch; the mist grew thicker than ever. Twig could barely see his hand in front of his face. 'What do you want of me?' he whispered.

'Want of you? Want of YOU?' The voice broke into raucous laughter. 'It's what you want of *me,* Master Twig. After all, you did summon me.'

'I s . . . s . . . summoned you?' said Twig, the faltering words weak and muffled in the dense fog. 'But how? When?'

'Come, come,' the voice complained. 'Don't act the innocent little woodtroll with me. "Oh, Gloamglozer!" it said in a desperate voice that Twig recognized as his own. "*Please. Please. Please. Let me find the path again.*" Do you deny you called me?'

Twig trembled with horror as he realized what he'd done. 'But I didn't know,' he protested. 'I didn't mean . . .'

'You called me, and I came,' said the gloamglozer, and there was a menacing edge to the voice now. 'I followed you, I looked after you. More than once I led you out of the perilous situations you had got yourself into.' There was a pause. 'Did you not think that I was listening, Master Twig?' it went on, more gently now. 'I'm always listening: listening for the stragglers, the loners, the ones who don't fit in. I help, I guide, and eventually . . .'

'Eventually?' Twig murmured.

'They come to me,' the voice announced. 'As you have come to me, Master Twig.'

The mist thinned once more. It floated in the air like flimsy twists of cobweb. Twig discovered that he was kneeling next to the edge of a cliff. Inches away from him the ground fell away into pitch blackness. Behind him were the rolls of pungent cloud, and in front . . . Twig cried out in fear and alarm. In front, hovering over the void, was the hideous grinning face of the gloamglozer itself. Calloused and warty, with thick tussocks of hair sprouting out of its long snarling face, it leered at Twig and licked its lips.

'Come to me,' it coaxed. 'You called me and here I am. Take that final step, why don't you?' It held out a hand towards him. 'You belong with me.'

Twig stared back, unable to tear his gaze away from the creature's monstrous face. Two horns curled to thin sharp points; two yellow eyes fixed him in a hypnotic stare. The mist grew still thinner. Around the gloamglozer's shoulders was a greasy grey cloak which fell away into nothingness.

'One small step,' it said softly, and beckoned. 'Take my hand.' Twig stared down at the bony taloned fingers. 'That's all it takes – for someone like you, Master Twig – to join me,' the voice continued seductively, and the yellow eyes grew wide. 'For you are special.'

'*Special*,' Twig whispered.

'Special,' the gloamglozer repeated. 'I knew that from the moment I first heard your call. You had an overwhelming longing; an emptiness inside which you yearned to be filled. And I can help you. I can teach you. That's what you really want, isn't it, Master Twig? You want to know. To understand. *That's* why you left the path.'

'Yes,' said Twig dreamily. 'That's why I left the path.'

'The Deepwoods aren't for you,' the gloamglozer went on; flattering, insistent. 'Not for you the huddling together for safety, the hiding in corners, the fear of everyone and everything outside. Because you are like me. You're an adventurer, a traveller, a seeker. A listener!' Its voice became hushed and intimate. 'You too could be a gloamglozer, Master Twig. I can instruct you. Take my hand and you'll see.'

Twig moved a step closer. His ankle jarred. The gloamglozer – still hovering in mid-air just beyond the Edge – trembled. Its monstrous face contorted with pain. Tears welled in the corners of its yellow eyes.

'Oh, what a time you've had of it,' it sighed. 'Constantly on the look-out. Never out of danger. Always frightened. But the tables can be turned, Master Twig. If you'll just *take my hand*.'

Twig shuffled awkwardly from one foot to the other. There was a rattle and a clatter as a flurry of dislodged rocks bounced down into the chasm. 'And look like *you*?' he said.

The gloamglozer threw back its head and roared with mirthless laughter. 'But have you forgotten, my vain little one?' it said. 'You can look how you will. A mighty warrior, a handsome prince . . . Anything. Imagine it, Master Twig,' it went on enticingly. 'You could become a goblin or a trog,' and as it spoke Twig found himself face to face with a succession of characters he recognized only too well. There was the gyle goblin who had led him from the colony,

the flat-head who had helped him out of the mire,

the trog who had tripped Mag and pointed the way to the air shafts.

'Or how about this one,' the gloamglozer purred. Twig stared back at a red-faced individual with fiery hair.

'Didn't I hear you thinking how *nice* it would be to stay with the slaughterers?' it wheedled. 'Or perhaps you'd prefer to be a banderbear,' it said, shifting its shape again. 'Big, powerful – no-one messes with a banderbear.' It sniggered unpleasantly. 'Except wig-wigs, of course.'

Twig shuddered. The hovering creature knew everything. Absolutely everything.

'I've got it!' the gloamglozer cried, turning itself into a squat brown creature with knotted hair and a button nose.

'A woodtroll. You could go home. You could fit in. Isn't that what you wanted all along?'

Twig nodded his head mechanically.

'You can be *anyone,* Master Twig,' the gloamglozer said, resuming its own form. 'Anyone at all. You can go anywhere, do anything. Simply take hold of my hand, and all this shall be yours.'

Twig swallowed. His heart beat furiously. If the gloamglozer was right, he would never have to be an outsider again.

'And just think of the things you'll see,' the gloamglozer purred enticingly. 'Think of the places you could go, shifting your shape, appearing as others want to see you, always safe, listening in corners; always one step ahead. Think of the power at your command!'

Twig stared at the outstretched hand. He was standing at the very edge of the cliff. His arm moved slowly forwards, brushing against the spiky hammelhornskin waistcoat.

'Go on,' said the gloamglozer, its voice like oil and honey. 'Take that step forwards. Reach out and take my hand. You know you want to.'

Yet Twig still held back. It wasn't as if all his encounters in the Deepwoods had been bad. The banderbear had saved his life. So had the slaughterers. It was they, after all, who had given him the jacket that had caught in the bloodoak's gorge, which now bristled so sharply. He thought of his village and Spelda, his own dearest Mother-Mine, who had loved him like her own since the day that he was born. Tears welled up in his eyes.

If he accepted the gloamglozer's tantalizing offer, he would not really turn into them. No matter what I *look* like, he thought. Instead, he would become what they all feared most. A gloamglozer. No. It was impossible. He would never again be able to return. Never. He would have to remain apart, aloof – alone.

'It is fear which makes us reluctant to be on our own,' the gloamglozer said, reading his thoughts. 'Join me, and you need never be frightened again. Take my hand and you will understand. Trust me, Master Twig.'

Twig hesitated. Could this truly be the terrible monster that all the forest dwellers so feared?

'Have I let you down so far?' the gloamglozer asked quietly.

Twig shook his head dreamily.

'Besides,' it added, almost as an afterthought. 'I thought you *wanted* to see what lay beyond the Deepwoods.'

Beyond the Deepwoods. The three words rang round inside Twig's head. *Beyond* the Deepwoods. Twig held out his hand. He stepped over the edge.

With a screech of terrible laughter, the gloamglozer grabbed Twig's wrist, its talons biting into his flesh.

'They all fall for it,' the gloamglozer cried triumphantly. 'All the poor little goblins and trolls, waifs and strays; they *all* think they're special. They all listen to me. They all follow my voice . . . It's pathetic!'

'But you *said* I was special,' Twig cried, as he dangled from the gloamglozer's bony grasp over the yawning space below.

'Did I really?' the gloamglozer sneered. 'You little fool. Did you honestly think you could ever be like me?

You are as insignificant as all the rest, *Master* Twig,' it said scornfully. 'You are nothing. NOTHING!' it screeched. 'Do you hear me?'

'But why are you doing this?' Twig wailed desperately. 'Why?'

'Because I am a gloamglozer,' the beast cried out, and cackled wickedly. 'A deceiver, a trickster, a cheat and a fraud. All my fine words and fancy promises count for nothing. I seek out all those who have strayed from the path. I lure them to the Edge. AND I DISPOSE OF THEM!'

The gloamglozer released its grip. Twig screamed with terror. He was falling. Down, down, he went, over the Edge and into the bottomless depths of darkness below.

.CHAPTER FOURTEEN.

BEYOND THE DEEPWOODS

Twig's head spun as he tumbled through the air. The uprush of wind set his clothes billowing and snatched his breath away. Over and over he rolled. And all the while, the gloamglozer's cruel words echoed round and round his head.

You are nothing. NOTHING!

'It's not true!' Twig howled.

The side of the cliff blurred past him like a streak of smudged paint. All that searching. All the trials and tribulations. All the times he had thought he would never make it to the end of the Deepwoods alive. To find his long lost father, only to lose him again – and then, worst of all, to discover that the whole treacherous journey had been a part of a cruel and complicated game devised by the deceitful gloamglozer. It was so, so monstrously unfair.

Tears welled in Twig's eyes. 'I'm *not* nothing. I'm not!' he wailed.

'I'm *not* nothing. I'm not!' Tears welled in his eyes.

Further and further he fell, down into the swirling mist. Would he fall for ever? He screwed his eyes shut.

'You're a liar!' Twig screamed back up to the top of the cliff.

Liar, liar, li . . . The word bounced back off the rock.

Yes, thought Twig, the gloamglozer *is* a liar. It lied about everything. Everything!

'I *am* something!' Twig called out. 'I am some*one*. I am Twig, who strayed from the path and travelled beyond the Deepwoods. I AM MEEEEEEE!'

Twig opened his eyes. Something had happened. He was flying, not falling, high above the Edge, in and out of clouds.

'Am I dead?' he wondered out loud.

'Not dead,' replied a familiar voice. 'Far from it. You still have far to go.'

'Caterbird!' cried Twig.

The caterbird's talons tightened their grip around Twig's shoulders; its great wings flapped

rhythmically through the cold thin air.

'You were at my hatching, and I have watched over you always,' it said. 'Now you truly need me, here I am.'

'But where are we going?' asked Twig, who could see nothing but open sky.

'Not "we", Twig,' said the caterbird. 'But you. Your destiny lies beyond the Deepwoods.'

With that the talons released their grip and, for a second time, Twig was falling. Down, down, down and . . .

CRASH!

Everything went black.

Twig found himself running down a long dark corridor. He dashed through a door into a dark room. In the corner was a wardrobe. He opened the door and stepped into the deeper darkness inside. He was looking for something; he knew that much. There was a coat hanging from a hook inside the wardrobe. Twig felt for the pocket, and climbed into the even deeper darkness inside. It wasn't here, whatever it was he was looking for, but there was a purse at the bottom. He opened the clasp and jumped into the even-deeper-still darkness within.

Inside the purse was a piece of cloth. Its touch was familiar. He felt the chewed and twisted corners. It was his scarf, his shawl. He picked it up and held it to his face, and there – staring back out of the darkness of the material – was a face. *His* face. It smiled. Twig smiled back.

'Me,' he whispered.

'Are you all right?' asked the face.

Twig nodded.

'Are you all right?' it said again.

'Yes,' said Twig.

The question came a third time, and Twig realized the voice was coming not from the scarf, but from somewhere else. Somewhere outside. His eyelids fluttered open. In front of him loomed a huge red hairy face. It looked concerned.

'Tem!' Twig exclaimed. 'Tem Barkwater.'

'The very same,' nodded the sky pirate. 'Now will you answer me – are you all right?'

'I . . . I think so,' said Twig. He pulled himself up onto his elbows. 'Nothing broken, at least.'

'How is he?' Spiker called.

'He's OK!' Tem shouted back.

Twig was lying on a soft bed of sailcloth on the deck of the sky ship. He pulled himself up and looked round. Apart from the Stone Pilot, they were all there: Spiker, Stope Boltjaw, Slyvo Spleethe, Mugbutt (chained to the mast), Hubble and, standing closest of all, the captain, Quintinius Verginix. Cloud Wolf. His father.

Cloud Wolf stooped and touched Twig's scarf. Twig flinched.

'Easy,' said the captain in a low voice. 'No-one's going to hurt you, lad. Seems we're not to be rid of you after all.'

'Never seen anything like it, cap'n,' broke in Tem Barkwater. 'Just dropped out of the sky, he did – straight onto the aft deck. This is strange sky we're in and no mistake . . .'

'Stop your chattering,' the captain said harshly. 'And get back to your posts, all of you. We must make Undertown by nightfall.'

The crew dispersed.

'Not you,' said the captain quietly, laying a hand on Twig's arm as he, too, made to leave.

Twig looked round. 'W . . . why did you leave me?' he asked, his mouth dry, his voice cracking.

The captain stared back, his mask-like face betraying no emotion. 'We didn't need an extra crew member,' he said simply. 'Besides, I didn't think that a pirate's life was for you.' He paused. There was clearly something weighing on his mind.

Twig stood there waiting for the captain to speak again. He felt shy, awkward. He chewed the inside of his mouth. The captain's eyes narrowed as he leaned forwards. Twig shuddered. The man's breath was warm and noisy at his ear, the side whiskers tickled his neck.

'I saw the shawl,' he confessed, so that only Twig could hear. 'Your scarf. The one that Maris – your mother – made. And I knew you were . . . After all those years.' He fell silent. His lower lip was trembling. 'It was more than I could bear. I had to get away. I . . . I left you behind. For a second time.'

Twig squirmed. His face was hot and red.

The captain placed his hands on Twig's shoulders and stared into his eyes. 'It will not happen a third time,' he said softly. 'I shall never abandon you again.' He wrapped his arms around the boy and hugged him tightly. 'From now on our destinies lie together,' he whispered urgently, 'And you and I shall ride the skies together. You and I, Twig. You and I.'

Twig said nothing. He could not. Tears of joy welled in his eyes; his heart was beating ready to burst. He had found his father after all.

Abruptly, the captain pulled away. 'But you'll be a member of the crew, just like all the rest,' he added gruffly. 'So don't you go expecting any special favours.'

'No, f . . . captain,' said Twig quietly. 'I won't.'

Cloud Wolf nodded approvingly, straightened up and turned on the others, who had been watching, perplexed. 'Come on then, you idle rabble,' he roared. 'Show over. Raise the mainsail, lift the grappling rope, and let's get out of here.'

A chorus of 'aye-aye, cap'n's filled the air as the sky pirates set to work. The captain strode towards the helm with Twig beside him, and took the wheel.

Together at last, they stood side by side as the sky ship soared into the air and away, beyond the Deepwoods.

The captain turned towards his son. 'Twig,' he said thoughtfully, his eyes twinkling. '*Twig!* I mean, what kind of a name is that for the child of Quintinius Verginix, captain of the finest sky pirate ship that ever sailed the heavens blue? Eh? Tell me that.'

Twig smiled back. 'It's *my* name,' he said.

STORMCHASER

·CHAPTER ONE·

REUNION

It was midday and Undertown was bustling. Beneath the pall of filthy mist which hovered over the town, fuzzing the rooftops and dissolving the sun, its narrow streets and alleyways were alive with feverish activity.

There was ill-tempered haggling and bartering; buskers played music, barrow-boys called out unmissable bargains, beggars made their pitiful demands from dark, shadowy corners – though there were few who paused to place coins in their hats. Rushing this way and that, everyone was far too wrapped up in their own concerns to spare a thought for anyone else.

Getting from a to b as quickly as possible, being first to nail a deal, obtaining the best price while undercutting your competitors – *that* was what succeeding in Undertown was all about. You needed nerves of steel and eyes in the back of your head to survive; you had to learn to smile even as you were stabbing someone else in the back. It was a rough life, a tough life, a ruthless life.

It was an *exhilarating* life.

Twig hurried up from the boom-docks and through the market-place – not because he was in any particular hurry himelf, but because the frenzied atmosphere was contagious. Anyway, he had learned the hard way that those who don't adjust to the breakneck pace of the place were liable to get knocked down and trampled underfoot. Along with 'avoid all eye-contact' and 'do not display weakness', 'go with the flow' was one of the cardinal rules of Undertown.

Twig was feeling uncomfortably hot. The sun was at its highest. Despite being obscured by the choking, foul-tasting smoke from the metal foundries, it beat down ferociously. There was no wind and, as Twig dodged his way past the shops, stands and stalls, a bewildering mix of smells assaulted his nostrils. Stale woodale, ripe cheeses, burned milk and boiling glue, roasting pine-coffee and sizzling tilder sausages . . .

The spicy aroma of the sausages took Twig back, as it always did – back to his childhood. Every Wodgiss Night, in the woodtroll village where he had been brought up, the adults would feast on the traditional tilder sausage soup. How long ago that now seemed, and how far away! Life then had been so different: self-contained, ordered, unhurried. Twig smiled to himself. He could never return to that life. Not now. Not for all the trees in the Deepwoods.

As he continued across the market-place, the mouth-watering aroma of the sausages grew fainter and was replaced with a different smell – a smell which triggered a different set of memories altogether. It was the unmistakable scent of freshly tanned leather. Twig stopped and looked round.

A tall individual with the blood-red skin and crimson hair of a slaughterer was standing by a wall. Hanging round his neck was a wooden tray overflowing with the leather talismans and amulets on thongs which he was selling – or rather *trying* to sell.

'Lucky charms!' he cried. 'Get your lucky charms here!'

No-one was paying him any heed, and when he went to tie the charms around the necks of the passers-by each attempt was greeted with an irritated shake of the head as the goblin or troll or whatever hurried past.

Twig watched him sadly. The slaughterer – like so many of the Deepwoods folk who had listened to rumours that the streets of Undertown were paved with gold – was finding the reality quite different. With a sigh, he turned and was about to move on when, at that moment, a particularly mean-looking cloddertrog in tattered clothes and heavy boots brushed past him.

'Lucky charm?' the slaughterer said cheerily and stepped forwards, leather thong at the ready.

'Keep your murderous red hands off me!' the cloddertrog roared and shoved the outstretched arms savagely away.

The slaughterer spun round and crashed to the ground. The lucky charms went everywhere.

As the cloddertrog stomped off, cursing under his breath, Twig hurried over to the slaughterer. 'Are you all right?' he asked, reaching down to help him to his feet.

The slaughterer rolled over and blinked up at him. 'Blooming rudeness,' he complained. '*I* don't know!' He looked away and began gathering up the charms and returning them to the tray. 'All I'm trying to do is scratch an honest living.'

'It can't be easy,' said Twig sympathetically. 'So far away from your Deepwoods home.'

Twig knew the slaughterers well. He had once stayed with them in their forest village, and to this day, he still wore the hammelhornskin waistcoat they had given him. The slaughterer looked up. Twig touched his forehead in greeting and reached down with his hand once again.

This time, with the last of the charms back in place, the slaughterer took a hold and pulled himself up. He touched his own forehead. 'I am Tendon,' he said. 'And thank you for stopping to see whether I was all right. Most folk round here wouldn't give you the time of day.' He sniffed. 'I don't suppose . . .' He checked himself.

'What?' said Twig.

The slaughterer shrugged. 'I was just wondering whether *you* might care to buy one of my lucky charms.' And Twig smiled to himself as, unbidden, the slaughterer selected one of the leather talismans and held it out. 'How about this one? It's extremely potent.'

Twig looked at the intricate spiral tooled into the deep-red leather. He knew that, for the slaughterers, the individual designs on the charms each had its own significance.

'Those who wear this charm,' the slaughterer went on as he tied the thong around Twig's neck, 'shall be freed from fear of the known.'

'Shouldn't that be the *un*known?' said Twig.

The slaughterer snorted. 'Fear of the unknown is for the foolish and weak,' he said. 'I had not taken you for such a one. No,' he added, 'for my money, what is known is generally far more frightening. And speaking of money, that'll be six quarters.' Twig reached into his pockets. 'Unless,' the slaughterer added in a conspiratorial whisper, 'you've got any phraxdust.' He looked at the silver ball-shaped medallion hanging round Twig's neck. 'A speck would do.'

'Sorry,' said Twig, dropping coins into waiting blood-red palm. 'I have none to spare.'

The slaughterer shrugged with resignation. 'Just a thought,' he muttered.

With the latest charm nestling amongst the others he had accumulated over the years, Twig continued on his way through the labyrinth of tiny winding alleyways.

He was passing a pet shop – heavy with the odour of damp straw and hot fur – when all at once, a small vicious-looking creature rushed towards him, teeth bared. Twig started back nervously, then laughed as it reached the end of its leash and began leaping up and down on the spot, grunting excitedly. It was a prowlgrin cub, and it wanted to play.

'Hello, boy,' he said, crouching down and rubbing the frolicsome creature beneath its hairy chin. The prowlgrin gurgled with pleasure and rolled over onto its back. 'You big softie,' said Twig. He knew it wouldn't last. Fully-grown prowlgrins were both beasts of burden and the favoured guardbeasts of those with anything worth guarding.

'Hey!' came a rasping, yet insistent whisper. 'What are you wasting your time with that bag of leechfleas for? Come over here.'

Twig looked round. Besides the prowlgrin, the front of the ramshackle shop had countless other creatures on display: furry, feathered and scaled, as well as some of the lesser trolls and goblins which were chained to the walls. There wasn't one of them that looked as if it had just spoken.

'Up here, Twig,' the voice came again, more urgently now. A shiver ran up and down Twig's spine. Whatever *had* spoken also knew him. 'Over *here*!'

Twig looked up, and gasped. 'Caterbird!' he said.

'The very same,' the caterbird whispered, and shifted round awkwardly on its perch to face him. 'Greetings.'

'Greetings,' said Twig. 'But . . .'

'Keep your voice down,' the caterbird hissed, and its right eye swivelled round to the entrance of the shop. 'I don't want Flabsweat to know I can talk.'

Twig nodded, and swallowed away the lump in his throat. How had so noble a creature ended up in such squalid surroundings? The caterbird that had watched over Twig ever since he had been present at its hatching – who had dared to capture it? And why had it been placed in a cage barely larger than the poor creature itself so that it had to squat down on its perch, with its magnificent horned beak sticking out through the bars, unable to straighten up, unable to flap its wings?

'I'll soon have you out of there,' said Twig, pulling his knife from his belt. He thrust the thin blade into the keyhole of the padlock, and began jiggling it around feverishly.

'Hurry,' urged the caterbird. 'And for Sky's sake, don't let Flabsweat see what you're up to.'

'Any second now . . .' Twig muttered through clenched teeth. But the padlock remained stubbornly locked. 'If I can just . . .'

At that moment, the air suddenly resounded with a deafening CRACK! Twig immediately stopped what he was doing and spun round in alarm. He knew what had happened. It happened all the time. The emergency chains which helped to hold the floating city of Sanctaphrax in place were always breaking.

'Another one's gone!' someone screamed.

'Look out!' screeched another.

But it was already too late. The chain which had snapped was already tumbling back to earth with an incongruously gentle jingle-jangle. Down on the street, everyone was dashing this way and that, bumping into one another – getting nowhere.

The chain crashed down. A scream went up. Then silence.

As the dust settled, Twig surveyed the scene. The roof of the ironmonger's opposite had been stoved in. Two stalls were flattened. And there on the street lay an unfortunate creature, crushed to death by the weight of the falling metal.

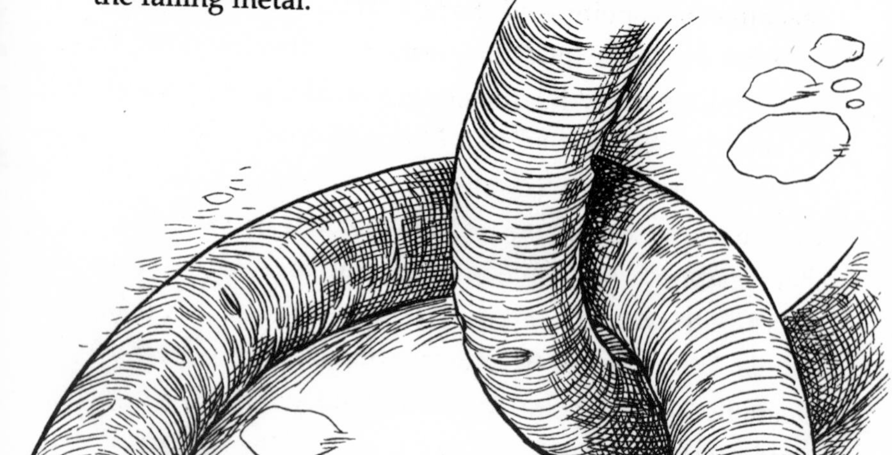

Twig stared at the tattered clothes and familiar heavy boots. It was the cloddertrog. Perhaps you should have listened to the slaughterer after all, he thought, and fingered the amulet at his neck. Now it was too late. For the cloddertrog, luck had run out.

'Ah, me,' he heard the caterbird sigh. 'The situation is reaching crisis point, and that's a fact.'

'What do you mean?' Twig asked.

'It's a long story,' he said slowly. 'And . . .' He paused.

'What?' said Twig.

The caterbird remained silent. It swivelled one eye meaningfully round towards the entrance of the shop.

'Oy!' came a gruff voice. 'Are you intending to buy that bird, or what?' Sliding the knife up his sleeve as he did so, Twig turned. He was confronted by a heavy-set character who was standing with his legs apart and his hands on his hips.

'I . . . I just dodged in here when the chain broke,' he said.

'Hmm,' said Flabsweat, looking round at the damage that had been caused. 'A bad business it is, all this chain-breaking. And all for that bunch of so-called academics. What good do they ever do us? Parasites, the lot of them. You know what? If it was up to me, I'd cut *all* the chains and let Sanctaphrax fly off into open sky. And good riddance!' he added bitterly, as he patted his glistening head with a dirty handkerchief.

Twig was speechless. He'd never heard anyone talk ill of the academics of the floating city before.

'Still,' Flabsweat went on, 'at least none of my property's been damaged, eh? *This* time. Now, are you interested in that bird or not?' he asked wheezily.

Twig glanced back at the bedraggled caterbird. 'I was looking for a talker.'

Flabsweat chuckled mirthlessly. 'Oh, you'll get nothing out of that one,' he said scornfully. 'Thick, it is. Still, you're welcome to try . . . I could let you have it for a very reasonable price.' He turned abruptly. 'I'm with another customer at the moment,' he called back. 'Give me a shout if you need any help.'

'Thick, indeed!' the caterbird exclaimed when Flabsweat had gone. 'The cheek! The audacity!' Its eye swivelled round and focused on Twig. 'Well, don't just stand there smirking,' it snapped. 'Get me out of here – while the coast is clear.'

'No,' said Twig.

The caterbird stared back at him, nonplussed. It cocked its head to one side – as far as the cage would allow. 'No?' it said.

'No,' Twig repeated. 'I want to hear that "long story" first. "The situation is reaching crisis point", that's what you said. I want to know why. I want to know what's happened.'

'Let me out, and then I'll tell you everything,' said the caterbird.

'No,' said Twig for a third time. 'I know you. You'll fly off the moment I unlock the cage door, and then I won't see you again till Sky knows when. Tell me this story first, and *then* I'll set you free.'

'Why, you insolent young whelp!' the caterbird shouted angrily. 'And after everything I've done for you!'

'Keep your voice down,' said Twig, looking round nervously at the doorway. 'Flabsweat will hear you.'

The caterbird fell still. It closed its eyes. For a moment, Twig thought that it was going to remain stubbornly silent. He was on the point of relenting, when the caterbird's beak moved.

'It all started a long time ago,' it began. 'Twenty years, to be precise. When your father was little older than you are now.'

'But that was before you were even born,' said Twig.

'Caterbirds share dreams, you know that,' it replied. 'What one knows, we all know. And if you're going to interrupt the whole time . . .'

'I'm not,' said Twig. 'Sorry. I won't do it again.'

The caterbird humphed irritably. 'Just see that you don't.'

·CHAPTER TWO·

THE CATERBIRD'S TALE

'Picture the scene,' the caterbird said. 'A cold, blustery, yet clear evening. The moon rises over Sanctaphrax, its towers and spires silhouetted against the purple sky. A lone figure emerges from the bottom of a particularly ill-favoured tower and scurries across the cobbled courtyard. It is an apprentice raintaster. His name, Vilnix Pompolnius.'

'What, *the* Vilnix Pompolnius?' Twig blurted out. 'Most High Academe of Sanctaphrax?' Although he had never seen the lofty academic, his reputation went before him.

'The very same,' said the caterbird. 'Many of those who attain greatness have the humblest of origins – in fact he used to be a knife-grinder in Undertown. But Vilnix Pompolnius was always ruthlessly ambitious, and never more so than on that night. As he hurried on, head down into the wind, towards the glittering spires of the School of Light and Darkness, he was plotting and scheming.'

Twig shuddered, and the fur of his hammelhornskin waistcoat bristled ominously.

'For you see,' the caterbird explained, 'Vilnix had the ear – and an indulgent ear, what's more – of one of the most powerful Sanctaphrax scholars at that time. The Professor of Darkness. It was he who had sponsored Vilnix through the Knights' Academy. And when Vilnix was later dismissed for insubordination, it was he who had secured his place in the Faculty of Raintasters rather than see him cast out of Sanctaphrax completely.'

The caterbird took a breath, and continued. 'Once inside the opulence of the professor's study, Vilnix held up a glass beaker of liquid dramatically. "The rain coming in from over the Edge is becoming more acidic," he said. "This is due to an increase in the number of sourmist particles in the raindrops. It was thought you might be interested," he added slyly.

'The Professor of Darkness *was* interested. Very interested. The presence of sourmist particles could presage the arrival of a Great Storm. "I must consult with the windtouchers and cloudwatchers," he said, "to determine whether they have also identified signs of an approaching Great Storm. Good work, my boy."

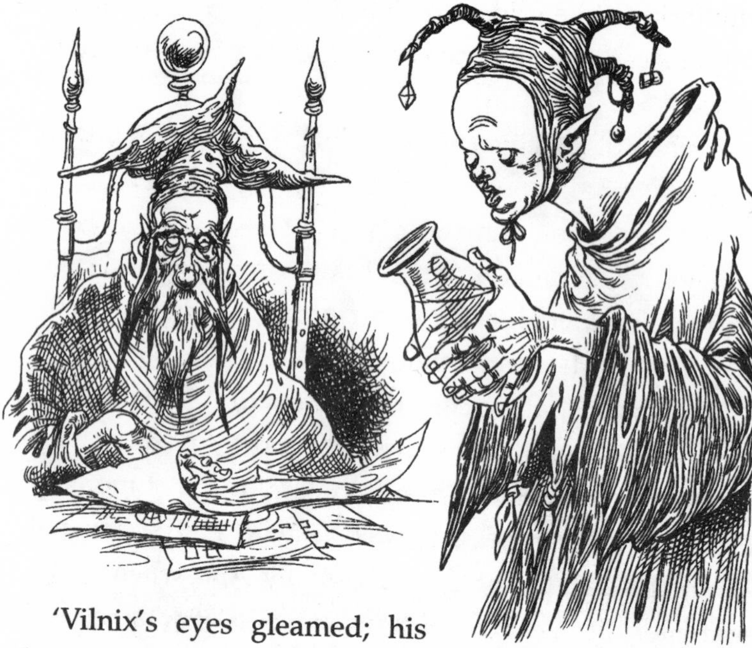

'Vilnix's eyes gleamed; his heart missed a beat. Things were going better than he had hoped. Taking care not to arouse his suspicions, he drew the old professor on. "A Great Storm?" he said, innocently. "Does this mean that a Knight Academic will be sent in search of more stormphrax?"

'The professor confirmed that it did. He tapped the papers in front of him. "And not before time, either, if these figures are correct," he said. "The great rock which Sanctaphrax stands upon is still growing – larger and larger, more and more buoyant . . ." His voice trailed away. He shook his head in despair.

'Vilnix watched him out of the corner of his eye. "And you need more stormphrax in the treasury to weigh it down – to . . . to . . ."

'The professor nodded vigorously. "To preserve the equilibrium," he said, and sighed. "It is so long since a Knight Academic returned with fresh supplies of stormphrax."

'A smile played over Vilnix's curled lips. "And which knight is to be sent on this occasion?" he asked.

'The professor snorted. "The Professor of Light's protégé. Quintinius . . ." He frowned. "Quintinius . . . oh, what's his name?"

'Vilnix winced. "Quintinius *Verginix*," he said.'

'My father!' Twig exclaimed, unable to keep quiet a moment longer. 'I didn't realize he knew the Most High Academe. Nor that he was ever in the Knights' Academy . . .' He paused thoughtfully. 'But then there's much I don't know about his life before he became a sky pirate,' he added.

'If you'd just hold your tongue for a moment,' the caterbird said impatiently, 'then perhaps . . .' It was cut short by the sound of frantic yelping which came from inside the shop.

The next moment, Flabsweat appeared at the doorway, white as a sheet and babbling on about how a vulpoon – a straggly bird of prey with a viciously serrated beak and razor-sharp talons – had just slipped its tether and laid into a hapless lapmuffler.

'Is it all right?' asked Twig.

'All right?' Flabsweat wheezed. 'The lapmuffler? No it's *not* all right. Guts everywhere, there are. And you can get good money for a lapmuffler. I'll have to fetch the animal-quack,' he muttered. 'Get it stitched up again.' He looked at Twig, as if seeing him for the first time. 'Are you trustworthy?' he asked.

Twig nodded.

'Hmm,' Flabsweat mumbled. 'Well, since you're still here, would you mind watching the shop while I'm gone? There could be something in it for you.'

'That's fine,' said Twig, trying not to sound too eager.

The moment Flabsweat was out of earshot, the caterbird immediately asked once more to be set free. But Twig was adamant. 'All in good time,' he said. 'After all, there's nothing worse than a tale which ends half way through its telling.'

The caterbird grumbled under its breath. 'Where was I, then? Ah, yes. Vilnix and your father . . . The pair of them entered the Knights' Academy on the very same morning and yet, from that first day, Quintinius Verginix outshone all the other young hopefuls – Vilnix included. In swordplay, archery and unarmed combat, he was unmatched; in the sailing of the stormchasers – the sky ships especially designed to chase the Great Storms – he was peerless.'

Twig beamed proudly, and imagined himself chasing a Great Storm. Pitching and rolling as the ship locked on to the whirling wind and then breaking through to the stillness within . . .

'Pay attention!' hissed the caterbird.

Twig looked up guiltily. 'I am!' he protested.

'Humph!' said the caterbird dubiously, its neck feathers ruffling. 'As I was saying, the professor explained to Vilnix that, if the Great Storm *was* confirmed, then – as tradition demanded – Quintinius Verginix would be knighted and despatched to the Twilight Woods. Sky willing, he would return with stormphrax.

'Vilnix smiled that smile of his. Inscrutable, reptilian. Now, at last, the time had come to touch upon the subject he had wanted to enquire about all along. "This . . . stormphrax," he said, in as off-hand a manner as he could manage. "When I was in the Knights' Academy, it was often talked about as the most wonderful substance that ever existed. We were told that the shards of stormphrax are in fact pure lightning," he continued, his voice oily, treacherous. "Can this possibly be true?"

'The Professor of Darkness nodded solemnly, and when he spoke again it was as though he was reciting from an ancient text. "That which is called stormphrax," he proclaimed, "is created in the eye of a Great Storm – a mighty maelstrom which is formed far beyond the Edge once every several years, which blows in on parched and sulphurous winds, which howls and sparks as it crosses the sky towards the Twilight Woods. There, the Great Storm breaks. It delivers a single mighty lightning bolt that scorches through the heavy twilight air and plunges into the soft earth beneath. In that instant it turns to solid stormphrax, gleaming in the half-light. Honoured is he who should witness such a sight."

'Vilnix's eyes gleamed greedily. Pure lightning! he thought. What power must each piece of stormphrax contain. He looked up. "And . . . errm . . . what does it look like exactly?"

'The professor's expression became dreamy. "Of unsurpassed beauty," he said. "A crystal that fizzes, that glows, that sparks . . ."

'"And yet it is heavy," said Vilnix. "Or so I learned. But how heavy?"

'"In the twilight of its creation it is no heavier than sand. Yet in the absolute darkness of the treasury at the centre of Sanctaphrax, a thimbleful weighs more than a thousand ironwood trees," the professor told him. "It provides the counter-balance to the buoyancy of the rock itself. Without it, the floating city would break its moorings and fly off into open sky . . ."

'Vilnix scratched his head theatrically. "What I don't understand is this," he said. "If the crystals and shards are so heavy, then how is the stormphrax brought through the darkness of the tunnels to the treasury in the first place?"

'The Professor of Darkness surveyed the youth gravely. Perhaps,' said the caterbird, interrupting his own story, 'just for a moment, he doubted the motives of the young apprentice. I'm not sure. Nor can I say what finally decided him to entrust Vilnix with the information. But entrust him, he did. It was a decision which was to change the course of history in Sanctaphrax. "It is transported in a light-box," he explained, "with the light it emits calibrated to approximate twilight itself."

'Vilnix turned away in order to hide his glee. If a light-box could be used to get the stormphrax in, then surely, he reasoned, it could also be used to get some out. "Perhaps I could see some for myself?" he suggested tentatively.

'"Absolutely not!" the Professor of Darkness barked – and Vilnix knew he had gone too far. "None may set eyes upon stormphrax," the professor said. "None save the Knights Academic and the guardian of the treasury –

who happens to be myself. It is blasphemy for unworthy eyes to feast upon the purity of stormphrax," he ranted. "An action, Vilnix, punishable by death."'

The caterbird paused dramatically. 'At that moment, the wind abruptly changed. The floating rock of Sanctaphrax drifted to the west and jerked violently as all the chains went taut.

'"I understand," said Vilnix humbly.

'"Ah Vilnix," the professor continued more gently. "I wonder if you truly do understand. There are many out there who covet stormphrax for themselves. Unscrupulous windtouchers and traitorous cloudwatchers who would not think twice at observing . . . at touching . . ." A violent shudder passed through his body. "At *experimenting* on stormphrax – if they thought it would serve their own ends."'

The caterbird fell silent for a moment before continuing with his tale. 'Early the following morning,' it said, 'the treasury guard would have seen a gangly figure creep furtively along the corridor from the treasury – had he not been dozing at his post. There was a light-box clutched in the intruder's bony hands. Inside the box were several fragments of stormphrax.'

Twig gasped. Vilnix *had* stolen some.

'Vilnix scurried back to the Apprentices' Laboratory at the top of the Raintasters' Tower,' the caterbird continued. 'Triumphantly he placed the box down in front of an eagerly waiting group of young raintasters and, with a flourish, opened the lid. The crystals of stormphrax sparkled and flashed like nothing they had seen before. "Pure lightning," said Vilnix. "If we can unleash and harness its energy then we'll become the most powerful academics Sanctaphrax has ever known."

'Hour after hour the raintasters worked, yet no matter what they tried – be it dissolving, freezing, melting or mixing the crystals with other substances – none discovered how to unlock the power of the stormphrax.

'Outside the window, the sun went down. The light turned a golden orange.

'Suddenly overcome with frustration, Vilnix raised the pestle and brought it down hard, crushing the fragment in his fury. A moment later, he was overcome with remorse. He had destroyed the priceless stormphrax.'

The caterbird's eye narrowed. 'Or so he thought at first. When he looked more carefully, though, Vilnix saw the result of his action. The crystals had turned to a sepia powder which moved in the bottom of the bowl like quicksilver. "I don't know what it is," Vilnix told the others, "but let's make some more."

'A second shard was taken. It was placed in a second mortar. A second pestle was raised. Outside, the light faded. Then, with the exception of Vilnix himself, who was busy pouring his own liquid dust into a jar, all the apprentices gathered round. The pestle was brought down and – BOOM!'

Twig started back in surprise.

'The power of the lightning had been unleashed all right,' the caterbird snorted. 'But with the direst of consequences. The explosion ripped through the tower, reducing half of it to smouldering rubble; it rocked Sanctaphrax to its core and jarred the ancient Anchor Chain to the very edge of breaking. The apprentices were all killed in the blast. All, that is, save one.'

'Vilnix Pompolnius,' Twig whispered.

'Precisely,' said the caterbird. 'There he lay, on the floor, barely alive but still clutching the jar to his chest. The scent of almonds hung in the air. Dazed and confused, Vilnix stared down at the stormphrax dust. What had gone wrong this second time? he wondered. What had happened?

'As he pulled himself up on his elbows, a drop of blood fell from a gash in his cheek and into the jar. The instant it made contact with the dust, the thick, red blood turned to crystal-clear water . . .'

The expression on the caterbird's face grew deadly serious. 'Crisis now hung over lofty Sanctaphrax,' it said solemnly. 'Thanks to the arrogant young raintaster's folly, the ancient chain was now perilously close to breaking point. Worse still, the theft of the stormphrax had left the treasury depleted. With the buoyancy of the rock increasing every day, and less to weight it down, the upward pressure on the rock became intolerable.

'There was just one glimmer of hope: the wind-touchers and cloudwatchers had confirmed that a Great Storm was indeed approaching. Accordingly, an Inauguration Ceremony was hurriedly arranged. Quintinius Verginix was to be knighted and would set off to chase the Great Storm to the Twilight Woods in search of stormphrax.

'Meanwhile,' the caterbird continued, 'Vilnix lay in his sick bed, his mind working furiously. He might have failed to harness the power of the lightning, but he realized that the stormphrax dust he'd created was itself miraculous – a single grain dropped into the foulest water instantly purified it. What would the inhabitants of filthy, fetid Undertown not give for his wonderful dust? "Anything," he whispered greedily. "Anything at all!"

'Without waiting to be discharged, he left his hospital ward and returned to the dilapidated tower of the rain-tasters – or rather rain*taster*, since he was the only one left. There, he busied himself. Everything had to be ready for the great day.

'Finally that day arrived. The sun rose, and shafts of light streamed in through the eastern arch of the Great Hall where the Sanctaphrax council was already assembled.

'The Professors of Light and Darkness – in white and black robes respectively – sat at the front of the hall

behind a table, upon which were a sword and a chalice. Before them, seated in rows, were the academics of Sanctaphrax. Every discipline was represented: the College of Cloud, the Academy of Wind, the Institute of Ice and Snow; the airsifters, the mistgraders, the fog-probers ... And, on crutches, the single remaining member of the Faculty of Raintasters.

'A tall, powerfully built young knight crossed the floor and knelt down in front of the Professor of Light. "By the powers invested in me – oh, thirst for knowledge, oh, sharpness of wit," the professor announced, raising first the chalice and then the sword, "I offer up for your approval Quintinius Verginix of the Knights' Academy."

'The professor looked down at the kneeling figure. "Do you, Quintinius Verginix, swear by all that is wise, that you will serve the Order of Knights Academic with heart and mind, forswearing all loyalties other than to Sanctaphrax."

'Quintinius trembled. "I do," he said.'

Twig's heart swelled with pride. My father! he thought.

'"And do you swear also that you will dedicate your life to the finding of stormphrax? That you will chase the Great Storms? That ..." The professor breathed in, slowly, deeply. "That you will not return until and unless you have completed your sacred quest?"'

The caterbird turned and fixed Twig with its unblinking gaze. 'His father – your grandfather – Wind Jackal, was a sky pirate captain. How furious Quintinius had been with him when the old fellow had offered him up for service at the Knights' Academy, for he had wanted to follow in his footsteps. Yet now . . . Now! Words could not describe how honoured he felt at receiving the highest accolade that Sanctaphrax could bestow. "Quintinius," he heard the professor gently say, "do you swear?"

'Quintinius Verginix raised his head. "I do!" he said.

'The Professor of Light then leaned forwards and handed the chalice to Quintinius. "Drink!" he said. Quintinius raised the chalice to his lips. The Professor of Light took up the sword, held it high above his head, and waited for Quintinius to drain the chalice. And waited and waited . . . But Quintinius remained motionless, unable to drink the thick, foul-smelling liquid.

'All at once, there was a flurry of movement in the rows of benches. It was Vilnix, leaping up noisily onto his crutches and making his way to the front of the hall.

'The Professor of Darkness sat forwards uneasily in his throne. What was the young fool doing now? he wondered. He watched Vilnix raise one of his crutches and tap the chalice lightly. "The good waters of the Edgewater River are no longer what they used to be," he chuckled, then turned to address the hall. "So, isn't it time we stopped fooling ourselves? All this nonsense about Knights Academic. About 'stormchasing'. About 'sacred stormphrax'." He sneered unpleasantly. "When did a Knight Academic last return? Tell me that? What has happened to all those others?"

'A murmur went round the hall. Garlinius Gernix? Lidius Pherix? Petronius Metrax? Where were they now? The murmuring increased. "Seven years ago, the last Knight Academic set sail," Vilnix went on, "Screedius Tollinix, his name . . ."

'"It was eight years ago," someone cried out.

'"Nearly nine," called another.

'Vilnix smiled slyly. He knew he had got them. "Nearly nine years," he announced, his voice echoing round the hall. He turned to Quintinius Verginix and pointed accusingly. "And we are pinning all our hopes on *him*!" He paused dramatically. "Why should he succeed where others have – so tragically – failed?"

'Just then, the Great Hall lurched violently. "Nine years!" Vilnix cried out again. "We need to do something now!" The hall lurched a second time. "But what?" Dust fell from cracks in the ceiling. "The answer is simple, my friends," Vilnix announced. "We must build more chains."

'There was a gasp, then the hall fell still. The plan was indeed simple. It was also outrageous. There had only ever been one chain: the Anchor Chain.

'A senior reader from the Faculty of Air Studies was the first to break the silence. "The production of chains would mean more factories, more foundries, more forges," he said. "The Edgewater River is already polluted." He nodded towards the chalice, still clutched in Verginix's hands. "We run the risk of making the water completely undrinkable."

'All eyes turned to Vilnix, who smiled benevolently. Then, making a mental note to reward the senior reader with a full professorship for his question, he hobbled back to Verginix and seized the chalice. With his free hand, he pulled a silver ball-shaped medallion from his gown and dipped it into the muddy liquid. Instantly, the water turned crystal clear. He returned the chalice to Verginix, who sipped. "It's sweet," he said. "Pure. Clean. It's like the water from the Deepwoods springs."

'The Professor of Light grabbed the chalice and drank, too. He looked up, eyes narrowed. "How is this possible?" he demanded.

'Vilnix returned the professor's gaze impassively. "It is possible because of an amazing discovery," he said. "*My* amazing discovery." He tapped the medallion. "Inside this pretty bauble is a substance so powerful that a single speck is enough to provide a person with drinking water for an entire year." He turned to the rows of incredulous academics. "This stor . . ." He stopped himself. "This substance, which I call *phraxdust* in honour of our beloved floating city, signifies a new beginning. Now we can ensure the future of Sanctaphrax by building those chains we so badly need, safe in the knowledge that we will never go thirsty."

'A cheer resounded around the hall. Vilnix lowered his head modestly. When he looked up again, his eyes were blazing with the excitement of impending victory. "My associates in the League of Free Merchants are merely awaiting the go-ahead to get started on the chains," he said. A smile flickered over his lips. "Naturally," he said, "they will deal only with the Most High Academe – the *new* Most High Academe, that is."

'He swung round and stared at the Professors of Light and Darkness. "For what would you have – this pair of buffoons who, between them, have brought Sanctaphrax to the very edge of destruction with their arcane rituals and pointless traditions? Or will you have someone who offers change, a fresh start, a new order?"

'Cries of "a fresh start" and "a new order" began to echo round the Great Hall. It lurched again. "And a new Most High Academe – Vilnix Pompolnius," the soon-to-be Professor of Air Studies proclaimed. The others took up the chant. Vilnix closed his eyes and bathed in their adulation as the chanting grew louder.

'Finally, he looked up. "Let your will be done!" he cried. "I, your new Most High Academe of Sanctaphrax, shall speak with the leaguesmen. The chains will be built. And Sanctaphrax, teetering on the brink of oblivion, will be saved!"'

The caterbird looked sadly at Twig. 'One person alone remained unmoved,' it said. 'One who, at the last possible moment, had seen everything he'd aspired to cruelly snatched away. Your father, Quintinius Verginix. His face hardened. There was something they would not take away: the sky ship that had been constructed especially for him. The *Stormchaser*.

'He spat with disgust and strode across the floor. At the door, he paused, turned. "If I, Quintinius Verginix cannot prove myself as a Knight Academic, then I shall prove myself as Cloud Wolf, the sky pirate," he bellowed. "And I make you this promise, Vilnix Pompolnius. You and your treacherous friends in the leagues will rue this day for so long as you shall live."

And with that, he left.'

The caterbird shook its head sadly. 'Of course, nothing is ever that simple,' it said. 'Despite your father's parting words, it was many moons before his defiant promise came true. His first ill-fated voyage almost saw the end of both him and his ship – indeed the only good that came of it was his initial meeting with the Stone Pilot. He was forced to lay low, to store the *Stormchaser* in a safe berth and take up a position on a league ship until he had gained sufficient money and inside information of the Leagues to try again.' Its eye swivelled and narrowed. 'The league captain he ended up serving was the notorious Multinius Gobtrax . . .'

'It was upon his ship that *I* was born,' said Twig thoughtfully. 'But what about Sanctaphrax itself?'

The caterbird snorted. 'For all Vilnix's fine words of *a fresh start* and *a new order,* the situation rapidly worsened. Nowadays, as you know, the Undertowners labour like slaves in the foundries and forges, making chains and weights to support the Anchor Chain. They manage to keep Sanctaphrax in place – but only just. It is a never-ending task. And all the while, the waters of the Edgewater River are becoming more and more polluted. It is only because of the particles of phraxdust, supplied to the loyal leaguesmen by Vilnix Pompolnius, that Undertown hasn't already choked to death on its own filth.'

Twig shook his head in dismay. 'And Vilnix?' he asked. 'What does he get out of it all?'

'Wealth and power,' the caterbird replied simply. 'In return for drinkable water, the leagues shower Vilnix and his new Faculty of Raintasters with everything they could possibly want – and more. Just so long as the specks of phraxdust keep coming.'

'But surely the situation cannot last for ever,' said Twig. 'When the phraxdust runs out Vilnix Pompolnius will have to take more stormphrax from the treasury.'

The caterbird nodded. 'That's precisely what he does do,' he said. 'And the Professor of Darkness is powerless to stop him. What's more, the production of more phraxdust has proved elusive. Despite a thousand attempts – many tragic – no-one has been able to reproduce the results of that first experiment.'

'But it's crazy!' said Twig. 'The more stormphrax that's taken from the treasury, the more chains they need to manufacture. The more chains that are manufactured, the worse the pollution in the water gets. And the worse the pollution in the water, the more phraxdust they need to purify it!'

'It's a vicious circle,' said the caterbird, 'that's what it is. A terrible, vicious circle. And twenty years after that momentous meeting in the Great Hall, the situation is looking bleaker than ever for both Sanctaphrax and Undertown. Wrapped up in their own concerns, both the raintasters and the leaguesmen remain blind to what is going on around them. But if nothing is done – and done soon – then it is only a matter of time before everything falls apart.'

'But what *can* be done?' said Twig.

The caterbird shrugged and turned his head. 'That is not for me to say.' It swivelled a purple eye round towards him. 'Right,' it said, 'my story is complete. *Now*, will you release me?'

Twig started guiltily. 'Of course,' he said, and retrieved the knife from his sleeve. He began jiggling the narrow blade about in the padlock again. There was a soft click. The lock was undone. He unclasped the padlock and pulled the door open.

'OY!' came an angry cry. 'You said you were trustworthy! What in Open Sky do you think you're doing?'

Twig spun round and gasped with horror. It was Flabsweat, back at last with the animal-doctor, and bearing down upon him like a madman.

'I can't . . .' he heard the caterbird complaining. 'Help me, Twig.'

Twig looked back. The caterbird had managed to get its head and one wing out of the cage, but the door was small, and its other wing was twisted back and jammed. 'Go back in and try again,' Twig instructed.

The caterbird did as it was told, folded its wings up and thrust its head back outside. Flabsweat was almost upon them, a heavy club swinging at his side. Twig reached up and, with his hands round the creature's neck and shoulders, pulled gently. Flabsweat raised the club. The caterbird pushed its legs hard against the perch.

'Come on!' Twig urged it desperately.

'Almost there . . .' the caterbird strained. 'I . . . Made it!' It flapped its wings experimentally – once, twice – then launched itself off from the edge of the cage and soared up into the air, apparently none the worse for its confinement.

It was time for Twig to make himself scarce, too. Without looking round, he turned on his heels and sped away into the thronging street. As he set off, the club glanced against his shoulder. A second earlier, and it would have smashed his skull.

Faster and faster Twig ran, barging through the crowds, elbowing dawdlers out of his way. Behind him, Flabsweat screamed with rage.

'Thief! Scoundrel! Netherwicket!' he roared. 'CATCH HIM!'

Twig ducked down into a narrow alley. The shouting grew fainter, but Twig kept going, faster than ever. Past pawnbrokers and tooth-pullers, barbers and inns, round a corner – and slap-bang into the arms of his father.

Cloud Wolf shook him roughly by the shoulders. 'Twig!' he bellowed. 'I've been looking for you everywhere. We're ready to set sail. What have you been up to?'

'N . . . nothing,' Twig faltered, unable to return Cloud Wolf's furious gaze.

High in the sky, behind his father's head, Twig saw the caterbird flapping off into the setting sun – past Sanctaphrax, out of Undertown, and away. He sighed enviously. The caterbird might be gone, but its doom-laden words remained with him. *A vicious circle, that's what it is. If nothing is done then it is only a matter of time before everything falls apart.*

And for a second time, Twig found himself wondering, But what *can* be done?

·CHAPTER THREE·

CRIES AND WHISPERS

i
In the Twilight Woods

It was twilight. It was always twilight in the woods, with the sun permanently setting. Or was it rising? It was difficult to tell. Certainly none who entered the Twilight Woods could ever be sure. Most, however, felt that the golden half-light between the trees whispered of endings not beginnings.

The trees, majestically tall and always in full leaf, swayed in a gentle breeze which endlessly circled the woods. They, like everything else – the grass, the ground, the flowers – were coated in a mantle of fine dust which glittered and glistened like frost.

Yet it was not cold. Far from it. The breeze was balmy, and the earth itself radiated a soothing warmth which rippled through the air above so that everything swam slightly before the eyes; nothing was quite in focus. Standing in the Twilight Woods was like standing under water.

There was no birdsong, no insect-rustle, no animal-cry, for none of these creatures inhabited the woods. Yet, to those with ears to hear, there were voices – and not simply the whisperings of the trees. They were real voices – muttering, mumbling, occasionally crying out. One was close by.

'Hold steady, Vinchix,' it said wearily, though not without hope. 'Nearly there. Hold steady, now.'

The voice came from high up in the air, where a wrecked sky ship was skewered on a jagged treetop, its broken mast pointing accusingly up at the sky out of which it had dropped. Dangling from a harness was a knight, seated upon his prowlgrin charger and silhouetted against the golden sky. Inside the rusted armour, their bodies were skeletal. Yet both the knight and his mount were alive, still alive.

The visor creaked, and the ghostly voice repeated its words of encouragement, words of command.

'Nearly there, Vinchix. Hold steady!'

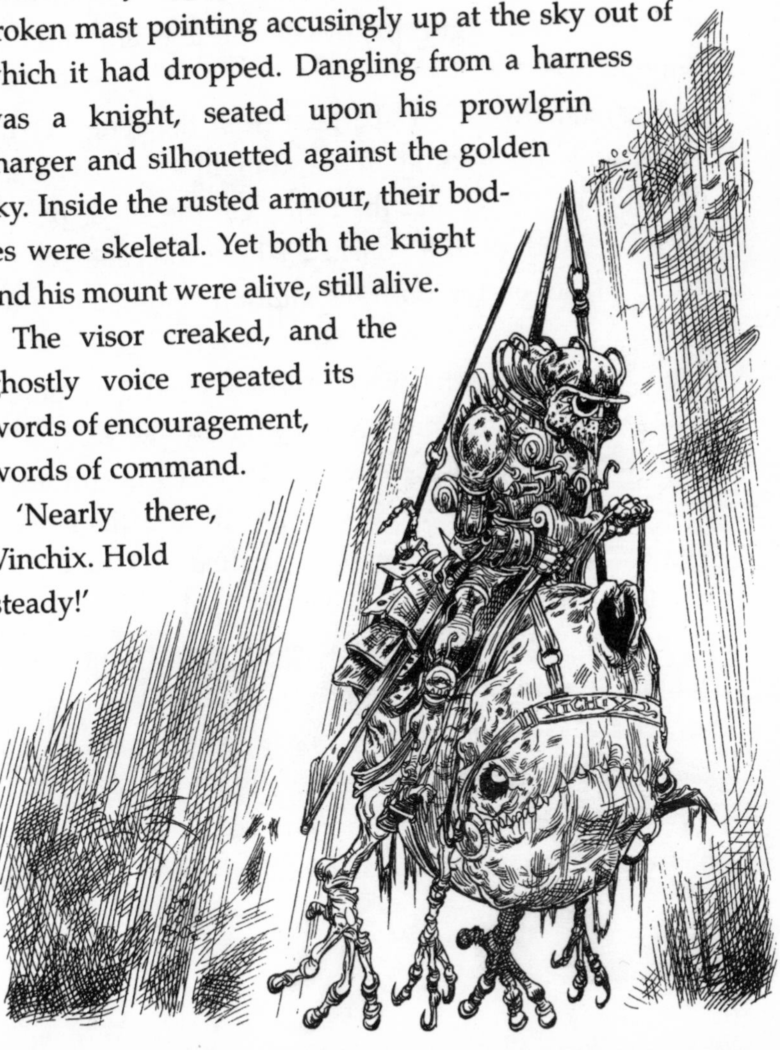

ii
In the Palace of the Most High Academe

The chamber – or Inner Sanctum, as it was known – was truly sumptuous. The floors were carpeted with snow-white fur, the ceiling embossed with gold, while those areas of wall not lined with bookcases were panelled with blackwood and silver, and encrusted with precious stones. Ornaments cluttered every surface – porcelain vases and ivory figurines, ornate carvings and intricate time-pieces.

A crystal chandelier sparkled from the centre of the room, unlit, but glinting in the sunlight – shooting darts of brilliance all around the room. On the silver panels, they flickered; on the polished tables, the cabinets, the grand piano; on the portraits and mirrors – and on the gleaming pate of the Most High Academe of Sanctaphrax himself, who was stretched out on an ottoman next to the long arched window, fast asleep.

He looked out of place in the opulent surroundings. The black gown he wore was faded, and there were sandals on his feet – modest, scuffed. Likewise, his angular body and sunken cheeks spoke of a life of abstinence rather than indulgence; his shaven head, of humility and rigour – yet also a degree of vanity. After all, why else would a person have his personal monogram – **ViP** – stitched into the hem of his hair-shirt?

A high-pitched rasping vibrated throughout the chamber. The person stirred and rolled onto his side. His hooded eyes snapped open. The rasping sound came again, louder than before. He sat up and peered through the window.

Situated at the top of one of the tallest, and certainly the most magnificent tower in Sanctaphrax, the Inner Sanctum offered breathtaking views across Undertown and beyond. The Most High Academe looked down. Between the billowing clouds of smoke, he could just make out half a dozen or so Undertowners busy securing the latest chain to the side of the great floating rock.

'Splendid,' he yawned, and climbed stiffly to his feet. He stretched, scratched, rubbed a hand absentmindedly over his head, and yawned again. 'Things to be done.'

He strode over towards a massive ironwood chest which stood in the corner of the room, pulled a heavy iron key from the folds of his robes and crouched down. At sundown, he was to have a meeting with Simenon Xintax, the current Leaguesmaster. Before then, he wanted to weigh the remaining phraxdust and calculate just how long the precious specks would last.

The lock released with a soft click, the lid creaked open and the Most High Academe stared down into the gaping darkness within. He bent down, retrieved a glass phial, held it up to the window – and sighed.

Even *he* could see the liquid dust was all but gone.

'A problem, certainly,' he muttered, 'but not yet an emergency. Better get it weighed, though. Work out just how many particles of phraxdust remain. Bargaining with Xintax from a point of ignorance would be fatal . . .' He wriggled round irritably. 'But first I have got to do something about this intolerable itching.'

Thankfully, thoughtful to the last, Minulis his manservant, had remembered the back-scratcher. A pretty thing it was, with a solid gold handle and claws of dragon ivory. The Most High Academe squirmed with pleasure as he scraped it up and down his back, reminded – as he always was – that the greatest pleasures in life are often the simplest. He lay the scratcher down and – deciding to postpone his calculations a little longer – poured himself a glass of wine from the decanter which Minulis had also thought to bring.

He walked across the room and stopped in front of a full-length mirror, smiled, straightened up and lifted his head. 'To you, Vilnix Pompolnius,' he said, raising his glass. 'The Most High Academe of Sanctaphrax.'

At that moment, the drilling began again – louder than ever. The floating rock trembled, the Inner Sanctum rocked and the mirror shook. The Most High Academe was so startled that he let the glass slip from between his fingers. It broke with a muffled *clink* and the spilt wine spread out over the white fur like blood.

The Most High Academe turned, and stepped away in disgust. As he did so, he heard a breathy whooshing sound behind him, followed by an almighty crash. He froze. Turned back. And there, lying on the floor in a thousand pieces, was the mirror. Crouching, he picked up a piece of glass and turned it over in his hand.

What was it his grandmother used to say? *A broken looking-glass, a sorrow come to pass*. He stared at the dark eye staring back at him from the jagged fragment, and winked. 'It's a good job *you're* not superstitious,' he said, and cackled with laughter.

iii
In the Mire

The leader of the gnokgoblins – a short, stocky female by the name of Mim – sniffed the air, fingered the collection of talismans and amulets around her neck and stepped forwards. She winced as the soft mud oozed up between her stubby toes.

Screed Toe-taker watched her scornfully. 'Still think you can make it across the Mire on your own?' he said.

Mim ignored him and waded on. *Squellp, squellp, squellp* went the pale sticky mud as it covered first her ankles, then her calves, then her knees. She stopped and looked up. The Mire seemed to stretch out for ever in front of her. Even if she, by some miracle, could make it

across to the other side, she knew that neither old Torp nor the young'uns would stand a chance.

'All right,' she said, and turned angrily – sinking down still further in the process. 'Perhaps we *could* be doing with a guide after all.' She hitched her skirt up. The mud crept higher. 'Help us out of here,' she said.

Screed stepped forwards and held out a bony white hand. Like the Mire which was his home, every inch of his body had been bleached the colour of dirty sheets. He pulled the goblin back to safety, and stared down at her, hands on hips.

The goblin rummaged inside her bag. 'Fifty, per person,' she said. 'That's what you said. Which makes . . .' She counted out the coins. 'Five hundred in all.'

Screed shook his head. 'The price has gone up,' he said, his voice nasal, mocking. 'A hundred each. That's what it's going to cost you now.'

'But that's all our savings,' she gasped. 'What are we ever supposed to live on when we do make it to Undertown?'

Screed shrugged. 'That's your problem,' he said. 'I'm not forcing you to come with me. If you can cross the Mire with its sinking-mud and poisonous blow-holes – not to mention the muglumps, oozefish and white ravens that would rip you apart as soon as look at you . . . Well, it's your choice.'

Mim stared glumly at the rest of her family group, huddled together on the bank. The choice was simple, she realized. Either they arrived in Undertown with nothing, or they didn't arrive at all.

'A thousand it is,' she sighed, handing over the money. 'But your price is very high, so it is.'

Screed Toe-taker snatched the money and dropped it into his pocket. He turned away, muttering under his breath. 'My price is higher than you could ever imagine, dear lady.' And he set off into the bleached and sticky landscape.

The family of goblins collected up their sacks of belongings.

'Come on then,' Screed called back impatiently. 'Look lively. Keep together. Walk where I walk. And don't look back.'

iv
In the Tower of Light and Darkness

The Professor of Light was angry. 'Accursed chains, accursed drilling, accursed Vilnix Pompolnius,' he growled between clenched teeth. 'Must we now destroy Sanctaphrax in order to save it?' He heaved himself up, with an armful of books, and began returning them to the shelves.

It was always the same. Every time a new chain was attached to the floating rock, the vibrations wreaked havoc in his humble study. Priceless apparatus was damaged, invaluable experiments ruined – and his entire library of books ended up on the floor.

With the last book back in place, the professor returned to his desk. He was just about to sit down when he noticed something out of the corner of his eye. Something most unwelcome. At that moment, however, there was a knock on the door and the Professor of Darkness burst in. 'We must talk,' he said.

The Professor of Light didn't move. 'Look,' he said glumly.

'What?'

'There,' he said, pointing. 'Light!'

The Professor of Darkness laughed. 'You should be pleased,' he said. 'Light is, after all, your field of study and expertise.'

'As yours is darkness,' the Professor of Light snapped. 'Or rather, the *absence* of light. But there is a place for everything. And just as the darkness in the heart of your erstwhile protégé, Vilnix Pompolnius, is misplaced, so too is light appearing through cracks in the middle of my wall.' He turned back and poked at the mortar. 'See that,' he said. 'It's all crumbling away.'

The Professor of Darkness sighed miserably. 'My study's just as bad,' he said.

The first thing Vilnix had done when he became Most High Academe, was to take the palatial School of Light and Darkness for himself, while relegating the two professors and their departments to the dilapidated Raintasters' Tower. The explosion had caused bad structural damage. Each time a chain was attached to the rock, that damage increased. It was merely a matter of time before the tower collapsed completely.

'Well, it can't go on like this,' said the Professor of Light. 'Which is why . . .'

'Which is why we need to talk,' the Professor of Darkness butted in.

'Which is why,' the Professor of Light continued, 'I have already spoken to someone about how one might change the situation.'

The Professor of Darkness stared at his colleague with a mixture of admiration and resentment. Despite their reduced circumstances, the old rivalry between the two academics remained. 'You have already spoken to whom?' he demanded.

'Mother Horsefeather,' came the reply.

'Mother Horsefeather!' The Professor of Darkness was astounded. 'That greedy old bird-woman. She'd sell her own eggs if the price was right. Do you seriously think we can trust her?'

'Oh, yes,' said the Professor of Light. 'We can trust her to do everything in her power to deceive us. That knowledge will be our strength.'

V
In the Backstreets of Undertown

'In here,' said Slitch, stopping abruptly next to a ramshackle hut on his left. He unlocked the door, and disappeared inside. His companion followed him. He pushed the door to and waited while the gnokgoblin located the lamp and lit it. 'My word,' Slitch shuddered, as he turned round and the pale light filled the room. 'You slaughterers *are* red.'

Tendon shuffled about awkwardly. 'Have you got any phraxdust, or what?' he said. 'If you haven't . . .'

'The best phraxdust in Undertown,' Slitch assured him. 'Potentially.'

'Potentially?'

'I have acquired some black-market stormphrax,' he explained. 'All you have to do is grind it down and, Hob's your goblin!'

Tendon stared at him impassively. 'You must think I'm daft,' he said at length. 'Stormphrax explodes when you try and grind it. Everyone knows that. His high-and-mighty Acadimwit is the only one with the secret . . .'

'I, too, now have that secret,' said Slitch. He took a bowl down from a shelf and placed it on a small table. Then he pulled a wad of velvet from his inside pocket, carefully unfolded it and removed a glistening, sparkling shard of stormphrax, which he held up between his middle-finger and thumb – the others all being missing – and placed it gently down in the bowl.

Tendon remained dubious. 'What's the secret, then?'

'This,' said Slitch, removing a leather pouch from his belt. He loosened the drawstring for Tendon to see inside.

'But what is it?' he said.

'Powdered deadwood bark,' said Slitch conspiratorially. 'The finest money can buy.'

Tendon pulled back nervously. It was the stuff Undertown doctors used to anaesthetize their patients for an operation.

'The numbing qualities of the deadwood counteract the volatility of the stormphrax,' Slitch explained. 'The explosion is *paralysed*, so to speak.'

'You're sure about that?' said Tendon.

'Oh, for Sky's sake!' said Slitch impatiently. 'Didn't you tell me you were sick of spending all your hard-earned cash on drinking water? Didn't you say you'd do *anything* to get hold of some phraxdust of your own. The deadwood will work, I assure you,' he said as he sprinkled a liberal quantity into the bowl. 'There will be no explosion and you, my friend, will have phraxdust to last you for the rest of your life.'

Tendon fingered the charms around his neck anxiously. Despite his misgivings, however, the gnokgoblin's offer proved too tempting to resist. He paid over the hundred quarters they had agreed upon, picked up the pestle and raised it above his head. With the money safely in his pocket, Slitch scuttled off to the far end of the hut, and crouched down behind a metal stove.

'Strike now!' he cried. 'It *will* work!'

And Tendon, gripping the handle as tightly as his sweaty hands would allow, brought the pestle sharply down with all his strength.

The explosion blew the roof of the hut right off. Tendon was hurled back against the far wall where he collapsed, a lifeless heap.

Slitch crawled out of his hiding place and climbed shakily to his feet. He looked down at the body of the dead slaughterer.

'Or then again,' he sighed, 'maybe it won't.'

vi
In the Bloodoak Tavern

Mother Horsefeather sat at a table by the door of the heaving Bloodoak tavern. Perched on a bar-stool beside her was Forficule, the nightwaif she employed. The pair of them were watching the rowdy groups of drinkers plunge their tankards into the communal trough of frothy woodale, one after the other. The illicit brewery concealed in the cellar was a nice little earner – particularly when the weather was so hot.

The door opened and three leaguesmen swaggered in. Mother Horsefeather clacked her beak with distaste. 'A good evening to you,' she said, avoiding their gaze. She removed three tankards from the shelf behind her and placed them on the table. 'That'll be twenty quarters apiece.'

'You can drink as much as you like,' the first leaguesman – a regular to the Bloodoak – explained to the others. 'Is that not right, Mother Horsefeather?'

Mother Horsefeather scowled. 'Indeed it is,' she said. 'But remember the rules.' She nodded over to a sign nailed to the wall. *No swearing. No fighting. No vomiting on the premises.*

'We need no reminding,' said the leaguesman, as he handed her a single gold coin worth twice the asking price. 'Keep the change, dear lady,' he said, and winked.

Mother Horsefeather stared down at the till. 'Thanking you kindly, sire,' she said, and slammed the drawer shut. Only when he had turned away, did she look up. You worm-ridden lump of hammelhorn dung, she thought bitterly.

'Now, now,' said Forficule gently, his huge bat-like ears twitching. Mother Horsefeather swivelled her head round and glared furiously at the nightwaif.

'*Heard* that, did you?' she snapped.

'I hear everything,' Forficule replied. 'As you well know. Every word, every whisper, every thought – for my sins.'

Mother Horsefeather snorted. The feathers around her neck were standing on end, her yellow eyes glinted. 'Well he is!' she said sourly, and nodded towards the table of leaguesmen. 'They all are. With their fine clothes, big tips and fancy manners. Hammelhorn dung, the lot of them!'

Forficule tutted sympathetically. He understood his employer's loathing of the leaguesmen. Because of their alliance with Vilnix Pompolnius – building chains in return for phraxdust – their dominance in the drinking-water market had left them unassailably powerful. If it wasn't for her black-market dealings with the sky pirates, Mother Horsefeather would have gone under long ago.

'Ah, the sky pirates,' Forficule sighed. 'Those intrepid

skyfaring brigands who will kow-tow to no-one. Where would we be without them?'

'Where indeed?' Mother Horsefeather nodded, her neck feathers finally lying down smooth. 'Speaking of which, Cloud Wolf and his crew should be back soon. I hope to goodness he's had as profitable a trip as he led me to believe. Otherwise . . .' The conversation she'd had with the Professor of Light abruptly came back to her, and an idea appeared, as if from nowhere. Her eyes twinkled. 'Unless . . .'

Forficule, who had been listening in to her thoughts, chuckled. 'Heads you win, tails he loses, eh?'

Before she had a chance to reply, the Bloodoak tavern suddenly rocked with the force of a nearby explosion. Forficule clutched at his ears and squealed with pain.

'Lawks-a-mussy!' Mother Horsefeather cried out, and the ruff of feathers shot back upwards. 'That sounded close!' As the dust settled, Forficule removed his hands, and shook his head from side to side. His massive ears fluttered like two enormous moths.

'Two more poor fools trying to grind their own phraxdust,' he said sadly. He cocked his head to one side and listened intently. 'The dead one is Tendon, a slaughterer.'

'I remember him,' said Mother Horsefeather. 'Often in here, he is – was. Always stank of leather.'

Forficule nodded. 'The survivor's name is Slitch,' he said, and shuddered. 'Ooh, a horrible piece of work, he is. He'd tried mixing stormphrax with deadwood dust and got Tendon to do his dirty work for him.'

Mother Horsefeather frowned. 'Everyone is so desperate to get hold of phraxdust,' she said. Her yellow eyes sparkled malevolently. 'If anyone's to blame for what happened,' she added, nodding her beak towards the table of rowdy leaguesmen, 'it's them! Oh, what I wouldn't give to wipe that smug expression off their loathsome faces once and for all!'

·CHAPTER FOUR·

THE CARGO OF IRONWOOD

It was late afternoon and, having successfully concluded a deal with some woodtrolls for a massive consignment of ironwood, the crew of the *Stormchaser* were heading back to Undertown. The atmosphere on board the sky pirate ship was buoyant, and Twig – the hero of the hour – was feeling particularly pleased with himself.

Although he hadn't personally known any of the woodtrolls they'd encountered, the fact that he'd been brought up in a woodtroll village meant that Twig was familiar with their ways. He knew when their *nos* meant *yes*. He knew when to haggle and, more importantly, when to stop – for if a woodtroll is offered too little for his wood, then he will take offence and refuse to sell no matter what. When Twig saw the tell-tale signs in their faces – a pursing of the lips and twitching of their rubbery noses – he had nodded towards his father. The deal was as good as it possibly could be.

Afterwards, to celebrate, Cloud Wolf had cracked open a barrel of woodgrog and handed round tots of the fiery liquid to each member of his motley crew. 'To a job well done,' he proclaimed.

'A job well done!' the sky pirates roared back.

Tem Barkwater, a hairy giant of an individual, slapped Twig on the back and squeezed his shoulder. 'Without this lad's knowledge of the Deepwoods folk, we would never have got the wood at such a price,' he said and raised his glass. 'To Twig!'

'To Twig!' the sky pirates chorused.

Even Slyvo Spleethe the quartermaster, who seldom had a good word to say to anyone, spoke generously. 'He did indeed do well,' he conceded.

Only one person failed to join in the congratulations: Cloud Wolf himself. In fact, when Tem Barkwater had proposed his toast, the captain had turned away abruptly and returned to the helm. Twig understood why. None of the crew knew that he was Cloud Wolf's son. To avoid any accusations of favouritism, the captain preferred it that way. Accordingly, he treated the lad more harshly than the other crew members and never betrayed any affection he might feel.

Understanding the reason for Cloud Wolf's surliness was one thing. Liking it, however, was another. Every slight, every injustice, every harsh word cut Twig to the quick and left him feeling that his father was ashamed of him. Swallowing his pride now, Twig joined Cloud Wolf on the bridge.

'When do you think we'll be back?' he asked tentatively.

'Nightfall,' said Cloud Wolf, as he locked the wheel and made minute adjustments to the hanging weights. 'If the winds remain favourable, that is.'

Twig watched his father in awe. Sky ships were notoriously difficult to sail, yet to Cloud Wolf it came as second nature. He understood his ship as though it was a part of him. Having heard the caterbird's story, Twig knew why. 'I guess you learned all about sky sailing and . . . and stormchasing in the Knights' Academy . . .'

Cloud Wolf turned and stared at him curiously. 'What

do you know about the Knights' Academy?' he demanded.

'N . . . nothing much,' Twig faltered. 'But the caterbird told me . . .'

'Pfff!' Cloud Wolf said dismissively. 'That scraggy blabbermouth! It is better to live in the present than dwell on the past,' he said sharply. And then, clearly eager to change the subject, he added, 'It's high time *you* learned the rudiments of skysailing.'

Twig's heart fluttered. He had been with the sky pirates now for more than two years. Like them, he wore one of the heavy pirate longcoats with its numerous hanging accoutrements – the telescope, the grappling iron, the compass and scales, the drinking vessel . . . Like them, his front was protected by an ornately tooled leather breastshield, while on his back was a set of parawings. In all that time, however, Twig's duties on board had been restricted to the most menial of tasks. He scrubbed. He cleaned. He was the all-purpose gofer. Now, it seemed, that was to change.

'The flight-rock, when cold, gives us natural lift,' Cloud Wolf explained. 'Balance, forward thrust and manoeuvring have to be achieved manually. Through these,' he said, and pointed to two long rows of bone-handled levers, each set at a different angle.

Twig nodded keenly.

'These levers here are connected to the hanging weights,' he said. 'The stern-weight, prow-weight, starboard hull-weights, small, medium and large; port hull-weights, ditto, mid-hull, peri-hull, neben-hull, and klute-hull-weights . . .' he said, rattling off the names. 'And *these* levers on the other side are attached to the sails. Foresail, aftsail, topsail,' he said, tapping the levers, each in turn. 'Mainsails – one and two – skysail, staysail, studsail, boomsail, spinnaker and jib. Got that? It's just a matter of keeping everything in balance.'

Twig nodded uncertainly. Cloud Wolf stood back. 'Come on then,' he said gruffly. 'Take the wheel, and let's see what you're made of.'

At first, it was easy. The adjustments had already been made and Twig merely had to grip the wooden wheel to hold a steady course. But when a sudden gust from the north-east caused the ship to dip, the task suddenly became more complicated.

'Up the medium starboard hull-weight,' the captain instructed. Twig panicked. Which lever was it? The eighth or the ninth from the left? He grasped the ninth and yanked. The *Stormchaser* tipped to one side. 'Not *that* much!' Cloud Wolf snapped. 'Up the staysail a tad and down the large port hull-weight . . . The *port* hull-weight, you idiot!' he roared, as the sky ship tipped over still further.

Twig yelped with terror. He was going to crash the boat. At this rate, his first attempt at skysailing would also be his last. He clung on to the helm grimly – brain feverish, hands shaking, heart thumping fit to burst. He mustn't let his father down. Pulling himself forwards, he seized the ninth lever for a second time. This time he moved it gently, downing the weight only a couple of notches.

And it worked! The boat righted itself.

'Good,' the captain said. 'You're developing the touch. Now, up the skysail,' he instructed. 'Down the prow-weight a fraction, realign the small and medium starboard hull-weights and . . .'

'League ship to starboard!' Spiker's strident voice cried out. 'League ship to starboard – and approaching fast.'

The words echoed round Twig's head. He felt short of breath; he felt sick. The rows of levers blurred before his eyes. One of them would almost certainly make the sky ship accelerate forwards – but which one? 'League ship getting closer,' Spiker announced. And Twig, in his blind panic, broke the first rule of sky ship sailing. He let go of the helm.

The wheel spun back viciously the moment his sweaty hands loosened their grip, sending him skittering across the deck. Instantly, the sails crumpled, and the *Stormchaser* went into a sudden spinning descent.

'You halfwit!' Cloud Wolf roared. He seized the wheel and, bracing himself against the deck, frantically tried to stop it turning. 'Hubble!' he bellowed. 'Here. Now!'

Twig was just stumbling back to his feet when Hubble brushed past him. It was only the most glancing of blows, but the albino banderbear was a colossal mountain of a creature – and Twig went flying.

The next moment, the spinning stopped. Twig looked up. The wheel was clasped, motionless, in the banderbear's massive paws. And the captain, freed up at last, was running his hands over the levers – now here, now there – as surely as an accordion-player darting over the keys.

'League ship, one hundred strides and closing,' called Spiker. The captain's silent playing continued. 'Fifty strides! Forty . . .'

All at once, the *Stormchaser* leapt forwards. The crew roared their approval. Twig staggered to his feet at last, muttering heartfelt thanks to Sky above. They'd made it.

Then Cloud Wolf spoke. 'There's something wrong!' he said quietly.

Wrong? thought Twig. What could be wrong? Hadn't they escaped with their illicit cargo of ironwood after all? He squinted behind him. Yes, there was the league ship, miles away!

'Something *very* wrong,' he said. 'We've got no lift.'

Twig stared at Cloud Wolf in horror. His stomach felt empty. Was this some kind of joke? Had he chosen this moment to tease him like a father? One look at the man's ashen face as he jiggled, jerked and yanked at a lever with more and more force confirmed that he had not.

'It's . . . it's the bl . . . blasted stern-weight,' he spluttered. 'It's jammed.'

'League ship gaining once more,' Spiker called out. 'And from the flag I'd say the Leaguesmaster himself was on board.'

Cloud Wolf spun round. 'Hubble,' he said, but then

had second thoughts. The massive creature was ill-suited to clambering over the hull. As were Tem Barkwater and Stope Boltjaw. And the oakelf, Spiker, though willing, would never be strong enough to release the great iron weight. Slyvo Spleethe would have been ideal if he wasn't such a coward. While Mugbutt, the flat-head goblin, though fearless in battle and everything else, was too stupid to remember what he was supposed to do. 'I'd better see to it myself,' he muttered.

Twig leaped forwards. 'Let me,' he said. 'I can do it.' Cloud Wolf looked him up and down, his thin lips tightly pursed. 'You need to stay here, at the levers,' Twig went on. 'For when I've released it.'

'League ship at two hundred strides,' Spiker called.

Cloud Wolf nodded briefly. 'All right,' he said. 'But be sure not to let me down.'

'I won't,' said Twig grimly, as he hurried off to the back of the ship. There he seized a tolley-rope and pulled himself up onto the rail. A flash of forest green blurred past him far, far below.

'Don't look down!' he heard Tem Barkwater shouting to him.

Easier said than done, thought Twig as he lowered himself carefully onto the hull-rigging, which hugged the bottom of the ship like cobwebs. The further down and round he went – slowly, carefully – the more upside down he became. The wind tugged his hair and plucked at his fingers. But he could see the stern-weight now – all tangled up in a loop of pitched rope.

He kept on, whispering words of encouragement to himself as he went. 'Just a little bit further. Just a teeny bit more.'

'How's it going?' he heard his father call.

'Nearly there,' he shouted back.

'League ship back on one hundred strides, and closing,' came Spiker's latest update.

Trembling with anticipation, Twig reached forwards, and pulled the clump of rope hard to one side. The weight should be swinging free. If he could just . . . He inched forwards and pushed the back of the huge knot with the heel of his hand. Suddenly it gave, the rope came loose, the weight swung down and . . . fell completely away. Twig gasped in absolute horror as the huge, round circle of iron tumbled off through the air, down to the forest below.

'What have you done?' came a voice. It was Cloud Wolf, and he sounded furious.

'I . . . I . . .' Twig began. The sky ship was rolling from end to end and reeling from port to starboard, completely out of control. It was all Twig could do to hang on. What *had* he done?

'You've only gone and released the rudder-wheel!' Cloud Wolf yelled. 'For Sky's sake, Twig! I thought that Mugbutt was stupid!'

Twig quaked under the barrage of insults and recriminations. Scalding tears welled in his eyes, tears he couldn't wipe away for fear of losing his grip. Then again, he thought miserably, wouldn't it be better simply to let go, to disappear? Anything, rather than face his father's wrath.

'Twig! Can you hear me, lad?' came a second voice. It was Tem Barkwater. 'We're going to have to ditch our cargo. That means opening the hull-doors. You'd better get yourself out of there sharpish!'

Ditch the cargo! Twig's heart sank and his tears flowed more freely than ever. The ironwood which had taken so much effort – and money – to acquire would have to go. And all because of him.

'Come on!' Tem screamed.

Twig climbed feverishly back along the hull-rigging, hand over hand, foot over foot, until he was climbing upright once more. He looked up. Tem Barkwater's huge red hand was reaching down for him. He grasped it gratefully and gasped as he was pulled back onto the deck. 'Right-ho, cap'n!' Tem cried.

Twig went to smile his thanks, but the sky pirate had already turned away, unable to meet his gaze. No cargo meant no wages. And, though squalid, Undertown was not the place to be with neither money nor the means to make it.

'Open the hull-doors!' Cloud Wolf commanded.

'Aye-aye, cap'n,' came the voice of Stope Boltjaw from the hold. Then, from deep within the bowels of the ship, there came the clanking of chains, followed by a rumbling *thud-thud-thud*.

Twig looked away guiltily. It was the ironwood logs tumbling, one after the other, through the gap beneath the hull as the doors were slowly cranked open. He glanced over the side. As he did so, the rest of the load was abruptly discharged. A strange and deadly precipitation, it tumbled back down to the Deepwoods from where it had come.

On seeing what was taking place just in front of them, the league ship immediately gave up the chase and swooped down after the falling logs. A load that size was not to be sniffed at. Twig's misery was complete. The *Stormchaser*'s loss had turned to the league ship's gain.

'Can't we go down and battle it out with them?' Twig asked. 'I'm not afraid.'

Cloud Wolf turned on him with a look of utter contempt. 'We have no rudder-wheel,' he said. 'No control. It's only the flight-rock keeping us skyborne at all.' He turned away. 'Raise the mainsheets,' he bellowed. 'Square the bidgets – and pray. Pray like you've never prayed before. An untimely squall and it won't be just the cargo we lose. It'll be the *Stormchaser* itself.'

No-one spoke a word as the sky ship limped back to Undertown. It was the slowest and most nail-biting trip that Twig had ever endured. Darkness had fallen by the time the fuzzy lights of Sanctaphrax came into view. Below it, Undertown seethed and gagged beneath a heavy pall of smoke. And still the silence continued. Twig felt wretched. It would have been better if the sky pirates had ranted and raved, called him every name under the Sky – anything but this deathly hush.

There were patrol boats around, but none took any notice of the crippled sky ship as it headed in towards the boom-docks. With its hull-doors still open, the craft clearly had nothing to hide.

Cloud Wolf steered the *Stormchaser* into its concealed berth, Stope Boltjaw dropped anchor, and Spiker jumped down onto the raised jetty to secure the ship's tolley-ropes to the tether-rings. The crew disembarked.

'Outstanding, Master Twig!' Slyvo Spleethe hissed as he passed him by. Twig shuddered, but the comment was only to be expected. Spleethe had never liked him. Worse, by far, were the averted eyes of the others. He shuffled miserably after them towards the gangplank.

'Not you, Twig,' said Cloud Wolf sharply. Twig froze. Now he was for it! He turned round, hung his head – and waited. Only when the last sky pirate had departed, did Cloud Wolf speak.

'That I should live to see the day when my son – my own son – should scupper a sky ship,' he said.

Twig swallowed hard, but the tears would not go away. 'I'm sorry,' he whispered.

'Sorry? What good is sorry?' Cloud Wolf thundered. 'We've lost the ironwood, the rudder-wheel – we almost lost the *Stormchaser* itself. And I still might.' His eye glinted like hard flint. 'I'm ashamed to call you my son.'

The words struck Twig like a blow to the back of the neck. 'Ashamed to call me your son?' he said and, as he spoke, his distress turned to anger. He looked up boldly. 'So, what's new?' he demanded.

'How dare you!' Cloud Wolf raged, his face turning purple.

But Twig did dare. 'You've never acknowledged to anyone, ever, that you're my father,' he said. 'Does that mean you've always been ashamed of me, ever since the moment we first found each other? Does it? Well, does it? Tell me it does and I'll leave, now.'

Cloud Wolf remained silent. Twig turned to go.

'Twig!' said Cloud Wolf. 'Wait.' Twig stopped. 'Turn and face me, boy,' he said. Twig turned slowly round. He stared up at his father defiantly.

Cloud Wolf stared back, a twinkle in his eye. 'That was well said,' he told him. 'You are right. I have not acknowledged who you are on board the ship. But not for the reason you suppose. There are those who would mutiny given half a chance, and take the *Stormchaser* for themselves. If they found out what . . .' He paused. 'How important you are to me – for you *are* important to me, Twig. You should know that.'

Twig nodded and sniffed. The lump in his throat was back.

'If they found that out, it would put your own life in the gravest danger.'

Twig let his head hang. How could he ever have doubted what his father felt for him? Now *he* was the one who felt ashamed. He looked up and smiled sheepishly. 'Can I stay, then?' he said.

Cloud Wolf's face creased up with concern. 'I meant it when I said I still might lose the *Stormchaser*,' he said.

'But how?' said Twig. 'Why? It's your sky ship, isn't it? I thought you took it on the day of your inauguration.'

Cloud Wolf snorted. 'It costs a lot to keep a sky ship

aloft,' he said. 'And ever since that infestation of woodbugs, the *Stormchaser* has been in debt up to the top of her pretty caternest. I was depending on the ironwood to pay off some of the money I owe. No,' he sighed, 'if anyone owns the *Stormchaser*, it's Mother Horsefeather. She's the one who finances us. And rakes off most of the profits into the bargain,' he added with a scowl. 'And now I can't pay her, she might well decide to take back what's rightfully hers.'

Twig was appalled. 'But she can't,' he cried.

'Oh, but she can,' said Cloud Wolf. 'What's more, she'd make sure I never got credit anywhere else. And what is a sky pirate captain without a sky ship, Twig? Eh? I'll tell you. Nothing. That's what he is. Nothing at all.'

Twig turned his head away, distraught. His father – once the finest Knight Academic Sanctaphrax had ever seen, now the greatest sky pirate in the Edge – was staring ignominy in the face. And he, Twig, was to blame. It was *all* his fault.

'I'm . . .'

'Just don't say you're sorry again,' Cloud Wolf interrupted. 'Come on. Let's go and get this over with,' he said gruffly. 'I just hope the old buzzard's not in too greedy a mood. And remember,' he said, as he strode off towards the gangplank, 'when we're sat down talking with Mother Horsefeather in the Bloodoak tavern, you be careful what you say – or even think. I swear the walls in there have ears!'

·CHAPTER FIVE·

THE BLOODOAK TAVERN

Creak, creak, creak, the tavern sign protested as it swung to and fro in the gathering wind. Twig glanced up and flinched. The sign was – as might have been expected – an artist's impression of a bloodoak, a terrible flesh-eating tree. And a very good impression it was, too, Twig admitted with a shudder. The glistening bark, the glinting mandibles – every time he saw the picture of the tree, he could almost *smell* the rank, metallic stench of death oozing from it.

For Twig knew all about bloodoaks. Once, lost in the Deepwoods, he had fallen victim to a particularly gruesome specimen. It had swallowed him whole and would have eaten him alive had it not been for his hammelhornskin waistcoat, which had bristled at the danger and jammed in the monster's throat. Trembling at the memory, he asked himself why anyone would want to name a tavern after so disgusting a creation.

'Are you going to stand there gawping all night?' Cloud Wolf snapped impatiently as he pushed past his son. 'Let's go in.'

As he threw the door open – BOOF! – a burst of energy exploded from the room. Heat. Noise. Light. And a heavy cocktail of smells, both fragrant and foul. Twig reeled backwards from the blast. No matter how many times he visited the Bloodoak tavern, he would never get used to the shock of that first moment.

The tavern was like a miniature version of Undertown itself, reflecting the incredible diversity of the place. There were flat-head and hammer-head goblins; oakelves, mobgnomes, black-dwarfs and red-dwarfs; trolls and trogs of every shape and every size. There were leaguesmen and sky pirates, tinkers and totters, raggers and royners, merchants and mongers . . . It seemed to Twig, as he stared in through the open door, that there was not a single Edge creature, tribe or profession not represented in the throbbing room.

The cloddertrog on the door recognized Cloud Wolf at once. He informed them that Mother Horsefeather was 'somewhere hereabouts' and waved them through. Sticking close to him as Cloud Wolf carved a route across the room, Twig tried hard not to knock anyone's drinks as he went. Flat-heads were notoriously volatile and throats had been slit for far less than a tankard of spilled woodale before now. Jostled and crushed in the sweaty, steaming surge of bodies, it occurred to Twig that *the Bloodoak* was exactly the right name for the tavern after all.

The owner of the tavern was over by the rear exit. She looked up as Cloud Wolf approached.

'Mother Horsefeather,' he said. 'I trust I find you well.'

'Well enough,' came the guarded reply.

She turned and stared down at Twig questioningly.

'Ah yes,' said Cloud Wolf. 'This is Twig. Twig, Mother Horsefeather. I want him to sit in on our meeting.'

Twig trembled under the ferocious gaze of the creature

in front of him. Of course, he'd seen Mother Horsefeather before, but always at a distance. Close up, she was imposing, intimidating.

As tall as Cloud Wolf himself, she had beady yellow eyes, a sharp hooked beak and a ruff of crimson feathers around her neck. Her arms, too, were fringed with feathers which, since she was standing with her taloned hands clasped together, hugged her like a purple and orange shawl. Twig found himself wondering whether, under the voluminous yellow dress, her whole body was covered with the same magnificent plumage.

All at once, he became aware of someone sniggering to his right. He turned. And there, perched on a bar-stool, was a slight, almost luminous creature, grinning from ear to huge bat-like ear.

Mother Horsefeather raised a feathery eyebrow and glared at Twig menacingly. 'This is Forficule,' she said, and returned her unblinking gaze to Cloud Wolf. 'He, too, will be present during our little talk,' she told him.

Cloud Wolf shrugged. 'It's all the same to me,' he said, then added as if Forficule were not there, 'What is it? Looks like the runt of an oakelf litter.'

Mother Horsefeather's beak clacked with sudden amusement. 'He's my little treasure-weasure,' she whispered. 'Aren't you, Forfy? Right then,' she announced to the rest. 'Follow me. We'll find it much easier to talk in the quiet of the back room.' And with that, she turned on her talon-toes and disappeared through the door. Cloud Wolf and Twig followed her, with Forficule bringing up the rear.

The room was hot, airless, clammy; it smelled of decay. And as Twig took his place at the small, square table, he felt increasingly uneasy. To his left was his father; to his right, Mother Horsefeather; while opposite him sat Forficule, eyes shut, ears trembling. The fur of his hammelhornskin waistcoat prickled beneath Twig's fingers.

Mother Horsefeather placed her scaly hands in front of her, one on top of the other, and smiled at Cloud Wolf. 'Well, well,' she said pleasantly. 'Here we are again.'

'Indeed,' said Cloud Wolf. 'And may I say how hale and hearty you are looking tonight, Mother Horsefeather – and how much yellow suits you.'

'Oh, Wolfie!' she said, preening despite herself. 'You old flatterer!'

'But I mean every word,' Cloud Wolf insisted.

'You, too, are as dashing as ever,' Mother Horsefeather clucked admiringly.

Twig looked at his father. It was true. In his ornate sky pirate regalia – with its ruffs and tassels and gleaming golden buttons – Cloud Wolf looked magnificent. Then, with a sudden shiver, Twig recalled how angry his father's face had turned when he had let go of the helm; when the *Stormchaser* had gone into a downward spin. How he had cursed when their precious cargo of iron-wood had tumbled down out of the sky.

He looked up. Forficule was staring at him intently. *Be careful what you say – or even think,* that was what his father had told him. Twig stared back at the quivering-eared nightwaif and shivered with anxiety.

'The rudder-wheel, eh?' he heard Mother Horsefeather saying. The pleasantries were clearly over. 'It sounds important.'

'It is,' Cloud Wolf agreed.

'And therefore costly?'

Cloud Wolf nodded.

'Well, I'm sure we can come to some agreement,' she said brightly. 'So long as the quality of the ironwood lives up to my expectations.'

Twig felt the blood drain from his face as the enormity of what he had done suddenly struck home. Because of him, the *Stormchaser* would never fly again. His heart pounded loudly. And when Forficule leaned across and whispered to Mother Horsefeather behind his hand, it pounded louder still.

The bird-woman's eyes gleamed. 'So, Wolfie,' she said, '*will* it live up to my expectations, do you think?' She leaned forwards and thrust her beak into his face. 'Or is there something you'd like to tell me?' she demanded, her voice suddenly clipped and hard.

'Tell you? I . . .' he began, scratching behind his eye-patch. 'That is . . .' He glanced round at his son. Twig had never seen him look so weary, so *old* before.

'Well?' Mother Horsefeather demanded.

'We did have rather an unfortunate set-back,' Cloud Wolf agreed. 'But nothing that can't be put right on our next voyage . . .'

'You seem to forget,' she interrupted brusquely, 'that you owe me ten thousand already. And that's before interest. Plus, of course, the cost of a new rudder-wheel . . .' She paused dramatically, and began preening her neck feathers carelessly. 'I'm not sure there should *be* a next voyage.'

Twig shrivelled up inside.

'Unless,' she went on slyly, 'it is on my terms.'

Cloud Wolf did not flinch. 'And those terms would be?' he said calmly.

Mother Horsefeather pulled herself to her scaly feet and turned around. She clasped her hands behind her. Cloud Wolf and Twig stared at her back expectantly. A half-smile played over Forficule's lips.

'We go back a long way, Cloud Wolf; you and I,' she said. 'Despite your current, unfortunate financial problems, you are still the finest sky pirate captain there is – after all, it was hardly your fault that the *Stormchaser* became riddled with woodbugs.' She stepped forwards. 'Therefore it is to you that I come with what will surely prove to be your greatest challenge. If you are successful, your debts will be cancelled at a stroke.'

Cloud Wolf eyed her mistrustfully. 'And what's in it for you?'

'Oh, Wolfie, Wolfie,' she said, and cackled with

laughter. 'You know me so well.' Her beady eyes glinted. 'A great deal, that's all I am prepared to say for now.'

'But . . .'

'Save your questions until I have explained,' Mother Horsefeather interrupted sharply. She breathed in. 'I have been approached,' she said, 'by the P . . .'

Forficule coughed loudly.

'. . . by . . . a Sanctaphrax academic,' Mother Horsefeather continued. 'He wishes to get his hands on some stormphrax – lots of it – and he will pay handsomely for the privilege.'

Cloud Wolf snorted. 'If he needs stormphrax, then why doesn't he simply raid the treasury,' he said. 'From what I've heard, everyone else does these days.'

Mother Horsefeather stared at him impassively. 'It is to replenish the depleted stocks in the treasury that the stormphrax is needed,' she said. 'Too much has been taken for phraxdust already,' she continued, glancing down at the silver medallion around her own neck. 'Not that anyone has actually been successful – but if nothing is done, then the floating rock will break its moorings and Sanctaphrax will drift off. Into open sky. For ever.'

'Pah,' Cloud Wolf spat. 'Sanctaphrax. What good has that place ever done me?'

Mother Horsefeather clucked with irritation. 'Sanctaphrax is an integral part of all our lives,' she snapped. 'Its scholars are the weather-diviners, the map-makers, the sifters of mists and phantasms that come in from beyond the Edge. It is they who read the patterns which bring order from chaos. Without them,

Undertown itself could not exist. You, of all people, Wolfie, should understand this.'

'I know only that Sanctaphrax stole the years of my prime and then cast me out,' Cloud Wolf said.

Mother Horsefeather's eyes sparkled. 'You felt cheated – you still do,' she said. 'And rightly so.' She paused. 'That is why I offer you now the possibility to avenge yourself on the usurpers.'

Cloud Wolf stared back at her, as it finally occurred to him what the devious bird-woman was after. 'You mean you want me to sail to the Twilight Woods in search of fresh stormphrax,' he said.

'I *mean,*' said Mother Horsefeather, 'that I am giving you a second chance. You will be able to utilize all that training you were given in the Knights' Academy; you will show that Cloud Wolf is more than a mere cut-throat and outlaw. At long last,' she said as she puffed out her breast feathers, 'the magnificent *Stormchaser* will be used for the purpose it was originally built. Not lugging ironwood around like some glorified tug-ship. But stormchasing!'

Twig's heart thrilled at the sound of the word. Stooorm-cha-sing! he whispered, savouring every syllable. He smiled excitedly. *Stoooooorrm-cha-sing.*

The next moment, any dreams he might have had were shattered. 'Out of the question,' Cloud Wolf snapped.

'Oh, but Wolfie,' Mother Horsefeather wheedled, 'think of the acclaim that will be heaped upon your head when you arrive back triumphant, with enough stormphrax to weigh down the floating rock of Sanctaphrax for a thousand years. Think of the glory – think of the *power*,' she added softly.

Twig willed his father to agree. Cloud Wolf shook his head.

'For, of course, with the treasury weighted down once again,' Mother Horsefeather went on, 'the accursed link between the raintasters and the leaguesmen will at last be broken.' Her eyes glinted. 'New alliances will have to be forged – a new hierarchy established. Think how high in the pecking-order you could find yourself. You and me, Wolfie. Just you and me, up there at the top.'

But still Cloud Wolf remained unmoved. 'Many long years have gone by since I left the Academy,' he said. 'And the *Stormchaser* is not the sky ship she once was . . .'

'Wolfie! Wolfie!' Mother Horsefeather chided him. 'Such false modesty! Quintinius Verginix was the most outstanding knight the Academy had ever seen, and the skills you learned there have been honed to razor sharpness as Cloud Wolf, the finest sky pirate captain ever.' Twig heard his father snort. 'And as for the *Stormchaser*,' she went on, 'we will have it repaired, realigned, refurbished – the works. She will fly as she has never flown before.'

For a moment, Twig thought this would sway it. Surely his father would be unable to resist such an offer. Cloud Wolf smiled and played with his waxed side-whiskers.

'No,' he said. He scraped the chair noisily backwards and stood up from the table. 'And now if you'll excuse me . . .'

Mother Horsefeather began scratching at the floor in a sudden fury. 'Excuse you?' she screeched. 'No I will *not* excuse you.' Her voice grew more and more shrill. 'You have no choice! I have something you need – and you have something I need. You *will* do what I say!'

Cloud Wolf merely chuckled to himself as he made for the door. In an uncontrollable rage, Mother Horsefeather flapped and thrashed about. The table tipped over. The chairs went flying. Twig, dodging back out of her way, caught sight of Forficule. He was staring intently at the door, ears quivering and a smile twitching at the corners of his mouth.

'You're finished!' Mother Horsefeather was screaming. 'Finished! Do you understand? I'll see you never so much as set foot on a sky ship again. I'll . . .'

There was a muffled knock. Mother Horsefeather froze. The door opened. 'You!' she exclaimed.

'My lord,' Cloud Wolf gasped, and fell to his knees.

Twig stared at the newcomer in confusion. He was old – very old – with long white hair and a stout staff to aid his unsteady gait. With his broken sandals, his fingerless gloves and his patched and threadbare gown, he looked as wretched as any alley-vagrant. Yet there was his father kneeling down before him.

Twig turned to Forficule for an explanation, but the nightwaif had moved away. It was up on the table, urgently whispering into Mother Horsefeather's ear behind its pale and bony hand. Twig would have given anything to know what was being said but, strain as he might, he could hear nothing but a conspiratorial *hssp-psss-psss*.

Twig groaned, returned his attention to his father – and groaned again. If he had been disappointed by Cloud Wolf's reaction to Mother Horsefeather's proposal, then he was mortified to find his father still kneeling.

Will you stand up and fight? he wondered bitterly. Or do you intend to remain on your knees for ever?

·CHAPTER SIX·

SCREED TOE-TAKER

The journey across the Mire was proving to be as harsh as anything Mim had ever experienced. And if the leader of the gnokgoblin family was finding the going tough, then the others were all but at the end of their strength. Mim's concern was growing more acute with every passing minute.

Screed had given strict instructions that they should all keep together, yet the further they went on across the endless muddy wasteland, the more separated they were becoming.

Mim squelched back and forth along the long straggling line as fast as the gluey mud would allow. From the young'uns up at the front to old Torp, who was bringing up the rear, and back again, she went – offering words of encouragement as she passed.

'Not far, now,' she assured them. 'Nearly there.' The

rank, stagnant stench of the Mire grew stronger. 'Forget where we are now and keep your thoughts on the wonderful place for which we're bound – a place of plenty, a place of opportunity, a place where goblins are respected and the streets are paved with gold.'

The gnokgoblins smiled back at her weakly, but none made any attempt to reply. They didn't have the energy. Even the young'uns, who had started out so enthusiastically – gambolling ahead like lambs – were now dragging their feet painfully slowly. Mim knew it would not be long before the first of her party gave up completely.

'Hey!' she cried out to the gaunt figure up ahead. 'Slow down a bit.'

Screed turned. 'Now what?' he snapped irritably.

Mim strode towards him. The burning sun beat down ferociously. Screed waited for her to catch up, hands on hips, leering. 'We need a rest,' she panted.

Screed looked her up and down, then squinted up at the sky. 'We keep on till sundown,' he said. 'Then we'll rest for the night. It's too dangerous travelling by darkness – what with the sinking-mud and poisonous blow-holes . . .'

'Not to mention the muglumps, oozefish and white ravens,' Mim interrupted tartly. 'Not that we've encountered any so far.'

Screed pulled himself up to his full height, and stared down his nose at her scornfully. 'Forgive me,' he said, his voice loaded with sarcasm, 'I was under the impression that you employed me as a guide to *avoid* these dangers.

If I'd only *known* you wanted to see them for yourselves . . .'

Mim looked down sheepishly. 'I'm sorry,' she said. 'It's just . . . Well, some of us are finding it difficult to keep up with the pace you're setting.'

Screed glanced back along the line of goblins. 'You paid for a two-day crossing,' he said sharply. 'Any longer than that and it'll cost you.'

'But we haven't got any more money,' Mim cried out.

Screed's yellow teeth gleamed against the bleached paleness of his lips. 'Like I say,' he said, turning and walking away. 'It'll cost you.'

Darkness had fallen by the time Screed Toe-taker called it a day. He stopped on an outcrop of rocks and placed the lantern down. 'We'll stop here,' he called back through cupped hands.

One by one, the goblins started to arrive.

'Keep that infant still!' Screed shouted at a young female with a squawling babe-in-arms. 'It'll attract every muglump for miles around.' He lifted the lantern and peered back the way they'd come. 'And where are the others?' he snapped. 'Just my luck if they've already gone and got themselves lost.'

'No, look! Over there!' one of the young'uns cried, and pointed back towards a curious, squat figure which was shuffling towards them out of the low, swirling mist. As it grew closer, the one figure became three. It was Mim, trudging purposefully on with a youngster on her back and an arm around old Torp.

Screed smiled. 'All present and correct,' he said.

Buoyed up by the gleeful cheers of the others, Mim staggered across that last stretch of sucking quicksilver mud and up onto the rocky outcrop. Old Torp released himself from her supporting arm and sat down. 'Well done, old-timer,' she whispered breathlessly. 'You made it.' She pulled the sleeping youngster from her back, laid him gently down on the ground and covered him with a blanket. Then, groaning with the effort, she pulled herself upright and looked round.

'Well, it's certainly not the most comfortable place I've ever spent the night,' she said. 'But it's dry. And that's the main thing. So, thank you, Screed, for bringing us to this place.'

'My pleasure,' he said, ignoring the sullen faces of the others – it was, after all, an expression he had seen a thousand times before. 'And now,' he said, 'you must all get some sleep.'

The gnokgoblins didn't need telling twice. Within seconds, all of them were rolled up in their blankets, like a row of woolly cocoons – all, that is, except for Mim. 'And yourself?' she asked Screed.

'Me?' he said loftily, as he perched himself on the top of the tallest rock. 'Oh, don't you worry about me. I have little need of sleep.' He gazed round the flat landscape, glinting and glistening like burnished silver beneath the moon. 'Besides, someone has to keep watch.'

Mim was reassured. Despite what she'd said earlier, she hadn't liked the sound of the muglumps, oozefish or white ravens one tiny little bit. She wished Screed a good night, snuggled up between two of the young'uns and, by the time dark clouds rolled over the moon a couple of minutes later, she was, like all the others, fast asleep.

Screed listened to the rasping chorus of snoring and smirked to himself. 'Sleep well, little dwarves,' he whispered, 'or goblins – or whatever you are.'

He brought the lantern nearer as the clouds rolled in, and pulled a knife from his belt which he began sliding gently back and forwards over the smooth rock. Occasionally he would spit on the metal, and inspect the blade in the yellow light. Then off he went again, slowly, methodically – *whish, whish, whish* – until every point along the blade was sharp enough to split a hair in two.

Woe betide the creature that thought it could get the better of him. Screed stood up, lantern in one hand, knife in the other. Woe betide *any* who fell into his clutches.

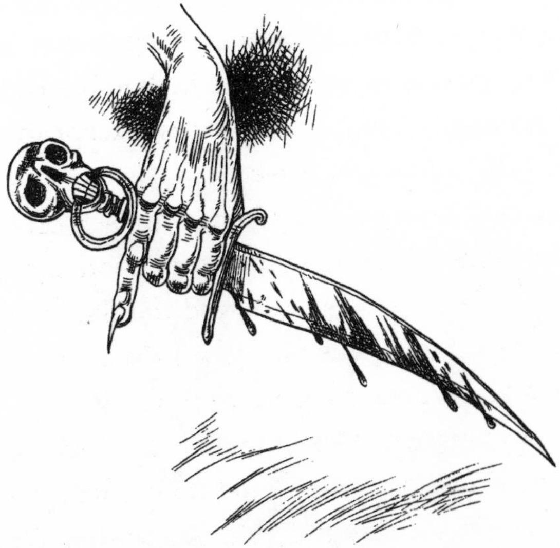

Abruptly, the clouds rolled back, and the bright moon shone down on the grisly scene, turning everything to black and white.

White blankets. Black blood.

White bony body, lurching on into the mud. Black shadow, stretching back across the rocks.

White ravens, already scavenging. Black deeds. Monstrous deeds.

With his leather bag full of bloody booty clasped in his bony hand, Screed Toe-taker picked his way across the Mire. Far away in front of him, the moon glinted on the wreck of a sky ship which lay half-buried in the mud like a giant skeleton. Unblinking, Screed kept his eyes fixed on the glinting ribs of the broken hull. Closer and closer he came. Not once did he falter. Not once did he look back.

'At last,' Screed muttered as he made it to the wreck. He glanced round for any tell-tale sign of intrusion and, when he was satisfied there was no-one and nothing there, he scuttled into the shadowy recesses of the lop-sided shipwreck.

If some intruder *had* taken the opportunity to investigate the place during its owner's absence, he, she or it would have been left shaking with disbelief at the horrors the ship concealed. The dank air, for a start, was thick with the pungent stench of death. And then there were the walls – studded their length and breadth with mummified toes, nailed to the wood.

There were big toes, small toes, hairy toes, scaly toes, toes with razor-sharp talons, toes with claws, toes with webbing – all of them shrivelled and black. And these were just a fraction of the total number – the select few – for at the far end of the hull in a massive wedge-shaped drift, were thousands upon thousands more.

Screed sloshed his way along the sky ship. He didn't register the gory trophies lining the walls, neither did he notice the awful stench; to Screed Toe-taker, the wreck of the *Windcutter* simply smelled of home.

He hung the lantern on a hook above a huge chest of ironwood and glass, opened the lid, crouched down and set to work. One by one he pulled the severed toes from his bag and, like an insane manicurist, scraped beneath the nails with a small file. Tiny particles of dust – some glistening white, some tinged with sepia – dropped down into the chest with the rest. And when he was satisfied that every speck had been removed, he tossed the toes on to the great heap with the others.

Finally done, Screed stared down with dreamy contentment into the chest. It was more than three-quarters full of the toe-nail scrapings. 'Oh, my beea-oootiful looty-booty,' he whispered. 'One day you will fill the chest, right up to the top. One day soon, Sky willing. And on that wondrous day, then maybe – just maybe – shall my quest be at an end.'

Screed stood up, slammed the lid shut, and stepped outside. The long night was over. To his left, the tell-tale purple clouds of a gathering storm were rolling in from the retreating darkness. To his right and far away in the distance, was a sky ship, silhouetted against the rising sun.

Both were coming closer.

·CHAPTER SEVEN·

ASSENT AND BETRAYAL

Mother Horsefeather watched uneasily as the ancient figure approached Cloud Wolf. She knew from bitter experience that it could be disastrous to allow the different parties – the supply and demand, so to speak – to meet. Far better to remain in the middle: fixing the deal, pulling the strings. And yet, as Forficule had pointed out, since she had singularly failed to persuade Cloud Wolf to embark on the journey, the newcomer was their only hope.

He leaned forwards and tapped Cloud Wolf with his staff. 'Arise, Quintinius Verginix,' he said.

Twig watched his father climb to his feet and look up. He saw his eyes gleaming with reverence, with respect, and at that moment, Twig knew with absolute certainty who the old, shabbily dressed person must be. It was his father's erstwhile patron and mentor, the Professor of Light.

'It has been a long time, Quintinius,' he said. 'The finest Knight Academic in a hundred generations, you were – yet . . .' He paused and looked at Twig, seeing him for the first time. 'Who is this, Horsefeather?' he demanded.

'The lad is with me,' Cloud Wolf answered for her. 'Anything you have to say to me can be said in front of him.'

'Are you sure?' the professor asked.

'Quite sure,' said Cloud Wolf, polite yet firm.

The Professor of Light nodded resignedly. 'We failed you, Quintinius Verginix. I appreciate that. Now, we come to you, cap in hand. We need your help.'

Watching his father shuffling about under the professor's penetrating gaze, Twig was reminded of himself. And when Cloud Wolf spoke, it was his own faltering tones that Twig heard in his voice.

'I . . . errm . . . that is . . . Mother Horsefeather has already outlined the . . . the problem.'

'Indeed,' said the professor, surprised. 'Then you will understand the gravity of the situation – or should that be the *lack of gravity* of the situation,' he added, chuckling at his little joke.

Cloud Wolf smiled weakly. 'Sanctaphrax is truly in danger then?' he said.

'It could break free of its moorings at any moment,' the professor said. 'We must have fresh supplies of stormphrax.'

Cloud Wolf listened in silence.

'The windtouchers and cloudwatchers have already

confirmed that a Great Storm is imminent,' the professor continued. 'By the time it arrives, someone must be ready to chase it to the Twilight Woods so that he might retrieve the stormphrax it creates. And that someone, my dear Quintinius Verginix,' he said, 'is you. There is not another soul alive equal to the task. Will you help us or will you see Sanctaphrax cast for ever into open sky?'

Cloud Wolf stared back impassively. Twig couldn't begin to guess the thoughts spinning round his head. Yes? Or no? Which was the answer to be?

Then Cloud Wolf gave the slightest of nods to the Professor of Light's proposal. Twig's heart pounded with excitement. No matter how minimal the response, his father had accepted.

They were to go stormchasing.

On the other side of the door with his ear pressed against the wood, someone else was excited to hear of the proposed voyage to the Twilight Woods. It was Slyvo Spleethe, the *Stormchaser's* quartermaster. He listened carefully to the plans being made, memorizing each and every detail mentioned. There were those who would pay well for such information.

At the sound of chairs being pushed back, Spleethe pulled away from the door and slipped back into the bar-room. He couldn't be caught eavesdropping now. The good captain would discover soon enough that his plans had been overheard.

By Undertown standards, the Leagues Chamber was luxurious – that is, there were floorboards rather than trodden earth underfoot and there was glass in the majority of the windows. Most of the room was taken up with a giant ring-shaped table, at which were seated all the senior leaguesmen who had been available at such short notice.

In the circular hole at the centre of the table was a swivel stool. And upon this sat Slyvo Spleethe.

Simenon Xintax, the Leaguesmaster, rapped loudly on the table with his gavel. 'Order!' he bellowed. 'Order!!'

The Leagues Chamber fell silent, and all eyes turned towards him. Xintax arose from his chair.

'Tricorn mitres on!' he said, and there was a flurry of activity as each of the leaguesmen picked up their head-gear and put it into place. Xintax nodded approvingly. 'I declare open this emergency session of the Undertown League of Free Merchants,' he announced. 'Let the questioning commence.'

The leaguesmen remained silent, waiting for Xintax, as chairperson, to frame the first question, the most important question – the question that would set the tone for all subsequent questions. For truth, as the leaguesmen were well aware, was a slippery thing. It had to be approached with care if it was not to change into something completely different.

Xintax took his seat. 'If we were to ask you, Slyvo Spleethe, whether you be – an honest individual,' he began, in the contorted form that tradition demanded, 'how would you verily reply?'

Spleethe gulped. Now that's a difficult one, he thought. Certainly he intended to answer the leaguesman's questions honestly. But as to whether he himself was honest, well, an honest person would not have been eavesdropping in the first place. He shrugged, and wiped away the droplets of sweat from above his top lip. 'It's like this, you see . . .' he began.

'You will answer the question with a yes or a no,' Xintax interrupted. 'You will answer *all* questions with a yes or a no. Nothing more, nothing less. Is that quite clear?'

'Yes,' said Spleethe.

Xintax nodded approvingly. 'So, I repeat. If we were to ask you, Slyvo Spleethe, whether you be an honest individual, how would you verily reply?'

'No,' said Spleethe.

A ripple of surprise went round the table. Then all the leaguesmen thrust their arms up into the air. 'I. I. I. I,' they called, each one trying to grab the chairperson's attention.

'Leandus Leadbelly, Gutters and Gougers,' he said.

Leandus, a short angry-looking character with one dark eyebrow which ran the width of his heavy brow, nodded towards Spleethe. 'If we were to ask you whether you have information concerning your captain, Cloud Wolf, the former Quintinius Verginix, how would you verily reply?'

Spleethe swivelled round to face his questioner. 'Yes,' he said.

'Farquhar Armwright,' said Xintax. 'Gluesloppers and Ropeteasers.'

'If we were to ask you whether the *Stormchaser* was currently skyworthy, how would you verily reply?'

'No,' said Spleethe, swivelling back again.

'Ellerex Earthclay, Melders and Moulders.'

'If we were to ask you whether, should the need arise, you would be prepared to kill one of your fellow crew-members, how would you verily reply?'

Spleethe breathed in sharply. 'Yes.'

And so it continued. The leaguesmen put their questions and Spleethe answered them. One after the other after the other. There was no order to the questions – at least, if there was, then Spleethe was blind to it. As far as he was concerned it would have made far more sense if he'd been allowed to tell them precisely what he'd overheard. But no. The interrogation continued, with the questions coming thicker and faster as the time went on.

Little by little, the entire story was revealed – and not just the bare facts. By pursuing the information so obliquely, the leaguesmen managed to build up a picture, complete in every single detail – and, with it, the knowledge of precisely what to do.

Simenon Xintax arose for a second time. He raised his arms. 'The questioning be concluded,' he said. 'If we were to ask you, Slyvo Spleethe, to swear allegiance to the Undertown League of Free Merchants, forswearing all other ties and pledging obedience to our will, how would you verily reply?'

Spleethe's head was in a whirl. From the questions they had framed, he guessed that untold wealth was on offer. Plus a sky ship of his own. *Plus*, most important of all, league status. But he also knew precisely what was expected of him – and for such a feat, Spleethe wanted more than wealth. He wanted power.

'I answer this question with a question of my own, be it permitted,' he began. Xintax nodded. 'If I were to ask you whether, for the successful conclusion of this hazardous endeavour, I might become the new Leaguesmaster of the Undertown League of Free Merchants, how would *you* verily reply?'

Xintax's eyes narrowed. He had learned much about Slyvo Spleethe through the questioning. The quartermaster, he knew, was a greedy creature, treacherous and self-important – his question came as no surprise. 'Yes,' he answered.

'In that case,' Spleethe smiled, 'my answer be also yes.'

On hearing his reply, the leaguesmen all climbed solemnly to their feet, clutched their tricorn mitres to their breasts and hung their heads. Simenon Xintax spoke for them all.

'We have asked, you have answered, and a deal has been struck,' he said. 'But be sure of this, Spleethe. If you should attempt to dupe, deceive or double-cross us, we shall not rest until you have been hunted down and destroyed. Do you understand?'

Spleethe stared back grimly. 'Yes,' he said. 'I understand. But be aware, Xintax, that what is true for the woodboar is also true for the sow. Those who cross *me* do not live long enough to tell the tale.'

Back in the stuffy room behind the bar of the Bloodoak tavern, a mood of optimism held sway. Once business had been concluded – with the flurry of double-handshakes that ritual required – Mother Horsefeather had rung a bell to summon her servants. It was time for the feast which had been prepared to celebrate the successful conclusion to the deal.

The food was delicious and plentiful, and the woodale flowed freely. Twig sat in contented silence, listening with only half an ear as the others talked on and on. *Stormchasing. Stormchasing.* It was all he could think about, and his heart thrilled with anticipation.

'I still think it was very forward of you to assume that we'd come to an agreement,' he heard Cloud Wolf chuckling as he tucked into his succulent hammelhorn steak.

'Who is to say I would not have provided a meal even if we had not?' Mother Horsefeather said.

'I say so,' said Cloud Wolf. 'I know you, Mother Horsefeather. *'If you do anything for nothing, do it for yourself* – isn't that how the saying goes . . .?'

Mother Horsefeather clacked her beak with amusement. 'Oh, Wolfie!' she said. 'You are a one!' She rose to her feet and lifted her glass. 'Since, however, the matter *has* been settled to everyone's satisfaction, I would like to propose a toast. To success,' she said.

'To success!' came the enthusiastic response.

The Professor of Light turned to Cloud Wolf. 'I am so very glad you have consented,' he said warmly. 'After all, I would not have liked to entrust so valuable a cargo to a lesser person.'

'You mean the stormphrax,' Cloud Wolf said. 'We've got to find the stuff first.'

'No, Quintinius, not the stormphrax,' the professor said, and laughed. 'I was talking about myself, for I shall be accompanying you. Together, with your skill and my knowledge, we shall return with enough stormphrax to end the current madness of chain-building once and for all.'

Cloud Wolf frowned. 'But won't Vilnix be suspicious should he get wind of it?'

'That's where *we* come in,' Mother Horsefeather said, and nodded towards the nightwaif. 'Tomorrow morning, Forficule will pay a visit to Sanctaphrax to announce the Professor of Light's tragic accident and untimely death.'

'I see that, between you, you've thought of everything,' said Cloud Wolf. 'There is, however, one last thing *I* have to say.' He turned to Twig.

'I know, I know,' Twig laughed. 'But it's all right. I promise I won't mess up on this voyage – not even once.'

'No, Twig, you will not,' said Cloud Wolf sternly. 'For you are not coming with us.'

Twig gasped. His face fell; his heart sank. How could his father say such a thing? 'B . . . but what will I do? Where will I go?' he asked.

'It's all right, Twigsy,' he heard Mother Horsefeather saying. 'It's all been sorted. You're to stay with me. . .'

'No, no, no,' Twig muttered, hardly able to take in what was happening. 'You can't do this to me. It's not fair . . .'

'Twig!' his father barked. 'Be still!'

But Twig could not be still. 'You just don't trust me, do you?' he shouted. 'You think I'm no good at anything. You think I'm useless . . .'

'No, Twig,' he broke in. 'I do not think you are useless, and one day, Sky willing, you will become a formidable sky pirate captain – of that I am sure. But, at the moment, you lack experience.'

'And how will I gain that experience if you leave me behind?' Twig demanded. 'Besides,' he said hotly, 'no-one alive has any experience of stormchasing. Not even you.'

Cloud Wolf did not rise to the bait. 'I have made my decision,' he said calmly. 'You can accept it with good grace, or you can rant and rave like a child. Either way, you are not coming, and that is an end to it.'

·CHAPTER EIGHT·

DEPARTURE

'Setting sail?' Tem Barkwater exclaimed.

'That's what the Stone Pilot reckons,' said Spiker.

'But that's admirable news,' said Tem. 'Why, three days ago, after all the trouble with the ironwood, and then losing the rudder-wheel like that, I had truly feared that the *Stormchaser* might never set sail again. Yet now look at her – all fixed and ready, and raring to go. I en't never seen the brasses gleam so bright.'

'And it's not just the brasses,' said Stope Boltjaw. 'Haven't you noticed the sails and ropes? And the rigging? Brand spanking new, the lot of them.'

'And the weight-workings have been tuned to perfection as well,' said Spiker.

'We must be about to embark on something very important,' said Tem Barkwater, stroking his beard thoughtfully.

'You don't need to be a genius to work that one out,' said Stope Boltjaw. 'The question is, what?'

Tem shook his head. 'I'm sure the cap'n'll tell us when he's good and ready,' he said.

'Aye, well,' said Stope Boltjaw. 'If we *are* to set sail then we'd do well to leave now, under the cover of darkness.'

'On the contrary,' said Tem Barkwater. 'We should bide our time and wait until morning.'

'What, and set off in full view of the leagues patrols?' said Stope Boltjaw. 'Have you taken leave of your senses?'

'Not I, Stope,' Tem retorted. 'It is you who has forgotten that, with the *Stormchaser* as she now is, we could outrun any and every league ship they might care to send after us.'

'Yes, but . . .' Stope protested.

'And anyhow,' Tem Barkwater went on, 'the Mire is a treacherous place at the best of times – crossing it in darkness is madness. What with them poisonous blow-holes erupting all round about. And nowhere to attach the grappling-irons in a storm. Not to mention that it's impossible to see where the sky ends and the ground begins. I remember once – I couldn't have been much more than a lad at the time – we were on our way back from . . .'

He was interrupted by Spiker. 'It's the captain,' he hissed. 'And he's not alone.'

Tem Barkwater fell silent, and he, Stope Boltjaw and Spiker turned to greet the two figures climbing the gangplank.

'Cap'n,' said Tem warmly. 'Just the person I wanted to see. Perhaps you could settle a little dispute for us. Stope, here, maintains that . . .'

'No, Tem, I can't,' Cloud Wolf snapped. He peered round into the darkness. 'Where's Hubble?'

'Below deck, cap'n,' said Tem. 'With Mugbutt. I believe the pair of them are helping the Stone Pilot make his final adjustments to the new rudder-wheel.'

Cloud Wolf nodded. 'And Spleethe?'

The sky pirates shrugged. 'Spleethe, we haven't seen,' said Tem Barkwater. 'We lost him in Undertown. He must still be on shore.'

Cloud Wolf turned on him furiously. 'He what?' he roared. 'How many times do I have to tell you that Slyvo Spleethe is never *ever* to be left to his own devices? Who knows what he might be up to now?'

'One minute he was with us in the Bloodoak,' Stope Boltjaw explained. 'The next minute he was gone.'

Cloud Wolf shook his head in disbelief. 'Spleethe is our quartermaster,' he explained to the Professor of Light. 'A slippery character with a mutinous heart. I've half a mind to set sail without him. Trouble is, he's good at his job. And with Twig staying behind, that'll put us at two crewmen down.' He shook his head. 'I can't risk it.'

'Twig's staying behind?' Tem Barkwater said, surprised. 'Has the lad fallen ill?'

'No, Tem, he has not,' Cloud Wolf said angrily. 'Though it is no concern of yours *what* has happened to him.'

'But . . .'

'Enough!' he shouted. 'I will not have such insubordination in front of our guest.' He turned to the Professor of Light. 'Now, if you'd like to follow me, sire, I'll show you to your quarters myself.'

'Thank you, I should like that,' the professor said. 'There are a few last-minute calculations I need to work on before we set sail.'

'Quite, quite,' said Cloud Wolf, and ushered the professor away before he could say too much about the proposed voyage.

The three sky pirates looked at one another in confusion. Who was this old character? Why was Twig not coming with them? And where *were* they going? Cloud Wolf suddenly spun round. 'Idle speculation is the pastime of the fool,' he remarked, causing them all to look down guiltily at the deck. 'You will inform me the moment Spleethe returns,' he said.

'Aye-aye, cap'n,' came the reply.

*

Twig stared down miserably into his glass of woodfizz. Mother Horsefeather had poured the drink long ago – 'to raise his spirits' as she'd commented to Forficule. Now it was warm and flat.

All round him, the drunken revelry continued at full-throttle. There was raucous laughter and loud swearing; tales were told, songs were sung, violent arguments broke out as the flat-head and hammer-head goblins became increasingly volatile. At the stroke of midnight, a lumpen she-troll started up a snake dance and, within minutes, the whole tavern was squirming with a long line of individuals, winding its way round and round the room.

'Oy, cheer up, mate,' Twig heard. 'It might never happen.'

He turned and found himself face to face with a grinning mobgnome standing beside him. 'It already has,' he sighed.

Puzzled, the mobgnome shrugged and returned to the dance. Twig turned back. He placed his elbows on the bar, rested his head in his hands with his fingers clamped firmly over his ears and closed his eyes.

'Why did you have to leave me here?' he whispered. 'Why?'

Of course, he knew what his father would reply. 'I'm only thinking of your well-being' or 'One day, you'll thank me for this' or, worst of all, 'It's all for your own good.'

Twig felt his sadness and regret shifting, by degrees, to anger. It was not good for him; not good at all. Life on the *Stormchaser* was good. Being with his father, after so long a separation, was good. Sailing the skies in pursuit of wealth and riches was good. But being placed in the charge of Mother Horsefeather in her seething, seedy tavern while the *Stormchaser* and its crew set off on so wonderful a voyage was unutterably bad.

Torturing himself all the more, Twig thought of everything he was missing. He imagined how it must feel to be sucked along in the wake of a Great Storm. He tried to envisage the single lightning bolt as it froze in mid-air and turned to solid stormphrax. And he asked himself what it must be like inside the notorious Twilight Woods. For, although the *Stormchaser* had often passed above them, none of the Sky Pirates had ever risked venturing down.

Would they be like the Deepwoods of his childhood? he wondered. Endless, luxuriant forest. Teeming with life. Filled with all manner of trees, from humming lullabees to the flesh-eating bloodoaks, and home to countless tribes and villagers and creatures of every kind . . .

Or were they indeed as mysteriously treacherous as the legends described? A place of endless degeneration. A place of confusion and delusion. A place of madness. *That* was how the storytellers spoke of the Twilight Woods, as they passed their tales on, word of mouth, down the generations.

Twig sighed. Now he would never know. What should have been the greatest adventure of his life had been snatched cruelly away by his own father. Even if it had been done for his own safety, because he was, as Cloud Wolf had put it, 'important to him'; even if that *was* the case, the fact remained that to Twig, it felt like a punishment.

'And it's just not fair!' he complained.

'What is not fair?' came a voice at his elbow. Twig started. If it was the ridiculous grinning mobgnome trying to get him to dance again, he would give him what for! He swung round angrily.

'Spleethe!' he said.

'Master Twig,' said Spleethe, his narrow lips curling to reveal a set of stained and crooked teeth. 'I thought it was you. Just the person I was looking for – though it saddens me, of course, to see you so down in the mouth,' he added.

Twig frowned. 'You were looking for *me*?' he said.

'Indeed I was,' Spleethe purred as he rubbed his chin thoughtfully, and Twig swallowed queasily at the sight of the quartermaster's hand, with its missing fingers and mess of puckered skin. 'You see, I couldn't help noticing that you were present during the discussions between the good captain and the bird-woman.'

'What if I was?' said Twig suspiciously.

'It's just that, well . . . although, naturally, the captain has filled me in on all the details of our little venture . . .'

Twig was surprised. 'He has?'

'Of *course* he has,' Spleethe said. 'Chasing the Great Storm to the Twilight Woods. The quest for the sacred stormphrax . . . I know it all. It's just that . . . One's memory, you understand . . . That is . . .'

Spleethe was fishing. The Leaguesmaster had demanded even more of him than he'd expected – taking the *Stormchaser*, killing Cloud Wolf, delivering the stormphrax. His task would be difficult and he had kicked himself for leaving the Bloodoak tavern so hastily before. After all, if he was to be successful, he needed to know *everything* about the meeting – including the part which took place after his departure.

'Silly of me, I know,' he continued slyly, 'but I cannot for the life of me remember how Cloud Wolf said the meeting was concluded.'

Twig's reaction took the quartermaster by surprise.

'Concluded?' he said angrily. 'I'll tell you how it was concluded. I was told to remain here, in Undertown, with Mother Horsefeather, while the rest of you go sailing off to the Twilight Woods.'

Spleethe's brow furrowed. 'Remain here?' he repeated softly. 'Tell me more, Master Twig,' he said. 'Open up your heart.'

Struggling to fight back the tears, Twig shook his head.

'But Master Twig,' Spleethe persisted, his voice whiny and wheedling, 'a problem shared is a problem halved. And of course, if there's anything that *I* can do, anything at all . . .'

'It's the captain,' Twig blurted out. 'He says he's worried about my safety, but . . . but . . . I don't believe him. I can't believe him. He's ashamed of me, that's what it is!' he sobbed. 'Ashamed to have such a gangly, blundering oaf for a son.'

Slyvo Spleethe's eyebrows shot upwards with surprise. Cloud Wolf, the lad's father? Now that *was* interesting – very interesting indeed – and his head spun with ways in which he could use this latest piece of information to his advantage. Composing himself, he laid his hand on Twig's shoulder.

'The captain has a good heart,' he said softly. 'And I am sure he has your best interests in mind. Yet . . .'

Twig sniffed, and listened.

'Yet there is a fine line between being protective and being *over*-protective,' he said. 'Why, the trip to the Twilight Woods would be the making of you.'

Twig scowled. 'Not now it won't,' he muttered. He shook Spleethe's bony hand off his shoulder, and turned away. 'Why don't you just go?' he said.

For an instant, a smile flickered at the edge of Spleethe's mouth; then it was gone. 'Master Twig,' he said. 'I do not intend to return to the *Stormchaser* alone. I believe – and here I must speak frankly – I believe that Cloud Wolf has erred in his judgement. Of *course* you must accompany us on our Twilight Woods adventure. This is my plan,' he said, and brought his face close to Twig's. His breath was stale and sour. 'We will smuggle you aboard. You can stow away below deck in Mugbutt's berth – no-one will ever suspect you of hiding there.'

Twig continued to listen in silence. It all sounded too good to be true. Yet he knew well enough that Cloud Wolf would find him eventually. There would be trouble when he did!

'It'll all be fine, you'll see,' Spleethe's nasal wheedling continued. 'When the time is right I myself shall reveal your presence to Cloud Wolf. I'll talk him round. I'll make him see sense. You just leave it all to me.'

Twig nodded. Spleethe squeezed Twig's elbow with his hard bony fingers. 'Come on, then, let's go,' he said. 'Before I change my mind.'

*

All was not well on board the *Stormchaser*. The crew stood nervously by while their captain paced up and down the quarterdeck, purple with rage.

The Professor of Light – freshly kitted out with a pirate longcoat and parawings – had informed the captain that the Great Storm could strike 'at any minute'. That was several hours ago. Yet the sky ship had still not set sail.

Cloud Wolf ceased his pacing, seized the side rail and bellowed into the night. 'SPLEETHE, YOU MISERABLE EXCUSE FOR A MANGY SKYCUR, WHERE ARE YOU?'

'At your service, cap'n,' came a familiar voice.

Cloud Wolf spun round to see the quartermaster emerging from the aft-hatch. He stared in disbelief. 'Spleethe!' he spluttered. 'You're here!'

'I thought you called me,' he said, innocently.

'I've been calling you for three hours or more!' Cloud Wolf raged. 'Where have you been?'

'With Mugbutt,' Spleethe replied. 'A wound to his foot has become infected. Septic and swollen it is. The poor creature was quite delirious.'

The captain breathed in sharply. It seemed he had found his quartermaster only to lose his finest fighter. Mugbutt was fearless in any battle and had got them out of more scrapes than Cloud Wolf cared to remember.

'How is Mugbutt now?' he asked.

'I've left him sleeping,' said Spleethe. 'Sky willing, he will be back to his old self when he wakes.'

Cloud Wolf nodded. Setting sail for the treacherous Twilight Woods without Mugbutt was a risk. And yet, with the Great Storm imminent, it was a risk he had to take.

He raised his head. 'Gather round,' he called. 'I have something important to tell you all.'

The sky pirates listened, open-mouthed, as Cloud Wolf outlined the plans. 'Stormchasing,' Tem Barkwater whispered reverently.

'The Twilight Woods,' Spiker shuddered.

Cloud Wolf continued. 'And our quest will be, as it ever was, to retrieve stormphrax for the treasury of Sanctaphrax.'

'Stormphrax!' Slyvo Spleethe – feigning surprise – exclaimed with the rest.

'Yes, stormphrax,' said Cloud Wolf. 'That is why the Professor of Light is travelling with us. He understands its properties. He will ensure we travel safely with our precious cargo.'

Spleethe frowned. So *that* was who the newcomer was. If only he'd known before.

'Right then, you scurvy skycurs,' Cloud Wolf announced. 'To your posts. We set sail at once.' While the sky pirates scurried this way and that, Cloud Wolf strode to the helm. 'Release the tolley-ropes,' he cried.

'Aye-aye,' Spiker called back. 'Tolley-ropes, released.'

'Unhook the grappling-irons!'

'Grappling-irons, unhooked.'

'And weigh anchor.'

As the heavy anchor was winched up, the *Stormchaser* leapt from its moorings and up into the sky.

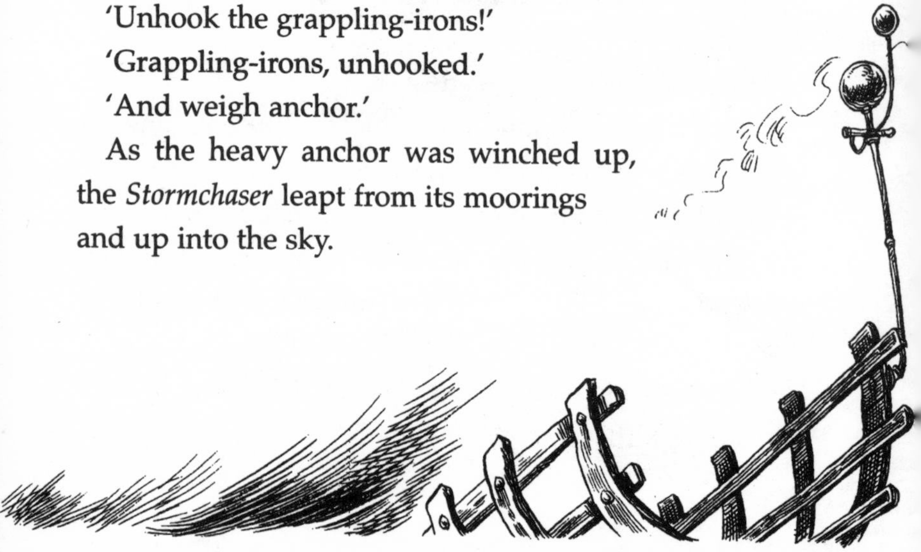

'Come on, my lovely,' Cloud Wolf whispered to his sky ship as it bucked and lurched, responding to the lightest touch of the weight and sail levers. 'My, but you're frisky once more. Just like you were when you were first built. Forgive me for all the times I used you as a common tugship. I had no choice. But now, my wonderful chaser of storms, your time has come.'

As the dawn broke – and keeping both Tem Barkwater *and* Stope Boltjaw happy – the *Stormchaser* sailed majestically out of Undertown, unchecked. Wispy wings of pink and orange fanned out across the morning side of the sky. A moment later, the sun appeared above the horizon on the starboard side. It rose slowly, bright red and tremulous.

Cloud Wolf sighed impatiently. The weather looked unpromisingly good. What *had* happened to the Great Storm that the windtouchers and cloudwatchers had predicted; that the Professor of Light himself had confirmed?

Just then, Spiker let out a yell from his look-out. 'Storm to port!' he cried.

The captain spun round and peered into the distance. At first, he could make out nothing unusual in the featureless darkness of the receding night. But then there was a flash. And another. Short, dazzling bursts of light in the shape of a circle – a circle which, when the lightning faded, still remained. Black on indigo. Growing larger with every passing second.

The lightning flashed again, and Cloud Wolf saw that it was not a circle, but rather, a ball – an immense fizzing, crackling ball of electrical energy, darkness and light combined, which was rolling headlong across the sky towards them.

'It's the Great Storm,' he roared, above the howl of the rising wind. 'Unfurl the mainsail, batten down the hatches and rope yourselves securely. We're going stormchasing!'

·CHAPTER NINE·

STORMCHASING

It had seemed like a good idea at the time, stowing away on the sky ship. Now Twig was not so sure. As the *Stormchaser* pitched and tossed, he retched emptily. Sweat beaded his ice-cold forehead; tears streamed down his burning cheeks.

Mugbutt sniggered unpleasantly. 'Feeling queasy?' he sneered. 'Too rough for you, is it?'

Twig shook his head. It wasn't the flight that was making him ill, but having to breathe the warm, fetid air he was sharing with the goblin. No flat-heads were known for their cleanliness, and Mugbutt was a particularly filthy specimen. He never washed, his bed of straw was wet and fouled, and remnants from the meat he had gleaned from the dinner table lay all around in various stages of decomposition.

Covering his nose with his scarf, Twig breathed in

deeply. Slowly, the nausea subsided, and with it the awful clamouring in his ears. He breathed in again.

Outside, he could hear the familiar noises of Undertown as the *Stormchaser* sped through the busy boom-docks, over the early-morning markets and past the foundries and forges. Bargains, banter, hog-squeal and hammer-blow; a cackle of laughter, a chorus of song, a muffled explosion – the intricate cacophony of life in Undertown which, even this early in the day, was already in full swing.

Soon, the sounds faded away and were gone, and Twig knew they must have left the bustling town and were heading out across the Mire. Now he could hear the *Stormchaser* itself. The creaking, the groaning; the hissing of air as it rushed past the hull. From below him, came the squeaking and scratching of the ratbirds that lived in the bowels of the sky ship; from above – if he strained – the murmur of voices.

'Oh, how I wish I could be up there with them,' Twig whispered.

'And face the captain's wrath?' Mugbutt growled. 'I don't think so.'

Twig sighed. He knew the flat-head was right. Cloud Wolf would surely skin him alive when he discovered that he had been disobeyed. Yet remaining hidden below deck was torture. He missed the feel of the wind in his hair, of soaring through the air, with the places of the Edge spread out below like an intricate map, and above the yawning expanse of endless open sky.

All through the childhood he'd spent in the Deepwoods, Twig had longed to rise up over the forest canopy and explore the sky above. It was as if, even then, his body had known that this was where he belonged. And perhaps it had. After all, Cloud Wolf, himself, had said on more than one occasion that sky-piracy was 'in the blood' – and with such a father . . .

Twig could hear him now, bellowing commands, and he smiled as he imagined the crew hurrying to obey him. For Cloud Wolf kept a tight ship. He was harsh, but just, and it was to his credit that, with him as its captain, the *Stormchaser* had suffered fewer casualties than any other sky pirate ship.

It was, however, the harshness of his justice which now kept Twig cowering in the flat-head's berth, too nervous to appear until Slyvo Spleethe had spoken up for him. He had no option but to wait.

'Storm to starboard, and advancing,' came Spiker's shrill cry. 'Three minutes to contact, and closing.'

'Belay that skysail,' roared Cloud Wolf. 'And check all winding-cleats.'

As the sky ship pitched abruptly to the left, Twig clutched hold of the main stanchion and clung on tightly. He knew the turbulence was a mere foretaste of what was to come. Normally at this point, with a storm so close, the *Stormchaser* would descend, drop anchor and remain there until it had passed. But not today.

Today, the sky ship would greet the storm up in the sky. It would tack closer and closer, until it was drawn into the hurricane-force slip-stream and be whisked away. Ever faster the *Stormchaser* would fly, inching its way round to the head of the storm. Then, when Cloud Wolf judged the moment to be right, it would spin round and pierce the outer shell of the maelstrom.

This was the most dangerous moment of all. If the *Stormchaser* flew too slowly, it would break up in the violent air. If it flew too fast, then there was always the risk that they would pass straight through the storm, emerge on the other side and watch helplessly as the Great Storm continued without them. In either event, their quest for stormphrax would be over.

No, Twig had heard that there was only one way to penetrate the inner calm of a Great Storm safely, and that was to hold the sky ship at a thirty-five degree angle against the windspin – at least, that was the theory. Yet, as the sky ship bucked and turned and Twig held on for grim death, the *Stormchaser* struck him as absurdly small and fragile for so daunting a task, no matter what angle they chose.

'One minute to contact, and counting,' Spiker shouted above the oncoming roar.

'Secure that spinnaker!' Cloud Wolf screamed. 'And Spiker, get down from the caternest, NOW!'

Twig had never heard such urgency in Cloud Wolf's voice before. What must it look like, he wondered, this Great Storm which filled his father – the esteemed Quintinius Verginix – with so much terror and awe? He had to see for himself.

Hand over hand, he pulled himself along a crossbeam towards the hull. Although there were no portholes down this deep in the sky ship, the cracks between the curving planks of lufwood were, in places, wide enough to see through. Wedge-shaped chinks of light sliced through the gloom. Reaching the hull at last, Twig knelt down and peered into the cracks.

Below him, he saw the featureless wasteland of the Mire stretching out in every direction. The white mud rippled in the wind, as if the entire wasteland had been transformed into a vast ocean. And there, to complete the illusion, was a ship.

'Except it's not sailing,' Twig muttered as he squinted at the distant shipwreck. 'And probably never will again.'

As the *Stormchaser* sped onwards, Twig realized that the ship had not been abandoned. There was someone there: a tall, thin figure, brandishing his fist at the sky. As colourless as his surroundings, he was well camouflaged. Twig wouldn't have noticed him at all had it not been for the bright lightning of the approaching storm glinting on the dagger clenched in his fist.

Was it the storm he was cursing? Twig wondered. Or was it the sight of the *Stormchaser* itself, passing over-

head, that had filled the curious bleached individual with such anger?

The next instant, both he and the shipwreck were gone. Lightning-dazzle briefly lit up the flat-head's disgusting quarters. The air crackled and hissed. Twig struggled to his feet and peered through a chink higher up the hull, wincing as the onrush of air stung his eyes. He wiped his tears away on his sleeve and squinted back through the gap in the wood.

'Sky above!' he cried out.

Directly in front of the sky ship, and obliterating everything else from view, was a rolling, tumbling, heaving wall of furious purple and black. The noise of the blast was deafening – like a never-ending explosion. Louder still, was the creak and groan of the *Stormchaser* itself.

As Twig maintained his gaze, so more lightning was discharged. It streaked across the curving surface of the Great Storm like a network of electric rivers, and imploded in circles of pink and green.

The din grew louder than ever; the lightning, brighter still. And all the while, the *Stormchaser* shook and rattled as the seconds to impact ticked unstoppably past. Twig wrapped both arms around the beam to his left, and tensed his legs.

Five . . . four . . . three . . .

Wheeeiiiiiiiii whistled the wind, its high-pitched whine rising to an ear-splitting scream.

Two . . .

The sky ship had never travelled so fast before. Twig clung on for dear life as it hurtled onwards.

One . . . And . . .

WHOOOMPH!!

Like a falling leaf in an autumn gale, the *Stormchaser* was abruptly seized and whisked off by the spinning wind. It listed hard to port with a fearful lurch. Twig was torn from the beam and hurled back across the straw-strewn floor.

'Aaaii!' he cried out as he flew through the air. He landed heavily, with a thud; his head jerked sharply back and struck the side of Mugbutt's berth with a loud *crack*.

Everything went black.

Mugbutt looked down and smirked. 'That's it, *Master* Twig,' he said, 'you stay here by my side where I can keep an eye on you.'

*

Above deck, it was all the captain and his crew could do to keep the *Stormchaser* airborne. While Hubble held the wheel in his powerful grasp, Cloud Wolf's fingers played over the keyboard of levers.

Twenty years it was since he had studied in the Knights' Academy; twenty years since he had learned about the finer points of stormchasing – and twenty years is a long time in which to forget. As Cloud Wolf raised this weight a fraction and lowered that sail a tad, it was instinct rather than memory that guided him.

'Stormchasing!' he murmured reverently.

On and on, they were drawn, whistling across the sky in the slip-stream of the Great Storm. Slowly, slowly and little by little, Cloud Wolf used the dry, turbulent currents to inch his way along the outer edge of the storm and on towards the front.

'Whoa, there, my beauty,' he whispered to the *Stormchaser*. 'Easy now.' Tentatively, he lowered the prow-weight – a fraction of a degree at a time. The sky ship bowed forwards.

'Raise the mainsail!' he ordered. Tem Barkwater and Stope Boltjaw stared at one another in confusion. What madness was this to raise the mainsail in such a wind? Surely they had misheard. 'RAISE THAT ACCURSED MAINSAIL, BEFORE I HAVE YOU SKY-FIRED!' the captain raged.

Tem and Stope Boltjaw leapt to it. And as the sail flapped and billowed, Cloud Wolf offered up a little prayer that he would be virtuous for ever more – if the sailcloth would just hold.

'Now, let's see,' he muttered through clenched teeth as he returned his attention to the weight-levers. 'Up with the peri-hull-weights, and down with the port hull-weights, small . . .' The *Stormchaser* trembled. 'Medium . . .' It leaned to the left. 'And large . . .'

As the third weight was lowered, the *Stormchaser* – still held in place by the raised mainsail at the front of the driving storm – began slowly to turn. Cloud Wolf stared down at his compass. Bit by bit the sky ship was shifting round to the thirty-five degree angle required to penetrate safely to the centre of the storm.

Forty-five degrees, he read off. Forty. Thirty-seven . . . Thirty-six . . .

'LOWER THE MAINSAIL!' he bellowed.

This time neither Tem Barkwater nor Stope Boltjaw needed telling twice. They unhitched the rope. The sail fell. The sky ship slowed, and was instantly swallowed up by the dense billowing clouds of purple and black. They were entering the Great Storm.

The air was blinding, choking. It crackled and fizzed. It smelled of ammonia, of sulphur, of rotten eggs.

All around them, the wind thrashed and battered. It pummelled the hulls and threatened, at any moment, to snap the creaking mast in two.

'Just a little further, my lovely one,' Cloud Wolf urged the *Stormchaser* gently. 'You can do it. You can bring us safely to the centre of the Great Storm.'

Even as he spoke, however, the sky ship shuddered as if to say, no, no it could not. Cloud Wolf threw an anxious glance at the compass. It was back at forty-five degrees. The wind was hitting them full on. The juddering grew more violent. Much more, and the sky ship would be shaken to pieces.

With trembling hands, Cloud Wolf raised the three starboard hull-weights as high as they would go. The *Stormchaser* swung back. The fearful judders subsided.

'Thank Sky,' Cloud Wolf said, as he seized the opportunity to wipe the sweat from his brow. He turned to Hubble by his side. 'Hold tight,' he instructed. 'Any second now and . . . YES!' he yelled – for at that moment, the compass point swung round to thirty-five degrees and the *Stormchaser* plunged through the violent, violet storm and into the eerie stillness within.

'RAISE THE MAINSAIL!' he bellowed, his voice echoing as if he was standing in a huge cavern. If they were not to fly out the far side of the storm, the sky ship's momentum would have to be brought under control. The sail should – if he had remembered his studies accurately – act like a brake. 'RAISE *ALL* THE SAILS!'

At first nothing seemed to happen to the sky ship as it continued to hurtle on towards the back of the storm. The flashing fingers of lightning which fanned out before them, came closer and closer. Tem Barkwater, Stope Boltjaw, Spiker and the others leaped to the ropes – even the Professor of Light joined in. Together, they hoisted the sails up, one after the other after the other. And as the sail-sheets rose, so the *Stormchaser* finally slowed down.

Before they came to a complete standstill, Cloud Wolf lifted the port hull-weights, lowered the starboard hull-weights and – when they had turned right about – pulled the prow-weight back to its original position.

Now facing the way the Great Storm itself was travelling, the *Stormchaser* sailed on within it. All around him, Cloud Wolf could hear the excited cheering of his crew. But he knew better than to celebrate too soon. Pin-point accuracy was essential if the *Stormchaser* was to maintain its position – one weight too low, one sail too high, and the sky ship would hurtle to one side of the storm and be spat into open sky.

'Hold a steady course, Hubble,' the captain said. 'And Spiker,' he called, 'how long before we cross into the Twilight Woods?'

''Bout twelve minutes,' the oakelf called back.

Cloud Wolf nodded grimly. 'I want you all – each and every one – to keep a watchful eye for the lightning bolt,' he commanded. 'If we are to retrieve the stormphrax, we must see exactly – and I *mean* exactly – where it lands.'

Back below deck, Twig slithered this way and that over the hard, wooden floor as the *Stormchaser* continued to pitch and toss. Every jolt, every jerk, every judder which was felt above deck, was magnified a hundredfold by the time it reached the bowels of the sky ship where he lay. Yet all the while Twig had not stirred. It was only at that moment when the *Stormchaser* finally pierced the wild outer edges of the turbulent storm that his eyelids had fluttered.

He became aware of voices behind him. Hushed and plotting voices: familiar voices. Taking care to remain as still as possible, Twig listened.

'. . . and I don't think the captain will put up much of a fight when he discovers what will happen to his captive son if he does,' Slyvo Spleethe was whispering. 'So, for the time being, Mugbutt, I want you to keep him down here.'

'Down here,' the flat-head whispered back.

'Until I come for him,' said Spleethe. He paused. 'I'll have to choose my moment very carefully.'

'Very carefully,' Mugbutt repeated.

'After all, stormchasing is a hazardous business,' Spleethe continued. 'I shall wait until Cloud Wolf has retrieved the stormphrax – before disposing of him.' He laughed unpleasantly. 'Let him do all the hard work, and then reap the rewards.'

'The rewards,' said Mugbutt.

'And what rewards they are to be!' Spleethe said. 'Captain of a sky pirate ship *and* Leaguesmaster! You stick with me, Mugbutt,' he added breathlessly, 'and you shall have wealth and power beyond your wildest dreams.'

'Wildest dreams,' the flat-head chuckled.

'And now I must leave you,' said Spleethe. 'I don't want the captain to become suspicious. And remember, Mugbutt. Keep Twig well guarded. I'm depending on you.'

As the sound of the receding footsteps faded away, Twig trembled with horror. What a fool he had been to listen to so shiftless a rogue. The quartermaster was intent on mutiny and – if he had understood him correctly – was planning to use Twig against his father to ensure that his wicked plans bore fruit.

Somehow, before that happened, he would have to warn Cloud Wolf – even if it did mean having to confront his father's wrath.

He opened one eye slightly, and peered out at the ferocious flat-head goblin. The question was, how?

·CHAPTER TEN·

CONFESSION

A sound, unfamiliar to the Inner Sanctum, echoed round the gold-embossed ceiling of the chamber. It was the sound of humming. Although utterly tuneless, it bounced along with unmistakable joy and optimism.

The servants – and there were many who tended to the Inner Sanctum and its important occupant – were under strict instructions to maintain complete silence at all times. And music of any kind – humming, singing, whistling – was particularly frowned upon. Only the week before, old Jervis – a loyal servant for more than forty seasons – had been caught crooning a lullaby under his breath. (He had recently become a great-grandfather.) For this moment of mindless contentment he was dismissed on the spot.

It was not, however, a servant humming now. The sound came from the thin lips and pudgy nose of the

Most High Academe of Sanctaphrax. For Vilnix Pompolnius was feeling exceedingly pleased with himself.

'Hmm, hmm, hmmm. Pom pom pom pom,' he continued as he busied about. 'Pom pom pom . . .' He paused and chuckled as the details of the previous evening came back to him. He had been dining with Simenon Xintax, and a most illuminating meal it had proved to be.

As a rule, the Leaguesmaster was far from his favourite dinner guest. He was, as far as Vilnix Pompolnius was concerned, an ill-mannered oaf – he slurped his soup, he chewed with his mouth open, and he belched loudly after every course. Yet it served Vilnix well to keep him sweet. If it wasn't for the support he received from the leagues, his own grip on power would soon evaporate.

As always, Xintax had eaten and drunk too much. Not that Vilnix objected. In fact he positively encouraged the Leaguesmaster's gluttony, piling seconds and thirds onto his plate and keeping his glass constantly topped up with Xintax's favourite woodbrew. After all, as his grandmother had so often said, *a full stomach and a loose tongue oft go hand in hand*. The Leaguesmaster's tongue had started to loosen during dessert. By the time the cheese and crackers were served, he was practically babbling.

'Mother Horsefeather, she's the one, she... *bwurrrp*... 'Scuse me!' He paused to wipe his mouth on his sleeve. 'She's only gone and organized a trip to the Twilight Woods, hasn't she? Her, the Professor of Light, and a sky pirate captain – can't remember his name just now ... Anyway, they're all in it together. They're ... *bwulchh* ... Whoops.' He giggled. 'They're planning on returning with a whole cargo of stormphrax,' he explained and pressed his finger to his lips conspiratorially. 'It's meant to be a secret,' he said.

'Then how have you come by this information?' Vilnix Pompolnius demanded.

Xintax tapped his nose knowingly with his finger. 'A cry in the spew,' he slurred and giggled again. 'I mean, a spy in the crew. Spleethe. Told us everything, he did.' Then he had leaned forwards, seized Vilnix chummily by the sleeve and grinned leerily up at his face. 'We're going to be rich beyond belief.'

'Pom pom pom pom,' Vilnix hummed, as the words came back to him. Rich beyond belief! At least, he thought, *one* of us is.

At that moment, there was a respectful knock at the door and the tousled head of his personal manservant, Minulis, appeared. 'If you please, your Most High Academe,' he said, 'the prisoner has been prepared and awaits your attention.'

'Ah, yes,' Vilnix nodded, and smiled unpleasantly. 'I shall be there, directly.'

As Minulis closed the door behind him, Vilnix rubbed his hands together gleefully. 'First Xintax spilling the beans, now this Forficule character dropping into our lap – my my, Vilnix, aren't *we* the lucky Most High Academe!'

He strode across the room to the mirror – the new mirror – and looked at himself. Unlike its predecessor, this mirror had not been hung. Instead, it leaned up against the wall at an angle. It was safer – it was also more flattering. His reflection smiled back at him.

'Oh, no,' he chided. 'That will never do. Whatever should the nightwaif think if I entered the Hall of Knowledge in so effervescent a mood? Prepare yourself, Vilnix,' he said dramatically, and let his dressing-gown fall to the floor. 'Make yourself ready.'

And doing what he always did before an important encounter, the Most High Academe of Sanctaphrax dressed himself up in the specially fashioned garments of high office – clothes which would help focus his mind, heighten his senses and darken his mood.

First, he pulled on the hair-shirt over his bare, scaly skin. Then, wincing as the protruding nails dug into the soles of his feet, he stepped into his sandals and bound them tightly. Next, he rubbed a stinging unguent over his freshly shaven head, and lowered the steel skull-cap onto his head until the internal spikes pressed into his scalp. Last of all, he took his shabby roughspin gown, swung it over his shoulders and raised the hood.

With each item of clothing he put on, the Most High Academe's good humour gradually drained away. By

the time the rough material of the hood grazed the back of his red-raw neck, his mood was as dark as the Sanctaphrax treasury itself and he, himself, capable of any cruelty.

He returned his gaze to the mirror and glared approvingly at his reflection. Seldom, if ever, had Vilnix Pompolnius looked so gaunt, so imposing. He arched one eyebrow.

'So, Forficule, my little messenger bird,' he said. 'I am ready for you now. How I am looking forward to hearing you sing!'

The Hall of Knowledge – as the interrogation chamber was euphemistically known – was situated at the top of a tower in the west-wing of the vast palace. The only access was through a concealed door in the upper corridor, and up a circular stone staircase.

With every step he climbed, the nails in his sandals dug sharply into his feet. By the time he reached the top, Vilnix Pompolnius was cursing under his breath. He threw the door open and strode inside. 'Where is the horrible little pipsqueal, then?' he demanded.

Minulis trotted over, closed the door and ushered the Most High Academe across the room. Despite its airy position, the windowless chamber was as dark and dank as any dungeon. The only light came from the two flaming torches fixed to the wall, and a golden glow which gleamed on the array of polished pokers, pincers, and pliers laid out ready.

Forficule himself was seated in an upright chair, so large it seemed almost to be swallowing him up. His ankles were bound, his wrists had been tied to the arm-rests, and his neck secured to a head-support by a leather strap: he could not move. As Vilnix Pompolnius approached him, Forficule glanced up. An icy shiver ran the length of his body.

'Ah, *there* you are,' said Vilnix. 'So good of you to drop by.' He sneered. 'I trust you're sitting comfortably.'

As he moved closer, Forficule shuddered. Behind the harmless words were thoughts no person should ever have.

'I understand you are a nightwaif,' Vilnix continued.

'No, no,' said Forficule, and laughed nervously. 'Many have made the same mistake. I am an oakelf,' he said. 'The runt of the litter.'

Vilnix Pompolnius sighed as the spikes of the steel skull-cap bit into his scalp. 'You will have noticed the interesting design of the chair,' he continued, running his fingers over the concave bowl of burnished silver which was fixed over Forficule's head. 'It amplifies sound,' he said, and flicked it lightly.

The metal chimed and Forficule, whose head had been secured at the point where the sound waves collided, winced with pain.

'I would advise you *not* to lie to me,' said Vilnix, and flicked the metal bowl a second time.

'I . . . I don't understand. Why have you brought me here?' Forficule trembled as the ringing in his ears slowly subsided. 'I came to Sanctaphrax from Undertown, in all good faith, to inform you about the tragic death of the Professor of Light . . .'

'Forficule, Forficule,' Vilnix purred. 'This is not good.'

He turned away and selected a pair of pincers. Forficule quivered with horror as he overheard precisely what the Most High Academe was thinking of doing with them. Worse and worse the imagined tortures became, until Forficule could stand it no more.

'Stop it!' he pleaded, his ears fluttering with distress.

Vilnix spun round, pincers in one hand, tapping them in the other. 'Oakelf, eh?' he said.

Forficule sniffed. 'I *am* a nightwaif,' he confessed.

Vilnix Pompolnius nodded. 'That's better,' he said,

and added – in his thoughts alone – from now on, I want the truth and nothing but the truth. He brandished the pincers, and imagined them smashing hard against the metal bowl above the chair. Do you understand me?

'Yes,' said Forficule simply.

'Now, who sent you?'

'I came of my own accord,' said Forficule.

Without saying a word, Vilnix strode up to him, and struck the bowl sharply. Forficule howled with pain.

'No, no,' he whimpered.

'Then tell me who?' barked Vilnix.

'Mother Horsefeather,' said Forficule. 'She thought you ought to know – the professor being an academic of Sanctaphrax, and all. He . . . he was in her tavern – the Bloodoak – when he had a . . . a seizure. Keeled over, he did. We did everything we could to revive him.'

'But, nevertheless, you failed,' Vilnix said.

'Sadly, yes,' said Forficule.

Vilnix narrowed his eyes. 'And where is the good professor's body now?' he asked.

'I . . . errm . . . that is, with it being so hot and all, Mother Horsefeather thought he should be buried as soon as possible.'

'You have interred a professor of Sanctaphrax in the ground?' Vilnix gasped. 'Do you not know that it is the right of every academic of our great floating city to have his body ceremonially laid out in the Stone Gardens, where the white ravens will pick his bones? How else is his spirit to rise up to open sky?'

'I . . . we . . .'

'But then, of course, the situation will not arise,' said Vilnix thrusting his head forwards into Forficule's face until his shining skull-cap grazed the tip of the night-waif's nose. 'Because he isn't dead. Is he?'

'Yes, yes,' said Forficule. 'He is.'

Vilnix straightened up abruptly, raised the pincers and slammed them against the metal bowl. 'Lies! Lies! Lies! Lies!' he screamed in time to the deafening hammer blows. 'And more and more and *more* lies!'

After seven blows, he let his arm fall limp. 'Now will you tell me the truth,' he said.

Forficule didn't answer. Although he had seen the angry lips move, he hadn't heard a single word above the pounding, crackling, screeching cacophony of noise inside his head. It was several minutes before he could make out any sounds again, and even then, the echoing din continued in the background.

'THIS IS YOUR FINAL CHANCE!' Vilnix was bellowing.

Forficule lowered his gaze. He shivered miserably. There was a saying among the fragile nightwaifs. *Better dead than deaf.*

'All right,' he whimpered. 'I'll tell you everything I know.'

And that was what he did. He told Vilnix every detail of the meeting which had taken place in the back room of the Bloodoak tavern. Of the entrance of the Professor of Light, and how the sky pirate captain had fallen to his knees. Of the plan the three of them had hatched up. Of the Professor of Light's decision to accompany the sky pirates on their quest to the Twilight woods.

'The treacherous cur,' Vilnix spat. 'And this captain?' he said. 'Has he a name?'

'Cloud Wolf,' said Forficule promptly. 'Though the Professor of Light addressed him by a different name.'

'Which was?'

'Quintinius Verginix,' came the reply.

Vilnix nodded. 'Now, there's a name to conjure with,' he said thoughtfully.

The nightwaif's thorough, if belated, confession had proved very interesting to Vilnix Pompolnius. Not only did it confirm what he suspected about the Professor of Light, but he now also knew that Xintax had lied to him the night before. *No-one* could forget the name of Cloud Wolf – the sky pirate captain was infamous. The Leaguesmaster himself must be planning something underhand.

Vilnix chuckled to himself. There were many other ambitious leaguesmen who would be only too happy to strike a deal with the Most High Academe.

He turned back to Forficule. 'And this youth you mentioned,' he said. 'This Twig. What is he to the assembled gathering?'

Forficule swallowed. Although he hadn't known Twig long, he had liked what he heard in the boy's head. His thoughts were decent and honest, loyal and true. He would hate to think that something he said might mean that the boy came to harm.

Vilnix dangled the heavy pincers in front of his face. Forficule nodded, as much as the leather strap would allow, and continued. 'He is a crew-member on board the *Stormchaser*,' he said.

'And?' said Vilnix Pompolnius, sensing he was on to something.

'He was born and raised in the Deepwoods,' he said.

'And?'

Forficule shuddered. If he made it clear that Twig was not relevant to the plan, perhaps the youth would be left in peace. 'He is not to accompany the pirates on this particular trip,' he said. 'He is to stay with Mother Horsef . . .'

Vilnix cut him short. 'There is something you're not telling me,' he said, and raised the pincers threateningly.

Forficule looked down. Tears welled up in his eyes. He was not a bad creature – but neither was he brave. The pincers hovered in the torchlight next to the metal bowl. Better dead than deaf.

'He . . . he is . . .' he faltered. 'That is . . . Cloud Wolf is his father.'

Vilnix breathed in sharply. 'A son,' he hissed. 'Quintinius Verginix has a son. And he has left him behind,' he smirked. 'How very careless.' He turned to Minulis. 'We must introduce ourselves to the lad forthwith,' he said. 'We shall invite him back here to Sanctaphrax, to await the return of his valiant father.'

He turned back to Forficule. 'What a splendid little bargaining chip you have given us,' he said, as he returned the heavy pincers to the shelf. 'I can't tell you how grateful we are.'

Forficule felt wretched. His attempt to protect Twig had failed, and now the youth was in mortal danger. And yet – Sky forgive him! – he couldn't help but be relieved that the Most High Academe seemed so pleased with the information.

'Am I free to go, then?' he asked.

Vilnix looked round at him, and smiled. Forficule stared back, hoping. With his head still echoing from the deafening noise of metal crashing on metal, he was unable to hear the dark thoughts lurking behind the Most High Academe's smiling face.

'Free to go?' Vilnix Pompolnius said at last. His eyes twinkled. 'Oh, yes. Quite free.'

Forficule gasped for joy.

Vilnix nodded to Minulis. 'Unbind him and throw him out,' he said. Then, as the hair-shirt itched and the spikes and nails dug into the Most High Academe's head and feet, he added, 'But first, cut off his ears.'

·CHAPTER ELEVEN·

THE EYE OF THE STORM

Twig lay some way from Mugbutt's filthy straw-covered quarters. He was still pretending to be unconscious. Each time the *Stormchaser* pitched and tossed he would roll over a little further, hoping that the flat-head would assume it was the movement of the boat shifting him across the floor. Slowly – painfully slowly – he was manoeuvring himself towards the staircase. One chance at escape, that was all he would get.

Stupid! Stupid! Stupid! he told himself. *Not only had he disobeyed his father, but he'd left him at the mercy of treacherous mutineers – just as Cloud Wolf had feared might happen.*

The sky ship lurched sharply to the left and Twig rolled over twice. The stairs were getting closer.

It was so obvious that Spleethe was up to no good, Twig continued angrily to himself. *He never liked you.*

You should've realized why he was being so friendly! 'Oh, Sky above,' he murmured. 'What have I done?'

The sky ship listed to starboard and Twig had to brace himself against the floor to stop himself being propelled back to Mugbutt's berth. Through the crack in his eyelids he watched the flat-head snuffling through the soiled straw for any bits of meat he might have missed.

Disgusting creature, he thought, and trembled. And a formidable fighter . . .

At that moment, the *Stormchaser* reared up like a prowlgrin charger, tilted abruptly to port and dropped in the sky. With his heart in his mouth, Twig rolled the last few yards towards the bottom of the stairs. There he hesitated and looked back. The sky ship reared up a second time and there was a loud crash as Mugbutt lost his balance and tumbled to the floor.

Now! Twig said to himself. Get out while you can.

He leapt to his feet, gripped the wooden rails fiercely and climbed the steep set of stairs as quickly as his trembling legs would allow.

'OY!' Mugbutt bellowed, when he realized what was happening. 'Where are you going?'

Twig didn't wait to reply. 'Come on!' he urged himself desperately. He was halfway up the stairs, yet the hatch at the top looked no nearer. 'Come *on*!'

Already, Mugbutt had climbed to his feet, vaulted over the bars which enclosed his berth and was racing headlong towards him. Six more steps he had to go, and Mugbutt was there at the bottom. Five . . . four . . . Twig could feel the entire staircase tremble as the heavy

flat-head hurried up behind him. Three . . . two . . .

'Nearly there,' Twig muttered. 'One more step and . . .' All at once, he felt the horny hand of the flat-head goblin grasping at his ankle. 'No!' he screamed and kicked back with both legs.

Shoving the hinged hatch open with shaking hands, Twig launched himself up and pulled himself through

the narrow opening. He knelt down beside the hole. Mugbutt's spatula fingers appeared at the rim. Twig leaned forwards, seized the hatch door and slammed it down with all his strength.

There was an agonizing cry. The fingers disappeared from view and from below the hatch came the muffled sound of Mugbutt tumbling back down the staircase. Twig had done it! He'd escaped – yet already, he could hear the flat-head pounding back up the stairs.

With his heart thumping, Twig slid the heavy bolts across the hatchway and, to make doubly sure, heaved a huge barrel of pickled tripweed across the floor until it came to rest on the hatch door. Then, leaping to his feet, he headed for the next flight of stairs – the flight which would take him up on to the deck itself. As he began climbing, the sound of furious hammering and cursing exploded behind him.

Let the hatch hold, Twig prayed. Please!

Up on deck and completely unaware of the drama that had been unfolding below them, the captain and crew of the *Stormchaser* were struggling to keep the sky ship airborne as the mighty ball of cloud crackled and flashed across the sky.

'Double bind the tolley-ropes,' Cloud Wolf bellowed as the Great Storm hurtled on towards the Twilight Woods. It was essential that he maintain the *Stormchaser*'s position at its very centre. 'Draw in the studsail. Untangle those jib lines!'

The atmosphere was, in every sense, electric. Tiny filaments of hissing blue light fuzzed the outline of the sky ship. They fizzed. They sparked. They danced on every surface, from bowsprit to rudder-wheel, masthead to hull. They danced on the sails, the ropes, the decks. And they danced on the sky pirates themselves – on their beards, their clothes, their fingers and toes; setting their entire bodies tingling.

Tem Barkwater was turning a handspike. 'Can't say as I like this over-much,' he grumbled as the sparking blue light played all round his hands.

Stope Boltjaw looked up from the skysail he was busy repairing. 'It's *ah* playing ha-*ah*-voc with my *ah* jaw,' he gasped.

Tem grinned.

'It's not *ah* fu-*ah*-nny!' he complained.

'But it is!' Tem Barkwater chuckled as his shipmate's lower jaw continued to open and close with a will of its own.

Years earlier, Stope Boltjaw had lost his lower jaw during a fierce battle between his sky pirate ship and two league ships. A notoriously ruthless leaguesman by the name of Ulbus Pentephraxis had crept up on him with his hunting axe, and struck him a savage blow which had caught him sideways on, just below his ear.

When he recovered, Stope had fashioned a replacement from a piece of ironwood. So long as he remembered to keep the bolts well oiled, the false jaw served him well enough – at least, it had done up until now. From the moment the *Stormchaser* penetrated the Great Storm, the curious electrical force had caused it to gape wide and slam shut, time and again – and there was nothing Stope Boltjaw could do to stop it.

'How *ah* much longer *ah* is this going on?' he groaned.

'Till we get to the Twilight Woods, I reckon,' said Tem Barkwater.

'Which will be in approximately . . . nine minutes,' Spiker called down from the rigging.

'Nine minutes,' Slyvo Spleethe repeated gleefully under his breath. The quartermaster, who had been sent to check that the mooring-cleats were holding up, but was now leaning against the poop-deck handrail gazing idly into the hypnotic swirl of the clouds all round them, glanced round.

'Keep it up, Quintinius Verginix,' he sneered. 'Complete your journey to the Twilight Woods. Recover the stormphrax. Then I shall make my move. And woe betide anyone who . . .' He gasped. 'What in Sky's name?'

The sight of Twig, standing in the doorway of the little cabin above the staircase, filled Spleethe with an uncontrolled rage. If Cloud Wolf should also see him, then all would be lost. Without a moment's thought, Spleethe dashed off towards him.

Twig looked about him in a state of bewildered excitement. His narrow escape from the flat-head goblin had left him breathless and edgy. Now, as he took in his surroundings, his heart clamoured more urgently than ever.

The air was purple; it smelled of sulphur, of burnt milk. All around the sky ship, the enveloping clouds boiled and writhed and crackled with blinding lightning. His body tingled as tentacles of blue light wrapped themselves around him, causing every hair to stand on end.

This was stormchasing!

The crew were feverishly busy, with Hubble, the ferocious albino banderbear, tethered to the helm, and Cloud Wolf fully occupied with the sail and weight levers as he struggled to maintain both speed and lift. What a time to have to reveal that he had stowed away on board; what a moment to have to break the news of the impending mutiny.

'Yet I have no choice,' Twig muttered grimly. Already, he could hear the wooden hatchway splintering below him. It was only a matter of time before Mugbutt emerged on board. Twig knew that if he didn't speak up now then his father would surely end up dead. He shuddered miserably. 'And it'll all be my fault!'

Bracing himself for the short yet perilous journey from stair-head to helm, Twig was about to set off when a heavy hand slammed down on his shoulders and yanked him back. An ice-cold blade pressed hard at the base of his neck.

'One move, one sound, *Master* Twig, and I'll slit your throat,' Spleethe hissed. 'Understood?'

'Yes,' Twig whispered.

The next instant, he heard a click behind him and found himself being shoved roughly into a store-cupboard filled with buckets and mops, lengths of rope and spare sailcloth. He tumbled backwards and landed heavily in the corner. The door slammed shut.

'Five minutes and counting!' the oakelf's strident voice announced.

Twig climbed shakily to his feet and pressed his ear against the locked door. He could just make out two voices speaking in conspiratorial whispers above the continuing roar and rattle. One was Spleethe's. The other was Mugbutt's.

'I'm not to blame,' the flathead was whining. 'He'd escaped before I had a chance to stop him.'

'You should have kept him tied up,' came Spleethe's irritated reply. 'Curse that Twig!' he said. 'Someone's bound to find him before the stormphrax has been retrieved . . .'

'I could finish him off now,' Mugbutt suggested coldly.

'No,' said Spleethe. 'We need him alive, not dead.' He growled with mounting rage. 'The meddlesome little whelpersnapper has forced my hand and that's a fact. But all is not lost, Mugbutt. Come on. Let's see if we can't turn the situation to our advantage after all.'

As the pair of them departed, Twig felt his heart hammering harder than ever. There he was inside a Great Storm, hurtling on towards the Twilight Woods in search of stormphrax. Finally he was doing what, for so long, he had only dreamed about. And yet, because of him, the dream had become a waking nightmare.

Above him, Spleethe and Mugbutt had made it to the helm. He could hear Spleethe's voice – though not what he said. Twig swallowed nervously and hammered on the door.

'Let me out!' he cried. 'Tem! Spiker! Boltjaw! Oh, why won't you hear me? Let me...'

At that moment Cloud Wolf shouted out. 'What?' he bellowed. 'But this is mutiny!'

Twig shuddered, and hung his head. 'Oh, Father,' he whimpered. 'If we ever get out of this alive will you ever forgive me?'

Confronted by the captain's rage, Spleethe remained icily calm. Apart from his eyes, which glinted beadily behind the steel rims of his glasses, his face betrayed not a hint of emotion.

'Not mutiny,' he said, as he drew his sword from its sheath. 'Merely a redistribution of power.'

Hubble growled ominously.

'This is leaguesman's chatter,' Cloud Wolf snorted. 'Has it really come so far, Spleethe?'

Just then, the *Stormchaser* lurched to the left, and abruptly lost speed. The rear of the storm raced up to meet them. Cloud Wolf lowered the stern weight and raised both the fore and aft sails. The sky ship leapt forwards again.

He turned back to Spleethe. 'Do you seriously imagine for a moment that you could sail the *Stormchaser*? Eh?'

Spleethe hesitated for a moment.

'You are a fool, Spleethe!' Cloud Wolf continued. 'What use have the leagues for stormphrax? Tell me that! It is phraxdust they need, and no-one knows the secret of how to make it safely.'

'On the contrary,' Spleethe replied. 'The League of Free Merchants is prepared to pay highly for a cargo of stormphrax. Very highly indeed. And since you are so reluctant to deliver it to them, then *I* shall. I think you'll find the others are behind me when they realize how much is at stake.'

Mugbutt made a move forwards. Hubble's ears fluttered. Cloud Wolf's hand gripped the hilt of his sword.

'Sky above!' the captain exclaimed. 'Did you not hear me? The leagues have no use for stormphrax. They simply wish to prevent it from reaching the treasury of Sanctaphrax – for if that happened, the floating city would again become stable and their lucrative alliance with the raintasters would fall apart.'

Slyvo Spleethe tightened his grip on his flashing sword.

'They have tricked you, Spleethe. They *want* you to fail.'

'You're lying!' Spleethe screamed, and turned to Mugbutt. 'He's lying!'

Cloud Wolf seized the opportunity. He drew his sword and threw himself at Slyvo Spleethe. 'You mutinous bilge-cur!' he roared.

But Mugbutt was too quick for him. As the captain lunged forwards, he raised his spear – as massive and heavy as befitted the powerful flat-head goblin – and leapt between them. The chiming sound of metal on metal filled the air as the captain and the flat-head launched themselves into deadly battle.

Clash! Crash! Clang! The fight continued, fast and furious. Cloud Wolf howled with rage.

'Blood and thunder!' he roared, 'I'll have the pair of you sky-fired!' He parried away the increasingly frenzied attacks from Mugbutt. 'I'll split your gizzards. I'll rip out your treacherous hearts . . .'

'Waah-waah!' the banderbear shouted out, and tore at the ropes that bound him to the helm.

The *Stormchaser* dipped and rolled. If it drifted towards the outer reaches, where the storm was raging at its wildest, the sky ship would be turned to matchwood in an instant.

'No, Hubble,' Cloud Wolf called out urgently. 'I . . . I'm all right. You must hold a steady course.'

The raised voices, the clash of metal, the pounding of feet – Twig could scarcely believe what he was hearing. Was his father fighting on his own? Where were the rest of the crew and why didn't they come to their captain's aid?

'TEM BARKWATER!' he bellowed, and beat his fists desperately against the locked door. 'STOPE BOLTJAW!'

All at once, the door burst open. Twig tumbled forwards and was immediately grasped by Slyvo Spleethe. 'I told you to keep your mouth shut,' he hissed as he wrenched Twig's arm up behind his back with one hand and pressed the knife to his neck with the other.

'Wh . . . what's happening?' Twig said.

'You'll find out soon enough,' Spleethe spat as he frogmarched Twig across the sparking deck. 'Do exactly what I say,' he instructed, 'and you won't get hurt.'

Quaking with terror, Twig was bundled round the

skirting-deck and up the narrow flight of stairs which led to the helm. The scene which greeted him filled him with sickening dread.

Cloud Wolf and Mugbutt were locked in mortal combat. Eyes blazing, jaws set, the pair of them were fighting for their lives. Their weapons clashed together with such ferocity, that spark after dazzling yellow spark jumped up out of the fizzing blue.

Twig wanted to leap forwards and fight by his father's side. He wanted to slay the wicked mutineer who dared to raise his hand against Captain Cloud Wolf.

'Easy now, Master Twig,' Spleethe hissed in his ear, and increased the pressure on the dagger at Twig's neck. 'If you value your life.'

Twig swallowed anxiously. The fight continued. He couldn't look; he couldn't turn away. Now Mugbutt seemed to be winning, now Cloud Wolf had the upper hand. And all the while, the surrounding storm gathered strength. The lightning flashed again and again, illuminating the curdled clouds and glinting on the flashing blades.

There was no grace to the fight, no finesse. Mugbutt, as the stronger of the two, was content to hack and slash away, battering the captain into submission. Twig tensed nervously as he watched Cloud Wolf being driven back towards the far wall.

Spleethe, fearing the youth was going to cry out, clamped his hand over Twig's mouth. 'Patience,' he whispered. 'It will soon be over. And then I shall take my rightful place as captain of the *Stormchaser*. *Captain*

Spleethe,' he mused. 'It has a nice ring to it.'

Oh, Father, Twig thought desperately as Cloud Wolf battled gallantly on. *What have I done to you?*

'Tem!' he heard him crying out above the rumble of the thunder and clashing of the heavy blades. 'Stopejaw. Spiker.'

But none of the sky pirates heard him. They were too busy keeping the increasingly unstable sky ship airborne.

'The sails are working their way loose,' Tem bellowed, as he heaved round on the sail-wrench. 'Stope, realign the spinnaker bidgets while I try to secure the mainsail. Spiker, see to that tolley-rope.'

'The flight brackets are jammed,' Spiker shouted back, as the sky ship continued to toss and turn. 'Stope, can you help me?'

'I've only got *ah* the *ah* one pair of hands,' Stope grumbled. 'And if I don't *ah* untangle this *ah* nether-fetter soon, we'll all be goners.'

At that moment, a particularly violent gust of wind struck the port bow. Stope Boltjaw cried out as the sky ship listed, and the matted mass of rope and sail was snatched from his hand. At the other end of the sky ship,

Cloud Wolf lost his balance and staggered across the deck.

'Waah!' cried the banderbear. If the other crew members could not come to his captain's aid, then surely he should do something.

'No, Hubble!' Cloud Wolf said breathlessly, as the sky ship lurched back to starboard. 'Keep hold of the helm, or we will all perish. That's an order.'

Tears welled up in Twig's eyes. Even now – as his father's arms grew weak – Cloud Wolf was more concerned with his crew than he was with himself. How valiant he was. How knightly. He, Twig, did not deserve such a father.

Clash! Crash! Hack and slash! Mugbutt's spear slammed down time and again, and with such force and speed, that Cloud Wolf could do nothing but defend himself. All at once, the sky lit up with a sudden flash of blinding light, the *Stormchaser* gave another awful lurch and the whole sky ship pitched forwards.

'The mast is cracking!' Spiker screamed.

'Secure the main-fetter!' Tem roared. 'Lower the sails!'

Cloud Wolf, with his face to the stern, stumbled back. Mugbutt was quick to seize the advantage. He leaped forwards and swung savagely with his spear.

Cloud Wolf ducked. The heavy blade missed him by a fraction. Mugbutt roared with fury and lunged again. Twig gasped – then sighed with relief – as Cloud Wolf knocked the flat-head's weapon away just in the nick of time and countered with a sudden attack. His sword thrust forwards at Mugbutt's chest.

Yes! Yes! Twig thought, urging the sword on.

But it was not to be – for at that moment a terrible sound of splintering wood ripped through the air as the mast snapped off, a third of the way up, and came tumbling down.

It crashed onto the deck and tipped over the side, where it remained, suspended in mid-air below the port side. The sky ship listed sharply to the left and threatened to roll right over.

'Cut the ropes,' Tem yelled, as he began slicing through the main-fetter. 'NOW.'

Stope and Spiker leaped to his side and began slashing and slicing at the tangled ropes and rigging. With half the ropes cut, the rest abruptly broke as one under the heavy weight, and the mast dropped down through the sky. The *Stormchaser* rolled back to starboard.

Twig let out a muffled cry as he and Spleethe toppled backwards, and he felt the knife nick the soft skin at his throat. His father was faring even worse. Not only had the sudden jolt thrown Mugbutt out of reach of the thrusting sword, but now Cloud Wolf was staggering towards him, off-balance, sword flailing and utterly defenceless. Twig froze as the flat-head grabbed his spear again and raised it up. Another second and his father would impale himself on the great jagged blade.

'WAAAH!' Hubble roared as he too saw what was about to happen. He tore furiously at the ropes which bound him to the wheel.

Mugbutt, startled by the noise, glanced up and realized, to his horror, how close to the tethered bander-

bear he had ended up standing. One of his mighty arms was raised. Hubble roared again and swung out savagely. Mugbutt leaped desperately to his left – fast, but not fast enough.

The blow caught the flat-head on the arm. It sent the spear spinning off across the deck, and Mugbutt himself hurtling to the floor. Cloud Wolf was on him like a shot. Without a moment's hesitation, he brought his sword down, hard and sharp, severing the goblin's head with a single blow. Then, bloodied sword raised, he turned murderously on Spleethe.

'And now you,' he stormed. 'You . . .' He fell silent. His eyes widened; his jaw dropped. 'Twig!' he muttered.

Slyvo Spleethe sniggered as he pulled the blade oh-so-gently across Twig's throat. 'Drop your weapon,' he said. 'Or your *son* gets it.'

'No,' Twig cried. 'Don't do this for me. You must not.'

Cloud Wolf tossed his sword aside and let his arms drop defencelessly. 'Release the boy,' he said. 'You have no quarrel with him.'

'Maybe I will. Maybe I won't,' Spleethe teased. He put away his dagger, but drew his own sword in a flash. 'Maybe I'll . . .'

The sky cracked and flashed, and the *Stormchaser* pitched wildly, first to one side, then to the other. The sky ship was drifting perilously close to the edge of the storm – and there was nothing Hubble could do to stop it.

Then all at once and before anyone realized what he was doing, Spleethe let go of Twig. He shoved him to the floor and raced headlong at the captain, sword raised.

'Aaaaaa!' he screamed.

The sky ship shuddered violently. Every beam, every plank, every joint creaked in protest.

'Two minutes, and counting,' Twig heard Spiker calling – then, with sudden alarm, 'Tem! Boltjaw! The captain's in trouble!'

At long last the others had noticed that something was wrong. But too late. Far too late. Already Spleethe's sword was slicing down through the air towards Cloud Wolf's exposed neck.

Below the hull, one of the port hull-weights was being shaken loose. Abruptly, it broke free and tumbled down through the sky. The *Stormchaser* keeled to starboard.

The sword landed heavily, missing its target, but burying itself deep in the top of Cloud Wolf's arm – his sword arm. Slyvo Spleethe's lip curled. 'You were lucky that time,' he said. 'You will not be so lucky again.' He raised the sword a second time. '*I* am captain now!'

'Hubble!' Twig cried out desperately. '*Do* something!'

'Wuh-wuh!' the banderbear bellowed, and gripped the wheel. The captain had told him – *ordered* him – to stay put.

For a moment, their eyes met. 'Wuh-wuh,' said Twig.

'WAAH!' Hubble roared. Mind made up, his eyes blazed and his hair bristled as he ripped the ropes from their moorings, and tore them to pieces as if they were made of paper. 'WAAAH!'

A shaggy white mountain, he stormed towards Spleethe in a flurry of flashing claws and bared teeth. He seized the scurrilous quartermaster round the waist, raised him up in the air and slammed him furiously back down onto the deck. Then, before Spleethe could so much as move a muscle, the banderbear roared again and came crashing down on the quartermaster's back.

There was a thud. There was a crack. Slyvo Spleethe was dead – his spine broken in two.

Twig climbed shakily to his feet, and desperately clung hold of the balustrade as the storm-tossed sky ship pitched and rolled, totally out of control. The mutinous usurpers might have been dealt with and his father's life spared – but the situation was grim.

With no-one now at the helm, the wheel was spinning, while the sails that remained flapped uselessly overhead. Below the hull, two more of the balance-weights shook themselves loose. The *Stormchaser* tossed and twisted, bucked and dived. Round and round it spun, threatening at any moment to tip upside down and scatter the hapless crew to certain death below.

Cloud Wolf struggled to pull himself up with his one good arm, wincing with pain as he did so. Tem Barkwater who, with the others, had finally made it to the bridge, struggled to get to him.

'Leave me!' Cloud Wolf cried fiercely.

A blinding flash tore across the sky, lighting up the *Stormchaser* and revealing the true extent of its damage. Any second now, it would break up completely. Cloud Wolf spun round to face his crew.

'ABANDON SHIP!' he bellowed.

The crew stared back at him incredulously. What madness was this? Abandon ship, when they were on the verge of reaching their destination?

At that moment, the air all round them exploded with the clamour of countless small birds as they billowed up from the bowels of the ship. Their triangular wings and whiplash tails, all frantically beating, flashed black against the dazzling background. Thousands of them,

there were, yet they flew with single intent. When one turned, they all turned. Squawking, squeaking, screeching, the flock wheeled this way and that as if to the command of some unseen choreographer.

'Ratbirds,' Tem murmured with horror. He knew – as did every sky pirate – that ratbirds only abandon a sky ship that is truly doomed. He spun round. 'You heard the cap'n,' he bellowed. 'Abandon ship!'

'And alert both the Stone Pilot and the professor,' Cloud Wolf called out.

'Aye aye, cap'n,' said Tem Barkwater, and staggered off to do the captain's bidding.

Spiker was the first to go. As he threw himself from the balustrade he called back, 'We are crossing into the Twilight Woods . . . Now!'

The rest of the crew soon followed him. Despite the awful danger of remaining on the *Stormchaser* a moment too long, one by one they knelt down and kissed the deck, before climbing reluctantly up onto the side and leaping off into the purple air. Stope Boltjaw. The Stone Pilot. Tem Barkwater and the Professor of Light. As the blast of air struck them, so the spring mechanism of their

parawings leapt up, the wind pockets inflated with air and they glided off and away.

Back on the bridge, Cloud Wolf was making his way to the helm, step by agonizing step, as the sky ship continued to judder and jolt.

'You too, Hubble,' he shouted at the steadfast banderbear. 'Leave your post. Go!' The great beast surveyed him dolefully. The sails fluttered and tore. 'Now!' roared Cloud Wolf. 'Before the sky ship goes down.'

'Wuh-wuh,' he cried, and lurched off to obey. As he moved away, Cloud Wolf saw that the banderbear had been shielding a second member of the crew who had not yet left the sky ship.

'Twig!' he barked. 'I told you to go.'

The swirling clouds squirmed. The *Stormchaser* shuddered and creaked.

'But I can't! I won't leave you!' Twig cried out. 'Oh, forgive me, Father. This is all my fault.'

'Your fault?' Cloud Wolf grunted as he struggled to take control of the helm. 'It is *I* who is to blame – leaving you at the mercy of that scoundrel Spleethe.'

'But . . .'

'Enough!' roared Cloud Wolf. 'Leave now!'

'Come with me!' Twig pleaded.

Cloud Wolf said nothing. There was no need. Twig knew that his father would sooner lose his own life than his ship.

'Then I'll stay with you!' he said defiantly.

'Twig! Twig!' Cloud Wolf cried, his voice barely audible above the rush and rumble of the storm. 'I may lose my ship. I may yet lose my life. And if that is my fate, then so be it. But if I lost you . . . It would . . .' He paused. 'Twig, my son. I love you. But you must leave. For you and for me. You understand, don't you?'

Tears welling in his eyes, Twig nodded.

'Good boy,' said Cloud Wolf. Then, lurching awkwardly from one side to the other, he hurriedly unbuckled his sword-belt, wrapped it round the scabbard and thrust out his hand. 'Take my sword,' he said.

Twig reached forwards. His fingers grazed his father's hand. 'We will see each other again, won't we?' he sniffed.

'You can depend on it,' said Cloud Wolf. 'When I regain control of the *Stormchaser* I shall be back for you all. Now go,' he said, and abruptly returned his attention to the rows of weight and sail levers.

Sadly, Twig turned to leave. When he reached the outer balustrade, Twig looked round and stole a final look at his father. 'Fare fortune!' he cried to the blasting wind, and launched himself into the air.

The next instant he screamed out in terror. He was dropping like a stone. The parawings must have been damaged when Spleethe had thrown him into the store-cupboard. Now they were jammed. They would not open.

'Father!' he screamed. 'FA-THER!'

·CHAPTER TWELVE·

Into the Twilight Woods

Twig screwed his eyes tightly shut as he fell, faster and faster. If ever he had needed the caterbird – who, since Twig had been there at its hatching, had sworn to watch over him – then surely it was now. Yet, as he continued to tumble through the sky, the caterbird failed to appear.

The air sped past Twig, snatching his breath away. He had all but abandoned hope when, suddenly, he heard a loud click. The mechanism on the parawings sprang up, the wings flew open and – *whooopf* – the silken pockets billowed out. Caught by the wind, Twig was tossed back upwards like a leaf in a gale.

He opened his eyes, and struggled to right himself. It was the first time Twig had had to perform a real emergency leap, yet when he pushed his legs back and his arms forward, as he had been taught, he found

himself gliding effortlessly with the wind. 'Flying,' Twig cried excitedly, as the wind sent his hair streaming back behind him. 'I'm flaaaah-ying!'

All round him, the air crackled and hummed. Something was happening. Something new; something bizarre. The lightning which, up until that moment, had been confined to the surrounding wall of cloud, suddenly began darting forwards to the centre of the storm in long, wispy threads. They danced and spiralled and began weaving themselves together in a ball of electric light.

Twig gazed in wonder. 'This is it,' he whispered excitedly. 'The Great Storm must be about to discharge its single mighty lightning bolt.' His hair stood on end; his head thrilled with anticipation. 'This is what it has all been building up to. This is what we came to see – the creation of stormphrax.'

The ball of light grew larger and larger, and larger still. Twig winced. He couldn't tear his eyes away – yet neither could he look without blinking. And when he did blink, he noticed something small and dark at the centre of the pinky-green afterglow.

'The *Stormchaser*,' he gasped.

He blinked again. There was no doubt. The sky ship was in the middle of the lightning ball which was, itself, in the middle of the Great Storm. And there at the very centre of it all, was his father, Cloud Wolf: Quintinius Verginix – the finest scholar ever to have passed out from the Knights' Academy – still valiantly holding his beloved *Stormchaser* on course. Twig's heart swelled with pride.

The humming noise grew louder and higher. The light grew more intense. The charged air itself seemed to tremble with foreboding.

What was going to happen?

Behind him, Twig felt sudden turbulence that heralded the rear of the Great Storm. It buffeted at his back and set him dipping and diving. His parawings creaked and strained, and Twig could do nothing but hold on and pray that they would not be torn from his shoulders.

Above him, the dazzling streaks of lightning were gradually fading as the electrical force was drained from the clouds. Twig's hair abruptly lay flat. All the energy of the storm was now encapsulated in that single ball of lightning. It hovered in mid-air, throbbing with energy, pulsing with light, roaring with life.

Twig held his breath as he continued to glide slowly downwards. His heart was pounding, his palms were wet. 'Sky protect me,' he murmured anxiously.

Then, all at once and without any warning at all –

BOOM!!! – the lightning ball exploded with an almighty crash and a flash of blinding light.

Shock waves rippled outwards across the sky. Twig quaked with terror. The next instant he was thrown backwards by the ferocious blast, and tossed into the oncoming bank of cloud.

'Aaaaggh!' he screamed, as the roaring, swirling wind tossed him around. He kicked out desperately and tried to flap his arms – but in vain. The wind was too powerful. It was trying – or so it seemed to Twig – to rip him limb from limb. All he could do was abandon himself to the overwhelming force of the turbulent air.

Over and over he tumbled. The silken pockets of the parawings were blown inside out, and he cried out in alarm as he found himself spinning round and down

through the rolling purple clouds.

'NOOO!' he screamed.

Further and further he dropped, arms limp and legs akimbo, too frightened to try realigning the parawings in case the wind caught them awkwardly and snapped them in half. His neck was twisted. His back was bent double.

'No more!' Twig whimpered. 'Let it be over.'

And, at that moment, it *was* over. Finally reaching the back of the cloud, Twig was spat out of the wild and thrashing frenzy of the Great Storm like a woodsap pip. In all, the entire terrifying ordeal couldn't have lasted for more than a few seconds. To Twig, it might have been a hundred years.

'Thank Sky,' he whispered gratefully.

An eerie stillness fell. It was as if the very air had been exhausted by the passing maelstrom. Twig shifted round and, as his parawings righted themselves once more, he continued his slow gliding descent. Ahead of him, he saw the Great Storm retreating. It slipped across the clear blue sky, beautiful and majestic, and glowing like a massive purple paper-lantern.

'Is that it?' Twig murmured. 'Have I missed the bolt of stormphrax itself?'

He hung his head in disappointment and was looking down at the Twilight Woods when all at once he heard another noise. It sounded like paper tearing, like hands clapping. Twig raised his head sharply and stared ahead. Protruding from the base of the purple storm was a point of brightness.

'Here it is!' he exclaimed. 'The bolt of lightning. The stormphrax itself!'

Longer and longer the jagged shaft grew, yet impossibly slowly – as if the clouds themselves were holding it back. Twig was starting to wonder whether it would ever be released when, all of a sudden, a resounding CRACK! echoed through the air. The bolt of lightning had broken free.

Like an arrow, it sped down through the sky, scorching the air as it passed. It crackled. It sparked. It wailed and whistled. A smell like toasted almonds filled Twig's nostrils, setting them quivering.

'It's . . . it's wonderful,' he sighed.

Down, down the lightning bolt hurtled. *Zigger-zagger,*

zigger-zagger. Through the upper canopy of leaves – hissing and splintering as it passed – and on to the ground below. Then, with a crackle, a thud and a cloud of steam, it plunged into the soft earth. Twig stared at the shaft of lightning standing tall amongst the trees below him, and trembled with awe and wonder.

'Stormphrax,' he whispered. 'And *I* saw it being formed.'

The Great Storm was by now nothing more than a distant blur of purple, low on the horizon and speeding out of sight. Now it was gone, Twig could hardly recall what it had been like trapped inside, tossed and thrown by the violent winds.

The air was sluggish, moist, heavy. It clung like damp cloth.

For Twig, still so high up, this was not good.

With a little breeze behind them, the parawings were wonderfully manoeuvrable. When the air was as still as it now was, however, parawinging was perilous. Steering was quite impossible. It took every ounce of skill to ensure that the silken wing-pockets remained filled with air. One awkward movement, and the wings would collapse and he would plummet to the ground below.

'It's like sailing a sky ship,' he recalled his father once saying. 'You have to maintain an even keel at all times.'

'Father!' he gasped. How could he have forgotten? he asked himself guiltily. Surely the *Stormchaser* could never have survived so great a blast. 'And yet, perhaps . . .' he murmured, hoping against hope. 'After all, I saw no sign of wreckage, no falling debris . . .'

Lower and lower Twig drifted; closer and closer came the stormphrax. Unable to dive down, he'd hoped that good fortune might bring him in to land near the precious substance. But it was not to be. Twig was still high up in the sky when he glided over the glistening bolt of solid lightning. He sighed with disappointment as it slipped back between his feet and disappeared behind him.

Too frightened to swoop, or even to look, round, Twig could do nothing but hang on, hold tight and remain as still as he possibly could. The patchwork of treetops, drenched in golden half-light, was coming nearer with every passing second. Sooner or later, he would have to land. He fingered the various talismans and amulets around his neck.

'Into the Twilight Woods,' he whispered, scarcely daring to guess what he might find there.

The further he descended, the more sluggish the air became. It grew warmer, heavier – almost suffocating. Droplets of water sparkled from every inch of his body. Faster and faster he dropped. The parawings fluttered ominously. Suddenly, and to his horror, Twig realized that he was no longer gliding at all . . . He was falling.

'No,' he cried out. This couldn't be happening. Not now. Not after everything he'd been through. 'NO!'

His voice echoed forlornly as down, down, down, he went. Tumbling round in the golden light. Crashing through the upper canopy. Bouncing against the branches and . . . THUD!

He landed heavily, awkwardly, and cracked the side of his head against the roots of a tree. The soft twilight glow instantly went out. Twig found himself in absolute darkness.

How long he remained unconscious, Twig never discovered. Time has no meaning in the Twilight Woods.

'Hold steady,' he heard. 'Nearly there.'

Twig opened his eyes. He was lying on the ground beside a tall, angular tree, gnarled with age. He looked round, and everything seemed to swim before him. Rubbing his eyes made no difference. It was the air itself – thick and treacly – that was distorting his vision.

He climbed groggily to his feet, and gasped. There in front of him was a knight on a prowlgrin charger, caught up in a tangle of leather harness straps, dangling a few feet from the forest floor.

Twig's eyes travelled from the rusting figure, up the snarl of twisted ropes, to the great skeletal hulk of a wrecked sky ship, speared on a jagged treetop. Ancient winding gear poked out from the ship's side like an angry metal fist. The knight swayed in the torpid air.

'Wh . . . who are you?' asked Twig tentatively.

From deep within the knight's visor, the voice came again.

'Hold steady, Vinchix,' it said. 'Nearly there. Hold steady, now.'

The white bones of the prowlgrin protruded from its papery, mummified skin, its empty eye-sockets stared out from the metal helmet bridle on which, in gold letters, the word *Vinchix* could just be picked out. It whinnied pitifully.

Twig swallowed hard. 'Can you hear me?' he asked the knight, his voice thin and quavery.

'Hold steady, Vinchix,' came the words again.

Twig stretched out a hand and touched the visor. Flakes of red rust fell away. Gently, scarcely daring to breathe, Twig raised the knight's visor.

Twig screamed in horror and recoiled. He spun round and, driven by blind panic, sped off into the heavy, golden depths of the Twilight Woods. No matter how fast or far he ran, however, the vision of the knight – decomposing, yet not dead – remained seared into his brain. The parchment skin shrunk tight on the grinning skull; the lifeless staring eyes; and, worst of all, the thin bloodless lips of the knight, still moving. 'Nearly there, hold steady, now.'

On and on Twig went, alone and lonely, searching for the bolt of stormphrax, hoping and praying that his fellow crew-members were doing the same.

The half-light of the Twilight Woods confused his eyes. One moment it glowed a rich golden yellow, the next it shimmered in black and white. Deep shadows, pools of brightness. Charcoal and chalk. The chiaroscuro of darkness and light which confused everything it fell upon.

Ancient trees, with their gnarled trunks and twisted branches, seemed to writhe in the liquid air, taking on shapes of goblins and ogres and gruesome giants.

'They're just trees,' Twig reminded himself. 'Just trees is all they are.' The words sounded musical, and oddly reassuring as he repeated them. 'Just treesy-weesy trees. That's all, just . . .'

'Twig!' he shouted, and shook his head from side to side. He must pay attention, he must remain in control.

He continued over the soft mattress of fallen leaves, staring down at his feet. The ground was covered with tiny sparkling crystals, like a sprinkling of salt, like a skyful of stars. Twig smiled to himself. 'See how they glitter,' he whispered. 'See how they glisten. See how they glimmer. See how they gleam . . .'

'TWIG!' he bellowed once again. 'Stop it!' And he slapped his face on both sides, once, twice, three-four-five times. He slapped it until it was pink and smarting. 'Keep your mind on the task at hand,' he said firmly. 'Don't let it wander.'

But this was easier said than done for the Twilight Woods were enchanting and seductive. They whispered, they echoed – they enticed. And as Twig made his way deeper and deeper into the woods, he was terrified to discover just how simple it was for his mind to drift away . . . to wander off . . . to disappear on distant flights of fancy . . .

'You are Twig, son of Cloud Wolf the sky pirate captain,' he reminded himself sharply. 'You are in the Twilight Woods, brought here by the Great Storm. You are searching for stormphrax, for the crew of the *Stormchaser* – for a way out.'

So long as he could hold on to these truths, he would be all right. But with every step, it was becoming harder. The woods seemed to be closing in around him, impinging on his senses. They filled his eyes with their liquid distortion, his ears with their echoing whispers, his nose and mouth with lushness – and decay.

As he stumbled on, he thought he glimpsed something out of the corner of his eye. He looked furtively over his shoulder, then frowned with confusion. There was nothing there.

'But I could have sworn . . .' Twig muttered anxiously.

Time after time, it happened. Something *was* there. He was sure of it. Yet no matter how fast he spun round, he never caught sight of whatever it was.

'I don't like this,' he shuddered. 'I don't like it at all.'

Behind him he heard a faint *clip-clop* sound. It caught him unawares and, before he knew it, Twig was back in the woodtroll cabin of his childhood. Spelda

Snatchwood – the woodtroll who had raised him as her own – was busying herself around the cabin, her bark sandals clipping and clopping on the wooden floor. The memories were so clear, so vibrant. He saw lufwood burning in the stove and smelt the pickled tripweed on Spelda's breath. 'You are my mother-mine,' he whispered. 'And you are Twig, my beautiful boy,' she whispered back.

Twig started at the sound of his name. He stared ahead, unable for a moment to make sense of the shimmering gloom. Were those eyes staring at him whenever he turned his head away? Were those claws and teeth glinting just out of sight?

'You are Twig, son of Cloud Wolf,' he told himself. 'You are in the Twilight Woods. You are searching for your crew-mates – for a way out.' He sighed. 'A way out of this nightmare.'

A soft squeaking-squealing sound filled his head. Metal on unoiled metal. Twig smiled. It was supper-time on board the *Stormchaser*, and the sky pirates were all seated round a long bench tucking into a meal of baked snowbird and earthapple mash. It was silent apart from the regular *squeak squeak squeak* of Stope Boltjaw's iron-wood jaw as he chewed. 'Sounds like we've got a woodrat in our midst,' Tem Barkwater noted and laughed. 'Eh, Twig? I said, it sounds like . . .'

Twig grimaced. It had happened again. How long before the treacherous woods robbed him of his mind completely? 'You are Twig,' he said, uncertainly. 'You are in the Twilight Woods. You are searching for . . . for . . .'

Just then, from his right, there came the unmistakable sound of a prowlgrin whinnying. Twig groaned. He must have been going in a huge circle. All that walking – all that *concentrating* – only to find that he had come right back to the same spot.

He scoured the tops of the trees for any sign of the wreck of the sky ship – but found none. Puzzled and uneasy, Twig chewed at the end of his scarf. Perhaps I imagined it, he thought. Perhaps . . .

Panic rose in Twig's throat.

'St . . . stay calm,' he told himself. 'Concentrate on what's ahead. Don't look round. You'll be fine.'

'Steady, Bolnix, you'll be just fine,' wheezed an ancient voice.

Twig looked up sharply. His eyes focused – and his heart missed a beat.

·CHAPTER THIRTEEN·

THE SEPIA KNIGHT

In front of him was a second knight. He was encased, from top to toe, in rusting armour, and seated upon a prowlgrin. As he moved round in the saddle, the heavy metal plates clanked and rattled; the gauges clicked, the pipes whistled softly.

'Hold steady now, Bolnix,' said the knight, his cracked voice reedy, sibilant.

Twig saw two eyes glinting from behind the helmet visor. He shivered apprehensively, and looked away. The prowlgrin, old and weak, shifted from foot to foot agitatedly.

'Steady, Bolnix,' said the knight again. 'Not too close, now.'

Wheezing with effort, the knight pulled off a gauntlet. Twig stared at the hand which was revealed. It was as gnarled as the branches of the ancient trees. Clunking and clanking, the knight raised his arm and began fumbling with the visor.

'Steady now,' he said.

Twig froze as the visor creaked rustily, and slowly swung open. He found himself staring into a pair of startlingly blue eyes, sunk, like half-excavated jewels, deep into an ancient, craggy face.

'Is that you, Garlinius? I have searched for so long.' The voice was as ancient as the face – and twice as melancholy.

'No,' said Twig, approaching the figure. 'Please sir, I've been shipwrecked. The *Stormchaser* . . .'

The knight recoiled, the pipes and gauges on his armour rattling alarmingly. The prowlgrin snorted with unease. 'You speak to me of stormchasing, Garlinius! You, who robbed me of the *Storm Queen*, and never returned. Oh, Garlinius, I searched for you so long. If you only knew.'

'Please,' said Twig, taking a step closer. 'I am not Garlinius. I'm Twig, and I . . .'

'Garlinius!' cried the knight, his mood suddenly improved. Returning the gauntlet to his hand, he leaped from the prowlgrin and grabbed Twig by the shoulder. 'It's so good to see you!' he said. 'We parted on bad terms. We knights should never do that. Oh, but Garlinius, I have suffered since. I've wandered these woods, searching and searching.'

The knight was staring into Twig's face, his eyes burning an iridescent blue. The metal gauntlet tightened its grip.

Twig winced, and tried to pull away. 'But I'm not Garlinius,' he insisted. 'I'm Twig. I am searching for my crew-mates, my . . .'

'Lost and searching,' the knight howled. 'I too. I too. But it matters, now, not a jot. For we are reunited once more. You and me, Garlinius,' he said, gripping Twig's shoulder still more tightly. 'Me and you.'

'Look at me!' Twig cried desperately. 'Listen to what I am telling you. I am *not* Garlinius.'

'If you only knew how long I searched,' the knight sighed. 'Searching, always searching.'

'Leave me alone!' Twig shouted. 'Let me go!'

But the knight would not let go. And no matter how much Twig squirmed or wriggled, he could not break free from the pincer grip of the heavy gauntlet.

Instead, and to his intense horror, he found himself being drawn closer and closer to the knight until he could feel the ancient creature's warm, fetid breath in his face. The knight raised his other hand, and Twig shivered with revulsion as he felt the bony, crepey fingers exploring every inch of his head.

'Garlinius,' said the knight. 'The aquiline nose. The high forehead. How well we are re-met.'

Up so close, Twig saw that the knight's armour was coated in a fine layer of sepia dust. It moved over the metal breastplate almost like a liquid. Now he could see his reflection in the metal underneath; now his face was gone again.

'If you only knew how lonely I've been, Garlinius,' the knight cried out. 'How long I've searched.'

Twig was beginning to panic. 'I must break free,' he muttered through gritted teeth. 'I must get away.'

He reached up, grabbed the gauntleted hand that gripped his shoulder and pulled with all his might.

'Garlinius!' protested the knight pitifully.

Twig brought his knee up hard, and connected with the knight's breastplate with a loud clang. The knight fell back and landed heavily with an echoing clatter on the crystal-covered ground. A cloud of sepia dust flew up into the air. Twig fell to his knees coughing violently.

'Garlinius!'

The knight was back on his feet. In his hand he held a long saw-toothed sword, vicious-looking despite the rust that cloaked it.

'Garlinius,' he said again, his voice suddenly thin and menacing. His blue eyes looked straight into Twig's, their clear intensity mesmerizing him for an instant. The knight raised the sword.

Twig stopped breathing.

The knight's wizened face creased with confusion. 'Garlinius?' he called out. 'Where are you?'

His eyes bore into Twig's.

'Come back, Garlinius,' he implored. 'We can be friends again. If you only knew how long I've searched. Garlinius! Please . . .'

Twig shuddered with pity. The knight was quite blind. The Twilight Woods had robbed him of his senses, every one; of his wits, of his reason – yet left him with his life. He would never rest. He would never find peace. Instead, he was doomed to continue his never-ending search for ever and ever. Nothing in the Deepwoods was as cruel as this place, thought Twig. I must get out! I won't let the evil Twilight Woods have *my* wits, *my* sight . . . I will escape.

The knight, hearing no reply, turned regretfully away. 'So near,' he whispered. 'Always so near, and yet . . .'

He whistled softly through his rotten teeth and the prowlgrin padded obediently to his side. Wheezing and panting, the knight clambered back into the saddle.

'I will find you, Garlinius,' he cried in his frail, cracked voice. 'A quest is a quest for ever. Wherever Vinchix takes you, Bolnix and I will follow.'

Twig held his breath and remained absolutely still as the knight shook his fist in the air, tugged on the reins and rode off into the depths of the Twilight Woods. The golden light gleamed on the back of his armour as he faded into the confusing patchwork of light and shade. The creaking grew softer, the clip-clop footfalls fading away to nothing.

Finally, Twig let out his breath, and gasped for air. As he did so, he felt a sharp pinch at his shoulder. The sepia knight's gauntlet still held its grip.

·CHAPTER FOURTEEN·

Louder Cries. Softer Whispers

i
In the Mire

Screed Toe-taker patted his stomach. The oozefish had tasted as vile as ever – bitter, bony and oily – but they had taken the edge off his hunger. He leaned forwards and dropped the bones into the fire where they crackled and burst into flames; the heads and tails, he tossed to the scavenging white ravens which had been hopping round the wrecked ship expectantly ever since the first wisps of fishy smoke had risen into the air.

'There you are, my lovelies,' he rasped.

The birds squabbled noisily over the scraps of food – pecking, scratching, drawing blood – until, one by one, they each seized a piece that suited them, leaped up into the air and flapped away to eat it in peace.

'Oozefish,' Screed snorted, and spat into the fire.

It was years since Screed had first set up home in the bleached wasteland, yet he had never got used to the taste of the food the Mire had to offer. Occasionally, of course, he would pilfer the provisions brought by the hapless goblins, trolls and the like, whom he would lead to their deaths. But their supplies of stale bread and dried meat were scarcely any better. No. What Screed Toe-taker craved was the food he had once eaten every day – hammelhorn steaks, tildermeat sausages, baked snowbird . . . His mouth watered; his stomach groaned.

'One day, perhaps,' he sighed. 'One day.'

He picked up a long stick and poked thoughtfully at the embers of the fire. The weather was calm this morning, with little wind and no clouds – unlike the previous day, when the sky had churned and rumbled with the passing storm. It had looked like a Great Storm. And he remembered the sky ship he'd seen speeding towards it like a flying arrow.

'Stormchasing,' Screed muttered, and sneered. 'If they only knew!' He cackled with laughter. 'But then, of course, by now they *will* know. The poor fools!' he said, and cackled all the louder.

The sun rose higher in the sky. It beat down fiercely, causing a swirling mist to coil up out of the swampy mud.

'Come on then,' Screed said, as he wiped his mouth on his sleeve. 'Can't sit round here all day.'

He heaved himself to his feet, kicked wet mud over the smouldering embers and ashes and surveyed the horizon. A broad smile spread across his face as he stared across the hazy Mire to the Twilight Woods beyond.

Who would arrive next, desperate for a guide to lead them across the Mire? he wondered, and sniggered unpleasantly. 'Looty-booty,' he whispered, 'here I come!'

ii
In the Palace of the Most High Academe

Vilnix Pompolnius yelped with pain and sat bolt upright. 'Imbecile!' he shouted.

'A thousand, nay, a million apologies,' Minulis cried out. 'I slipped.'

Vilnix inspected the injured finger and licked away a drop of blood. 'It's not too serious,' he said, and smiled. 'Anyway, a little bit of pain never did anyone any harm.'

'No, sire,' Minulis agreed eagerly.

Vilnix settled himself back on the ottoman and closed his eyes. 'You may continue,' he said.

'Yes, sire. Thank you, sire. At once, sire,' Minulis babbled. 'And you may be sure, it won't happen again, sire.'

'It'd better not,' Vilnix snarled. 'There are many who would leap at the opportunity of becoming personal manservant to the Most High Academe of Sanctaphrax – should the post suddenly become free. Do I make myself clear?'

'*Crystal* clear, if I might make so bold,' said Minulis ingratiatingly.

With the utmost care, he lifted the bony hand once more and resumed the manicure. The Most High

Academe liked his nails filed to needle-points. They enabled him to scratch his back most satisfyingly.

'Minulis,' said Vilnix Pompolnius at length, his eyes still closed. 'Do you dream?'

'Only when I sleep, sire,' he replied.

'A good answer,' Vilnix replied. 'And one that illustrates the difference between you and me.'

Minulis went on with his filing in silence. The Most High Academe did not like to be interrupted.

'The only times *I* dream is when I am awake.' He opened his eyes. 'I dreamed of all this,' he said, sweeping his free hand round the sumptuous Inner Sanctum in a wide arc. 'And lo and behold, my dreams all came true.'

Minulis nodded. 'The Council of Sanctaphrax is lucky indeed to have so wise and venerable a scholar as its Most High Academe.'

'Quite so,' said Vilnix dismissively. 'And yet, since reaching the pinnacle of success, I have missed my dreams.'

Minulis tutted sympathetically.

Abruptly, Vilnix sat up and leaned forwards conspiratorially. 'I'll let you into a little secret, shall I?' he whispered. 'Following my supper with the Leaguesmaster and my little chat with that nightwaif creature, I have started dreaming again. Wonderful dreams,' he said softly. 'Dreams more vivid than any I have ever had before.'

iii
In the Backstreets of Undertown

Deaf, destitute and on the street, Forficule had sunk just about as low as it was possible to sink. No use to anyone, least of all Mother Horsefeather – who he knew wouldn't now give him so much as a second glance – he sat cross-legged on a threadbare blanket, his head swathed in bloody bandages, watching the good citizens of Undertown scurry past him without a second look.

'Spare a little change?' he cried out at intervals, and rattled his tin cup. 'Help save a poor soul less fortunate than yourselves.'

His words, however, fell on ears as deaf as his own. After eight hours of begging, the cup still contained no more than the brass button that he himself had placed there that morning. By sundown, Forficule was about to leave when somebody did finally pause beside him.

'Spare a little change,' he said.

'A little change?' the newcomer said softly. 'Come with me and I'll make you rich beyond compare.'

Forficule made no reply. He hadn't heard a single word. Slitch – reluctant to repeat his offer any louder – crouched before him and rubbed his thumb and middle-finger together. Forficule looked up and concentrated on the gnokgoblin's lips.

'Money,' Slitch mouthed. 'Wealth. Riches. Come with me.'

If Forficule had been able to hear Slitch's thoughts – or

even his voice – he would have recognized him at once as the unscrupulous goblin who had caused the death of the unfortunate slaughterer, Tendon. But Forficule could hear neither. Like a baby, he had to take the smiling goblin's words at face value. He climbed to his feet, tucked the grimy bundle of rags under his arm, and let himself be led away.

Perhaps it was his desperation that left Forficule as blind as he was deaf. Or perhaps he didn't want to remember what he had seen before. At any rate, he did not remember the familiar scene in the hut, of mortar, pestle and crystal.

'Stormphrax,' Slitch mouthed, and smiled as he handed the nightwaif the pestle.

Forficule nodded.

'But hang on a moment,' Slitch went on. He turned and removed a phial of deep yellow liquid from the shelf. 'Dampseed oil,' he explained, and removed the cork stopper. 'If we pour a little into the bowl with the crystal, then . . .' He stopped. 'What are you doing? NO!' he screamed and lunged at the nightwaif.

But it was too late. With his eyes fixed on the glistening, sparking shard of stormphrax, Forficule had heard nothing of Slitch's explanation. He gripped the pestle firmly in both hands. 'Here we go,' he whispered, and brought it sharply down.

BOOM!

CRASH!

The crystal of stormphrax exploded with terrifying force, taking the hut with it. The roof flew off, the walls flew out and the floor became a massive crater. As the dust settled, two bodies could be seen, locked together in a fatal embrace.

iv
Outside the Bloodoak Tavern

'What in Sky's name was that?' the Professor of Darkness exclaimed.

Mother Horsefeather shook her head. 'You academics,' she chided. 'Heads in the clouds in your castles in the air. You've got no idea, have you?'

The pair of them were taking an early evening stroll together. They had urgent business to discuss and, since the Bloodoak tavern had proved to be so open to eavesdropping, had taken their conversation outside.

'So, tell me,' he said. 'What was that noise? It sounded like an explosion.'

'It *was* an explosion,' she said, her ruff of neck feathers bristling. 'Every time some poor fool tries to turn stormphrax into phraxdust there is an explosion.'

The Professor of Darkness started with surprise. 'But where do they get this stormphrax?' he asked.

Mother Horsefeather clacked her beak impatiently. 'The black-market is flooded with the stuff,' she said. 'Word has it the Most High Academe himself is authorizing it in the hope that someone, somewhere, will unlock the elusive secret to safe phraxdust production, though . . .'

'But . . . but this is outrageous!' the Professor of Darkness spluttered. 'I had no idea . . . No wonder the treasury is so depleted.' He shook his head. 'I curse the day I first laid eyes on that traitorous usurper, Vilnix Pompolnius.'

'Yesterday is over,' said Mother Horsefeather curtly. 'Tomorrow is still to come.'

'I know, I know,' said the professor, 'but what can we do? I've already told you that both Vilnix *and* the Leaguesmaster now know that Cloud Wolf has set off in search of stormphrax. Both await his return. Both have the means to confiscate his cargo – and if one fails, then the other will surely succeed.'

'On the contrary,' said Mother Horsefeather, her eyes twinkling. 'Both will fail, you mark my words. I know Cloud Wolf for the wily old skycur that he is. While his two enemies are battling it out, he will slip between them and bring the cargo of stormphrax to me, just as we agreed.' Suddenly, her eyes narrowed. She spun round. 'Anyway, how do *you* know so much, eh?' she said. 'Are you now privy to the Most High Academe's thoughts?'

'No, I . . .' the professor began. 'I see your ignorance of Sanctaphrax equals my own of Undertown. Intrigue, whispers, gossip – the black-market of our noble floating city is flooded with the stuff!' he said, and smiled.

'Forficule,' said Mother Horsefeather, 'was it . . .?'

'Forficule told Vilnix everything,' the professor said.

Mother Horsefeather hawked noisily and spat on the ground. 'No wonder the little squit was too ashamed to show his face,' she squawked.

'Tortured, he was, until he did,' the professor explained. 'He had no choice. But no, I didn't learn of the Most High Academe's plans from Forficule.'

'Then who?' Mother Horsefeather demanded to know.

'From someone who has sworn allegiance to the position of power, rather than the individual who holds it,' the professor explained. 'His name is Minulis,' he said. 'He is personal manservant to Vilnix Pompolnius – and he senses that changes are coming.'

Mother Horsefeather cackled with delight. 'Then it's up to us to ensure that he senses right!'

·CHAPTER FIFTEEN·

DEAD OR ALIVE

Twig stopped mid-stride and peered up into the golden sky. Had he noticed something moving, something flying overhead? Or was it just another illusion, another cruel trick of the watery light?

'Father,' he cried out. 'Is that you?'

'You . . . you . . . you . . .' the woods cried back.

Twig shuddered miserably. There was nobody there – there was *never* anybody there. The mocking faces that he saw, sneering and jeering at him out of the corners of his eyes, vanished each time he turned to confront them. Nothing remained but wraith-like twists of mist. He was alone. Quite alone.

And yet, as he turned back and continued on his solitary journey, the feeling of being watched persisted. It gnawed at his mind relentlessly.

'Over here,' someone or something whispered. 'Here!

Here!' Or was it just the sound of the rising breeze, warm and oily, lapping at the ancient trees?

Twig felt dizzy, disorientated, unable to trust what his ears or his eyes were telling him. The trees swayed and the branches reached out towards him, their long woody fingers plucking at his clothes, pulling his hair.

'Leave me alone!' Twig howled.

'Alone . . . alone . . .' the woods called back.

'I won't stay here for ever!' he screamed.

'For ever . . .'

Twig thrust his hand into the knight's gauntlet, reached round and pulled his father's sword from its scabbard. Grasping the hilt helped him to hold on to who he was – Twig, son of Cloud Wolf. In the Twilight Woods, he needed all the help he could get to remember even that. Yet the sword brought with it guilty memories, shameful memories.

Cloud Wolf had blamed Slyvo Spleethe for kidnapping him and dragging him reluctantly on board the *Stormchaser*. Twig knew that wasn't what happened. He had gone willingly. More than that, it was he who had revealed to the treacherous quartermaster that Cloud Wolf was his father. In so doing, he had betrayed the captain's greatest weakness. He might as well have stabbed him in the back.

'I didn't mean to,' he mumbled. 'Really, I didn't. Oh, Father, forgive me for my wilful ignorance, for my utter stupidity, for my lack of thought . . .'

The gleaming eyes and glinting teeth emerged from the shadows and hovered at the edge of his field of vision once more. Twig raised his gauntleted hand and rapped it sharply against his head. It didn't pay to dwell on *lack of thought* in the Twilight Woods.

As he lowered his arm, he watched the coating of fine dust slip around on the polished surface of the gauntlet, and fall from the metal fingers like droplets of liquid. It was only by this piece of armour which had been left behind, that he knew his encounter with the sepia knight had been more than a mere figment of his imagination.

'You are searching for stormphrax,' Twig told himself as he set off once more. 'You are searching for the crew of the *Stormchaser* – you are searching for a way out.'

On and on he stumbled. On and on and on. So far as Twig was concerned, time might as well have stopped completely. He didn't feel hungry. He didn't feel thirsty. He didn't feel tired. And yet, as he continued on through the bright and shadowy depths, in the grip of the enchanting torpor, Twig's apprehension grew.

'Twilight Woods,' he snorted. '*Nightmare* Woods, more like it.'

The wind rose higher, rustling the leaves and sending their coating of glistening crystals showering down to the glittering ground below. Twig stared, mesmerized by the scintillating display. And as they fell, he became aware of a sound – light and delicate – like the soft tinkling of wind-chimes.

As it grew louder, Twig stopped and cocked his head to one side. What could be making such sweet and melodious music? It seemed to be coming from his left.

'I am Twig,' he reminded himself as he raised his sword in his gauntleted hand. 'I must leave this place. I will not become like the sepia knight.'

'... like the sepia knight...' the woods whispered back.

Twig followed the unearthly music, picking his way through the trees and undergrowth, trying his best to ignore the cries of disbelief that echoed just out of earshot. Up ahead, a bright, silvery light gleamed from the shadows. Twig broke into a run. He slashed impatiently at the undergrowth with his sword. He held back the razor-sharp creepers with the gauntlet. Closer and closer he got. A sweet almond-like perfume wafted around him. The light intensified, the jangled music grew louder.

And then he saw it...

There, with one end buried deep in the ground and the other rising zig-zag high up into the air, was a tall and magnificent crystal. It was the bolt of lightning, now solid, which Twig had watched being discharged from the Great Storm.

Twig gasped. 'Stormphrax,' he whispered.

Close to, the lightning bolt was even more remarkable than he had imagined. Flawless, unblemished and as smooth as glass, it pulsed with a pure white glow. The noise, he realized, was coming from the top of the jagged bolt, far above his head.

'It's cracking,' he murmured in alarm. 'It's . . . breaking up!'

At that moment, there came a loud sound, like bells tolling, and a huge chunk of the crystal hurtled down through the air towards him in a shower of tiny glittering particles. Twig leapt back, fell to the ground and stared in horror as it landed, with a heavy thud and a puff of sepia dust, exactly where he had been standing.

The bell-like ringing sounded again and two more, even larger pieces of stormphrax landed beside the first. They too embedded themselves in the ground, and all three promptly disappeared.

'They're burying themselves,' Twig realized.

He remembered, of course, that in absolute darkness a thimbleful of stormphrax was as heavy as a thousand ironwood trees – now he could see what this meant in practice. The dark and immeasurably heavy underside of each of the giant pieces of crystal was dragging the rest down.

Thud, thud, thud. Thud. Thud-thud. Several more blocks fell. Twig scuttered backwards on his hands and feet, terrified that one of them would land on him. Some were small. Some were very large. All of them buried themselves where they landed, deep down in the absolute darkness below.

Then, in a grinding symphony of noise, the lightning bolt gave a lurch, and Twig saw that it, too, was sinking beneath the surface. It was this downward movement which was causing the top to splinter and crack – and the more crystal that disappeared into the darkness, the stronger the pull became.

Twig shook his head in dismay. Even if the *Stormchaser* had been anchored right there above the clearing, how difficult it would have been to retrieve the pieces of stormphrax. Suddenly, with a final *shwooohk-POP*! the final section of stormphrax sank down out of sight.

'Gone,' he whispered.

He stood up and looked around the clearing. Apart

from the burnt and broken branches, there was no sign that the bolt of stormphrax had ever been there. Distant laughter echoed.

'Gone,' he said again, hardly able to believe his eyes.

All those years of waiting for a Great Storm. And all the dangers that chasing the storm had involved. The broken mast. The abandoning of the sky ship. The loss of his father. And for what? For a bolt of lightning which had disappeared within hours of reaching its destination – and almost killed him in the process!

Except, thought Twig with a shudder, it wouldn't have killed me, would it? A piece could have broken my back or stoved in my skull – but I wouldn't have died. Icy fingers strummed up and down Twig's back at the macabre thought of what *might* have happened.

'And now, all that's left is this,' he said, kicking angrily at the sprinkling of crystals, too small to sink with the rest, which rested on every surface like frost. A cloud of glittering dust flew up into the glinting air. Twig felt sick. He wanted to cry. He wanted to scream. 'Stormchasing!' he cursed bitterly. 'A fool's errand, more like.'

'Yet oddly appealing for all that,' came a cracked, reedy voice from behind him.

Twig started, then raised his eyes impatiently to the sky. The sepia knight was the last person he wanted to meet again.

'Twig,' came the voice again. 'It is Twig, isn't it?'

'Yes,' Twig snapped as he spun around. 'It's . . .' He stopped short. It was not the sepia knight; neither was it a phantom, a ghoul, a trick of the light. 'YOU!' he exclaimed.

'Indeed it is,' the Professor of Light said as he peered up at him awkwardly. 'Though slightly the worse for wear, I fear. I couldn't quite get the hang of those parawings,' he explained. 'Had quite a tumble.'

Twig stared back at him in open-mouthed horror.

'Do I really look that bad?' he said, and sighed wearily. 'I do, don't I?'

Twig felt a lump coming into his throat. 'Your neck,' he whispered. 'It's . . .'

'Broken,' said the professor. 'I know.' He raised his hands, clamped them to either side of his head and pulled it up until his eyes met Twig's. 'Is that better?' he asked, and smiled weakly.

Twig nodded. The next moment, however, the professor sneezed on the dust, and the whole lot flopped forward again. Twig tried hard to swallow away the rising feeling of nausea.

'We need to fix it in place, somehow,' he said, and turned round – ostensibly to look for something that he might use, but actually to avoid eye-contact with the terrifying sight of the professor's lolling head. 'A stick,' he muttered busily. 'Hang on,' and he dashed off into the trees.

The next minute he was back, carrying a long and – for the ancient trees of the Twilight Woods – straight branch, which he had broken off a nearby tree.

'This ought to do the trick. If I place it against your back, like so. And bind it tightly with my rope like . . . so. That's it.'

He stepped back to check his handiwork. From the back, it looked as though the professor had a young sapling growing out of his spine.

'Now, for the head itself,' he chattered on, as he pulled a length of bandage from a pocket. 'That ought to be enough. Let's just see.'

The professor, whose chin was resting against his chest, glanced up as far as he could. 'What are you going to do?' he asked.

'I'll show you,' said Twig. 'If you raise your head again then I'll secure it to the branch at the back. To stop it falling forwards again.'

'Excellent idea,' said the professor enthusiastically. He lifted his head up for a second time, and rested it gently against the branch.

Twig wound the bandage round and round the professor's forehead and the makeshift support, clamping the two together. When the bandage was all but used up, he tore the end in two and tied a double-knot. 'There,' he said at last.

The professor removed his hands. His head remained upright. Twig breathed a deep sigh of relief.

'Outstanding piece of improvisation,' the Professor of Light exclaimed. 'I must say, that Tem Barkwater was right. You are indeed an ingenious young fellow.'

Twig started with surprise and delight. 'Tem?' he said. 'Is Tem here or . . .?' The spectral air flickered gleefully and chimed with unpleasant laughter. Twig's stomach sank as he realized his likely mistake. 'Or were you talking to him on the *Stormchaser*?' he said.

'No, no,' replied the professor. 'We hardly exchanged a word on board ship. No, he is here, in the Twilight Woods . . .' A look of bewilderment passed over his face. 'We were together, only a moment ago. We . . . I was looking at . . .' He turned round awkwardly and stared at Twig. 'I can't remember what I was looking at.'

Twig nodded, and glanced round uneasily at the shifting shadows. 'This is a treacherous place,' he said softly. 'There's something here . . . Or someone – or maybe, many. I don't know. But I see faces I can't focus on, hear voices that fade away when I try to listen.'

'That's it,' the professor said dreamily. 'Questions searching for answers. Theorems looking for proof . . .'

'Why,' Twig went on, and raised the sword high in his gauntleted hand, 'if it weren't for these . . . The sword reminds me of where I came from and who I am. The gauntlet, of what I must never become. Without them, I fear I would lose myself completely. Oh, Professor, we have to leave these woods as soon as we can.'

The professor sighed, but did not move. 'Twig,' he said softly. 'My neck was broken in the fall. It was only because I landed in this place that I am still alive. I cannot leave the immortality of the Twilight Woods,' he said. 'I would die in an instant if I did.'

Twig shook his head miserably. The professor was right, of course.

'But it's not so bad. Now I can study stormphrax for ever.' He smiled. 'And what more could a Professor of Light ask for?'

Twig smiled back, but his heart chilled at the words. If the professor could not go, then where did that leave him? Alone again? Abandoned? The thought was more than he could bear.

'Professor,' he said tentatively. 'You will help me find the others, won't you?'

The professor turned and surveyed him gravely.

'What type of a person do you take me for?' he said. 'We academics of Sanctaphrax are not all as rotten as that traitorous foulpox; that upstart knife-grinder, Vilnix Pompolnius – no matter what you may have heard to the contrary.'

'Sorry, I didn't mean . . .' said Twig. 'It's just . . . I couldn't . . . I can't . . .'

'Hush now, Twig,' said the professor.

'I've got to leave!' Twig cried out. 'I've got to. Before it's too late.'

'. . . too late . . . too late . . .' the woods taunted.

The professor wrapped his arm awkwardly round Twig's shoulder. 'I give you my word,' he said. 'I shall not abandon you. After all,' he said, nodding back at the branch which was supporting his head, 'one good turn deserves another.'

'Thank you,' Twig sniffed, and looked up. 'I . . .'

The professor was staring into mid-air, a smile playing over his lips. Once again, his mind had been lured away by the treacherous spectres and phantasms that haunted the darkest corners of the woods. The crystals sparkled. 'Light incarnate,' he whispered dreamily. 'Light made whole.'

'Professor,' Twig shouted, anxiously. 'Professor! You gave me your word!'

·CHAPTER SIXTEEN·

CAPTAIN TWIG

'Professor!' Twig screamed into his companion's ear. 'It's me, Twig. You must help me.'

But the professor merely turned away, raised his arm and began scrutinizing the back of his hand. 'See how the crystals cling to each individual hair,' he marvelled. 'And how the light illuminates its entire length, from follicle to split end.'

Twig nodded. The hairs were indeed shining. But, so what? 'Professor,' he tried again, 'listen to me.'

'You're right, my old and trusty friend and rival,' the professor said. 'It does seem to soak up the light. Trust you to notice the particles of sepia dust in-between. Such a substance must indeed have purifying qualities . . .'

Shaking his head, Twig turned away. Just as the sepia knight had mistaken him for his old compatriot, Garlinius, so the professor was now seeing and hearing him as the Professor of Darkness. It was hopeless. Utterly hopeless.

Twig fought back his tears. 'You come with me,' he said, as he took the professor gently by the wrist and led him away. 'Come on. Two heads are better than one – even if one of them *is* broken and empty.'

They hadn't gone more than a dozen paces when the Professor of Light stopped and turned on Twig. 'What exactly do you mean by "broken and empty"?' he demanded.

Twig burst out laughing. 'Professor!' he exclaimed. 'Welcome back!'

'Oh, Twig,' the Professor of Light said softly. 'What a remarkable place this is.'

Twig smiled uncertainly and, as the unlikely pair continued their search for the rest of the crew of the *Stormchaser,* he kept quiet as the professor rambled on and on about the stormphrax crystals.

'Light in physical form,' he enthused. 'Solid energy. Can you imagine such a thing, Twig? Volatile in bright light, stable in the twilight glow, yet heavy beyond reason when cloaked in darkness. Stormphrax is a wondrous substance and no mistake.'

Twig nodded. That much, at least, he knew to be true.

'But then weight, as Ferumix demonstrated so well, is relative,' the professor went on. 'x equals y + z over pi, where x represents weight, y, the surface area of the crystal and z, its translucency.' He frowned. 'Or do I mean radiance?'

Twig stared at him uneasily. Did the professor's

calculations prove that he still had his wits about him – or was he simply uttering meaningless gibberish. 'There's certainly a lot of the stuff,' he commented, as he glanced about him.

'Indeed!' the professor exclaimed. He turned stiffly round to look at Twig. His eyes glinted wildly. 'And I intend to count it all – every last particle – thereby allowing me to establish just how many Great Storms it has taken to produce this number of crystals, and how long. Epochs. Millennia,' he whispered reverently. 'Aeons.'

Twig shook his head. All this talk of time spinning away endlessly troubled him. The air rippled, and voices whispered to him from the harlequin shadows. Gentle, soothing voices. Enticing voices.

'You are Twig,' they murmured. 'You are sixteen years old. How much you have seen and done in that short space of time . . .'

And, as Twig continued to stare into the flashing diamonds of light and shade, he saw scenes he recognized, places and people he knew. Taghair, the oakelf, who had shown him his name. Hoddergruff, a woodtroll neighbour. On board the *Stormchaser* with the sky pirates. In the back room of the Bloodoak tavern. Mother Horsefeather, Forficule – Cloud Wolf.

'How much more has the eternity of the Twilight Woods to offer,' the voices lulled.

Twig stared at the face before him. 'Father?' he murmured, and took a step forwards.

Cloud Wolf's spectral form slipped back and hovered

just out of reach. 'Farther than you think,' he replied, his voice low and resounding. 'But stay awhile,' he said. 'Search and you will find me. One day, Twig. Just keep on searching, and one day . . .'

'NO!' screamed Twig. 'You're not my father. Not my *real* father.' He gripped the gauntlet round the hilt of the sword and pulled it from its scabbard. 'Leave me, whatever you are!' he shouted, and began slashing frantically all round him.

The air crackled and curdled. The faces retreated. They jeered and gesticulated and poked out their tongues.

'Stay awhile? I will not stay here!' he cried out.

'. . . stay here . . .'

'Be gone, I say,' roared Twig. 'Be gone!'

'. . . gone . . .'

And they were. Twig found himself staring into the troubled eyes of the Professor of Light. His gnarled fingers gripped him firmly by the shoulders.

'Can you hear me, lad?' he shouted. 'Twig!'

'Yes,' he said. 'I can hear you . . . Oh, Professor,' he whimpered, 'if I don't leave the Twilight Woods soon, then I must surely stay here for ever.' He tightened his gauntleted grip on the sword and brandished it in the air. 'TEM!' he bellowed. 'SPIKER! STOPE! HUBBLE! WHERE ARE YOU?'

His words echoed and faded away to nothing. Twig hung his head. It was hopeless. It was . . . but wait. He cocked his head to one side.

'What is it?' asked the professor.

'Sssshh!' Twig hissed, and closed his eyes to concentrate all the harder. And there it was again. Low and plaintive – the faint but unmistakable sound of a banderbear yodelling its greetings.

As a child, Twig had often lain in bed listening to the massive solitary creatures calling to one another across the vast distances of the Deepwoods. So far as he knew, there were no banderbears in the Twilight Woods – save one.

'HUBBLE!' he cried, and yodelled back as best he could. 'Wa-ah-ah-ah!'

'Wa-ah-ah-ah-ah!' came the reply, closer now.

Gripping his sword – just in case – Twig broke into a run.

'Wuh-wuh!' he called excitedly.

'Wuh-wuh!' The voice was closer than ever. The next moment there came the sound of cracking and splintering wood, and Hubble himself – the giant albino banderbear – came crashing out of the shadowy trees towards him.

'Hubble!' Twig exclaimed.

'T-wuh-g!' roared the banderbear, and the pair of them fell into each other's arms and hugged warmly.

'I feared I would never see you again,' said Twig at length, as he pulled himself away. As he did so, he realized they were not alone. Just as the Professor of Light had followed him, so the rest of the crew had followed Hubble. Twig wiped his tears away, and smiled round at the circle of grinning faces.

'Tem,' he said. 'Spiker. Stope, Stone Pilot – it is *so* good to see you all.'

'And it warms my heart to discover that you, too, are safe, Master Twig,' said Tem Barkwater. He paused. 'I . . . that is, we hoped the captain might be with you.'

Twig shook his head. 'Cloud Wolf refused to abandon the *Stormchaser*,' he said. 'The last I saw of him, he had regained control of the sky ship and had steered it to the very centre of the Great Storm.'

'Good old cap'n Cloud Wolf,' said Tem Barkwater. 'The bravest sky pirate I ever met, and that's a fact. He'll be back to find us soon enough, you see if he isn't.'

Twig nodded, but said nothing. Now was not the time to mention the ball of lightning he had seen surrounding the sky ship, nor the explosion that followed. There was no point in crushing the sky pirates' hopes. On the other hand, waiting around for Cloud Wolf to return could prove fatal. In the event, it was the Professor of Light who came to his aid.

'You must all leave here as soon as you can,' he said.

The sky pirates turned to look at him. 'Without the cap'n?' said Tem, horrified.

'We have no way of knowing where the captain is,' said the professor. 'And in his absence, I recommend we elect a new captain. Someone to whom we all pledge our allegiance, someone who will lead us to the edge of the Twilight Woods.'

Tem shuffled about awkwardly. 'Who then?' he said gruffly.

'Why, Twig, of course,' said the professor. 'Who else? As the erstwhile captain's son and heir . . .'

The sky pirates gasped as one. Tem Barkwater shook his head in disbelief. 'Son and heir?' he exclaimed. 'What, young Twig? But, he can't be.'

'Are you doubting my word?' the Professor of Light demanded stiffly.

'No . . . Yes . . . I mean . . .' Tem bumbled.

'Quintinius . . . that is, Cloud Wolf told me himself,' the professor said. 'That is why he intended leaving the lad back in Undertown. For his own safety.'

Tem whistled through his teeth. 'I remember the cap'n once telling us about a child born to him and the lady Maris,' he said. 'They had no choice but to abandon him to his fate in the Deepwoods . . .' He turned to Twig, who nodded.

'I was that child,' he said.

Tem stared for a moment, nonplussed. Then, abruptly, he drew his sword, raised it high and fell to his knees. 'To you, Captain Twig, son of Cloud Wolf, I pledge my life.'

Seeing his example, Spiker, Stope Boltjaw and the Stone Pilot followed suit. Twig reddened. It was all happening so quickly. Sky pirate captain – and he didn't even have a sky ship! Nevertheless, as custom required, he drew his own sword and crossed it with the raised swords of the sky pirates, one after the other.

'And I to you,' he said. 'And I to you.'

The sky pirates replaced their swords, raised their heads and cried out, 'Captain Twig, we await your word.'

'Yes, well, I . . .' Twig faltered. His face turned redder still.

They had all suffered injuries during their emergency escape. Spiker's arms and face were badly bruised, Tem Barkwater's nose looked broken, the Stone Pilot was limping awkwardly, while Stope Boltjaw had lost his makeshift lower jaw, leaving his head gaping open in a permanent, empty grin. Worst of all, however, was Hubble.

At their initial reunion, Twig had been too overjoyed to notice. But now, as he looked at the banderbear, he saw that he was in a sorry state. The white fur down his front was stained and matted with blood, and he wheezed noisily with every step he took. Twig could only pray that his old friend's injuries were not as bad as they appeared.

Twig turned back, and checked they were still heading towards the star. 'It was good of you to accompany us,'

'There is a star,' the Professor of Light interjected. 'The East Star. Not only is its light a constant amidst the shifting passage of the constellations, but it is also bright enough to be seen by twilight.' He bent his knees and looked up awkwardly into the sky. 'There,' he said, pointing. 'There it is.'

The sky pirates all turned and looked. One after the other, they too saw the East Star, twinkling softly in the golden glow. Twig nodded. It was time for him to assume the control he had been given.

'If we keep the star in front of us,' he said, 'it will ensure that we are walking in a straight line. Sooner or later, we are bound to reach the edge of the Twilight Woods. Are you with me?'

'Aye aye, cap'n,' they replied. 'We are with you.'

'Then let us go,' Twig said. 'Professor, you walk with me. Hubble, you bring up the rear. Make sure no-one straggles or strays.'

'Wuh-wuh,' the banderbear replied.

They set off once more, with Twig feeling more confident than at any other time since his arrival in the Twilight Woods. He had a purpose now: an aim, a destination. What was more, he had responsibilities beyond himself. He glanced back at the crew as they waded after him through the thick, liquid air.

he said to the professor.

'Ah, well,' he said. 'My motives were not altogether selfless, for I too need to find the edge of the Twilight Woods.'

Twig was surprised. 'But I thought you intended staying here,' he said.

'Indeed I do,' said the professor. 'But if I am to calculate the number of Great Storms I must first establish the total area of the Twilight Woods. And I can't do that by remaining somewhere in the middle.'

'No,' said Twig absent-mindedly. 'I suppose you can't.'

Something had occurred to him – something worrying. Assuming they did make it to the edge of the Twilight Woods, what then? The Mire was notoriously dangerous even to fly over; how much more dangerous

it would be to cross on foot. What was more, as captain, he would be responsible for his crew's well-being. Shivering with anticipation, Twig turned back to the professor for advice.

'What the . . .!' he exclaimed. The professor was not there. He spun around in a panic, and saw him several paces back, crouched down stiffly on a bank beside a tree.

'To see a world in a grain of stormphrax,' he was saying. 'To hold infinity in the palm of one's hand . . .'

'Professor!' Twig shouted, and shook him firmly by the shoulder.

The Professor of Light turned and stared into Twig's eyes. Slowly, slowly, there was recognition. 'Twig,' he said. 'I . . . I am so sorry,' he said. 'Let us continue,' he said.

'Thank you, Professor,' said Twig. 'I . . .' He paused and turned to the others. 'This is too hazardous,' he said. 'We must make sure that none of us wanders off – even if his mind does.'

'A rope,' said Spiker.

'Of course!' said Tem Barkwater enthusiastically, as he swung his own coil of rope down from his shoulder. 'We must all tie ourselves together in a line.'

Twig nodded and supervised the operation. He kept Hubble at the back, tying the rope right round his immense waist. Next, at regular intervals, he made slip-knots, got the sky pirates to put their left hands through the loops and tightened them around their wrists, one after the other. Tem Barkwater, Spiker, Stope Boltjaw, the

Professor of Light. Lastly, he tied the remaining length of rope around his own waist.

'Right,' he announced. 'Onwards!'

Bound together, the ramshackle crew continued through the Twilight Woods, on towards the distant star twinkling far, far in front of them. Twig shuddered. 'I hope the end is not *too* far,' he whispered.

'. . . too far . . .' the air whispered back.

Just then, a sudden commotion erupted behind him. Twig spun round and looked down the line of sky pirates. Someone was missing.

'Where's Stope Boltjaw?' he demanded, as he strode angrily towards the empty slip-knot.

'Gone,' said Spiker.

'Gone?' said Twig.

'Kept muttering about how he couldn't, how he *wouldn't* leave his precious jaw behind. The next thing I know, he's trotting off into the undergrowth.' He pointed. 'Over that way.'

Twig shook his head and turned on the others furiously. 'How could you have let this happen?'

'Wuh-wuh, wuh,' the banderbear explained.

It was then that Twig realized Hubble was not merely standing beside Tem Barkwater, but was holding him tightly. He, like Stope Boltjaw, had broken away from the rope.

'What is it? What happened?' he said. 'Tem? What's the matter?'

But Tem would not return his gaze. 'Leave me be!' he snarled. 'Let me go.' His eyes suddenly focused on something to his left. 'Cal!' he shouted out. 'Don't go without me.'

Twig turned, but there was no-one there – at least, no-one visible to him.

'Cal!' Tem shouted. 'Wait for me. Oh, my poor, wonderful brother – it has been so long.' He thrashed violently in Hubble's arms. 'LET ME GO!' he roared. 'NOW!'

Twig stared at the huge, red-faced sky pirate struggling in Hubble's arms like a toddler in the middle of a tantrum, and shook his head in dismay. The Twilight Woods were taking their toll on the crew's sanity far more quickly than he had thought possible.

'My brother,' Tem was ranting. 'I have searched so long . . .'

'It's an illusion, Tem,' Twig said. 'A trick. There's no-one there.'

'Cal!' he cried out. 'Cal, answer me,' and he began struggling all the more violently. 'LET ME GO!' he boomed.

Twig bit into his lower lip. Ever since he had first met up with the sky pirates, Tem Barkwater had always been so good to him – how could he now abandon him to the Twilight Woods? Yet, in his present state, he was a danger to them all. Certainly Hubble, injured as he was, would not be able to hold him for much longer. He turned to the banderbear sadly.

'Let him go, Hubble,' he said.

The moment Hubble released his grip, Tem calmed down. He looked round about him blindly for a moment – then smiled. 'Cal,' he cried, and trundled back the way they'd come. 'Cal, wait for me.'

As Twig watched him lumbering away, tears welled up in his eyes. Big old dependable old Tem Barkwater was going. 'Bye bye, my friend,' he called. 'And may you find who you are looking for.'

He felt a soft but heavy hand on his shoulders. It was Hubble. 'Wuh-wuh,' the giant creature said softly.

'I know,' said Twig. 'We'll *all* miss him.'

Down in number, and in spirit, the party continued in the direction of the East Star – Spiker, the Stone Pilot and Hubble, with the Professor of Light and Twig up at the front. They walked in silence. They walked alone. The abandoned rope lay on the ground far behind them, already gathering dust. Twig gripped his sword and gritted his teeth.

How did such a fearful place ever come to exist? Twig wondered miserably. He turned to the others. 'Come on,' he urged. 'Keep up. It can't be far now.'

'Right behind you, cap'n,' said Spiker, breaking into a trot.

'Wuh-wuh,' added Hubble and lumbered wheezily after him.

The Stone Pilot, on the other hand, must have misunderstood what Twig had said. He stopped and began waving his arms and stomping his feet as much as the heavy overcoat and heavier boots would allow. Sepia dust rose up in clouds. The glass eye-panels set into his hood gleamed dazzling gold.

'Oh, no,' Twig sighed. 'Not you, too.'

The Stone Pilot – the most practical and loyal of all the sky pirates – had also ended up succumbing to the immortal madness of the Twilight Woods.

'Wuh-wuh?' said Hubble.

'I don't know,' said Twig. He approached cautiously. With the Stone Pilot's head completely hidden beneath his long heavy hood, it was difficult to guess what might be going on in his mind. 'Can you hear me?' he bellowed. 'Are you all right?'

A gruff and muffled grunt emerged from the hood, and the Stone Pilot pushed Twig roughly aside and pointed.

'I know,' said Twig. 'I have also seen . . .'

'GRURRGH!' the Stone Pilot grunted impatiently. He spun Twig round and grasped him by the head.

'What the . . !' Twig exclaimed. 'Have you gone mad? Hubble! Help!'

The Stone Pilot grunted again, and twisted Twig's head around, forcing him to look where he'd been pointing. Hubble came trundling headlong towards them. 'WUH!' he roared.

'Gruuh grunh!' the Stone Pilot's muffled voice insisted.

'Oh!' gasped Twig as he finally realized what the Stone Pilot had seen.

Hubble lunged awkwardly at the Stone Pilot.

'It's OK!' Twig screamed. 'Look!'

All of them turned and stared ahead. And there, between a gap in the trees directly beneath the East Star, shone a patch of bleached brightness.

'It's the Mire,' Twig whispered. He turned to the others excitedly. 'We've made it! We've reached the edge of the Twilight Woods and . . .' He paused. Were his eyes deceiving him once again, or was there someone there? He peered more closely. Yes. There was no doubt. A gaunt, angular figure, hands on hips and legs astride, was standing silhouetted against the brightness beyond.

Hubble sniffed the air and growled uneasily, his wispy ears fluttering with suspicion. Unaware of the banderbear's misgivings, Twig strode ahead with the Professor of Light.

'I'm leaving!' he called into the dancing patterns of light and shade. 'And I won't ever come back.'

'... come back ... come back ...' the woods called back, coaxing, cajoling.

Twig fixed his gaze giddily on the stooped figure up ahead. The air whispered and shimmered as, all round, the squirming, swirling mist of ghostly creatures struggled to steal him away once and for all.

'... come back ... come back ...' they echoed.

'Never,' Twig cried, and fumbled for his sword. 'Never!'

'... ever ... ever ... ever ...' the woods replied.

·CHAPTER SEVENTEEN·

THE MIRE TAKES ITS TOLL

Screed Toe-taker watched the approaching party from under hooded eyes. A mixture of amusement and disdain played on his thin, white lips.

'Well, well, well,' he rasped. 'What *have* we here?'

As a rule, the travellers who passed his way journeyed in groups of their own kind. A gang of darkridge goblins, a gaggle of barkelves, a family of woodtrolls – or, he remembered with a smirk – gnokgoblins.

But this shower!

He stooped and squinted. There was a youth. And an elderly character – perhaps his grandfather – who looked as if some tree or other had taken root in the back of his white robes. Then a small creature – an oakelf, by the look of him. And someone or something in heavy hooded clothing. And . . . Screed groaned. 'A banderbear,' he muttered huskily.

Screed Toe-taker was wary of banderbears, and with good reason. Not only were the creatures prodigiously strong, but they were also oddly intuitive. Only once before had he tried to take a banderbear's toes – it had almost cost him his life.

Screed smirked. 'Almost!' he whispered for, as always, the element of night-time surprise had proved too much for his victim. 'Mind you,' he said, 'he wasn't nearly as big and mean-looking as this character. I'm going to have to watch my step.'

Those last few steps were proving the most challenging of all for Twig. As he stumbled onwards the spectres, wraiths and ghouls taunted him wickedly. 'Your father, Cloud Wolf,' they whispered. 'Will you leave him here? Alone? Without his only son?'

'I have no choice,' Twig muttered tearfully.

'Come on,' he heard the professor saying. 'Put on your gauntlet and raise high your sword. You can make it, Twig. You can break free of the Twilight Woods.'

'Yes . . .' Twig said uncertainly. He did what the professor had told him. 'Yes, I can – I *will* make it.' He paused. 'Are the others with us?'

'We're all still here,' Spiker confirmed.

Twig looked up ahead. At the end of the long swirling tunnel of his vision hung the star. Below it stood the pale, angular figure. Step followed faltering step as Twig kept on towards them both.

'Not far now,' the professor said encouragingly. 'Soon be there.'

Twig spun round to face him and grasped him by the arm. 'Then you must stop,' he said. 'If you go too far you will die.'

From his position at the edge between the Mire and the Twilight Wood, Screed Toe-taker was growing impatient. 'Oh, for Sky's sake, what's going on now?' he grumbled angrily. 'If it isn't one of them, it's the other.' Then, noticing how the banderbear's ears were fluttering, he changed tack.

'Come on!' he yelled. 'I only want to help you – before it's too late.'

As the words from outside the Twilight Woods echoed round Twig's head, the spectral voices and visions finally released their hold over him. His ears cleared. His eyes unmisted. He recognized the woods for what they were – a tawdry place, glittering yet gloomy, heavy with torpor and the reek of decay.

The Professor of Light looked up at Twig. 'I'm all right to go a little further,' he said.

'Are you certain,' said Twig.

The professor nodded. 'Quite certain,' he said, and turned away. 'Come on.'

Remembering that he was captain, Twig straightened

up and called back as Cloud Wolf would have done. 'Greetings!' he said. 'I am Twig, sky pirate captain. State your name and business.'

Screed sniggered unpleasantly. 'A whelp with the words of a woodwolf,' he muttered under his breath. He raised his head. 'My name is Screed,' he replied. 'And my business is to guide travellers across the treacherous Mire.'

The banderbear snarled ominously.

'Though perhaps you have no interest in my services,' Screed continued, his eyes skittering back and forth under lowered lids. 'Perhaps you already know all about the Mire, with its sinking-mud and poisonous blow-holes, its muglumps, oozefish, white ravens . . .'

'No, no,' said Twig. 'I might well be interested.'

He walked the last few yards of the Twilight Woods and halted at the very edge. Screed – one step away – was standing in the Mire. Between them lay an invisible line separating the two places. For a moment, they stared at one another in silence. From far away over the bleached wasteland came the sound of raucous cawing.

'White ravens,' said Screed. 'Fighting over a carcass – the smell of blood drives them to a frenzy.'

Behind him Twig was aware of the others' unease.

Screed smiled craftily. 'Sometimes they don't wait until you're dead to attack,' he rasped.

Twig winced. The Mire was – as he well knew – a harsh and perilous place, yet he did not trust this Screed character with his deathly pallor and sly bloodshot eyes.

Oh, Sky above – some sky pirate captain I am! thought

Twig miserably. And he found himself wishing once again that his father was here with him. *He'd* know what to do.

For the third time since Twig had been elected captain, it was the Professor of Light who came to his aid. Stepping forwards, he stood next to Twig.

'So how much do you charge, per individual?' he said.

Charge! thought Twig in alarm. The thought of paying for the guide's services hadn't even occurred to him, yet of course the curious bleached creature would want rewarding. Twig, however, didn't have a bean to his name. None of the crew did.

'Tell you what,' Screed said, rubbing his chin thoughtfully. 'Special offer for sky pirates.' He looked at them askance. 'Two hundred each.'

Twig trembled. With four of them planning to cross the Mire, that was eight hundred – eight hundred he hadn't got.

The professor, however, seemed unconcerned. 'A thousand in all,' he said. 'I can cover that.'

Now Twig was really confused. 'But . . .' he began. 'I thought . . .'

The Professor of Light turned towards him. 'After much consideration, I have decided to go with you,' he announced. 'If you'll have me, that is.'

'Yes, yes, of course,' said Twig uncertainly. 'But you said . . .'

'I will take my chances,' the professor said. 'Who knows, perhaps my neck will mend . . .' He paused. 'At any rate, I cannot stay here.'

'But you were so sure,' said Twig. 'You said . . .'

'I know what I said,' the professor interrupted. 'I thought I'd be able to research stormphrax if I remained. But I was wrong. Although the Twilight Woods would indeed give me the time to study, they would also rob me of the ability to do so.'

Screed Toe-taker tutted impatiently.

Ignoring him, the professor went on. 'I am an academic, Twig,' he said. 'Why, in Sanctaphrax I am known for the sharpness of my intellect. I can recite Dilnix's ancient *Treatise on the Properties of Light*, I know *The Thousand Luminescent Aphorisms of Archemax* by heart . . . Yet here, in this terrible mind-numbing place, I can barely remember who I am.'

'So, you mean . . .'

'I mean, I would rather die a dignified death than suffer the ignominy of an eternity of ignorance.' He pulled a leather pouch from the folds of his gown and handed it to Twig. 'There's five hundred in there,' he said. 'He can have the rest when we arrive.'

Twig turned to Screed, and shuddered as he caught the gangly individual staring down at the professor's feet, licking his lips. 'If you agree to the terms,' he said, offering the leather pouch, 'we have a deal.'

Screed looked up and smirked. 'Very glad to hear it,' he said. He took the pouch in one hand, slipped it down the front of his jerkin and reached out again to shake Twig's hand.

Twig shuddered at the touch of the dry, bony fingers. 'Come then,' said Screed, and he pulled him gently but firmly across the invisible line, out of the Twilight Woods – and into the Mire.

Twig stopped and turned back. The Professor of Light hadn't moved. Despite his resolve, it was a hard step to take – after all, it might be his last.

'Come on,' said Screed irritably. 'We haven't got all day.'

'You take as long as you like, Professor,' said Twig.

Screed snorted, and turned away in disgust. Twig put out his arm for the professor to steady himself upon.

'Thank you, Twig,' said the professor. 'Whatever may happen, my boy, it has been an honour and a pleasure getting to know you. One day you will be a fine sky pirate captain. With your own ship. I know you will.'

And, so saying, the professor took that all-important step forwards. Twig, who was expecting him to collapse at any moment, moved to support him. But the professor did not collapse. He winced with pain as he crossed into the Mire. He cried out. He stumbled a little. But he remained standing.

From behind him, Spiker, Hubble and the Stone Pilot cheered with delight. 'Well done, Professor,' they said.

'Yes, well done!' Twig beamed. 'You'll be as right as rain once we get you back to Sanctaphrax.' The professor smiled weakly. His face had turned a deathly shade of grey. Twig's face clouded with concern. 'H . . . how *are* you feeling?' he asked him anxiously.

'Alive,' the professor groaned. 'Just about. But I'm afraid I'm going to be rather slow. Perhaps it would be better if . . .'

'No,' said Twig resolutely. 'You're coming with us. We'll all take it in turns to help you.' He turned to the others. 'Come on, then, you lot. Let's go.'

'And not before time, either,' said Screed waspishly.

As the remaining crew-members shambled forwards, Screed turned and strode off. Twig followed after, with his arm around the professor's back.

'Look lively!' Screed called back. 'And remember, keep together, walk where I walk – and don't look back.'

Twig's heart sank as he looked ahead and saw just how far they had to go. The Mire seemed to stretch on for ever. If he had been on his own, the journey would have been daunting. With the professor leaning heavily against him . . .

'One step at a time,' the professor wheezed, as if reading his mind. Twig nodded, and looked down at the white mud as it oozed around his feet. The professor was right. They were out of the Twilight Woods, and *that* was what mattered, for although the Mire was as perilous as it was vast, it too had boundaries. And, thanks to their fortuitous encounter with a guide . . .

'Cap'n! Cap'n!' he heard Spiker shrieking with alarm. For an instant Twig forgot that the oakelf was addressing *him*. He looked round automatically for Cloud Wolf. 'Cap'n Twig!' Spiker screamed. 'You must come quick. It's Hubble!'

Twig glanced ahead. The albino banderbear was lying in a heap on the soft ground.

'You go,' said the professor. 'I can stand unaided.'

Twig didn't need telling twice. He raced through the thick, sucking mud and fell to his knees beside his friend. 'What is it?' he said. 'Hubble, what's wrong?'

'Wuh . . . wuh-wuh,' the banderbear groaned. He clutched at his chest, and turned his massive head away.

'Hubble!' Twig cried, his eyes filling with tears. 'Hubble, speak to me. Tell me what to do.'

'Wu-uuh,' the banderbear moaned softly, and was suddenly racked with a fearful gurgling cough that sent spasms of pain shooting through his body.

Twig struggled to hold back his tears. The injuries Hubble had sustained during his descent from the *Stormchaser* were internal – and far more serious than Twig had realized. His breath came in short wheezing pants. Twig stroked the creature's neck, whispering all the time that everything would all be all right, everything would be fine. The banderbear smiled weakly and closed his eyes.

'T-wuh-g. Wuh-wuh. Fr-uh-nz . . .'

Suddenly, a trickle of blood – dazzling red against the thick white fur – welled in the corner of his mouth, over-flowed and ran down his cheek. Hubble coughed again, trembled, spluttered – and fell still.

'NO!' Twig wailed, and threw himself round Hubble's neck. 'Not you. Not now. You can't be dead!' he howled. 'You seemed so . . . so well . . .'

'It happens to the best of them,' came a mocking voice from behind him. Twig froze. 'One minute they're fine,' he continued. 'The next, dead as . . .'

'Screed!' Twig roared, as he leaped to his feet and drew his sword. 'One more word and, so help me, I shall slice you in two.'

Screed sneered. 'And condemn your crew to certain death?' he said. 'I don't think so.' He turned away, leaving Twig quivering with impotent rage.

'Come, Twig,' said the Professor of Light. 'You can do no more for your friend.'

'I know,' said Twig. He sniffed. 'But . . .'

'Come,' the professor repeated. 'Before that scoundrel, Screed, gets too far away.'

·CHAPTER EIGHTEEN·

TOE-TAKING

Screed Toe-taker could hardly believe his luck. When the banderbear had collapsed, it was all he could do not to leap about with delight. Struck down the moment it had left the immortality of the Twilight Woods, the most dangerous member of the group was a danger no longer.

'And the others will be easy pickings,' he whispered to himself, and wheezed with wicked laughter. 'The old fellow will slow them down nicely.' He paused, and rubbed his jaw thoughtfully. 'Still,' he added, 'it does seem a shame to let good toes go to waste. Particularly such large and hairy ones.'

He looked round to see where the rest of the group had got to, and was pleased to discover that – despite his advice – they were already strung out in a long line. Far away at the back was the oakelf. He was clearly in trouble.

'Not long now, little one,' Screed whispered menacingly. 'And not much longer for you either,' he said, turning his attention to the heavily-clothed figure limping along in the middle of the line. 'And as for you two,' he said, as he focused in on the youth and the old person on his arm, 'you, my twinkly-toed friends, will be the glitter on the icing!'

He raised his arms and cupped his bony, parchment fingers to his mouth. 'Hey!' His cracked voice echoed round the bleached landscape like the cawing of the white ravens. Neither of them paid it any attention.

'Hey, you!' Screed bellowed. 'Captain Twig!'

This time the youth looked up.

'What is it?' he called back, his voice fluttering on the wind.

'We're nearly half-way,' Screed shouted. Then he pointed behind him. 'You see that jagged bit on the horizon. It's the mast of a wrecked ship. That's where we're headed. When we get there, we can all rest up a bit.'

'We must rest now!' Twig shouted back.

Screed smiled to himself. 'Out of the question, I'm afraid. This whole area is infested with the worst type of oozefish. Eat you alive as soon as look at you.'

There was a pause.

'Well, can you at least go a little slower?' Twig called.

'Course I can, Captain,' Screed called back amiably. 'But I shan't!' he added under his breath. He raised his hands to his mouth again. 'Now, you just keep right on till you get to that shipwreck,' he said. 'You'll be all right so long as you keep going in a straight line. But watch out. There are poisonous blow-holes on both sides, and the sinking-mud is treacherous. So, don't stray from the path.'

'We won't,' he heard Twig calling back.

'Oh, and one last thing,' Screed shouted. 'Although it looks flat, the Mire is quite bumpy. Don't panic if you can't see me or the ship for a couple of minutes. Just keep going.'

'OK!' shouted Twig.

Screed chuckled to himself. What an obliging young fellow this Captain Twig was proving to be. He turned away contentedly and continued across the fetid waste-land. The white sun glinted on the distant shipwreck. Screed knew that although it was nearer than it looked, it was also farther than any of the guileless party of sky pirates would ever get.

'Muglumps, oozefish and white ravens,' he snorted. 'They are as nothing compared with me. For I, Screed Toe-taker, am the most dangerous creature in all this great white wilderness – as you will discover to your cost, *Captain* Twig,' he sneered.

Screed's words echoed round and round Twig's head. *Don't stray from the path.* It was what Spelda and Tuntum, the woodtrolls who had brought him up as their own, were always telling him. Yet if he hadn't strayed from the path then, he would still be living in the Deepwoods to this day. This time, however, Twig knew that the advice was sound, for if the professor slipped or stumbled, it could prove fatal.

With his head fixed to the branch at his back, the injured professor could not look down, and so it was left to Twig to keep an eye on where they were stepping – and that meant looking away from their destination. Each time he glanced up again, he found they had drifted to one side or the other.

'Must I do everything?' Twig complained irritably. 'Why don't you tell me when we're wandering off course?'

'I can't,' said the professor. 'My eyes are closed.'

'Well open them!' Twig snapped impatiently.

'I can't,' he repeated wearily. 'With my head fixed at this angle, my eyes are set towards the sun. If I stare at it too long, I'll go blind.' He snorted miserably. 'And what use is a Professor of Light who cannot see? I'd end up begging on the streets of Undertown.'

Twig turned away guiltily. 'I'm sorry,' he said. 'I . . .'

'Oh, my dear boy,' said the professor, 'you are the last person under Sky who should apologize. You stuck by me in the Twilight Woods; you are sticking by me now. I am, and shall remain, eternally grateful to you.' He paused. 'It's that Screed character I'd like to tear off a strip. He *said* he'd slow down.'

Twig nodded, but said nothing. Perhaps the guide *had* slowed down. He and the professor were making such painfully slow progress that it was difficult to tell.

The journey was taking on the never-ending quality of a nightmare. Every yard was like a mile, every second seemed to take an hour.

'Sky above!' the professor moaned. 'How much further to go? I don't think I can take much more of this.'

'You're going to be fine,' Twig assured him as he glanced over his shoulder to check that Spiker and the Stone Pilot were still following them. 'It can't be that far now.' He turned back and looked up ahead – and gasped with horror.

'What is it?' said the professor, his eyes snapping open.

'Screed,' said Twig, as he unhooked his telescope with one hand and frantically scoured the horizon. 'He's not there!'

The Professor of Light squinted into the distance. 'He warned us this might happen,' he said.

'I know, but . . .'

'Come now,' said the professor. 'I am old and in pain. I am allowed to be disheartened. But not you, Twig. You have your whole future in front of you.'

Twig stared ahead glumly. 'Mud,' he muttered, 'that's all I can see in front of *me*. Oh, Professor. If only I hadn't disobeyed my father, none of this would have happened. But no. I wouldn't do as I was told. Stubborn and stupid, I had to sneak back on board the *Stormchaser*. This is *all* my fault.'

'Twig, my boy,' said the professor gently. 'What's done is done. I am not about to apportion blame. The important thing now is how you deal with the consequences of your actions. If you . . . WAAAAAH!' he screamed, as at that moment and without any warning, a scalding blow-hole erupted between the two of them.

'Professor!' Twig cried, as he was torn from his side.

He stared up in horror at the thick column of seething mud which shot up into the air like the trunk of a great white tree. Higher and higher it rose, loudly roaring, before folding over on itself and tumbling back to earth in a shower of thick, sticky globules.

'Professor!' Twig cried again. 'Where are you?'

'Over here,' came a quavering voice from the far side of the column of mud. 'I'm stuck.'

'Just hold on,' Twig called back. 'I'm coming to get you.'

As the mud spewed forth from the hole, clouds of noxious steam billowed up all round Twig. Coughing and spluttering, eyes streaming, he staggered forwards. The heat shimmered. The mud gushed. Twig raised his arm to his face, but nothing could keep out the breath-snatching stench.

'Can't . . . find . . . you . . .' he gasped.

'Here,' the professor's frail voice replied. It sounded close. Twig stopped, wiped his eyes and peered through the dense mist. And there, staring back at him, was the professor, not three strides ahead.

'Stop!' he was shouting. 'Not a step further.'

For a moment, Twig could make no sense of what he saw. Clearly, the professor had not landed on his back for, although his head was most definitely at ground level, it was staring ahead, not up at the sky. And then he understood. The Professor of Light had fallen into a patch of quickmud. It was already up to his armpits.

Twig pulled his scarf from around his neck and tied it over his mouth and nose as a makeshift mask. Then, he removed his sky pirate's coat, knelt down at the edge of the sinking-mud and, with the collar and shoulders gripped tightly in his hands, tossed the other end towards the professor.

'Grab hold of it,' he gasped. 'I'll pull you out.'

The professor clung on. Twig braced his legs, leaned backwards – and pulled as he had never pulled before.

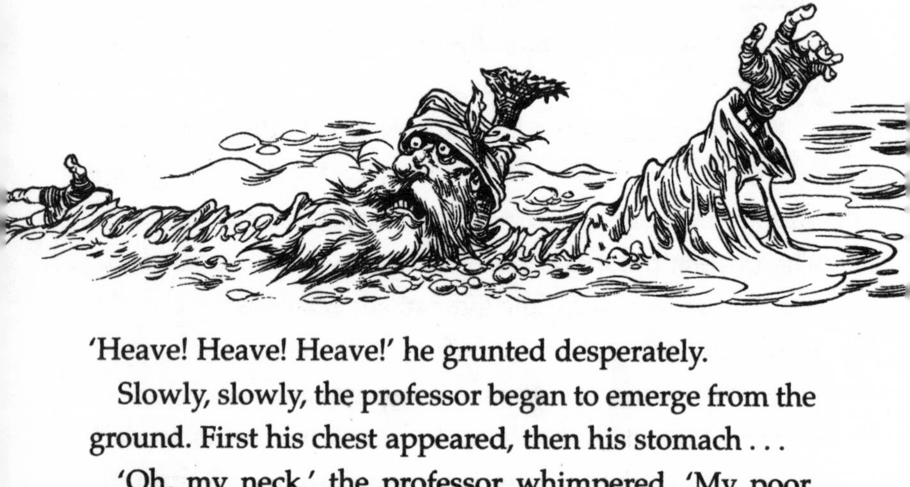

'Heave! Heave! Heave!' he grunted desperately.

Slowly, slowly, the professor began to emerge from the ground. First his chest appeared, then his stomach . . .

'Oh, my neck,' the professor whimpered. 'My poor, poor neck.'

'Nearly there,' Twig gasped. 'Just . . .'

Squellssh . . . POP!

The sucking mud had released its grip on the professor's legs. He lay on his front, head down.

'Professor,' said Twig urgently, as he rolled him onto his back and wiped the claggy mud from his face. 'Professor, can you hear me?'

The professor's thin, cracked lips parted. 'Yes,' he croaked faintly. 'I can hear you . . . You saved my life.'

'Not yet I haven't,' said Twig. 'But I shall. Climb on my back.'

'Oh, Twig,' the professor protested. 'I couldn't . . . *You* couldn't . . .'

'We won't know until we try,' said Twig. He slipped his coat back on, turned and hunkered down. 'Put your arms around my neck,' he instructed. 'That's it.'

Then, with a grunt of effort, he straightened up, grasped the back of the professor's bony legs with his hands and set off. Away from the quickmud, he trudged. Away from the blow-hole with its poisonous mist and fountain of scalding mud. On and on through the bleached and boggy landscape. The temperature dropped. The air cleared.

'Still no sign of Screed,' the professor muttered at length. 'A deceitful individual if ever there was one. Takes our money, he does, and then abandons us to our fate. Probably sat in that shipwreck right now, with his feet up.'

Twig raised his head and stared out across the Mire. The shipwreck was, at last, looking nearer.

'To Open Sky with that scurvy cur,' Twig cursed, and spat on the ground. 'With or without Screed's help, Spiker, the Stone Pilot, you and I are going to survive this ordeal. As captain of this crew, I give you my word.'

Screed was not in his wrecked sky ship home. The moment he was sure that no-one would notice, he had ducked down out of sight behind a rock and rolled in the mud until he was covered from head to foot in the bleached sludge.

'Make myself disappear, I shall,' he said, and chuckled throatily.

Then, satisfied that he was perfectly camouflaged, Screed climbed to his feet and doubled back across the Mire as fast as he could, keeping parallel to the path the sky pirates were taking. Although he could see them, they couldn't see him.

'Keep to the path, you addleskulls,' he hissed as he passed Twig and the old fellow. 'Don't want you getting swallowed up by the Mire, do we? At least, not yet.'

On and on he loped. Past the curious figure in the heavy clothes; past the oakelf – now down on his hands and knees – and on towards the body of the banderbear. As he drew close, he saw that he was not the first on the scene. The white ravens were already tearing into the carcass with their beaks and claws.

'Be gone, you bleached devils!' Screed roared as he raced towards them, arms flapping wildly.

The white ravens bounced back on their springy legs, furiously cawing – but did not fly away. Screed crouched down. Although much of the body had already been consumed by the scavengers, the feet – huge, hairy and rapier clawed – were still intact. As he tilted his head to one side, the sun glinted on the countless minute crystals trapped in the fur between the toes.

'Such beea-oootiful looty-booty,' Screed smirked.

He drew his knife from his belt and, with the detached precision of a surgeon, sliced off the toes and slipped them into his leather bag. The white ravens screeched and squawked in a frenzy of frustration.

'There,' he told them. 'All yours now.' And with that, he swung the bag onto his shoulder and loped off again. 'One down,' he chuckled. 'Four to go.'

Spiker was the first he came to. The oakelf was still down on his hands and knees – yet no longer able to crawl. His breath came fast and wheezing. Screed stood, hands on his hips, looking down at the pitiful creature. The next moment he wrapped his arm around the oakelf's shoulders and pulled backwards. The blade of his knife glinted for an instant. The oakelf gurgled, clutched at his throat – and collapsed.

'Did him a favour, really,' Screed muttered to himself as he set to work on the toes. 'Putting him out of his misery like that.' He stood up and looked ahead at the figure with the hood, still struggling painfully on.

'Ready or not,' he muttered. 'Here I come!'

The exhausting trek was taking its toll on Twig. Although little more than skin and bones wrapped up in a gown, the Professor of Light's weight seemed to be increasing as Twig lugged him, without a break, across the squelching, stagnant mud.

'Almost there,' the professor said. 'Just a few steps more.'

Suddenly, Twig found himself crossing into shadow. The air was instantly cooler. He looked up. The wreck of the great ship towered high above him.

'Thank Sky!' he gasped.

'Thank *you,*' said the professor.

Twig released the professor's legs and gently eased him off his back. 'Aaah!' he sighed, and his arms floated upwards as if by themselves. 'I feel as if I could fly!'

The professor tutted sympathetically. 'Was I really such a burden?'

'For a while back there, I thought we weren't going to make it,' Twig admitted. 'But we're here now.' He looked round. 'Screed!' he shouted.

'Screed . . . Screed . . . Screed . . .' the name echoed unanswered into the distance.

Twig shook his head. 'Where is he? What's he playing at?'

The professor snorted. 'I wouldn't put anything past that scoundrel,' he said.

Twig started with sudden alarm. Spiker and the Stone Pilot! He'd been so intent on rescuing the professor that he'd forgotten all about the rest of his crew.

He scampered over the overturned hull of the ship, leaped across to the mast and began shinning up. Even though the boat was resting at a perilous angle on the white mud, the caternest was still by far the highest landmark in the Mire. He looked back the way he had come.

Far away in the distance, he saw something. Brown on white. Motionless. Trembling with fearful anticipation, Twig unhooked his telescope from the front of his coat and put it to his eye.

'Spiker,' he gasped, as the terrible scene came into focus.

'What's happened?' he heard the professor calling up to him.

'It's ... it's Spiker,' he called back. 'He's dead. Murdered.'

'And the Stone Pilot?' the professor asked.

Twig swung the telescope round, sweeping the glistening white plains for any sign. 'I . . . I'm just trying to find him,' he blustered. Suddenly, a dark blurred shape filled the centre of the glass as it emerged from behind a bleached rock. His sweaty hands, shaking uncontrollably, slipped as he tried to adjust the focus. 'Yes!' he cried. 'It's him. And he's quite near.'

'Alive?'

Twig nodded. 'Just,' he said. 'But he's dragging his right leg badly. He can barely walk. I . . .' He gasped.

'What was *that*?'

Some way behind the Stone Pilot, he had seen movement. White on white, yet visible for all that – as if the Mire itself had grown a body and a head. Someone or something was moving towards the Stone Pilot.

'What is it?' Twig trembled. 'A mud-demon? A mire-monster? The terrible muglump?'

He re-focused the telescope. The creature came into sharp relief – the gangly arms and legs, the stooping back, the skull-like head with its tight skin that plucked at the mouth and eyebrows. Twig quivered with rage. This was no mud-demon or mire-monster.

'Screed,' he hissed. 'I might have known.'

The Stone Pilot stopped. Turned. And Twig heard a muffled cry of anguish as the Stone Pilot screamed and staggered backwards. A dazzling flash of light slashed across Twig's eyes.

'And he's got a knife!'

Twig snapped the telescope shut, scrambled down the mast, over the hull and ran back into the Mire.

'Where are you going?' called the professor.

'To help the Stone Pilot,' he called back. 'Before it's too late.'

With sweat pouring and his body aching, Twig stumbled on as fast as he could. Screed and the Stone Pilot were rolling about in the mud. Closer he got. The knife glinted. Closer and closer. Now the Stone Pilot had the upper hand; now Screed was on top. If he could just . . . All at once, the Stone Pilot's head fell back, struck by a savage blow. The knife glinted again.

'SCREED!' Twig screamed.

The bony white figure instantly leapt away from his prey, and turned on the youth like a cornered animal. His yellow teeth gleamed. 'Well, well,' he rasped, as he drew a long evil-looking sickle from his belt. 'Saved me the bother of coming to you, have you? *Most* considerate.' He bounced the sickle up and down in his bony hand. The blade gleamed along its razor edge.

The colour drained from Twig's cheeks. He had so little first-hand experience of one-armed combat.

'Come on then, *Captain* Twig,' Screed taunted, and beckoned with his free hand. 'Let's see what you're made of.' He scuttled closer like a mud-crab. 'Or perhaps you'd prefer to turn and run – I'll give you a head start,' he added and cackled mirthlessly.

Twig drew his sword and stared defiantly into Screed's bloodshot eyes.

'I will stay and fight you, Screed,' he announced, praying that the wicked creature would not notice how his voice trembled, how his arm shook. 'What's more,' he said boldly, 'I will defeat you.'

Screed stared back, but made no reply. He stooped lower and began swaying from side to side. Back and forwards flashed the sickle as he tossed it from hand to hand. And all the while he kept his unblinking gaze fixed on Twig's eyes. Then he jumped.

'Waah!' cried Twig, and leaped back. The curved blade sliced through the air, low and deadly. If he hadn't moved when he did, the sickle would have ripped his stomach wide open. Again the blade came at him.

He's toying with me, Twig told himself. Driving me back towards the sinking mud. Fight back! Fight back – or die!

He braced himself. Suddenly the sickle swooshed down towards him – fast, low and wickedly glinting – Twig held his breath, gripped his sword fiercely and brought it up to meet the sweeping blade.

'Unnh!' he grunted, as the crashing blow juddered up his arm and jarred his whole body.

'Come, come, captain,' Screed leered, as he bobbed and weaved around in front of him. 'Is that the best you can do?'

Suddenly, the air was whirling with the terrifying dance of the curved sickle. It spun, it plunged, it darted and dived. Heart in his mouth, Twig thrust his sword out. It clashed against the sickle again. And again and again . . .

I will defeat you! Twig's voice screamed in his head. *For Spiker. For the Stone Pilot . . . For myself.*

Screed darted abruptly to the left, and lunged forwards. Twig was too fast for him. He side-stepped out of danger, deflected the sickle harmlessly away and thrust his sword at Screed's scraggy neck.

'Now!' he roared as he blundered forwards. 'You . . .' His foot slipped down the side of a concealed pothole. 'Aaaaaiii!' he squealed as his ankle went over.

As Twig crashed heavily to the muddy ground, the sword slipped from his grip and landed in the soft mud – just out of reach. Screed was on him in an instant. He pinned down Twig's gauntleted arm with his foot and tickled him under the chin with the point of the merciless blade.

'Fancied your chances with Screed Toe-taker, did you, *Captain* Twig?' he said, his face twisted with contempt.

He lifted the sickle high above his head. It was silhouetted against the sky like a black moon. The blade glinted.

'SCREEDIUS TOLLINIX!' The professor's thin, reedy voice echoed across the Mire. 'What has that creature done to you?'

Screed froze, and turned his head. 'What the . . .?' he murmured.

Without a second thought, Twig wrenched his trapped arm free, rolled over, seized his sword and struck Screed a savage and penetrating blow in the centre of his bony chest. Thick red blood poured down the sword. It met Twig's gauntlet and turned to clear, sparkling water which splashed down his arm.

The sickle dropped to the ground with a soft *plattsh.* Screed looked down. He seemed almost surprised to see the sword protruding from his chest. His puzzled gaze met Twig's.

Twig gasped. The expression on Screed's face was changing before his eyes. Away went the evil leer; away the sneering lips and wild eyes. From the barbaric blood-thirsty maniac who, only seconds before, had been intent on tearing him to pieces, Twig watched Screed transform into someone quite different; some-one calm, thoughtful – noble, even. His eyes sparkled with a faraway look and a smile

played around his mouth. The lips parted, and a single word slipped out from between them.

'Sanctaphrax.'

The next moment, he fell to the ground, dead.

Twig climbed shakily to his feet. He stared at the motionless body. 'I've killed somebody,' he murmured as he closed Screed's eyes with his trembling finger-tips.

He looked at peace now and, as in those last moments of life, oddly majestic. A lump rose in Twig's throat. What had happened to turn him into so loathsome a creature? His gaze fell on the bag strung around the dead guide's shoulders. Might his personal belongings offer a clue? Twig leaned forwards, loosened the draw-strings and looked inside.

'Whoooaargh!' He retched emptily. Tears filled his eyes, but the sight of the cluster of toes lingered. He tossed the bag away, bent over double and took long deep breaths. 'Why?' he gasped at last and stared at Screed in horror. 'What kind of a monster were you?'

But he had no answers left to give. Twig pulled himself to his feet. As he turned away, the white ravens were already gathering. It was only then that he looked at the gauntlet.

·CHAPTER NINETEEN·

SCREED'S LOOTY-BOOTY

With his sword cutting a swathe through the growing flock of scavenging birds, Twig hurried towards the Stone Pilot's body. The inside of the glass eye-panels set into the hood were misted up. Did this mean the Stone Pilot was still breathing? Could he still be alive after the savage blow that Screed had dealt him?

'If only I could get these things off,' Twig muttered as he tugged in vain at the set of bolts which held the hood and gloves in place. He knelt down and pressed his ear against the heavy coat, searching for a trace of a heartbeat. A broad grin spread over his face, for there it was – faint, but regular – the Stone Pilot's beating heart.

'Now, don't you worry,' Twig said as he leapt to his feet. 'I'll soon have you back at the shipwreck. It's cool there.' He slipped his hands under the Stone Pilot's arms and round his chest. 'You're going to be . . . *wheeoo!* . . .'

he groaned as he lifted the shoulders off the ground, '... just fine!'

With every gruelling step, Twig's body cried out for rest – yet he did not ease up, not even for a moment. If the Stone Pilot died, then Twig would have lost his entire crew and that was something he would not allow to happen.

'Almost there,' he muttered breathlessly. 'Not long now.'

The Stone Pilot made neither a sound nor a movement, but Twig knew that his heart must still be beating, for the white ravens were leaving them alone. The moment it stopped, they would attack in an instant.

At last, he found himself bathed once again in the long shadow cast by the shipwreck. Twig gazed up at the merciless white sky and offered silent thanks.

'Professor,' he called, looking about him. 'Professor?'

'In here,' came a weary voice from inside the shipwreck. Twig turned. To his left was a large hole in the side of the hull. 'In here,' the professor said again, his voice little more than a whisper.

As Twig dragged the Stone Pilot through the broken entrance, he was struck by the breathtaking smell of decay. He laid the Stone Pilot down beside the far wall and found the professor propped up against a fallen beam on the opposite side. The branch at his back was still keeping his neck poker-straight. He was alive – yet even in the gloom, it was clear that he was in a bad way.

'He killed him,' the professor was groaning. 'He murdered him.'

'No,' said Twig. 'He's injured – and perhaps badly, but he's still alive.'

The professor sighed weakly. 'Not the Stone Pilot,' he wheezed and swept his arm round. 'This ship,' he said. 'I found the name plate. It's the *Windcutter*. It was captained by Screedius Tollinix. Screedius Tollinix!' he wailed. 'A fine and valiant knight.' His eyes burned with rage. 'Until that loathsome guide got his hands on him, that is,' he added and collapsed in a fit of coughing.

Twig stared back at the professor. Of course! When the professor called out, Screed had recognized his own name. That was why he'd paused . . . And Twig had killed him. He hadn't the heart to tell the professor that Screedius Tollinix and their guide were one and the same.

He crouched down beside him. 'Try to get some sleep,' he said.

'No, no,' the professor said agitatedly. 'There will be time for sleep soon enough. There are things we must elucidate, explain: things we must discuss . . .' For a second his eyes went blank. When they focused again, they looked bewildered, frightened. 'Twig, my boy,' he said, his voice low and breathy. 'You must listen. And listen well. I must tell you about stormphrax.'

'But . . .' Twig began.

'After all, that is why I am here,' the professor went on. 'That is why your father insisted I travel with you all. For I know everything there is to know about the sacred crystals. Their value. Their properties. Their power.' He paused. 'Since stormphrax is too heavy to move when in darkness and too volatile in direct sunlight, we must . . . *you* must engineer a constant but dim light to accompany it until it has reached its resting place at the heart of the floating rock of Sanctaphrax. And when *that* happens . . .'

'But what's the point of all this?' Twig blurted out. 'We haven't got any stormphrax. We weren't able to retrieve any from the Twilight Woods. Or had you forgotten, Professor? We failed.'

'Twig, be quiet!' the professor insisted. He raised his arm and pointed to the far end of the hull. 'Over there,' he wheezed.

Twig turned. His eyes had grown accustomed to the darkness by now and, as he stared into the shadows, he saw a large chest half sunk in the mud. 'W . . . what is it?' he asked.

'Go and see,' said the professor.

As Twig crossed the oozing floor towards the chest, the smell of rotting flesh grew stronger. 'Woaagh!' he gasped, and gagged at the sight of the thousand miniature trophies nailed to the wooden walls. 'Bwwwoorrgh!' he heaved again, as the huge sloping pile in the corner revealed itself to be countless thousands more of the amputated toes.

'What in Sky's name?' he muttered, and looked back at the professor for some explanation.

The professor waved him on impatiently.

Twig stopped next to the glass and ironwood chest and looked down. The top was closed, but not locked. He hesitated. What if it was full of more body parts? What if Screed also had a thing for eyeballs, or tongues?

'Open it!' he heard the professor insist.

Twig leaned forwards, took a deep breath, and threw the lid open. A silvery light gleamed from within. Twig stared down and trembled with awe at the sight of the multitude of flashing, sparking crystals. 'Stormphrax!' he gasped.

'And more than enough for all our needs,' said the Professor of Light.

'But how?' said Twig. 'I . . .' He cut himself short. 'The toes!' he exclaimed.

'Precisely,' said the professor. 'As the hapless goblins, trolls, trogs or what have you set off from the Deepwoods for Undertown, their journey took them through the Twilight Woods. There, particles of stormphrax collected under their toenails and claws, do you see? Then, when they reached the Mire, they encountered Screed – that most foul of individuals – who stole their money, slit their throats and took their toes.' He sighed wearily. 'Though why?' he moaned. 'That is the question. What use could such a degenerate soul have had for so wonderful a substance?'

The words of the sepia knight popped back into Twig's head. *A quest is a quest for ever.* And he shuddered with horror as he realized what must have happened.

Even though Screedius Tollinix had wrecked his ship, he had not been able to abandon his quest. After all, like Garlinius Gernix and Petronius Metrax before him and Quintinius Verginix after, he would have pledged to dedicate his life to the finding of stormphrax and sworn never to return to Sanctaphrax until and unless he had completed that sacred quest.

Unable to return to Sanctaphrax empty-handed, Screedius Tollinix had single-mindedly pursued his goal no matter what that involved. The noble Knight Academic, whom Twig had glimpsed at the moment of death, must have been driven insane by his desire to fulfil the promises he had made at the Inauguration Ceremony – no matter how much he amassed, it could never be enough.

'And I wouldn't like to guess how many had perished to satisfy the wicked creature's hideous lust,' the professor was saying.

Twig stared down at the glittering crystals. Each one, he now knew, had been paid for in blood. Trembling almost uncontrollably, he reached forwards, seized the lid and slammed it shut.

'It's not fair!' he stormed. 'I dreamed of returning – successful and victorious – with enough stormphrax to stabilize the floating city of Sanctaphrax for a thousand years.'

'But you still can,' the professor wheezed.

Twig rounded on him furiously. 'Not like this!' he shouted. Behind him, the Stone Pilot muttered drowsily. 'I wanted to discover new stormphrax, pure stormphrax,' he continued. 'Fresh from a Great Storm. In the Twilight Woods. Not this . . . this evil treasure-trove scraped from the toes of the dead.'

'Ah, Twig,' the professor groaned. 'Twig, my boy . . .' He began coughing again, a low rasping sound that rattled in the back of his throat. 'Ends and means,' he wheezed. 'Ends and . . .' The racking cough returned, more heart-rending than ever.

'Professor!' Twig ran towards him. His face had turned a pale shade of yellowy-grey. His eyes were sunken, his cheeks hollow. Every breath was an effort. Twig took his hand. 'Professor, are you all right?'

The professor stared at Twig's gauntleted hand. Weakly, he drew his finger across the metal knuckles. Sepia dust clung to his fingertip. 'Of course,' he whispered, barely audibly. 'Phraxdust . . .' He paused.

'Yes,' said Twig, 'when Screed's blood touched it, it turned to pure water.' He bent down until his ear was all but pressing against the professor's quivering lips. The warm breath in his face smelt of decay.

'The secret . . .' the professor whispered. 'I know how to produce phraxdust. Safely.' He gasped and brought his hands to his throat. 'The Twilight Woods were telling us all the time.'

'Go on,' said Twig, and swallowed away his tears. 'In your own time, Professor.'

A smile played over the professor's lips. 'Time!' he croaked. 'Time . . .' His eyes rolled in his head. 'Stormphrax breaks down in the twilight of the woods. The twilight, Twig! Not darkness, not light – but twilight. Slowly it crumbles over the centuries, ground down by the pressure of twilight. Ground down, Twig, for hundreds upon hundreds of years, into dust. Phraxdust. The phraxdust that coats the armour of those poor lost knights – that coats the glove you wear.'

Twig looked down at the gauntlet and the fine layer of sepia dust. 'But the secret?' he whispered. 'I don't understand.'

The professor sighed and summoned up the last of his strength.

'Don't you see, Twig? What it takes hundreds of years for the Twilight Woods to do naturally, we can do with a single crushing blow. But that blow can only, *must* only, fall at the very moment of . . .'

'Twilight!' gasped Twig.

The professor let out a long, pitiful sigh. 'Tell . . . Professor of Darkness,' he whispered. 'You can . . . trust . . . him . . .'

He fell silent. The warm breath ceased. Twig straightened up and looked down at the wise old face.

The Professor of Light was dead. Already, the white ravens were screeching noisily outside. Twig heard them scrabbling overhead, scraping at the wood; he saw the boldest of them poking their heads through the hole in the side of the hull and peering round with their beady scavenging eyes.

'Be gone with you!' he cried.

The birds retreated, but only for a moment and not very far. Twig knew he would have to bury the professor's body at once. As he dragged it outside, the white ravens flocked round him, screeching with rage.

'You shan't have him!' Twig screeched back.

With the sun now low in the sky, he followed his lengthening shadows across the path, towards a circular patch of quickmud. There, at its edge, he lay the professor down. The white ravens flapped and fluttered in a frenzy of excitement. Twig tried hard to think of some words to mark the solemn occasion.

'Professor of Light,' he murmured. 'Venerable academic of Sanctaphrax. A wise and noble individual. This place is not good enough for your final resting place . . .' He faltered, then took a deep breath. 'Rest in peace.'

And with that, he pushed the body forwards. The feet went into the sinking-mud first, followed by the legs and the torso. The white ravens, beside themselves with rage, were swooping, diving, yet unable to get at the dead body. The mud crept up the professor's chest. His arms. His fingertips. Tears streamed down Twig's face.

'Farewell,' he whispered, as the head disappeared from view.

For a moment, all that could be seen to mark where the professor had been, were the uppermost twigs of the branch that Twig had secured to his neck. Then they too slipped down out of sight. A bubble of air plopped on the surface. Then stillness. Calmness. Peace.

Twig knelt on one knee, reached forwards with his gauntleted hand and dipped it into the pool of warm sinking-mud as a mark of respect. As he did so, it abruptly changed. Twig gasped. Before his very eyes, the thick white mud turned to water, as crystal clear as the babbling brooks which meandered through the

Deepwoods. Far below him, he could see the professor's body spiralling down deeper and deeper in its watery grave.

Twig sat back on his haunches and stared at the heavy gauntlet. The sepia dust, so fine it moved like liquid, was still slipping over the polished silver.

'Phraxdust,' he whispered reverently, as he picked himself up and looked around.

Far, far away in the distance he could make out the lights of Sanctaphrax, twinkling in the air. Below it, the squalid sprawl of Undertown squatted under its blanket of filthy brown smoke. The inhabitants of both places would benefit from the contents of the glass and iron-wood chest. The stormphrax would restore equilibrium to the floating rock, while the phraxdust would purify the festering Edgewater River.

Ends and means, the professor had said. Twig was unsure whether the lives that might be saved in Sanctaphrax and Undertown by the crystals could ever justify Screed's massacre of so many individuals. What he did know was that if he failed to return with the chest of stormphrax, then they would certainly all have died in vain.

'I must try,' he said to himself. 'For the sake of the living. For the sake of the dead.'

Just then, he heard a troubled groaning coming from inside the hull of the shipwreck. It was the Stone Pilot. He was finally coming round.

·CHAPTER TWENTY·

THE STONE PILOT

The first thing Twig did on re-entering the shipwreck was to light the lantern which Screed had hanging on a nail by the opening. A warm honey-like glow filled the gloomy interior, and Twig saw that the Stone Pilot was sitting up.

'Thank Sky you're still alive,' he said.

The Stone Pilot nodded. 'But only just,' came a timid, muffled voice from inside the heavy suit. There was a pause. 'I can't feel my right leg at all.' Twig stared back in shocked silence. 'I was attacked by that so-called guide of ours,' the Stone Pilot went on. 'Must have knocked me senseless. I don't know how I ever got here.'

'I . . . I brought you here,' Twig explained.

The Stone Pilot nodded again. 'And Screed?'

'Screed is dead,' said Twig. 'By my sword. He . . . I . . .' He crouched before the Stone Pilot, confused. 'You can *speak*,' he said.

'I can.'

'But, I didn't know ... I mean, forgive me, but I always assumed you were dumb.'

'I don't waste my words,' he said. 'The world is wide and treacherous. These clothes and my silence are my protection.' He paused. 'Your father understood this well.'

'My father?' said Twig, surprised. 'He knew you could talk?'

'He knew *everything*,' said the Stone Pilot and, with these words, began squirming and wriggling until he had manoeuvred his right arm up out of its sleeve. Through the glass panels, Twig saw the surprisingly delicate fingers fiddling with the inner set of bolts which secured the hood to the shoulders. One by one, the catches clicked open.

Twig was spellbound. Not only had the Stone Pilot revealed that he could talk, but now – for the first time – he was about to show his face. Twig held his breath. What horrible disfigurement or affliction could the poor creature be suffering from, that he had gone to such lengths to conceal himself? What terrible secret lurked within that cumbersome suit of clothes?

As the hood was lifted, a neck came into view, pale and slender. Twig bit into his lower lip. The next moment, a mass of thick orange hair cascaded over the face. The Stone Pilot raised a hand, and swept it away.

Twig gasped. 'You're ... you're ...' he blustered.

'A girl,' the Stone Pilot replied. 'Are you surprised?'

'Of course I am!' said Twig. 'I had no idea. I thought you were going to be some kind of ... monster ...'

The Stone Pilot scowled and looked away. 'Perhaps it would be better if I were,' she said quietly. 'The most deformed and hideously scarred creature in the Deepwoods cannot be as lost and alone as I, now that I have lost Cloud Wolf – and the *Stormchaser*. It was the only place where I felt safe, and even there I still needed this.' She tapped the discarded hood.

'Cheer up,' said Twig, trying to sound reassuring. 'We'll get out of this.'

'It's no use,' cried the Stone Pilot. 'We're going to die in this great wide place. I know we are.'

'You mustn't talk like that,' said Twig sternly. Then, trying to distract the distressed girl, 'According to a story my father once told me, you were there at my birth,' he said. 'On board a sky ship, it was – a sky ship captained by the notorious . . .'

'Multinius Gobtrax,' the Stone Pilot interrupted. 'I recall it well,' she said, her voice thick with tears. 'We were over the Deepwoods in the middle of a terrible storm when Maris, your mother, went into labour.' She shook her head. 'I've never known up-currents like it. The sky ship was sucked up above the forest before anyone had a chance to down anchor or secure the grappling-irons.'

'Yet you managed to save the sky ship,' said Twig. 'I remember Cloud Wolf telling me how you doused the buoyant wood-burners, released the balance-weights, and climbed over the side to chip away at the flight-rock itself.'

The Stone Pilot looked down. 'I did what needed

to be done,' she said quietly.

'And I'm glad you did,' said Twig. 'After all, if you hadn't, then I wouldn't be here now.'

The Stone Pilot managed a smile. 'And who would have saved me from Screed if you weren't?' she said. 'We'll call it quits, shall we?'

'Yes,' said Twig uncertainly.

'But?' said the Stone Pilot.

'Nothing,' said Twig. 'It's just ... Well, that was sixteen years ago. How come you ...'

'Look so young?' she said, finishing his question for him.

Twig nodded.

The Stone Pilot looked away; a pale and slender hand reached for the hood. Twig stared thoughtfully at the seemingly ageless girl with her pale, almost translucent, skin and her shock of orange hair. She looked so familiar . . . And then he remembered.

'Mag!' he exclaimed.

'I beg your pardon,' said the Stone Pilot, surprised.

'That's who you remind me of,' he said. 'Someone I met a long time ago. She was a termagant trog girl. She . . .'

'What do you know about termagant trogs?' the Stone Pilot asked hesitantly.

Twig shrugged. What *did* he know about the termagants? He knew that Mag – a similarly pale-skinned and red-haired girl – had caught him and kept him as a pet in their underground caverns. He knew that, when she'd come of age, Mag had drunk from the sacred roots of the bloodoak tree and been transformed into a hulking great beast of a woman like Mumsie, her mother. He knew, too, that if he had not escaped when he did, he would have been torn to pieces.

'A pet?' said the Stone Pilot.

Twig nodded. 'She kept me on a long tether. She pampered and patted me.' He winced. 'And she used to spend hours beading and braiding my hair.'

'Until she turned termagant?'

'Exactly.'

The Stone Pilot fell silent and stared down stony-faced at the ground. When she looked up, Twig saw the tears welling in her eyes. 'That was one good thing about wearing the hood,' she said, hugging it to her body. 'Nobody ever saw me cry.' She sniffed. 'As you can see, I never turned termagant.'

Twig nodded, relieved that she hadn't. Watching his sweet, loving Mag turning into the fearful, bloodthirsty creature had been one of the most distressing incidents of his entire life.

'When my time came and the Mother Bloodoak bled for me, I was not there,' she explained sadly. 'And those who miss their appointed moment can never turn, but are condemned to remain as you see me now, until the day they die.'

'But . . . but why did you miss it?' Twig asked.

The trog girl sighed. 'It was on the day before I was due to turn termagant,' she said. 'I was outside the cavern walking my pet, a prowlgrin pup, when I was surrounded by a pack of trained whitecollar wood-wolves. They tore my pet to pieces but left me to their master. A slaver from Undertown,' she said, spitting out the words. 'He shackled me along with woodelves, trolls, goblins, and marched us off to a Deepwoods slave market. That's where your father found me – filthy, ragged and half out of my mind.'

'He bought you?' said Twig, wide-eyed.

'He saw the state I was in,' she said. 'He seized that miserable slaver's whip from him and nearly flayed him alive. Then he took me by the hand and said, "Come, little one, Maris will fix you up." And I went.'

Twig crouched back down beside her. 'It . . . it must have been awful for you,' he said sympathetically.

The Stone Pilot nodded. 'I could never find my cavern home,' she said. 'Sky knows, I've searched over the years. But in due course Cloud Wolf even gave me a home.'

'The *Stormchaser*,' said Twig.

'Yes,' replied the Stone Pilot. 'And a trade. I'm the best Stone Pilot in the skies. Or was. Now I've got nothing.'

'You've got me,' said Twig, stretching out a hand.

The Stone Pilot looked up at him and, hesitantly, took his hand in hers.

'If we're going to stay here, then we'll need to find some food,' said Twig brightly.

'Stay here?' said the Stone Pilot.

'Of course,' he said. 'How else are we going to make the ship skyworthy again? We'll never get out of the Mire if we don't.'

Twig looked round at the broken hull of the wreck. Getting the sky ship airborne again would be a formidable task – particularly since the Stone Pilot's injured leg meant he would have to do the work on his own. Then again, what choice did he have?

'The repairs don't have to be perfect,' said the Stone Pilot, following Twig's gaze. 'So long as you can locate the flight-rock, I think I can get the *Windcutter* flying again. Cloud Wolf taught me well.'

Twig smiled. 'I don't even know your name.'

The Stone Pilot stared back at him for a moment, eyes narrowed in thought, her hands gripping the protective hood. Finally, she spoke. 'My name is Maugin,' she said.

*

On that first morning, the rising sun woke Twig early. He left the sleeping Maugin to rest and made a thorough inspection of the entire sky ship. It was soon clear that the sun would rise above the fetid Mire many times before the *Windcutter* was skyworthy again.

The hull was not only broken in places but also rotting on the starboard side that rested in the mud, the mast was cracked and, though several of the hanging weights were in place, many were missing. The flight-rock had split in two. One half lay trapped beneath a heavy beam in the warm mud. The other half was nowhere to be seen.

'First of all,' he said, 'I must see whether there are any tools on board. If I can't find a hammer and some nails then I won't be able to repair anything.' He hesitated. 'On the other hand, what's the point of doing that before I find the other half of the flight-rock.' He turned. 'Then again, if there are no supplies on board, we'll starve to death anyway.' And with that, he returned the way he'd come.

Yet wherever Twig looked, he drew a blank. The 'tween-deck store-room, stock-room and stowing-room were all empty. The cabins and steerage had been stripped bare. And he already knew there was nothing in the hold where he and the Stone Pilot had spent the night.

'We're done for,' he sighed. 'I'd better break the news to Maugin.' And he headed down the stairs that would take him back down to the hold.

On reaching the bottom, Twig frowned with confusion. Where was the Stone Pilot? Where was the chest of stormphrax and the gruesome display of toes? As his eyes got used to the darkness, he realized he was in a different part of the hold altogether – the forehold rather than the mainhold. He looked round, first gasping, then grinning, then whooping with delight.

'Twig?' came a voice from the other side of the wooden wall. 'Is that you?'

'Yes!' Twig shouted back. 'And I've found it. I've found Screed's store and sleeping quarters. And . . . and . . . there's everything here we need,' he said. 'Plates and goblets, knives and spoons. Oh, and here are his fishing-rods, and hooks and lines. Candles and lantern oil. And a large box of ship's biscuit. And a barrel of woodgrog. And . . . Oh, Maugin! He's been sleeping on the sails.'

'And ropes?' called Maugin. 'We'll need ropes to raise them.'

Twig poked around under the mattress of folded sails. 'Yes!' he exclaimed. 'Coiled up as a base underneath, all the ropes we could possibly want. And . . . here! A huge chest, full of tools. We'll be able to get started right away.' He paused. 'How's your leg?'

'Not so bad,' Maugin called back, but Twig could hear pain in her soft voice.

Twig set to work eagerly. Hour after hour, he toiled, carrying out the instructions of the Stone Pilot, who – although she would have denied it – was suffering constant pain from the angry gash on her leg. But the *Windcutter* really was a wreck. Every spar seemed rotten, every plank ready to crumble. Although he did the best he could, patching here, trimming there, the task seemed hopeless. When the sun sank down below the horizon, he looked round, dismayed by how little he had actually achieved.

'I'm never going to get this finished,' he complained.

'Don't worry,' Maugin reassured him in her soft, shy voice. 'Find the other half of the flight-rock and we'll make her fly.'

Twig shook his head. 'But the flight-rock is buoyant,' he said. 'Won't it simply have floated away?'

'I don't think so,' the Stone Pilot replied. 'As you know, cold rock rises, hot rock sinks. Assuming it landed

somewhere in the warm Mire mud, it should still be there.'

Although the Stone Pilot had been badly injured when descending from the *Stormchaser*, her leg had, thankfully, not been broken. With regular cleansings in the phrax-dust-purified water, the swelling went down, the redness faded and the angry wound slowly began to heal. They had been there ten days when she first climbed shakily to her feet.

'That's amazing, Maugin!' said Twig, and took her by the arm. 'See if you can put some weight on it.' The Stone Pilot stepped tentatively forwards onto her right leg. It wobbled. She winced – but persevered. 'Excellent!' Twig enthused. 'It'll soon be as good as new.'

'It'll never be that,' said Maugin, smiling bravely. 'But I daresay it'll serve me well for a few more years. Now how's supper coming along?' She looked up and sniffed the air.

'Supper!' Twig exclaimed. 'I forgot all about it,' and he dashed outside to seize the metal griddle from the fire. 'Just how I like them!' he called back.

'You mean, burnt,' said Maugin, smiling as she peered through the hole in the hull.

Twig looked up and grinned. The Stone Pilot's shyness was slowly disappearing. 'So you won't be wanting any?' he said.

'I didn't say that,' came the reply. 'What have we got today, anyway? No, don't tell me. Oozefish!'

'Hammelhorn steaks, actually,' said Twig. 'With fresh crusty bread and a nice side salad.' Maugin's mouth dropped open. 'Only kidding,' said Twig as he handed her a platter with her daily ration of three oozefish, a slab of hard tack and a handful of dried woodsap segments arranged upon it. 'The perfect diet,' he said.

'If you say so,' said Maugin with a smile. She eased herself down onto a rock and began nibbling at a corner of the rock-hard biscuit.

Far away in the distance, the massive orange sun sank down below the horizon and the sky glowed pink and green. Twig and Maugin watched the lights of Sanctaphrax appearing, one by one. Behind their heads, the stars were already sparkling and – as they sat eating in silence – the night spread across the sky like an opening canopy.

'I love the evenings,' said Twig as he rose to light the lantern. 'It's so peaceful out here, with nothing and no-one for miles around and only open sky above.'

Maugin shuddered. 'It gives me the creeps,' she said.

Twig did not reply. He knew that, despite her years as a sky pirate, being a termagant trog Maugin still yearned for her life underground. It was – like Twig's own desire to sail the skies – in the blood.

'By the way,' he said, 'I've got some good news.'

'What?'

'I found the other half of the flight-rock.'

'You did?' said Maugin excitedly. 'Where?'

Twig swallowed hard. He had found it in the purified pool where the Professor of Light was buried. The previous evening, he had gone there in despair to talk to the old professor. And there it was, bobbing in the clear warm water, just beneath the surface.

'Oh, not far from here,' said Twig. 'Do you think you can join it together?'

'I've mended worse,' said Maugin.

Twig looked across at her and smiled. 'We've been lucky so far, haven't we?'

'Luckier than I ever dared to hope,' Maugin admitted.

At that moment, far up in the twinkling depths of the night, a shooting star blazed across the sky with a soft hiss. Twig lay back and watched it. 'It's so beautiful,' he sighed.

'Shhh!' said Maugin. 'And make a wish.'

Twig turned and looked at her. 'I already have.'

·CHAPTER TWENTY-ONE·

The Flight to Undertown

For the next two days, Twig and Maugin worked harder than ever. Having completed the nauseating task of removing Screed's collection of rotting toes, Twig cleared the mud away from the bottom of the ship. Next, he bound the cracked mast, completed the repairs to the hull-rigging and, with wood taken from the redundant cabins, began sealing the largest holes in the hull. Maugin bound the two halves of the flight-rock together in an intricate latticework of ropes, bound in wet mire mud and baked hard into place in the sun. Then the two of them began the arduous business of dragging the ropes and sails from the forehold to the decks.

Although made of woodspider-silk the sails were cumbersome to manoeuvre and half rotted with age. Every gust of wind set them fluttering and flapping, and small tears appeared that had to be patched.

'Hold on tight!' Twig ordered below, as the studsail he was holding billowed out. He was halfway up the mast at the time, and struggling to attach it to a sliding-cleat. 'Do you really think these will get us to Undertown?'

'Have faith,' Maugin called up, 'and a light touch on the sail levers. The flight-rock will do the rest.'

Twig smiled. There was something in Maugin's calm manner that reassured him. He was beginning to depend on this quiet, serious girl more and more. 'Come on,' he said. 'Only the staysail and the jib to rig up, and we're done.'

As the setting sun signalled the end of yet another day, Twig checked the knots for a final time, balanced his way back along the creaking bowsprit and jumped down onto the deck.

'There,' he announced. 'Finished.' He surveyed his handiwork nervously. 'Shall we go for a trial run?'

'It's getting dark,' said the Stone Pilot. 'We should leave it until morning.'

'You know best,' said Twig, somewhat relieved. 'Let's go and have a tot or two of woodgrog to celebrate. We've earned it.'

The following day, Twig was woken before the sun had risen. 'Get up,' Maugin was saying as she shook him by the shoulders.

Twig opened his eyes and looked round groggily. His head was thumping. Too much woodgrog, he realized miserably.

'We must leave now, before the wind changes,' said Maugin. 'I'm going down below deck to see to the flight-rock. You take the helm. I'll call up to you when I'm ready,' she said.

Twig washed, dressed, drank enough of the phraxdust-purified water to quench his thirst and clear his head, and made his way to the helm. There by the wheel – freshly aligned and greased – Twig stared at the two long rows of bone-handled levers. 'Stern-weight, prow-weight, starboard hull-weights, small, medium and large,' he muttered, ticking them off in his head. 'Then, mizzensail, foresail, topsail,' he said, turning his attention to the second row of levers. 'Skysail . . . No, studsail. Or is it the staysail . . .? Blast!'

'Ready to launch!' came Maugin's calm voice, echoing up the staircase from the bowels of the ship. 'Raise the mizzensail.'

'Aye-aye,' Twig called back, his own voice sounding shrill and more nervous than he'd have liked.

With his heart in his mouth, he leaned forwards, seized the mizzensail lever and pulled. The sail billowed and filled with air. At first, nothing happened. Then, with a judder and a creak, the *Windcutter* lifted slightly, and almost imperceptibly began to right itself. The rotten timbers groaned horribly.

'Down the port hull-weights,' Twig muttered. 'Up the large starboard hull-weight a tad and . . . Whoa!' he cried as the ship listed sharply to port. The sound of tearing sailcloth filled his ears.

'Careful,' called the Stone Pilot steadily.

Twig tried to remain cool. He raised the port hull-weights a fraction, and compensated by lowering the stern-weight. The sky ship stabilized and, with a long and rasping squelch, it rose arthritically up from the sucking mud.

'YES!' Twig cried out. The wish he had made as the shooting star flew across the sky had come true. The *Windcutter* was skyborne. They were on their way back to Undertown.

'Easy as she goes!' the Stone Pilot called.

Twig nodded as he turned the wheel slowly to the left. 'Stay calm,' he told himself. 'Keep a steady course – and concentrate.'

The sky ship keeled to port. Twig's head spun. There was so much to remember. With the wind coming from the south, the starboard hull-weights needed to be raised higher than the port hull-weights – but not too high, or else the sky ship would go into a spin. His task was made no easier by the lack of the neben-hull-weights and the constant nerve-racking creaking of the old rotten hull.

'You're doing fine!' the Stone Pilot called up encouragingly.

Am I? Twig wondered. He hoped so. That last time he had tried to sail a sky ship, it had ended in disaster – and that was with his father there to take over when things got too difficult for him. Now there was no-one to come to his aid. Twig was on his own.

'You can do it,' he urged himself. 'You *must* do it!'

At that moment, he glanced up to see a dark cloud speeding towards them. As the *Windcutter* rose higher, the cloud descended. They were on collision course.

'What is it?' Twig gasped. Trembling with unease, he spun the helm to the left. The cloud, too, shifted direction. 'And what's going to happen when it strikes?' he shuddered.

Closer and closer, it came. Twig became aware of a curious noise – a squawking, squeaking, screeching noise – that grew louder, and louder still. All at once, he saw the cloud for what it really was. A flock of birds; all flashing wings and lashing tails. The ratbirds were returning.

As one, the flock wheeled round the sky ship once, twice, three times, darting between the sails in figures of eight, before swooping down out of view beneath the hull. Through the many cracks they flew, and into the base-hold of the ship where they took up residence. The familiar sound of twittering and scratching filtered back up to the deck.

'Ratbirds!' Twig whispered, his face beaming with delight. It was a good sign. Even if it was an old wives' tale about ratbirds abandoning a doomed sky ship, Twig was as glad to see them arrive as Tem Barkwater had been dismayed when they left. And, as he raised the remaining sails and the sky ship lurched forwards, his heart soared. Like his father, his father before him, and his father before him, Twig – *Captain* Twig – was in charge of his own sky pirate ship.

Far below him – and farther all the time – the shadow of the sky ship skudded across the glistening white mud of the Mire. Now and then Twig would lean forwards and adjust one or two of the hanging weights. It was coming more easily now. He was beginning, as Cloud Wolf had put it, to develop *the touch*.

On and on they sailed, running before the wind. Ahead, the horizon melted away in a bank of swirling mist and the distant floating city of Sanctaphrax vanished. Below, the shadow abruptly disappeared too, as clouds – real clouds this time – swept across the sun. All round him, the air was filled with the creaking and whistling of a gale-force wind as it tugged and strained at the sky ship. Every now and then, a plank would splinter and fall away. The *Windcutter* was slowly falling to bits, but still she flew on.

'Don't panic,' Twig whispered in a vain attempt to still his thumping heart. He fiddled feverishly with the levers. 'Lower the sails a little. Raise the hanging weights. Gently. Gently.'

'We should be there before darkness falls,' came a voice at his shoulder.

Twig turned. It was Maugin. 'Shouldn't you be tending to the flight-rock?' he asked anxiously.

'There's nothing to do for the time being,' Maugin assured him. 'Not till we come in to land. I've been checking round the ship. We'll have to take it slowly.'

'And the stormphrax?' said Twig. 'The lantern needs to be burning at a sort of twilight brightness,' he reminded her.

'The stormphrax is fine,' she said. 'Everything's fine.' She paused. 'Except . . .'

'What?'

'I'm not sure,' she said. 'But I have the horrible feeling the mast-bindings we secured are giving way. We must sail with the wind until we absolutely have to tack against it to make Undertown. Otherwise the mast will break. It means we'll be taken over the Edge. We must keep our nerve until the last minute.'

Twig tensed. His palms were wet and his mouth was dry. Just the thought of sailing over the Edge into the uncharted sky beyond, where even the sky pirates never dared to venture, filled him with dread. Yet, if the Stone Pilot was right about the mast, they had no choice. They would have to sail with the wind until they were level with Undertown, and then turn, dash back towards land – and pray.

'Is the Mire still below us?' he said.

Maugin went to check. 'Yes,' she called back from the balustrade. 'But the Edge is approaching. Keep the lights of Sanctaphrax in view.'

'I know!' Twig snapped as he raised the starboard hull-weights. The boat lurched and listed; the mast creaked ominously.

'Go with the wind,' said Maugin. 'Let her have her head.'

Twig nodded grimly. His hands gripped the helm, white knuckled; he drew blood biting into his lower lip. The sky ship listed even further. If he wasn't careful it would roll over completely.

'Easy!' Maugin called, as the ship dipped savagely. Twig lowered the stern- and prow-weights. The sky ship steadied momentarily. Twig sighed – but his relief was short-lived. 'Twig,' she said, her voice as calm and steady as ever. 'We've gone over the Edge.'

An icy chill coursed through his veins. The wind had taken them towards the mysterious nether-regions beyond the Edge where dragons and monsters were said to roam, where few had visited and none had returned. To a place known only for the weather it conjured up – Great Storms, of course, but also mad howling whirlwinds that warped the mind and filled sleeping heads with visions; thick, suffocating fogs that stole the senses; driving rain, blinding snow, sulphurous dust storms that coated everything in a fine layer of particles – now green, now grey, now red.

'Got to keep sight of the lights of Sanctaphrax,' he murmured. 'Wait till they're level with us. Keep your nerve, Twig. Keep your nerve!'

Tearing herself away from the mesmerizing mists which writhed and swirled beneath her, Maugin ran back to the helm. 'I'll take the wheel,' she said. 'You concentrate on the levers.'

The wind gathered force. The tattered sails screamed as it tore through the fresh rents in the sailcloth. The groaning timbers of the hull grew shrill with splintering.

Twig's hands danced over the levers. Lifting here, lowering there, steadying the mast jib. And all the while, the lights of Sanctaphrax drew nearer on the starboard bow, glinting tantalizingly from solid ground.

Beneath the crumbling hull of the *Windcutter* was the inky blackness of the void. Panic rose in Twig's throat. He wanted to pull the ship about, straight into the teeth of the gale that gripped them, and make a dash for the grey cliff face of the Edge. If they crashed over land, at least they'd stand a chance of surviving. But here, beyond the Edge, they could fall for ever.

His hand jerked out for the starboard hull-weight lever. He felt an iron grip. Maugin's slender hand held him at the wrist. 'Not yet,' she whispered, mouth close to his ear. 'Have faith. Wait for the lights to come level. Wait, Twig. Wait.'

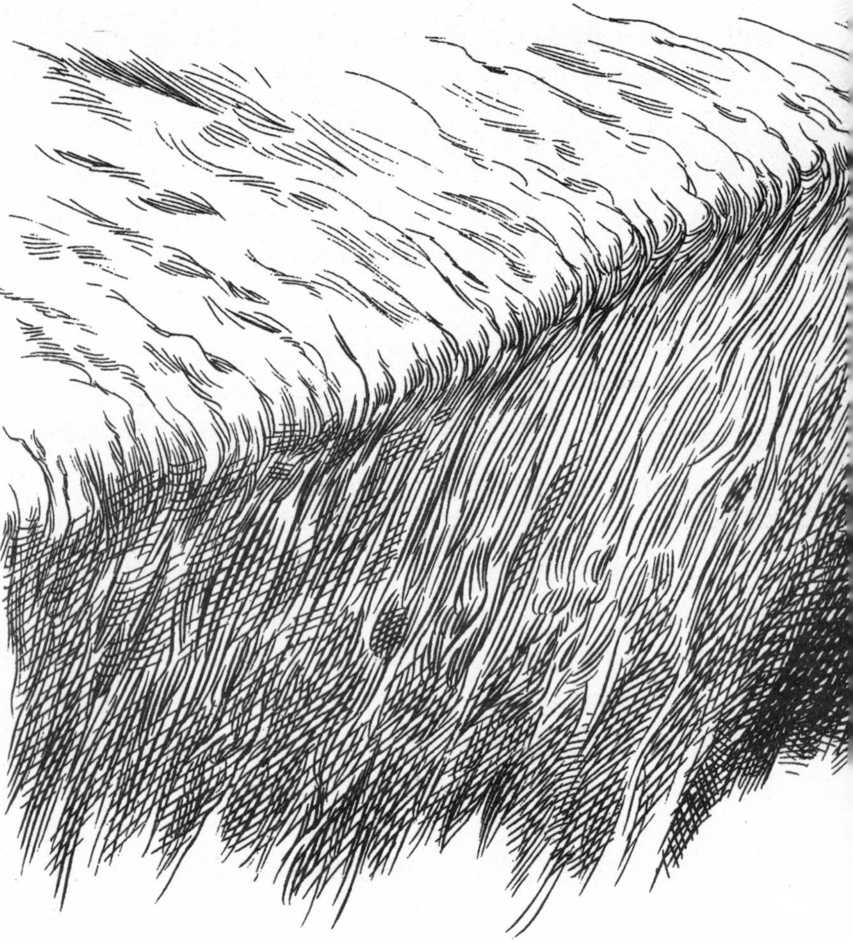

Twig's panic receded. But he was drenched with sweat, and shivering violently – with cold, with anticipation. All at once, a sickening crash split the air behind them and the aft-spar flew past, down into the darkness, dragging its sail with it.

'It's all right,' Twig shouted, as he steadied the rudder-wheel to bring the bucking sky ship back under control. 'I've got her.'

Maugin surveyed the horizon. 'Now!' she shouted.

Twig's hand immediately shot out for the starboard hull-weight lever for a second time. This time Maugin did not stop him. He pulled down with all his might. As the heavy boom swung about, the *Windcutter* jarred as if hit by a giant hammer, and tacked into a blast of icy wind.

The mast screeched under the strain, its sails ripping apart and flying past him like phantoms. Then, with an ear-splitting splintering, the entire mighty upright began to buckle.

'Don't break,' Twig implored. 'Not now!'

With an agonizing screech, the mast folded backwards. The teeth of the gale bit deep into its rotten centre and . . . CRASH! It split in two and the top half slammed past the bridge.

Twig threw himself on the Stone Pilot as the great column swished past their heads like Screed's evil scythe.

'We're done for!' he screamed as the sails fell limp and the *Windcutter* began to drop through the air. Abruptly, the lights of Sanctaphrax were snuffed out. 'We're lost!'

'No!' Maugin was screaming back. 'The flight-rock. The flight-rock will save us. Cool the flight-rock and we float. Twig, we float!'

They clawed their way to the stone-cradle, with the wind whistling through their ears as the ship fell in a vertical spin.

'Pull that iron ring, Twig!' screamed the Stone Pilot. 'Pull it with me. One. Two. Three. Now!'

Together, they hauled back the great iron ring of the stone cradle and a loud hiss spat out from the bars as cold earth fell on the stone encased within. The roaring in Twig's ears grew less. The *Windcutter* was slowing. It was steadying. Twig opened his eyes. The wreck of the sky ship was righting itself as, with growing buoyancy, the flight-rock strained at the bars of the stone-cradle and pulled them upwards.

'Listen now, Twig.' Maugin's voice was tense and urgent. 'When we rise above the Edge, we *must* have sail – any sail. To take us forwards; to take us back over land.'

'I'll give you sail,' said Twig. He was strangely calm. They hadn't come this far to fail now.

The glow of the stormphrax chest cast a ghostly light over the tangled mess of rigging and tattered sail. Twig scanned the wreckage. The mast was broken – but it would have to do. He threw himself into the task of raising a makeshift sail with feverish intensity.

They were rising with increasing speed when suddenly, yes, there were the lights of Sanctaphrax, and Undertown, straight ahead in the distance. Twig pulled on the sail ropes with all his might, the coarse fibres biting into his flesh, drawing blood.

Then the wind struck. The jolt ran through Twig's body. He gasped with pain – but the tattered sails billowed. The old *Windcutter* gasped with Twig, and dragged itself back towards the Edge.

'Raise the starboard hull-weights,' Twig instructed himself, as he dashed back to the helm. 'Lower the port weights. And align the stern- and peri-hull-weights. That's it. Now raise the studsail a tad – easy does it, gently, and . . .' The heavy boom swung wildly round. Twig looked up nervously. The broken mast was hanging on; the makeshift sails were holding.

They were going to make it. Limping, splintered; tattered, cracked and wind-battered. But they were going to make it.

·CHAPTER TWENTY-TWO·

TO THE HEART OF SANCTAPHRAX

Twig moved forwards in his chair. 'You have no choice!' he said. 'I have something you need – and you have something I need.'

Mother Horsefeather permitted herself a little smile. The youth was certainly bold.

'You are your father's son,' she said, and clacked her beak. 'Coming here in that creaking wreck of a sky ship, giving ultimatums.' Her beady yellow eyes glinted. 'Might I remind you that if it hadn't been for my backing, the *Stormchaser* would never have set sail in the first place.'

'I know that,' said Twig, 'but . . .'

'Now you tell me that it is lost. With Cloud Wolf aboard. Yet there you are, shouting out your demands. It is *I* who should be making demands of you, *Captain* Twig,' she said.

'No, I . . .' said Twig uncertainly.

'Fifteen thousand it cost, plus interest. As you know, I'm not in the business of giving money away. I want a return on my investment . . .'

At that moment the Stone Pilot who, back inside her protective disguise, had been standing patiently at Twig's shoulders, strode forwards. She slammed her gloved hand down on the table.

'Hold your beak, bird-woman!' she roared. 'Let the captain speak.'

Mother Horsefeather clucked nervously, and smoothed down the ruffled feathers around her neck. She fixed Twig with a fearsome glare. 'Your father,' she sniffed, 'was a gentleman.'

Twig nodded and swallowed noisily. 'This is what I want,' he said. 'One, all debts incurred by my father, Cloud Wolf, are to be written off. Two, you are to supply me with a new sky ship, packed with supplies and ready to sail. I shall call it *Edgedancer*.'

'*Edgedancer*?' Mother Horsefeather sneered.

'And three,' Twig continued without a break, 'you will pay for a crew of my choosing to sail her. I'll take a pouchful of gold now, as a sign of your good faith.'

Mother Horsefeather's expression darkened, 'you ask a great deal, Captain Twig,' she said, thrusting her beak towards him. 'And what do you offer in return that is worth so much?'

Twig sat back in his chair and twiddled with his hair. 'I thought you'd never ask,' he said. 'I will give you the secret of safe phraxdust production.'

Mother Horsefeather's jaw dropped. A curious chirruping sound rattled at the back of her throat. 'But but but . . .' she gurgled. 'You mean . . . But I'll corner the water market,' she squawked.

Twig nodded, and stared at the bird-woman in disgust as her face contorted with joy and villainy and naked greed.

'I'll control it all!' she cackled. 'I'll be more powerful than that glutinous Leaguesmaster, Simenon Xintax. *And* the odious upstart, Vilnix Pompolnius. I'll be more powerful than the whole lot of them put together.' She turned on Twig suspiciously. 'You are sure you know the secret?' she said.

'I am,' said Twig. 'And when you fulfil my demands I shall prove it to you. You shall become powerful. And rich beyond your wildest dreams.'

Mother Horsefeather ruffled her feathers and fixed Twig with cold unblinking eyes. 'You have a deal, son of Cloud Wolf,' she said, pulling a leather pouch of gold coins from the pocket of her apron and tossing it across the table. 'But remember this, Captain Twig. If you double-cross me, I shall personally see to it that the leagues hear of your impudence.' Her beady eyes narrowed. 'The League of Torturers will be particularly interested to hear that they have a new subject to study – and at such great length!'

It was late afternoon by the time Twig left the Bloodoak tavern. With the Stone Pilot, he returned to the boom-docks, lugged the heavy chest up from the hold of the *Windcutter* and, together, the pair of them set off through Undertown.

The narrow, dirty streets were hot and sultry, and many of the stall-holders and shop-keepers had shut up their premises and retired for an afternoon nap. They would open again at sundown. One establishment, however, had not closed and, as Twig and the Stone Pilot struggled past with the chest of Stormphrax, its fat and glistening owner emerged from inside.

'Oy! It's you!' Flabsweat cried, and made a lunge at Twig.

Without even thinking, Twig drew his sword. 'Back off,' he said calmly, 'or it will be the worse for you.'

Flabsweat retreated, fear in his eyes. 'I . . . I didn't mean no offence . . .' he blustered.

Twig stared at the frightened shopkeeper uneasily. Is this what the quest had done to him? Is this what he had become? He looked down, removed the gauntlet from his hand and held it out. 'Here,' he said. 'Take it.'

Flabsweat reached forward. 'Wh . . . what is it?' he said.

'A trophy from the Twilight Woods,' said Twig. 'It is coated with phraxdust – enough to produce fresh water for you, your family and all your animals for the rest of your lives.'

Flabsweat traced his finger over the liquid-like sepia dust. 'Phraxdust,' he gasped. 'Why, thank you. Thank you.'

'I trust that you will now consider the matter with the caterbird closed,' said Twig.

'Oh, quite closed, absolutely closed, completely and utterly closed,' Flabsweat babbled. Twig turned to go. 'And if there's anything I can do for you,' he said. 'Any of the more *exotic* species you might like me to procure . . . I can get hold of anything. As a gift. Just you say the word.'

Twig paused and looked back. 'I might hold you to that,' he said.

Twig and the Stone Pilot continued on their way and, as Sanctaphrax came nearer, Twig's heart beat furiously. He didn't know whether he was nervous or excited. Only when they were at last directly beneath the massive floating rock did Twig look up. He saw a large basket suspended far above his head. 'Is there anyone up there?' he called. 'I wish to visit Sanctaphrax.'

The small, angular face of a gnokgoblin appeared at the edge of the basket, and peered down. 'At whose invitation?' he said.

'We are to visit the Professor of Darkness,' Twig replied.

The gnokgoblin's eyes narrowed. 'The Professor of Darkness, eh?' he said. The basket began to descend.

Twig turned to the Stone Pilot and smiled. 'So far, so good,' he whispered.

The basket came to rest just in front of them and the gnokgoblin looked them up and down. 'I hope that chest's not too heavy.'

'Nowhere near as heavy as it will be,' Twig said. 'But we could do with a hand.'

Together, the three of them hefted the chest into the basket and jumped in beside it. Then the gnokgoblin bent down, grasped the winch-handle and began turning. The basket wobbled and lurched, and rose slowly up into the air.

'Interesting individual, the Professor of Darkness,' the gnokgoblin said, his voice nasal and whining. 'Never abandoned his opposition to the Most High Academe.' He looked askance at Twig, gauging his opinion before continuing.

Twig snorted. 'A usurper is a usurper,' he said.

The Stone Pilot shuffled about uneasily. There were spies everywhere in Sanctaphrax.

'Well, he *is*,' Twig snapped.

''Tis the mind of many in the venerable floating city,' the gnokgoblin said, nodding sagely. He looked up and met Twig's questioning gaze. 'I'm not one to listen to rumours, you understand,' he said, 'but word is that the days of Vilnix Pompolnius are numbered.'

Twig listened in silence.

''Course, it's his own fault. How did he expect the leagues to react when he cut off their supplies of phrax-dust? Eh?'

'Perhaps he has no more to supply them with,' Twig offered.

'Which is my point entirely. If he's no use to the leaguesmen *nor* the academics, then how much longer can he cling on to power? Eh? You tell me that.' He drew a deep breath. 'If you ask *me*, it'll be those leaguesmen who get to him first. Don't like being double-crossed, they don't,' he said, and ran his finger sharply across his exposed throat. 'If you take my meaning?'

Twig nodded, but offered no comment. It occurred to him that if Vilnix Pompolnius ever got his hands on the stormphrax in the chest, not only would his current problems be over, but his position of corrupt power would become unassailable.

They continued in silence to the top, where the gnokgoblin leaped onto the landing stage to help Twig and the Stone Pilot with their heavy cargo. 'Just follow that path to the very end, and then turn left,' he said. 'The old Raintasters' Tower is straight ahead. You can't miss it.'

'Th . . . thanks,' Twig said, and shook his head. The splendour of the city which spread out before him was overwhelming.

For a start, what the gnokgoblin had called a path was in fact a wide avenue, paved in intricate patterns with red, black and white tiles and bordered on both sides with towers that gleamed like gold in the light from the sinking sun. And what towers!

Each one was different yet equally as wonderful as its neighbour. Some had minarets, some had spires; some were domed with intricate mosaics of mirrors and semi-precious stones. Some had clock towers, others belfreys. One had large windows, paned with crystal; another had clusters of diamond-shaped openings. One was so slender it swayed in the wind; another was squat and robust.

The design of each tower, of course, depended on which faculty or school it belonged to. As did the various instruments and pieces of paraphernalia attached to the sides. There were pin-wheels and wind-socks and canti-levered scales on one; sun-dials, weather vanes, plumb lines and brass calibraters on another. While on a third, an intricate system of suspended bottles – each one a different shade of blue – tinkled in the breeze.

Twig stared round him, open-mouthed. The finery, the elegance, the perfect proportions – wherever he looked. It was too much to take in. A line of ornate pillars. An intricately carved portico. The statues, the fountains – how *did* you make water fly like that? The sweeping staircases. The curving passageways. The delicately arched bridges.

'It's incredible,' he sighed.

All round him, the gowned academics were scurrying this way and that. Over the bridges, up and down the stairs, in and out of the towers they went: some alone, some in twos, some in huddled, whispering groups – all

with their heads down, engrossed in their own concerns and as oblivious to the sumptuousness of their surroundings as they were to the presence of the youth and the hooded character who struggled slowly past them with the heavy chest.

Twig had expected Sanctaphrax to be a subdued place of learning, reserved and reverent – yet the professors and lecturers and readers were behaving anything but. Sanctaphrax was thronging. The atmosphere was charged with secretive intrigue, with furtive anticipation and, as the academics passed him by, he caught snatches of troubled conversation.

'. . . perilously near the end . . .' '. . . chains won't hold much longer.' 'Vilnix Pompolnius, he's the one to blame . . .' 'I shall put your suggestions to the Professor of Fogprobing, perhaps . . .' 'Open sky – for ever . . .' 'Something must be done . . .'

'Something *is* being done,' Twig muttered as he and the Stone Pilot finally made it to the end of the long, curving avenue. They turned left. Before them stood a dilapidated tower.

Untouched since that darkening evening when Vilnix, the then apprentice raintaster, had carried out his fateful experiment, the residence of the Professor of Darkness was all but in ruins. The right side of the tower had been blown clean away, leaving staircases exposed and chambers permanently open. What remained pointed accusingly up at the sky.

Twig and the Stone Pilot stumbled over the shattered paving-stones which led up to the door. They went inside and lugged the chest up the stairs. There was a light fanning out across the landing of the second floor. Twig walked towards it. A modest plaque nailed to the door confirmed that they had come to the right place.

Twig knocked softly.

'Oh, what is it *now*?' came a weary voice. 'I've already told you all I know.'

'Professor,' Twig called urgently.

'I am old and frail,' the voice complained. 'And so so tired. Just leave me alone.'

'Professor, we must speak,' Twig persisted and tried the door. It was not locked and, despite the professor's continued protests, he and the Stone Pilot entered. The moment she was inside, Maugin abruptly dropped her end of the chest and sat down on the lid with an exhausted grunt. Twig lowered his end, looked up at the person behind the desk – and gasped.

Apart from the fact that he was wearing black robes, rather than white, the Professor of Darkness was the Professor of Light's double.

'Who in Sky's name are you?' he demanded, and leaped to his feet. 'I thought it was the guards back again.'

Twig smiled. 'You don't seem so old and frail now, Professor.'

'Bwuh . . . bwuh . . . bwuh . . .' the professor blustered, totally at a loss for words.

Twig stepped forwards. 'I am Twig,' he said. 'This is the Stone Pilot. Together we have completed the quest upon which my father, Quintinius Verginix, was recently sent.'

The professor's jaw dropped. 'I . . . that is, you . . .' His eyes twinkled. 'You mean to tell me . . .'

'We have returned with stormphrax,' said Twig.

The professor leaped to his feet and hurried across the room towards them. 'Stormphrax!' he said. 'Are you certain?'

'Quite certain,' said Twig. 'Your colleague, the Professor of Light, confirmed it.'

'Bah, that old buffoon!' he said gruffly, but Twig noticed the wateriness in his eyes. 'What's the bally-buzzard up to, anyway?' he asked.

Twig looked down. 'I'm afraid the Professor of Light is dead,' he said gently.

'Dead!' the professor gasped.

'His dying words were that I should tell you about the stormphrax,' said Twig. 'That I can . . . trust you.'

'My old friend, dead,' the professor said sadly. He smiled weakly. 'Come, then. Let's see what you've got there.'

The Stone Pilot climbed wearily to her feet and limped to one side. Twig stepped forwards and raised the lid. The Professor of Darkness looked inside. 'Why, the old woodgoat!' he squealed with delight. 'It *is* stormphrax! This is wonderful! Quite wonderful! But how in Sky's name did you come by so much? And why are the crystals all so small?'

'It's a long story,' said Twig.

'And one I look forward to hearing,' the professor said. 'But first we must get the stormphrax to the treasury . . .'

'No, Professor,' said Twig firmly. 'First there is something else I must show you. It is time to put an end to this phraxdust madness, once and for all.' He glanced out through the window at the sun, already deep orange and low in the sky. 'But we must be quick. I'll need a mortar and pestle.'

'But . . .'

'*Now*, Professor,' Twig insisted. 'Please!'

The professor pointed him towards a marble work-surface at the far end of the chamber. 'You'll find everything you could possibly need over there,' he said. 'But . . .'

'Thank you,' said Twig.

He seized a metal beaker and hurried back to the chest. As he passed the professor, he nodded towards the window. 'How long to go until twilight?' he asked. '*True* twilight.'

'Ah, true twilight,' the professor said dreamily. 'That mystical moment between light and darkness. So fleeting. So fine . . . It was the only aspect of our studies about which the Professor of Light and myself could ever agree upon . . .'

'Professor!' Twig snapped, as he passed him on his way back. 'How long?'

The professor marched towards the window and performed a quick calculation in his head. 'One and a half minutes,' he said huffily.

'Less time than I thought,' Twig muttered. He hurried over to the bench and selected a mortar. 'Gently, gently,' he whispered to himself as he poured some crystals down into the bowl. Next, he picked the heaviest pestle from the rack, and raised it above his head. 'Professor,' he called out, 'you must tell me when that moment of true twilight occurs. Do you understand?'

The professor looked round. He saw Twig standing above the bowl of stormphrax with the pestle raised above his head.

'No,' he gasped. 'Are you mad? You'll blow us all to open sky!'

'Have faith, Professor,' Twig said. 'And keep your eyes to the sky. Remember, not a moment too soon and not a moment too late.'

The chamber throbbed with silence for what seemed

like an eternity. Twig's arm began to ache – and doubts to niggle. What if the Professor of Light had been wrong after all? The shaft of golden light pouring in through the window shifted a shade.

'Now!' the Professor of Darkness cried out, shattering the awful silence.

Twig held his breath and brought the pestle down as hard as he could into the waiting mortar. There was a thud. A crunch. A sparkling brilliance. But no more. And, as the golden light at the window turned to amber, Twig looked down at the bowlful of sepia powder sliding round like liquid.

'It worked,' he whispered. He spun round to the professor. 'It worked!'

The Professor of Darkness trotted towards him, beaming with delight. He looked down into the bowl. 'First stormphrax! Now phraxdust! Wait, I must pinch myself to check I'm not dreaming.'

'This is no dream,' said Twig. 'The stormphrax will restore equilibrium to Sanctaphrax and the phraxdust will purify the drinking water once more.' He turned and stared boldly into the professor's eyes. 'And now I know it works, there is something else to do, Professor,' he said, his voice hushed and earnest. 'I have a plan to ensure that the secret of safe phraxdust production shall never fall into the wrong hands. But I'll need to ask for your help if it is to work.'

'Ask away, Twig, my boy,' said the Professor of Darkness. 'Ask and it shall be done.'

With darkness falling, Twig and the Stone Pilot followed the professor from his chamber. Back down the spiral stairs they went, grunting and groaning as the heavy chest bumped against the walls. At the bottom, instead of going out through the door, the professor took them down a further flight of stairs, through a narrow archway and on into a tunnel. It was dark and dank there, with only the dim light from the lantern in the chest to show them which way to go.

'Daren't risk lighting the torches in case it destabilizes the stormphrax,' the professor called back.

On and on they walked. This way, that way, down stairs and ramps, gradually making their way to the very centre of the floating rock. Behind him, Twig could feel the Stone Pilot getting slower and slower. He knew that she was nearing the end of her strength.

'Is it much further to go?' asked Twig.

'We're almost there,' said the professor. 'Just round this next corner and . . .'

'HALT! WHO GOES THERE?'

The professor stopped in his tracks. Twig – who was finding it difficult to see the black robes in the dark tunnels anyway – walked slap-bang into him. Maugin grunted with alarm and dropped the chest – onto her foot – and grunted again, this time with pain. Out of the confusion came the professor's frail voice.

'Is that you, Bogwitt?' he said. 'It is I, the Professor of Darkness. I must have access to the treasury.'

'Can't,' came the surly reply from the guard.

'I . . . I . . . I beg your pardon,' the professor spluttered. 'Do you dare to deny me entrance?'

'By order of the Most High Academe.'

'What?' exclaimed the professor. 'But both you and I know that our worthy leader, Vilnix Pompolnius, would never *dream* of including me in such an order. So let me pass. At once.'

'No-one is to enter the treasury,' said Bogwitt with sudden ferocity. 'Neither leaguesman nor academic.' He lifted his lamp to the professor's face. 'And especially not you. Those was my orders from Vilnix Pompolnius himself. What's more, you're to surrender your key.'

'Surrender my key? Over my dead body!' the professor huffed.

'If that's what you want, so be it,' came the chilling response.

The lamp was placed on the ground with a clatter, and

Twig heard the *swoosh* and *thwip* of a sword and dagger being unsheathed. He peered round over the professor's shoulder at the guard blocking their view.

'A flat-head,' he muttered to himself. 'I might have known.' As he stared at the swaggering goblin – all glinting ear-rings, gold teeth and blades – fury and loathing rose up in his throat. How dare this barbaric flat-head goblin stand in their way when they had come so far and achieved so much – when they were so near to their final destination?

'My dear Bogwitt,' the professor was saying. 'This must all be some kind of a misunderstanding. If you could just let us inside the treasury for a moment. No-one would ever know and . . .'

At that moment Twig's rage exploded. He wrested his own sword from its scabbard and leaped forwards.

'Let us pass, curse you!' he roared.

For a moment, the flat-head looked surprised – but only for a moment. With a leering smile playing over his lips, he squared up and lunged abruptly forwards, his sword thrusting towards Twig's neck. Twig stepped sharply back, and parried. The two swords clashed ferociously and – stunned by the awful force of the blow – Twig reeled backwards. Bogwitt was on him in a trice, sword thrusting and dagger slashing.

Twig trembled before the onslaught of wild, thrashing blows. Panting with effort, he staggered backwards, defending himself as best he could, but weakening with every second. Suddenly, the flat-head jumped to the right and swung his heavy sword in from the left. Twig was caught unawares. He stumbled to the side and struck his elbow on the wall.

'Aaaoow,' he howled, as searing pain shot up his arm and down his spine. His sword clattered to the stone floor.

Bogwitt stepped forwards, eyes glinting. He raised his own sword. 'Silly little fool,' he hissed. 'Did you really believe that you could defeat me – personal bodyguard to Vilnix Pompolnius himself – the fiercest and most feared guard in Sanctaphrax?' He gripped the hilt of his sword till his knuckles went white. A glistening purple tongue flicked across his thin lips; his eyes gleamed. 'I shall enjoy this.'

'Stop!' Twig cried out. 'Do not strike.'

The flat-head sneered. 'So the big brave bear was a

timid wee woodmouse all the time, was it?' he said, and laughed unpleasantly.

'Hear me out,' said Twig, and reached inside his jacket.

'What treachery is this?' the flat-head roared. 'Remove your hand at once, before I pin it to your heart.'

Twig slowly pulled out his hand, bringing with it the pouch which Mother Horsefeather had given him. He jingled it lightly in his palm. 'Gold, Bogwitt,' he said. 'Ten gold pieces could be yours.'

'Of course it could,' said Bogwitt. 'Or I could slit your pretty throat and take it all.'

'You could,' said Twig, standing his ground. 'But it wouldn't do you any good.'

The flat-head hesitated for a moment. 'What do you mean?' he asked gruffly.

'He to whom you have pledged your allegiance is about to be dethroned,' he said.

'What, Vilnix Pompolnius? Don't make me laugh!' said the flat-head. 'The Most High Academe?'

'The scurrilous usurper,' the Professor of Darkness muttered under his breath.

'The leaguesmen are against him,' Twig continued. 'The academics are against him.'

'But . . . but why?' demanded the flat-head.

'Why?' the Professor of Darkness broke in. 'Because he has run out of both the phraxdust which secured his alliance with the leaguesmen and the stormphrax which holds the floating city in place.'

Bogwitt looked confused. 'But there is stormphrax in

the treasury,' he said. 'That is what Vilnix ordered me to guard.'

'Why don't you take a look then?' suggested the professor, and handed him a heavy key.

The flat-head goblin's eyes narrowed. 'If this is some kind of a trick . . . ?'

'Just look!' snapped the professor.

With his sword still raised, Bogwitt picked up his lamp and crossed over to the treasury door. There, he turned the key in the lock, twisted the handle and pushed. He stuck his head in and stared round in disbelief. Anger rose in his throat.

'Empty,' he snarled. 'The lying, cheating, no-good . . .

It's completely empty!'

'Vilnix lied to you,' the professor said simply. 'As he lies to everybody.'

'You backed the wrong side, Bogwitt,' Twig said, spelling it out for him. 'And now there can be no place for you in Sanctaphrax. However . . .'

'But I didn't know!' Bogwitt blurted out. 'I was only doing my job. I . . .'

'*However,*' Twig repeated, 'there is one possible way out of all this.' He paused. 'You are a good fighter, Bogwitt.'

'The best,' he nodded.

'And clearly loyal,' said Twig.

'I am, I am,' the flat-head agreed eagerly.

Twig nodded. 'Then this is what I propose,' he said. 'You join the crew of my sky pirate ship. But not as a slave. There will be no bondmen or galley-slaves on board the *Edgedancer*.' He glanced down at the leather pouch. 'What do you say?'

For a moment, the flat-head goblin remained silent. Then, slowly, a smile spread across his broad face. He met Twig's gaze. 'I says yes,' he replied.

Twig slowly counted out ten pieces of gold into his hand. 'But if you try to cross me, Bogwitt, it will be the worse for you,' he added threateningly. 'There are many, both in Undertown and Sanctaphrax, who would like to get their hands on Vilnix Pompolnius's former bodyguard.'

'You can rely on me, Captain Twig,' said Bogwitt.

'I believe I can,' said Twig, and he slapped the coins down into the palm of his hand. 'Welcome aboard, Bogwitt,' he said.

The professor, who had been watching the exchange

with some confusion, stepped forwards. 'Come,' he said, 'let us complete our task.'

Twig nodded. 'Bogwitt,' he said, 'will you take the other end of that chest.' The flat-head did not move. 'Bogwitt!' Twig snapped. 'I trust that this is not the first indication of a mutinous nature.'

'No, no,' said Bogwitt, and approached the chest. 'Not at all, sir, but . . .' He shuddered. 'Why does the box glow so strangely?'

'Stormphrax,' Twig answered. 'We have brought stormphrax. Equilibrium is about to be restored to the empty treasury of Sanctaphrax.'

A minute later, the treasury was no longer empty. In the middle of the circle which had been carved at the very centre of the chamber, stood the chest of stormphrax.

'But why has nothing happened?' asked Bogwitt.

'Only when it's in darkness, pure and absolute, does the stormphrax attain maximum weight,' the professor explained. He raised the lid of the chest and removed the twilight lantern. 'Come,' he said. 'It is time.'

In a line, with the professor in front and Twig bringing up the rear, the four of them made for the door. As they went, the lantern and the lamp swung, sending dark shadows swooping round the chamber and across the chest. The stormphrax grew heavy, then light again – then heavier than ever. And as *that* happened, so the floor of the treasury rocked and trembled.

'Quick!' the professor cried, and broke into a run.

The others followed, stumbling and staggering as the

floor continued to judder. When he reached the door, Twig glanced back for one last look. The chest seemed absurdly small in the centre of the enormous chamber. Could it really be enough to stabilize the mighty floating rock?

'Twig!' said the professor sharply.

Twig stepped outside, seized the heavy iron handle and slammed the door shut behind him, the sound echoing back along the dark tunnels. At the same time, the floor beneath his feet abruptly dropped away.

His stomach lurched. His heart leapt into his mouth. Terrified, he cried out.

The next instant, the movement jerked to a halt. There was silence. There was stillness. Twig turned to the Professor of Darkness.

'Is that *it*?' he said.

'That is it,' the professor confirmed. 'The perfect amount.'

Twig shook his head in disbelief.

'Trust me,' said the professor. 'Deep down here at the centre of the rock, the effect is minimal. Up on the surface, however, in the city itself, the consequences will be cataclysmic. In fact, you must believe me when I say to you that Sanctaphrax will never ever be the same again.'

·CHAPTER TWENTY-THREE·

SHOWDOWN

Vilnix Pompolnius was waking from a deep dreamless sleep when the floating rock first trembled. He opened his eyes, glanced round the luxurious Inner Sanctum and smiled a self-satisfied smile.

'How wonderful this all is,' he muttered. 'And how exquisitely clever I am to have made it mine.'

He threw back his covers, climbed out of bed and walked to the window. The sun – large and red and wobbling like an immense bowl of dellberry jelly – had just risen up above the horizon. Pink, feathery light spread across the sky. Vilnix yawned and rubbed his hand over his stubbly scalp.

'The start of yet another delightful day,' he said, and threw the window wide open.

A blast of refreshingly dewy air struck him in the face, snatching his breath away. Behind him, the glass

droplets of the crystal chandelier tinkled like wind-chimes. Vilnix leaned out and pulled the window shut again – he didn't want them to shatter. But the chandelier continued its insistent jangling music.

Vilnix frowned and looked round, puzzled. 'What in Sky's name . . .?' he muttered.

At that moment, the rock lurched and the mirror – the second mirror, the mirror which was leaning up against the wall – abruptly slid back, over the thick white carpet and down to the floor. Vilnix sighed. At least it hadn't smashed. But what had caused it to fall in the first place? The weight-fixers and chain-clampers weren't due to start work for another two hours and anyway, the floating rock was now gripped by judders and jolts far more severe than anything their drills could cause.

Horrified, Vilnix Pompolnius clung on to the window sill as the Inner Sanctum shook more violently than ever. Priceless objects were crashing to the floor all round the chamber – the porcelain vases and ivory figurines, the ornate carvings and the time-pieces, the leatherbound books.

Is it a storm? Vilnix wondered. Or an earthquake? Or has the floating rock finally become so buoyant that it is tearing away from its moorings?

At that moment, there was a loud cracking sound and the chandelier abruptly broke free from the ceiling moulding and hurtled to the floor. It landed with an almighty crash – on the mirror. Shards and splinters of crystal and glass flew all over the chamber, embedding themselves in the panelled walls.

'What is going on?' Vilnix screamed. 'Minulis! MINULIS!'

But, on this occasion, the personal manservant to the Most High Academe failed to appear.

'Minulis, where are you?' stormed Vilnix, and strode furiously towards the door of his servant's spartan antechamber. He'd show the impudent wretch that he wouldn't be kept waiting!

Vilnix hadn't got more than half-way across the glass-strewn carpet when, all at once and with no warning, the entire chamber dropped down. He stumbled and fell to the floor. Above his head, a crack opened from one side of the ceiling to the other, and a massive section of gold-embossed plaster came crashing down about him.

When the dust settled Vilnix raised his head, stood up and shook the powdery fragments from his robes. Sanctaphrax, he realized, was now steady again. Rock steady. 'And yet for a moment we were falling,' he whispered. 'Which can mean but one thing . . .' His sallow face reddened with fury. 'That odious sky pirate must have returned with the stormphrax undetected.'

His head spinning with decisions and imperatives, Vilnix pulled his gown of office over his hair-shirt, fixed the spiked steel skull-cap into place and swept from the chaos of the chamber.

'I'll show him,' he muttered furiously. 'I'll show them all! They'll see what happens to traitors who meddle in the affairs of the Most High Academe.'

It wasn't only the Inner Sanctum which suffered damage. In every corner of every room of every tower of

Sanctaphrax, the story was the same. Instruments slipped from worktops; books fell from shelves. Walls cracked, windows broke, stonework and plaster tumbled to the ground as the vibrations had grown more violent.

Shrieks of terror and howls of pain rose up above the rumbling, crashing roar, and the citizens of Sanctaphrax – young and old, venerable and lowly – spilled out from the towers and into the squares and streets. For a moment they stood there, at a loss to know what to do as minarets and castellations came crashing down around them.

'What's happening?' 'What's going on?' they screamed at one another. ''Tis the end of Sanctaphrax!' Then someone called out, 'To the Great Hall!' and, as one, they all surged along the main avenue towards the oldest and most solid building in all of Sanctaphrax, the place where they always took to in an emergency.

The crowd arrived at the hall, angry and loud. They poured inside and were outraged to discover that even this ancient place of sanctuary had not been spared the consequences of the terrible shaking that had gripped their floating city. Fallen blocks of stone littered the cracked marble floor; a pillar lay on its side while a second one looked ready to topple at any moment. And, as they watched, a jagged crack zig-zagged its way up across the back wall from the foundations to the roof.

'Not here,' they cried out. 'Not the Great Hall!'

By the time those at the back of the crowd were at last entering the building, the rock was once again still – yet no-one's rage had abated. Not a jot. From the academics, crushed together at the front of the hall, to the servants and guards, packed in around the walls, the cries were the same.

'Where's Vilnix?' they demanded. 'He's the cause of all this.' 'That sanctimonious scoundrel!' 'That accursed usurper!' 'That treacherous villain who cannot see beyond the lining of his own pockets!' 'Where *is* he?'

Then, as two figures strode out on to the podium, the questions abruptly changed. 'What's the Professor of Darkness doing up there?' 'And who is that with him?'

The professor raised his arms and appealed for quiet. 'Friends,' he cried. 'Friends.' A hush fell. 'I understand your distress. I share your pain that our beloved Sanctaphrax has been so sorely wounded. And yet,' he went on, 'there was no way that it could have been avoided.'

A growl of discontent rumbled round the room. This wasn't what they had come to hear. Twig stared at the sea of angry faces before him and trembled. If the professor wasn't careful, the crowd would rip them apart first and ask questions afterwards.

'What about my laboratory?' demanded the Professor of Windtouchers.

'And who's going to replace the windows of my observatory?' added the Professor of Cloudwatchers.

'Buildings can be repaired,' the professor continued, undaunted. 'And now there is no further need for chains, there will be hands enough to effect those repairs.'

An anxious muttering started up. 'No chains?' everyone was saying to everyone else. What madness was this? Of course they needed chains!

'No chains save the one ancient Anchor Chain which keeps us from drifting,' the professor explained.

'Clarify!' called the Professor of Cloudwatchers.

'Elucidate!' demanded the Professor of Windtouchers.

'What do you mean?' a gruff voice shouted from the back.

'I mean this,' the professor said. 'That the crisis which has been hanging over our heads for so long is, at long last, over. Sanctaphrax is once more in equilibrium.'

His words were greeted with absolute silence. Could it be true? they all wondered. Could it *really* be true?

'But what about all that jolting and juddering?' asked the Professor of Cloudwatchers.

'And the shaking and shuddering,' added the Professor of Windtouchers.

'That,' said the professor, turning to them, 'was the rock being weighed down by the cargo of stormphrax.' He looked up. 'It will not happen again for as long as any of us shall live. Of that, I give you my word.'

A murmur went round the hall; a murmur which grew louder and louder, until everyone seemed to be talking at the same time. Then a solitary cheer went up from the back. Others joined in. And the next moment, the entire hall was resounding with the exultant whoops and cries of unbounded joy.

'To the Professor of Darkness!' someone yelled.

'Yes, to the new Most High Academe of Sanctaphrax!' cried the Professor of Cloudwatchers, waving his arms in the air.

'Or should that be, to the *old* Most High Academe?' said the Professor of Windtouchers.

'Old or new, I would be honoured to resume my responsibilities as the Most High Academe,' the Professor of Darkness announced, to rapturous applause. 'And yet,' he continued, 'it is not I you have to thank for all that has taken place. I was not the one who ventured forth to the Twilight Woods and who risked all to return to Sanctaphrax with a cargo of precious stormphrax.'

'Then who? Who?' the crowd called out. Surely not the bony youth who hovered by his side.

The professor took a step towards Twig, seized him by the wrist and raised his arm high in the air. 'Professors, academics, citizens,' he announced. 'I give you Captain Twig. *He* is the person you must thank.'

Twig turned as red as a woodsap as the crowd whooped and whistled and cheered, overwhelmed by the waves of gratitude that washed over him.

'Thanks to this brave and valiant youth, we will no longer have to lie in our beds, quaking with fear that the floating-rock might break its moorings and fly up into open sky,' the professor said, raising Twig's arm still higher.

'Hooray!' cried the delighted crowd.

'Thanks to him, we have been freed from our dependence on the greedy leaguesmen for our well-being.'

'*Hooray!*' they bellowed, louder still.

'By all that is wise, he served us with heart and mind, forswearing all loyalties other than to Sanctaphrax,' the professor announced.

Twig trembled at the words. Where had he heard them before? he wondered. Why were they so familiar?

'He dedicated his life to the finding of stormphrax. He chased a Great Storm and did not return until he had completed his sacred – aye, Twig, your *sacred* – quest.' The professor smiled. 'Kneel my boy,' he said.

That was it! Twig remembered. They were the words used at his father's Inauguration Ceremony. 'But . . . I . . . you . . .' he blustered, and swallowed hard. Then, lowering his eyes to the floor, he dropped down onto his knees.

The crowd fell silent as the Professor of Darkness walked towards the back of the hall and removed the ceremonial sword from the cracked wall. Twig was trembling; he was trembling so badly he was sure everyone must be able to hear his teeth chattering. The next moment, the professor returned with the sword and stood before him. Twig looked up to see the great gold blade coming down slowly through the air as it dubbed him, first on his right shoulder, then on his left.

'I pronounce you to be an honorary Knight Academic,' the professor said. 'Arborinus Verginix be your name. Arise!'

For a moment, Twig did not move. He could not. His legs had turned to jelly. Only when the professor reached down and took his hand did Twig manage to climb shakily to his feet. A mighty, clamouring din was echoing round the Great Hall, so loud it made his head spin.

'Hooray! Hooray! Hooray!' the assembled company yelled, and they skipped and jumped and danced for joy, academics with servants, professor with professor, each putting away their grudges and grievances – at least for this one wonderful moment.

'We shall be able to engage in our lofty pursuits once more,' the Professor of Cloudwatchers exclaimed, and slapped his old rival on the back.

'We shall be able to indulge our intellect again,' the Professor of Windtouchers agreed. 'To calibrate the infinite subtleties of the wind . . .'

'And clouds,' the Professor of Cloudwatchers put in.

'From the whisper of a zephyr to the roar of a mighty hurricane . . .'

'Cirrus, stratus, cirrostratus, cumulonimbus . . .'

The Professor of Windtouchers drew breath sharply. 'If it wasn't for the wind,' he snapped, 'your clouds wouldn't even move.'

'It is only because of the clouds,' the Professor of Cloudwatchers replied hotly, 'that we see the wind blowing at all . . .'

But the Professor of Windtouchers was no longer listening to his colleague and rival. 'Look!' he gasped, and pointed to the front of the hall.

All around the Great Hall, his action was being repeated until the chamber was silent and all eyes were on the tall menacing figure who stalked across the stage and up the steps to the raised pulpit.

There he stood, stooped and angular, his hands gripping the sides of the wooden support. All round him

were his personal guards: a dozen hulking flat-heads, legs astride, arms folded. Vilnix tugged at his sleeves, readjusted his skull-cap, and slowly surveyed the gathering from under hooded eyes. His lips curled with contempt.

'What is the meaning of this?' he said, his voice soft, yet threatening. 'Can I not turn my back for a moment?'

The crowd shuffled about uneasily.

Vilnix sneered and leaned out over the pulpit. Then, with his back arched and the skull-cap gleaming, he pointed accusingly at the Professor of Darkness. 'Will you listen to the lies of this false prophet?' he roared. 'This senile old fool who brought Sanctaphrax to the very brink of ruination before, and now seems intent on finishing the job off?'

Twig shook his head. No, no, that wasn't how it was at all. Yet, with every word Vilnix spoke, the crowd was becoming more restive.

'In cahoots with renegade sky pirates he was,' Vilnix said, spitting out the words.

The murmuring in the Great Hall grew louder, more insistent as the mood turned uglier. Eyes glinting triumphantly, Vilnix returned his gaze to the crowd.

'He and those he has duped into believing in him are traitors, collaborators, knaves. Guards!' he screamed. 'Seize him – seize them both – these verminous bugs that must be crushed . . .'

Two of the flat-heads strode towards them.

'It takes one to know one,' a shrill voice called out from the back. It was followed by a ripple of nervous laughter.

Vilnix spun round and peered furiously into the shadows. His heart began to pound. 'Who said that?' he demanded. 'Come on, who was it?' A servant, dressed all in white, stepped forwards. 'Minulis!' Vilnix gasped. 'Is that you?'

'The Professor of Darkness spoke the truth,' Minulis

shouted defiantly. A muttering went round the walls of the Great Hall. 'Unlike you!'

'How *dare* you!' screeched Vilnix. 'Guards, seize him too!'

Two more of the flat-heads jumped down off the stage, and began wading through the crush of bodies. But they didn't get far. For once the academics worked as one, linking arms, pushing back – allowing Minulis to continue.

'Many's the whispered conversation I overheard. The crooked deals you struck with the Leaguesmaster. The bribery. The corruption. *You* are the traitor!' he cried boldly. 'I am only sorry that when I was shaving your scurvy head I had not courage enough to slit your scrawny throat!'

White with rage and shaking, Vilnix screamed at him to be silent. 'Will you let your Most High Academe be slandered in this way?' he demanded of the crowd.

'You are not our Most High Academe,' came a voice. It was the Professor of Windtouchers.

'Not any more,' added the Professor of Cloudwatchers.

Vilnix's jaw dropped. Could he, who prided himself on his manipulation of a situation, have gauged the mood so badly?

'Guards, guards . . .' he cried. Two of the flat-heads took a step forwards, but then stopped. The crowd jeered and booed and hissed. 'Go on, then!' Vilnix screamed. But the flat-heads were having none of it. What was more, now that the natural reticence of the academics had been broken, their taunts and accusations came thick and fast. That he had abused his power, colluded with criminals, poisoned the river, desecrated the stormphrax – that he had threatened the very existence of Sanctaphrax.

'He wants stringing up!' someone screamed.

'Hanging's too good for him!' shouted another.

Vilnix didn't wait to hear any more. As the crowd surged towards him, he suddenly spun round, hitched up his robes and sped off.

A furious cry went up. 'After him!'

Down the steps at the edge of the stage, Vilnix ran, with Twig hard on his heels. The crowd raced to meet him.

'I'll cut him off,' someone shouted.

'Oh, no you won't,' Vilnix muttered as he dodged out of the way of the reaching arms and sped to the side wall. Behind a tapestry was a door. Vilnix was through it before anyone even realized it was there.

'He's getting away!' an angry voice shouted.

Twig was first through the door after him. He looked left. He looked right – and there was Vilnix, gown still up around his waist, tearing away down the central avenue. 'Stop!' he yelled. 'Stop!'

Faster and faster Twig ran, with the furious crowd following closely behind. Up an alley, over an arched bridge, through a tunnel and on, they ran. Vilnix Pompolnius knew Sanctaphrax like the back of his hand and, time and again, Twig lost precious seconds as he took a wrong fork or ran past a turning. Yet he was gaining. Slowly, but surely, he was catching up.

'You can't get away,' he bellowed, as Vilnix abruptly jumped down off an overhead walkway, and made a dash for the edge of the rock.

'Just watch me!' Vilnix cried, and cackled with laughter.

Twig looked up to see the gnokgoblin from earlier standing next to his basket and beckoning at Vilnix. 'This way, sire,' he said. 'You'll be down in a trice, so you will.'

Twig groaned as Vilnix strode to the end of the landing stage. He *was* getting away, after all.

'Let me give you a hand,' the gnokgoblin said obligingly.

'I can manage on my own,' Vilnix said gruffly, pushing the gnokgoblin to one side. He put his hand on the wicker side and jumped into the basket.

The next instant, there was the sound of tearing. Twig saw a look of horror flash across Vilnix's face. Then he, together with the basket, disappeared and hurtled down to the ground below.

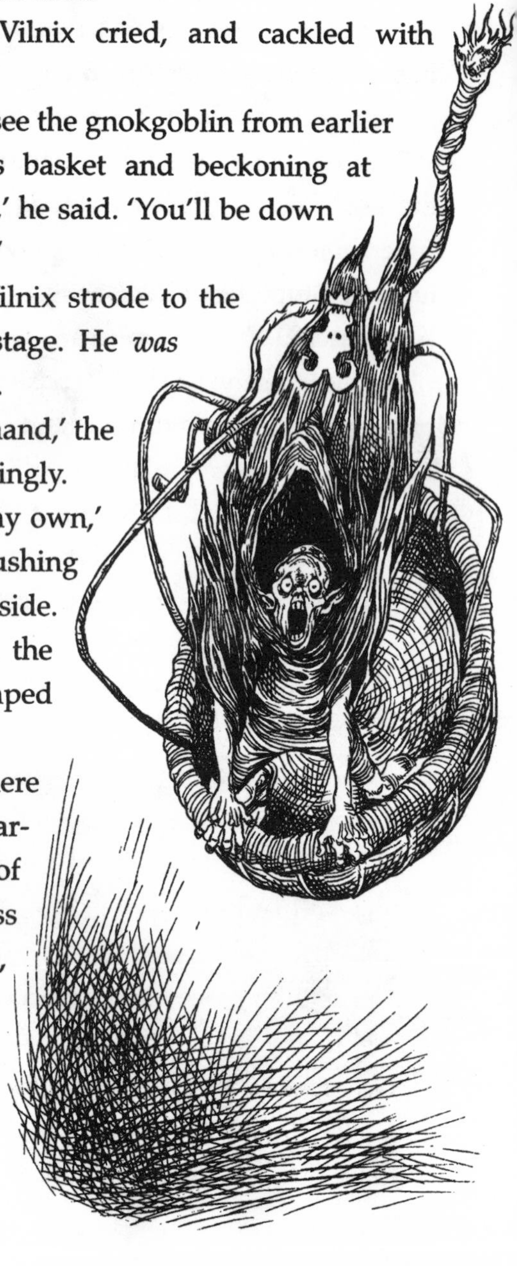

'AAAAaaarggh!' Vilnix screamed, halting everyone in their tracks. Desperate, frenzied, chilling, the cry faded – then stopped abruptly.

Far, far below on the ground, the body of Vilnix Pompolnius lay draped across a knife-grinder's wheeled stall. His arms were outstretched, his legs akimbo, the skull-cap so badly dented it would never be prised from his shattered skull. Millcrop, the knife-grinder, looked into the lifeless face of the former Most High Academe.

'Well, well,' he said. 'If it isn't old Villy. Should have stuck to knife-grinding, like me.'

Back up in Sanctaphrax, Twig reached out for the rope which had broken. Although a few of the strands were frayed, the rest had clearly been sliced through with a knife. He turned, and his gaze fell on the dagger tucked in at the gnokgoblin's belt. 'You,' he said.

The gnokgoblin shrugged. 'I told you the leaguesmen would see to him.' He jingled a pouch of coins in his hand before slipping them inside his jerkin. 'And good payers they are, too,' he smirked.

Twig climbed to his feet and walked past the gnokgoblin. 'Vilnix Pompolnius is dead,' he announced to the crowd.

A shout of joy and derision went up. 'He's gone! He's gone!' they all cried. 'And good riddance!'

Twig looked away uneasily. He was as relieved as anyone else that Vilnix Pompolnius was gone, yet the manner of his death disturbed him. It had been an underhand execution, and all the more dishonourable for that.

'*There* you are, captain,' came a voice.

It was Bogwitt. The Stone Pilot was standing beside him. Twig nodded to them. 'Come,' he said. 'Let us leave this place.'

·CHAPTER TWENTY-FOUR·

THE EDGEDANCER

In the event, their departure was delayed by the Professor of Darkness who, catching up with them at one of the alternative baskets, tried everything he could to persuade Twig to stay.

'Where will you go?' he said. 'What will you do? There could be such a fine and venerable future for you here, my boy, if only you would take it.'

But Twig shook his head. 'I can't,' he said. 'I . . . I am a sky pirate captain. Like my father, and his father before him. It's in the blood.'

The professor nodded regretfully. 'But if you ever change your mind . . .' he said, 'the title of *Professor of Light* would sit comfortably on so valiant a pair of shoulders.'

Twig smiled.

'Ah, well,' the professor sighed. 'One can but try. Now

about the matter we discussed in my study,' he said. He stepped back to reveal two bulging sacks on the ground behind him. 'I think you'll find everything in order. Envelopes. Instructions. Crystals. Just as we agreed. And I will see to it that the bell rings every evening. It's always good to have a new tradition.' He smiled. 'Officially, it shall be in honour of your return from the Twilight Woods.'

Twig reached out and shook the professor's hand warmly. 'Until the next time, Professor,' he said.

Back in Undertown once more, Twig found that they had come down within spitting distance of the Bloodoak tavern. Yet a further two days were to pass before they crossed Mother Horsefeather's threshold. It took that long to assemble a crew.

That first morning, they paid Flabsweat a visit. Unfortunately for the fat, glistening proprietor, a fresh consignment of creatures had just arrived from the Deepwoods. If Twig had been alone, he might have withdrawn his offer, but the presence of the fierce flathead and the ominous hooded creature persuaded him to honour the promise he had made.

Just as Cloud Wolf had taken on the Stone Pilot all those years ago to give her back her freedom, so Twig left with three individuals who should never have been in a pet shop in the first place.

The first was Spooler, an oakelf with wide eyes that twitched nervously. Although a fragile-looking specimen, Spooler had valuable experience of skysailing.

The second was Goom, an adolescent banderbear who still bore the wounds of the spiked pit it had been trapped in. As Twig looked the creature up and down, it leaned forwards and touched the banderbear tooth around his neck.

'Wuh?' it said questioningly.

'Wuh-wuh,' Twig explained.

'T-wuh-g?' it said.

Twig nodded. Even though the banderbear was young, it knew all about the boy in the Deepwoods who had once cured a banderbear of toothache.

And the third crew-member . . . Twig would not even have noticed the scaly creature with its reptilian tongue and fanned ears had it not spoken. 'You are looking for crew-members,' it hissed. 'How useful it would be to have someone aboard who can hear thoughts as well as words – Captain Twig.' It smiled and its fan-ears snapped shut. 'I am Woodfish.'

Twig nodded. 'Welcome aboard, Woodfish,' he said as he handed him his ten gold pieces.

Six strong, they were now. With a couple more the crew would be complete. Yet with Woodfish now amongst them, the finding of two suitable crew-mates proved difficult.

Every time Twig approached and talked to likely-looking characters in the inns and markets, Woodfish would listen in to their deepest thoughts, and was soon tutting critically and shaking his head. This one was too cowardly. This one, too careless. This one had mutiny in his heart.

It wasn't until late afternoon on the second day that they stumbled across the next crew-member in a seedy inn. At first he looked the least likely of them all, a stocky red-faced slaughterer, drunk at the bar and weeping into his woodale. But Woodfish was adamant. 'There is sorrow in his head, but his heart is good. What's more, he understands the rudiments of skysailing. Go and speak with him, captain.'

In the conversation that followed Twig discovered that the slaughterer's name was Tarp – Tarp Hammelherd – and that he had come to Undertown in search of his brother, Tendon, who had run a small lucky-charm business. That evening, not two hours since, he'd learned that Tendon was dead, blown up in some stupid accident with stormphrax – because he was thirsty.

'And it's not right,' he wailed.

Woodfish was correct. Tarp Hammelherd's heart *was* good and, having calmed him down, Twig offered him ten gold pieces and a place on the *Edgedancer*. Tarp accepted.

'Forgive me,' came a strident voice from behind them. 'But am I correct in understanding that you are looking for crew-members. If that is the case, then look no further.'

Twig turned round. The person before him was thin yet wiry, with a pinched and pointed face, a hooked nose and small, sticking-out ears. 'And you are?' he asked.

'Wingnut Sleet,' he replied. 'The finest quartermaster this side of the sky.'

Twig glanced at Woodfish, but the scaly eavesdropper merely shrugged.

'I have a head for heights, a mind for numbers and an eye for a bargain,' he announced, his restless blue eyes glinting behind steel glasses.

'I . . . I . . . Wait a moment,' said Twig, and took Woodfish aside. 'Well?' he whispered.

'I'm not sure, captain. Certainly, every word he spoke was the truth. And yet. I don't know . . . there is something. Something pent-up about him. Something that might snap at any moment – or never at all.'

Twig sighed, exasperated. 'We could go on searching like this for ever,' he complained. 'And this Sleet character sounds good. If we take him on then we've got ourselves a complete crew.' He glanced out of the window. 'We could go to Mother Horsefeather at once.' He tipped the final ten pieces of gold from the pouch and turned to Woodfish. 'I'm going to take a chance on him.'

Woodfish nodded. 'Your decision, captain,' he said. 'Your decision.'

'The *Edgedancer* is ready and awaits you somewhere safe,' Mother Horsefeather said. 'But first, the secret.'

'Ah, yes,' said Twig. 'The secret.' Mother Horsefeather drew closer as Twig pulled a crystal of stormphrax from his pocket and placed it on the table before him. 'A mortar and pestle, if you please,' he said.

'But ... but ...' Mother Horsefeather clucked anxiously. 'This is what everyone tries – and you know what happens.'

Twig drummed his fingers impatiently. Mother Horsefeather fetched the mortar and pestle.

'Thank you,' he said. 'Now, observe. I place the crystal in the bottom, so. I raise the pestle and I wait.'

Feathers rustling, Mother Horsefeather stared at the youth as he whispered strange words under his breath.

'What are you saying?' she demanded. 'Is it some kind of incantation.'

Far above them, the sonorous bell of the Great Hall tolled. Twig brought the pestle down. The stormphrax turned to phraxdust with no more than a fizz and a glimmer.

'Yes, oh, yes!' Mother Horsefeather exclaimed and wrapped her huge padded wings warmly around Twig. 'Excellent. Excellent. But what *were* the words. You must tell me.'

Twig laughed. 'I was counting off the seconds,' he explained. 'The secret is that stormphrax can only be turned safely to dust at the exact moment of true twilight. Not a moment before. Not a moment after.'

'Twilight is twilight as far as I'm concerned,' said Mother Horsefeather. 'And it lasts a whole sight longer than a moment.'

Twig smiled. 'To you and me,' he said. 'And yet to the Professor of Darkness, that fragment of time which separates light from darkness is as plain as . . . as the beak upon your face.'

Mother Horsefeather clacked with irritation. 'And how am *I* to determine that fragment of time?'

'The Professor of Darkness will sound a bell every evening at the precise moment,' he explained. 'All you have to do is be ready.'

The bird-woman's eyes narrowed. 'The Professor of Darkness?' she said, suspiciously.

'It's not what you think,' said Twig hurriedly. 'He is doing it in celebration of my return from the Twilight Woods. He . . .'

'If you have breathed a word of this to him, then our deal is off,' Mother Horsefeather snapped. Her eyes glinted. 'In fact,' she said, 'since you have already told me so much . . .'

Twig stood up abruptly from the table. 'Consider how awful it would be if, one day, the bell rang either a moment too early or a moment too late,' he said coldly. 'I have kept my side of the bargain, Mother Horsefeather. My crew are waiting outside. Now I want my gold and my sky ship.'

Mother Horsefeather pulled a key from her apron and tossed it down on the table. 'The boom-docks,' she said. 'Wharf 3. The gold is on board.'

'Are you sure?' said Twig. 'Remember the bell.'

Mother Horsefeather clucked miserably. 'It will be by the time you get there,' she said.

The new crew fell in love with the *Edgedancer* the moment they clapped eyes on it.

'She's a beauty,' Tarp Hammelherd gasped, 'and no mistake.'

'A diamond,' murmured Sleet.

Twig beamed proudly as he stared up at the broad, white sails and criss-cross of spotless rigging. Together, they pulled the sky ship down the ramp-rollers, out of the ramshackle building and into the night. A full moon gleamed down on the polished masts and hull, on the silver lamps, on the burnished instruments and bone-handled levers.

'All aboard,' cried Twig, as he had heard his father cry so many times before. 'Take to your posts.'

The sky pirates leaped to obey. Twig went to the bridge, gripped the helm and waited for the Stone Pilot to signal that the flight-rock was ready.

The signal came.

'Unhitch the tolley-ropes,' Twig shouted. 'Raise the mainsail. Steady on the boom.' The *Edgedancer* began to rise. Gently, Twig realigned the stern- and prow-weights. The bow rose and the sky ship soared up into the air.

Twig laughed for joy. The sky ship handled like a dream. Unlike the *Windcutter*. He lowered the port hull-weights and adjusted the mainsail a fraction. And yet, he thought as the sky ship glided obediently round to the left, had it not been for that perilous journey across the Mire and over the Edge in the crumbling sky ship, he would never have learnt to master the controls. Now, with the experience of the *Windcutter* behind him, flying the *Edgedancer* was a piece of pie.

As they swooped down low over the Bloodoak tavern, Twig saw Mother Horsefeather peering up at him from the doorway. 'Tarp,' he called. 'Spooler. Start emptying the sacks.'

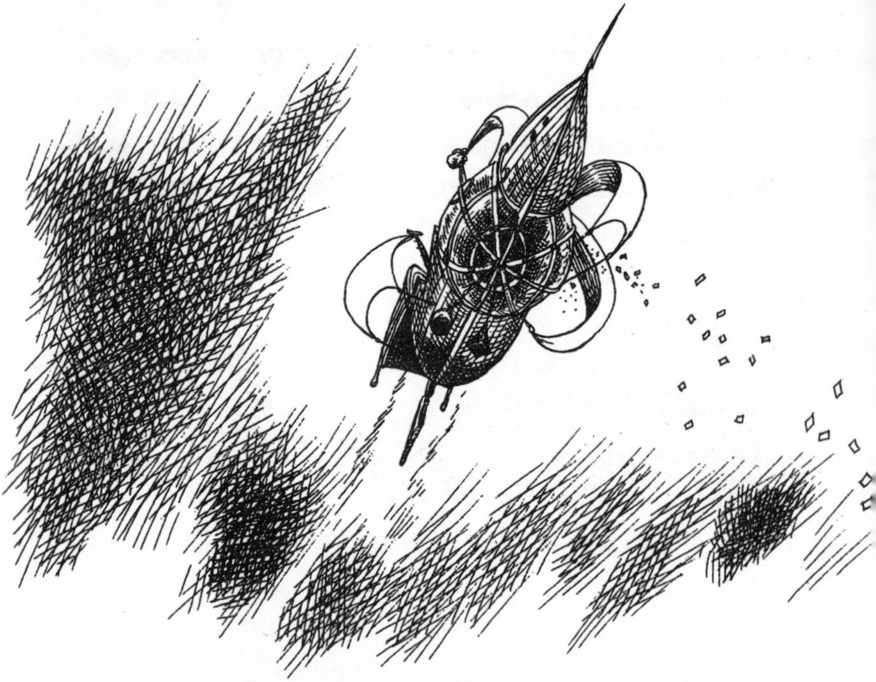

'Aye aye, captain!' they called back and, leaning over the back of the aft-deck, began throwing handful after handful of the envelopes to the air, where they fluttered, flapped and floated down to Undertown below. The sky pirates watched as the Undertowners ran this way and that in the oily, yellow lamplight, seizing up the curious folds of paper which had appeared as if from nowhere.

'Begging your pardon, captain,' said Tarp, as they circled the town for a second time. 'But what exactly are we doing?'

Twig grinned as the Bloodoak tavern came back into view. 'We are ending a monopoly.'

'Captain?'

'Each envelope contains a crystal of stormphrax and instructions for the safe production of phraxdust. It was the only way I could make sure that *everyone* would have access to pure, clean water once again.'

'Oh, I like that, captain,' Tarp cried. 'I like that a lot. That's fair, that is. My brother, Tendon, would most definitely have approved.'

'Which is more than can be said for Mother Horsefeather,' Sleet observed. 'She looks fit to explode.'

Twig laughed and replied to her clenched and shaking fists with a wave. 'It was high time for that avaricious bird-woman to get her come-uppance,' he said. 'She's ruled the Undertown roost for far too long.' He glanced round. 'How are those sacks coming along?'

'Nearly done, captain,' came the reply.

Twig smiled. He too was nearly done. With the stormphrax in place, the chain-building would cease, the pollution would stop and the Edgewater River would, once again, run clean enough to drink. The vicious circle gripping Sanctaphrax and Undertown was almost at an end.

As the last envelopes fluttered down, Twig turned the helm to port. It was time to sail away from Sanctaphrax, from Undertown. He raised the sails and lowered the stern-weights. The *Edgedancer* leapt forwards. And, with the wind gathering strength and singing in the rigging, Twig closed his eyes and threw back his head, giddy with elation.

He had done it! He had achieved what his father, Quintinius Verginix, had set out to do all those years earlier. Perhaps that was the way it was always meant to be . . . Who could tell?

Whatever, Twig had chased a Great Storm to the Twilight Woods in search of stormphrax and, although he had ultimately come by the sacred substance in a different place, come by it he certainly had. Having departed as a stowaway, he had returned as a captain – victorious and triumphant. A hero.

The wind caressed his face and tousled his hair. Could there be anything more exhilarating than soaring across the endless expanse of blue? A broad grin spread across his face. No, nothing, he realized. Nothing in the world. After all, he had been born to it.

And at that moment Twig felt himself to be the most fortunate person who had ever lived.

'Skysailing in my own sky ship,' he murmured, his chest bursting with pride. 'The *Edgedancer*.'

All at once, the air around him became loud with a great wheezing and flapping of wings. He heard the sky pirates cry out in fear and alarm. Twig opened his eyes.

'You!' he exclaimed.

'Indeed,' the caterbird replied, as it shifted round on the balustrade and thrust its beak forwards.

'Are you all right, captain?' came a voice. It was Tarp Hammelherd. 'Or should I sink an arrow in the creature's scraggy neck now.'

Twig spun round to see Tarp's crossbow lowered and pulled. 'Avast!' he screamed. 'All weapons down.'

The caterbird's eyes swivelled round. 'A fine welcome, Master Twig,' it sniffed. 'Yet perhaps it is in order, for I bring bad news.'

'News? What news?' Twig asked uneasily.

'It is Cloud Wolf,' it said. 'Your father is in grave danger.'

'Danger?' said Twig anxiously.

'The Great Storm never released him from its terrible grip,' the caterbird explained. 'When I last saw him, he was being carried off. I followed as far as I dared . . .'

'Where to?' said Twig.

'Far from here. Too far.'

'Not . . .'

The caterbird nodded. 'Over the Edge, Twig. Farther than anyone has ever been before, deep deep into uncharted sky.'

Twig stared ahead, heart thumping wildly. His father, out there, lost in the monstrous, misty wasteland beyond the Edge – it was too appalling even to consider.

'I must try to rescue him,' he said resolutely.

'It will be a perilous undertaking, Master Twig . . .' the caterbird began.

'*Captain* Twig,' Twig interrupted stiffly. 'And there are no perils great enough to keep me away. The *Edgedancer* is ready. The crew are ready. And so am I.'

'Then we will set forth at once,' said the caterbird.

Twig started with surprise. 'We?' he said. 'Do you intend to travel with us?'

'You were at my hatching,' the caterbird reminded him. 'I am bound to watch over you – always.' It sighed. 'Sometimes I wish it were not so . . . But enough of all this. We must make haste. Find a rope. Tether one end to the bowsprit, the other round my belly. I will track your father across open sky.' It paused and shuddered. 'It will mean flying further than even I have been before – but I will lead you to him. Sky willing we will not be too late.'

'Sky willing,' Twig repeated softly. Then, without another word, he lowered the starboard hull-weights and shifted the rudder-wheel.

'All set,' cried the caterbird. It leapt up from the balustrade and flapped off ahead. As the tether grew tighter Twig pulled down hard on the helm. The *Edgedancer* leapt forwards.

With the caterbird in front, the sky ship sailed closer and closer to the Edge. Below it, the water of the Edgewater River fell abruptly away and cascaded down for ever through dark sky. The wind blew, the sails billowed and the *Edgedancer* soared out – *over* the Edge and beyond.

'Sky protect us,' Twig whispered. 'Sky protect us all!'

MIDNIGHT OVER SANCTAPHRAX

·CHAPTER ONE·

OPEN SKY

Out in the vast cloudscape, a lone sky ship in full sail cut through the thin air. Ahead, at the end of a rope-tether, a gigantic bird flapped its mighty black and white wings as it led the ship ever further into that place of terror for all the creatures from the Edge – open sky.

'Weather vortex straight ahead,' the small oakelf shouted from the caternest at the top of the main-mast. His voice was shrill with fear. 'And it's a monster!'

Down at the helm of the *Edgedancer*, a young sky pirate captain in a hammelhornskin waistcoat raised his telescope to his eye with shaking hands. As he focused in on the dark, swirling air, his heart missed a beat. The approaching vortex was indeed monstrous. It was as if the great milky clouds were curdling and falling in on themselves, swirling into a great blood-red throat at the centre of which was an inky blackness that threatened to swallow the tiny sky ship whole.

'I see it, Spooler,' the young captain called to the oakelf. 'It's coming in at a rate of about a hundred strides per second, Captain Twig, sir,' Spooler shouted, panic plain in his voice. 'We've precious little time till impact.'

Twig nodded grimly. Already the currents of air around them were beginning to spin unpredictably. They were passing in and out of great banks of cloud; plummeting as they went in, soaring up again as they emerged on the other side. With the binding tether taut, the caterbird continued its steady, relentless flight.

'Surely this is madness!' complained the wiry weasel-faced quartermaster in the gaudy brocaded coat. He pulled the large tricorn hat from his head and wiped his sweaty brow. 'It's heading straight for the vortex.'

'We must follow where the caterbird leads, Sleet,' Twig shouted back.

'B . . . but . . .' stuttered Wingnut Sleet, his voice a thin whine.

'Sleet!' Twig called back. 'We are all in this together. Just make sure those tolley-ropes are securely cleated.'

Muttering under his breath, the quartermaster went to do the young captain's bidding. On the lower deck, he found a heavy flat-head goblin clinging to the rigging, its eyes white with fear.

'Nothing to worry about, Bogwitt,' Sleet said through gritted teeth. 'If our young captain really does believe that that great scraggy bird can lead us to his long-lost father rather than to certain death in the heart of the vortex, then who are we to argue?'

'Who indeed!' shouted a stocky figure with the telltale flame-red skin and hair of a Deepwoods slaughterer. 'You signed on with Captain Twig, just like the rest of us. And I reckon, just like the rest of us, you saw something special in him – like he saw something special in each of us. We're the chosen few, we are, and we'll see this through to the end.'

'Yes, well,' replied Sleet uncertainly. 'The end seems rather closer than I'd expected.'

'Vortex, a hundred thousand strides and closing,' came the nerve-racked voice of Spooler from the caternest.

'It's all right to be afraid, Sleet,' murmured a soft, hissing voice from the shadows behind them.

Sleet dropped the tolley-rope and turned. 'Reading my thoughts again, were you, Woodfish?' he said.

Woodfish recoiled. He was a slight, reptilian individual with webbed hands and feet and enormous fanned ears which were constantly aquiver.

'I can't help it,' he apologized. 'It's what we waterwaifs do. And I can tell you this, too. The young captain knows this caterbird well. He was there at its hatching, and for that the creature is bound to watch over him as long as they both shall live. It was the caterbird who discovered Twig's father marooned in a wreck of a ship in open sky. It enlisted Captain Twig's help, and he enlisted ours. We are behind him all the way. Besides,' he added, 'the caterbird knows what it's doing – even though its thoughts *are* a bit tricky to read.'

'Oh, well, that makes me feel *much* better,' Wingnut Sleet replied sarcastically.

'I know,' said Woodfish quietly. 'I can read *your* thoughts quite clearly.'

Sleet's smile froze, and his sallow cheeks reddened.

'The tolley-ropes, Sleet!' shouted Twig.

The young captain stared ahead into the great open void. The *Stormchaser*, his father's sky pirate ship was out there somewhere, deeper in open sky than any sky ship had ever sailed before, and he would find it, whatever it took.

They had already travelled for twenty days and twenty nights, with the caterbird out ahead, leading them on unfalteringly into the treacherous void. Now, as the pink light from the rising sun spread out across the sky on that twenty-first morning, the seemingly tireless creature was taking them still further. And all the while, the winds were becoming more and more unpredictable as the dominant south-westerlies collided with the tunnel of air coming in from the east.

'Take the helm, Goom,' Twig said to the great shaggy mountain of hair and tusks standing behind him. Every sky pirate captain needed a faithful lieutenant, and Goom the banderbear was Twig's. 'Hold a steady course. We've got to keep on after the caterbird.'

Goom grunted, his feathery ears fluttering.

Twig turned his attention to the two rows of bone-handled levers that controlled the sky ship. With dextrous expertise, his hands played over them – raising the stern-weight and lowering the prow-weight; lowering the starboard hull-weights, small, medium and large, as far as they would go, while raising their counterparts on the port side completely.

The sky ship dipped and listed sharply to starboard as Twig attempted to follow the caterbird's erratic path. Cries

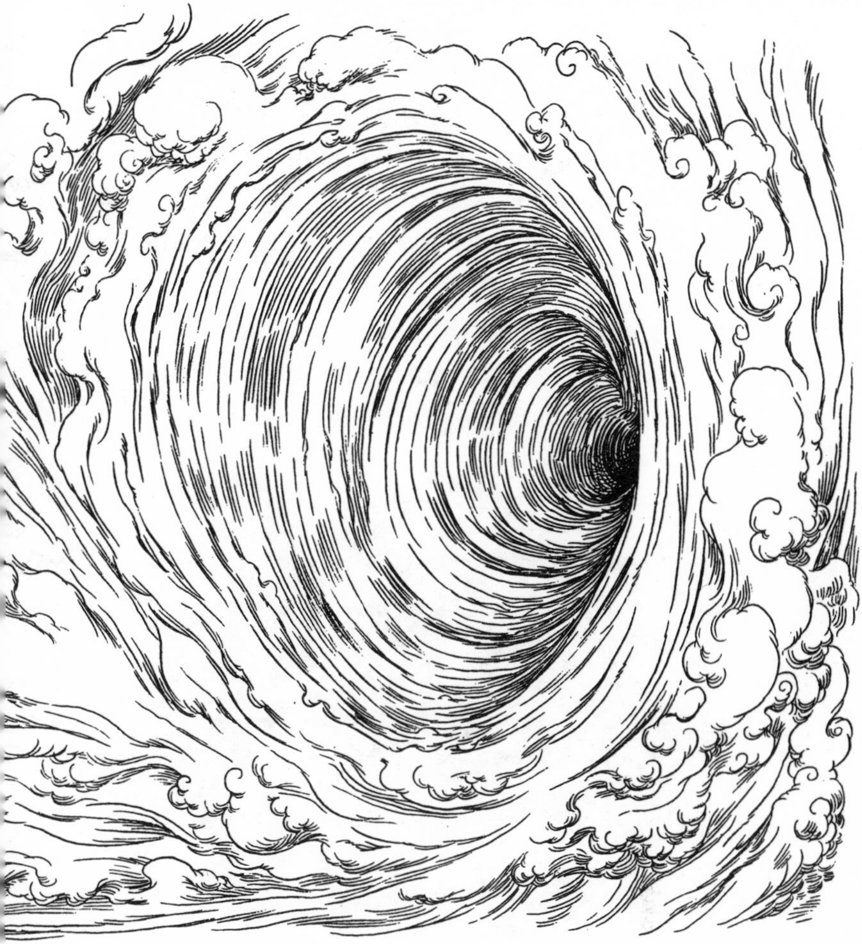

of alarm went up from the lower decks. Twig gritted his teeth and concentrated. Flying a sky ship was a difficult skill at the best of times, but with a vortex looming in from open sky, Twig was being tested to the limit.

With one hand, he positioned the neben- and klute-hull-weights. With the other, he adjusted the angles of the sails – tilting the staysail, slackening off the mainsail, bringing the jib gently round . . . Easy does it . . .

'Angle, speed and balance,' Twig muttered to himself.

They were the three fundamentals of skysailing. Yet as the wind became more turbulent with every passing minute, it was difficult to maintain any of them.

'Harder to starboard, Goom!' Twig bellowed, as he realigned the hull-weights. 'We've got to maintain the angle of . . .'

All at once a fearsome juddering went through the sky ship. The hull creaked, the masts trembled. Abruptly it flipped up and listed to the other side.

'Tether down!' Twig bellowed at his crew. At any moment, the *Edgedancer* could turn turvey – and, with no land below them, anyone who fell would fall for ever.

Spooler, the oakelf, disappeared into the caternest. Wingnut Sleet grabbed a tolley-rope and lashed himself to the fore-mast. Tarp Hammelherd the slaughterer and Woodfish the waterwaif clung to the bowsprit, while Bogwitt the flat-head goblin simply threw back his head and howled.

At the centre of the ship, on a platform above the flight-rock, a figure in a great pointed hood and coat stood, calm and still and silent. This was the last member of Twig's crew – the Stone Pilot.

The wind buffeted the sky ship violently: now on the port bow, now on the starboard. Twig raised the prow-weight completely and held his breath.

For a moment, the *Edgedancer* juddered more violently than ever. But it remained upright. Heartened by this, Twig made fine adjustments to the mainsail and jib. The sky ship listed slightly to port and leapt forwards. The tether slackened off. In the distance, the caterbird flapped towards the great gaping chasm of the vortex.

'Seventy-five thousand strides and closing,' Spooler shouted out.

'Stay tethered!' Twig cautioned his crew loudly. 'I don't want to lose anybody overboard.'

'Anybody?' Sleet mumbled. 'More like *everybody*! We're all doomed if we pursue this foolish course.'

Tarp Hammelherd glared round at him. 'Sleet!' he warned.

Sleet stared back at him defiantly. 'Someone's got to tell him,' he said. 'He's going to get us all killed.'

'The captain knows what he's doing,' said Tarp.

'Besides, we've come too far to turn back now.'

Hearing the developing dispute, Twig looked round. He saw his crew, each one now tethered securely to the tolley-ropes. The fear in their eyes was unmistakable. His gaze fell on Tarp.

'What's going on down there?' he said.

'Nothing, cap'n,' said Tarp, with a shake of his shaggy red head. 'Just Sleet here got a touch of the jitters.'

Wingnut Sleet turned and looked up. 'So far as I'm aware,' he said, 'no captain has ever steered his sky ship into a weather vortex and lived to tell the tale.'

The others listened but remained silent. They were all too loyal – and grateful – to the captain to question his commands, yet their fear of the approaching weather storm kept them from leaping to his defence. Twig looked at them sadly.

How different the scene before him was now compared with the night the *Edgedancer* had set off on its long journey. Then, under a bright full moon, the entire crew had sat down together on the lower deck to a hearty supper of roast snowbird, wood pumpkin and blackbread. Their spirits were high, the woodale loosened their tongues, and they regaled one another with stories of their lives before Twig had signed them up to sail with him.

For the crew of the *Edgedancer*, this was their first voyage together. There was Spooler the oakelf – small, wary, but with vision so sharp he could spot a white raven in the mire at a thousand strides.

Goom, the young banderbear, was already a giant, his tusks newly grown; a single blow from one of his massive paws could kill a hammelhorn. And then Woodfish, the reptilian creature from the black depths of the Deepwoods whose fan-like ears heard everything, spoken or unspoken. Twig had rescued all three from the clutches of Flabsweat, an unsavoury retailer in exotic pets, and earned their lifelong gratitude in the process.

Tarp Hammelherd, the slaughterer, was a Deepwoods dweller who had been lost to the taverns of Undertown.

Bogwitt, a flat-head goblin and fierce warrior, had once been a Sanctaphrax guard. Both had been treated harshly by capricious fate; both had been offered succour and a second chance on board the *Edgedancer*. Neither would ever forget the young captain's kindness.

And then there was Wingnut Sleet – who owed nothing to him – a clever, yet sly, quartermaster on whom Twig had taken a chance. Only the silent Stone Pilot had been known to Twig – and had sailed with him before.

'To our first adventure together!' Tarp had said, and raised his glass. 'And may the caterbird guide us quickly to the cap'n's father, and bring us all safely back to the Edge.'

A ripple of assent had greeted his words.

'To our first adventure,' the sky pirates had cried.

Now, three weeks later, that adventure was reaching its climax.

'Vortex, fifty thousand strides,' Spooler shouted above the roar of the approaching vortex.

'Listen up, all of you,' Twig called loudly. He turned to the banderbear at the helm, still holding a steady course despite the treacherous battering from the wind. 'You too, Goom,' he said. 'Can you all hear me?'

'Yes,' came the chorus of voices and the crew, as one, turned to look up at their captain.

All round them, the clouds writhed and squirmed, yellow and grey, with flashes of electric blue. The wind gusted treacherously as the weather vortex – with the gaping opening to the spinning tunnel face-on – drew closer. Twig looked up nervously, his hammelhornskin waistcoat bristling. The caterbird was still heading straight for it.

'I did not force any of you to come,' said Twig. 'Yet come, you did. And I am grateful for that – more grateful than you could imagine.'

Woodfish nodded his head knowingly.

'I thought I had lost my father for ever. Now I have been given a chance to find him. I shall never forget that it is you who have made this possible.'

'I would follow you to the end of open sky, cap'n!' Tarp Hammelherd shouted back.

'Wuh-wuh!' Goom agreed.

Wingnut Sleet lowered his head and shuffled around awkwardly.

'We have already come a long way together,' Twig continued. 'Now we are about to be tested to the limit. Sky willing, we will find Cloud Wolf and return to the Edge,' he said. 'But if . . .' He paused. 'If we fail, then I swear that so long as you are members of my crew, come what may, I will never abandon you. Never! As captain of the *Edgedancer*, I give you my word.'

Tarp Hammelherd looked up. 'I can't speak for the others,' he said, 'but I'm with you, cap'n, all the way.'

'Me, too,' said Woodfish.

A rumble of agreement echoed round the deck. Even Wingnut Sleet nodded.

'Though I still don't see why we have to make things so difficult for ourselves by sailing straight into the mouth of a weather vortex,' he grumbled.

'Have faith in the caterbird,' Twig replied. 'It knows what it's doing . . .'

'Vortex at twenty-five thousand strides,' cried Spooler. 'Approximately four minutes to impact.'

The *Edgedancer* flew into a bank of grey, sticky cloud. The gale-force gusts of wind tipped it this way, that way. While Goom gripped the helm, Twig ran his fingers over the bone-handled levers in a frantic effort to keep the sky ship steady. All round them, blue lightning forked and flashed. The cloud was so dense that the sky pirates could barely see their hands before their faces.

'Angle, speed and balance,' Twig muttered. For once the words offered no comfort. With the thick air in his eyes, his nose, his mouth, he felt his nerve beginning to go.

At that moment, the *Edgedancer* burst through the bank of cloud. To a crew-member, the sky pirates started back in horror. Twig gasped. Even the caterbird seemed surprised by the sight which confronted them. The swirling entrance to the vortex was suddenly there, directly in front of them. Its great blood-red mouth gaped so vast, it took up most of the sky.

'V . . . v . . . vortex, ten thousand strides and c . . . closing,' Spooler stammered.

'A little higher, Twig,' the caterbird's voice floated back to them as it soared upwards, pulling the tether taut once again. 'We must enter the vortex at the still point in the very centre of the spinning tunnel of air.'

Without giving the command a second thought, Twig's hands danced over the levers once more, raising the prow-weight, lowering the stern-weight and realigning the stud and staysails.

'That's it,' the caterbird shouted back. 'Now hold this course. So long as we remain at the centre of the weather vortex, we stand a chance.'

An icy shiver of unease ran the length of Twig's spine. The swirling vortex roared closer.

'Five thousand strides,' Spooler cried.

Hurricane-force winds battered the *Edgedancer* with immense power, threatening at any moment to send the sky ship into a fatal spin. The charged air smelt of sulphur and toasted almonds; it made the hair of the sky pirates stand on end.

'A thousand strides!'

The ship trembled and creaked. The crew grabbed onto anything they could. They held on desperately.

All at once, the frayed edge of the spinning vortex was swirling round the sky ship. It was like staring down a monstrous throat. There was no turning back now.

'Five hundred strides!' cried the oakelf. 'Four. Three. Two. One . . .'

'Brace yourselves!' Twig cried. 'We are entering the weather vortex . . . *now!*'

·CHAPTER TWO·

THE WEATHER VORTEX

It was a world of red they were plunged into. There was a blast of furnace-hot air, and a terrible screaming which filled Twig's ears. His stomach knotted, his breath came in gasps and, when he managed to half-open an eye, the wind caused scalding tears to course down his cheeks.

'Sky above!' he exclaimed.

They were inside the raging red gullet of the monstrous weather vortex. All round them, the swirling currents wailed and screeched. Yet here, at the central still point, there was a clammy, eerie calm.

'Heavy on the mainsail, Tarp,' Twig bellowed above the roaring air. 'And double-check that the tolley-ropes are secure.'

'Aye aye, cap'n,' he shouted back.

The weather vortex was vast beyond imagination. It was as if the sky itself had turned into a great voracious beast. And the *Edgedancer* was inside it: swallowed up, consumed.

'Hold fast!' Twig roared. 'Goom, chain yourself to the helm and keep us steady.'

The banderbear leapt to obey. Twig concentrated on the sail and hull-weight levers. With the wind spinning faster and faster – an angry red wall that surrounded them, constantly threatening to draw the sky ship off course and into its terrible turmoil – it was vital to maintain balance as they were sucked in deeper and deeper.

'What now?' Twig called out to the caterbird.

'There is no going back,' the bird boomed. 'We are entering the turbulent heart of the Mother Storm, the birthplace of tempests and tornadoes – a place of terrible madness. Yet at its very centre, there is ultimate calm and . . .'

'And?' Twig called back. The air had turned icy blue, and tiny vicious hailstones stung his face.

'And,' boomed the caterbird, half lost in a bank of swirling fog far ahead, 'it is there we shall find your father – if any of us survive.'

All of a sudden, Twig was gripped by a feeling of intense sadness. He fell to his knees, great sobs racking his body. Woodfish screamed with high, piercing sorrow. Sleet lay curled in a ball at the feet of a weeping Bogwitt. The tiny hailstones beat out a terrible rhythm on the decks.

What was happening? Twig wondered. What was this all-consuming sorrow? He hauled himself to his feet. It was almost too much to bear.

Tarp Hammelherd knelt on the ground, his head hung low, and bellowed like a wounded tilder. 'Why?' he howled, and his body convulsed with grief. 'Why did you have to die?'

Spooler swung down the mast and crouched down beside him. 'Tarp, my friend!' he implored.

But Tarp couldn't hear him. And when he looked up, his unseeing eyes stared past the oakelf.

'Oh, Tendon. My brother!' he cried. 'My poor, poor brother . . .' He collapsed on the deck, shielding his head from the hailstones.

Twig gripped the helm. Behind him, Goom the banderbear's loud howls drowned out all other sounds. Then the swirling green fog broke silently over the bow. Thick and evil, it coiled round the deck, cloaking the crew from sight. With the abrupt change in the weather, the sobs of the crew turned to howls of fear.

Twig shuddered as the green fog hit him. It pierced his skin, chilling him to the very marrow in his bones. Blind panic gripped him.

'We're doomed!' he screamed. 'We'll never escape. We're all going to die here in this terrible place. We . . .'

'After sorrow, fear,' the voice of the caterbird floated back. 'This too will pass. Be brave, Captain Twig.'

Twig shook his head. The fog thinned and the terror began to release its hold. A light drizzle was now falling, the raindrops glittering and shimmering like tiny jewels. Wingnut Sleet threw back his head and roared with laughter. Twig drank in the rain. His head swam. It was all so wonderful, so beautiful, so unutterably . . .

'*Aaaaargh!*' screamed Sleet.

Below him, Twig could see the quartermaster staggering back from the balustrade, clawing desperately at his face. Encasing his head and shoulders was a ball of lightning, with worm-like tendrils of light squirming over his terrified features. Woodfish screamed and dived for cover as more sparking twists of lightning crackled across the deck.

'Get down!' yelled Twig, all feelings of elation abruptly gone.

Wingnut Sleet, seemingly lifeless, was slumped on the deck next to the body of Tarp Hammelherd.

'Save us! Save us!' screamed Woodfish, his voice high and sibilant.

'We must go on!' Twig shouted back.

And then the red mist descended.

Thick, penetrating and acrid with the stench of wood-smoke, the mist blurred Twig's vision. He found himself consumed with rage. His eyes blazed. His nostrils flared. His teeth ground together.

'No going back!' he roared, pounding at the helm.

The *Edgedancer* bucked and juddered alarmingly. Twig hit out at the bone-handled levers, scattering them this way and that. The sky ship seemed to gasp as its weights and levers pulled in opposite directions. Beside him, even Goom was unable to resist the effects of the red mist.

'Wuh!' he bellowed as, gripped by a frenzy of rage, he tore at the balustrades and punched holes in the sides of the sky ship. 'WUUUUH!'

Twig's inner fury intensified. It was all the caterbird's fault, this turmoil, this madness: the fact that they had set off into open sky in the first place.

'Curse you!' he bellowed. 'May you rot in open sky!'

Behind him, the banderbear roared fiercely as he ripped at the doorways and battened-down hatches and tossed each wrenched-off piece of splintered wood over the side. Creaking and cracking, the *Edgedancer* was now out of control. At any minute the swirling vortex would tear it to pieces.

Twig raced down to the main deck and over to the bowsprit. The red mist filled his mouth, stained his eyes and filled his muscles with a wild and unfamiliar strength. The madness grew; his senses closed in. He became blind to what his eyes were trying to show him, deaf to what his ears could hear. With his sword in his hand, he was cutting, hacking, stabbing and all the while, the terrible roars of the banderbear screamed in his head.

Then everything went black.

Twig opened his eyes to find a milky whiteness all around him. The *Edgedancer* hung in space at a crazy angle, perfectly still.

'We made it,' he said quietly to himself. He looked about in astonishment. Everything suddenly seemed clearer and sharper than ever before.

Tarp Hammelherd lay in a heap, still softly sobbing. Wingnut Sleet, hands clasped to his face, didn't move. Bogwitt was unconscious, a section of mast pinning his right leg to the deck. Beside him, and utterly exhausted, the banderbear's great hairy form lay in the wreckage of mast and rigging, heavy rasping breaths showing that he lived still. One great paw rested against Spooler the oakelf. His whimpers revealed that he, too, was clinging to life. Woodfish sat in the bows, shaking his head from side to side.

'I can't hear a thing,' he repeated monotonously.

The Stone Pilot appeared at the top of the bridge staircase.

Twig smiled weakly. 'Look,' he said. 'I'm fine. Are *you* all right?'

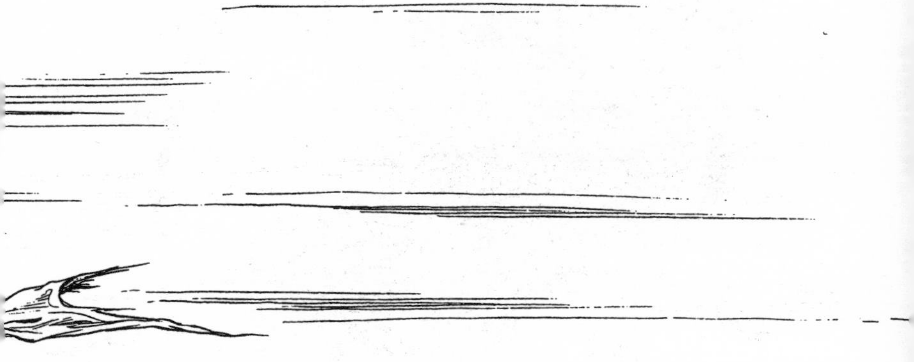

From deep inside the hood came a muffled voice. 'Oh, captain,' it said softly.

'What?' said Twig. 'I . . .' He followed the line of the Stone Pilot's pointing finger. It led to his own hands. He looked down, to see a piece of limp rope in one hand, his sword in the other. 'What have I done?' he murmured.

Slowly, fearfully, he pulled the rope-tether towards him. It offered no resistance. All at once, the end flicked over the balustrade and landed on the deck at his feet. It had been severed neatly.

'Caterbird!' Twig screamed. 'Caterbird, where are you?'

There was no reply. The caterbird – his guide and protector – was gone. Horrified, Twig turned to the Stone Pilot.

'What has happened?' he whispered.

'I . . . I tried to stop you,' the Stone Pilot said. 'But you were too strong for me. Swearing and cursing, you were. You seized the rope and tugged it towards you. The caterbird cried out as its wings clipped the bowsprit. Then you raised your sword and thrust forwards . . .'

Twig gasped. 'Did I kill it?' he asked.

'I don't know,' the Stone Pilot replied. 'The last thing I remember is Goom knocking me to the floor.'

'My crew, my crew,' said Twig, shaking his head. 'What is to become of them now?'

The great heavy hood of the Stone Pilot turned from side to side. Out of the corner of his eye, Twig saw something black and white sliding across the sloping deck. He looked round, just in time to see one of the caterbird's tail feathers sliding under the balustrade and slipping over the jutting ledge. As it fluttered away into the glistening void, Twig shuddered at the enormity of what he had done. The great caterbird, who had watched over him since its hatching, was gone, perhaps dead – and by his own hand. Twig was on his own now.

'What do I do?' he said miserably. He pulled out his telescope and looked all round him. The milky whiteness now glittered with all the colours of the rainbow: intoxicating, mesmerizing – red and orange and yellow and . . .

The Stone Pilot seized him by the elbow and cried out urgently. 'Look there!'

Twig pulled the telescope from his eye and squinted into the white light. 'What? I . . .' And then he saw it. There, looming from the mist, was a shadowy shape suspended in mid-air. It was almost upended; its mast was broken, the sails hanging limply like broken woodfly wings. Twig's skin tingled; his heart thumped.

'Oh, caterbird,' he murmured. 'You did not fail me, after all. You led me to the *Stormchaser*.'

With his heart in his mouth, Twig leaned over the balustrade. He cupped his hands to his mouth.

'Father!' he bellowed. 'Father, if you're there, answer me!'

But no sound came from the floating shipwreck save the creaking of its cracked hull and the *tap-tap-tap* of a loose tolley-rope knocking against the broken mast. The *Edgedancer* drifted closer to the wreck of the once-proud *Stormchaser*. Twig peered at the sky ship. It shimmered with a brilliance that hurt his eyes.

'I must know if my father is on board,' he said.

He seized one of the fore-deck grappling-hooks, swung the rope round his head and launched the heavy hook down through the air at the other sky ship. It seemed almost to pass through the *Stormchaser* until, with a shudder and the sound of splintering wood, it struck something solid – and held. The Stone Pilot secured the end of the rope to the bowsprit. Twig climbed up, placed a length of broken wood over the rope, and clutched it with both hands.

'Wish me good fortune,' said Twig, and with that he was gone – sliding off down the rope before the Stone Pilot could answer.

The descent was steep and fast, and Twig's arms felt as if they were being wrenched out of their sockets. Below him the gaping void blurred past as he gathered speed and – *crash* – thumped down onto the deck of the *Stormchaser*.

For a moment Twig remained still, scarcely believing he had made it in one piece. He looked about. The sky ship was battered almost beyond recognition. The wood and rigging seemed drained of colour. With a jolt, Twig realized that they were almost transparent, and he could see down deep inside the ship. Then he heard a voice.

'Twig? Twig is that really you?'

Twig swung round. A gaunt, pale figure sat beside the shattered helm. 'Father!' he cried.

Cloud Wolf looked older. His fine clothes hung in rags, his hair was white and his eyes were bluer than Twig remembered – unnaturally blue. Across his right shoulder were the raw scars from a recent wound. Twig ran towards him, his heart clamouring inside his chest, and fell at his side. 'Oh, Father,' he said tearfully. 'I have found you.'

'I have waited so long, my boy,' Cloud Wolf whispered wearily. He pulled Twig closer to him. 'You have come far to reach this place,' he said. 'The caterbird who found me said you would. He was right. No father has ever been prouder of his son than I am of you.'

Twig lowered his head modestly. Tears splashed onto his leather breastplate.

'So much emotion,' said Cloud Wolf gently. 'I know, I know.' His voice grew harder. 'Twig,' he said urgently. 'You must listen closely, for I shall say this but once. This is a dangerous place I have drawn you to.' He sighed. 'If I had known beforehand, I would never have asked the caterbird to enlist your help.'

'But, Father, I *wanted* to . . .'

'Don't interrupt, Twig,' said Cloud Wolf. His body glistened from head to toe. 'I don't have much time left. The perilous vortex has brought me – us – here to the very heart of the Mother Storm. It is a place of calmness, of enlightenment – yet there is a terrible price to pay for the knowledge she imparts.'

'Price to pay?' said Twig anxiously.

'Those who arrive here slowly become one with the Mother Storm, Twig,' his father continued gently. 'She enters through the eyes, the ears, the pores of the skin. She fills you with knowledge of the weather itself – knowledge which the academics of Sanctaphrax have, for centuries, been striving to attain – but she claims you for herself in the process.'

Twig gasped. 'You mean . . . ?'

'I have been becalmed here too long, my boy. I can't hold on to my thoughts for much longer . . .' Cloud Wolf waved a pale, almost translucent hand in front of Twig's face.

'Oh, Father,' Twig murmured. 'What is . . .?'

'I am disappearing, Twig – becoming one with the Mother Storm. My greatest sorrow is leaving you when we have only just been reunited. But before I do, there is something I must tell you – something I have learnt here. The Mother Storm will soon return.'

'To the Edge?' Twig gasped.

'Aye, Twig,' said Cloud Wolf. 'This mighty storm which first seeded the land with life is coming back, as she has done every several thousand years since the beginning of time itself. She will sweep in from open sky, pass over the Mire, the Twilight Woods and on to the highest point of the Deepwoods. Riverrise.'

'Riverrise?' said Twig. 'But surely the place is only a myth . . .'

'Riverrise exists,' said Cloud Wolf firmly. 'When she reaches it, the Mother Storm will rejuvenate its waters, the Edgewater River will flow vigorous and strong once more, and her energy will spread out all across the Edge, bringing new life, new hope – a fresh beginning.' He paused, and Twig looked down to see the pain in his father's eyes. 'At least,' he murmured, 'that is what *should* happen. But all is not well.'

Twig frowned. 'I don't understand,' he said.

Cloud Wolf nodded patiently. 'That last time the Mother Storm visited the Edge her journey to Riverrise was clear,' he explained. 'Now, there is something which stands in her way . . .'

Twig gasped. 'Sanctaphrax!' he said.

'Sanctaphrax,' whispered Cloud Wolf, his eyes misting over. 'Our floating city, with its shining spires and venerable institutions – once, long ago, when it was truly great, my home . . .' He cleared his throat. 'It lies directly in the path of the storm. It will be destroyed by the energy of the Mother Storm when they meet.'

'But . . .' Twig began.

'Hush,' said Cloud Wolf wearily, 'for there is worse to come. If the Mother Storm is blocked by Sanctaphrax, then she will never reach Riverrise to seed it with new life. The waters of the Edgewater River will dry up completely. And with their going, the darkness at the black heart of the Deepwoods will spread out like a vast fungus, until it has engulfed every inch of the Edge.' He looked up at his son. 'Twig,' he said. 'Sanctaphrax must not block the path of the Mother Storm.'

'But what can I do?' said Twig, searching his father's ghostly face for some clue.

'The Anchor Chain . . . it holds the floating city in place . . . it must be . . . severed,' Cloud Wolf told him, every word an effort.

'Cut the Anchor Chain?' said Twig, astonished. 'But . . . but . . .'

'Sanctaphrax will soar away and the Mother Storm will sweep on unhindered to Riverrise. The Edge will be saved, but . . .' His voice grew fainter. '. . . Sanctaphrax will be lost.'

As he spoke, his entire body began to glisten and sparkle.

Twig gasped, and started back. 'Wh . . . what's happening?' he stammered.

Cloud Wolf held up his hands and looked, bemused, as they shimmered like countless million dancing atoms. 'Finally, she has come for me,' he sighed.

'What do you mean?' said Twig. 'What's going on?'

'I told you, Twig. I have been here for too long,' his father whispered barely audibly. 'The Mother Storm has filled me with herself. That is how I know what is soon to take place. But with that knowledge, I have lost myself, Twig. The brighter I glisten, the fainter I get.' As he spoke, the glittering grew more intense, and the form of Cloud Wolf the sky pirate captain became more difficult to make out. 'She has claimed me for herself. I must leave you, Twig.'

'No!' said Twig. 'I shan't let you go!' He shifted round onto his knees and tried to sweep his father up in his arms. But it was like cradling light. 'Father!' he cried out.

'Be still, Twig,' said his father. 'You must know one last thing . . . *when* the Mother Storm will strike . . .'

'When, Father?' said Twig. 'When?'

Cloud Wolf's glittering mouth moved, but not a sound left his lips.

'Father?' Twig shouted desperately. 'When?'

Tethered together the two sky pirate ships circled each other slowly. Twig left the fading *Stormchaser* and swung back across the yawning void to the *Edgedancer* – brought lower in the sky by the Stone Pilot. He landed with a heavy thud on the deck. Behind him, the rope went limp. The *Stormchaser* had finally disappeared completely.

The Stone Pilot stared into Twig's ashen face. 'What happened?'

Twig struggled to clear his head. 'It . . . it was so strange,' he whispered. 'Unearthly . . .'

'Captain Twig,' said the Stone Pilot, shaking him by the shoulders. 'Snap out of it! Tell me what happened on the *Stormchaser*. Cloud Wolf, your father? Did you find him?'

Twig looked up as though hearing the words for the first time. Tears welled in his eyes. He nodded. 'Yes, but . . . Oh, I don't know what to think . . .'

Without saying a word, the Stone Pilot reached up and unfastened the internal bolts which secured the glass eye-panelled hood to the shoulders of the greatcoat. The catches opened and the Stone Pilot removed the hood to reveal the slight figure within. Her red hair fell down over her pale cheeks and slender neck.

'Twig, it's me, Maugin,' she said gently. 'Remember? You once saved my life.' She paused. 'Now calm yourself and tell me what happened over there.' She rolled the heavy Stone Pilot suit down off her shoulders and took him by the hand.

Twig shook his head. 'I did see my father,' he said, 'but he is gone now. For ever.' He sniffed and tried in vain to swallow the painful lump in his throat. 'Before he disappeared, he told me what I have to do. Sanctaphrax must be destroyed.'

'Sanctaphrax destroyed?' Maugin gasped. 'Why?'

Twig silenced her with his hand. 'We must return to Sanctaphrax so that I can warn the Most High Academe.'

'But, Twig,' said Maugin. 'We are becalmed in the middle of open sky.'

Twig clutched his head in his hands and rocked from side to side.

'Twig, you must tell me what you know,' Maugin persisted. 'Sky willing, at least one of us will survive to pass on your father's message.'

'Yes,' said Twig, pulling himself together. 'You are right.'

Maugin's eyes grew wider and wider as Twig began telling her what Cloud Wolf had told him.

'The Mother Storm,' she murmured. 'Riverrise . . . I had always thought such matters were merely the subject of legends.'

'I, too,' said Twig. 'I . . .' His jaw dropped. 'Sky above!' he exclaimed. 'What's happening now?'

The pair of them looked round. The glistening air seemed to be coalescing, and rushing in towards them.

'Quickly Twig,' said Maugin urgently. 'Tell me everything. Before it is too late.'

As the whiteness closed in, the air pressure increased. The pain in Twig's ears became intolerable.

'He told me . . . He said . . .'

All round him, the light intensified. His ears whistled. His head throbbed. Despite the intensity of his memories, the words of explanation wouldn't come.

'When, Twig?' said Maugin. 'When will the Mother Storm strike? Did he tell you or not?'

Twig clutched his head. The air grew denser, heavier. 'I . . . he . . .' he murmured. His eyes filled with bewilderment. 'When the water stops flowing . . .'

He fell silent and winced with pain as he struggled to

remember his father's last fateful words. His eyes throbbed. His head felt as though it had been clamped in a vice.

'When . . . when the very last drop falls, she will arrive. Dawn over Riverrise,' he whispered faintly. 'Midnight over Sanctaphrax . . .'

But Twig could not know whether Maugin had heard him or not, for a wind whisked his words away, whiteness filled his vision and a high-pitched whine whistled in his ears.

'Put . . . your hood on,' he shouted to Maugin, and stepped forwards to help her back into the heavy suit.

The air grew even whiter. Bright white. Dazzling white. It filled his eyes, shutting out everything else till he was utterly blind. The sky ship trembled. He fell away from Maugin and stumbled backwards – slowly, impossibly slowly – through the viscous air.

'Maugin!' he cried out – or rather, *tried* to cry out – for his voice could no longer escape his mouth.

He landed on the deck. Muffled noises echoed round him: splintering, cracking, crashing. The whiteness intensified. The high-pitched whine grew to a scream. Twig screwed his eyes shut, clamped his hands over his ears and rolled himself up into a tight ball.

But it was no use. He couldn't keep it out. The terrifying whiteness was inside him, as blinding and deafening within as without. It blunted his senses. It gnawed at his memory.

'Maugin,' Twig mouthed. 'My crew . . .'

Whoooooopff!

Unable to withhold the mounting pressure a moment longer, the white storm imploded in on itself. For an instant there was stillness. Then, with a cataclysmic thunderclap, the dazzling sphere – with the *Edgedancer* at its centre – exploded outwards with such force that the very sky juddered.

·CHAPTER THREE·

THE LOFTUS OBSERVATORY

Far away, the floating city of Sanctaphrax keeled and bucked in a fearsome storm. The Anchor Chain which moored it to solid ground was being tested to the limit. Inside the sumptuous buildings, its citizens – the academics and apprentices, the servants and guards – huddled together in silent groups of their own kind, terrified at the thought that the chain could snap.

Only the Professor of Darkness remained alone. As Most High Academe of Sanctaphrax, it was his duty to continue working while the others sought refuge. When the violent storm had first broken, he had hurried up the winding staircase to the top of the Loftus Observatory as fast as his frail, old legs would take him. The various pieces of measuring equipment which represented every academic discipline in Sanctaphrax awaited his inspection. He arrived to find them all going wild.

'Sky above!' he exclaimed as he entered the airy room.

He scratched his bushy beard and pushed his steel-rimmed spectacles up his nose as he took a closer look at the instruments. 'But such readings are unheard of.' He glanced out of the window of the high tower. 'And little wonder.'

The storm that night was greater than any he had ever witnessed before. Hurricane-force winds and driving rain were sweeping in from beyond the Edge, battering the jutting spur of land with unprecedented violence.

'Come on, now,' the professor muttered to himself. 'Readings must be taken. Calculations calibrated. Facts and figures logged.' He gripped his staff tightly as he crossed stiffly from one side of the swaying observatory to the other. 'But where should I begin?'

The brass anemometer was spinning furiously, registering wind speeds far in excess of any previously recorded. The rain-gauge was overflowing and bleeping loud the concentrated presence of anti-magnetic sour-mist particles.

The professor shook his head. 'Unbelievable,' he muttered. 'Quite un . . .' He paused. 'But never mind the anemometer or the rain-gauge!' he cried. 'What in Sky's name is the sense-sifter doing?'

The object of the professor's sudden feverish interest was a small, silver box which stood, at an angle, on a tripod. Each of its six sides was inlaid with a small square panel made of a soft, glimmering material derived from the wings of woodmoths. Like the creatures themselves, the material was sensitive to emotions, changing its colour according to the mood surrounding it. Anger would cause it to turn red; sadness, blue; fear, yellow, and so forth.

There were two sense-sifters in Sanctaphrax: one, here, in the Loftus Tower, the other in the rundown Department of Psycho-Climatic studies. Normally, the weather-sensitive apparatus glowed a neutral white. A particularly depressing downpour might tinge it with pale blue; a long stretch of balmy breezes and sunny skies might turn it a delicate shade of pink. But always pastels. Nothing extreme was ever registered. Certainly no more than would cause a slight sense of disappointment or an increased tendency to smile. For though the weather undoubtedly affected all the creatures of the Edge, its effects were always mild.

Until now!

As the professor stared at the sense-sifter, his jaw dropped and his heart pounded. The apparatus was pulsing with multi-coloured intensity. Flashing, sparking, fizzing. Now dazzling red, now ultramarine, now gleaming emerald green. And purple – deep, dark, crazy purple.

'A *mind* storm,' he gasped. He had read of such phenomena in the dusty tomes of *The Elemental Treatise*. 'No wonder my own mind has been in such turmoil.'

At that moment a bolt of lightning zigzagged down out of the swirling sky to the north. For a moment, night became day. The needle on the light-meter shot off the scale and jammed, while the sound-recorder shattered completely in the thunderclap that followed immediately after.

The professor stared at the broken instruments. 'What frauds we are, pretending to *understand* the weather,' he murmured, then checked furtively over his shoulders, in case someone was listening. There were many in Sanctaphrax, twisted with ambition, who would leap at the chance to exploit the Most High Academe's deepest misgivings. Thankfully, no-one was there to hear his blasphemous words.

With a sigh, the Professor of Darkness hitched up his black gown and climbed the ladder which led into the glass-domed attic. He pressed his eye to the viewfinder of the great telescope in the centre of the floor.

As he adjusted the focus, the professor found himself staring deeper and deeper into the dark void beyond the Edge. If he could just see that little bit further . . .

'What mysteries lie out there?' he wondered out loud. 'Wh . . . what in Sky's name is *that*?' A small dark fuzz had crossed his field of vision.

With trembling fingers, he readjusted the focus. The blurred object became solid. It looked like a sky ship. But what was a sky ship doing out there, untethered and so far away from land? Scarcely able to believe what he was witnessing, the professor pulled away, removed his pocket handkerchief and wiped his eyes.

'No doubt about it,' he muttered feverishly. 'It *was* a sky ship. I know it was. Unless . . .'

He glanced round at the sense-sifter. It was pulsing a deep shade of purple.

'No,' he shuddered. 'I can't have imagined it. I'm not mad.'

He spun back, grasped the telescope and peered back down the sight anxiously. There was nothing there in the swirling depths. With trembling fingers he played with the focus. Still nothing. And then . . . The professor gasped. From the point where the sky ship had been – at least, where he *thought* it had been – several bright balls of light were spinning off into the dark sky.

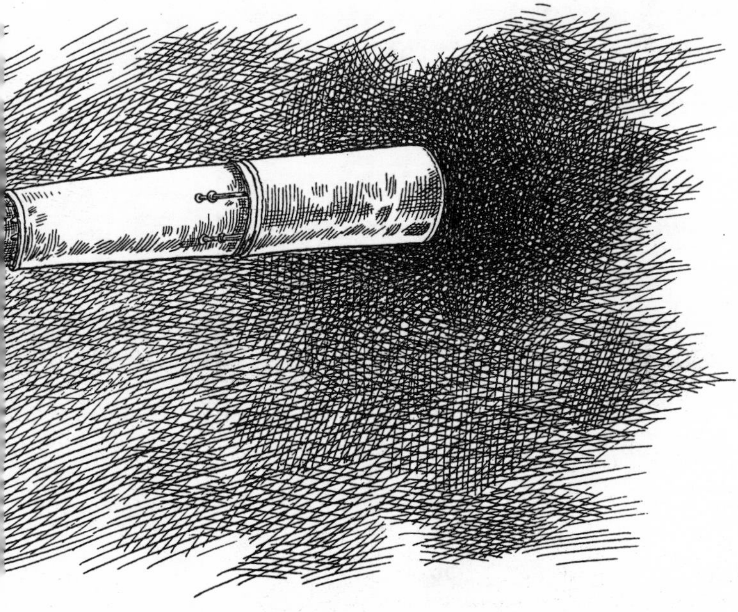

Perplexed, he let go of the telescope and hurried to the window.

'Shooting stars!' he cried.

One after the other, the dots of light flew up and hurtled across the night sky towards the Edge in wide flaring arcs. Seven in all there were, the professor noted. No, eight; two were flying close together. Apart from this pair, each of them was heading in its own direction, at its own speed and describing its own unique parabola.

The professor sighed. The characteristics of light were outside his field of expertise, yet he would like to have one of the shooting stars for himself to examine its make-up; to prove, once and for all, that it was darkness that lay at the heart of all light. The trouble would be in finding one where it landed.

Already the shooting stars were falling; some, quite near. Others continued over the Mire and on to the Deepwoods beyond. While one – shining more brightly than the rest – went on further than the professor could even see.

'Curious,' he whispered. The wind howled and the tower creaked. 'Very curious.'

Far below the battered floating city, the streets of Undertown had turned to a quagmire. Its hapless inhabitants squelched about the sucking mud, trying desperately to salvage something from the trail of destruction the maelstrom was causing.

'Sky above, what is to become of us all,' the frightened voice of a mobgnome cried out as a bright flash lit up the sky. 'Why were we not told about the arrival of so fearsome a storm?'

The wind screeched. The roof rattled. A shooting star hissed across the night sky above her head. Glancing up too late to see it clearly, she wiped the hair from her eyes and peered through the sheets of driving rain at the floating city. Her face twisted with rage.

'Why didn't the academics warn us?' she demanded.

'Academics? Don't make me laugh, Glim,' her companion shouted down angrily as he struggled to rope their flapping roof into place. 'Barkslugs, the lot of them! Slow, slimy and full of stinking . . .'

CRASH!

'TOG?' Glim shouted in alarm. 'Are you all right?'

There was no reply. Heart pumping with anticipation, Glim gathered up her skirt and climbed the ladder. The roof was empty. There was a gaping, jagged hole in the corrugated ironwood panels.

'TOG!' she cried again.

'I'm down here,' came a muffled voice.

Clutching tightly with trembling fingers, Glim pulled herself forwards across the roof and peered down into the hole. The sight which greeted her made no sense. A huge piece of wood lay in the middle of the floor. Beneath it lay Tog.

'Help me,' he whispered. 'Can't move. C . . . can't breathe.'

'Just hang on,' Glim shouted back. 'I'll be right with you.'

Shakily, she eased herself back down the roof and felt

for the top rung of the ladder with her feet. The wind tugged at her fingers. The rain lashed at her face. Slowly, carefully, she descended the ladder and ran inside.

'Oh, good gracious!' she exclaimed, and her fingers flew to the lucky amulets around her neck.

Close to, the piece of wood looked even bigger. It was curved and varnished, and along its side, gold letters gleamed in the lamplight. *EDGEDA* . . . The word ended abruptly in a jagged mass of splinters.

'It looks like a bit of a sky ship,' said Glim. 'Though why anyone would want to go skysailing in *this* weather . . .'

'Never mind all that,' Tog wheezed. 'Just get it off me!'

Glim started back guiltily. 'Yes, Tog. Sorry, Tog,' she said.

Brow taut with concentration, she tugged at the wood with all her might. It was heavy – much heavier than it looked. Despite all her efforts, it hardly moved. Yet move it did. And just enough for Tog to release his trapped legs and scramble backwards.

'Yes!' he cried.

'*Unnkh!*' Glim gasped, and the wood fell to the floor with a bang. 'Oh, Tog,' she said. 'Are you all right?'

The mobgnome inspected his body carefully, up and

down. 'I think so,' he said finally. 'Leastways, no bones broken.' He nodded towards the section of broken sky ship. 'Which is more than can be said for the crew of this thing, I dare say.'

'Do you think they were leaguesmen or sky pirates?' said Glim.

Tog ran his fingers over the fine wood and gold lettering. 'Hard to say, really,' he replied at last. 'But I'll tell you this for nothing. This sky ship must have been a real beauty when she was all in one piece.'

Glim shuddered. 'Oh, Tog,' she said. 'Can you imagine what it must be like being up in the sky when so terrible a storm strikes? Nowhere to run. Nowhere to hide . . .' She looked up at the hole in the roof. 'Puts our problems into perspective, don't it?' she said.

'Certainly does,' said Tog thoughtfully. 'I'd best get it repaired before the whole place floods.'

It wasn't only the mobgnomes who suffered damage. There were others, in various parts of Undertown, who lost their homes, their property, even their lives, to the falling debris.

In the main commercial centre, a broad section of hull flattened one side of the aviary run by Flabsweat the pet shop owner, killing half the captive birds outright and leaving the rest dazed but free to escape. The bowsprit flew down through the air like a spear, skewering an unsuspecting hammelhorn – penned up and ready for the following morning's sale – as it landed. The heavy main mast crushed a row of market stalls where it fell.

The west side of the town fared no better. A volley of falling hull-weights brought considerable damage to the opulent dwellings of several prominent leaguesmen. And the rudder-wheel – a great circular slab of rock which keeps a sky ship on an even keel – smashed through the roof of the Leagues' Chamber itself. It broke the ceremonial ring-shaped table in two, and killed three leaguesmen in the process.

The three unfortunates were later identified as Simenon Xintax, the current Leaguesmaster, Farquhar Armwright, a slight, nervous individual who represented the League of Gluesloppers and Ropeteasers, and Ulbus Pentephraxis – a bull of a leaguesman known more for his ferocity in battle with the sky pirates than for any business acumen: none of them had stood a chance.

Even Sanctaphrax itself suffered damage from the

wreck of the sky ship. First, a large section of poop-deck completely destroyed all the intricate apparatus on the high balcony of the Cloudwatchers' College. A moment later, a heavy fore-harpoon speared the side of the dilapidated – and thankfully abandoned – Raintasters' Tower and remained there, swaying precariously, half-way up the crumbling wall.

The noise from the blow was tremendous. It echoed round the entire city and juddered through the floating rock itself.

'That's it,' the Professor of Windtouchers groaned. 'We're all doomed now.' He turned to the Professor of Cloudwatchers who was crouched beside him beneath his desk. 'It has been an honour and a pleasure knowing you, my friend,' he said.

'The pleasure has been all mine,' the Professor of Cloudwatchers replied, beaming brightly.

The Professor of Windtouchers frowned. '*All* yours,' he said. 'If it was *all* yours, I wouldn't have derived *any* pleasure from our acquaintance. And I did.'

The Professor of Cloudwatchers nodded sagely. 'But I derived *more* pleasure.'

'Why, you obstinate, hog-headed . . .'

'Who are you calling hog-headed?'

A second, and louder, noise filled the air and, as the city rocked, the contents of every shelf and cupboard in the study tumbled down to the floor with a crash.

'That's it,' the Professor of Windtouchers groaned. 'We're certainly all doomed now.'

The third loud noise was the loudest of all. It boomed and thundered with such force that the two professors fell down flat on the floor. All over Sanctaphrax, academics and apprentices, servants and guards, did the same.

Only the Professor of Darkness, the Most High Academe of Sanctaphrax, knew what had happened. At the sound of the first crash, he had looked from the window of the Loftus Observatory to see a nearby tower swaying precariously, to and fro.

'The Raintasters' Tower,' he murmured, and swallowed nervously. 'Thank Sky I was not in it.'

Up until only a few days earlier, his own study had been situated at the top of the tower. But what had caused it to rock so? He looked down. And there, half-way up, he saw a gleaming spike of metal and wood buried deep in the shattered stonework.

The professor scratched his head. 'It looks like a sky ship harpoon, but . . . *whooah!*'

He stared in horror as the great harpoon juddered, slipped and, in a flurry of rocks and mortar, tumbled down through the air, landing with a loud crash on the roof of the covered cloisters far below. The first stone pillar crumpled; the rest toppled, one against the other like a line of dominoes, until all of them were down.

Then, just as the air was clearing, the weakened wall of the tower finally gave up the struggle to remain standing, and the whole lot came tumbling down to the ground in an explosion of rocks, rubble and dust.

The professor's jaw dropped. Deep furrows crisscrossed his brow. He was recalling the sky ship which had disappeared so mysteriously. The curious falling debris. The shooting stars . . .

The sound of insistent tapping interrupted his musings. He spun round and there, perched on the broad sill beyond the window, was a white bird with yellow eyes and a vicious-looking beak which it was hammering at the glass.

'Kraan!' said the Professor of Darkness.

Years earlier, he had found the bird as a bedraggled fledgling, half-dead in a snowstorm. He'd taken it back to his warm study where he'd both nursed it back to health and taught it the rudiments of speech. Now Kraan was fully-grown and powerful, and despite – or perhaps because of – its unpromising start in life, it had gone on to become leader of the flock of white ravens which roosted in the Stone Gardens, right at the tip of the Edge.

The professor hurried to the window and pushed it open. The gale-force wind burst in, ruffling his beard and setting his black robes flapping. 'Kraan, my loyal friend,' he said. 'How good to see you – but what has brought you here in such terrible weather?'

The white raven cocked its head to one side and stared at him with one unblinking yellow eye. 'Strange lights in sky,' it said, its voice raucous and rasping as it shouted above the noise of the storm.

'Shooting stars,' the professor nodded. 'I saw them too. I . . .'

'Shooting stars,' the white raven repeated. It turned its head and fixed him with the other eye. 'One in Stone Gardens.'

The professor started with surprise. 'You mean . . . You're saying . . .' A broad grin spread over his face. 'One of the shooting stars has come down in the Stone Gardens, yes?'

'Stone Gardens,' Kraan repeated.

'But this is wonderful news you bring,' the professor said.

'Stone Gardens,' Kraan called for a third time. It flapped its heavy wings, launched itself off from the sill and swooped away into the night.

'Quite so,' said the professor, as he hurried across to the top of the stairs. 'I must go and investigate for myself at once.'

·CHAPTER FOUR·

THE STONE GARDENS

The Stone Gardens lay at the very tip of the jutting Edge promontory. There were no plants there. No shrubs or trees. No flowers. Nothing grew in this ghostly place but the rocks themselves.

Seeded long long ago, they had been growing in the Stone Gardens for as far back as anyone knew. *The Elemental Treatise* itself made several mentions of *'The wondrous spheres of rock which do grow and, in their immensity, float skywards.'* The great floating rock upon which Sanctaphrax had been built had its origins there.

New rocks appeared beneath the old ones, pushing those above them higher as they grew. Over time, stacks had formed with the rocks standing one on top of the other, and each one larger than the one below. Strange eerie groans and deep sonorous rumblings accompanied the rocks' growth – noises which, combined with the towering silhouettes of the rock stacks, made the Stone Gardens a place of fear to Undertowners.

If left untended, the uppermost rocks would become

so large, so buoyant, that they would break free with a crumbling sigh and sail upwards into open sky. But the Stone Gardens *were* tended. The colony of great white ravens over which Kraan ruled – sleek descendants of their smaller, scraggier cousins in the Mire – had been roosting in the stone stacks for centuries. It was they who monitored the growth of the rocks.

Their sensitive talons could detect the shifts of a ripe flight-rock. Their acute ears could pick up the whisper of a rock about to float free. Once, occasionally twice, a season, the great flock would take to the sky and circle round the Raintasters' Tower. Then, like a great drift of snow, they would alight on the sloping roof of the Loftus Observatory, signalling to the academics of Sanctaphrax that the rock harvest should begin.

Under the watchful eye of the Most High Academe,

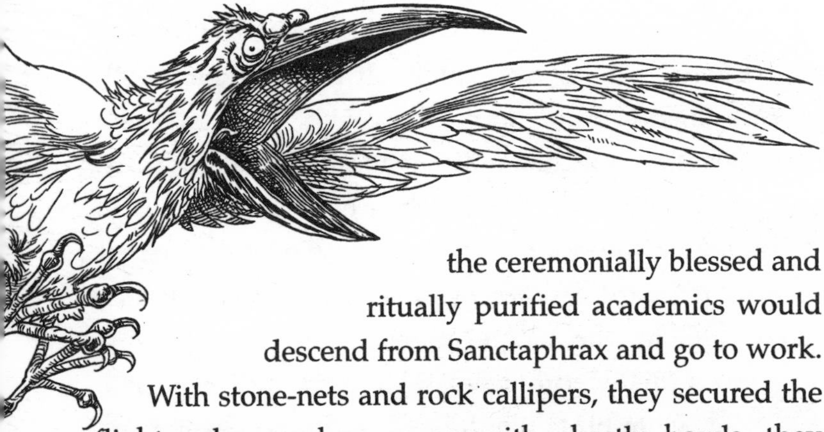

the ceremonially blessed and ritually purified academics would descend from Sanctaphrax and go to work. With stone-nets and rock callipers, they secured the flight-rocks one by one as, with ghastly howls, they broke free.

Superstitious at the sight of the great white flock – like a visitation of ghostly spirits from beyond the Edge – the Undertowners quaked with fear. The howling of the rocks and the shrieking of the ravens – known by most as *the chorus of the dead* – was almost too much to bear. It panicked the animals, it sent youngsters scurrying indoors with their ears stopped and struck terror into even the bravest of hearts. The Undertowners would clutch their best-favoured talisman or charm and whisper urgent prayers that death might spare *them* a while longer.

Yet, for all their fears and superstitions, the Undertowners would have been still more alarmed if the noise ever failed to come. For, terrifying as it was, the ghoulish clamour heralded the delivery of the flight-rocks upon which each and every one of them depended. If the supply of flight-rocks ever dried up, no ship would ever again be able to take to the sky.

Richly rewarded by Undertown for the flight-rocks,

the academics were only too aware of the importance of this material side to their duties. It brought them both great influence and enormous wealth, allowed them their elevated existence in the magnificent floating city, and enabled them to continue their own lofty studies.

Despite the importance of the rocks, the academics felt no need to guard the Stone Gardens. That task could be safely left to the white ravens. The moment the academics finally completed their work and departed, the great white birds would swoop down noisily from the Loftus Observatory to gorge on the hammelhorn and tilder carcasses left out for them – or, when death had visited Sanctaphrax, on the ceremonially laid-out bodies of the deceased academics themselves.

It was into this place of death, and growth – the Stone Gardens – that the shooting star had fallen. Above the sound of the wind which whistled in and out of the stone stacks, a faint hissing had been heard and the white ravens had looked up to see a tiny ball of light flying in from beyond the Edge.

As it came nearer the sizzling, spitting sound had grown louder; the light, bigger, brighter. Abruptly, a bank of dark cloud had blotted out the moon, but the Stone Gardens had become lighter, not darker, as the glowing ball of light had hurtled towards them. It had turned the water in the dips and hollows to black mirrors, and the stacks of spherical rocks to orbs of burnished silver.

The white ravens had flapped their ragged wings and screeched with terror. It was a shooting star, and it was heading straight for their rocky home.

Down, down, down and . . . CRASH! The object had landed with a loud muddy splash beside the highest stack of rocks. And there it had remained. Dazzling, yet motionless.

Hopping forwards inquisitively, the white ravens had formed a circle around the shiny object. Was it dangerous? Was it edible? They had screeched and flapped and stabbed at it nervously before Kraan had stopped them with an angry shriek.

'Waaaark!'

Any unusual intrusions into the Stone Gardens had to be reported to the Professor of Darkness without delay. And, as leader of the flock of white ravens, it had been Kraan's duty to do so.

'Waaaaark!' it had screeched a second time, as it flapped away.

The white ravens were to guard the shining object until his return.

*

'Faster, you addle-brain!' shouted the Professor of Darkness. 'Good grief, you must be the slowest barrow-driver in all of Undertown!' He leaned back and struck the lugtroll on the shoulder with his wooden staff. 'Faster,' he bellowed. *'Faster!'*

Instead of speeding up, the lugtroll stopped completely and lowered the wooden shafts to the ground. The professor slumped backwards, braced himself against the side rail and turned on the lugtroll furiously.

'What is the meaning of this?' he bellowed.

'This is as far as I go,' came the reply.

The professor looked round and was surprised to see that they were at the edge of the Stone Gardens. 'And not before time,' he said gruffly. 'But I'm not done with you yet. I need you to take me into the Gardens themselves.'

The lugtroll shook his head.

'Did you hear me?' the professor demanded.

Scuffing his bare feet in the dust, the lugtroll looked away. 'I'm not going another step,' he said firmly. 'I've already brought you further than I like coming.' He shuddered. 'I hate this place. Gives me the creeps, it does.'

'I see,' said the professor curtly. He climbed down from the barrow and straightened his robes. 'You will wait for me here,' he said.

'Oh, but . . .' the lugtroll whined.

'It will be the worse for you if you do not,' the professor warned him. 'If you are not here when I return, I shall see to it that you never push another barrow so long as you live.'

The lugtroll looked over his shoulders anxiously. 'All right,' he said at last. 'But . . . try not to be too long.'

The professor surveyed the grim, rocky landscape and shivered with foreboding. 'Believe me,' he muttered. 'I shall be as quick as I possibly can.'

Wrapping his gown tightly around him and raising his hood, the professor set off. His feet stumbled and squelched; his wooden staff tapped at his side. He felt weary and increasingly ill at ease. The Stone Gardens, groaning and creaking all round him, suddenly seemed uncomfortably immense – and the prospects of finding the fallen shooting star pitifully small.

Where should he try first? What should he look out for?

Looking round, as the low moon brightened and dimmed with the passing clouds, the professor caught a flash of flapping wings far ahead. His heart missed a beat. The savage birds that roosted in the Stone Gardens were both unpredictable and dangerous and, hearing their raucous cawing fill the air, he was about to head off in the opposite direction when a horrible thought struck him.

'Since it was Kraan who told me about the shooting star,' he said to himself, 'there is every likelihood that it is the shooting star they are all flapping around now. Ah me,' he sighed. 'Be brave now. Show no fear, or they will be upon you at once.'

As the moon sank down beneath the horizon, the temperature fell sharply. Mist, coiling up from the ground, swirled around the professor's shuffling feet and tapping staff.

'Sky protect me,' he murmured in a quavering voice as the screeching of the white ravens grew louder.

Guided only by the incessant noise of the raucous birds, he stumbled on over the uneven ground, half-blinded by the thick mist.

All at once, a tall stack of rocks loomed out of the misty shadows before him. He paused. Half a dozen of the great white ravens were perched on the boulder at the top, squabbling for position. Others clung to the sides. A dozen more – massive specimens, each of them – were down on the ground, wings outstretched, loping round in their strange, weightless dance. They were guarding something, that much was clear.

The professor took a step closer. His heart thudded – not only with fear, but also with excitement. Whatever the white ravens were clustered around, it was still glowing. He took another step. And another . . .

'*Waaaaark!*' the white ravens cawed furiously as their attention was grabbed by the intruder.

Those on the stack flapped their wings and rose up screeching into the air. Those on the ground loped forwards and thrust at him with gaping beaks and savage talons. They were angry – and hungry.

'D . . . do you not know me?' the professor cried. He held out the heavy gold seal of high office which hung from the chain around his neck. 'It is I, as Most High Academe who sees to it that you are fed, who . . .'

He fell still. The birds were paying no heed to his words.

They were all around him now in a wildly flapping circle, and beginning to test his strength. To keep them at bay was a hopeless task. Even while the professor was lashing away at those in front of him with his heavy wooden staff, others were snapping viciously at his back.

'Kraan!' he bellowed. Surely his old friend wouldn't let any harm come to him. 'KRAAN!'

From above his head came a flurry of wings as the largest and most powerful white raven of all spiralled down out of the sky. Its talons glinted. Its beak gleamed. It was Kraan. Staggering backwards, the professor watched it land on the back of an attacker and sink its beak in its neck. A loud shriek echoed round the Stone Gardens. Blood trickled down over white feathers.

'*WAAAARK!*' Kraan screeched menacingly.

The other white ravens fell back.

'Dangerous here,' Kraan croaked, spinning round to snap viciously at a bird that had ventured too close.

'The shooting star . . . ?' the professor stammered.

'Shooting star,' Kraan confirmed raucously, turning and cutting a swathe through the gathering of disgruntled white ravens. The professor followed him, nervous still. If the colony banded together they could overpower their leader in an instant.

As they approached the glowing object, the professor squinted down into the dense mist. He trembled, hardly daring to believe what he was seeing. It must be his imagination. Or a trick of the light and shade. He moved closer still, crouched down and reached out. His fingers confirmed what his eyes had already told him. This was no fallen star. No fireball. No blazing rock.

It was the body of a sky pirate, lying on its front, face turned away – and glowing from head to toe more brightly than a flaming torch.

'I knew I hadn't imagined seeing the sky ship,' he muttered. 'It must have exploded. And the shooting stars I saw, those eight balls of light . . .' He looked back at the glowing sky pirate. 'Could they have been the crew?'

The cawing of the white ravens grew louder than ever. Now the professor understood why they had been guarding their find so jealously, and why his arrival had aroused such fury. To them, the sky pirate who had dropped into their midst was a free meal – a free meal Kraan and this gowned intruder were preventing them from enjoying.

He reached forwards and seized the sky pirate by the shoulder. As he did so, his fingers brushed against something as sharp as needles. He pulled back and looked more closely.

'Hammelhornskin fleece,' he said thoughtfully. He noted the sky pirate's build, his youth – and the thick, matted hair. This time when he took hold of his shoulders he did so more carefully. He rolled him over and stared down at the face.

'You!' he gasped. The body pulsed with the eerie luminous glow. 'Oh, Twig, what has happened to you? What have you done?'

All around them, the white ravens screeched and squawked, the bravest of them hopping forwards to stab at Twig's legs with their cruel beaks.

'Twig!' the professor called desperately. The intrepid young sky pirate captain was alive still, but fading fast. 'Twig, wake up. I'll take you back to Sanctaphrax. *Twig!* You wouldn't listen to me. Oh no! "I'm a sky pirate captain," you told me. "Like my father, and his father before him," you said. "It's in the blood." And look where it's got you! Why, if your father, Quintinius Verginix, could see you now . . .'

At the sound of his father's name, Twig stirred. The professor smiled. The white ravens hopped back, squawling with fury.

Twig's eyelids fluttered. The professor observed the movement with excitement.

'Or, perhaps I should call him by his other name. The name of the most feared and respected sky pirate captain ever to sail the skies. Cloud Wolf . . .'

Twig's eyes snapped open. 'Father,' he said.

'No, Twig,' said the professor gently, 'not your father. It is I, the Professor of Darkness.'

But there was no sign of recognition in the eyes as they stared round, wild, unseeing. Nor did Twig speak another word. The professor shivered with apprehension. Apart from the strange glow it gave off, the young sky pirate's body appeared unscathed, yet his mind had clearly suffered.

The ravens moved closer once again. Kraan stabbed at the most inquisitive of the birds and turned to the professor. 'Go,' it said. 'Take shooting star, now!'

From the urgency in its raucous voice, the professor knew that Kraan would not be able to keep the other white ravens at bay for much longer. Trying hard to ignore the disconcerting confusion in those blindly staring eyes, the professor supported Twig under his arm and heaved him up.

'Now, walk,' he muttered. 'Come on. You can do it.'

The sky lightened to the east as the professor hobbled back through the Stone Gardens, one hand round Twig's shoulder and the other holding his staff.

'That's it, Twig,' he said encouragingly. 'Just a little further.'

·CHAPTER FIVE·

COWLQUAPE

'A shooting star!' The solitary figure of a junior sub-acolyte, a tousle-haired youth in ill-fitting robes, peered out into the night. 'How curious,' he murmured.

The storm had passed, and the academics were stirring from their numerous hiding places.

'What have we here?' came a sneering voice from behind the youth. 'A little runt of a leaguesman's son. Why aren't you in the library with your nose stuck in a scroll, Cowlquape?'

The voice belonged to a tall apprentice in the fur-lined robes worn by all those in the College of Cloud. Several others stood behind him, dusting off their clothes and sniggering.

'I thought . . .' mumbled the youth. 'I thought I saw something, Vox.'

'Leave sky-watching to those of us who are qualified,' Vox said nastily. 'Don't you have a latrine or something to slop out?'

'I . . . I was just going,' said Cowlquape, all fingers and thumbs as he gathered up his bundle of scrolls. He hurried off down the rubble-strewn walkway.

'Undertown scum!' Vox's voice floated after him.

Barely fifteen years old, Cowlquape was small for his age. He was lowest in the pecking order of Sanctaphrax – slopping out the latrines was just one of his jobs. He was at the beck and call of any who had a menial task that needed performing: running errands for the various sub-professors, mistsifting and windgrading, helping to maintain the spotless and gleaming appearance of the floating city.

Cowlquape, however, dreamt of better things. Whenever he could, he would seek refuge in the Great Library of Sanctaphrax – now sadly neglected – and immerse himself in the countless dusty old barkscrolls that were housed there.

The library wasn't fashionable. It had neither the glamour of the College of Cloud or the Academy of Wind, nor the power and influence of the School of Light and Darkness – but then Cowlquape himself wasn't fashionable. His father, a burly, overbearing bully of a leaguesman by the name of Ulbus Pentephraxis, had bought him into Sanctaphrax.

'You'll never make it in the leagues, you frightened little barkworm,' he had said. 'Perhaps those pompous weather-watchers up there can make something of you. It's certainly beyond my capabilities!'

And so he had secured sub-acolyte tenure for his son. At first, Cowlquape had been overjoyed. He was soon to discover though that the floating city could be as harsh a place to live as the streets of Undertown. For although they were undeniably wealthy, the leaguesmen were universally despised by the academics of Sanctaphrax, and those acolytes and apprentices who gained entrance to the floating city with their money were despised all the more.

As he hurried through the deserted avenues of the majestic floating city, Cowlquape paused to take in every detail of the splendour which surrounded him: the magnificent towers, with their minarets, domes and spires, gleaming pink in the glow of the rising sun, the ornately carved pillars, the statues and fountains, the sweeping staircases and arched walkways. He knew that he could never, ever take it for granted. It was all so elegant. So opulent. So grand.

Cowlquape sighed. It made him feel even smaller than usual to gaze up at it all. Vox's taunt came back to him. 'Undertown scum!'

Would he ever be accepted in this magnificent city, he wondered, or would he never be anything more than a frightened little barkworm?

One thing was for certain. He could never go back to Undertown. The noise, the filth, the blows and kicks

from his father – and the look of disappointment in his mother's eyes before she'd died. His life in Undertown had all but crushed him completely. No, come what may, Sanctaphrax was his home now. His father paid good money to the College of Cloud to keep him here. And he, Cowlquape, would earn the respect of those snooty professors!

'Be brave,' he whispered to himself. 'Be confident.'

He was rounding the corner of the Institute of Ice and Snow when he heard a voice from the landing-stage ahead of him.

'Crushed to death by objects falling out of the sky,' it was saying.

Cowlquape started, then shrank back into the shadows. A thickset gnokgoblin was talking to a fellow basket-puller on the jutting platform.

'Whatever next?' said the gnokgoblin's companion.

'I know,' said the gnokgoblin. 'I just come up here from Undertown a minute ago. Lucky to escape with my life, I can tell you. I was in the Bloodoak tavern when Mother Horsefeather – the old bird who owns the place – comes bustling in all of a quiver with news that a sky ship had been struck by the full fury of the storm. Smashed to smithereens, it was, with lethal bits of debris dropping down all over Undertown. 'Parently the giant rudder-wheel came smashing through the ceiling of the Leagues' Chamber – and flattened three bigwig leaguesmen.'

'No!' said his companion, wide-eyed with gory interest.

'On my mother's life,' said the gnokgoblin. He raised his hands and counted off the victims one by one. 'First, the Leaguesmaster,' he said. 'Simon or Simeon something or other. Then whassisname Armwright, the Rope and Glue character. And then . . .' He frowned thoughtfully. 'Ah, yes. Captain of one of them league patrol boats. Pentephraxis. Ulbus Pentephraxis.'

Cowlquape felt as if he had been hit by the full weight of the rudder-wheel himself. His father, dead! He could never mourn the loss of so unpleasant a father, yet his breath came in short, anxious gasps as the terrible implications of the news sank in.

When a leaguesman died, the League took everything. Even now his father's erstwhile colleagues could be stripping the family mansion of everything they could lay their hands on, like ravenous white ravens. And who was to stop them? Certainly not his weedy only son up in Sanctaphrax.

'Sanctaphrax!' Cowlquape groaned, his head in his hands. Who would pay his fees? The College of Cloud would throw him back on to the streets of Undertown as soon as the money dried up. He was finished, ruined – fit only to be fed to the ravens.

The journey from the Stone Gardens had taken longer than it should have and the sun was up long before the lugtroll finally made it back to Undertown. For a start, although no bones were actually broken, Twig's experiences in the storm had left him weak and slow. He'd had to stop for several rests as the professor steered him on towards the barrow. And when they arrived there, the lugtroll had insisted that the terms of their deal be re-negotiated since there were now *two* persons returning from the Stone Gardens, rather than the *one* he had taken there.

'Weigh more, pay more!' the lugtroll had insisted, and refused to budge until the professor gave way.

Then, when the amount had at last been settled and they set off, it was soon clear that the lugtroll had taken on a bit more than he could chew. On the flat he had puffed and panted as he crept along at a snail's pace, while on the hills he had wheezed so badly that the professor had wondered at times whether they were ever going to make it at all.

Twig, for his part, hadn't registered a single thing that was going on. Apart from that one word, he had not spoken. Withdrawn and passive, he had allowed the Professor of Darkness to bundle him into the barrow. And as the trip had got underway, the luminous glow which had drawn the professor to Twig in the first place had faded away.

'Soon be back,' the Professor of Darkness said encouragingly.

Twig gave no indication that he had heard.

'Do you remember how we first met?' the professor said, trying to stir Twig's memory. 'When you came to my old study at the top of the old Raintasters' Tower . . .' He chuckled. 'By Sky, Twig,' he added. 'You helped Sanctaphrax in her hour of need then. Now Sanctaphrax will help you. I swear this shall be so.'

He stared into Twig's troubled face and trembled with helpless sympathy.

'Oh, Twig,' he continued. 'What in Sky's name made you venture, untethered, into open sky in the first place? Did you not realize the perils you would have to face?' He gripped him by the shoulders. 'What happened out there?'

But Twig made no reply. The young sky pirate captain's head was clearly in turmoil. If he didn't receive attention soon, there was surely a danger that he could lose his mind completely. The professor looked round him and was gratified to find that they were just reaching the outskirts of Undertown. Five minutes later, the lugtroll lowered the shafts of the barrow to the ground.

'We're here,' he wheezed, and bent over double, gasping for breath.

As he climbed out of the barrow, the professor glanced up at the floating city hovering over them. One of the hanging baskets was directly above his head. He raised his arms and cupped his hands to his mouth.

'Anyone up there?' he shouted.

Still standing in the blustery shadows, Cowlquape stared up the broad paved avenue, his heart heavy, his eyes misting up. His gaze darted from building to magnificent building, each one designed to suit the school or college it housed.

'And I shall never see any of this again,' Cowlquape muttered, tears in his eyes. 'Soon I'll be a beggar on the streets of Undertown.'

Just then there was a commotion at the end of the platform. The Professor of Darkness stepped out of a basket as it came to rest on the landing-stage. He had someone with him – someone barefoot, bony, with matted hair and tattered clothes. Cowlquape forgot his troubles for an instant. Who was he? he wondered. And wasn't that the Professor of Darkness with him?

As the gnokgoblin lowered his basket again and disappeared from view, leaving the professor and the stranger on their own, Cowlquape stepped out of the shadows.

'You there, lad!'

'Who me, sir?' Cowlquape stammered, dropping his bundle of scrolls.

The Professor of Darkness looked him up and down. 'Yes, you,' he said. 'Help me to get Tw . . . er, my friend to the School of Light and Darkness and, er . . .'

'Of course, sir. At once, sir,' said Cowlquape, hauling the youth up onto his back.

'I take it that you can keep your mouth shut,' said the professor, leading the way. 'I don't want a lot of gossiping academics disturbing my friend.'

'Y . . . yes,' said Cowlquape softly.

The professor looked at him warily. 'What's your name, lad?' he asked.

'Cowlquape, if it pleases you,' came the reply. 'Junior sub-acolyte of Sanctaphrax.'

'Junior sub-acolyte of Sanctaphrax,' the professor repeated, his eyes narrowing. 'An Undertowner, by the look of you. Rich father in the leagues, I'll be bound.'

They had almost reached the entrance to the school.

Cowlquape nodded. 'Yes, sir. My father is . . .' He checked himself. '*Was* a leaguesman, sir.'

'Very good, very good,' said the professor absent-mindedly.

They arrived at the studded door of the School of Light and Darkness – for Cowlquape, all too soon.

'Thank you, my lad,' the professor said, as he bustled the stumbling figure inside the school. The great studded door slammed shut.

Cowlquape stood alone in the avenue, feeling lost. What now? He turned and wandered back the way they'd come. How long did he have? A day? A week? Probably no more than that, and then he'd be out, his few possessions in a bundle under his arm as he stepped into the basket to return to Undertown for ever.

'Well, Cowlquape,' he said to himself. 'Until then I'll find the darkest, dustiest corner of the Great Library and, who knows?' He smiled bravely. 'Just like all those barkscrolls, they may forget all about me!'

·CHAPTER SIX·

INSIDE AND OUT

The huge dinner gong clanged mechanically from the Refectory Tower. As one, the doors of the schools and colleges of Sanctaphrax burst open and a great throng of chattering professors, apprentices and acolytes streamed hungrily towards it. Head down and heart pounding, Cowlquape joined them. He slunk into the bustling refectory, took a brass bowl and platter from the racks and mingled with the seething crowd of those waiting for lunch.

Ten days had passed since the Professor of Darkness had asked for his help. In that time, Cowlquape had spent his time hiding, curled up in a dusty corner of the Great Library with his beloved barkscrolls, lost in the fantastic tales and legends they held. Nobody had disturbed him, and he had ventured out only to forage for food – a latrine cleaner's pie, an apprentice's tilder sausage dropped absentmindedly.

But it had been at least a day since he'd last eaten anything. When he had heard the dinner gong, his hunger had got the better of him. He was so ravenous that he was prepared to risk being caught by those in the College of Cloud and expelled from Sanctaphrax for ever for the sake of a hot bowl of delicious, spicy tilder stew.

At the long high tables, the senior professors were being waited upon. In the galleries lining the walls, academics and senior apprentices jostled noisily over large communal stew-pots. Whilst in the 'pit' below, a great clamour of acolytes jostled and shouted round the stew-pipes that snaked down from a huge central cauldron. As he made his way through the clamouring throng Cowlquape couldn't help but catch snatches of conversation.

'The Department of Psycho-Climatic Studies confirmed that it definitely was a mind storm the other night,' an apprentice was saying. 'And we're still feeling its after-effects.'

His colleague nodded. 'I know,' he said. 'I'm beginning to wonder if the skies will ever clear again.'

In the continuing gloom that had followed that fateful night, more treacherous weather had been blown in from beyond the Edge. Rain – registering deepest indigo on the sense-sifters both up in the Loftus Tower and in the garret of the Department of Psycho-Climatic Studies – had prompted an outpouring of communal grief across the region. A thick and oily mist had rendered the residents of some northern districts of Undertown temporarily deaf and dumb. While, the previous night, a

heavy downpour led to outbreaks of terrible violence amongst the cloddertrogs in the boom-docks.

The abrupt change in the character of the weather was bringing the hitherto insignificant Department of Psycho-Climatic Studies into the limelight. Its dean, a rotund pen-pusher by the name of Lud Squeamix, now sat self-importantly at the highest of the long tables, slurping stew up through his teeth, pausing only to belch loudly.

'I'm thinking of going for a place in the Department,' a third apprentice was saying. 'That's where the action is these days.' He looked round furtively. 'I hear that the windtouchers and cloudwatchers are forming an alliance.'

'*Pfff!* Fat lot of good it'll do them,' snorted his companion. 'Has-beens, the lot of them.'

All around the refectory the feverish conversations were the same. Plots and counterplots had become rife. And as if this wasn't enough, there were other rumours going round that even the most level-headed of academics could not ignore.

Up in the College of Rain gallery, a senior apprentice turned to his neighbour. 'And *I've* heard he's up to something,' he said. 'Something suspicious!'

Cowlquape's ears pricked up.

'Something suspicious?' said his companion. 'What, the Most High Academe?'

'That's the one,' the first senior apprentice replied. ''Cording to my sources in the School of Light and Darkness, he's got someone locked up in there. They say he was found in the Stone Gardens, and I can well believe it. He looks like a vagrant, and never speaks – though he can freeze your blood with one icy stare.'

'Absolute madman, by the sound of him,' an apprentice cloudwatcher in an upper gallery called down. 'He howls!'

'Howls?' said the apprentice raintasters as one.

'Like a woodwolf,' the cloudwatcher continued. 'Every night. 'Course, you wouldn't hear it from your faculty, but it echoes all round the College of Cloud. Spooky, it is.'

Cowlquape frowned. He, too, had heard the curious night-time howling from his hiding place in the library, but hadn't made the connection between that and the staring-eyed character he had encountered with the Professor of Darkness that blustery morning.

As he inched his way forwards to the stew-pipes, his thoughts stayed with the stranger.

Gossip had it that the mysterious individual was none other than Twig, the young sky pirate captain who had returned to a hero's welcome in Sanctaphrax only weeks earlier. It was said that he had done what no-one had ever done before – set out into open sky, untethered. Something must have happened to him out there, the stories maintained. Something unearthly, inexplicable; something that had left him both dumb and distracted. It was curious then that, according to the rumours, the Most High Academe had conferred upon him the title of Sub-Professor of Light.

The crowd shuffled towards the pipes. Behind

Cowlquape, two sub-apprentice windtouchers were bemoaning their lot.

'Windgrading, windgrading and more windgrading,' one of them complained. 'And the professor's such a tyrant!'

'The worst type,' came the reply.

Cowlquape sighed. At least your futures are secure, he thought bitterly. Unlike my own. He shuddered, and the brass platter slipped from his grip and clattered to the stone floor.

The raintasters and cloudwatchers around him looked at the thin, tousle-haired boy with amusement.

'Then again, at least we're not sub-acolytes,' one of the windtouchers commented sniffily.

'Undertowner!' said the other scornfully.

'Sky above!' a voice bellowed from the highest of the long tables, and all heads turned. It was Lud Squeamix and he was almost choking on his stew. 'Who'd have thought it?' he spluttered.

A flagon was dropped in surprise.

'Upon my word,' someone else exclaimed, 'it *is* him.'

Every eye looked towards the highest long table. There, where the most prominent academics were eating, the Professor of Darkness was to be seen ushering the mysterious, wild-eyed individual to an empty seat.

The apprentices forgot all about the junior sub-acolyte in their midst.

'I can't believe that's Twig,' Cowlquape heard one of them say. 'I mean, look at him!'

'Like a crazy one,' another agreed.

'And he's meant to be the new Sub-Professor of Light!' said a third. 'I wouldn't fancy being *his* apprentice.'

'Yeah,' laughed the first apprentice raintaster. 'Definitely a couple of raindrops short of a shower.' And they all burst out laughing.

All, that is, except for Cowlquape. While the apprentices were too empty-headed to see anything beyond his outward appearance, Cowlquape looked again. There was something about the young sub-professor – a fierce intelligence ablaze in those bright, staring eyes. Perhaps Twig hadn't lost his mind at all, Cowlquape thought with a sudden jolt. Perhaps he had simply turned his gaze inwards.

Beneath the stew-pipe at last, he pulled the lever, taking care that none of the steaming tilder stew missed his bowl. He grabbed a hunk of oak-bread from the basket beneath the pipes, soggy from stew others had let fall, and pushed his way towards the mass of low stools that sprouted like mushrooms beneath the galleries. Looking up, he could see Twig clearly.

The newly appointed sub-professor was staring into mid-air, oblivious to his surroundings. Occasionally, prompted by the nudging elbow of the Professor of Darkness, he would start picking at his food like a bird. But only for a brief moment – and never long enough actually to eat anything.

As Cowlquape continued to watch the twitchy young individual – only a few years older than himself – he asked himself what horrors Twig must have endured when the *Edgedancer* received the full brunt of the mind storm. After all, if a passing rain cloud could lead to the cloddertrogs attacking each other, then what must it have done to the sky pirate captain who had seen his ship destroyed?

Just then, a blanket of blackest cloud swept in across the sky and plunged the refectory into darkness. The Professor of Darkness – for whom the sudden gloom was of particular interest – pulled a light-meter from the folds of his gown. Concentrating intently, he failed to notice his young sub-professor get up from his seat and make his way down the wooden steps.

'Curious,' muttered Cowlquape.

A heavy hand landed on his shoulder almost knocking him off his stool. 'Well, well, well,' came a familiar mocking voice. 'If it isn't our favourite little Undertowner!'

'Vox!' gasped Cowlquape, looking up into the arrogant face of the tall cloudwatcher apprentice.

'I hear somebody hasn't been paying his fees,' he said. '*Tut, tut*. That won't do at all.'

Cowlquape trembled. 'Please!' he begged. 'It's just that my father, he . . .'

'Save it for the Professor of Cloudwatching, barkworm!' Vox's voice was hard, his grip vice-like on Cowlquape's shoulder.

Outside, a dismal angry drizzle began to fall. Rage at the unfairness of it all flared in Cowlquape's eyes. It wasn't his fault that his father had been killed!

'Professor of Cloudwatching?' he said. 'Professor of Cloudwatching?' His voice rose to a shout. Vox stared in amazement. 'You can give this to your Professor of Cloudwatching in place of payment!' And with that Cowlquape hurled the bowl of steaming stew into the tall apprentice's face.

'*Aaaargh!*' Vox shrieked, falling into a gaggle of mistsifters and sending bowls and stew flying everywhere.

Cowlquape took to his heels, ducking and dodging as he made for the door, and bowling a couple of indignant latecomers off their feet as he dashed from the refectory.

It was even darker outside than it had been inside and, away from the noise of the refectory, far more forbidding. Purple-edged black clouds twisted and swirled overhead like bubbling wood-tar. The wind was sulphurous. And even though he could not know how the sense-sifters were glowing orange, Cowlquape felt an unfamiliar tumult of emotions within him: anger, exultation, and a nerve-tingling fear as chaotic and swirling as the weather around him.

Chicker-chacker-cheeeesh. Crimson lightning darted this way and that across the sky, and the thunder which followed crashed all round the floating city, shaking it to its very core.

Head spinning, Cowlquape set off for the refuge of the Great Library. He kept to the shadows as he hurried silently across the greasy tiles. Around a corner, he halted. He looked back and forth. The coast was clear. From the guard turret to his right to the landing-stage far away on his left, the place was deserted.

As he set off again the sky lit up for a second time, and Cowlquape caught a sign of movement out of the corner of his eye. He spun round and squinted into the dim light. There was the young sub-professor. He was standing atop the stone balustrade of the landing-stage, legs apart, head up, arms outstretched and palms raised. All round him, the lightning cracked and splintered.

'Twig!' Cowlquape bellowed. He didn't know whether it was his own inner confusion or simply the madness of the weather that made him call out the professor's name. Could he really be going to jump? 'Stop! Stop!'

His urgent cries were drowned out by a second rumble of thunder. Twig tottered on the edge of the balustrade, flapping his arms.

'NO!' Cowlquape yelled. He raced forwards, heart in his mouth, and seized the hem of Twig's waistcoat. '*Ouch!*' he cried, as the hammelhorn fur turned instantly to sharp needles which pierced his skin. Droplets of blood welled up on his fingertips.

The lightning flashed again. The thunder rolled. And, as the wind grew stronger, a light sparkling rain began to shower down. All over Sanctaphrax, the mood changed to elation. Cheers echoed from the refectory. Cowlquape, gripped by a sudden feeling of intoxicating strength, grasped Twig's arm and pulled him off the balustrade. Twig fell to the ground.

'Forgive me, Professor,' Cowlquape whispered. 'I thought you were going to jump.'

Twig stumbled to his feet. 'You spoke?' he said.

Cowlquape's jaw dropped. '*You* spoke!' he said. 'They said you were dumb . . .'

Twig frowned and touched his lips with his fingers. 'I did,' he whispered thoughtfully. He looked round, as if seeing for the first time where he was. 'But . . . what am I doing here?' he said. 'And who are you?'

'Cowlquape, Professor,' came the reply. 'Junior sub-acolyte, if it pleases you.'

'Oh, it pleases me well enough,' said Twig, amused by the young lad's formality. Then he frowned. 'Did you say . . . *Professor*?'

'I did,' said Cowlquape, 'although Sub-Professor would have been more accurate. You are the new Sub-Professor of Light – at least, if the rumours are to be believed.'

A look of bemusement passed over Twig's face. 'This must be the Professor of Darkness's doing,' he said.

'He was the one who brought you to Sanctaphrax,' said Cowlquape. 'From the Stone Gardens, they say. He . . .'

'The Stone Gardens,' said Twig softly. 'So I didn't imagine it.' Looking lost and bewildered, he turned to Cowlquape. 'And yet . . .' He frowned with concentration. 'Oh, why can't I remember . . . ?' He scratched his head slowly. 'It's as if I've been in a dream. I remember my crew, the voyage, entering the weather vortex and then . . . Nothing!' He paused. 'Until just now, when you obviously stopped me from throwing myself to my destruction.' He smiled. 'Thank you. What did you say your name was?'

'Cowlquape,' said Cowlquape, 'and I don't know what came over me. I shouldn't have saved you at all.' He stared down at the ground disconsolately. 'I should have joined you. I have nothing to live for!'

'Come, come,' said the young professor gently. He laid his hand on Cowlquape's shoulder. 'You can't mean that.'

'I do,' said Cowlquape, hanging his head. 'I'm an Undertowner. My father is dead and I have no fees to pay for my apprenticeship. When they find me, they'll throw me out of Sanctaphrax. What have I got to live for?'

Twig looked at the bookish young acolyte. 'You saved me,' he said simply. 'I think I ought to repay the debt. You say I'm a Sub-Professor of Light.'

Cowlquape nodded.

'In that case, I hereby appoint you as my apprentice, Cowlquip.'

'Cowl*quape*,' said Cowlquape excitedly. 'Do you really mean it?'

'Of course,' said Twig, smiling. 'I'll need a smart young apprentice to look out for me now that I've finally woken up. I've got a lot to do.'

'I'll look out for you, professor,' said Cowlquape. 'You see if I don't.'

·CHAPTER SEVEN·

THE SHOOTING STAR CHART

Cowlquape strode out of the Great Library, brushing the dust from his fine new robes. The costly black material showed up every speck, and the fur trim seemed somewhat extravagant – but the clothes fitted splendidly. He clutched the ancient barkscrolls to his chest and hurried towards the School of Light and Darkness.

Turning into a narrow alley next to the Windtouchers' Tower, he stopped. There, blocking his way, stood Vox, the cloudwatcher, his face pasty with woodsalve.

'Alone at last,' the tall apprentice snarled.

Two more cloudwatcher apprentices appeared behind Cowlquape. He was trapped.

'I believe you and I have some unfinished business, barkworm,' said Vox, producing a mean-looking cudgel from the folds of his gown. He swung it through the air, catching Cowlquape a glancing blow to the side of the head, and sending him sprawling.

'Vox!' he gasped. 'You great big bully . . . *Unnkhh!*'

'Where's your so-called professor now, Undertowner, eh?' Vox sneered. 'Where's brave Captain Twig, saviour of Sanctaphrax?'

'Right here,' said Twig, seizing Vox's upraised arm and twisting it neatly up behind his back.

'*Aaargh!*' yelled the apprentice, dropping the cudgel.

Twig shoved him away. 'I believe my valued apprentice, Cowlquape, needs a hand,' he said.

'Y . . . yes, sir,' stammered Vox, cowering before the young professor.

'And dust off his robes while you're about it.'

Vox clumsily helped Cowlquape to his feet and brushed him down.

'Now be on your way,' said Twig. 'And don't ever let me catch you bothering him again or you'll find yourself on a one-way basket trip to Undertown. Do I make myself understood?'

Vox nodded sullenly and sloped off. His friends had long since fled.

'Thank you, Professor,' gasped Cowlquape.

Twig smiled. 'How many times do I have to tell you?' he said. 'Call me Twig.'

'Yes, Prof . . . Twig,' said Cowlquape.

'And Cowlquape.'

'Yes, Twig?'

'You dropped this.' The young professor handed the crumpled barkscrolls to his apprentice. 'And don't get bark dust all over your nice new robes.'

'No, Twig,' said Cowlquape happily; and followed the Professor towards the School of Light and Darkness.

Twig's study was situated at the top of the west tower in the School of Light and Darkness. It was a small room, yet with its soft hanging armchairs and blazing stove, a comfortable and cosy place. The wall was lined with shelves brimming over with rows of leather-bound books, stacks of papers tied up with ribbons, and intricate light-orientated scientific apparatus. A furry layer of dust covered it all.

Twig watched Cowlquape as his young apprentice sat with his nose in a barkscroll, reading avidly in front of the open-doored stove that glowed with purple flames. It must be lufwood he's burning, Twig thought, and was once again taken back to his childhood with the woodtrolls, when he would sit on the tilder rug before the fire listening to Spelda – his adoptive mother – as she recounted her tales of the dark Deepwoods.

The lufwood logs gave off a lot of heat but, being buoyant when burned, they had a tendency to fly out when the door to the stove was open. Every so often, Cowlquape would look up and nudge back into the stove a blazing log which threatened to escape.

'What's that you're reading?' Twig didn't hide the boredom in his voice. It was plain to his young apprentice that Sanctaphrax, and the stuffy confines of the School of Light and Darkness in particular, stifled the young sky pirate captain.

'An old barkscroll, Professor,' said Cowlquape. 'I found it in the Great Library – it's fascinating . . .'

'Call me Twig,' he said impatiently. Then, in a gentler voice, 'I envy you, Cowlquape.'

'Me, Twig? But why?'

'You can pick up a barkscroll and be transported off to goodness knows where. I've watched you sit there for hours, poring over some scrap of bark, half eaten by woodmoths and barkworms, as if in a trance. You're a born academic, Cowlquape. Whilst I . . .' He paused. 'I'm a sky pirate!'

Twig climbed to his feet, crossed the stuffy study and flung open the window. Icy rain splashed down on his upturned face and trickled down the back of his neck. 'That is where I should be,' he said, pointing beyond Sanctaphrax. 'Out there. Sailing the skies as captain of a sky pirate ship. Like my father and his father before him. It's in the blood, Cowlquape – and I miss it so.'

Cowlquape put down the barkscroll and caught an escaping lufwood log with the fire tongs.

'Oh, Cowlquape,' Twig continued, his gaze still fixed on the endless expanse of sky outside. 'You have never heard the wind singing in the rigging, or seen the world laid out below you like a map, or felt the rushing air in your hair as you sail across the sky. If you had, you would know what misery it is to be stuck in this poky study. I feel like a bird whose wings have been clipped.'

'I love Sanctaphrax,' said Cowlquape. 'I love its towers, its walkways; the Great Library – *and* this poky study. But I wouldn't be here if it wasn't for you.' He looked down, suddenly embarrassed. 'And I'd follow you anywhere, even . . .' He gestured to the open window. 'Even out there, into open sky.'

Twig flinched. 'There were others who followed me there,' he replied quietly.

'Your crew?' said Cowlquape.

'My crew,' Twig whispered sadly. He could see them all now, the diverse yet loyal bunch he had assembled: the flat-head goblin, the slaughterer, the oakelf, the waterwaif, the Stone Pilot, the banderbear and the bespectacled quartermaster. They had believed in him, followed him into open sky – and had perished there. 'I don't know how, but I killed them all, Cowlquape. You see how dangerous it can be putting your trust in me.'

'Are you sure they're dead?' said Cowlquape.

'Of course they're dead,' said Twig irritably. 'How could they possibly have survived?'

'*You* did,' said Cowlquape. Twig fell still. 'I mean, did you actually see what happened to them?'

'See?' Twig repeated. 'I can't remember!'

'Can you remember *anything* of that fateful voyage into open sky?' he prompted.

Twig hung his head. 'No,' he admitted glumly.

'Then how do you know they're dead?' Cowlquape persisted. 'How many were on board the *Edgedancer* when you set sail?'

'Eight, including myself,' said Twig. 'But . . .'

'The Professor of Darkness said eight shooting stars were seen flying through the sky,' Cowlquape blurted out.

Twig frowned. 'Cowlquape, what are you saying?'

'I've said too much.' Cowlquape stumbled over the words. 'The professor told me not to talk to you about your former life. He said that it would only upset you . . .'

'Upset me? Of course it upsets me!' Twig stormed. 'If I thought for an instant that any of them were still alive, I'd leave this place right now and find them, whatever it took.'

Cowlquape nodded. 'I think that's what the professor is afraid of,' said Cowlquape. 'Forget I spoke, Twig.'

'Forget!' Twig turned on him. 'I can't forget! Eight shooting stars, you say. One for each member of the *Edgedancer*. Cowlquape, think now, did the professor say where these shooting stars landed?'

'Well, I . . . I mean, I think . . .'

'I can answer that,' came a voice. The Professor of Darkness stood in the study doorway. 'I should have known I couldn't make a professor out of you, Twig, my boy,' he said sadly. 'You're just like your father, a born adventurer – and like him, you're probably destined to be lost for ever in open sky.'

Twig seized the professor's hand. 'My father?' he said. 'You know what happened to my father?'

The professor shook his head. 'Only that he was swept away in the Great Storm many weeks ago, and hasn't been seen since.' He looked deep into Twig's troubled eyes. 'Did you . . . ? Out there . . . ?'

'I don't know,' Twig said unhappily. 'I can't remember.' He grasped the professor's hand in his own and squeezed it tightly. 'Professor, you must help me find my crew. As their captain, I made a promise never to abandon them, come what may. If there is even the *slightest* chance that any of them are alive, then it is a promise I must keep.'

'But Twig,' said the professor. 'Even if . . .'

'And maybe,' said Twig, cutting through the professor's objections, 'just maybe, my crew might help me retrieve my memory.' He pulled away from the professor and looked into his eyes. 'For who knows what I might have forgotten – out there, in open sky. Something useful perhaps? To you, Professor. To Sanctaphrax.'

The professor nodded uneasily. Twig had a point.

Having sailed so far into open sky he had experienced what no-one before had ever experienced; what the aged academic himself had only dreamed of doing – namely, entering the source of the weather itself. What was more, Twig had survived and returned to tell the tale. For the moment, of course, his mind was shut tight, but if it could be unlocked . . .

'Very well,' said the professor. 'I can see your mind is made up. Go in search of your missing crew, Twig, and with my blessing.' He pulled a leather pouch full of gold pieces from the folds of his robes and placed it into Twig's hand. 'For your journey,' he said. 'Use it wisely. Now follow me to my study and I shall show you the chart I made the night you fell to earth. It shows the approximate position of the other shooting stars – if my calculations are to be trusted. A few fell not far, somewhere in Undertown. A couple fell farther off in the Deepwoods, Sky help them. And one – the final one – fell so far away that I couldn't track it with any certainty.'

'Show me, Professor!' said Twig excitedly. He turned to his apprentice. 'We're going to find my crew, Cowlquape. To be reunited . . .' He paused. 'Perhaps they will even be able to tell me about my father . . .'

'Twig,' said the professor sternly. 'Go charging off on this shooting star hunt if you must. And indeed, I see that you must. But for Sky's sake leave the lad here, safe in Sanctaphrax where he belongs.'

Cowlquape stepped forwards, grasped Twig's arm and faced the professor. 'I'm sorry, Professor,' he said. 'But I too have made a promise!'

·CHAPTER EIGHT·

THE LULLABEE INN

'Cowlquape,' said Twig gently. 'The basket will soon be here.' Cowlquape looked up from the old barkscroll he was examining. 'Trust you,' Twig smiled. 'We're just about to set off on an arduous, not to say possibly futile, quest and you've got your nose stuck in a scroll.'

'Sorry, Twig,' said Cowlquape. 'But this particular scroll really is fascinating.'

Twig smiled. 'You're dying to tell me about it, so go on then.'

'It's *The Myth of Riverrise*, Prof . . . I mean, Twig,' said Cowlquape excitedly.

'What, that old tale?' said Twig. 'Spelda, my mother – or rather the woodtroll who raised me as her own – used to tell it to me when I was a young'un.' A smile played on his lips as his eyes glazed over. '*Once upon a velvet blackness came a spark . . .*' Twig murmured. 'Oh, how my heart thrilled when she spoke those words. Of all the many tales she told, *The Myth of Riverrise* was always my favourite.'

'The spark turned. And the wind breathed. And the rain cried . . .' Cowlquape read.

Twig nodded. *'And the sun smiled. And the first minute of all minutes came to pass,'* they said together.

'You know it off by heart!' said Cowlquape, delighted.

'*The Myth of Riverrise* is told in every corner of the Edge,' said Twig. 'I heard it in the caverns of the termagant trogs, I heard it on board the *Stormchaser* – different versions, but essentially the same. What you've got there is the classic.'

'It makes sense of things,' said Cowlquape.

Twig tugged at the ends of the scarf around his neck. 'Sometimes there is truth buried in the old tales,' he said seriously.

'Do you think, then,' said Cowlquape, 'that somewhere out there is the place where it all began?'

'That *the Mother Storm did strike the highest point of that barren, jutting rockland and seed it with life*?' said Twig. 'Why not? I've seen many strange things out there in the Deepwoods, in the Twilight Woods . . .' He fell silent.

'What is it, Twig?' asked Cowlquape, concerned.

Twig was staring into the empty sky beyond the Edge. 'There *is* something,' he whispered. 'I'm sure of it. Something I can't remember.' His voice grew more urgent. 'Something I *must* remember . . .'

'Twig,' said Cowlquape, and nodded behind him. 'The basket-puller's arrived.'

Without another word, Twig and Cowlquape climbed into the basket. Cowlquape trembled giddily. The basket-puller, a gnokgoblin, unhitched the rope and began winching them slowly down from the floating city. 'A lot of weather we've been having recently,' he said, and looked at them askance. 'But then I'm sure I don't have to tell you two that.'

They were being pumped for information. Like all Undertowners, the gnokgoblin was desperate for any explanation of the treacherous weather that, of late, kept blowing in from beyond the Edge. Twig said nothing, and Cowlquape followed his example.

As the basket was lowered, Twig and Cowlquape removed their gowns and rolled them up, so that they could travel incognito. The smells of Undertown grew stronger, the lower they got. Pungent smells. Familiar smells. Roasting pinecoffee beans, burnt tilder oil, and, the sickly sweet scent that so many used to mask the stench of untreated sewage.

And noises. The clatter of ironwood wheels on cobblestones, the banter and badinage, the endless bustle of feverish activity.

The gnokgoblin brought the basket down in the artisans' quarter – a sprawling hotchpotch of ironmongers, leatherworkers and glassblowers.

Stepping out of the basket, Twig pointed down a winding alleyway to his left.

'This way, Cowlquape,' he said. 'We need to be methodical, so let's start by visiting all the taverns in the east of Undertown.'

'But I'm not thirsty,' said Cowlquape nervously.

'Nor am I, Cowlquape. But there's plenty that are – traders, slavers, merchants and skysailors. And when they drink, Cowlquape, they talk. And when they talk, we'll listen. And maybe, just maybe we'll hear something. Stay close,' Twig told him, 'and keep your eyes and ears open.'

'I'm a good listener,' Cowlquape smiled as he followed him into the crowd.

Cowlquape soon lost count of the inns, taverns and drinking dens they visited – the Running Tilder, the Rusty Anchor, the Hook and Eye – the names merged into one another. By the end of that first day, however, they had heard nothing! Weary and footsore, Cowlquape followed Twig out of the Redoak. Night had fallen long ago and the oil street lamps had all been lit. Cowlquape looked round, bleary-eyed. 'Which one should we . . .' He stifled a yawn. '. . . we try next?'

Twig smiled. 'No more for this evening,' he said. 'We'll take lodgings for the night and resume our search tomorrow.'

Cowlquape looked round uncertainly. 'You want to spend the night here in Undertown?' he said.

'We're on a quest to find my missing crew, Cowlquape,' Twig reminded him. 'We can't go scurrying back to Sanctaphrax every time we get cold or wet or tired, can we?'

Cowlquape shook his head. 'No,' he said a little sorrowfully. 'I suppose we can't.'

They secured lodgings that night in a small, dark room above the Redoak. It was simple, yet adequate. There were two straw mattresses against the walls, and a large pitcher of fresh water in the corner enabled them to swill out their mouths and wash away the smell of stale smoke.

'Goodnight, Cowlquape,' said Twig.

'Look for your roots, captain,' whispered a voice.

'What did you say? Cowlquape?' said Twig. But there was no reply. Cowlquape had fallen into a deep, dreamless sleep.

They woke late the following morning and, after a hearty breakfast, set off once more. And so it continued. For three days – from noon to midnight – they trudged round the eastern quarter of Undertown, resting up for the night in the tavern they had ended up in when the clock struck twelve. On the fourth day, they found themselves outside a tavern – the Lullabee Inn – in a particularly rough part of Undertown down by the boom-docks.

'The lullabee tree shares your roots,' said a soft, sibilant voice by Twig's ear.

Twig turned to Cowlquape. 'What do you know of lullabee trees?'

'Me?' said Cowlquape, puzzled. 'Nothing, Twig.'

Twig frowned. 'Well, we might as well try here,' he said.

Cowlquape looked up at the tavern sign of a Deepwoods tree with a broad knobbly trunk and fan-like upper branches. The artist had even painted a suspended caterbird cocoon hanging from its branches.

'Come on, look lively,' said Twig, stepping forwards. 'We . . .'

CRASH!

A heavy log bench came bursting through the window to the right of the door. Twig and Cowlquape ducked down. Just in time, for the next moment, a heavy barrel came hurtling through the glass in the door itself. It missed their heads by a fraction, struck the ground with a resounding *crack* and spilled its contents.

'Like I say, Motley, accidents can happen,' an angry voice shouted from inside.

'Yeah,' said a second voice menacingly. 'Troughs can get damaged. Barrels can get broke.' The statements were accompanied by the sounds of splintering wood.

'And faces can be rearranged,' hissed a third. 'If you get my drift.'

'Yes, yes,' came a fourth voice – a small and anxious voice.

Twig and Cowlquape pulled themselves up and peered cautiously through the broken door. Three hefty hammerhead goblins were standing round the hapless landlord, a slight character with tufted hair and mottled skin. His body was trembling from head to toe. 'Times are hard,' he stammered. 'Takings are down. I just d . . . don't have the money.'

Twig looked at Cowlquape, his eyes burning with indignation. 'How I hate to see the strong picking on the weak,' he said.

Cowlquape placed a hand on his arm. 'There are too many of them,' he whispered. 'You'll get hurt . . .'

But Twig brushed Cowlquape's hand aside. 'Perhaps I should also have left you to be beaten up by that apprentice cloudwatcher,' he said.

Cowlquape reddened with shame.

'It's OK, Cowlquape. You stay here if you want to,' said Twig. 'But I'm going in.' He climbed to his feet and pushed the broken door open.

The hinges creaked. The hammerheads spun round.

'Evening,' said Twig calmly. 'Evening, Motley. A goblet of your finest sapwine if you'd be so good.' He glanced round and a smile flickered over his lips; Cowlquape had followed him in after all. 'And one for my friend here, as well.'

'I . . . we're just about to close,' said Motley.

Twig glanced up at the cluster of customers skulking in the shadows at the back of the tavern, too cowardly or too inebriated to come to Motley's aid. None of them looked as if they were about to leave.

'No wonder business is bad,' the hammerhead said gruffly. 'Turning away your customers like that!' He looked Twig and Cowlquape up and down, and smirked. The dark-grey ironwood of his false teeth gleamed in the turquoise glow of the lullabee flames. 'Take a seat,' he said, pointing with a knife towards one of the benches that was still upright.

Cowlquape moved to obey the goblin. Twig laid a reassuring hand on the youth's shoulder.

'Sit down!' roared the hammerhead.

'Just do as they say,' said Motley weakly. 'I'll be with you directly.'

Twig and Cowlquape remained where they were.

'Did I not make myself clear?' the hammerhead growled between clenched teeth. The other two turned and made towards them, fists clenched and eyes blazing.

'Riverrise clear!' Twig replied steadily, and drew his sword with its great curved blade: the sword his father had thrust into his hands just before being swept away in the Great Storm. It flashed in the turquoise light.

For a moment, the surly goblins were stunned to silence. Then they turned, looked at one another and laughed with disbelief.

'You little pipsqueal!' the nearest one bellowed at the

young captain and drew his own weapon; an evil-looking sickle. 'Come on then,' he growled, sneering, beckoning, shifting his weight from foot to foot.

'Go on, Tabor,' the hammerhead with the knife grunted encouragingly. Motley seized the opportunity to slip away. 'That's it!' Stepping back smartly from the shadows, Motley swung his club. '*UNNKH!*'

The blow struck the hammerhead on the side of his head, felling him like a tree and sending his knife skittering across the floorboards. It came to rest at Cowlquape's feet. Cowlquape hesitated, then bent to pick it up.

The heavy knife felt strange in his grasp. Despite his father's best attempts to teach him, Cowlquape had never mastered the art of self-defence. He turned on the second hammerhead nervously. 'You'd better just watch it,' he said, as threateningly as he could. 'Don't make me have to use it.' His voice was thin and unconvincing.

Behind him, the sickle of the third hammerhead sliced through the air. Twig leapt to his young apprentice's side, sword raised. The sickle struck it with a ferocious blow that jarred the length of his arm. He held his ground.

'The uglier they are, the prettier the victory,' Twig muttered. He lunged forwards ferociously, once, twice, at the two hammerhead goblins.

The sickle hissed through the air again, low and from the side this time. Twig jumped back. The cruel tip to the blade missed his stomach, but snagged on the fastener of his hammelhornskin waistcoat. Cowlquape spun round and stabbed furiously at Twig's attacker.

'*Aaiii!*' the cloddertrog squealed, as the sharp blade cut into the thumb of his fighting hand.

'Attaboy,' Twig shouted out encouragingly. He raised his arm and thrust the sword forwards. It found its mark and the hammerhead's sickle clattered to the ground.

Cowlquape kicked it over to the side wall. Twig pressed his sword against the hammerhead's neck.

'Leave now,' he said coldly, 'or so help me, I shall finish the job off.'

The two hammerheads exchanged glances. 'Let's get out of here!' one of them bellowed, and they both spun round and beat a hasty retreat. Neither of them once looked back at their fallen comrade.

'Sky above,' Cowlquape muttered. He held out the hammerhead's knife to Twig.

Twig smiled. 'Keep it,' he said. 'You earned it. That was excellent, Cowlquape,' he said. 'I didn't know you had it in you.'

Cowlquape lowered his head bashfully, and slid the knife down behind his belt. Neither did he.

'Not exactly known for their loyalty to one another, hammerhead goblins,' Motley chuckled, as he hung the club back on the wall. He turned to Twig and Cowlquape. 'Yet dangerous for all that,' he said. 'Thank you for coming to my aid, gentlemen.' He righted one of the upturned benches. 'Take a seat. You shall drink of my finest barrel – and on the house, of course.'

Twig and Cowlquape sat down. Cowlquape was drenched in sweat, his hands shaking. He looked around the tavern for the first time.

The other drinkers, sipping and slurping in the shadowy corners, seemed unaware of the recent disturbance. Some sat beneath the rows of hexagonal barrels set into the far wall like woodbee honeycomb; some hunkered on low logs by the drinking troughs. In the corner, the covered brazier glowed turquoise and echoed with the melancholy singing of the burning logs.

'It sounds like lullabee wood,' Cowlquape remarked unsteadily. He still felt shaken.

'We *are* in the Lullabee Inn,' said Twig, and smiled. 'Takes me back to the Deepwoods when I was a boy. Spelda – the woodtroll mother I told you about – would put a lullabee log on the fire at bedtime. The mournful songs used to lull me to sleep.'

'They sound eerie to me,' Cowlquape shuddered.

Motley returned with three goblets brimming with golden liquid. He sat down between them.

'To your very good health,' he said, and they all raised

the sparkling sapwine to their lips. *'Aaaah!'* Motley sighed appreciatively. 'Pure nectar.'

'It's very good,' said Twig. 'Eh, Cowlquape?'

Cowlquape winced as the pungent liquor burnt his throat and sent stinging vapours up his nose. He placed the goblet down and wiped his eyes. 'Very nice,' he rasped. He frowned and turned to Motley. 'But aren't you afraid the racketeers will be back?' he said.

Motley chuckled. 'Hammerheads are cowards at heart,' he said. '*Once bitten* and all that. Once word gets round that the Lullabee Inn's no pushover they'll leave me alone – for the time being at least. And it's all thanks to you two!'

'Oi, Motley!' came a gruff voice from the far corner. 'More woodgrog, now!'

'Coming up!' Motley shouted back. He climbed to his feet and wiped his hands on his apron. 'No peace for the wicked,' he said. 'Give me a shout when you need a refill.'

Motley scuttled away. Twig turned to Cowlquape who was trying a second sip of the sapwine. 'Take your time,' he said. 'I may as well have a look round while we're here. Chat to some of the locals. See if anyone knows anything.'

Cowlquape placed the glass down for the last time, nodded eagerly and jumped to his feet. 'Good idea,' he said. 'I'll come with you.' He didn't fancy being left on his own in this rough, shadow-filled place with its strange mournful music.

There were a dozen or so individuals in the tavern all

told. Trogs, trolls and goblins: heavy drinkers with lined, leathery faces and blank staring eyes.

'Greetings, friend. Can I get you a drink?' said Twig, tapping the shoulder of a small figure hunched over the drinking trough. 'Interesting weather we've been having.'

The creature turned, revealing itself as a lugtroll. He focused in on Twig's face. 'What d'ya want?' he snarled.

Twig raised his hands. 'Just a drink,' he said. 'And a little conversation. Motley! Fill my friend's trough here. He looks thirsty.'

Several pairs of eyes looked round and stared at him blankly.

'Thank you, sir,' said the lugtroll. Twig had got his attention.

'Like I said, interesting weather – strange rains, hailstones as big as a goblin's fist, all sorts of things falling out of the sky. Why, I even heard tell of shooting stars falling to earth right here in Undertown.'

The lugtroll shrugged. 'I ain't seen nothing,' he said. 'Just got off a sky ship from the Great Shryke Market. Carrying slaves we were.' He grunted. 'Never again! The noise was horrible – screaming and moaning they was, all the way. Can't get it out of my head. I came straight here to forget.' He buried his face in the brimming trough and Twig moved on.

'Cap'n?' came a gruff, questioning voice to his right.

Twig spun round. Cowlquape peered into the shadows, trying to see who had spoken.

'Cap'n, is that you?' A heavy seat scraped back on the wooden floor and a stocky individual scrambled to his feet, rubbing his eyes as if he had just woken from a sleep. Twig stared as the figure approached. It was a Deepwoods slaughterer: hair wild and blood-red skin, deep purple in the shadowy darkness. His morose features twisted round into a grin. 'Cap'n Twig, it is you, isn't it?' he said. 'Tell me it is?'

'Tarp?' said Twig. 'Is that you, Tarp? Tarp Hammelherd? From the crew of the *Edgedancer*?' Twig cried out. 'Yes, it's me! It's me, your captain!'

The two of them fell into one another's arms.

'Oh, cap'n,' Tarp said, tears welling in his eyes. 'I feared I would never live to see this day.'

Twig broke away from Tarp's stifling embrace and gripped the slaughterer's arms. 'But you *did* live, Tarp! You're alive! You're really alive!' he said, his voice quivering with excitement. 'And now I have found you!' He turned to Cowlquape. 'Look, Cowlquape,' he said. 'We've found one of my . . .'

He fell silent. His young apprentice looked as if he had seen a ghost. He was standing stock-still, mouth open and eyes almost popping out of his head. At his side, Motley looked equally dumbstruck.

'Cowlquape, what in Sky's name is the matter?' said Twig.

'Y . . . you're b . . . both glowing,' came the stammered reply.

'Like a pair of tilder-oil lanterns,' said Motley, staring in awe.

Twig looked at Tarp. It was true. A luminous light was glowing brightly from the top of the slaughterer's blood-red hair to the tips of his tooled leather boots. He looked down at his own body. Chest, legs, arms, hands, wiggling fingers – they were all aglow.

All round them, the regulars were muttering to one another. They wagged their fingers, they shook their heads. The lugtroll next to Cowlquape fingered the amulets around his neck. 'Spirits,' he hissed. 'Spirits in the boom-docks. And now spirits here. It ain't natural, I tell you.'

A couple of mobgnomes climbed to their feet. 'I'm not staying here,' said one nervously, and scuttled to the door.

'Me neither,' said his companion. He turned to Motley as he hurried past. 'Things in Undertown are weird enough these days without spirits turning up at the Lullabee Inn!'

'Yeah,' muttered the lugtroll, hurrying after them. 'Spirits is where I draw the line.'

'But . . . but they were just leaving,' said Motley. 'Weren't you?' he added, as he ushered all three of them hurriedly to the door. 'Nothing personal,' he muttered to Twig. 'But you're upsetting the customers. And trade is trade you understand.' He pushed them gently but firmly outside.

As the door slammed behind them, Twig turned to the others. 'There's gratitude for you!' he chuckled. 'But who cares? You're *alive*, Tarp! That's what matters.'

'It's good to see you too, cap'n, but . . .' Tarp frowned. 'We did look a bit odd, glowing 'n all. It's enough to put the frighteners up anyone.' He frowned. 'I was glowing when I first landed back in Undertown,' he said, 'but it soon faded. Until just then,' he added uncertainly, 'when we met again.'

'It was the same with me,' said Twig. 'Yet there we were, reunited and glowing once more. Something must have happened out there,' he said, his voice low and breathy. 'Something which even now binds us together.' He seized Tarp by the arm. 'Do *you* remember what happened? To the rest of my crew? To my ship? And, my father! Do you know if we found Cloud Wolf . . .?'

But the slaughterer was shaking his great, shaggy red head sorrowfully. 'If only I *could* remember, cap'n,' he said. 'But I can't recall a darned thing after we entered that weather vortex.'

Twig smiled and squeezed his arm warmly. 'No matter,' he said. 'I have found you, Tarp, and that is a start. An excellent start! Now all we have to do is find the others.' His face clouded over. 'But where?'

'Spirits,' said Cowlquape softly.

'What was that, Cowlquape?' said Twig. 'Speak up.'

Cowlquape turned to him. 'I overheard that lugtroll saying that you must be a spirit.' He paused. 'Just like the ones in the boom-docks!'

'The boom-docks?' said Twig. 'Spirits in the boom-docks? Just like us?'

Cowlquape nodded. 'That's what I heard him say.'

'Oh, well done, Cowlquape!' Twig exclaimed with delight, and clapped him on the shoulder. 'That is where we shall go. To the boom-docks!'

Cowlquape lowered his head. 'I said I was a good listener,' he muttered happily.

·CHAPTER NINE·

THE CLODDERTROGS

The moment they had stepped outside, Twig and Tarp Hammelherd had stopped glowing. The sun, though low and golden in the late afternoon sky, was nevertheless bright enough to obscure their curious luminous glow.

And thank Sky for that! Cowlquape thought, as they set off.

They headed eastwards, through streets that they were getting to know well, and on down towards the swampy boom-docks beside the sluggish Edgewater River. Twig was in reflective mood.

'We've done well, Cowlquape, finding Tarp alive,' he said, 'but as for the others . . .' He fell silent. 'Do we really dare hope that these ghosts, these spirits, could possibly be . . . Who? Goom? Spooler? Wingnut Sleet perhaps, or Woodfish?'

'Well, the lugtroll did say *spirits* not *spirit,*' said

Cowlquape, 'so there must be at least two of them there.'

Twig pulled from his bag the scroll of paper the Professor of Darkness had given him, and opened it out. It revealed a map of the Edge annotated with lines and crosses which charted the trajectories and approximate landing places of the eight shooting stars. The cross drawn over the Stone Gardens had been circled. That was where Twig himself had landed. He took a charcoal-stick and circled one of the four crosses dotted around Undertown.

'One down,' he said, turning to Cowlquape. 'And three still to find.' He smiled hopefully. 'Maybe they're *all* down in the boom-docks.'

'Maybe,' said Tarp Hammelherd. 'Though, to be honest, cap'n, I'm not sure how much I give for their chances if they *have* ended up there. It's cloddertrog territory, and they don't take kindly to outsiders at the best of times.'

'And what with all those stories of fighting we've been hearing,' Cowlquape added, with a shudder.

'Courage, Cowlquape,' said Twig. 'Stories is probably all they are. If we stick together, we'll be fine. Trust me.'

Cowlquape smiled bravely. Since they had first arrived in Undertown he had been overwhelmed by Twig's determination. Although they might well have been on a fool's errand, not once had the young captain contemplated giving up. And now, with Tarp Hammelherd found, the young captain's determination had paid off. But what lay in front of them – bloodthirsty cloddertrogs – would test that determination to the limit.

Cowlquape shuddered again.

All round them, the cosmopolitan atmosphere of the thronging eastern quarter was coming to an end as they entered the hinterland of the boom-docks. The rows of shops and houses gave way to a maze of narrow alleys lined with ramshackle huts and shacks, each one overrun with huge families of cloddertrogs.

'Just watch your step,' Tarp Hammelherd cautioned, looking round furtively over his shoulder. 'Keep to the centre of the alleyways – cloddertrogs are suspicious of anyone going too near their property. And avoid eye-contact at all costs.'

Initially, Cowlquape complied with Tarp's instructions, yet as they continued through the noisy, bustling streets, he began to relax. The overspilling taverns were raucous but relaxed. The markets buzzed with friendly banter, while the cramped houses resounded with snatches of song, young'un-play, infant-wail and gales of infectious laughter. It was a poor area, certainly, but there was nothing about its atmosphere which struck him as threatening.

'I can't see what I was fretting about,' Cowlquape said, as he punted a stray bladderball back to a rowdy group of youngsters.

'Yeah, well,' said Tarp Hammelherd grimly. 'First impressions can sometimes be deceptive. Things can turn nasty in a moment . . .'

'*Wurrgh!*' Cowlquape cried out.

'What is it?' Twig asked.

Cowlquape turned away and pointed back into a dark

and empty doorway. Twig peered into the shadows. The sudden pungent smell of decay snatched his breath away.

'Bones,' Twig muttered.

Cowlquape gagged.

'See what I mean!' said Tarp Hammelherd darkly. 'Now be on your guard.'

Cowlquape looked round, suddenly seeing the lumpen trogs in a different light. He noticed how large their yellow teeth were, how bloodshot their eyes, and he saw the heavy, studded clubs they carried over their shoulders and the knives on their belts.

Sticking closer together than ever, he, Tarp and Twig headed off down a dark, rubbish-strewn alley which led to the river's edge. Here, the homely smells of stale woodale and boiling mire-cabbage were overwhelmed by the odour of rotting fish. Above them, the early evening sky darkened as thick, billowing clouds swept in.

At its end, the alley opened out into the sprawling filth of the boom-docks themselves. The dwindling Edgewater River lapped half-heartedly at the recently exposed mud-banks. A light, greasy drizzle began to fall. Even though the light was fading – oil lamps had been lit and shone dimly from the rotting clapboard warehouses which lined the banks – they could still see the bones scattered over the mud. Lots of them, large and small. Each one had been picked clean by scavenging white ravens and the piebald rats which splashed and squealed as they fought over the waste that the encrusted sewage-pipes discharged into the sluggish water.

'I don't like this one little bit,' said Cowlquape uneasily.

'Neither do I,' said Twig, shaking his head. 'It's a pity that lugtroll wasn't more specific about where the spirits had been seen.'

Cowlquape nodded. 'I . . .' He gulped. 'You're beginning to glow again,' he said. 'Both of you.'

Twig examined his outstretched arm and saw for himself the faint, yet discernible, light it was giving off. 'It must be because it's getting dark,' he said.

'Then we . . . we'd better split up,' said Tarp nervously.

'Split up?' said Twig.

'The closer we are, the brighter we glow. I noticed that back inside the Lullabee Inn . . .'

'No, Tarp,' said Twig. 'I told you, we stick together. Besides, as I noticed *outside* the Lullabee, if it's bright enough we don't glow at all.'

'But Twig . . .' Cowlquape began.

'Cowlquape!' said Twig sharply. 'We'll go on a little further. Together!'

They continued in silence, picking their way past stacks of boxes and piles of empty barrels, through towering mounds of rusting chains and rotting fish, and on underneath the raised jetties which creaked as the tolley-ropes of the cumbersome tug ships pulled at the tether-rings.

The drizzle stung as a wind got up. Cowlquape winced as, with every step, his boots sank deep into the slimy mud. 'This is hopeless. We're never going to find them here,' he said. 'And you're glowing even brighter.'

'We'll try this way,' said Twig evenly.

They turned away from the river and went back up through the narrow alleys. Beneath the street lamps, the curious luminosity was barely visible. Yet, as they went on, Cowlquape thought he noticed a difference in the reaction of the cloddertrogs they passed. Before, they had simply been ignored. Now – unless it was his imagination – they were being studiously avoided; eyes were averted and those approaching stepped to one side or disappeared into doorways until they had passed.

'I think they've noticed,' Cowlquape hissed.

'Come on,' said Tarp Hammelherd. 'Let's get out of here. We don't want to draw attention to ourselves.'

'It's a bit late to worry about that now,' Twig said out of the corner of his mouth. 'Look.'

They were standing at the edge of what seemed to be a junction, like the hub of a great spoked wheel, where dozens of the narrow alleyways met. At its centre stood an immense wooden vat, around which a seething mob of carousing cloddertrogs jostled together. The rowdy scene was bathed in the bright purple light of lufwood torches which cast grotesque shadows on the leering cloddertrog faces – and masked Tarp and Twig's luminous glow completely.

Shoved forwards by those just arriving, Twig, Cowlquape and Tarp Hammelherd found themselves being impelled deeper into the crowd and towards the great vat. The atmosphere of the place struck all three of them in the face like a blast of bad breath: hot, humid and foul. Cowlquape struggled hard not to heave.

'Fish,' said Twig. 'Rotten fish and . . .' His nose wrinkled up. 'Tripweed.'

From his childhood, Twig had always loathed the smell of the pickled tripweed on the woodtrolls' breath. Here, the stench was overwhelming. Pungent. Acrid. Fermenting. It seemed to be coming from the frothing vat.

'Tripweed beer,' he groaned.

'Three jugs, is that?' came a voice from beside the wooden vat. A squat cloddertrog with a filthy cloth draped over his arm motioned them to approach. They picked their way past the heaving bodies of drunken cloddertrogs asleep in the mud.

'I . . . errm . . . You haven't got any woodgrog, have you?' said Twig.

'Nah!' the cloddertrog scowled. 'This is a drinking pit. We don't cater for the hoity-toity here.'

Twig nodded. 'Then three jugs of tripweed beer it is,' he said amiably.

The cloddertrog climbed a wooden ladder and thrust three filthy jugs into the vat.

'Best to keep him happy,' Twig said to Cowlquape. 'Though I wouldn't drink it if I were you. It's fermented from rotted tripweed and the entrails of oozefish.'

Cowlquape shivered with disgust. The cloddertrog returned.

'There you go,' he said, thrusting the overflowing wooden jugs into their hands.

'Thanks,' said Twig, slipping a coin into the cloddertrog's outstretched paw of a hand. 'And tell me . . .'

But he had already turned his attention to a scrum of thirsty cloddertrogs who were standing to one side, cursing and swearing, demanding to be served. Twig nudged Cowlquape and nodded towards the jugs. 'Let's see if these can buy us some information.'

Taking care not to knock into anyone – '*spilled beer and spilled blood oft flow together*' as the cautionary saying went – they picked their way through the heaving mob.

The stench from the tripweed beer grew stronger. It steamed from the jugs, it hung in the air, it oozed from the pores of the cloddertrogs all round them.

One of them – a colossal individual – turned and peered at the outsiders with glassy-eyed interest. His gaze rested on the jugs in their hands.

'Are they for me?' he exclaimed, his voice booming and slurred. 'You're too kind!' He seized the jugs, swallowed long and deep and beamed back at them. 'Nectar of the clods,' he boomed, and roared with laughter. He threw the two empty jugs aside and started on the third. Behind him, a group of ruddy-faced individuals burst into song. A roar of laughter went up from the drinking pit.

'So what line of work are you in?' said Twig.

'Same as most round here,' the cloddertrog replied. 'Dock work. Loading. Unloading . . .' He grinned. 'Wouldn't swop it for the world.'

The cloddertrog beside him turned and punched him good-naturedly on his fleshy arm. 'That's coz your soft in the head, Grom,' he said. He turned to Twig. 'I'll tell you what, I for one wouldn't mind swapping places with one of them academical types up in Sanctaphrax. Living in the lap of luxury, they are.'

'*Pfff,*' said the first, and spat on the ground. 'I'd sooner be down here, Tugger, as you very well know – with a jug in my hand and surrounded by mates.'

'See?' said Tugger, turning to Twig and Cowlquape, and screwing a thick finger into his temple. 'Soft in the head. Finest sapwine they drink up there in the floating city, out of cut-glass goblets. Or so I've heard.'

'They certainly do,' said Twig. 'We were up there only the other day – on business,' he added. It seemed unwise to let the cloddertrogs know of their true connection with Sanctaphrax. 'You wouldn't believe the wealth.'

'Oh, I would,' said Tugger.

'Mind you, none of them seemed as happy as anyone here,' said Twig, looking round.

'Told you!' said Grom triumphantly. He drained his jug and folded his arms.

'In fact,' Twig went on, 'they all seemed rather distracted. Apparently reports have been coming in that spirits have been sighted in Undertown. In particular in the boom-docks . . . Mind you, it's probably all a load of nonsense,' he said. 'You know what they're like with their lofty ideas – it's what comes of living with their heads in the clouds the whole time . . .'

The two cloddertrogs exchanged glances. 'Yet maybe there is some truth in the stories this time.'

Twig's eyes narrowed. 'You don't mean . . .'

'I've seen them myself,' said Grom.

'Me, too,' said Tugger, nodding earnestly. 'Two of them.' He leant forwards conspiratorially. 'They glow!'

Cowlquape's heart began to thump. He looked Twig and Tarp Hammelherd up and down for any trace of their own tell-tale luminous light. Thankfully, the lufwood torches were blazing so brightly that there was none.

'Glow?' he heard Twig saying. 'How peculiar. But tell me, where exactly did you see them?'

'Once down by the river, glowing in the darkness,' came the reply. 'Once up in the market-place, late at night when all the lamps had been put out.'

Grom nodded. 'And once, at midnight, I seen them floating along an alley. There one minute, they were, then gone again.' He shrugged. 'Sky alone knows where they came from or where they go to – but they give me the heebie-jeebies, so they do.'

Tugger laughed heartily and slapped Twig on the back. 'Enough of this talk of spirits,' he said. 'I got a mighty thirst on this evening. Another jug?'

Twig smiled. 'I'm afraid not,' he said. He turned to the others. 'Come on Tarp, Cowlquape. If we're going to complete our business this side of midnight, we'd best be going.'

'Please yourself.' The cloddertrog turned away. 'Too good to drink with the likes of us,' said Grom, nudging Tugger.

Twig, Tarp and Cowlquape retreated. The light drizzle turned to great heavy drops of rain. Twig felt a surge of irrational anger welling up inside him. He fought against the feeling. Beside him, Tarp's and Cowlquape's faces were drawn and tense.

'*Waaargh!* You stupid oaf!' bellowed an angry voice.

'Me, stupid?' a second voice roared. 'You ridiculous dunderhead!' There was the sound of a clenched fist slamming into a jaw.

'It's . . . it's the weather doing this,' Twig muttered through gritted teeth, and grabbed Cowlquape by the arm.

The next instant, the whole place exploded into violence as each and every cloggertrog turned on one another. Fists flew. Teeth were bared. Clubs were drawn. Curses filled the air.

'Quickly, Cowlquape,' Twig said, steering him forwards. 'Let's get out of here.'

But there were cloddertrogs everywhere, gripped by rain-rage, blocking their way, lashing out blindly at any who came too near. Punching. Kicking. Snarling and biting.

The great vat was splintered and leaking. A scrum of half a dozen of the furious creatures fell screaming to the ground, where they squirmed and writhed in a flood of tripweed beer, still scratching and scraping and scuffling with each other.

'I'll rip off your head.' 'I'll tear you limb from limb!' 'I'll yank out your liver and swallow it whole!'

And all the while, the terrible rain grew heavier. It hammered down torrentially, flooding the narrow streets and dousing the blazing lufwood torches, one by one.

'Come on, Tarp,' Twig called as he and Cowlquape attempted to squeeze through the crush of thrashing bodies. 'I . . . *wurrrgh!*' he grunted as a particularly large cloddertrog seized him from behind and clamped a fleshy hand over his mouth. Another cloddertrog had hold of Cowlquape. A third pinned Tarp against a wall.

Half a dozen more torches sputtered and died. Then, all at once, the last of the blazing lufwood torches went out, and the whole area was plunged into darkness.

'WAAAAH!' the cloddertrog screamed in Twig's ear and shoved him roughly away. He careered into Tarp. Their luminous glow became brighter than ever.

'Spirits!' the cloddertrogs howled and fell back – enraged still, yet too terrified to attack.

'Quick,' Twig whispered to the others. 'Let's get out of here before they realize we might not be spirits after all.'

He grabbed hold of Cowlquape's arm, and the three of them made a dash for it. The cloddertrogs bellowed after them, but did not follow. Yet there were others out there on the streets – everywhere they looked – all driven to bloodthirsty violence by the madness of the weather.

'What do we do?' said Tarp, running first in one direction, then back again. 'We're done for! We're doomed!'

'*This way*,' hissed a voice in Twig's ear.

'Very well, this way!' he shouted and ran up the narrow alley, the others hot on his heels. 'Stick together!' he bellowed. 'And pray to Sky that . . .'

'*Aaaaargh!*' they all cried out in horror as the ground beneath them seemed to give way.

Falling. Down, down, down. Tumbling through the dark, fetid air, arms and legs flailing wildly. Above their heads there was a loud bang as a trapdoor slammed shut.

·CHAPTER TEN·

THE CISTERN

'Goodness!' Cowlquape gasped as the rapid descent came to an abrupt halt. Something soft, silken and oddly springy had broken his fall. With a cry of surprise he bounced back, and grunted with pain as Tarp Hammelherd crashed heavily into him. The two of them fell back down onto the bouncy mesh of fibres. Twig landed on top of them both.

All at once, there was a click. Then a thud. Then, with a hissing swish, a rope drawstring tightened up. The mesh-like material gathered around them, gripping them tightly and thrusting the three hapless individuals close together.

The first thing that hit Cowlquape was the incredible stench, so powerful it felt like the fingers of an invisible hand reaching down his throat and making him gag. Encased in the thick netting, the glow from Twig and Tarp was muted, but by the faint light that *did* penetrate outside, Cowlquape slowly began to make out his surroundings.

They were suspended high above a great, steaming underground canal. All around them, pipes protruded from the walls of the immense tunnel through which the canal flowed. A constant stream of filthy water poured from the pipes and into the foaming torrent below.

'The sewers,' Cowlquape groaned. 'I . . . *Ouch!* That hurts!' he yelped as Twig's bony elbow pressed sharply into his back. 'What are you doing?'

'Trying to draw my knife,' Twig grunted. 'Though I can't . . . seem to . . . move . . .'

'*OWWW!*' Cowlquape howled, still louder.

Twig gave up the struggle. 'It's hopeless,' he muttered. 'I just can't reach it.'

'Wouldn't do you much good if you could,' came Tarp Hammelherd's muffled voice from below them. His face was pressed into the bottom of the net. 'It's made of woodspider silk.'

Twig groaned. Woodspider silk was the material used in the manufacture of sky pirate ship sails – light as gossamer, yet tough enough to withstand the battering of the gales which swept in from beyond the Edge. His knife would be as good as useless against the thick spun fibres from which the net had been constructed.

'This is terrible, cap'n,' Tarp Hammelherd complained. 'I'd have sooner chanced my luck with those crazy cloddertrogs than ended up strung up like a great tilder sausage.' He winced miserably as the steaming vapours of the passing filth swirled up into his nostrils. Piebald rats sniffed the air and squeaked up with frustration at the glowing bundle dangling above them. 'Somebody, or something, set this trap,' he said, 'and we've fallen into it.'

'What do you mean, *something*?' said Cowlquape, alarmed.

'I've heard that muglumps live in the sewers,' came Tarp's hushed and muffled voice. 'Fearsome beasts they are. All claws and teeth. But clever, devious – perhaps one of them might have . . .'

'*Shhh!*' Twig hissed.

From far in the distance came a harsh, clanking sound.

'What's *that*?' Cowlquape whispered, dread setting the hairs at the back of his neck tingling.

'I don't know,' Twig whispered back.

The clanking grew louder. It was getting closer. Twig, pinned against Cowlquape, couldn't turn his head. Tarp, beneath them, couldn't see a thing. Only Cowlquape, whose head was fixed so that he could gaze back along the tunnel, faced the direction of the sound. He gulped.

'Can you see anything, Cowlquape?' said Twig uneasily. He knew that it wasn't only piebald rats and muglumps that lived in the sewers. There were trogs and trolls who had left their underground caverns in the Deepwoods for the promise of a better life in

Undertown, only to find that the frantic bustle above ground was too much to take. Some starved. Others had taken up residence in the sewerage system underground, where they scavenged a brutal existence.

The clanking was closer than ever now, harsh and clear above the gushing pipes. *Clang!* Metal scraped on metal. *Clang!* The pipes seemed to shudder.

And then Cowlquape saw it: a great metal hook which swung through the air, clanged against a pipe jutting out from the tunnel wall and took hold. The hook was fastened to a gnarled wooden pole around which two bony hands tightened their grip and pulled.

A shadowy figure standing awkwardly in a bizarre craft of lashed-together driftwood emerged from the gloom. He swung the hook again. *Clang!* It gripped the next pipe, and he pulled his barge against the current of the foaming canal, closer and closer.

Cowlquape gasped. 'I can see something,' he whispered.

CLANG!

The boat was almost beneath them now. A huge flathead leered up at him.

'Twig,' Cowlquape squeaked, 'it's . . .'

The hook sliced through the air in an arc, then ripped back, releasing the net. Like a hot flight-rock – with the three hapless individuals still bound up inside – it fell with a heavy thud into the bottom of the goblin's barge, just as the current took it underneath.

They hurtled along the stinking canal, buffeted by waves of filth, the driftwood craft dipping and rocking in the swell. The goblin, balanced expertly on the stern, loomed over them. In his bony hands was the long hook, now acting as a rudder and guiding the makeshift boat on its way. Faster and faster, and . . .

CLANG!

The boat jolted to an abrupt halt as the goblin's hook latched fast to a jutting pipe overhead. Twig, Cowlquape and Tarp struggled inside the net.

'What have we caught today, Bogwitt?' came a voice from above.

'Bogwitt?' breathed Twig.

Dagger in hand, the goblin reached down and pulled the slip-knot that held the top of the net. The net fell away. Twig leapt to his feet, glowing brightly. Mouth agape, the astonished flat-head goblin dropped his dagger.

'Sleet!' he yelled. 'He's glowing! He's glowing like us!'

'Don't you recognize me, Bogwitt?' said Twig, trying to sound calm as the barge rocked dangerously beneath his feet. 'It's me, Twig.'

'*I* recognize you, *Captain* Twig,' came the voice from above. 'Though I never thought to see you alive again, least of all in the sewers of Undertown.'

Twig looked up. There in the entrance of a wide, gaping pipe stood a gaunt figure dressed in the heavy longcoat and tricorn hat of a sky pirate. He, too, was bathed in the same luminous glow.

'Sleet!' cried Twig, almost losing his balance. 'Wingnut Sleet!'

But the former quartermaster of the *Edgedancer* had already turned away and disappeared into the pipe.

'Don't you mind him, captain,' said Bogwitt, clambering awkwardly from the boat, his right leg dragging behind him. 'I'm sure he's more pleased to see you than he's letting on. And as for me, I couldn't be happier.'

'Nor I, to see you,' said Twig. 'I can scarcely believe what's happening.'

He followed Bogwitt up the iron holds in the wall to the entrance of the pipe, high above. Unlike all the others, no foul water spewed from it. Cowlquape and Tarp followed them close behind. Then, pushing back a heavy hide curtain at the other end of the pipe, they found themselves in a wide chamber.

Wingnut Sleet stood to one side, his face half turned away. 'Welcome,' he said softly.

Cowlquape looked round in amazement. The place was a veritable smuggler's cave, stacked from top to bottom with boxes and crates overflowing with an array of costly items. There were rugs on the floor and hangings on the walls. There was furniture: two armchairs, a table, cupboards – and a small, ornately carved writing-desk. There were pots and pans, bottles and jars, crockery, cutlery, cruet . . . and the mouthwatering smell of tildermeat sausages.

'It used to be a water cistern,' Sleet explained. 'Now it is where we are forced to live.'

Twig nodded. 'I feared you might not be living at all,' he said.

'Aye, well, perhaps it would be better if I weren't,' Sleet muttered under his breath as he turned and crossed the cistern to where a skillet was sizzling on a stove.

'But Sleet . . .' Twig began.

'Oh, him and me get by all right down here,' Bogwitt broke in. 'We've been here weeks now. We forage and

filch – and you'd be amazed at the stuff we find in the nets some days . . . though we always take any creatures back to the surface – after relieving them of any valuables they may be carrying. And with light no problem . . .' He nodded towards Wingnut Sleet's back, hunched over the stove. 'So long as the two of us stick together.'

'The glowing, you mean?' said Twig.

'It was the same with us two when the cap'n found me,' said Tarp. 'And now here's the four of us all aglow.'

'Something must have happened out there to cause it,' said Twig. 'But I remember *nothing*. How about you, Bogwitt? Can you remember what happened to us out there in open sky?'

The flat-head goblin shook his head. 'No,' he said. 'We set off after the caterbird in search of your father, we entered the weather vortex – and then, not a thing.' He grimaced as he pointed to his right leg. 'All I know is that I was injured somehow.'

'And you, Sleet?' said Twig. The hunched figure remained silent. Twig frowned. The quartermaster's surliness was beginning to irritate him. 'Sleet!' he said sharply.

Sleet stiffened. 'Not a thing,' came the sullen reply. He laid down his spatula and turned slowly round. 'I know only that it did this to me.' He removed his tricorn hat.

Cowlquape gasped. Tarp Hammelherd turned away. Twig, eyes wide with horror, started back. 'Y . . . your face!' he breathed.

The hair was gone, as was the left ear – and the skin down that side looked as if it had melted like wax.

A white, sightless eye nestled in the molten folds. The quartermaster's hand moved up to the hideous scarring.

'This?' he scowled. 'This is how I found myself on my return from open sky. Not a pretty sight, eh?'

'I . . . I had no idea,' said Twig.

Sleet shrugged. 'There is no reason why you should,' he said.

'But you blame me for taking you inside the weather vortex?'

'No, captain,' said Sleet. 'I agreed to accompany you. It was my choice.' He paused. 'Though I confess to being disappointed that you don't know how we made it back to the Edge either.'

'I know only what I was told,' said Twig regretfully, 'that we looked like eight shooting stars as we sped back across the night sky. At least, that's how the Professor of Darkness described it.'

Sleet's one good eye narrowed. The scarred flesh quivered. 'The Professor of Darkness?' he said.

Twig nodded. 'Some he saw landing in Undertown – you, Bogwitt, Tarp Hammelherd; perhaps one other as well. The others travelled further. They came down somewhere in the Deepwoods. I vowed to find you all. And look, I've found three of you already. It's more than I'd ever dared hope for.'

'Hope,' said Sleet bitterly. 'I've learnt to live without it. After all, hope isn't going to heal this.' He ran his fingertips gently down the terrible scars.

Cowlquape turned away.

'I could bear neither the staring eyes . . .' Sleet glanced at Cowlquape and Tarp Hammelherd, 'nor the averted gazes of those who are repelled by my appearance. So I came down to the sewers, to hide myself away. And Bogwitt – to his credit – accompanied me.'

'Where he goes, I go,' Bogwitt growled loyally.

'We look out for each other,' said Sleet. 'It is necessary down here,' he added darkly.

'Like the professor – sorry, Twig – looks out for me,' said Cowlquape, turning back. 'It's sometimes necessary, even in Sanctaphrax.'

'Sanctaphrax,' said Sleet, more softly. His eyes misted over. 'I too once nurtured dreams of finding a position in the floating city of academics. But then, with that place, it isn't *what* you know, but *who* you know.' He sniffed bitterly. 'And I knew no-one.'

From the back of the chamber came the smell of burning. Bogwitt limped across the floor and seized the skillet from the stove. 'Supper's ready,' he announced.

'Tildermeat sausages,' said Sleet.

'My favourite,' said Twig, suddenly realizing how hungry he was.

Bogwitt shared out the sausages, sliced up a loaf of bread and returned with five plates balanced in his arms. He handed them out.

'And there's a flagon of excellent sapwine I've been saving for a special occasion,' said Sleet. 'Bogwitt, our finest goblets if you please.'

'To the crew of the *Edgedancer*,' Twig announced when each of them had a brimming glass in his hand. 'To those found and to those still to be found.'

The others chorused the toast in hearty agreement and everyone sipped at the sweet, golden liquid.

'*Aaah!*' sighed Tarp Hammelherd, wiping his whiskers on the back of his hand. 'Exquisite!'

Even Cowlquape appreciated the warm spicy flavours of the sapwine and a little later, when they were all tucking into the succulent tildermeat sausages he too realized just how hungry he'd become.

'Delicious,' he spluttered, tearing off a chunk of sausage and a hunk of bread. 'Absolutely deee-licious!'

Twig turned to his scarred quartermaster. 'I must say, Sleet, you've done well given the awful situation you found yourselves in. And you, too, Bogwitt. Very well. But you can't stay here in this terrible place, especially as you have both been injured on my behalf. One day I shall have a new ship and you shall be my crew again. But for now I must find out what has happened to the others.'

'We will go with you,' said Sleet.

Bogwitt nodded enthusiastically. 'Where you go, we go, Captain Twig,' he said.

'Not this time, Bogwitt,' Twig replied gently. 'Your leg needs time to heal, too.'

'Then we must stay here,' said Sleet sullenly. He nodded towards the vaulted roof. 'For there is nothing for us *up there*.'

'On the contrary,' said Twig. '*Sanctaphrax* is up there.'

'S . . . Sanctaphrax?' said Wingnut Sleet. 'But . . .'

'As you so rightly said, Sleet, it isn't what you know, but who. *I* know the Professor of Darkness. And *you* know me.'

Wingnut Sleet's mouth dropped open.

'I shall write you a letter which you will deliver to the professor himself.' He glanced round. 'I assume you have the means to do so,' he said.

'Oh, yes,' said Sleet. 'Paper and ink of the highest quality, and the finest snowbird quills. Something I picked up on one of our foraging trips.'

Twig smiled. 'You will stay in my study in the School of Light and Darkness and await my return,' he said. 'I would guess that the professor might wish to conduct a couple of experiments on you, concerning the way you glow – but otherwise, you will be left alone. How does that sound?'

'It sounds very good, captain,' said Wingnut Sleet. 'Very good indeed.'

'Indeed,' Bogwitt echoed.

'Yes, Bogwitt,' said Twig. 'As you once worked there as a guard, you must know Sanctaphrax like the back of your hand. Take the hidden alleys and secret passages on your way to the Professor of Darkness. Let's try and keep those gossipy academic tongues from wagging.' He turned to the slaughterer. 'Tarp,' he said, 'you must go with them.'

'Me?' Tarp cried out. 'Accompany them to Sanctaphrax?' He shook his head in disbelief. 'But I want to go with *you*, cap'n. I'm fit. I'm strong. You need someone like me on such a perilous quest.'

'I'm sorry, Tarp, but only Cowlquape can travel with me.'

'But why, cap'n?'

'Think about it, Tarp,' said Twig gently. 'How far do you think we'd get, glowing like tilder lamps? Whenever it is dark, we would begin to glow if together – and the fear of others would not help in our search.'

'But we could cover up,' Tarp persisted. 'We could wear thick hooded cloaks to conceal the light and . . .'

'And end up more conspicuous than ever!' said Twig. 'No, I must do this without you. Together, we would only fail – and that is something I must not do.'

The slaughterer nodded understandingly. 'You're right, Cap'n Twig,' he said. 'I should have thought.'

'Thank you, Tarp,' said Twig gratefully. He turned to Bogwitt and Sleet. 'It is agreed then. You three will await my return in Sanctaphrax, while Cowlquape and I journey on to find what has become of the rest of my missing crew.' He frowned with pretend impatience. 'So where is that paper and pen?'

·CHAPTER ELEVEN·

THE WESTERN QUAYS

Two weeks later, Cowlquape and Twig found themselves on the dockside of the western quays. Their previous night's lodgings had been infested with vicious dustfleas and, having been bitten half to death, they'd decided to cut their losses before sunrise and leave the filthy dormitory. Outside now, the first deep red feathers of sunrise were tickling the horizon. Twig yawned, stretched and rubbed his eyes.

'May this new day bring us the information we require,' he said, and sighed. 'Oh, why is the fourth crew member proving to be so elusive?' he wondered out loud.

'Mm-hmm,' mumbled Cowlquape. He was sitting on the jetty by Twig's feet, his legs dangling over the side. His nose, as always, was buried deep in one of the precious scrolls he kept in the bag slung over his shoulder.

Twig looked around him. Unlike the rundown boom-docks to the east, where only the lowliest of tug ships moored, the western quays were well-heeled. This was where the leaguesmen's sky ships were docked, and the shore behind was lined with their buildings – solid constructions with façades that were more than merely functional. Each one bore the coat of arms of the league it housed: the crossed sickle and chisel of the League of Gutters and Gougers, the piebald rat and coiled rope of the Gluesloppers and Ropeteasers, the pot and pliers of the Melders and Moulders . . .

Behind them all stood the lofty Leagues' Chamber, where the High Council of the Merchant League of Undertown sat. Always the most impressive building in the boom-docks, it looked more striking than ever at the moment, surrounded as it was by an intricate framework of scaffolding. Twig nodded towards it.

'They must be seeing to the roof,' he said.

'Mm-hmm,' Cowlquape mumbled again. He licked his finger and, without looking up, turned to the next barkscroll.

Twig turned back and stared at the river, flowing weakly past. The rising sun bounced oozy blobs of red over its crumpled surface.

The trouble was, their search for the fourth crewman in the leaguesmen's district had proved as unrewarding as their searches everywhere else in Undertown. The bustling streets, the noisy markets, the industrial quarter, the northern heights – Twig and Cowlquape had been to them all. Yet no matter how many taverns they visited, how many individuals they spoke to, how many enquiries they made, they had discovered nothing whatsoever about a falling shooting star or the sudden appearance of someone acting oddly.

'Perhaps the time has come for us simply to abandon our search here in Undertown and set forth for the Deepwoods,' said Twig.

'Mm-hmm,' said Cowlquape, his brow furrowed.

'Cowlquape!' said Twig. 'Have you heard a single word I've been saying to you?'

Cowlquape looked up, his expression puzzled, his eyes gleaming with excitement.

'Ever the studious academic, eh?' said Twig. 'You've been lost in those barkscrolls ever since we got here.'

'Oh, but it's . . . they're . . . just let me read you this,' he said. 'It really is absolutely fascinating stuff.'

'If you must,' said Twig resignedly.

'It's more about *The Myth of Riverrise,*' said Cowlquape eagerly. 'About the Mother Storm . . .'

Twig started as, for a fleeting moment, a memory from the fatal voyage into open sky flashed inside his head. 'The Mother Storm,' he muttered, but even as he said the words the elusive memory slipped away again. He looked up. 'Go on then,' he said. 'Tell me what it says.'

Cowlquape nodded and found the place with his finger. '*For as I write, it is now the commonly held belief that the Mother Storm has struck the Edge not once, but many times, destroying and recreating with each return,*' he read out. '*I . . .*'

'*I*?' said Twig. 'Who wrote these words?'

Cowlquape glanced up. 'They are a transcription of the original bark-writings that date back to the Time of Enlightenment in the Ancient Deepwoods,' Cowlquape explained. 'This version,' he said, stroking the scroll affectionately, 'was written down by a lowly scribe several hundred years ago. But the originals were much, much older.'

Twig smiled. The lad's enthusiasm was infectious.

'The Time of Enlightenment!' said Cowlquape. 'Oh, it must have been such a wonderful time to be alive. A glorious age of freedom and learning – long before our magnificent floating city of Sanctaphrax was even dreamed of. The Deepwoods emerged from darkness under the visionary leadership of Kobold the Wise. How I would love to have known him! He banished slavery. He united the thousand tribes under the lordly arms of the Trident and the Snake. He even oversaw the invention of the written word . . .'

'Yes, yes, Cowlquape,' said Twig. 'Very interesting. Is there a point to all this?'

'Patience, Twig,' said Cowlquape. 'All will soon be revealed. The Time of Enlightenment was abruptly snuffed out like a candle, Kobold the Wise's Union of a Thousand Tribes broke up, and the whole region descended into the barbarity and chaos that has reigned in the Deepwoods to this day.' He returned his attention to the barkscroll. 'Listen,' he said, 'this is what the scribe writes.'

Despite himself, Twig remained silent and listened attentively as Cowlquape read from the curled and yellowed scroll.

'Kobold the Wise grew old and weary. Madness walked the market glades and deep meadows. Tribe turned upon tribe, brother upon brother, father upon son, for the Sky had grown angry and stole the reason of all who dwelt beneath it.

'Thus did representatives of the Thousand Tribes gather at Riverrise, and say, "Kobold, you who see further into Open Sky than the greatest of us, tell us what to do, for, in our madness, we are devouring each other and the sky turns our hearts black."

'And Kobold raised himself up from his sick bed and said, "Lo, the Mother Storm returns. Her madness shall be our madness. Prepare yourselves, for time is short . . ." '

Cowlquape paused. 'There's a bit of a gap in the text here,' he explained. 'Wood-weevils have devoured the original bark.' He looked down again. 'This is how it continues.

'. . . The Mother Storm, she who first seeded the Edge with life, shall come back to reap what she has sown, and the world shall return to Darkness,' he said, emphasizing every word. 'Do you see, Twig? Kobold the Wise was describing *The Myth of Riverrise* and predicting the return of the Mother Storm – a prediction that came all too true, for the Deepwoods did indeed return to darkness. And now it is happening all over again.'

Twig turned away and stared up into open sky where

the Mother Storm had held him in her terrible grasp.

'The madness described is with us again,' Cowlquape said solemnly, 'blown in on the weather from beyond the Edge. The mad mists and heart-breaking rains – the terrible violence. What was it I read out?' He found the place again. '. . . *in our madness we are devouring each other*. Don't you see, Twig. It isn't a myth at all. The Mother Storm is returning.'

'The Mother Storm is returning,' Twig repeated quietly. The words chimed with familiarity. But how? Why? He shook his head with frustration. Something important had undoubtedly happened to him out there in the weather vortex far away in open sky. Why couldn't he remember what it was? Would he ever remember?

He looked at his troubled young apprentice. 'Come, Cowlquape,' he said. 'I think we can safely leave such matters to the academics of Sanctaphrax. For ourselves, it is time we abandoned – or at least postponed – our search for the fourth crew-member of the *Edgedancer*, and set forth into the Deepwoods. Let's go to the posting-pole and find ourselves passage on board a sky ship.'

Somewhat reluctantly, Cowlquape rolled up his precious barkscrolls, pushed them back into the bag and climbed to his feet. Then, together, he and Twig headed off along the quay to the central embarkation jetty. It was there that the posting-pole was situated.

The posting-pole was a tall, stout pillar of wood to which those sky ship captains with spare berths to announce would nail advertisements, written out on squares of shimmering cloth. It was the easiest way for those with no means of transport of their own to travel from one part of the Edge to another.

As Twig and Cowlquape reached the end of the embarkation jetty, the sun wobbled up above the horizon, crimson and majestic. Ahead of them, silhouetted against the sky, stood the posting-pole. With the countless fluttering pink-tinged scraps of material nailed along its length, it looked like a curious tree, its bark covered in blossom.

'I only hope that one of them is offering something suitable,' Twig muttered as he walked forwards.

Cowlquape went with him. 'How about this one?' he said a moment later, and read from the square of cloth. '*Raggers and Royners Leagueship. Departing for the Deepwoods this afternoon*. They've got a double berth spare. And the price seems fair.'

But Twig shook his head. 'No,' he said. 'No, it's not quite . . .' His voice drifted away as he raised and read announcement after announcement.

'What about this one, then?' said Cowlquape. 'A tug-master bound for the ironwood copses of the barktrolls is leaving later this morning and needs an extra two pairs of hands.'

But Twig paid him no attention as he continued to read down the list of vessels and their destinations. The *Stormfinder*, destination: the slaughterer camps.

A voice in his head said, *'No.'*

The *Cloudeater*, destination: the Great Hammelhorn Fair.

'No.'

The *Luggerbrill*, destination: the Goblin Glades.

'No.'

On down the list he went. *No, no, no,* until . . .

'Yes, this is the sky ship you must take,' the voice said, softly but clearly.

'Of course!' Twig exclaimed. 'Cowlquape, this is it. This is the one. Listen.

Two spare places going on board the Skyraider,
five gold pieces each.
Destination: The Great Shryke Slave Market.'

Twig looked up. 'What better place to resume our search?'

Cowlquape nodded uncertainly. His father, Ulbus Pentephraxis, had told him terrible stories about the Great Shryke Slave Market. 'Won't it be a bit dangerous?' he asked warily.

Twig shrugged. 'Undertown can also be dangerous,' he said. 'We must visit a place where creatures from all over the Deepwoods congregate.'

'Yes, but . . .' Cowlquape said. 'I mean, couldn't we go to that Great Hammelhorn Fair you mentioned. Or, look, there's a sky ship heading for the Timber Clearings of the woodtrolls. Wouldn't that do instead?'

'Cowlquape,' said Twig, 'there is no place in the Deepwoods like the Great Shryke Slave Market. Its denizens travel from every corner to be there. It is the obvious place to start our search.' He glanced down at the announcement once again and smiled. 'Thunderbolt Vulpoon,' he said. 'Now there's a name to conjure with.'

Cowlquape shivered. 'He sounds horrible,' he said. 'Isn't a vulpoon one of those vicious birds with a serrated beak?'

'It is,' said Twig.

'And Thunderbolt!' said Cowlquape. 'What kind of a monster would take the name of a bloodthirsty bird of prey *and* the most terrible and unpredictable feature of the weather?'

Twig snorted. 'A vain and foolish one,' he said. '*Name wild, captain mild,* as my father used to say. Those who select the most ferocious of names are without exception the ones least worthy of them.' His eyes misted up. 'Whereas the more gallant and valiant call themselves by less ostentatious names.'

'Like Cloud Wolf,' said Cowlquape quietly.

'Yes,' said Twig, 'like my father, Cloud Wolf, the most gallant and valiant sky pirate captain of them all.' He glanced back down at the announcement. 'Sky above!' he exclaimed.

'What?' said Cowlquape, alarmed.

'The departure time!' said Twig. 'The *Skyraider* is due to set sail in less than a quarter of an hour.'

*

'This is hopeless!' Twig cried out. 'Where is it?'

Ten minutes had passed since he'd stuffed the cloth announcement into his back pocket – ten minutes spent dashing along the quay, racing up and down the jetties, looking at the names of the sky ships. An old lugtroll had just assured them that the sky ship they were searching was at the second jetty, but they were there now and, despite looking twice, had drawn yet another blank.

'You don't think it might have left early, do you?' said Twig breathlessly.

'If the two spare places have already been filled, maybe so,' said Cowlquape, secretly hoping that it had.

'But it *can't* have,' said Twig. He paused and looked up and down the docks.

There were so many sky ships there – elegant league ships, sturdy merchant tug ships, streamlined patrol ships, as well as the occasional sky pirate ship – yet the *Skyraider* itself was nowhere to be seen.

'Perhaps we should return to the posting-pole and . . .'

'No,' said Twig. 'There isn't time.' He called to a group of dock-workers standing with their backs turned, deep in conversation. ''Scuse me,' he yelled. 'Do *you* know where a sky ship by the name of *Skyraider* is berthed?'

Without even deigning to turn round, one of them shouted back. 'Nineteenth jetty. Bottom right.'

Cowlquape turned to Twig. 'But we've just come from that end of the quays,' he said.

'I don't care,' said Twig. 'This could be our last chance.' He grabbed Cowlquape by the arm and dragged him forwards. 'Come on, Cowlquape,' he shouted. 'Run!'

Along the quayside promenade, they dashed. With Cowlquape close on his heels, Twig barged blindly through groups of haggling merchants, upending boxes of fish and barrows of fruit. Cowlquape glanced back over his shoulders. 'Sorry,' he called. On they sped, past jetty after numbered jetty which stuck out into mid-air, high above the Edgewater River. The eighth, ninth and tenth jetties flashed past.

'Faster, Cowlquape!' Twig shouted breathlessly, as the voice in his head urged him on.

Twelfth ... thirteenth ... Cowlquape's heart was pounding, his lungs burning, yet still he drove himself on. Seventeenth ... Eighteenth ...

'The nineteenth jetty!' Twig exclaimed. He skidded round, jumped down the five stairs in one leap and pounded along the wooden platform. 'And look!' he cried. 'How in Sky's name did we miss it before?'

Cowlquape looked up and followed Twig's pointing finger to a magnificent sky pirate ship tethered to the end of the raised jetty on the left.

'The *Skyraider*!' said Twig. 'We've found it, but ... Oh, no!' he gasped.

The mainsail was up, the grappling-hooks had been raised and a small figure was crouched over the tether-ring, unfastening the tolley-rope. The sky ship was about to depart.

'STOP!' Twig roared, as he doubled his speed and hurtled headlong along the jetty. Although he could not explain it, something told him he *had* to board the *Skyraider*. No other ship would do. 'WAIT FOR US!'

But the crew-member – a mobgnome – paid him no heed.

'*STOP!*' Twig shouted again.

He could hear the mobgnome muttering irritably as he tugged at the snagged rope, then sigh with relief as it came free.

Nearly there . . .

The mobgnome tossed the rope onto the deck and, in the same movement, jumped aboard himself. Tantalizingly slowly at first, the sky pirate ship began to float up and away from the jetty.

'NO!' screamed Twig.

The gap between jetty and sky ship widened.

'Are you with me, Cowlquape?' he cried.

'I'm with you,' came the reply.

'Then, jump!' yelled Twig and, as the pair of them reached the end of the jetty at last, they launched themselves at the departing sky ship. Together they flew through the air, arms outstretched, willing themselves on.

'*Unkhh!*' Cowlquape grunted as his hands gripped the safety-rail and his body slammed into the hull. The next instant, Twig landed beside him.

Winded, the pair of them clung on for grim death. They would have to catch their breath before pulling themselves up on to the deck. But it didn't matter. The important thing was that they had made it, just in the nick of time.

'Well done,' whispered a voice in his ear.

'We're on our way, Cowlquape,' Twig murmured. 'To the Deepwoods and the Great Shryke Slave Market.'

'Twig, I . . . I . . .'

'Cowlquape?' said Twig, twisting his head round. 'What is it?'

'My hands . . . all slippery,' Cowlquape mumbled, and Twig watched helplessly as his young apprentice struggled desperately to pull himself up. 'Can't . . . can't hold . . . *aaaargh!'* He was falling. Away from the *Skyraider*, out of the sky and down to the pleated mud below . . .

·CHAPTER TWELVE·

THUNDERBOLT VULPOON

Twig heaved himself up, swung his leg over the safety-rail and rolled over onto the deck. Then, without pausing, he jumped to his feet and peered back down, over the side.

'Cowlquape!' he bellowed. Certainly he had heard no splash and, though he peered closely at the muddy river-bed below, he could see no sign of his young apprentice. 'Cowlquape!' he cried out again. 'Where are you?'

'Down here,' came a weak voice.

Twig's heart gave a leap. 'Where?'

'On the hull-rigging,' said Cowlquape. 'But I don't know if I can hang on for much longer.'

'Yes, you can!' Twig urged him. 'You've got to, Cowlquape.'

Far below now, the Edgewater River gave way to the Mire.

'It . . . it's no good,' Cowlquape whimpered. 'I can't get a foothold and my arms . . . so weak . . .'

Twig looked round desperately for help, but the *Skyraider* was oddly deserted. The mobgnome had disappeared, and there was no-one else in sight apart from a squat and somewhat flamboyant figure standing up at the helm.

'Help!' he bellowed. 'Help! Someone's fallen overboard!'

Lost in the mechanics of skysailing, the helmsman seemed unaware of the drama unfolding behind him. The sky ship soared higher.

'There must be someone here!' Twig roared. 'HELP ME!'

'What, what, what?' came a nervous, twittery voice by his side. It was the mobgnome, back again. An ancient-looking gnokgoblin with bow-legs and white whiskers stood behind him.

Twig groaned. Neither of them looked up to much. 'My companion fell,' he explained hurriedly. 'He's clinging on to the hull-rigging. Get me a rope and a stave-hook. Now!'

The two crew-members nodded and disappeared. A moment later, they were back. Twig tied one end of the rope to the main aft winding-cleat and tossed the rest over the side. Then, with the stave-hook under his arm, he lowered himself down the rope.

'*Whoa,*' he gasped, as the sudden rush of wind snatched his breath away. 'Keep your nerve,' he told himself. 'Easy does it.'

With the rope twisted between his feet, Twig carefully

let himself slip down. Hand over hand, he went, past the portholes, past the winched grappling-hooks. Further and further. As the hull curved in and away from him, he found himself dangling in mid-air.

'Don't look down, whatever you do,' Twig heard.

He twisted round. And there was Cowlquape, half-way down the side of the sky ship, clutching hold of the hull-rigging for dear life. He'd managed to loop one leg through the criss-cross of ropes, but there was blood all round his fingers from his blistered palms. Every second he remained there the rope dug in deeper.

'Hold tight Cowlquape!' Twig yelled across the airy gap. 'I'm going to try swinging closer.'

By constantly shifting his weight Twig set himself in motion – not back and forwards as he'd hoped, but in a series of widening circles. The sky ship soared higher still. Far below him, the bleached mire glistened like the surface of an ocean of milk. As the circles grew wider still, Twig passed closer and closer to the hull-rigging until finally, with the stave-hook outstretched, he managed to hook a piece of rope and pull himself in.

'There,' he grunted, as he grabbed hold of the rigging to Cowlquape's right. 'We'll have you back on board in no time.'

He twisted round, and tied the rope firmly around Cowlquape's waist. As he was securing the knot, he saw just how badly the lad's hands had been chafed. The blood was dripping from his shaking fingertips.

'Hang on, Cowlquape,' he said. 'I . . .'

The stave-hook slipped from his grasp and tumbled down to the ground below. The sky ship was by now too high for them either to see or hear it landing. Twig squeezed Cowlquape's shoulder.

'I'm going to climb back up on deck,' he said. 'When I give the word, let go. We'll pull you up.'

Cowlquape nodded, but could say nothing. His face was white with fear.

Twig darted up the hull-rigging and leapt back onto the deck. The mobgnome and the old gnokgoblin were still there.

'Grab the rope and take the strain,' he ordered. The two crew-members did as they were told. Twig joined them.

'Let go, Cowlquape!' he shouted down.

The rope lurched and grew heavy.

'Right,' Twig grunted to the others. 'Now, pull! Pull as if your lives depended on it.'

Slowly – painfully slowly – the three of them tugged and heaved, inching their way back across the deck. Suspended below them, Cowlquape felt as if nothing was happening. It was only when he twisted round and looked back at the hull that he saw he was indeed rising up towards the deck.

'Nearly there,' Twig said encouragingly. 'Just a little bit more and . . . Yes!' he exclaimed, as the tousled head of his young apprentice abruptly came into view. While the mobgnome and the gnokgoblin braced themselves, Twig secured the end of the rope to the tether-post, rushed back to the balustrade and seized hold of Cowlquape's wrist. 'Got you!' he grunted.

Cowlquape tumbled down onto the deck. Twig slumped down beside him, exhausted.

'Well, well, well, what have we here?' came a syrupy voice. 'Scurvy stowaways, is it?'

Twig looked up. It was the squat figure he had seen at the helm. He climbed to his feet. 'We're no stowaways,' he said, and pulled the small piece of cloth from the posting-pole out of his pocket. 'We wish to travel with you to the Great Shryke Slave Market – I take it you are Thunderbolt Vulpoon.'

'*Captain* Thunderbolt Vulpoon,' came the reply, as the fastidious little person tugged at the ruffs around his wrists and twirled the points of his waxed moustache. A great ring of keys jangled at his belt. 'Indeed I am.' His eyebrows arched and curled like the sound holes on a wood-lute. 'But this is against all the laws of skysailing,' he said. 'Surely you must know that nobody may board a sky ship without its captain's permission. How else can a potential passenger be vetted before setting sail? I don't even know your names.'

'I am Twig,' said Twig and, ignoring the puzzled flicker of half-recognition which passed across the captain's ruddy face, he turned to his apprentice. 'This is Cowlquape.'

The captain sniffed dismissively. 'Riff-raff by any other name would smell as rank.' He turned. 'Grimlock!' he bellowed.

The towering figure of a brogtroll, clothed in filthy rags, emerged from a trapdoor in the floor behind them. 'Grimlock be here, master,' he rumbled.

'Grimlock, seize these wretches!'

With awful purpose, the captain's brutal sidekick strode towards Twig and Cowlquape, arms outstretched. Twig held his ground.

'We are not riff-raff, *Captain* Vulpoon,' he said. 'We apologize for our rather hasty boarding, but yours was the only ship bound for the slave market, and we didn't want to miss it. Call your minder off.'

Grimlock lurched closer.

'We can pay,' said Twig, reaching inside his shirt for the leather pouch the Professor of Darkness had given him. 'Five gold pieces each, wasn't it?'

The captain paused. He looked them up and down.

'Perhaps I've been too hasty,' he said with a smile. 'You have the look of academics about you. From Sanctaphrax, no doubt – I'm sure you could manage fifteen.'

'But . . .' Twig began.

Grimlock seized Cowlquape by the shoulders and lifted him off his feet.

'All right!' shouted Twig. 'Fifteen it is.'

Captain Thunderbolt Vulpoon smirked as the coins jangled down into his pudgy hand. 'Put him down, Grimlock,' he said.

Cowlquape sighed with relief as he felt the reassuring solidity of the deck beneath his feet once more. He watched the flabby captain spit into his right palm and shake hands with Twig, then turn and grab his own hand and . . .

'*Aaa-oww!*' he howled, and pulled away.

The captain looked down. 'Oh, would you look at that,' he said as he saw Cowlquape's upturned palms. 'Like two raw hammelhorn steaks! We'll have to get you patched up.' His dark eyes gleamed. 'A fine specimen like you.'

Cowlquape squirmed uneasily. 'A specimen?' he wondered out loud.

'Did I say *specimen*?' said the captain. 'Sorry, I meant to say, a fine figure of a lad.' Cowlquape recoiled as the captain scrutinized him closely. 'Bright eyes, strong teeth, broad shoulders . . .' He smiled. 'And bound for the Great Shryke Slave Market.'

Twig nodded. 'We have important business there,' he said.

Thunderbolt Vulpoon smiled all the more broadly. The sun glinted on his silver teeth. 'Indeed you have,' he said softly. 'But first things first.' He turned to the old gnokgoblin. 'Jervis,' he said sharply, his face hardening. 'Show our guests to their quarters. And Teasel,' he barked at the mobgnome. 'Tell Stile there will be two extra mouths to feed – and get something from the medical supplies for the lad's wounds.'

Jervis and Teasel jumped to it nervously.

'And you,' he shouted at the brogtroll. 'Go down and still the . . . the cargo.' He nodded up at the main-mast, which was swaying precariously from side to side. 'They're getting too restless.'

'Grimlock go,' the brogtroll muttered, and lumbered off.

Vulpoon raised his eyes theatrically to the sky and swept a limp hand across his powdered forehead. 'Worst crew I've ever captained,' he complained. 'Still,' he went on, affable and charming once again, 'we shall endeavour to ensure that your voyage is a comfortable one.'

The rolling from side to side grew more and more extreme until everyone on deck – the captain included – had to grab on to something or risk being tossed off the side of the sky ship. Vulpoon grinned sheepishly.

'Live cargo!' he said, and snorted. 'Trouble is, once they get the jitter up, the whole boat's thrown out of kilter.'

'Live cargo?' Twig queried, as the sky ship leaned sharply to port, and then lurched back again.

'Hammelhorns,' said Vulpoon, his eyes flickering round his swaying ship. 'To satisfy the catering needs of the slave market.'

Twig nodded, his thoughts already elsewhere. At that moment a plaintive howling went up. It cut through the air and sent shivers of unease darting up and down Cowlquape's spine. The sky ship righted itself. The howling abruptly ceased. And, with the mainsail billowing, the *Skyraider* soared forwards.

'*That's* better,' said Thunderbolt Vulpoon, his fat face creasing into a smile as he rubbed his pudgy hands together. 'So, Jervis, jump to it.' He turned to Twig and Cowlquape. 'And if there's anything you need, don't hesitate to ask. Supper will be served in an hour's time.'

*

Their quarters were comfortable enough, and the days passed with a frustrating sameness – the two companions seldom leaving their cabin. But Cowlquape still felt uneasy. Lying on his front one day, unable to concentrate on the barkscroll in front of him, he looked up from his hammock. 'I just don't trust him,' he said.

'What's that?' said Twig.

'Thunderbolt Vulpoon,' said Cowlquape. 'I don't trust him. Or that hulking great bodyguard of his.'

Twig turned from the porthole of the cramped cabin and looked at the anxious lad.

'What's more,' Cowlquape continued, 'I still don't understand why he's taking a cargo of hammelhorns to the slave market. It can't be profitable.' He frowned. 'I reckon I know what his live cargo is.'

'What?' said Twig.

'Slaves,' said Cowlquape darkly.

'Out of the question,' said Twig. 'Sky ships from Undertown don't carry slaves, you know that.'

'But . . .'

'Undertown is a free town, Cowlquape,' said Twig. 'And the punishment for attempting to enslave the least of its inhabitants is death. No-one would willingly serve on such a ship.'

Cowlquape shrugged. 'I still think hammelhorns is an unlikely cargo,' he said stubbornly. 'Anyway, we'll see when we get to the market, won't we? Though when *that* will be, Sky alone knows! Nine days we've been sailing now. Nearly ten . . .'

'The Deepwoods is vast,' said Twig. He gazed back

Bang! Bang! Bang!

Cowlquape's eyes snapped open. The cabin was in darkness. He looked round blindly.

Bang! Bang! Bang! BANG!

'Yes?' Cowlquape shouted.

The cabin door opened and there, silhouetted against the light in the corridor, was the dishevelled figure of Jervis. 'Come to see to your dressings,' he said.

'Oh, yes,' said Cowlquape. 'I didn't realize it was so late.'

Jervis closed the door behind him and crossed the floor. He set a small box down on the ledge, closed the porthole and lit the lamp. Cowlquape sat up and swung his legs down the side of the hammock. Jervis stood before him, then began unwinding the first bandage. The peppery scent of the hyleberry salve grew more intense.

'I think they're almost better,' said Cowlquape.

The scab came away with the final twist of lint. Below it, the skin was smooth and soft. Jervis examined the hand critically in the lamplight before pronouncing it 'good as new'.

'Are we approaching the Great Shryke Slave Market yet?' Cowlquape asked, as Jervis set to work on the second bandage.

'Not approaching, as such,' said Jervis, responsive for once. 'But we're on-track, sure enough. Look-out spotted a market burn-out at sundown, so he did. Signs indicated the great market had flocked north-north-west. That's where we're heading.'

The left hand had healed just as well as the right,

Jervis was pleased to see. He ran a horny finger over the soft, pale skin. The sky ship listed abruptly to port and a beam of moonlight streamed in through the porthole. It passed over Cowlquape's outstretched hands.

'S'posed to be lucky, that is,' said Jervis. 'The moon crossing your palm with silver. Back where I come from they say it means you'll live a long and prosp . . .' He stopped, and Cowlquape thought he could see sorrow in the ancient goblin's expression. Abruptly he rose and left, fear obvious in his eyes, as if he had been about to say something unwise.

Cowlquape stared at the closed door nervously. Why had Jervis seemed so fearful? What had he been too afraid to say?

The soft oil lamplight bathed the cabin in shadowy orange. Cowlquape climbed to his feet, crossed to the porthole and flung it open again. Warm, luscious air – heavy with pinesap and lullabee mist – flooded inside. Cowlquape breathed in deeply and poked his head out through the circular window.

Below him, the canopy of trees stretched out as before like a vast sparkling sea in the bright moonlight. Cowlquape didn't know how far they had travelled nor how far there was still to go. He knew only that, if Jervis's pronouncements proved correct, he would soon be down there in the suffocating darkness beneath its leafy surface – in a place he'd never imagined he would ever visit. A shiver of fear and excitement ran through him. The dream was still fresh in his mind.

'I can't wait to leave this great rolling sky ship,' he

muttered to himself, 'and get my feet back on solid ground. It's . . .' He fell still, and squinted into the distance.

Before him, gleaming in the moonlight far ahead like a great bleached canker in the luxuriant green of the forest canopy, was a ragged patch of land where everything was dead. Cowlquape trembled. He had never before witnessed such barren desolation.

As the *Skyraider* drew closer, Thunderbolt Vulpoon bellowed out his orders to 'fly in low'. Sails were lowered, hull-weights realigned, and the sky ship slowed to a woodslug's pace.

Cowlquape poked his head out of the porthole and looked down uneasily. The line separating the living forest and the lifeless clearing was crossed. 'Sky above!' he exclaimed.

Every single tree beneath him was dead. Some had been burned, some had been hollowed – others looked as if they had simply died, and stood now with their skeleton leaves clinging to their branches. Vast tracts had been scorched back to bare earth. Nothing lived there; nothing grew.

With the *Skyraider* flying down so close to the scarred, bleached forest, the area seemed unimaginably immense. All round, as far as the eye could see, the terrible desolation continued.

'So the Great Shryke Slave Market has done all this,' Cowlquape whispered tremulously.

When the sky ship was passing over the remains of a forest settlement, the captain commanded that they go in especially close, for it was in the decimated villages such as this – in the stonefall and woodburn – that clues to the market's next resting place were to be found.

Cowlquape trembled with horror. Every tree had been felled, every well destroyed, every building had been razed to the ground. As for those who once inhabited the place – the gnokgoblins, mobgnomes, woodtrolls, or whatever – they were now all gone, captured by the bird-creatures and sold on as slaves. Now, only piles of rubble and heaps of charred wood indicated that a thriving village had once been here: that and the network of paths which radiated out from its former centre.

It was there – at the central-most point and sticking up out of the scorched ground like some giant black insect – that a gibbet of burnt timber stood, a bleached white skeleton strapped to its black crossbeam. A bone finger

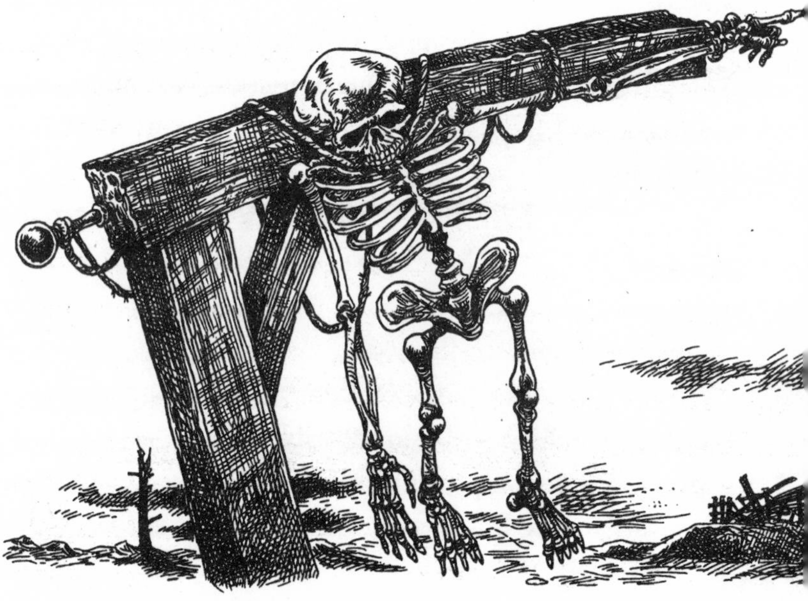

pointed towards the moon, low on the horizon.

All at once a cry went up. 'East-north-east!'

'East-north-east!' Cowlquape heard the captain repeat, and the *Skyraider* abruptly swung round to port and soared back up into the sky.

Beneath him, as the sky ship gathered speed, the dead area of forest receded and was finally left far behind. Cowlquape shuddered miserably. Having seen for himself the awful devastation it caused, the Great Shryke Slave Market was the last place in the Edge he now wanted to visit.

'I think I'd sooner stay on board the *Skyraider*,' he muttered. Just then, the sky ship hit a patch of squally air and dipped sharply, rocking from side to side as it did so. Cowlquape groaned. His stomach gurgled ominously. 'Then again . . .' he murmured queasily.

BANG! BANG!

The two heavy thuds on the door sounded as though someone was trying to batter it down. Cowlquape jumped and, remembering the look in Jervis's eyes, drew his dagger.

'Wh. . . who i . . . is it?' he asked.

The door was flung wide open. The great ragged brogtroll was standing in the corridor.

'Oh, it's you,' said Cowlquape.

'Grimlock it be,' came the reply as, stooping low, he shuffled into the cabin. He was carrying a tray, with an earthenware jug and two goblets on it, dwarfed by his massive hands. He looked round the cabin. 'Where's the other one?'

'Just stretching his legs,' said Cowlquape, concealing the knife behind his back, but not returning it to its sheath. 'He'll be back in a minute.'

Grimlock nodded. 'Is good,' he said. 'The master said this be for the pair of you.' He held the tray out. 'Finest woodgrog gold can buy. Help you get a good night's sleep, he says.'

'Th . . . thank you,' said Cowlquape, eyeing the murky brew suspiciously. It was the first time Thunderbolt Vulpoon had concerned himself with the quality of their sleep. 'If you just put it on that shelf over there I'll tell Twig directly he returns. As I say, he shouldn't be . . .'

At that moment Twig himself appeared in the doorway. 'Cowlquape,' he said breathlessly 'We've got to talk . . .'

'Twig!' Cowlquape interrupted. 'Just the person I was

hoping to see. Grimlock here,' he said, flapping his hands towards the figure standing in the shadows, 'has just brought us a jug of the captain's finest woodgrog.' Twig nodded towards the brogtroll and smiled. 'It's to help us get a good night's sleep,' added Cowlquape meaningfully.

'I'm sure it is,' said Twig brightly.

'Shall Grimlock pour some?' the lumbering creature asked hopefully.

'No,' said Twig. 'No, I think I shall save it for when I'm about to turn in. But thank you for offering, Grimlock.' He crossed the cabin and sniffed at the jug. 'Mmm, I'll look forward to that,' he said, and looked up at the brogtroll. 'The captain is too kind.'

Grimlock shook his head glumly. 'Oh, no,' he said, 'the master's not kind. Not him. He starves Grimlock, he does. Won't let him eat the cargo – not even the little-'uns.'

Twig looked at the great mountain of muscle in front of him. 'You don't look starved,' he said. 'Could do with a new set of clothes maybe . . .'

'Grimlock's always cold,' the brogtroll complained. 'The master sells the cargo's clothes.'

Cowlquape's jaw dropped. He turned to Twig, who nodded and frowned; he should remain silent.

'Grimlock never gets them,' the brogtroll continued. 'Grimlock likes pretty clothes, he does. Nice pretty clothes to keep Grimlock warm. Grimlock likes your clothes.'

He reached out a meaty paw to brush Twig's hammelhornskin waistcoat. It bristled defensively.

'*Ouch!*' Grimlock wailed, and clutched his finger where the spiky hair of the waistcoat had drawn blood. 'Not pretty!' he exclaimed.

'No,' said Twig, smoothing down the ruffled fur. 'This wouldn't suit you at all. In fact, I'd have thought a nice embroidered coat and a hat with a feather would be much more suitable.'

'Yes, yes!' said the brogtroll excitedly.

'Grimlock!' roared the captain's voice from above. 'The cargo's getting restless again. Go and sort it out!'

'Grimlock's starving,' said the brogtroll. 'Grimlock's cold. Grimlock would like a hat with a feather. Pretty.'

'You'd better go,' said Twig. 'Thank the captain for the woodgrog.'

The brogtroll shuffled out. The door shut. Cowlquape turned immediately to Twig. 'Clothes!' he exclaimed. 'He talked about the cargo's clothes. And how many hammelhorns do you know that wear clothes?'

Without answering, Twig picked up the heavy earthenware jug and emptied its contents into the two goblets. Then he tipped them both out of the porthole. 'Full of powdered sleeping-willow bark,' he muttered. 'Cowlquape, we are in great danger . . .' He placed the empty jug back on the shelf. 'I overheard a conversation between Teasel, that mobgnome, and Stile,' he continued. 'That dead grove we recently passed over had a black gibbet with a skeleton strapped to its crossbeam. It meant one thing and one thing only. Our next stop will be the Great Shryke Slave Market itself.'

'B ... but that's good, isn't it?' said Cowlquape uncertainly.

Twig sighed. 'It should have been,' he said. 'Oh, Cowlquape, I feel so bad about bringing you into all this.'

'What do you mean?' said Cowlquape anxiously. 'What else did you overhear?'

'I've been stupid. Stupid and blind,' Twig said. 'All I could think about was finding my lost crew, and now ...' He gripped his young apprentice by the shoulder. 'You were right all along, Cowlquape,' he said. 'The cargo we're carrying is not hammelhorns. It *is* slaves.'

Cowlquape took a sharp intake of breath. 'I knew it,' he said.

Twig sighed. 'Just our luck to have stumbled across the most villainous of sky pirate captains ever to have taken to the air. Five dozen or more wretches he's got chained up in the lower hold of the ship,' he said. 'Mobgnomes, flat-head goblins, cloddertrogs ... All bound for the market where they will be sold on to the highest bidder.'

'And us?' said Cowlquape. 'Why didn't the captain simply have us thrown into the hold and clapped in irons with the rest?'

Twig looked away. 'We're too valuable for that,' he said quietly. 'He doesn't want us damaged – the moment he saw us he must have made up his mind. He's a crafty one, I'll give him that.' He turned back to Cowlquape. 'We are to be sold to the roost-mother herself.'

'The roost-mother?' said Cowlquape.

'The leader of the bird-creatures which rule the market,' Twig replied. 'She goes by the name of Mother Muleclaw. Apparently she is offering to pay highly – *very* highly – for specimens such as us. It's not every day that a Sanctaphrax academic is sold in the slave market!'

'That was why he was so interested in our well-being,' said Cowlquape. He stared down gloomily at the pale new skin on the palms of his hands. 'And why he was so keen that my wounds should heal.'

Twig nodded. 'And why the food has been so excellent,' he said, and shuddered. 'He's been fattening us up!'

· CHAPTER THIRTEEN ·

MUTINY

Twig stared out of the porthole as the *Skyraider* lurched and swayed onwards, tacking against the wind in the east-north-easterly direction the gruesome sign had pointed them in. A breeze got up. The moon sank low in the sky, sparkling on the forest canopy as the wind rippled its leafy surface. There was no sight of the slave market.

All round him, he could hear the sounds of the sky ship in flight. The whispering of the sails. The rhythmical tapping of the tolley-ropes. The creaking boards. The whistling rigging. The squeak and scurry of the ratbirds, deep down in the bowels of the ship. And something else . . . A deep, sonorous sound . . .

'Listen,' he said, turning away from the porthole.

Cowlquape looked up from his hammock. 'What?'

'That noise.'

'What noise?'

Twig motioned Cowlquape to be silent. He crouched down on the floor and placed his ear against the dark varnished wood. His face clouded with sorrow. '*That* noise,' he said.

Cowlquape rolled off the hammock and joined Twig on the floor. As his ear touched the wooden boards, the sounds became clearer. Groaning. Howling. Hopeless wailing.

'The cargo?' Cowlquape whispered.

'The cargo,' said Twig. 'The mobgnomes, the flat-head goblins, the cloddertrogs . . . the sound of misery and despair – the sound of slavery. Thank Sky we are forewarned and know what the captain is planning . . .'

His words were shattered by a bare-knuckled rapping at the door.

'Quick,' said Twig. 'Into your hammock. Pretend to be asleep.'

A moment later, Twig and Cowlquape were curled up in their hammocks, eyes shut and mouths open, snoring softly. The rapping at the door came a second time.

'We're asleep, you idiots,' Cowlquape muttered under his breath. 'Just come in.'

'*Sshhh!*' Twig hissed.

The door-handle squeaked as it was slowly turned. The door creaked open. Twig rolled over with a grunt and continued snoring, though he sneaked a peek into the cabin from the corner of one eye.

Two heads peered round the cabin door. One was Teasel's. The other belonged to an individual Twig had not seen before: a burly cloddertrog. The pair of them were frozen to the spot, anxiously watching to see if

Twig was about to wake up. He obliged them with a snoozy murmur, and settled back down.

A cloddertrog, he thought unhappily.

'I think they must have drunk it,' said Teasel, crossing the room. He sniffed at the goblets, and peered into the jug. 'Yeah, all gone.' He looked at the two hammocks. 'Sleeping like babies, so they are,' he giggled. 'Right, then, Korb. You tie up the little'un. I'll see to this one.'

The pair of them pulled lengths of rope from their shoulders and advanced to the two hammocks. Cowlquape trembled as the foul-smelling cloddertrog came close. He quaked as the great looming creature tossed the end of the rope over his feet. He was about to be tied up inside the hammock. Rigid with fear, he felt the rope bite as it was pulled tight around his ankles.

'Easy there,' said the mobgnome. 'The captain said *no marks*. And you know what happens if you cross the captain . . .'

The cloddertrog scratched his head. 'I don't want him wriggling free when he wakes up though.'

'Don't worry,' the mobgnome assured him, as he went to secure his own rope around Twig's neck. 'He'll be out till . . . *Aaaaargh!*' he wailed as a sharp elbow slammed into the base of his nose with a sickening crunch. Blood gushed in a torrent. The mobgnome clutched his hands to his face and staggered backwards.

Twig sat up, swung round and leapt forwards, sword drawn. 'Drop your knife first,' he shouted at the cloddertrog. 'Then your cutlass.'

The cloddertrog stumbled back in surprise. The mobgnome was still on his knees, clutching his nose. Cowlquape loosened the rope around his legs, climbed off his hammock and stood by Twig's side.

'Knife, Cowlquape,' said Twig, nodding to the hammerhead's dagger. Shakily, Cowlquape drew it from his belt. 'And you,' Twig told the cloddertrog. 'Just use your thumb and forefinger.'

'Thumb and forefinger it is,' he said.

Twig watched. The blade of the knife appeared from its sheath. 'Now, drop it!' he said.

The cloddertrog glanced down at his hand.

'Drop it!' shouted Twig.

'All right, all right,' said the cloddertrog. His knuckles

whitened. 'I just . . .' As he spoke, he flicked his wrist and the knife spun through the air.

Twig recoiled. Too late! '*Aaargh!*' he screamed as the spinning knife sank its razor-sharp point into his side. His sword clattered to the floor.

As Twig toppled backwards the cloddertrog drew his evil-looking cutlass and lunged forwards.

'Twig!' shouted Cowlquape, leaping on the cloddertrog's back.

The heavy cutlass splintered the wooden wall, inches above Twig's head.

'Geddoff me!' roared the cloddertrog, tearing the lad from his shoulders and tossing him aside.

Cowlquape went flying back across the cabin and crashed into the still kneeling Teasel. The mobgnome was knocked senseless.

The cloddertrog sneered. 'I don't care what the captain says,' he said. 'You're going to get what's coming to you!' He raised the fearsome cutlass high above his head and . . .

BOOF!

Cowlquape brought the heavy earthenware jug down with all his strength on the cloddertrog's skull. The cloddertrog keeled forwards, landed heavily on the floor and lay still.

'Now that's what I call a sleeping draught,' said Cowlquape with a shaky smile.

'Thank you, lad,' said Twig, as he struggled to his feet. Although his hammelhornskin waistcoat had prevented the knife penetrating too far, the wound was throbbing. He hobbled across to his sword, picked it up and turned to Cowlquape.

'Come, Cowlquape. We have an appointment with Captain Vulpoon.'

Taking care not to make a sound, Twig and Cowlquape made their way through the sky ship. They passed store-rooms and stock-cupboards, the galley, the sleeping berths. At each door and corridor they came to they paused, looked round furtively and listened for any sound. Apart from a low snoring from the crew's quarters – where Jervis and Stile were sleeping – there was nothing.

They were about to make their way up to the helm itself when Cowlquape noticed a narrow, black and gold lacquered staircase set back in an alcove. He looked at Twig questioningly.

Twig nodded and stepped forwards. He began climbing the narrow stairs. 'Well, well, well!' he exclaimed a moment later as he stepped into the room above. 'We've struck lucky.'

Cowlquape joined him. He looked round the ornate chamber with its gold trappings, luxurious carpet and inlaid woodwork, its huge mirrors and crystal chandeliers – its vast, sumptuous four-poster bed.

'We must be in Vulpoon's quarters,' he said. 'It's . . . magnificent!'

'There's certainly profit to be had from the misery of others,' said Twig sourly.

He began opening the mirrored doors to the many wardrobes which lined the room, and rifled through the gaudy clothes which packed every inch within. From the third wardrobe, he pulled out a particularly foppish jacket. Long and quilted, it was a deep magenta colour with navy and gold brocade. There were feathers around the collar and at the cuffs. Semi-precious stones, set into the embroidered threads, sparkled enticingly. Twig slipped the jacket on.

'What do you think?' he said.

'Well, it's . . .' Cowlquape started. He shook his head. 'I don't know what we're doing in here.'

Twig laughed. 'You're right, Cowlquape,' he said. 'It's time we left. Come on.' And with that he strode across the room and back down the stairs. Cowlquape followed close behind.

Up on deck at last, Twig breathed the crisp, cold air deep down into his lungs. A broad grin spread across his face.

'Ah, Cowlquape,' he said. 'Fresh air. A following wind. The sheer exhilaration of soaring across the endless sky.'

Cowlquape laid a hand on Twig's arm and pointed up the wooden staircase to the helm. The captain and the brogtroll, Grimlock, were silhouetted against the greyness of the sky. Twig nodded and raised his finger to his lips.

They advanced, keeping to the shadows cast by the low moon on their port bow. Around the skirting-deck, they went. Up the stairs. Slowly. Stealthily. All at once, the whole sky ship was bathed in purple light.

'*Waah!*' Grimlock cried out.

Twig and Cowlquape froze.

'*Fire!*' the brogtroll bellowed. 'Grimlock see fire!'

'Be still, you fool!' the captain cried. 'It's not fire. It's the signal flare.'

'Signal flare?' said Grimlock blankly.

The captain groaned. 'Oh, Grimlock, Grimlock, there really isn't a lot going on in there, is there?' he said, waving his lace handkerchief at the brogtroll's head. 'The signal flare alerts the guards at the slave market that there are slaves on board!' He rubbed his plump pink hands together. 'And what a lot of slaves we've got. Mother Muleclaw will be so pleased with me.'

'Mother Muleclaw,' Grimlock growled. He remembered her well enough. Beaten him, she had. Beaten poor Grimlock when he'd once strayed from the ship.

'Aye, the roost-mother herself,' said Vulpoon. 'She's the one our two fine young gentlemen are going to.' He chuckled. 'I wonder if they'll last any longer than the last lot?'

Twig's eyes rested on the finery of the captain's clothes – the elegant embroidered silk frock coat with its intricate pattern of costly marsh-gems and mire-pearls, the highly-polished knee-length boots, the ruffs at his collar and cuffs, the fluffy purple vulpoon feather in his tricorn hat. He was a dandy. A fop. Twig had never seen a sky pirate captain like him before, and it turned his stomach knowing how this unpleasant individual had come by such wealth. 'So when is our estimated time of arrival in the slave market?' he asked, stepping from the shadows.

Vulpoon spun round, his face a picture of horrified shock. 'You!' he blurted out. 'What are you doing here? Where are Teasel and Korb?'

'Sleeping soundly,' said Twig, a smile playing over his lips.

'But this is an outrage!' the captain roared. His eyes bulged. His face turned crimson in the purple light. 'You're meant to be . . .'

'Asleep?' said Twig. He drew his sword. 'Bound and gagged? All trussed up for market?' He began to circle the captain.

'I . . . You . . . It's . . .' Thunderbolt Vulpoon blustered. 'And that's *my* jacket you're wearing!' he shrieked. 'GRIMLOCK! SEE TO THEM!'

Grimlock blundered forwards.

Twig calmly ran his hand up and down the jacket, his fingers hovering over the jewels. 'See, Grimlock,' he said.

Grimlock halted in his tracks. 'Pretty clothes,' he said, his eyes lighting up.

'Grimlock!' bellowed Vulpoon furiously.

But Grimlock did not hear him. Mesmerized by the dazzling beauty of the wondrous jacket, he drooled.

'It could be yours, Grimlock,' Twig said. 'All yours.' He slowly slipped an arm out of a sleeve and let the jacket drop down his shoulder. 'Would you like it, Grimlock?' he said. 'Shall I give you the pretty jacket? Shall I?'

Grimlock's eyes widened with confusion. He looked at the captain. He looked at the jacket. His brow furrowed. Twig slipped off the second sleeve and held the jacket in his left hand.

'Grimlock, obey!' Vulpoon screamed. 'Do as you're told!'

A smile spread over Grimlock's clodden features. He

took a step forwards. Twig held the jacket out. 'Take it,' he said.

Grimlock reached out, snatched the jacket and slipped his arms down inside the sleeves. 'Pretty jacket!' he said, grinning from ear to ear. 'Grimlock pretty!'

Twig pointed his sword at Vulpoon. 'It would have taken so little to ensure the loyalty of your crew,' he said. 'And after all, you have so much.' He turned away in disgust. 'Remove his keys and tie him up, Cowlquape.'

'Please, please,' the captain pleaded. 'No, don't do that, I implore you. I didn't mean anything. Really . . . It was all a misunderstanding . . . *Please!*'

Twig grimaced. 'And gag him, Cowlquape!' he said. 'I'll listen to no more of this creature's spineless whining.'

While Cowlquape bound and gagged the former captain of the *Skyraider*, Twig took to the helm and raised his telescope to his eye. Far in the distance and slightly to starboard, a patch of the unending Deepwoods seemed to be glowing with an oily yellow light. He focused the glass.

'We've found it, Cowlquape,' he breathed. 'We've found the Great Shryke Slave Market.'

With nimble fingers, Twig raised the mainsail a fraction, realigned the studsail and lowered the port hull-weights. The great sky ship swung gently round until the faint, but growing, yellow glow was directly before them. He raised the port hull-weight, lowered the stern-weight and shifted the rudder-wheel a tad to starboard. The *Skyraider* was on course.

Cowlquape joined Twig at the helm and, as the slave market drew ever closer, the pair of them were overwhelmed by the sounds, the smells, the sights emanating from the curious agglomeration of life stretching over a vast area of the forest. For if the places the market had left behind were dead, then this – this raucous, pungent, seething mass of activity – was more vibrant than any place either of them had ever experienced before.

A thousand odours filled the air: pine-smoke and pole-weasel perfume, mothballs and woodgrog, and hammelhorns spit-roasting over roaring flames. Below it all, however – noticeable only when the currents shifted the more pleasant scents away – was the omnipresent

stench of rotting, of decay: of death.

Cowlquape shuddered involuntarily.

Twig turned to him. 'You're right to be apprehensive,' he said. 'For all its glitter and dazzle, the Great Shryke Slave Market is a terrible place. It claims for itself the unwary, the foolish . . .' He placed his hand reassuringly on Cowlquape's shoulder. 'But not us, Cowlquape,' he said. 'We shall not fall into its clutches.'

'A thousand strides, and closing,' the look-out called down from the caternest.

Twig readjusted the hull-weights and shifted all the sail-levers down a fraction. The sky ship glided downwards through the sky.

'Five hundred strides!' the look-out announced. 'Landing-stage on the port bow.'

Cowlquape squinted ahead. In front of them he saw an aerial jetty, jutting out from the top of a stripped tree. At the far end, closest to them, stood one of the bird-creatures: a stocky individual with dowdy feathers and a beak and claws which glinted in the purple light of the flare it was waving as it guided them in. Cowlquape swallowed.

'A shryke,' he murmured softly.

Twig raised the neben-hull-weights and lowered the stern-weight. The sky ship slowed and dipped. He lowered the sails, one by one: the flight-rock would do the rest.

'One hundred strides!'

As if in response to the look-out's cry, Jervis and a gangly individual with a markedly twisted spine – Stile the ship's cook, Cowlquape presumed – appeared on the deck. They looked round, eyes wide, mouths open. The sky ship docked.

There were the passengers, sailing the ship. Grimlock was primping and preening by the bowsprit in a frock-coat. And the captain was trussed up on the floor . . .

'What in Sky . . . ?' Jervis muttered.

Just then, there was a loud thud behind them as the end of the gangplank dropped down onto the stern. Twig and the others turned to see a dozen or more of the formidable shrykes marching across the board and advancing towards them.

'What have you got to trade?' their leader – a stout

bird-creature with multi-coloured beads plaited into her drab, tawny feathers – asked as she reached the bridge.

'Not much, I'm afraid,' said Twig. 'Bit of a mix-up in Undertown. We ended up carrying hammelhorns instead of slaves.'

The shryke narrowed her cold, glinting eyes and tilted her head to one side. 'Do you mean to tell me there are only free citizens on board?' she squawked indignantly.

'Except for one,' said Twig. He prodded Captain Vulpoon in the back with his foot and smiled at the shryke. 'A prime specimen,' he said. 'Links with academics, or so I understand.'

'Really?' said the shryke, her neck feathers ruffling up. She turned to her second in command. 'The roost-mother might be interested.'

'My thoughts entirely,' said Twig.

'How much are you asking?' asking the shryke.

Twig's head spun. 'A hundred and fifty,' he said, plucking a figure from the air.

The shryke's eyes narrowed. 'Roundels or docklets?' she demanded.

'R . . . roundels,' said Twig. The shryke tutted and turned away. 'I mean, docklets. A hundred and fifty docklets.' He smiled. 'I'm sure Mother Muleclaw won't be able to resist getting her claws into him.'

The shryke hesitated for a moment. Then, she turned back and stared at Twig with one yellow eye. 'The price is still high,' she said. 'But . . . it's a deal.'

The crew of the *Skyraider* gathered on the main deck all gave a cheer as the shryke grasped the bundle before her. Captain Thunderbolt Vulpoon had treated them all like slaves. There were no tears for the avaricious tyrant as – wriggling like a barkslug – he was hefted up onto the feathery shoulders of his captors and carried away.

'*Mffll bwfll blmmf!*' His muffled oaths were lost to the gag.

'The same to you!' Jervis called after him. 'And good riddance.' He turned to Twig. 'What's to become of us now, though?'

'Of you?' said Twig. 'You're all free. You can do what you want, go where you want . . . Back to Undertown for a start, then who knows?'

'Please, young master, take us back,' pleaded Jervis, his gnarled hands reaching out and clutching Twig's. 'We need a captain if we are to sail the ship.'

'No, I . . .' Twig muttered. 'It's not possible. We . . . that is, Cowlquape and I have business to attend to . . .'

Cowlquape leant across, raised his hands and whispered in his ear. 'The cargo, Twig. Don't forget the cargo.'

'Don't worry, Cowlquape. I haven't forgotten,' said Twig. He raised his head and addressed the motley crew before him. 'When I said "you're all free", I meant it. *All* those on board the *Skyraider* – each and every one – are free.'

'You mean . . .?' Jervis began. 'The . . . the slaves?'

'Yes, old-timer,' said Twig. 'Those you helped to waylay and transport to this terrible place are as free as yourself. And I warrant that there'll be creatures amongst them who have some skill in skysailing.' He turned to his young apprentice. 'Come, Cowlquape. Let us go and release Vulpoon's prisoners.'

Cowlquape followed Twig back below deck, and down deep into the dark bowels of the sky ship. He couldn't help but feel a warm glow of pride inside him. Twig could simply have walked from the *Skyraider* and left its occupants to their fate. But no. Even now, though they were on a quest to search for Twig's lost crew, the young captain could still spare the time to assist others. Cowlquape remembered his dream, and winced with embarrassment. If anyone was fit to wear the mantle of Kobold the Wise it was the young captain, not himself.

As they clattered down the final flight of stairs – their boots echoing on the bare boards, the air, fetid and foul, chinks of light penetrating the gloom from broken hull planks – a cry went up from the chained prisoners. With a shudder, Cowlquape recognized the sound he'd heard earlier.

'Is there someone there?' they shouted. 'Water! Water!' 'Something to eat.' 'Korb! Korb, is that you?' 'Have mercy on us, I beg you!'

Twig shook his head. There was no knowing when the poor wretches had last eaten or drunk anything and Twig's blood boiled at the monstrous injustice of it all. He strode towards the door, took the ring of keys from Cowlquape, selected the largest and pushed it into the keyhole. The key scraped in the lock like an angry rat-bird. Inside, the voices fell still.

'*Pfwooah!*' Cowlquape gasped as Twig pushed the door open and a blast of foul air struck him full in the face.

'Hide your revulsion,' Twig whispered back at him. 'It is not the prisoners' fault that their conditions are so disgusting.' He stepped inside. 'It is the greed that led to their imprisonment that is to blame for this foul place.'

A raucous clamouring immediately began. 'Where's Korb?' 'Where's our food and water?' 'What's going on?' 'Why aren't we sailing any more?'

Twig looked around at the miserable assembly of flat-heads and gnokgoblins, cloddertrogs and woodtrolls, and raised his hands for quiet.

'Friends, your ordeal is over!' he called. 'The *Skyraider* is to return to Undertown! And you will travel with it, to be reunited with your families!'

The prisoners looked at one another in confusion.

'You are going home!' Twig announced. He raised the ring of keys above his head and shook them. 'As free citizens! You, and the crew that tyrant enslaved. There will be no slaves at all on board this sky ship ever again!'

For a moment, there was absolute silence. Then a flathead goblin gave a mighty cheer, and the hold exploded in whoops and cries of tumultuous joy. The sky ship trembled and lurched as the trolls, trogs and goblins – their chains clanking – danced round with delight.

Twig waited for the noise to subside before continuing. 'Now, I need volunteers to crew this ship,' he said. 'How many of you have experience of skysailing?'

Half a dozen arms shot up into the air.

'We've done our bit, Cowlquape,' said Twig with a smile. 'They'll be able to get back safely to Undertown. Our quest lies in the slave market.' He turned back to the prisoners. 'You will all be unshackled,' he said. 'Be patient. Your turn will come.'

Twig divided the keys up between himself and Cowlquape. One by one, the pair of them matched key to lock, unfastened the manacles and set the prisoners free. They streamed out of the dark, filthy hold, away from their prison and up on deck to taste the clear air and look at the stars. There was laughter and much hand-shaking; there were tears and heartfelt thanks. At last, wiping sweat from his brow, Cowlquape peered into the gloom of the farthest corners of the hold.

Only two shackled prisoners remained. A young pinched-looking gnokgoblin with an eye-patch and, at the opposite end of the cavernous chamber, a small figure bundled up in a ragged cloak.

Cowlquape approached the bundle. It let out a faint sigh as he fumbled with the key in the lock of the manacle around its leg. The mechanism failed to click.

He tried again, but it was no good.

'I can't seem to unlock this one,' Cowlquape called across the room. 'It must be the key – or the rusty lock. Or something.'

'Let me try my key,' Twig called back. 'I won't be a minute,' he said to the gnokgoblin as he pulled himself up and crossed the filthy straw which covered the floor. 'Let me see,' he said to Cowlquape, putting the key in the lock. 'Ah, yes, I think I've got it.' He frowned. 'Cowlquape?' he said. 'What's the matter?'

Cowlquape shook his head. 'I don't believe it!' he gasped. 'Look, Twig, look!'

'What is it, Cowlquape?' said Twig. 'Tell, me . . .'

But Cowlquape was not listening. 'It's fate, Twig! It's fate!' he babbled excitedly as he stared unblinking at the young captain's outstretched hand. 'Fate itself must have brought us to this place!'

'Cowlquape,' said Twig sharply. 'What are you talking about?'

And then he saw. His hand, his arm – they were glowing. His entire body was aglow with the same bright light that had illuminated him before. When he had met up with Tarp Hammelherd, and Bogwitt, and Wingnut Sleet . . .

He turned and looked at the bundle of rags cowering immediately before him, his raised arm shielding his sensitive eyes from the sudden light. 'It can't be. Can it? Spooler?' he said. 'Can it really be you?'

The oakelf started back. He lowered his arm – an arm that was also glowing. 'Captain Twig?' he whispered.

'Captain Twig!'

'Spooler!' Twig exclaimed, and he embraced the oakelf tightly, lifting him up off the ground in his excitement. 'It *is* you!' He turned to Cowlquape, beside himself with joy. 'It's Spooler!' he exclaimed. 'The fourth missing member of my crew. Oh, Spooler,' he said, releasing his grip on the oakelf and looking him deep in his eyes. 'I hoped ... but I never dreamed ... But tell me, how did you end up in this terrible place?'

The oakelf looked down. His brow furrowed. 'I . . . I'm not sure, Captain. It's all a blur,' he whispered.

'We were on board the *Edgedancer*,' Twig reminded him gently. 'Tethered to the caterbird. We set off into open sky in search of my father, Cloud Wolf.'

'Yes, yes,' said Spooler. 'That I remember.' He shuddered. 'And I remember seeing the weather vortex from the top of the caternest, coming closer and closer . . .'

'Yes?' said Twig eagerly.

'And then, nothing,' said Spooler. 'The next thing I knew I was lying in the gutter in the Undertown fish market.'

Twig hid his disappointment.

'A mobgnome found me,' Spooler continued. 'He

offered me somewhere to spend the night; he gave me something to drink. Woodgrog . . .' His face clouded over. 'And then . . . And then, *this*!' he wailed, and sobs of misery wracked his frail body.

'It's all right, Spooler,' said Twig softly. 'You're safe now. We've found you – though Sky alone knows how. And now this sky ship will take you back to Undertown.'

'But what is there for me in Undertown?' the oakelf wailed.

'You must make your way to my study in Sanctaphrax,' Twig said. 'The others are waiting for me there: Tarp, Bogwitt, Sleet. They will be delighted to see you. You can wait with them. Cowlquape and I shall return when we have discovered what has happened to the rest of the missing crew.' He took the oakelf's bony hands in his own. 'And we must travel on alone, Spooler. We can't take you with us. It was the same with the others. The glow that we create when we are together makes us too conspicuous.'

Spooler pulled away with surprising force. 'No,' he said firmly. 'No, captain. I cannot spend another moment on this evil vessel.' There was a desperate urgency in his voice.

'But Spooler,' said Twig, 'I've explained . . .'

'I can be useful to you,' Spooler persisted. 'On the long voyage here I gleaned a considerable amount of information – vital information – about the slave market from some of my fellow-prisoners.'

'But, Spooler . . .' Twig began again.

'Besides,' Spooler went on, 'I am an oakelf. Observant. Sensitive. My faculties are sharp. And like all other oakelves I know how to read the signs in the behaviour of others. I will be able to determine how the slave market operates.'

Twig shook his head.

'And as for the glowing,' Spooler continued without taking a breath, 'apparently, there are all sorts in the market. *All* sorts! Including creatures that glow – the glimpelt when its fur gets wet, the fritts when they're frightened, the lumhorn when it's attacked . . . No-one will give us a second look.'

Twig glanced up at Cowlquape, who shrugged.

'If you transgress just one of the unwritten laws of this place, then you're done for,' said Spooler, drawing a finger across his exposed throat. 'Believe me, captain, without my help in the Great Shryke Slave Market, you won't last ten minutes.'

'He's got a point,' said Twig.

Cowlquape nodded vigorously. 'He certainly has!' he said. The thought of falling into the clutches of the cold, glinting-eyed shrykes filled him with horror.

'Then it's decided. We shall continue as three,' said Twig.

'I think this was meant to be,' said Cowlquape. He looked down, suddenly serious. 'I read something in the barkscrolls the night before last, something that I think is important. It is what Kobold the Wise said to his followers as they gathered at Riverrise to await the Mother Storm. *"We are all but puppets, waiting for our strings to*

spheres woven from woodwillow and sallowdrop twigs which hung from their branches, while wooden walkways, slung from tree to tree and strung with smoking oil lamps, formed a network of paths. The noise was cacophonous and unbroken; the stench, repellent.

'This is the place,' a voice in Twig's head whispered. *'Let Spooler guide you.'*

Twig turned to the oakelf. 'Spooler,' he said, 'do you really think you can guide us safely through this terrible place?'

Spooler nodded. 'I shall do my best,' he said. 'First of all, we must see about some white cockades. Come, let us go. And Sky protect us all.'

Twig's heart missed a beat as he followed Spooler over the wobbling plank of wood. He hadn't realized how high up they were for, although docked, the *Skyraider* was still some fifty strides above the forest floor.

'The whole market is raised up,' Spooler was saying. They had reached the other side and were stepping through the outer canopy of leaves. 'Everything is fixed to, or suspended from, the great trees.'

Twig stared ahead of him, open-mouthed. 'It's stranger than I ever imagined it would be,' he whispered.

'And vast,' said Spooler. 'Searching for an individual in this lot . . .' His voice faded away and he flapped his hands at the thronging walkways, creaking and groaning under the weight of the crowds that snaked their way along them.

'We'll manage,' said Twig. 'Somehow. Eh, Cowlquape?' There was no reply. Twig spun round.

'Cowlquape?' he called. 'Where are you?'

'*Wuurgh!*' came a small groan from back the way they'd come.

'Cowlquape!' shouted Twig. He ran back through the curtains of foliage and along the landing-stage. And there was his young apprentice, down on his hands and knees in the middle of the bouncing gangplank, eyes tightly closed, shaking like a leaf and unable to move. 'It's all right,' Twig said. 'I'll come and get you.'

'NO!' Cowlquape wailed. 'I can't get up. I'll fall. I know I will.'

Born and raised in Undertown, the youth had never liked heights. Living on the floating city of Sanctaphrax had been fine because it was so vast – though he'd avoided the higher walkways and always shut his eyes in the baskets. Skysailing had scared him at first, but again the ship had been large and, when up on deck, he'd taken care not to look down. But this – wobbling about on a thin gangplank in mid-air – this was almost as petrifying as dangling on that rope from the *Skyraider*. In some ways it was worse. At least boarding the sky ship had been over rapidly; he'd just had to hold on. But here, the walkways went on for miles.

How would he ever cope with them?

'Crawl,' he heard Twig instructing him. 'Grip the sides of the plank and crawl forwards.'

Cowlquape's head spun. His breath came in short, sharp gasps. 'I can't,' he muttered. 'I just can't.' Even though his eyes were still clamped shut he could *feel* the space between him and solid ground.

'You can!' said Twig. 'You can't stay here! Besides, if you fall, what would become of your precious barkscrolls?'

Cowlquape groaned. He felt for the sides of the board with his hands, then shuffled forwards on his knees. His toes dragged along the rough surface of the plank.

'That's the way!' Twig shouted encouragingly. 'Just a little bit further.'

Arms trembling and teeth clenched, Cowlquape moved forwards again. And then again. Moving without thinking. All at once, hands gripped his jacket and he felt himself being dragged forwards. His legs turned to jelly and he fell with a thud on something hard – the walk-way shuddered. He opened his eyes. Twig was crouching down beside him.

'This is a fine place for me to discover about your head for heights, Cowlquape,' he said. 'The whole market's strung up in the trees.'

'Just give me a moment ... I'll be all right,' said Cowlquape bravely, climbing shakily to his feet. He followed Twig along the landing-stage. 'It was just that gangplank. No sides.' He shuddered. 'Nothing to hold on to ...'

At that moment, an ear-piercing squeal ripped through the air, followed by a torrent of curses. Twig, Cowlquape and Spooler ran across to the wooden rail and looked down. Cowlquape gulped nervously.

The noise was coming from a small platform with a red and white striped canopy some way below them. A bandy-legged goblin was leaping around and brandishing a massive fist at the air below him. Beside him was a blazing stove suspended on chains from the branch above.

'Blast you to open sky for wriggling free like that!' he was screaming. 'You've ruined me! Ruined me, do you hear?'

Cowlquape squinted below. There was something there – silent now – bouncing from branch to branch down to the ground. He turned to Twig. 'What is it?' he said.

Twig shrugged.

'A woodhog, probably,' said Spooler. He nodded towards the goblin, still jumping up and down on the platform in uncontrollable fury. 'There are hundreds of vendors like him all over the slave market, living from hand to mouth . . .'

Suddenly, there was a sharp creak and, with a splintering of wood, the platform broke away from the tree-trunk it was anchored to. The goblin screamed and clutched wildly at the hanging stove. For a moment he swung wildly. Then – his fingers hissing and smoking with the intense heat – he let go.

Cowlquape stared in horror, appalled, yet unable to tear his gaze away as the second creature tumbled down after the first. Screaming with terror, the goblin struck a thick branch with a thud, the body – limp now and twisted, with arms and legs akimbo – continued down, down, down . . .

'Sky above!' Cowlquape cried out. 'What are *they*?' He pointed down at the ground, where dozens of fluffy orange creatures were gathering, their bear-trap jaws agape.

Twig and Spooler peered down. 'Wig-wigs,' they said in unison.

Twig shuddered. 'Terrible creatures. They hunt in packs and devour their victims, dead or alive.'

'Here, they don't even need to hunt,' said Spooler. 'They live well enough off the discarded waste from the slave market . . .' The body of the goblin crashed down onto the ground and was immediately pounced upon by the ferocious wig-wigs. 'And anything else that drops down. Accidentally or otherwise,' he added.

'And when they've finished, there's nothing left,' said Twig. 'Not a scrap of fur or a splinter of bone.'

Cowlquape blanched. 'They . . . they can't climb trees, though,' he said anxiously. 'Can they?'

Twig shook his head. 'No,' he said. 'No, they can't.' And from the look which came into his eyes, Cowlquape guessed that the young captain was speaking from experience.

'Come,' said Spooler urgently. 'We must find a tally-hen and buy our white cockades at once. Without them we could be seized by a slave-trader and put on sale at any moment.' His huge black eyes darted round the shadows. 'I heard that there's usually one near the end of each landing-stage,' he said. 'Yes, look.' He pointed to a tall, narrow hut secured to a tree. 'There's a tally-lodge.'

Twig looked. It was one of the turret-like constructions he'd seen earlier. 'What are we waiting for then?' he said.

Together, the three of them crossed the gently swaying hanging walkway. Too terrified to look either left or right, Cowlquape kept his gaze fixed on the hut as he shuffled across. They approached the door.

Close up, the building was a small triumph of Deepwoods architecture. Constructed from buoyant lufwood, it was sturdy yet almost weightless, and artfully curved to minimize wind resistance. A lantern above the door illuminated a gold-lettered plaque: *Tally-Hen Mossfeather*. Twig raised his fist and knocked.

'Enter,' came a raucous voice.

As Twig went to lift the latch, Spooler stayed his hand. 'Be sure to wait for her to speak first,' he hissed. 'It is the way here.'

Twig nodded and opened the door, and the three of them walked into the dark room. Acrid smoke from the tilder-oil lamps around the walls immediately caught in their throats and made their eyes water. A swarthy shryke with metallic grey-green feathers and ivory-white talons stood before them, her back turned, busily moving coloured discs around a numbered tally-board.

Twig stepped forward and waited.

'Fifty-seven, fifty-eight, plus time-penalties,' the shryke muttered to herself. 'Can't you see I'm busy?' she snapped.

'We wish to buy white cockades,' Twig replied boldly.

The shryke paused. '*Buy*, did you say? Not beg, borrow or barter?' She spun round. 'And what do you intend buying them with? We don't take tokens or vouchers. It's two gold pieces per person.'

Twig reached inside his jacket, undid the leather pouch and counted out six gold pieces. He handed them over. Without saying a word, the shryke took one of the coins and bit into it with her savage-looking hooked beak. She looked up.

'Three cockades, you say?'

'One for each of us,' said Twig.

The shryke nodded sullenly and turned towards a locked door in the back wall, which she opened to reveal a dark safe carved into the living tree itself. She lifted the lid of the box inside and removed three woodthistle-shaped white rosettes.

'Here,' she said. 'The cockades ensure free right of passage for three days and three nights. After that, the material rots away. If you are caught without cockades you will be seized and sold as slaves.'

'Three days in this place will be more than enough,' said Twig.

The shryke snorted unpleasantly. 'That's what they all say. But I'm warning you,' she said, 'the days and nights bleed into one another in the Great Shryke Slave Market. Our visitors are always complaining about the uncommon haste with which time passes . . .'

'Which is why we must thank you and bid you farewell,' said Twig promptly. 'We have much to do.' With that, he spun round and left the room, the others following after. The door slammed shut.

'Surly creature,' Cowlquape commented.

'Shrykes aren't exactly known for their graciousness,' Spooler scowled. 'Yet those who are made tally-hens generally act with more integrity than most.' He frowned. 'Attach your cockade to the front of your jacket where you can keep an eye on it. The slave market is full of light-fingered individuals, and hats with cockades upon them have a horrible habit of going missing.'

With the white cockades positioned and secured to

Spooler's satisfaction, the oakelf turned and set off into the slave market. The others followed.

'And keep close,' Spooler instructed. 'Even as cockaded free citizens you risk being picked off by some unscrupulous merchant who would lock you away till the cockade rots and then claim you as his – or her – own.'

Twig's top lip curled with contempt. 'Is there no honour at all amongst slave-traders?' he said.

'You can't buy and sell honour, captain,' said Spooler. He smiled ruefully. 'And money is the only thing that matters here.'

Twig frowned. If any of the crew they were searching for *had* ended up in the slave market, what chance would they have stood in so mercenary a place?

'There is an auction in the slave market,' Spooler was saying. 'The Grand Central Auction. I thought we might try there first.'

Twig nodded. 'Come on, then,' he said wearily. 'But let's keep ourselves to ourselves – and our eyes and ears open.'

Back in Sanctaphrax, a ferocious storm was raging. High winds and driving hail battered the floating city. Above it, the sky was a cauldron of seething, swirling clouds tipping down bolt after bolt of jagged lightning. Up in Twig's study in the opulent School of Light and Darkness, the purple glow from the stove played on the fidgety faces of three sky pirates.

'It's all this waiting around that I can't stand,' Wingnut Sleet complained as he paced up and down the small room.

Bogwitt, who was sprawled out in a chair trying to dislodge some meat from his teeth with a fingernail, looked up. 'It's all them academics ever seem to do,' he growled. 'Idle bunch of slackers the lot of them.'

'Mind you,' said Sleet, wincing uncomfortably with every flash of lightning, 'I wouldn't fancy being out on a night like this. You know, I swear the weather's getting worse.'

Tarp Hammelherd shivered and crossed the room to warm his hands at the stove. 'Goodness knows what it must be like in the Deepwoods,' he said. 'I hope Captain Twig's safe.'

Sleet turned to him, his scarred flesh quivering. 'And what if he never returns?' he said. 'Are we to be expected to spend the rest of our lives in this poky little room?'

'The captain looked after us,' said Tarp. 'The least we can do is wait for him.'

'Yes, but for how long?' Sleet persisted.

'As long as it takes,' said Tarp firmly. A volley of hailstones drummed against the pane of glass, drowning him out. Tarp shuddered and looked out through the window. 'Sky protect you, Captain Twig,' he murmured. 'May you be successful on your quest to find those other crew-members less fortunate than ourselves . . .'

'And get back here as quickly as you can!' added Wingnut Sleet.

The Great Shryke Slave Market was like nothing either Twig or Cowlquape had ever experienced before: a sprawling labyrinth that extended further than any creature could walk in a day and a night – not that such terms had much meaning in a place lit by glowing lamps and sputtering torches, where the sunlight never penetrated.

Over aerial bridges, up rope-ladders and down, they hurried. This way and that. Onwards and inwards. It was as though they had been swallowed up by a huge and monstrous beast, and were now lost within its cavernous innards. Above, below and on every side, there was feverish activity as life coursed through its veins. The air was stale, orange-red, and throbbed like a beating heart. Chaotic, it had seemed at first, yet a closer look revealed that underlying it all was order, purpose.

They passed business after small business – shops, stalls, makeshift trestle-tables – each one with its owner shouting out never-to-be-repeated bargains, trying to catch their eye. One that did was up on a platform just above their heads – a solitary lugtroll, her white cockade pinned to a tall plumed hat, hawking glittering jewellery.

'Look,' Cowlquape gasped. 'It's *alive*!'

Twig looked closely. The lad was right. Each of the necklaces, bracelets and brooches was sparkling, not with precious stones, but with live firebugs which had been fixed into position with filaments of wire twisted round their glowing abdomens.

Spooler nodded at their own bodies, glowing ever so faintly in the dimly-lit gloom. 'Best get out of here before she decides to use us two!' he said.

And on they went. Past hanging cages laden with huddled birds, crates of reptiles and insects, and dying hollowed trees with bars at the gaping holes, forming

cages to woodbears and white-collar wolves; past rows of sleeping oakbats, their ankles tethered to the branches with leather jesses.

A while later, Twig stopped at a food stall, where a vendor – like the hapless goblin he'd seen earlier – had tilder sausages and woodhog steaks sizzling on a hanging stove. He bought three steaks and three hunks of oak bread, handed them round and they continued walking, eating as they went.

'Something to satisfy your thirst, too?' came a voice soon after.

Twig paused. Cowlquape and Spooler stopped beside him. The creature who had spoken to them was a gabtroll. She was stooped, with warty skin, drooping pink ears and, most bizarre of all, bulbous green eyeballs swaying at the end of long eye-stalks, which her long slurping tongue kept moist and clean. She looked up from her steaming pot.

'I've the finest herbal teas in the whole of the slave market,' she told them, her eyes swaying on their rubbery stalks. 'You,' she said, the eyes focusing in on Cowlquape, 'for you, I would recommend an infusion of hairy charlock and oak-apple. It emboldens the timid of heart. And is excellent for vertigo.' She smiled at Spooler, and her tongue slurped noisily over the peering eye-balls. 'For you, wood-comphrey, I think. It's a general pick-me-up.' She smiled and slurped again. 'And you certainly look as though you could do with one.'

She turned to Twig. Her face twitched with surprise and her eyes bounced in and out on their stalks.

'What?' said Twig, somewhat taken aback. 'Do you not know what *I* should drink?'

'Oh, I know all right,' the gabtroll said softly. Her eyes stared directly into his own. 'Bristleweed,' she said.

'Bristleweed,' Twig repeated. He turned to the others and laughed. 'Sounds delicious.'

The gabtroll's eyes retracted. 'Its name sounds common enough, I'll grant you,' she said. 'Yet bristleweed is one of the rarest herbs in all the Deepwoods.' Her voice lowered to a hushed whisper. 'It grows in purple clumps among the skulls and bones at the base of the flesh-eating blood-oak tree. Harvesting it is a nightmare,' she added, and her eyes peered closely into Twig's once more. 'As I'm sure you can imagine.'

Twig nodded. He'd had first-hand experience of the monstrous tree, as the gabtroll seemed to sense.

'You are a seeker, a searcher,' the gabtroll continued, without taking a breath. Her rubbery brow creased with concentration. 'Looking for others . . .'

'Perhaps,' said Twig.

'Yet there is someone else you do not realize that you seek,' said the gabtroll, and smiled. 'And bristleweed will help you.'

'It will?' said Twig.

The gabtroll nodded. She sprinkled a spoonful of the powdered purple herb into a wooden mug, ladled in warm water from the pot and stirred it round with a wooden spoon. 'Here,' she said. 'Take it. Don't expect immediate results, but in time it will help you find the one you are looking for.' She paused. 'Yourself.'

'Find myself?' said Twig, disappointed. 'But *I'm* not lost.'

The gabtroll, busying herself with Cowlquape and Spooler's drinks did not look up. 'Are you sure?' she said softly. 'Is there not *something* missing?'

Twig fell still. The curious creature was right of course. Something *was* missing. That memory of his time spent on board the *Edgedancer*, in the middle of the weather vortex. *That* was what was missing.

What *had* happened to him there?

Twig raised the cup to his lips and drank the sweet, fragrant tea down in one go. The others did the same and, having paid for their drinks, they set off once again into the vast three-dimensional maze, slung out between the trees.

'So how's that timid heart of yours, Cowlquape?' Twig said with a chuckle as they were crossing a hanging walkway some while later.

Cowlquape smiled. 'Believe it or not, Twig, I reckon the tea must have helped.' He stopped, clutched hold of the rope hand-rail and looked down. 'My fear of heights isn't nearly so bad as it was.'

Twig nodded. Gabtrolls were renowned for their understanding of herbs and roots. 'And you, Spooler?'

he said to the oakelf, scuttling on ahead of them.

'Never felt better, captain,' came the cheery reply.

Cowlquape turned to Twig as they continued after him. 'And what about you?' he said. 'Has the bristle-weed tea helped you to find yourself?'

Twig shook his head. 'Not yet, Cowlquape,' he said. 'Not yet . . .'

All round them the air grew more and more stifling and the noise louder. Howling. Wailing. Chatter and squawk. Whipcrack and chain-rattle. The hopeless moaning of a band of waifs, wraiths and the lesser trolls, roped to tether-rings. Roars of triumph. Cries of defeat. And orchestrating the whole terrible cacophony, the raucous flocks of flightless bird-creatures who inhabited the slave market: the shrykes.

They came in all shapes and sizes, from the hefty patrol

leaders to the scrawny little snitches and snoopers. All were female – the few miserable male shrykes there were kept penned and treated like slaves themselves.

The colour of the shrykes' plumage also varied. Most of the guards were tawny; the tally-hens, metallic slate-grey. But there were others. Mottled and striped, piebald and spotted. Some woodnut brown, some ironwood grey, some snowbird white. And some were brightly coloured.

Greater in stature than the others and with a certain air of nobility about them, the roost-sisters, as those with real power were called, were answerable only to Mother Muleclaw herself. Despite the apparent frippery of their dress – the gaudy aprons, the ornate headdresses, the golden rings through their beaks – the roost-sisters were greatly feared. Cold and ruthless, they were also terrifyingly unpredictable.

Twig looked up to see one of them now, strutting arrogantly across a crowded upper parapet, wings swinging, beak in the air, and striking out with her leather flail at random as she went. Twig turned away in disgust.

'The whole accursed place should be razed to the ground,' he said angrily. 'Wiped out. Burned down.'

Cowlquape's expression clouded over. 'I dare say it will be, one day,' he said. 'But not before those beyond the slave market decide they have no more need for pets and servants and bound workers. In the Deepwoods. In Undertown. Yes, and in Sanctaphrax, too.'

Twig turned towards his young apprentice. 'Cowlquape, are you saying that it is in some way *our* fault that this place exists?'

Cowlquape shrugged. 'Perhaps,' he said. 'We demand, they supply. And as Kobold the Wise said . . .'

'Mind your backs!' came a chorus of shrill voices. 'Make way! Make way!'

Twig turned to see half a dozen tawny shryke guards, flails and clubs drawn, marching along a walkway parallel to their own. They were split up into three pairs. Each pair was dragging along a protesting prisoner, beating him savagely as they went.

'We didn't notice!' one of them moaned.

'We can explain!' protested another.

'What's happening?' Cowlquape asked Spooler anxiously. 'What have they done wrong?'

Spooler nodded towards them. 'No cockades, see?' he said. 'They've rotted away. And now they're about to pay the penalty.'

'I wouldn't like to be in their shoes,' said Twig with a shudder.

'Neither would I,' said Cowlquape, nervously checking his own cockade. It was reassuringly fresh. 'I do wish we'd hurry up and find that wretched auction place.'

Twig looked round him. 'Me, too, Cowlquape,' he said. 'Me, too.'

They were passing through a section of the slave market where the more exotic Deepwoods creatures were kept. There were fromps coughing and quarms squealing from behind the bars of the hollowed trees, and razorflits, bound by the legs and suspended upside down from hooks, screeching with fury. A rotsucker, imprisoned in a cage far too small for it, oozed a green bile from the end of its tubular mouthpiece that hissed where it dropped and gave off coils of foul-smelling vapour; a muzzled halitoad crouched in a mist of its own noxious breath.

'It . . . it's disgusting here,' said Cowlquape, his voice muffled by the hand he'd clamped over his mouth.

'Yet no less popular for that,' Twig commented with a weary sigh.

He'd already noticed that the whole area was bustling with particularly eager buyers. The sound of their haggling reached fever pitch as they all tried to secure deals which would, in turn, make them a pretty profit.

'Come on,' he said, lengthening his stride. 'Let's find that auction once and for all. I don't want to stay in this vile, parasitic place a moment longer than we have to.'

An hour later – just as they were about to give up – they saw it: the Grand Central Auction.

Situated on a large, terraced platform, the auction consisted of a long windowless building, a raised stage and a lectern. The whole lot was lit up with heavy hanging glass balls, each one containing a live firebug which gleamed like a candle-flame as it flew round its tiny prison, looking for a way out. They illuminated the auction area so brightly that Twig and Spooler's faint glow faded away completely.

'Twenty-five? Do I hear twenty-five?' The auctioneer – a tall noble-looking shryke with pink and purple plumage – clutched her blackwood hammer and scanned the crowd. 'I'm asking twenty-five for this trio of flat-head goblins. At the peak of their physical con-

dition, they are. Ideal bodyguards or mercenaries. Twenty-five? Thank you. Thirty. Do I hear thirty?'

Twig stared at the scene, his heart beating furiously. Could any of his missing crew be here? The three ragged flat-heads, shackled to one another, stood morosely at the front of the stage. Four tawny shryke guards stood with them, flails and clubs drawn and ready to punish any misdemeanour. The auctioneer stood at the lectern to their right.

'Forty,' she said. 'Do I hear forty?' She nodded. 'Forty-five?'

Below her, on a log, sat a stooped, slate-grey tally-hen with a clipboard clutched in her claws. Between licks at the end of her crayon, she was noting down the rising amount.

Cowlquape nudged Twig. 'Recognize anyone?' he said.

Twig shook his head. 'No,' he said. He peered back into the dark shadows at the back of the stage where an assortment of Deepwoods creatures stood huddled together, waiting their turn to come under the hammer. There were cloddertrogs, mobgnomes, a gnokgoblin with a young'un at her breast, a gangly lugtroll and a couple of unfamiliar wiry, matted-haired trolls from the darkest reaches of the Deepwoods where Twig had never ventured.

'No-one,' he said disappointedly.

'Going once,' the auctioneer cried out 'Going twice . . . Sold!' she announced, and the blackwood hammer cracked down heavily on the top of the lectern. 'Sold to the flat-head with the crimson jerkin.'

Twig snorted. Flat-heads buying flat-heads! What kind of a place was this where free-citizens and slaves could only be told apart by cockades? He turned to Cowlquape and Spooler. 'Come,' he said. 'It was worth a try, but we're clearly wasting our time here. Let's go.'

Cowlquape turned to leave. He was as disappointed as the others. In fact the longer he remained in the slave market, the more uneasy he was becoming. If it were up to him, they would cut their losses and depart at once.

'Lot Nine,' the auctioneer cried. 'A waterwaif.'

Twig started. A waterwaif? He'd seen no waterwaif. He turned round and stared back at the stage. And sure enough, there – cowering behind the cluster of cloddertrogs – was a slight, scaly creature with fanned ears and a darting, reptilian tongue. One of the tawny shrykes jabbed him sharply in the back. The waterwaif groaned and hobbled wearily to the front of the stage.

'I thought we were going,' said Cowlquape.

'Wait,' said Twig.

He stared at the individual before him, then at Spooler, then back at the waterwaif – then back at Spooler.

'Well?' he said.

'I . . . I'm not sure,' the oakelf replied. There was excitement in his voice. 'It *could* be . . .'

'Could be what?' said Cowlquape.

'Not what, but *who*,' said Twig. 'It could be Woodfish.'

'From your crew?' said Cowlquape.

Twig nodded.

Just then, the auctioneer's bidding got underway.

'Ten!' she announced. 'Who'll offer me ten.'

Twig raised his hand.

The auctioneer glanced at him. She nodded and turned away again.

'Fifteen,' she said. 'Do I hear fifteen?'

'Fifteen,' came a gruff voice.

'Twenty?' said the auctioneer, turning back to Twig.

Twig glanced round at the character who had bid against him – an evil-looking individual with a metal eye-patch, who was leering at the waterwaif with his one good eye and licking his lips ominously.

From the emblem embossed into his heavy leather coat, Twig could see he was a leaguesman – though the symbol was none he recognized. He raised his hand a second time.

The auctioneer nodded again. 'Twenty-five?' she said. 'Do I hear twenty-five.'

Twig glanced around again. This time, his gaze met that of the one-eyed leaguesman, who was glaring back at him furiously. 'Twenty-five!' he bellowed.

'Thirty!' shouted Twig.

'Thirty-five!'

'Fifty!'

The leaguesman hesitated for a moment, then – as Twig looked round – his mouth cracked open and his gold teeth glinted in the glow from the imprisoned fire-bugs. ''S all yours,' he sneered.

'Sold to the individual in the hammelhornskin waistcoat for fifty,' the auctioneer announced. 'Come forward to pay the tally-hen and lot number nine is yours.'

Twig stepped up onto the stage. Cowlquape held his breath. Was the waterwaif the crew-member Twig was searching for or not? The next moment, the air resounded with a screech of surprise.

'You want to do *what*?' the tally-hen demanded, her voice loud and incredulous. 'You want to buy it a cockade?'

Cowlquape's heart leapt. So it *was* Woodfish after all! He moved closer to the stage, the better to hear what was going on.

'I think you'll find the amount correct,' Twig was

saying as he handed over a cluster of gold pieces. 'Fifty for the purchase and an extra two for a white cockade.'

The tally-hen glanced up at the auctioneer questioningly.

'If he wants to waste his money on fine gestures . . .' she sniffed, and her beak clacked with contempt.

The tally-hen shrugged. Fifty-two gold pieces were fifty-two gold pieces after all. She slipped the money into the chest, reached inside the pocket of her pouch and removed a white cockade.

'Here,' she said.

Twig took it and handed it over to the waterwaif. He smiled. 'For you, fellow free-citizen,' he said.

'Th . . . thank you,' the waterwaif said uncertainly.

'Even though you are not the one I hoped you would be,' said Twig quietly.

Cowlquape gasped. *Not* the one? What did he mean?

The waterwaif frowned, and listened in on Twig's thoughts. 'Oh, I see,' he said. 'You thought I was your missing crew-member, Woodfish.' His fan-like ears fluttered. 'I'm sorry to disappoint you.'

Twig shrugged. 'It's not your fault,' he said. Then, smiling grimly, he reached out and shook the scaly hand of the waterwaif.

'Lot number ten!' the auctioneer bellowed above the rising swell of angry voices in the crowd. She looked down impatiently. 'Will those involved in the previous sale kindly leave the stage.'

Cowlquape and Spooler helped the still somewhat bewildered waterwaif down onto the platform. Twig jumped down after him. The four of them slipped back through the crowd.

On the other side, Twig turned to the waterwaif. 'Anyway,' he said, 'I'm glad to have been of help. Live long and fare well,' he said formally, and turned away – to be confronted with the furious face of the thwarted leaguesman pressed closely into his own.

'What do you think you're playing at?' he said.

'Playing at?' said Twig.

The leaguesman seized him by the shoulder and pulled him close. 'You heard me,' he spat. 'Do you realize how long I've been searching for a waterwaif?' the leaguesman hissed into Twig's ear. His breath was warm, moist and made fetid by the rotten meat trapped between his gold teeth. 'Thirty-six cockades-worth!' he said. 'Thirty-six dumping cockades-worth! This was the first I'd found. And then you come along!'

With that, he drew his dagger. Twig stumbled. The blade glinted. Crying out, the waterwaif leapt between them. The knife plunged into his chest.

A curious look of serenity passed over the waterwaif's face as he tumbled back to the wooden platform. It had all happened so quickly, but he had read the leaguesman's murderous thoughts in an instant. His eyes misted over; his ears fell still.

Astonishment turning to rage, Twig drew his own sword. But as he stepped forwards, half a dozen of the tawny shryke guards brushed him aside and fell upon the leaguesman.

Shrieking with fury – eyes glinting and feathers erect – they tore the cockade from his lapel and seized him in their vicious claws. The leaguesman struggled in vain as he was bundled away.

'It was him!' he protested. 'Let me go!'

'Oh, we'll let you go, all right!' came the gleeful reply. 'We'll let you go under the auctioneer's hammer.'

'No, not a slave,' the leaguesman shouted, and struggled all the more desperately. 'You can't sell me as a slave. Do you not realize who I am . . . ?' His voice was drowned out by the sound of scornful laughter as the shrykes dragged him away.

Twig shakily approached the dying waterwaif. He crouched down. 'I'm so sorry,' he said tearfully. 'Ending up a slave would have been better than . . . than this.'

The waterwaif's ears fluttered weakly. 'No,' he whispered. 'Nothing is worse than that,' he said. 'You saved my life, and I am happy I was able to save yours . . .' His eyes widened abruptly as a spasm of pain racked his body. 'And there is one last service I can do you . . .'

As Cowlquape and Spooler watched on, Twig lowered his head and listened intently.

'You are looking for the missing crew of the *Edgedancer*,' the waterwaif whispered hoarsely. 'I read it in your thoughts.'

'Yes,' said Twig.

The waterwaif clutched at him weakly. 'One of those you remember in your thoughts, well . . . I have seen him here . . . in the market.'

'You have?' Twig exclaimed. 'Who is it? And where can I find him?'

'He . . . he . . .' His voice gurgled. Twig held the waterwaif up and put an ear to his mouth. 'The Wig-Wig . . . Arena,' he whispered, and his body juddered. There was a gasp. A whimper. And the light in his eyes flickered and died.

Twig laid the waterwaif back down and closed his eyelids. Cowlquape and Spooler crouched down beside him.

'It wasn't your fault,' said Cowlquape.

'Yet he's dead, for all that,' said Twig. He sighed. 'What should we do with the body?'

'The shrykes will take care of it,' said Spooler. 'Come, captain. There's nothing more you can – or may – do here.'

With heavy-troubled hearts, the three of them left. Cowlquape, who was last in line as they crossed over the nearest hanging walkway, glanced back to see that the tawny guard shrykes had returned to the scene. Two of them hoisted the dead body onto their feathery shoulders, and all six of them scuttled off. Cowlquape turned away.

On the far side of the hanging walkway, Twig stopped and looked round him. More than ever, he felt that the Great Shryke Slave Market was nothing less than an evil wood fungus, sucking the life out of its host, the Deepwoods, and all who dwelt in her. He couldn't wait to leave. He looked at Cowlquape and Spooler and knew that they felt the same way. But they couldn't leave. Not yet.

'The Wig-Wig Arena,' he said to Spooler. 'Does that name mean anything to you?'

The oakelf's dark eyes widened with unmistakable fear. 'Oh, yes, captain,' he said, his voice trembling. 'It certainly does. I know all about the Wig-Wig Arena.' He shuddered. 'I only wish I didn't.'

· CHAPTER FIFTEEN ·

THE WIG-WIG ARENA

Cowlquape suddenly looked up, breaking the silence that had followed the oakelf's words. His face was deathly pale. 'Twig,' he trembled. 'It's started.'

'What's started?'

Cowlquape lightly touched his woodthistle-shaped rosette. 'My cockade,' he said miserably. 'The material is starting to wilt.'

'Are you sure?' said Twig. 'It looks all right to me.'

Cowlquape shook his head angrily. 'Look!' he said. 'It's gone all limp at the edges. I can't believe we've been here long enough for that to happen.'

'That tally-hen did warn us to keep track of time,' Twig reminded him.

'Yes, but three days!' Cowlquape exclaimed hotly. 'We can't possibly have been here for three days. It's all a con, a trick to enslave more unsuspecting free citizens . . .'

'Cowlquape, calm down,' said Twig. 'It hasn't rotted away yet. And anyway, what's done is done. We must look forwards.' He turned to Spooler. 'Time's running short,' he said. 'This Wig-Wig Arena,' he said. 'Can you take us there?'

The oakelf nodded and looked round about him slowly, thoughtfully. 'By reading the signs in the market crowds, I can,' he said. 'Look over there at those merchants. See the greed in their faces? Follow them and they'll lead us back to the Grand Central Auction. Whereas over there, those gnokgoblins. See the way they stop, look around, then go on a few steps? They're browsers. They'll lead us to the livestock-traders and trinket-sellers.'

'Yes, yes,' said Twig impatiently. 'But what about the Arena? How do we know who to follow there?'

'Bloodlust,' said Spooler. 'Look for bloodlust in the faces of the crowd.' He continued scanning the milling groups of trogs and trolls, goblins and gnomes, leaguesmen and sky pirates. 'There!' he said at last, and pointed at a gaggle of goblins. 'That looks a likely group. Look at the purpose in their stride. The violence in their gestures. The glint in their eyes.' He sniffed the air and shuddered. 'I can *smell* their lust for blood, oozing from every pore. Oh, they're heading for the Wig-Wig Arena, all right,' he said. 'I'd stake my life on it.'

'That's good enough for me,' said Twig. 'We'll follow them. And Sky willing we will find the crew-member the waterwaif saw there. Come on, Cowlquape. Before we lose sight of those goblins.'

They set off in pursuit. Ahead of them the group of goblins was becoming increasingly rowdy and, as that happened, so the numbers heading in the same direction increased as more and more, attracted by the noise, came to swell their ranks. Twig, Cowlquape and Spooler surrendered themselves to the stream. Past a tattooing-stall they went, a whip-merchant's, a leech-doctor's; past a corral of roosting prowlgrins, a flock of tethered vulpoons – impelled ever onwards by the excited crowd. They couldn't have escaped the forward surge now even if they'd wanted to.

'I'll say this for the roost-mother,' a shrill gnokgoblin piped up. 'She certainly knows how to put on a spectacle.'

His companion nodded vigorously. 'Nothing beats a contest with a banderbear pitted against the wig-wigs,'

he said. 'It's an absolute classic!'

Twig gasped. A banderbear? Pitted against wig-wigs!

'Wasn't there a banderbear on board the *Edgedancer*?' Cowlquape said in Twig's ear, whilst all the time fighting to keep up in the jostling scrum. 'You think it might be the one that the waterwaif saw, don't you?'

'Perhaps,' said Twig. 'I cannot leave until I know one way or the other.'

'Still,' Cowlquape went on, as he stumbled forwards. 'A big strong creature like a banderbear can defend itself against wig-wigs, surely?'

Twig shook his head seriously. 'I once saw what a pack of wig-wigs can do to a banderbear.' He pulled a pendant from the folds of his jacket and held it up for Cowlquape to see. It was a tooth. 'This is all that is left of that banderbear,' he said.

'But . . . *Whoooah!*' Cowlquape exclaimed as the crowd abruptly squeezed in on him from all sides and surged forwards. He was carried towards a narrow archway. **THE WIG-WIG ARENA**, he read, in gold letters, as he was swept beneath the arch and on to a broad platform. He looked round. His mouth fell open.

'Amazing, isn't it?' said Twig.

'Unbelievable,' said Cowlquape. 'The architecture, the planning – the *size* . . .'

They were in a bright clearing, encircled by huge trees. Tier upon tier of curved terraces had been suspended from the branches above to form a vast amphitheatre. At its centre, far below them, lay a deep torch-lit pit, ringed by mesh-like netting.

'Move along there,' came an irritated voice from behind them. 'Move right down into the arena.'

Cowlquape recognized the shrill tone of a guard shryke at once. His head buzzed with fear as, without turning round, he did as was told, stepping down off the platform and onto the first of the circular terraces that extended far down below them. Twig and Spooler followed him.

Down, they went; one terrace after another. Cowlquape took it all in, as they picked their way through the countless groups of chattering goblins and trolls.

The Wig-Wig Arena was like a giant funnel rising up from the forest floor at the bottom, where the bloody contests would take place, to the forest canopy at the top. One tree, even more massive than its neighbours, dominated the arena. It was directly opposite the terrace where Twig, Cowlquape and Spooler found themselves jostled into seats – a colossal ironwood tree, its black, spade-like leaves in sharp relief against the blondwood steps rising up behind it. Cowlquape looked more closely.

Attached to the tree's sturdy branches were several constructions: square platforms for the armed guard shrykes dotted here and there; a small, squat building beside a raised stage; cogs, pulleys and winding gear; a plank jutting out from the main trunk, leading nowhere. Further up the tree was a broad podium, with the brightly-coloured roost-sisters standing along its balustrade in a row. And above this – suspended from a network of heavy ropes – was an ornate royal-box. Inside it sat a solitary figure.

It was the roost-mother herself: Mother Muleclaw. She was resplendent in her crested head-dress, her firebug jewels and a diaphanous silver cloak which hung loosely over her rainbow plumage. No finery, however, could conceal the wickedness in her eyes. From her box, she had a perfect view of every inch of the arena.

As she cast her malevolent gaze round Cowlquape quaked, and his hand shot up to conceal his wilting cockade. Twig noticed the movement.

'Cowlquape,' he said gently. 'Calm yourself.' He swung his arm round in a wide arc. 'There are hundreds, perhaps thousands, of individuals here,' he said. 'They're not interested in us when there's so much money to be made.'

He nodded towards the slate-grey tally-hens already scuttling about taking bets from the growing swell of spectators. Cowlquape watched them for a moment.

'No, I suppose not,' he said hesitantly. 'All the same . . .' He looked across the arena and shuddered. 'There's someone in there,' he said, pointing to the squat construction below the podium.

Twig looked. He saw fingers clutching the bars at the locked door. Some poor wretch was about to meet his death – yet it was not a banderbear . . .

At that moment, a fanfare of trumpeting cut through the air. A roar of approval went up round the crowd. Cowlquape looked up into the ironwood tree to see a dozen striped shrykes perching in the upper branches, with long tasselled horns at their beaks. The fanfare was repeated. This time, the crowd fell still. All eyes fell on the royal-box.

Mother Muleclaw arose slowly. Her beak clacked noisily. 'We are gratified to see so many here,' she announced. 'We know you will not be disappointed by this evening's contest. It isn't every night we get to see a banderbear in battle.'

The crowd roared its agreement. Mother Muleclaw raised her multicoloured wings for quiet.

'Before the main event, we have a little surprise for you. The appetizer, so to speak,' she said, and her beak clacked with amusement. She leant down from the box. 'Release the prisoner,' she demanded.

The guard shryke saluted with its tawny wing and stepped forward to unlock the door of the prison

beneath the podium. A portly individual appeared at the doorway and looked round with obvious confusion.

'What? What? What?' he blustered.

Cowlquape stared in disbelief – at the ornate jacket with its marsh-gems and mire-pearls, at the tricorn hat with the purple vulpoon feather, at the waxed moustache, the arched eyebrows, the pink, pudgy hands. 'Thunderbolt Vulpoon,' he breathed, and clutched hold of Twig's arm. 'This is what he had planned for us!' he whispered, his voice low with dread.

'If I'd known,' said Twig, 'I'd never have handed him over to the shrykes. Not even a slave-trader deserves this.'

The crowd watched in silence as the guard shryke cracked her flail and drove the sky pirate captain towards the plank jutting out over the pit below. The yellow torchlight gleamed on his quivering features as he looked up at the hanging royal-box. 'Why?' he cried out. 'For the love of Sky, why are you doing this?'

Mother Muleclaw squawked with irritation, and the shryke's heavy flail cracked Vulpoon around the head.

'We had promised you a leaguesman from Undertown for your delectation,' said Mother Muleclaw, addressing the crowd.

The crowd cheered happily.

'Or perhaps even a Sanctaphrax academic,' she said.

The cheering of the crowd grew louder still.

'Unfortunately, due to circumstances beyond our control, this will not now be possible . . .'

The crowd booed and hissed. Mother Muleclaw

glared down at Vulpoon. 'All I can offer you is this miserable specimen. Still I am sure he'll put on an excellent show for you.' Her voice became a raucous screech, that echoed round the arena. 'I give you Thunderbolt Vulpoon, the sky pirate captain.'

A deafening roar went up. Cowlquape looked round in disgust at the rapt expressions on the spectators' faces as they watched the hapless Vulpoon being prodded forward with a sharp pike onto the plank. A chant started up, and was soon echoing all round the arena.

'Down! Down! Down! Down!'

Vulpoon stumbled forwards. For an instant, his body hung there at the end of the plank as if held by invisible ropes. Then there was movement again, and Thunderbolt Vulpoon was toppling forwards –

rolling over

and over

as he fell,

before landing in a bed of soft moss at the bottom of the pit. The crowd roared its approval.

For a moment, the sky pirate captain didn't move. Then, with a shake of his head, he climbed to his feet and drew his sword and dagger. He looked round – at the heavy curtain of netting that enclosed the pit; at the small holes cut into it every ten metres, allowing access from the forest floor outside. The crowd looked too, scrutinizing the shadowy openings for that first tell-tale flash of orange.

'There!' someone screamed. 'Over there!'

It was the first of the wig-wigs. It dashed across the arena floor, looking no more frightening than an orange floor-mop. Until the creature opened its mouth! The crowd gasped as one as the powerful jaws snapped wide open to reveal the rows of razor-sharp teeth.

All round the arena, the arrival of the first wig-wig had prompted a flurry of betting. Tally-hens and tote-fledgers darted among the crowds, shouting out ever-changing odds and exchanging gold pieces (each one, checked with a sharp clack of the beak) for betting-slips.

'Twenty-five on twelve minutes!'

'Fifty on forty-seven dead wig-wigs.'

'A hundred that he's got a maximum of ten seconds left!'

Sickened, Cowlquape turned away and buried his face in his hands.

At last, a roar went up.

'YES!'

Louder and louder it became, until the terraces themselves were trembling with the noise. Above the uproar came the trumpeting of the horns. And still the clamour did not abate. One of the tally-hens trotted to the ironwood tree and a message was passed up to the roost-mother.

Mother Muleclaw rose to her feet once more. A hush fell.

'The sky pirate captain managed to kill forty-three wig-wigs before his demise,' she announced. 'And twenty-seven more were wounded.'

The winners cheered. The losers – of whom there were many more – groaned.

'The contest lasted for precisely ten minutes and . . .' she hesitated. The spectators clasped their betting-slips tightly. 'Ten minutes and forty seconds. That's four-o. Forty.'

Again, the few excited whoops of delight were drowned out by a general groan of disappointment. Mother Muleclaw clacked her beak.

'But now, my friends, we must proceed,' she announced. 'It is time for the evening's main event.' She nodded at the shryke guard on the platform below her, who began turning a great handled wheel. The pulleys creaked. The ropes shifted. From above the hanging royal-box, the bottom of a heavy, ironwood cage began slowly to descend from the dense grey-black foliage.

'A classic contest!' the roost-mother shrieked. 'The ultimate confrontation! Power versus perseverance. The mighty versus a multitude.' She tossed back her plumed head. 'For your delectation and delight, a genuine . . . an extremely rare . . . in the prime of physical fitness . . .'

The crowd went wild with feverish anticipation; waving their arms, stamping their feet. And, as the cage came lower – revealing the fierce, furious beast pounding at the bars of its hanging prison – their bloodthirsty cries became more and more tumultuous. Mother Muleclaw smirked with self-satisfaction, and when the cage was hanging directly next to the royal-box, she nodded down at the shryke for a second time. The turning stopped. The cage juddered to a halt. Mother Muleclaw raised a great taloned hand.

'I give you . . . a BANDERBEAR!' she screeched.

Twig gasped. It wasn't just *a* banderbear. It was Goom.

There wasn't any doubt. Even if he hadn't recognized his face, the tell-tale scars from the spiked pit that had once trapped him gleamed on his left flank.

Clucking softly, Mother Muleclaw reached out and stroked the claws of the banderbear which stuck out between the bars of the hanging cage. 'I know he's going to give those wig-wigs a run for their money,' she said, her voice oily.

The crowd – whipped up to a frenzy by the thought of the ensuing confrontation – had begun chanting once again.

'Down!' they demanded. 'Down! Down! Down!'

Cowlquape's whole body shuddered with revulsion.

'We must act quickly,' said Twig urgently. 'Go back to that prowlgrin corral we passed. Buy four prowlgrins,' he said, giving Cowlquape a handful of gold coins. 'The largest and strongest you can find. Then meet me round the other side of the arena, on the walkway directly beneath the branches of the ironwood tree.'

'But Twig . . .' Cowlquape began.

'*Now*, Cowlquape,' said Twig firmly and, before his young apprentice could say another word, he dashed off through the crowd.

Cowlquape stared after him for a moment, then turned to Spooler.

'We'd best see about those prowlgrins,' the oakelf said.

Cowlquape nodded. He only hoped Twig knew what he was doing.

The arena was thick with feverish betting as Twig made his way towards the ironwood tree.

'Thirty gold pieces on twenty-eight minutes and nine seconds.'

'Fifty each way on at least two hundred and fifty wig-wigs copping it.'

'Seventy-five gold pieces!'

'A hundred!'

Ignoring the yelps of pain and cries of anger as he elbowed his way through the jostling crowd, Twig finally arrived at the point where the trunk of the great tree emerged from behind the top terrace. He stopped, pulled the sky pirate grappling-hook from the front of his heavy longcoat and glanced round.

The atmosphere was now approaching fever-pitch and no-one – neither shryke nor spectator – noticed the young sky pirate standing in the shadows. Taking the rope in his hand, Twig swung the hook into the branches above and, when it took securely, scrambled up.

'And now,' Mother Muleclaw screamed above the din, 'the moment you've all been waiting for!' She nodded down at the shryke guard: she should begin to lower the banderbear into the pit below.

Twig reached a broad, flat branch high in the iron-wood tree and crept carefully along it. He stopped when he was directly above the royal-box and hanging cage. Below him, Mother Muleclaw raised her wings.

'And so,' she announced, 'let the contest begin . . . *Whurrggh!*'

As one, the crowd let out a gasp of astonishment at the sight of the young sky pirate dropping down into the royal-box and seizing the roost-mother. An arm grasped her round the throat; a hand pressed the glinting blade of a knife against her ruffled neck.

'Stop lowering the cage!' Twig bellowed. 'Bring it up level with the royal-box again – or the roost-mother gets it!'

With a squawk of indignation, the tawny shryke paused and fixed Twig with an astonished stare. Then slowly, she reversed the direction of her turning. The roost-sisters were in uproar, shifting about on their podium, screeching and squawking. Other shrykes – tawny guards and great, serrated-beaked slavers – closed in on the tree from the walkways menacingly.

'Back off!' Twig roared. 'Tell them,' he hissed into Mother Muleclaw's feathery ear. 'Tell them now.'

'St . . . stay back,' said Mother Muleclaw, in a strangulated voice.

'And tell them to drop their weapons!' Twig increased the pressure of the knife.

'Do as he says!' she squawked.

'That's better,' said Twig. Then, still maintaining the

pressure on the knife, he reached over to the cage and unclasped the lid at the top. One of the banderbear's massive paws appeared.

Suddenly, the crowd seemed to realize what was happening. Up until that moment, the spectacle of the youth threatening the roost-mother had held them captivated. Now they saw what he had in mind, and were incensed.

'He's released it!' they roared furiously. 'He's letting it go!'

Twig dragged the cowering Muleclaw to the far end of the royal-box as the banderbear heaved himself up out of the cage. He watched, heart in his mouth, as the great, clumsy creature grasped at a branch above his head for support, and stepped across the yawning chasm below.

As the banderbear fell into the royal-box, the crowd exploded with anger. 'It's getting away!' they raged.

The roost-sisters below craned their necks round to see what was happening.

Twig watched the banderbear climbing to his feet. 'Goom,' he said. 'I knew it was you.'

'Wuh?' the great beast asked. 'T-wuh-g?'

'Yes, Goom,' said Twig. 'Didn't I promise that I'd never abandon my crew.' He glanced upwards. 'Pull yourself up onto that branch above our heads. Then pull me up beside you.'

The banderbear shuddered nervously, making the royal-box shake. Mother Muleclaw cried out as Twig's knife nicked the scaly skin beneath the feathers. The crowd howled with dismay as the great lumbering creature reached up, sunk its claws into the overhead branch and swung its tree-trunk legs up into the air.

'A hundred and fifty says he doesn't make it,' a voice rang out above the din.

'Two hundred says we'll be looking at a new roost-mother before the night is out!' yelled another.

The crowd went wild.

At his third attempt, Goom managed to swing his legs over the edge of the branch and drag himself up. He crouched down on the broad branch and lowered a great arm.

'Wuh!' he said.

Twig grabbed hold of the banderbear's wrist. Goom pulled, and Twig was whisked up clear of the royal-box. The instant her attacker was gone, Mother Muleclaw cried out.

'Seize them!' she shrieked, jumping up and down in the box in a fever of rage. 'No-one threatens the roost-mother and lives! Guards ... *Aaargh!'* she screamed, as one of the banderbear's razor-sharp claws sliced through several of the ropes that kept the royal-box in place. The box swung wildly. Her sharp talons gripped the wooden sides. 'No,' she whimpered. 'Have pity ...'

'Pity?' Twig shouted. 'The only pity is that this was not done long ago.' And with that, he reached down and sliced through the last ropes.

The royal-box plummeted down through the air, with Mother Muleclaw screaming all the way.

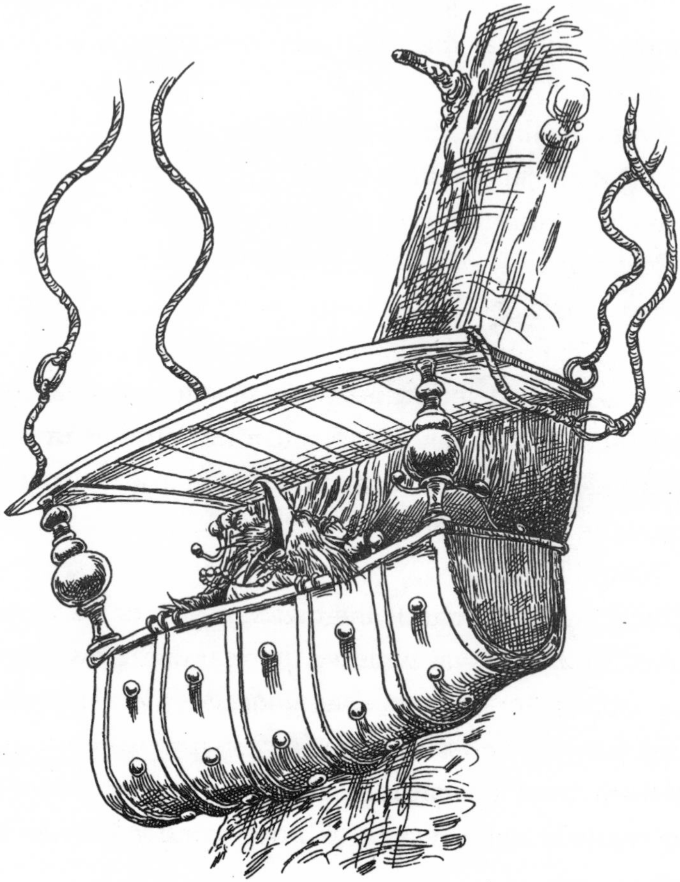

The crowd roared with delight. This was even better than a banderbear. This was the roost-mother herself. As the first of the wig-wigs emerged from the dark openings in the stockade, the noise became deafening. Whooping. Wailing. Cheering and shouting. 'A hundred on . . .' 'Five hundred that . . .' 'A thousand!'

Twig turned to the banderbear. He seized him by a quivering paw.

'Edge your way along this branch,' he shouted, 'then down onto that one, there.' He pointed to a broader, flatter branch growing out of the trunk behind him. 'It's almost as wide as the walkways. And then, when I say jump, jump!'

'Wuh!' the banderbear grunted in alarm.

The noise all around them was deafening: a great screeching from the shrykes and the roar of the bloodthirsty crowd.

'Trust me,' said Twig, struggling to make himself heard. He turned and made his own way along the branch, arms raised to keep his balance as the heavy banderbear anxiously lumbered after him. The leaves quivered. The branch swayed. Below him, Twig saw the boards of the wooden walkway come closer.

'Jump!' he shouted.

'WUH!' cried the banderbear, and the pair of them leapt from the branch and down to the walkway below. Scrambling to his feet, Twig looked around wildly. Angry shrykes on the adjacent walkways were running at them from every side, shoving their way through the crowds who were still thronging towards the extraordinary spectacle unfolding in the pit.

'Twig! Twig!' came an urgent voice.

Twig spun round to see Cowlquape and Spooler on a broad platform just ahead, pushing towards them through the crowd. They both held a tether in each of their hands, at the end of which were four startled prowlgrins.

'Well done, Cowlquape!' he shouted.

Just then, four shryke guards dropped onto the walkway from above. They landed between them, cutting Twig and the banderbear off from escape. In a split second the banderbear was on them. With a mighty blow from his paw, he swept two shrykes from the walkway in a flurry of feathers. The other two dropped their clubs and flails, and fled with terrified screeches.

'They were the biggest ones I could find,' panted Cowlquape, as he and Spooler finally reached the others. The prowlgrins bucked and whinnied from the end of their tethers.

'Ideal,' said Twig. 'Goom, take the biggest. Climb up, all of you.' He grabbed the reins and leapt onto his own prowlgrin.

Goom remained still. 'Wuh-wuh!' he groaned miserably.

'It's the *only* way,' said Twig. 'Come on!'

Already more shrykes were gathering. For the moment they hung back, but when there were enough of them, they would rush forward. There was murder in their yellow eyes.

Reluctantly, the massive banderbear clambered up onto the waiting prowlgrin. The creature groaned under the heavy weight, and locked its bow-legs.

'All right?' said Twig.

The banderbear nodded unhappily.

'Let's get out of here!' Twig shouted.

Gripping the reins tightly, he kicked hard into the prowlgrin's flanks. The others did the same. The next instant – as if in some strange dance – the four beasts reared up, pawed the air with their fore-legs and leapt forwards.

Clutching on for dear life, Twig and Cowlquape, Spooler and Goom found themselves charging along the walkway away from the ironwood tree and the terrible arena. They knocked spectators and shrykes aside. Cowlquape held on desperately. He'd never ridden a prowlgrin before, and never wanted to again. It was terrifying.

The walkways swayed and shuddered beneath them, market-stalls crashed as they careered past – but the prowlgrins were as sure-footed as they were swift. The market sped by in a hazy blur of colour and oily lamp-light. Suddenly, they were approaching the end of a walkway that gave way to nothing. It was the edge of the slave market. The astonished face of a slate-grey shryke peered out from a tally-booth directly ahead.

Now what? thought Cowlquape, his heart pounding.

Without a moment's hesitation, the prowlgrin beneath him launched itself off from the end of the walkway and into mid-air. Cowlquape sank his heels deep into its belly as the wind whistled past. He gripped the reins, white-knuckled.

Below him, the forest opened up like a gaping chasm. Falling. They were falling. His stomach leapt up into his mouth; he screwed his eyes shut. This was worse than the Sanctaphrax baskets, worse than the sky ship, worse than . . .

Ker-dunk!

His whole body jarred as the prowlgrin grabbed a branch with its fore-paws and, in an instant, kicked off again with its hind-legs. Cowlquape gripped the reins tighter still. Again, the forest opened up. And again, the prowlgrin landed, sure-footed on a branch before kicking down hard with its powerful hindquarters and leaping again.

The prowlgrin was well trained. Even though Cowlquape had never ridden before, all he had to do

was hold on as it forged its way through the forest from tree to tree. *Ker-dunk – whoosh! Kerdunk* . . . Little by little, it became easier. Cowlquape was learning when to tense his stomach and when to relax; when to lean forwards, when to sit back.

But what of the others?

Cowlquape stole a hurried glance back over his shoulders. Twig and Spooler were close behind him. And behind them was the banderbear. Despite the weight on its back, Goom's prowlgrin was managing to keep up. Then, with a jolt, Cowlquape saw a flurry of movement behind the banderbear. Half a dozen or more of the tawny shryke guards, on prowlgrins of their own, were close on their heels.

'What do we do, Twig?' Cowlquape shouted out.

'They're catching up.'

'Courage, Cowlquape!' Twig called breathlessly. 'Prowlgrins are beasts of the Deepwoods. They're used to travelling through the dark forest. But shrykes are roost creatures. They seldom stray far from the flock.'

Quite suddenly, the lights of the slave market disappeared and they were plunged into gloom. Cowlquape cried out with fear and screwed his eyes tightly shut.

'It's all right!' he heard Twig shouting happily. 'Cowlquape, open your eyes. It's all right.'

Cowlquape did as he was told and was relieved to discover that, though the forest itself was indeed pitch black, the sky pirates he was travelling with were glowing brightly in the darkness. Twig, Spooler and Goom; all three of them were bathed in the strange luminous light.

On they went, without easing up for a moment, from branch to dark, looming branch; fleet and sure-footed.

Then Twig called out. 'They've stopped!'

Cowlquape glanced round a second time. He saw the group of prowlgrins with their shryke riders perched on branches in the shadows, some distance behind them. They seemed in no hurry to continue the chase into the depths of the black forest. He saw something else; his cockade had disintegrated completely. All that remained was the pin.

'Thank Sky!' he murmured. 'We've beaten them! We . . . *whooah!*' he gasped as he slipped in the saddle.

'Careful, Cowlquape,' said Twig. 'We might have escaped the Great Shryke Slave Market, but there are still wig-wigs below on the forest floor.'

Cowlquape gripped the reins grimly. And as they continued on their flight and the slave market was left far behind, he kept his gaze fixed firmly on the forest ahead.

They did not stop, nor even slacken their pace. Before they could descend to the forest floor to rest up for the night, they had to ensure that they were well away from the voracious wig-wigs that had been attracted by the slave market. Cowlquape grew weary as they pressed on.

'How much farther?' he shouted after Twig.

'Just a little,' Twig shouted back. 'We must . . .'

'Captain!' shouted Spooler. The agitation in his voice was unmistakable. 'Captain Twig, it's Goom's prowlgrin.'

Twig spun round. 'Oh, no,' he muttered. The poor creature was suffering under the burdensome weight on its back. Its strength was all but used up. Each leap was laboured, each landing a gamble. As for Goom himself, the banderbear's glowing face was contorted with fear as his mount struggled on, ever more precariously.

'Wuh,' it was groaning. 'Wuh-wuh.'

Twig sighed. There was nothing for it. Wig-wigs or no wig-wigs they would have to descend. Sky willing, they had already put enough distance between them and the vicious orange creatures.

'Down!' he bellowed, and tugged on the reins of his own prowlgrin. 'We're going down.'

Their slow descent coincided with a thinning of the trees. As they leapt down, from branch to branch, lower and lower, Cowlquape scoured the forest floor for any tell-tale flash of orange.

There was none. He sighed with relief.

They landed in a tussocky glade of greatgrass. First Twig, then Spooler and Cowlquape, and finally Goom. His prowlgrin slumped to the ground, panting with exhaustion. Goom rolled off and lay beside it. The others dismounted, too. Spooler led the prowlgrins to a nearby tree and tethered them to a low branch. Twig crossed over towards the banderbear and crouched down next to him. He wrapped his arm around the creature's great neck and Goom rose, lifting Twig right off his feet.

The two figures lit up the glade with their eerie glow.

Cowlquape ran over to join them.

'You did it!' he exclaimed. 'You did it!'

Twig turned his head and smiled at his young apprentice. '*We* did it,' he said. 'You and me and Spooler, and Goom himself. We all did it!'

·CHAPTER SIXTEEN·

THE WELL-TRODDEN PATH

Having ridden so far and for so long, the four travellers were weary. Twig knew there was no point in forging on any further that night.

'We'll stop here,' he said 'and set off again early tomorrow morning. Cowlquape, Spooler, get a fire going. Goom and I will see about something to eat.'

'Aye, aye, captain,' said Spooler.

Cowlquape shivered as he watched Twig and the banderbear setting off into the darkness of the great forest. They looked so small against the massive trees: so insignificant, so vulnerable.

'Take care,' he muttered, and busied himself collecting sticks and branches from the surrounding undergrowth – taking care himself not to stray too far.

'Good,' said Spooler when he returned. 'Make a pile over there.'

Cowlquape dropped the huge bundle of wood and

watched Spooler coaxing a flame from something grey and fluffy. 'What's that?' he said.

'Barkmoss,' said Spooler, between blows. 'Excellent tinder. Usually.' He blew some more. His face was red and gleaming. 'The accursed stuff's damp though.' He blew harder still. Abruptly, the moss burst into flames. Spooler placed it gently down on a flat rock and turned to Cowlquape. 'Get me some small twigs,' he said. 'Dry ones.'

Cowlquape leapt to the pile and returned with a handful. He handed them to Spooler, who arranged them in a pyramid-shape above the flames. They too caught, and the pair of them stoked up the blaze with larger logs. Soon, they had a huge fire burning.

While Spooler sorted through their provisions for pots, plates and mugs, Cowlquape sat himself down next to the fire. With the night-sounds all around – a screech here, a squawk there – he felt safer there next to its protective flames. He reached into his bag for his beloved barkscrolls.

At that moment, there was a crashing noise to their left, and Goom came blundering back through the forest. Twig followed close behind, keeping to the trail the banderbear had carved out. He approached the fire and emptied a sack of fruits and roots onto the ground. 'Oak-apples, dellberries, yarrowroots,' he said, 'and numerous other delicacies especially selected by Goom with his sensitive banderbear nose, as being both nutritious and delicious!'

'Wuh!' said the banderbear, nodding his head in agreement. He lowered his great shoulder and lifted off the body of a young tilder. An arrow stuck out from its neck.

'Did you shoot that, Twig?' said Cowlquape, impressed.

'With my improvised home-made bow and arrow,' Twig laughed. 'It's been a long time, but I haven't lost my touch,' he said. 'Steaks for us and the rest of the carcass for the prowlgrins.'

A sudden fit of spluttered coughing echoed round the trees just above. Cowlquape ducked down and covered his head with his hands – only to see the others laughing at him.

'It's just a fromp,' said Twig. 'Quite harmless . . .'

'*Wa-iiiiii-kakakakaka* . . .'

The mating call of a night-lemuel cut him short. Cowlquape ducked down for a second time.

'Cowlquape,' said Twig softly. 'You're right to be cautious, for the Deepwoods is a dark and dangerous place. But I'm afraid you're just going to have to get used to the sounds it makes.'

Cowlquape nodded sheepishly. He didn't mean to keep reacting the way he did. 'I think I need some more of that gabtroll's special tea,' he said.

Twig smiled. 'Perhaps that could be arranged. We've got the oak-apples.' He turned to Goom. 'Did you find any hairy charlock?'

The banderbear rummaged through the pile of fruit and roots with surprising delicacy for one so huge. He selected a stubby root with a topknot of feathery leaves. 'Wuh,' he announced, holding it up together with a bunch of sugar grass.

'There,' said Twig. 'All the ingredients we need.'

By the time the moon rose, plump and bright, the four of them were sitting round the fire tucking into their tilder steaks and sweet rootmash, while the prowlgrins, apparently none the worse for their long ride, devoured the tilder carcass noisily. Cowlquape sipped at the tea Twig had put together.

'Not bad,' he said. 'The gabtroll's was sweeter, but . . . not bad at all.' All round him, the Deepwoods echoed with the rising crescendo of noise. Coughing, squealing, screeching . . . Cowlquape smiled. 'And what's more,' he said, 'it seems to be doing the trick.'

Twig yawned. 'Glad to hear it, Cowlquape, I . . .' He yawned again.

'Why don't you get some sleep,' said Cowlquape generously. 'I'll take first watch.'

'I'll join you,' said Spooler.

Twig nodded, too tired to argue. 'We'll rest up till dawn,' he said. 'Make an early start.' And with the old, familiar Deepwoods sounds ringing in his ears, he lay down by the fire, curled up and drifted off to sleep. Goom did the same. Spooler got up to check the prowlgrins.

Cowlquape crouched down by the fire and poked the glowing embers into life with a greenwood stick.

'Who'd have thought that *I* would ever end up inside the Deepwoods, the ancient home of Kobold the Wise?' he muttered. He laid the stick down and pulled the ancient barkscrolls from his pack. 'Of all places!'

*

Far away in the floating city of Sanctaphrax, a cold, heavy mist swirled round its avenues and alleyways. Vox, the tall young apprentice from the College of Cloud, shuddered, wrapped his fur-lined gowns tightly about him and lengthened his stride. He was already late for his secret meeting with the newly-appointed Professor of Psycho-Climatic Studies.

'Out of my way, scum!' he cursed, as an unfortunate sub-acolyte blundered into him in the mist.

'S . . . sorry, Vox,' the youth stammered, and Vox was gratified to hear the respectful nervousness in his voice. He cuffed him about the head, twice.

'Just watch it in future,' he snarled as, gown flapping in the icy wind, he strode away.

CRASH!

The ground behind him shook. Vox started with alarm, then spun round angrily, sure that the impudent youth had thrown something at him. But he was wrong. He stared down shakily at the huge chunk of shattered masonry which had been dislodged by the treacherous winds high above his head. It had missed him by a hair's breadth.

'The whole place is falling to bits,' he muttered bitterly. 'Time was when an apprenticeship in Sanctaphrax meant a secure future.' Several more pieces of rock and mortar peppered

down onto the walkway, sending Vox scuttling away.

These days, nothing was secure in Sanctaphrax; the ferocity of the weather saw to that. Storm after storm had been blowing in from beyond the Edge of late, each one worse than the one before – thunderstorms, wind-storms, fire and ice-storms; great storms and mind storms. No-one had ever known anything like it. Repairs to the damaged buildings couldn't be made quickly enough, while all academic studies had ground to a halt. Something was brewing out there in open sky, that much was clear – yet there wasn't a single academic, not even the Most High Academe himself, who knew what.

'And how can an ambitious young apprentice know who to make alliances with when the conditions are so unpredictable?' Vox asked himself. Was the Professor of Psycho-Climatic Studies likely to prove any more influential than the Professor of Cloud in the end?

He paused on a bridge and, gripping the balustrade, looked at the clouds tumbling in from beyond the Edge.

'That little runt, Cowlquape, had the right idea, disappearing from Sanctaphrax when he did,' he muttered. Refectory gossip had it that the youth had set off with Twig, the wild-eyed madman that the Professor of Darkness had taken under his wing. Even stranger, the professor now had three more peculiar guests . . . Vox gritted his teeth. Despite his words, he *had no intention of leaving Sanctaphrax.*

'Come what may, I shall turn the current situation to my advantage,' he murmured. He traced his fingers over the scar on his cheek left by the bowl of steaming tilder stew. 'And woe betide Cowlquape if our paths should ever cross again.'

*

A soft drizzle fell in the Deepwoods as the four travellers packed up the following morning. It dampened everybody's mood. Twig, Cowlquape and Spooler mounted their prowlgrins and set off. Goom, to save the strength of his prowlgrin, alternately rode or loped after them, the tether of the fourth prowlgrin wrapped round one massive fore-paw.

They continued through the dense, green forest in silence. It was no coincidence that, as clouds overhead grew darker and the rain fell heavier, niggling doubts began to gnaw at each and every one of them. They'd been lucky so far – very lucky – but now their luck had run out. They all knew that finding any further crew-members in the vast Deepwoods was an impossible task. The best they could hope for now was to find a village settlement, somewhere leaguesmen or sky pirates might visit to trade – then buy their passage back to Undertown. But out here in the perilous forest, even that was a formidable task.

Yet when the sky brightened and the warm sun burst through the canopy, their moods improved. Cowlquape breathed in the rich smells of the surrounding woodland: the dark, loamy soil, the juicy foliage, the fragrant fruit. It was all so different to the stale, smoky odour which tainted everything in Undertown.

'How's it going?' Twig asked him.

'It's all so beautiful,' Cowlquape said, with a sweep of his arm. 'Especially now the sun's shining.'

'Beautiful but deadly,' said Twig in a low voice.

They travelled far that first day, eating the fruit and

berries that Goom sniffed out as edible as they went. (The prowlgrins would have to wait until they put up for the night before their meal.) And as they rode further, Twig pointed out some of the more exotic Deepwoods creatures that he recognized.

To Cowlquape, each one sounded grimmer than the last and the hairs at the back of his neck were soon tingling uncomfortably. There were halitoads, with their foul, choking breath; feline mewmels, with spiky tails and poisonous spit; mannilids – sticky, brain-shaped creatures which hung disguised in bulbul trees and lived off the oakhens who came in search of bulbul berries. A rotsucker flapped slowly across the sky far above their heads, while a skullpelt – with its yellow claws and hooked teeth – dined on a quarm it had charmed from the trees.

Despite everything they encountered, however, by the time evening came around again, they had not seen a single trog or troll or goblin – no-one who might be able

to help them. Twig seemed increasingly worried.

'I know the Deepwoods,' he said. 'I was brought up amongst woodtrolls. They taught me never to trust the forest, always to be on the alert for danger.'

Cowlquape looked up from the oak-mallows he was toasting in the dancing flames of their fire. His mug of tea stood on the ground beside him. 'We are going to be all right, Twig,' he said nervously, 'aren't we?'

'Sky willing, Cowlquape,' Twig replied softly. He turned to the youth and smiled. 'Course we are,' he said reassuringly. 'Now drink your tea.'

On their tenth morning in the Deepwoods though, having still not met any creature who could help, no amount of the hairy charlock and oak-apple tea was enough to raise Cowlquape's spirits. The prowlgrins had gone.

'I just can't believe it,' he groaned. 'I'm sure I checked them before I went to bed. They did seem jumpy – but I thought they'd be all right.'

Twig was alarmed. 'Something must have scared them in the night and they pulled free of their tethers.' He looked at Cowlquape. 'Didn't I tell you to double-knot the tether-ropes?'

Cowlquape stared at the ground. 'Sorry,' he said, in a whisper. He looked up sheepishly. 'So – what do we do now, without the prowlgrins?'

'We go on,' said Twig angrily. 'On foot.' With a sinking feeling in the pit of his stomach, Cowlquape saw fear in his eyes.

Twig set off at a furious pace and Cowlquape was soon puffing and panting.

'Why can't we rest?' he wheezed. 'Or at least slow down a bit?'

Twig laid his hand on the young apprentice's shoulder. 'You've still got a lot to learn about the Deepwoods, Cowlquape,' he said. The fear remained in his eyes. 'They might look peaceful and idyllic, but behind every tree there lurks danger – and we still don't know what may have upset the prowlgrins. We must find a settlement as soon as we can, or we will surely perish.'

'But Twig, a few minutes' rest can't hurt, can it?' pleaded Cowlquape.

All at once, a series of piercing screams cut through the air. 'Aaargh! *Aaaargh!* AAAAARGH!'

Up ahead, the banderbear was leaping about in the middle of a glade of long swaying grass, like a creature possessed. The oakelf was nowhere to be seen.

'Wuh!' Goom bellowed, as he scythed furiously at the waving green fronds.

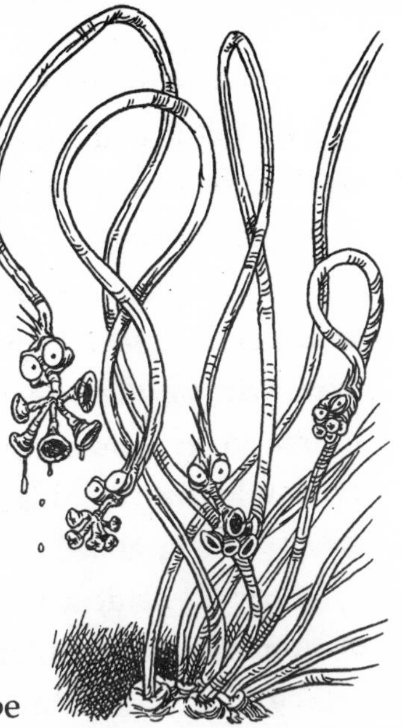

'What's the matter with him?' Cowlquape gasped. 'And where's Spooler?'

'This is the Deepwoods, Cowlquape!' said Twig. He drew his sword and raced towards the banderbear. 'I told you – there is danger everywhere!'

Dagger in hand, Cowlquape followed close behind as they entered the dappled glade. All round them, greatgrass grew thick and long. Goom, up ahead, waved his arms and shouted at them. Even to Cowlquape – who couldn't understand a single word the creature said – the meaning was clear. They should go back. The banderbear was telling them to escape while they still had the chance.

Suddenly Twig began slashing all around him. 'I should have guessed!' he shouted back. 'We're in a bed of reed-eels, Cowlquape. They must nest all round here. No wonder the prowlgrins fled. Protect yourself . . .'

For a moment, Cowlquape couldn't move. Where the tall grass ought to have been, there was instead a great mass of green worm-like creatures protruding straight up from holes in the ground. They had small deep-set orange eyes and, for a mouth, petal-shaped suckers which swayed towards him as he passed by, trying to attach themselves to his skin.

'Get off!' he screamed as, twisting and turning, he stabbed all round with the dagger.

As the blade came close, the lithe reed-eels retracted, sliding from view down inside their holes – only to pop up a moment later. Cowlquape swung his knife backwards and forwards. He couldn't afford to let up for an instant. When he caught up with the others, Goom had the oakelf over his shoulders and was beating a hasty retreat. Twig grabbed Cowlquape by the arm.

'Hurry,' he said, sweeping his sword round in a long low arc. 'We must get out of here. The reed-eels are in a feeding frenzy.'

Cowlquape didn't wait to be told a second time. With his dagger slicing wildly at anything that moved, he dashed ahead. The reed-eels were cunning. They plaited themselves together to bar his way. They slithered across the ground at his ankles.

'Cowlquape, be careful!' Twig shouted, and slashed at a loop of twisted eels.

'Deepwoods,' Cowlquape muttered. 'Danger . . .' He stumbled on. Beneath his feet, there was greatgrass once again. He double over and gasped for breath. 'That . . . was . . . close,' he panted. 'I . . .'

'*Too* close,' he heard Twig saying. He looked up. Twig was kneeling next to Spooler's body, Goom by his side.

'Is he . . .?' Cowlquape said.

Twig nodded. 'Dead,' he said. 'The fangs of the reed-eels have spread their venom through him.'

Cowlquape stared down in horror at the petal-shaped

marks all over the oakelf's exposed skin; at his discoloured face, his swollen body. 'Blast you!' he howled, and threw back his head. 'Blast you, Deepwoods!'

Twig pulled his young apprentice to his feet. He spoke softly and urgently. 'Take care, Cowlquape. The Deepwoods have ears. Believe me, I know.'

Cowlquape looked into Twig's eyes and fell silent. He had, indeed, so much to learn about the Deepwoods.

Having buried Spooler deep within the roots of a lullabee tree as oakelf tradition demanded, Twig, Cowlquape and Goom set off once again. Their spirits were lower than ever. Twig cursed himself for not insisting that the oakelf return with the *Skyraider*. All round them, the forest seemed deeper and darker than before.

On and on they tramped. Up steep, grassy banks, through marshy flats, over hillocks and hummocks and rocky outcrops. Cowlquape was overwhelmed with an aching tiredness that made every step an effort. Brambles scratched his legs, branches slapped his face. His legs ached. His stomach churned.

Overhead, the sun set on yet another day. The sky darkened and the moon rose. Suddenly Twig stopped. He stood stock-still, a look of wonder on his face.

'Shall I get some firewood?' said Cowlquape.

Twig shook his head. 'I don't believe it,' he murmured.

'Wh . . . what?' said Cowlquape, his eyes darting round nervously.

Twig pointed to the ground at their feet. 'Look! There!' he said.

'I can't see anything,' said Cowlquape. 'Twig, are you all right?'

'It's a path, Cowlquape,' said Twig. 'A *woodtroll* path.'

Cowlquape frowned. 'A woodtroll path?'

'Yes,' said Twig. 'I'd know it anywhere. The path has been flattened by generations of passing woodtrolls. See there, baked into the mud: it's a footprint. Look at the broad heel, the low arch, the stubby toes. Unmistakable. This is definitely a woodtroll path!' He looked up at Cowlquape, tears in his eyes. 'Once, long ago, I strayed from a path just like this. It was a mistake yet, as I came to learn, my destiny lay beyond the Deepwoods.' He sighed. 'Now I seem to have come full circle.'

'You think *this* is the path you strayed from?' said Cowlquape incredulously.

'All woodtroll paths join up,' said Twig. 'They form a network through the Deepwoods – to the lufwood groves, to the market clearings. They connect village to woodtroll village. If we stick to this path – *the* path – we will come to a woodtroll settlement. And woodtrolls trade with sky pirates! We're saved, Cowlquape! We're saved!'

'Well, what are we waiting for?' said Cowlquape, turning away. 'Let's follow the path!'

'I just can't believe it,' Twig whispered. 'After so many years, I've found the path again!' He looked up. 'Hey, wait for me, you two!' He stepped onto the path and hurried after Cowlquape and Goom.

The path wound and twisted, but never disappeared. With the moon shining down, it glistened brightly like the slimy trail of a barkslug. Often they came to forks in the path, sometimes to junctions where several paths met. At each one, Twig always chose which way to go without the least hesitation.

'All paths lead to other paths that lead to woodtroll villages,' he assured them. 'We can't go wrong.'

Cowlquape nodded. Yet the further they went, the more it seemed to him that the young captain was taking them in a specific direction.

Suddenly Twig stopped. 'Smell the air,' he said. 'That aromatic smoke is from scentwood. It's what woodtrolls burn in their stoves when they want to dream, and when . . .' He paused and cocked his head to one side. 'And can you hear that?' he whispered.

Cowlquape listened, and yes – there, behind the sounds of the night-creatures, was something else. 'Music,' he said, surprised.

'We must be very near a village,' said Twig.

They walked on a little further. The sound of sad singing voices filtered through the trees. Then the wind changed, and the lament faded away – only to return, louder than ever, a moment later. Deep voices, high voices, singing their own tunes yet all bound together by the sad underlying melody.

'Wuh-wuh!' said Goom.

'I know this music,' said Twig, a strange, haunted look on his face. 'Someone has died.' He turned to Cowlquape. 'They are performing their Ceremony for the Dead.'

Drawn on by the mournful song, the three of them continued along the path. Left, they went. Then left again. Then right. Abruptly, through the dense undergrowth, the flickering yellow of torchlight appeared. Twig stopped in his tracks and trembled.

Cowlquape had never seen him like this before. Young. Uncertain. The years seemed to have fallen away, leaving the inexperienced woodtroll-lad within, exposed. His eyes glistened with tears and there was a sad smile on his face.

'Twig,' said Cowlquape, concerned. 'Is there something the matter? Do you want to turn back?'

Twig shook his head. 'No,' he said. 'I'll be all right. It's just that I'd forgotten so much. I grew up in a village like this one, Cowlquape.' He peered ahead at the familiar woodtroll cabins secured high up in the trees. 'I lived in a lufwood cabin just like those . . . Still, enough!' Twig seemed to pull himself together. 'Keep close to me. And if anyone stops us, I'll do the talking. Woodtrolls can be very suspicious about uninvited arrivals – especially on so solemn an occasion.'

They were on the edge of a clearing dominated by a huge lullabee tree from which hung a caterbird cocoon. It was in such cocoons, hatching places of the great caterbirds, that the wise ones of the village – oakelves normally – took up residence. Sleeping in the warm, aromatic cocoons enabled them to share the dreams of the widely-travelled birds.

It seemed as if every single woodtroll villager was out there in the clearing, flaming torch in hand, as they gathered round the tree. The music was coming from the midst of the crowd directly beneath the cocoon.

As Twig and the others stepped forwards, the ceremonial song reached its climax – a discordant howl of grief that rose higher and higher. Twig hesitated. Row after row of woodtrolls stood before him, their backs turned, their heads bowed. The song came to an abrupt end. The silence which followed was broken by a voice. It came from the caterbird cocoon.

Twig gasped. He'd know that rich, cracked voice anywhere. 'No,' he murmured. 'No, it can't be.' He strained to get a better look over the bowed heads in front. An ancient oakelf was sitting in the suspended caterbird cocoon, high up in the great, spreading lullabee tree.

'Taghair!' he breathed.

'You know him?' Cowlquape said.

'I . . . I can hardly believe it,' said Twig. 'It's like a

dream, Cowlquape. I have indeed come full circle. This isn't any old woodtroll village. This . . .' He swallowed away the painful lump in his throat. 'This is *my* village, Cowlquape. I've come home.'

'From the sky we come and to the sky we go,' the oakelf was reciting. *'Descending and ascending. This night we are here to commend to open sky, that his unencumbered spirit might once again fly free, the body of our beloved Tuntum, husband, father, friend . . .'*

'Tuntum? Did he say, Tuntum? No, it can't be true!' Twig wailed.

The woodtrolls spun round to see a tall, gangly individual with matted hair and a furry waistcoat hurtling

towards them. Outraged by the intrusion, yet too timid to confront the wild-eyed stranger in their midst, the crowd parted to let him pass.

Twig stopped in front of the lullabee tree, beneath the cocoon. Before him stood the bereaved family. Huddled together in their grief, they turned angrily as one to face the unwanted intruder. Twig hardly dared believe it but, yes, he knew them all – Snodpill, Henchweed, Poohsniff – the half-brothers and sisters he never imagined he would ever meet again. And there, looking smaller than he remembered, was Spelda, the kindly woodtroll who had taken him as a foundling-infant into her home and raised him as her own.

'Mother-Mine!' he sobbed and ran towards her, arms open wide.

Spelda's jaw dropped. Her eyes grew wide. 'Twig?' she said. She gaped at his longcoat and parawings, the accoutrements of a sky pirate. 'Can it truly be you?'

Twig nodded, tearfully, bending to clasp her hands between his own.

'You came back,' Spelda whispered.

They stayed silent for a long time: the tall, young sky pirate and the little old woodtroll. At last Spelda drew back.

'I know you and he didn't always see eye to eye,' she said, 'but he never stopped loving you, Twig.' She sniffed and wiped her rubbery button-nose. 'Right to the very end.'

Twig looked down at the platform of bound scent-wood logs by his feet; the sky raft of buoyant lufwood which, when lit, would rise up into the sky. He looked at the shrouded bundle which was tethered to it.

'Can I see him?' he asked.

Spelda nodded. Twig stepped forwards and pulled aside the shroud of woodspider silk at Tuntum's head.

'He looks so peaceful,' said Twig quietly. 'How did he die?'

'In his sleep,' said Spelda. 'He'd been ill for several moons.' She smiled bravely. 'He was a good husband, and father . . .'

'The time is upon us,' came the oakelf's voice from above them.

Twig bent over and kissed Tuntum's forehead lightly, then fastened the shroud.

'Who will touch the pyre with the celestial flame?' asked the oakelf.

Snodpill stepped forwards and handed a burning torch to Spelda. She looked at it for a moment then, with a soft sigh turned to Twig. 'Can you still remember the words?' she said.

Twig nodded. He took the torch from Spelda's hand and raised it to the sky. Behind him the woodtrolls pressed their hands together in prayer.

'From the first lightning bolt you came, O, Sky flame!' Twig said.

'O, Sky flame!' the others murmured.

'Sky fire, light the pyre, return to open sky again, O, Sky flame!'

'O, Sky flame!'

Twig stooped and touched the burning torch to the base of the sky raft. There was a crackle and hiss; the next instant the entire construction was engulfed in sheets of purple flame.

'Return to open sky,' he murmured, as the blazing platform rose and hovered in front of them. The flames blazed all the more fiercely and the buoyant sky-raft with its precious cargo soared up towards the forest canopy and away into the endlessness of open sky. Twig watched it become a ball, a dot, a speck, unable to tear his eyes away as it flew – like a shooting star – across the sky and away.

'Twig, lad,' came a voice. 'Come over here. And close your mouth if you don't wish to swallow a woodmidge.'

Twig looked up. The ancient oakelf's wise and kindly face was smiling down at him. He turned to Spelda, who nodded. 'Go to him, Twig,' she whispered.

'Greetings to you, Taghair,' Twig called back, and bowed low.

'Oh, such polite phrases and pretty graces,' Taghair replied. 'Let me get a closer look at you, lad.'

Twig stepped forwards.

'Come, we must talk,' he said, and nodded towards the suspended sling-chair. 'I take it you still remember how to use it.'

'Of course,' said Twig. He'd done it a hundred times or more as a youngster. He fastened himself into the hanging seat, pulled the rope and raised himself up into the air until he was high above the ground and face to face with the ancient oakelf himself, peering out of his caterbird cocoon.

'So,' said Taghair, slowly. 'You have come a long way, Twig. I've been expecting you.'

Twig's eyes lit up. 'You dream caterbird dreams, don't you?' he said. 'Was it the caterbird who told you to expect me?'

'No, Twig,' said Taghair. 'It was not your caterbird who informed me that you were on your way.' He leant down and touched Twig's glowing hand. His eyes twinkled. 'It was another who has been calling you – ever since his return from open sky.'

Taghair shifted across to one side of the opening. As he did so, an eerie luminous light streamed out from the depths of the cocoon.

'Captain Twig,' said a voice.

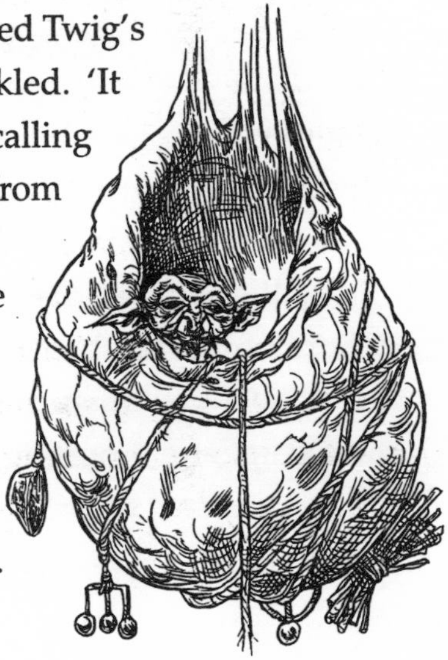

Twig peered in. His jaw dropped. 'Woodfish!' he cried out. 'It's you! But how . . . ? When . . . ? Where . . . ?'

Taghair chuckled. 'Always were a one for questions, weren't you?' he said.

Woodfish the waterwaif leant forwards. His fan-like ears fluttered. 'At your service, captain,' he said. 'I knew you'd make it!'

'B . . . b . . . but how is this possible?' Twig spluttered. He looked from one to the other.

Taghair breathed in noisily. 'I believe it was no accident that Woodfish's *shooting star* fell so close to the woodtroll village where his beloved captain grew up. He was drawn to it, you might say,' he explained. 'The woodtrolls found him and brought him to me. He has been here ever since. Waiting.'

'Waiting?' said Twig.

'Waiting for you,' said Taghair.

'I can read thoughts, as you know,' Woodfish broke in. 'All waifs can. But Taghair, here, taught me how to dream.'

'And he proved an excellent pupil,' said Taghair solemnly. 'He dreamt of you lying, broken, in the Stone Gardens below faraway Sanctaphrax.'

'You did?' said Twig.

Woodfish smiled. 'Yes, Captain Twig,' he said. 'And I dreamt of the others, too: Tarp in the taverns, Wingnut Sleet and Bogwitt in the sewers, poor Spooler on the slave ship, and Goom in the hands of the shrykes. My dreams touched all of them.'

'He guided you to them, Twig,' said Taghair. 'With a

whisper here and a word there, he told you which way to go. And then he guided you here.'

Twig's jaw dropped. 'You!' he said to Woodfish. He remembered the little sibilant whisper he'd heard so many times – urging him into the Lullabee Inn, drawing him away from the cloddertrogs, helping him to select the *Skyraider* from the numerous sky ships on offer at the posting-pole, guiding him along the woodtroll path. 'It was *you* all the time!'

Woodfish nodded. 'Every step of the way, captain,' he said. 'Though I couldn't have done it by dreaming alone. I needed your courage, your stubbornness and most of all, your loyalty. We *all* needed that.' His rubbery mouth broke into a smile. 'And we still do.'

Twig stared back. 'You discovered *all* the crew?'

'I did,' Woodfish confirmed.

'So the last crew-member,' said Twig excitedly. 'The Stone Pilot. Is the Stone Pilot alive?'

'Yes,' Woodfish said simply.

'Where?' said Twig. 'Tell me where, Woodfish. We must set forth at once.' His head was in a spin. 'And do you remember what happened out there in open sky?' he pressed. 'What happened to the *Edgedancer*? And my father – Woodfish, did we find my father?'

'I don't know,' said Woodfish, the barbels at the corners of his mouth quivering as he shook his head. 'I remember nothing of what happened after we entered the weather vortex. But I know what lies ahead.'

'What does lie ahead, Woodfish? Tell me,' said Twig urgently.

'When I dream of it,' said Woodfish, 'my dreams go dark. We must go into the darkness, Captain, and beyond that. At the very edge of my dreams, the Stone Pilot is waiting.'

'But where, Woodfish? Where?' Twig was almost shouting now.

Woodfish looked at Taghair, then back at Twig. 'On the other side of the deepest, blackest part of the Deepwoods,' he said, 'where all creation began . . . *Riverrise*!'

·CHAPTER SEVENTEEN·

THE DEEPWOODS' DARK HEART

Despite Spelda's best endeavours, Twig could not be persuaded to stay in the woodtroll village a moment longer than necessary. He was packed up and ready to leave long before sunrise.

'I shall come back, Mother-Mine,' he said. 'Now that I've found you, I won't lose you again.'

'You promise?' said Spelda.

'I promise,' said Twig.

Spelda nodded sadly, and wiped away a tear. 'Take these,' she said. 'Some extra provisions for your long journey. Food and drink. Warm cloaks.' She sniffed. 'Your father's axe.'

Twig held the familiar axe in his hands. 'Thank you,' he said.

Spelda smiled bravely. 'Tuntum always hoped that you might one day have it.' She rummaged in the pockets of her dress, and pulled out a talisman on a leather thong. 'And this is from me,' she said tearfully. 'A charm.' She reached up and tied it around his neck. 'It will protect you in those dark places you must go . . .' She shivered. 'And guide you safely back to me.'

'Begging your pardon, captain, but we must go,' said Woodfish. 'We have a long journey ahead.'

Twig bent down and kissed Spelda on her forehead. 'Bid farewell to Taghair for me,' he said. 'And don't worry!'

Spelda nodded. 'And don't you go forgetting your promise,' she said. She wiped her tears away. 'Go now,' she said. 'And Sky protect you.'

Twig turned away. The others were already heading out of the village back towards the path. He walked steadily after them. He didn't look back.

'She loves you very much,' said Cowlquape, when he caught up. The glow from the village lanterns and the babble of woodtroll voices faded away behind them.

'Spelda?' said Twig. 'She was the finest mother anyone could hope for. And, looking back, Tuntum loved me also – he just found it harder to show it.'

Cowlquape smiled weakly. He thought of his own bully of a father, Ulbus Pentephraxis, who would beat him as soon as look at him. Yet here was Twig, with *two* fathers – Tuntum and Cloud Wolf – and he was about to tell Twig how much he envied him his memories when Woodfish came to an abrupt halt. They were standing in front of a gnarled tree, festooned with hooks and rings.

'The Anchor Tree,' said Twig. 'This marks the

woodtroll village boundary.'

'Woodfish nodded. 'We must strike out on our own from here.'

A single bolt of lightning darted across the sky, followed by an ominous rumble of thunder. Rain – heavy and warm – began to fall. Twig fingered the amulet Spelda had just given him.

'Time for me to stray from the path once again,' he said softly.

The forest grew denser as they went further from the woodtroll path into the Deepwoods. The rain eased off and high up above their heads the sun rose on another day. And another. And another – until they seemed to have been walking for ever. Beneath the forest canopy, it remained dark and gloomy. Cowlquape hated it. The air was close, windless, and he was continually panting to keep up with Twig and the others.

The Deepwoods were as menacing as ever. Flesh-eating pods snapped at him greedily as he scurried past. Scaly tree-creatures bared their teeth at him from the branches overhead, the spikes down their back quivering menacingly. A bulging, yellow wood-python – basking in a shaft of sunlight after a recent meal – slithered into the undergrowth as he stumbled close. And all the time, the forest itself grew more and more impenetrable as the days passed. Cowlquape gritted his teeth and struggled on, deeper and deeper.

Now, up ahead, Goom began having problems

hacking through the undergrowth. The thorny brambles which had been dogging their way for an hour or more were becoming thicker, more tangled; their barbs, the size of daggers. One of the banderbear's shoulders was already matted with blood.

'Ease off, old friend,' said Twig. 'Those thorns are sharp.' He pulled Tuntum's axe from his belt. 'Let Woodfish and me go first.'

Woodfish drew his cutlass. 'And keep your wits about you,' he warned. 'Even this inhospitable forest of thorns is home to dangerous predators.'

Cowlquape shivered, and glanced round nervously. He followed Twig and Woodfish into the tunnel they were hacking out. His senses were on fire – ears listening for any suspicious sound, nose twitching, eyes peeled. Progress was painfully slow. Every step they advanced was a struggle. They rested up increasingly often, and for longer periods of time.

'This is hopeless,' Cowlquape complained as, for the third time in as many minutes, Twig let his axe fall limp at his side. 'We're lost in this terrible thorny place. We'll never find our way out.'

Twig turned to him, his face shiny with sweat.

'Woodfish is our guide, Cowlquape, and we must trust him. We are in his world now.'

The waterwaif shook his head. 'This is merely the beginning of the Nightwoods,' he said. 'True waif country lies beyond the great thorn forests.' He sighed. 'I thought I'd escaped it for good. It is an evil place.'

Cowlquape frowned. 'You speak harshly of the place you were born and raised,' he said.

Woodfish returned his puzzled gaze. 'Life in waif country is a short and brutal affair,' he explained. 'A hand-to-mouth existence with none of the things you take for granted, Cowlquape. Hot meals, comfortable beds . . .' He smiled. 'Ancient barkscrolls. Besides,' he went on, 'I daresay I am not the only one to take little pride in his origins.'

Cowlquape nodded sadly. 'And beyond the waif country?' he said.

'The Dark Heart of the Deepwoods,' said Woodfish. 'And perhaps Riverrise.'

'*Perhaps* Riverrise?' said Cowlquape. 'You mean you don't know.'

'I have never been to Riverrise,' said Woodfish. 'Nor has any soul I've ever heard of. But you know that, Cowlquape. It is written in those barkscrolls you treasure. Riverrise has been lost, forgotten since the passing of Kobold the Wise. Yet it is said that it lies at the very heart of the Deepwoods.'

'But you can't know that for sure, for all your dreaming and waif ways,' wailed Cowlquape.

Twig smiled and lifted his axe over his head. 'Don't let

your courage fail you now, Cowlquape,' he said. The axe came crashing down, slicing through half a dozen of the thick woody brambles. 'After all, we can't abandon our search here. Woodfish did dream that the final member of the crew is at Riverrise waiting for us. It must exist – and now we must find it.' The axe crashed down again. 'And wouldn't you love to actually see Riverrise – to walk where Kobold the Wise once walked?'

'Yes,' said Cowlquape meekly. 'Yes, I would.'

They went on. The sun passed unseen across the sky and set. Later, the moon rose. It was only when the splinters of moonlight pierced through the thorn-bushes that Twig realized how much time had passed. He laid his axe aside, heavy with fatigue, dripping with sweat.

'We'll rest up here,' he panted.

Cowlquape looked round. With the thorn-bush surrounding them and the uneven boulders beneath their feet, it didn't look too promising. But once Twig and Goom had hacked out a larger clearing, and they'd all removed the rocks and laid out their cloaks on the sand below, it wasn't too bad. Of course, a hot, bright fire would have been nice, but with the bushes all round them so dry, they dared not light one. One spark and the whole lot was likely to go up. Thankfully, it was a warm enough night, and the glowing sky pirates themselves provided enough light to see by. Cowlquape wondered once again what it was that made Twig and his crew shine so brightly. Something *must* have happened to them all out there in open sky. But what?

Woodfish heard his thoughts. 'It is a question I have

air was brittle with eerie stillness. There was no bird-song. No creature-cry. Every time a twig was cracked by a passing boot, or a pebble kicked, the sound ricocheted from tree to tree, and off into the darkness.

Cowlquape stumbled blindly on. His sodden feet had blistered and swelled. His face and hands were criss-crossed with cuts from spiny creepers he never saw until it was too late. Reduced to eating the bark and fungus that Goom selected as edible, Cowlquape's stomach cried out for food; proper food – yet he did not complain.

By night, they slept in makeshift hammocks fashioned from their cloaks and ropes, strung out between the branches of the trees. By day they walked. And walked and walked. It was on the seventh day that Woodfish discovered running water.

'Look at it,' he said, staring down at the tiny stream trickling through the centre of a broad river basin. 'This used to be a raging torrent. No wonder we've seen no sign of life for so long.'

Cowlquape crouched down at the sandy edge. 'So long as it quenches my thirst, I don't mind how little there is.' He cupped his hands and slurped at the clear water.

Woodfish turned to Twig. 'The running water marks the beginning of true waif territory.' His fan-like ears trembled. 'They are all around us. I can *hear* them.'

'I can't hear anything,' said Cowlquape, looking up.

'Yet, they are there,' said Woodfish nervily. 'Waterwaifs. Flitterwaifs. Barkwaifs. Nightwaifs . . . Put your cloaks on, all of you. Raise the hoods over your

asked myself a thousand times,' he said. 'Perhaps it is to remind us of something important that happened.' He shrugged. 'Sadly, as I told the captain, I have no memory of what took place after we entered the weather vortex.' He nodded at Goom and Twig. 'And unfortunately, neither have they.'

'We can worry about the past later,' said Twig. 'For now, we must get some sleep.' He laid himself down on the soft sand and wrapped about him the thick cloak, which abruptly extinguished the glow from his body.

Cowlquape turned to Woodfish. 'When will we get to waif country?'

'Sleep, Cowlquape!' said Twig, without looking up. 'The more tired you are, the longer it'll take.'

All round them the thorns clicked as a chilly breeze blew through the surrounding bushes. Cowlquape lay down between Twig and Goom, and pulled his cloak up around his shoulders. Woodfish settled himself last. Awake or asleep, the waterwaif would hear any intruders. As he wrapped his cloak around him, the whole clearing was plunged into darkness.

Refreshed and rested, the four travellers were up early the following morning, and taking it in turns to hack at the wall of thorns once more – first Twig and Woodfish, then Cowlquape and Goom. They made good headway and at midday, Woodfish announced that their ordeal was almost over.

'Let me take over,' said Twig, seizing his axe off Cowlquape. And he began chopping at the thick brambles like a creature possessed. 'Yes!' he called back a moment later. 'I can see it. I can see the end of the thorn-bushes.'

Half a dozen well-positioned swings of the axe later, and Twig was through.

'So far, so good,' he panted.

The others crawled through the narrow gap and straightened up. Cowlquape looked around and trembled with horror. The relief he'd felt at escaping the clutches of the thorn-bushes instantly melted away. Before them lay waif country.

It was a dreary place, marshy underfoot, foul-smelling, and so dark that Cowlquape would have been blind had it not been for his three glowing companions. As he stared about him at the gnarled trees, encruste with dripping moss and oozing fungus, which loome from the shadows like fearsome monsters, he almo wished he were.

'Where now, Woodfish?' he heard Twig asking.

The waterwaif was crouching down with his lar fluttering ears close to the ground. He looked up a pointed into the darkness of the dismal forest ahe 'The heart of the Deepwoods lies in that direction,' said.

It was a hard slog through the cold, dank forest. T

heads to dim your glow. We must not draw attention to ourselves.'

'It's so dark,' said Cowlquape nervously. 'How will we find our way?'

'We follow the stream,' said Woodfish. 'She will lead us to the heart.'

'But what if we lose one another?' Cowlquape whimpered.

'We'll rope ourselves together,' said Twig. 'Don't panic, Cowlquape.'

'No, don't panic, whatever you do,' said Woodfish. 'Waifs will be attracted by fearful thoughts.'

Cowlquape groaned. Now, on top of everything else, he had to pretend not to be scared.

'Follow me,' Woodfish told them. 'Stay close. And whatever voices you may hear, ignore them as best you can.'

Gripping the rope that was strung between them, the four of them stumbled on through the darkness, following the water upstream. Cowlquape fixed his thoughts on the stories he'd read in the barkscrolls and imagined what Riverrise might be like.

'This way,' whispered a voice. *'It's over here.'*

Cowlquape hesitated. He looked about. Two round eyes glowed in mid-air some way to his left, staring, unblinking. Woodfish tugged his cloak sharply.

'Keep going,' he warned. 'Don't let them into your thoughts.'

But the voices continued. Sometimes tempting, sometimes pleading; always soft and seductive.

'Come this way,' they crooned. *'You'll be all right. Trust*

us – please trust us. If you're not too timid. If you're not too scared.'

'Ignore them,' Woodfish's voice broke into their minds, calm and reassuring. 'We must keep going.'

The eyes glinting in the invisible branches increased in number. Twenty. Fifty. A hundred pairs stared down at them as they stumbled on through the dark forest.

'Follow us; follow,' the voices sighed, and in their soft invitation, Cowlquape heard the promise of something he couldn't ignore. *'Kobold the Wise came this way. Let us show you, Cowlquape.'*

He let go of the rope.

'Twig, Riverrise is so close. So close, Twig,' whispered the voices. Twig hesitated.

'Captain Twig!' Woodfish's voice in his ear was urgent. 'Do not listen to them, Cowlquape . . .'

'But they're waifs, Woodfish,' said Twig. 'Like your good self. Like Forficule, a nightwaif I once knew in Undertown . . .'

'We are not in Undertown now. These are *wild* waifs,

and they are hunting us. They're *hungry*, captain,' said Woodfish sharply. 'They're . . .' He peered back along the line and grimaced. 'Sky above! Where *is* Cowlquape?'

Twig looked about him, unable to see anything at all, apart from the gleaming eyes. 'Has he gone?' he said.

'He has,' said Woodfish, scanning the darkness. He crouched down, ears twitching. 'Wait, I think I hear him. I . . . Oh, no!'

'This way, Cowlquape, that's right,' chorused the unseen voices.

'Quick!' said Woodfish. 'He's still close by. You stick with me, Captain Twig,' he said as he seized him by the arm and dragged him away from the river-bed and off into the darkness. 'Stay close, Goom,' he called back.

They stumbled and groped their way through the dark forest.

'Calm your thoughts,' urged the waterwaif. 'I must listen.'

'Kobold the Wise once trod this ground, Cowlquape,' murmured the voices.

'Yes, there he is!' said Woodfish. 'This way!'

The terrain grew wilder, more treacherous. Black logs littered the forest floor, impeding their progress. Bindweeds and barbed knotweeds slowed them down still more.

'They're getting away with him,' Twig gasped as the light grew dim far in front of them. 'Oh, Cowlquape,' he whispered. 'Cowlquape.'

'Wuh-wuh!' grunted Goom.

'Quiet!' said Woodfish. He stopped to crouch low to the ground again.

'Just a little further, Cowlquape. That's right.'

Woodfish shuddered. 'We haven't much time!' he said.

They bounded on into the darkness, Woodfish now on Goom's shoulders in front, crashing through the undergrowth, carving out a path for Twig to follow. Ahead they could see countless pairs of eyes, dropping down from the trees onto the forest floor and gathering in a circle.

'Kneel down, Cowlquape. Rest your head. You're so tired, so very tired . . .'

'What's going on?' Twig panted.

'I told you,' Woodfish muttered. 'The waifs are hungry, and they're closing in for a kill.'

Goom burst onto the scene. The waifs darted back in alarm and flew into the surrounding trees, hissing and mewling. All, that is, apart from the ones already attached to Cowlquape's twisted body. Woodfish shuddered. 'Flitterwaifs,' he said. 'I might have known!'

Twig stared at the dark creatures. They had stubby legs, broad, membraned wings and flattened faces, with jagged fangs that jutted down at an angle from their top jaw. It was these fangs which were biting into Cowlquape's back, his leg, his neck . . .

'Get off him!' Twig roared. He drew his sword and dashed forwards. He plunged the blade through the flitterwaif on Cowlquape's back and, tossing it aside, slashed at the one on his leg. Spitting and snarling, the creature flapped its wings and flew up into the branches with the rest. The flitterwaif at Cowlquape's neck turned and fixed Twig with its blazing eyes. The jagged fangs glinted. Twig gripped the sword tightly. He would have to be careful not . . .

'. . . *to sever Cowlquape's neck,*' the flitterwaif completed for him. '*You wouldn't want to do that, captain,*' it said, and hissed malevolently.

Twig's eyes narrowed. Since the creature could read his thoughts he would have to act suddenly, to take it unawares . . . No! Don't think, don't think . . . just . . .

With a sudden *swoosh*, the great sword leapt forwards,

flew down through the air and sliced off the flitterwaif's head in one deadly movement. Twig breathed a sigh of relief and sank to his knees. He hadn't even scratched Cowlquape's throat – yet Cowlquape was in a bad way. He seemed to be unconscious.

'Help me move him,' Twig called to the others. 'Goom, can you carry him away from here?'

'Wuh,' the banderbear grunted, and picked Cowlquape up in his massive arms.

'You can't escape.' 'You'll never make it!' 'Leave the boy behind,' the flitterwaifs hissed furiously as they flapped around in the trees above them. They were ravenous. They smelt blood and sensed fear. Food so succulent was hard to find in the Nightwoods and they weren't about to surrender their prey without a fight. All at once, one of their number tilted its wings and dive-bombed. Others followed suit.

'Aaargh!' Woodfish screeched, as three sharp claws slashed at his face. He swung his cutlass. Twig gripped his father's great sword tightly. They took up positions on either side of Goom and staggered on blindly, stabbing and thrusting at the darkness – and as the flitterwaifs continued their frenzied bombardment, so the travellers' heads were filled with the shrill voices of their attackers.

'Give him up!' they screeched. *'Leave the boy. He's ours!'*

'What do we do, Woodfish?' said Twig nervously. 'We're never going to outrun them.'

Without saying a word, Woodfish crouched down and began heaping lumps of the claggy mud beneath his feet on top of one another. Then, reaching up to the youth in Goom's arms, he removed his cloak and wrapped it around the large shapeless form he'd constructed.

'Right, let's get out of here,' he whispered. 'And as we leave, I want you all to *think* about how sad it is that we have had to abandon Cowlquape to his fate.'

'Don't go. Not that way,' the flitterwaifs complained. *'Leave the boy, or you'll be sorry!'*

As Twig continued into the darkness he did as Woodfish had told him, concentrating on what an awful tragedy it was that his young friend had been left behind. Goom and Woodfish were doing the same. They hadn't gone more than a hundred strides when the flitterwaifs began to fall back.

'It's working,' came Woodfish's voice inside his head. 'Keep it up.'

I'm so sorry to leave you here, Twig thought. But we'll be back for you soon, Cowlquape. I give you my word!

Behind them now – and further behind with every step they took – the flitterwaifs were converging on the cloaked heap of mud. It sounded right. It smelled right. Yet the youth was not there. All at once, a far-off howl of rage echoed through the trees as the waifs realized that they had been tricked.

Woodfish turned and mopped his brow. 'We've lost them,' he said. The waterwaif knelt and listened again, ears close to the ground. 'I hear water. We're very close.'

'Close to what?' Twig asked.

Woodfish gestured ahead. 'The Deepwoods' black heart.'

*

At the top of the Loftus Tower in Sanctaphrax, the Professor of Darkness was close to despair. The barometer needle was rising and falling, seemingly at will. The tacheometer was broken, as were the dynamometer and anemometer, while the fragile woodmoth material of the sense-sifter was hanging in tatters. Every single one of his precious instruments was being battered to bits. And if he was unable to collect the relevant data, then what was he to tell the academics and apprentices who were relying on their Most High Academe to come up with a reason for the sudden change in the weather?

He crossed to the broken window and, shielding his eyes from the searing blast of air, looked down on his beloved floating city. There wasn't a single building which didn't bear the scars of the ravaging storms. Statues had been toppled. Towers had collapsed. Debris littered the ground. And there were gaping holes in every roof where slates had been torn away by powerful twisters which had swept in from open sky the previous night.

It was little wonder that there were whispers going round the dusty corridors about evacuating the floating city. To remain on the great floating rock, so exposed to the incoming storms, seemed more and more foolhardy by the day. Yet, for the Professor of Darkness, leaving Sanctaphrax was unthinkable. It was his sanctuary, his home – his life. And he had the three sky pirates to consider too. Tarp, the slaughterer, and Bogwitt, the goblin, were adamant that they were to stay until Twig returned – even if the weasely Wingnut Sleet did not seem so convinced . . .

'Oh, Sky preserve us,' he muttered unhappily to himself. 'Where is this all going to end?'

*

Drawn on by the sound of running water, Woodfish continued through the dark forest with the others following close behind. In Goom's arms, Cowlquape stirred.

'I'm sorry,' he moaned. 'I didn't mean to . . . They said Kobold the Wise . . . They said . . .'

'It's all right, Cowlquape,' said Twig. 'You're safe now. Do you think you can walk?'

'I think so,' said Cowlquape as Goom put him gently down. 'It's all my fault, Twig . . .'

'Quiet!' said Woodfish. His fan-like ears quivered. 'I sense great danger. We're not out of waif country yet.'

They edged forwards step by faltering step, each holding the shoulder of the one in front, with Woodfish leading the way. The forest was black and, with their hooded cloaks masking their luminous glow, the three sky pirates were invisible. Behind them followed Cowlquape, shivering with cold and weakened by the attack on him. Although he had no glow to mask, he missed the warmth of his abandoned outer cloak. A deep silence fell, as impenetrable as the darkness.

Then Twig saw them, just ahead – waif eyes glinting from the surrounding trees. He took a sharp intake of breath. How could they possibly survive another attack?

'This way!' cried Woodfish suddenly, his fan-like ears fluttering. 'Follow the sound of the water. And don't listen to the waifs!'

Stumbling wildly, the four travellers carried on through the lurching forest, the eyes dancing in the trees ever closer, and fearful whispers invading their thoughts again.

'You'll never escape! You'll never get away!'

'Stay! Stay here with us . . .'

'Twig!' Cowlquape moaned. 'I can't . . .'

'You must, Cowlquape!' Twig urged him breathlessly. 'Just a little further . . . I can hear the water now.'

'NO!' came an anguished cry, and the waterwaif disappeared from view.

'Woodfish!' Twig cried.

The next moment he and Cowlquape reached the edge of the dark, boggy ground. The land fell away abruptly before them, steep and strewn with boulders. And there was Woodfish, his faintly glowing figure tumbling down over the scree, far beneath them. Cowlquape groaned with dread.

Behind, the intensity of the whispers grew to a mounting crescendo. The air trembled with flapping wings.

'Wuh?' Goom grunted.

The bell-like sound of trickling water echoed up out of the gloomy abyss.

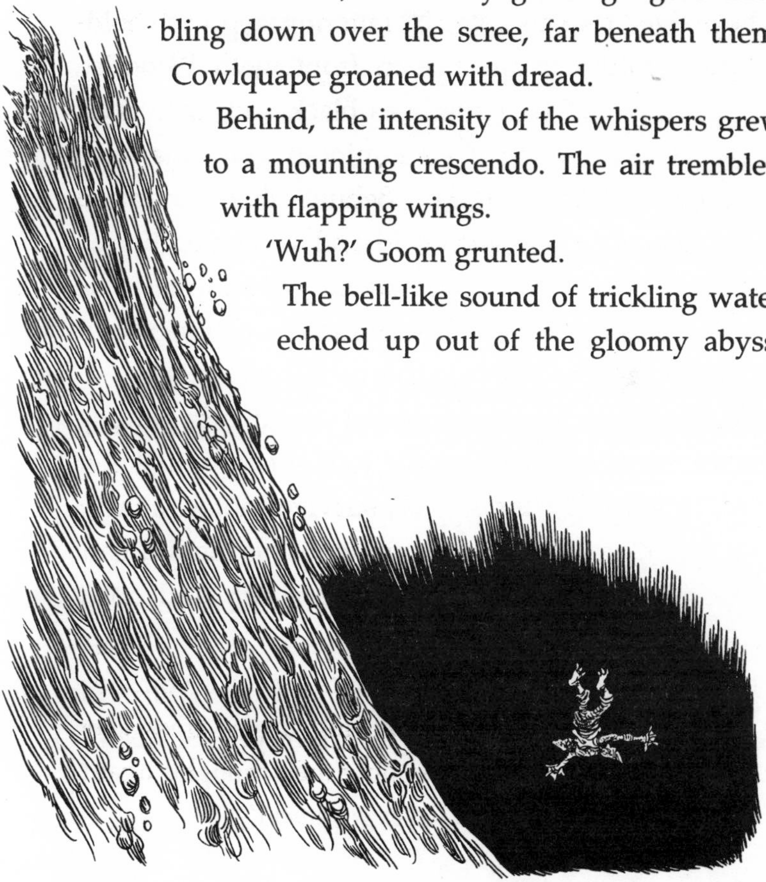

Cowlquape hesitated. 'This can't be right,' he shouted to Twig. 'This can't be Riverrise!'

'We must go on!' Twig cried. 'We must follow Woodfish!'

Before he knew what was happening, Cowlquape felt his arm being tugged, and he was pulled forwards onto the treacherous slope beside Twig. Down he hurtled, his feet slipping on the sliding gravel scree.

All round them, the desolate howl of the thwarted waifs echoed through the air. Even they would not venture down into the rocky abyss.

'Aaaaiii!' Cowlquape screamed with pain.

His ankle had gone over. He tumbled to the ground, but kept falling down the long, steep slope. Down, down, amid a tumbling mass of rock and stone. Bouncing. Crashing. His knee struck a boulder. His face and hands were cut. His head slammed down against the ground.

Then nothing . . .

'The water, Cowlquape,' came a voice. *'Go to the water, and drink.'*

Cowlquape looked up. There before him, standing next to a deep pool at the base of a mighty waterfall, was a tall, crowned figure with embroidered robes and a long plaited beard. His warm, sorrowful eyes seemed to stare right through into Cowlquape's spirit. Every inch of him ached; his head throbbed and a sharp pain stabbed up from his legs as he tried to move.

'You,' he murmured softly.

'Yes,' said Kobold the Wise. *'It is I, Cowlquape.'* He dipped his finger in the pool and wiped it along Cowlquape's lips. *'The water, Cowlquape,'* he said. *'You must drink the water. It will restore you. It is the water of Riverrise.'* He smiled. *'So much awaits you, Cowlquape,'* he said, as he turned and walked off behind the waterfall. *'But first, drink the water.'*

The dream ended. Cowlquape stirred. And back came the pain. Every bone in his body felt as if it had been snapped in two. His nails were ragged and torn. Blood, from deep gashes across his forehead, trickled down his face.

Then he heard water trickling, and opened his eyes. There *was* a pool there. It was smaller and darker than the one of his dreams, and the mighty waterfall no more than a trickle. *Drink the water*. The words of Kobold the Wise filled Cowlquape's head.

He looked round. The others lay near him. With a jolt, he saw that their motionless bodies were glowing no more.

Drink the water.

Wincing with agony, Cowlquape rolled onto his front. Slowly, painfully, he pulled himself along the ground with his one good arm, inch by terrible inch.

Drink the water.

At the edge of the pool at last, Cowlquape stared down at his battered reflection in the rippled water – the gash, the torn ear, the blood . . . He reached down and scooped at the water with his hand. It was cool and velvety. He brought it to his mouth, and sipped.

A shimmering warmth coursed through his veins in

an instant. He drank some more. The terrible racking pains vanished and the wounds stopped throbbing. When he'd drunk his fill, Cowlquape wiped away the blood and inspected his reflection a second time. There wasn't a scratch on him.

'The water of Riverrise,' he gasped.

Once, twice, three times, he cupped his hands in the pool and carried the cool, restoring water to his companions. He let it trickle down over their lips, into their mouths, and watched with unbounded joy as their eyes flickered and the soft familiar luminosity began to glow from their bodies once again.

Twig looked up, his eyes wild with fear. 'Cowlquape!' he gasped. 'Falling . . . falling . . .'

'Don't speak, Twig,' said Cowlquape, as he helped the young captain to his feet. 'Come with me to the pool, and drink.'

One by one, Twig, Woodfish and Goom slaked their thirst with the cool, life-giving waters. They drank away their injuries, their misgivings, their fears.

Twig looked up, and followed the thin trickle of water which threaded down the rock face from a jutting ledge far, far above their heads. 'What is this place?' he said.

'We are at the foot of Riverrise,' said Cowlquape excitedly. 'This, this is her water!'

Twig stared up at the vertical rockface.

'It's this way, Twig!' said Cowlquape, jumping down into the pool and splashing through it. 'Behind the waterfall – or what now remains of it. Yes, there!' he exclaimed. 'Look, Twig!'

A narrow crack in the cliff-face, like a knife cut, sliced back into the rock. Cowlquape scrambled out of the water and stared up into the shadowy gap. The others splashed across the pool to join him.

'You see,' said Cowlquape. 'And look here,' he said, fingering the two symbols carved into the rock at the entrance. 'The trident and snake of . . .'

'Kobold the Wise,' Twig breathed. He turned to Cowlquape. 'But how did you know? Was this also in those precious barkscrolls of yours?'

Cowlquape shook his head, and smiled. 'I dreamt it,' he said simply.

Twig nodded. 'Then let us follow your dream,' he said. 'Lead us, Cowlquape. Lead us to Riverrise!'

·CHAPTER EIGHTEEN·

RIVERRISE

At first, the going was hard. Fallen rock debris littered the ground, and even Goom was forced down onto his hands and knees as he scrabbled up the narrow cutting. The sound of shifting gravel and bouncing pebbles echoed round the steep walls on either side.

'It's getting easier here,' Cowlquape called back. 'The path is firm – like steps.' He looked down. 'They *are* steps,' he whispered.

Twig caught him up, and the pair of them paused for a moment to look ahead. Rising up was a long winding staircase, carved out of the rock by the passing of countless feet.

Cowlquape shuddered with excitement. 'I am treading where *he* trod,' he murmured as he hurried ahead. 'I am walking in the footsteps of Kobold the Wise.'

Higher and higher, Cowlquape climbed. Not once did he falter. Not once was he short of breath. Abruptly, the air grew light. Cowlquape looked round and his heart gave a leap. At last – at long, long last – he was above the terrible canopy of the stifling Deepwoods he had feared he would never leave.

He hesitated, and looked up. White and yellow clouds swirled high above his head, offering tantalizing glimpses of the tall mountain peak beyond. He felt Twig's hand resting on his shoulder, and turned towards him.

'Listen to the water, Cowlquape,' said Twig. Cowlquape cocked his head to one side. The tinkling sound of the trickling stream had stopped. In its place was a soft yet insistent *plink plink plink* as the water dripped down into the pool, far below them. 'It's drying up,' said Twig grimly. 'And when the waters of Riverrise stop flowing . . .' He paused, puzzled by the words he had uttered.

'Yes, Twig?' said Cowlquape.

'When the waters of Riverrise stop flowing . . .' Twig repeated. He clutched his head with his hands. 'Oh, Cowlquape, why can I hear my father speaking these words? I . . . I . . . No, it's no good,' he said, the frustration clear in his voice. 'I just can't remember.'

'Come on,' said Cowlquape. 'Perhaps the answer lies at Riverrise.'

The air grew warmer as they continued upwards. The clouds came closer and closer still. Swirling, wispy, bewildering. All at once, the bright sun burst through, bathing everything beneath it in golden shadows.

'We're above the clouds!' Cowlquape cried out with

joy. 'And look!' He pointed ahead. The end of their climb lay so close.

Cowlquape ran forwards, his heart thumping with anticipation. Twig trotted by his side with Goom and Woodfish following close behind.

Far in the distance, a great caterbird – no more than a ragged dot against the tangerine sky – wheeled round. Its gimlet eyes scanned the high mountain tops for a moment. Then it flapped its broad wings, and soared off.

As the heads of the four travellers emerged above the upper ridge of rock, the dazzling sun filled their eyes. They raised their hands to shade them and squinted ahead.

Cowlquape gasped and fell to his knees. 'Riverrise,' he trembled.

Behind him, the sound of water echoed up from the pool far below them. *Drip. Drip. Drip.*

Side by side, the four travellers stared ahead in awe and elation at the magnificent scene spread out before them. They were standing on a great white marble slab overlooking the wide bowl of a once mighty lake, now no more than a shallow pool, which was fringed with luxuriant vegetation.

There were emerald green trees, and bushes and shrubs, all laden with heavy fruit; and flowers – red and purple and yellow and orange and blue – which filled the air with a heady mix of perfumes.

'It's a huge garden,' Cowlquape breathed.

Before them, the quivering sun was sinking down

behind the western reaches of the lofty, gleaming pinnacles which ringed the whole area like a great, gold crown. Lengthening shadows raced towards them, down over the fertile gardens of the slopes and on across the shrunken, turquoise spring beneath their feet.

'Look there,' said Cowlquape, pointing. A jutting spur of rock stood out at the lake's furthermost point. 'That's where the water spills over into the pool below.' A single drip echoed up out of the stillness. 'This *is* Riverrise!'

The sun disappeared behind the marble rocks, silhouetting them against the dark red sky like a magnificent temple. Soon it would be dark. Twig turned to the water-waif.

'The Stone Pilot?' he said. 'Where is the Stone Pilot, Woodfish?'

Woodfish raised his hand for silence. His ears pricked up and quivered. He peered into the towering stacks of fluted marble down by the edge of the spring.

'What is it, Woodfish?' said Twig. 'Do you hear someone . . . ?'

And then he heard it too. A soft rustling stirring the stillness. His breath caught in his throat. He stepped forwards, his body faintly glowing with luminous light. As he did so, a figure appeared on the other side of the spring. And as it came closer – moving in and out of the trees – it became clearer, and also began to glow.

Cowlquape found himself staring at a slim girl with pale, almost translucent skin and a shock of fiery hair. His jaw dropped. Surely this could not be the remaining missing crew-member? Yet, she was glowing . . .

'Wuh-wuh?' Goom grunted.

'Twig?' said Cowlquape. 'Is this girl the Stone Pilot?'

Twig made no reply. The girl came closer.

'Captain Twig?' she said tentatively.

'Maugin,' Twig whispered. 'It *is* you.'

'Yes, captain,' the girl said, running forwards and throwing her arms around him. A single drop of water dripped down from the lip of the rock. 'I knew you would come for me.'

'Didn't I swear I would never abandon any of my crew?' said Twig, and smiled. 'You are the last, Maugin.'

Maugin pulled away. 'The last?' she said.

'Yes, Maugin,' said Twig.

Far below, the drop splashed into the dark pool.

Maugin looked up shyly at Woodfish and Goom. 'But where are the others? Tarp Hammelherd? Spooler?'

Twig looked away. 'Spooler is dead,' he said sadly. 'But Tarp, Bogwitt and Wingnut Sleet are waiting for us back in Sanctaphrax.'

Maugin started back in alarm. 'In Sanctaphrax?' she said. 'But are they all right?'

Twig chuckled. 'They've been resting up in my study in the School of Light and Darkness,' he said. 'Safe and sound.'

'But, captain,' said Maugin. Her face looked tense. Fine lines puckered the corners of her mouth. 'Do you not remember what Cloud Wolf told you?'

Twig froze. 'Cloud Wolf?' he whispered. 'I . . . I don't remember, no.'

Maugin frowned. 'He told you what you must do,' she

said. 'On the *Stormchaser*, far out in open sky,' she added gently, trying to jog his memory. 'Before the white storm struck . . .'

'*Stormchaser*? White storm?' said Twig, shaking his head. 'I don't remember anything. None of us do,' he said, looking round at the others. 'Nothing at all, from the moment we entered the weather vortex . . .' He turned back to Maugin. 'But *you* do. Because you were clothed in your heavy, hooded coat, the storm did not fog your memory . . . Tell me what happened, Maugin. Tell me what you remember.'

The sound of another drop splashing into the pool echoed up through the air. Maugin turned away.

'Tell me!' Twig shouted. 'I must know!'

'Yes, tell him the thoughts in your head,' said Woodfish. 'Or I shall!'

Maugin sighed. 'You leave me no choice.' She breathed in, noisily, and looked up. 'With the caterbird gone – cut from its tethers by your own hand – I feared . . .'

'I cut the caterbird loose?' Twig gasped.

Maugin nodded. 'Do you want me to continue?'

'Yes,' said Twig.

'. . . I feared we would never find the *Stormchaser*. Yet find it, we did, becalmed at the still centre of the weather vortex. Your father, Cloud Wolf was waiting for you there.'

'My father,' Twig whispered, as a distant recollection

stirred deep within his memory. 'He spoke to me.'

Maugin nodded. 'He told you that the Mother Storm – that mighty storm which first seeded the Edge with life – was returning.'

Cowlquape shuffled about excitedly. It was what he had guessed all along.

'He explained how it would sweep in from open sky towards Riverrise, at the highest point of the Deepwoods,' Maugin continued, 'to rejuvenate the dying spring.'

'Yes, yes,' said Cowlquape, unable to remain silent a moment longer. 'Just as it's written in the barkscrolls.'

'Hush, Cowlquape,' said Twig sharply. Fragments of memory were beginning to come together. He looked up at Maugin. 'But Sanctaphrax lies in its path,' he said. 'Yes, *now I remember* . . . Cloud Wolf . . . he told me to . . . to cut the great Anchor Chain, didn't he?'

Maugin nodded. 'If the Mother Storm wastes her energy destroying Sanctaphrax, she will never reach Riverrise to bring new life to her waters,' she said. 'Then the stagnant darkness at the black heart of the Deepwoods will spread out, until every inch of the Edge has been swallowed up!'

'Sky above,' Twig moaned. 'What have I done?' He looked into Maugin's eyes. 'I was *there,* Maugin. In Sanctaphrax. I could have told them. The way our bodies glowed should have reminded me . . . Oh, if only I'd remembered what I had to do.' He turned to the others. 'We'll set off back at once. Maugin, you must come with us.' Then his face paled and he staggered to one side. 'Maugin,' he said desperately. 'Did I tell you *when* this had to be done?'

She shook her head.

Twig moaned. 'You had part of the story, Maugin. And I needed to hear it to unlock my memory, and remember the rest . . .' He faltered. 'The Mother Storm will return when . . .' His father's words came back to him with awful clarity, '. . . when the waters of Riverrise stop flowing . . .'

Maugin suddenly drew away. Her whole body was rigid, her gaze fixed on the spur of rock jutting out from the edge of the Riverrise spring.

'Twig!' said Maugin, seizing him by the arm. 'Twig, listen!'

Twig fell still. He cocked his head to one side. 'What?' he said. 'I can't hear anything.'

'Exactly,' said Maugin. 'It is silent.'

Twig frowned. 'What do you mean? I . . .' An icy shiver ran the length of his spine. The regular *drip drip* of the Riverrise water had stopped.

'The Riverrise spring has finally died,' said Maugin in a low voice. 'It can mean only one thing . . .'

Twig looked up, his eyes wide. 'The Mother Storm is

on her way,' he said. 'I remember everything now. She should reach here at dawn. But that will never happen. Instead, she will strike Sanctaphrax at the stroke of midnight, expending her energy uselessly – and the Edge will descend into darkness. I've failed,' he said bitterly. 'I've failed Cloud Wolf. I've failed Sanctaphrax. I've failed myself.'

Woodfish stepped forwards. 'Yet, perhaps there is a solution, after all.' He looked at Maugin, and his eyes narrowed. 'I can read it in her thoughts.'

'What?' said Twig. 'What is she thinking, Woodfish?' He turned to Maugin. 'Is there something you're not telling me?'

She looked away.

'Maugin!' said Twig. 'Please!'

'Do you want *me* to tell him?' said Woodfish.

Maugin swallowed back her tears. 'There's only one way of getting back to Sanctaphrax in time,' she said quietly. 'But at terrible risk.'

Twig's jaw dropped. 'By midnight?' he said. 'How?'

'But it's madness,' said Maugin. She glared at Woodfish. 'Just a foolish thought.'

'Tell me!' Twig demanded.

Maugin sighed. And although she stared back at him evenly enough, when she spoke, her voice was no more than a tremulous whisper.

'By sky-firing.'

·CHAPTER NINETEEN·

FLIGHT TO SANCTAPHRAX

Sky-firing! Twig blanched. It was a method the more unscrupulous captains – both sky pirates and leaguesmen – had of dealing with mutinous crew-members. The offending individual was tied to a burning length of buoyant wood and launched off like a rocket on a one-way trip into open sky. It was a horrific punishment, feared by all who took to the skies in ships. Surely Maugin couldn't really mean . . .

'I know it sounds insane, captain,' said Maugin. 'But instead of launching a blazing tree-trunk upwards, it could just be possible to calculate an angle of ascent that would take you in a wide arc over the Deepwoods and on to Undertown. But the risks are appalling. You could fall short and land in the Twilight Woods or the Mire, or overshoot Undertown entirely and disappear over the Edge itself. And even if, by some miracle, you did reach Undertown, the chances are you'd be a charred corpse when you hit the ground.'

Twig looked back at Maugin steadily. 'That's a chance I'm prepared to take,' he said.

'But, Twig,' said Cowlquape. 'You heard what she said. It would be certain death!'

'I must try,' said Twig firmly. 'It'll be certain death for Sanctaphrax if I don't. And for every single creature in the Deepwoods if the river is not rejuvenated. I *must* try.'

Cowlquape grasped Twig's hand. He was trembling; his breath came in gasps. 'Let *me* go in your place. Let *me* be sky-fired to Sanctaphrax. I am younger than you. Lighter. And what's the life of a failed apprentice compared with that of the finest sky pirate that ever lived?' He paused. 'And . . . and you could tie a message to my back addressed to the Professor of Darkness, just in case I didn't make it there alive . . .'

Twig smiled. 'You are not a failed apprentice, Cowlquape; you have served me well.' He shook his head. 'I can't ask you to do this. It is my task.'

'But Twig!' protested Cowlquape, tears in his eyes.

'Thank you,' said Twig, 'but I won't hear another word on the matter . . .'

'And yet the idea of someone accompanying you is not a bad one,' Maugin said thoughtfully. 'A stout tree should bear the weight of two passengers, and it would mean that if one blacked out, the other would still have a fighting chance. *I* shall go with you, captain.'

'You?' said Cowlquape incredulously.

'I am a Stone Pilot,' said Maugin. 'I have the knowledge and expertise. I should be the one to accompany Twig.'

Twig smiled and bowed his head. 'I'm very touched,' he said. 'But I must go alone.'

'But, captain!' protested Maugin.

'I'm sorry, Maugin,' said Twig. 'You and the rest of the crew have followed me faithfully for long enough. I risked all your lives by sailing into open sky. I've already asked too much of you.' He paused. 'Give me your expertise, not your life.'

Maugin took his hand. 'You have my life already,' she said.

They searched the luxuriant gardens of Riverrise for the tallest, stoutest, most buoyant tree they could find. At last, they settled on a magnificent silver-grey lufwood standing proud at the very edge of the still water of the spring.

'It seems almost a shame to cut down such a beautiful tree,' said Cowlquape with a faraway look in his eyes. 'I wonder how long it has stood here, drinking the waters of Riverrise. Why, Kobold the Wise might himself have sat in its shade.'

'It's a fine choice, captain,' said Maugin. 'It'll burn long and bright.'

'Let's get to work,' said Twig impatiently. 'Time is running out. The Mother Storm is on her way – and midnight is drawing closer and closer over Sanctaphrax.'

Goom felled the great tree with massive blows of Tuntum's axe; splinters of ash-grey lufwood peppered the air. At last the tree fell with what, to Cowlquape at

least, seemed like a sad, creaking sigh, followed by a tremendous crash.

While Goom stripped the branches, till all that was left was the trunk itself, Twig and the others – under Maugin's close supervision – set about feverishly lashing together a launching ramp from the stoutest branches.

'We must align the ramp with the east star, for there lies Sanctaphrax,' said Maugin. 'And angle it carefully. The flight's path must not be too high, or you'll never return to earth.'

'But how can you possibly judge the distance?' asked Cowlquape, shaking his head.

'I can't,' said Maugin bluntly. 'But I was a Stone Pilot before you were born. Flight is my trade. It's all I know. I must use all my experience – though even then it only comes down to making a good guess.' She turned away. 'Twig, you will have to keep your wits about you. We'll rope you to the very tip of the trunk with slip-knots that you can pull to release yourself when Undertown appears beneath you.'

'I understand,' said Twig.

As the sky darkened, they set the log against the ramp, angled to Maugin's satisfaction, and bundles of the leafy branches were arranged around the base in a tight cluster. Twig buttoned up his longcoat and tightened the straps of his parawings. Then, at Maugin's insistence, he was smeared all over with a thick covering of the cooling Riverrise mud from the water's edge.

'The mud will protect you from the intense heat from the flames,' she explained. 'And take this,' she added, handing him a small bottle. 'It contains the restorative water of Riverrise – though, Sky willing, you will not have to use it.'

Finally, Twig was lashed to the underside of the great tree trunk. Maugin secured the final slip-knot.

'Farewell, Captain Twig,' she whispered.

Twig twisted his head round and watched as Maugin climbed down the launching ramp and jumped to the ground. He looked along the length of the tree-trunk behind him, straight and streamlined for flight; and at the bundle of leaves bound to its base that, even now, Woodfish was waiting to ignite with the flaming torch in his hand.

'Wait for my signal,' called Maugin. 'Light those leafy branches first, exactly at the places I point out.'

'Stop!' shouted Cowlquape. He was running from the water's edge, his clothes covered in mud, hastily daubed. 'I can't let you go alone, Twig,' he cried. 'I can't!'

He shinned up the sloping lufwood tree and clung tightly to the trunk.

'We don't have time for this!' said Twig impatiently.

'Then move over, Twig,' said Cowlquape. 'Maugin, tie me into place. You said yourself that two stand a better chance than one.'

'You would really do this for Sanctaphrax?' said Twig. 'Even though it could mean death?'

'Not for Sanctaphrax,' said Cowlquape. 'For you, Twig.' He smiled. 'And perhaps also for Kobold the Wise.'

Twig turned to Maugin. 'Do as he says,' he told her.

Finally they were ready. Twig smiled down at his loyal crew-members standing on the ground below him.

'Wuh-wuh, T-wuh-g!' Goom called.

'My dreams will go with you,' said Woodfish. He bent down to the branches Maugin pointed to, one after another, and touched them with the burning torch. The oily leaves exploded into flame.

'I will be back!' Twig shouted above the roar of the blaze.

White hot inside the blazing branches, the base of the trunk caught fire. It hissed. It steamed. It juddered and shook, and then . . .

Tearing away from its tethers, the great burning tree-trunk blasted away from the scaffold and soared up into the sky – leaving a fan of orange sparks in its wake. The top of the tree, with its two tethered passengers, soon disappeared into the darkness, until only the blazing base could still be seen – a dot of light that grew smaller and fainter as it sped off on its perilous journey.

'Sky protect you, Twig!' Maugin whispered.

When the blazing tree launched itself into the air the upward force was so strong that it stole Twig's breath away and left him gasping for air. Face to one side, eyes clenched shut, he gripped the ropes that bound him to the trunk, and prayed they'd hold.

And still they were accelerating. The pressure was intolerable. His stomach sunk down to his toes. The blood rushed from his brain. His mouth was tugged down at the corners. At unimaginable speed, the tree hurtled over the Deepwoods with its living cargo. Any forest-dweller noticing it would have wished upon a shooting star in vain.

Feeling sick and light-headed Twig saw the moonlit canopy of burnished silver blurring past beneath him.

He gritted his teeth. His temples throbbed, his neck ached, his stomach churned with fear.

'Don't black out!' he told himself grimly, and prayed again that the knots would hold.

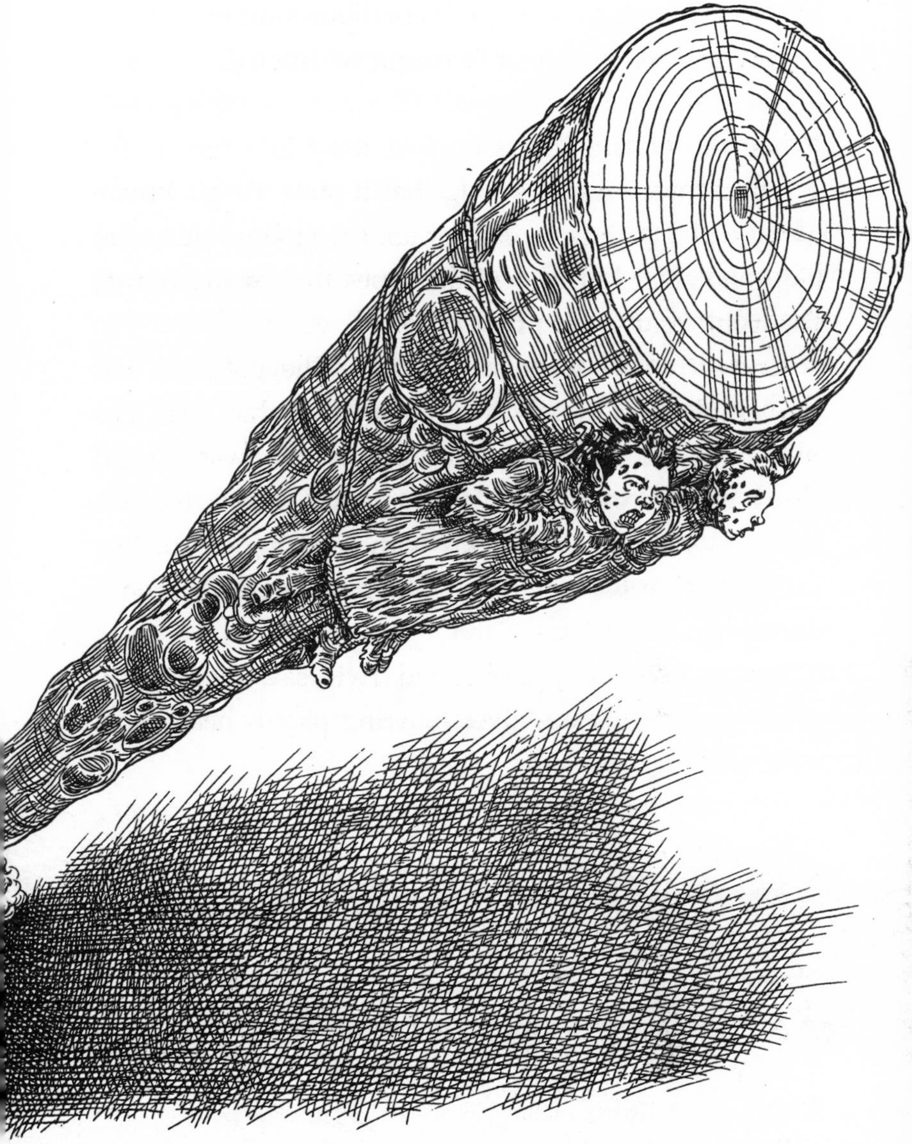

The caterbird's words of encouragement on board the *Edgedancer* came back to him. Crystal clear, as though his great wise protector had never left him after all, they whispered inside his head. *This too will pass,* they said. *This too will pass.*

Twig closed his eyes. Everything passes. Joy. Pain. The moment of triumph; the sigh of despair. Nothing lasts for ever – not even this . . .

Reluctantly, Twig opened his eyes. Travelling almost horizontally now, they seemed to be at the top of the flaming comet's great arc. The endless expanse of trees flashed past, far below him. Speed. Pressure. Unbearable heat. He heard Cowlquape groaning beside him.

The flames had consumed more than half of the great tree-trunk. Huge chunks of blackened cinder broke off and fell away and, as the flames came closer, the heat grew more and more intense. Neither Twig nor Cowlquape could stand it much longer. Their hearts thumped. Their hands trembled. Their bodies were bathed in sweat.

'Don't give up now,' Twig whispered. His head spun with weakness. 'Keep going . . .'

The great buoyant tree had passed its highest point, that much was certain. Grunting with effort, Twig peered ahead – and his heart gave a leap. Far in front of them, gleaming brightly beneath the silver moon, was the barren wasteland of the Mire. Twig had never been so happy to see the terrible, bleached landscape before. A moment later, they were above it – further off in the distance, the lights of Sanctaphrax glimmered.

Down, they were flying now. Lower and lower. The intense heat was staggering. Cowlquape's boots blistered. The hairs on Twig's hammelhornskin waistcoat shrivelled and fell limp.

Keep going, Twig urged himself again. Just a little longer . . .

Low in the sky, the great towers of Sanctaphrax gleamed in the moonlight. Beneath it, the squalid mess of Undertown sprawled down to and along the banks of the now waterless Edgewater River. It had dried up completely, Twig realized with a jolt. And now that the water from Riverrise had ceased to flow . . .

Cowlquape screamed.

The flames were roaring all round them and, despite the thick, protective layer of Riverrise mud, the pair of them were being baked alive. Twig turned to meet Cowlquape's panic-stricken gaze.

'Hold on,' he rasped. The boom-docks came into view. The farthest outskirts of Undertown passed below them. 'Now, Cowlquape!' Twig cried. 'Pull the ropes!'

The apprentice's eyes rolled back in their sockets and his head slumped forwards.

'COWLQUAPE!'

Beneath him, the great floating rock of Sanctaphrax passed by. Twig's head spun. What should he do? If he released himself, Cowlquape would hurtle on, over the Edge and into open sky. Yet if he tried to rescue him, Sanctaphrax itself might perish.

There was no choice.

Twig drew his knife and sliced through Cowlquape's binding ropes. They frayed and snapped, and the young apprentice was plucked from the stump of blazing wood by the wind. The parawings flew open and Cowlquape floated away.

Without missing a beat, Twig slipped the knot binding himself to the stubby remains of the once great tree, and flew up into the air after him. His parawings opened, and the silken folds billowed out behind him. Twig looked round nervously, half-expecting to see Cowlquape plummeting down to the ground. But no. There he was, gliding below him.

'Cowlquape!' he shouted and, by bringing his knees up and thrusting forwards, he tilted the angle of the parawings and swooped down towards him.

Cowlquape's face was as white as a sheet, but he was alive. And not only alive, but also – thank Sky – conscious once more.

'How do I steer these things?' he wailed.

'Don't even try,' Twig called back. 'You're doing fine. Just don't make any sudden movements!'

As they glided down, the last signs of ramshackle habitation fell away behind them. The land beneath became rocky and inhospitable. It sped up to meet them.

'There's no turning back now,' Twig cried. 'Prepare yourself for landing. Crumple and roll, Cowlquape!' he bellowed. 'Crumple and roll.'

The next moment Twig landed, followed immediately by Cowlquape. As they felt the ground beneath their feet, they let their legs relax and rolled over onto their sides. The baked mud cracked and fell away.

Twig was first up. He crouched down over the motionless body of his friend, unstoppered the little bottle Maugin had given him, and touched the Riverrise water to his lips.

Cowlquape opened his eyes at once and looked up.

'How are you?' Twig whispered.

'Apart from being burned and battered half to death, you mean?' said Cowlquape, sitting up.

Twig smiled. 'Can you walk?' he said.

'I . . . I think so,' said Cowlquape. 'Where are we?'

Twig looked round at the silvery stacks of rocks, each one larger than the one beneath. 'In the Stone Gardens,' he groaned.

Wisps of mist coiled up from the earth where the cold air touched the warm ground. A wind was getting up. Cowlquape shivered.

'The Stone Gardens,' he complained. 'But that's miles from Sanctaphrax!'

Just then, the air all round them filled with a flurry of wings. One by one, sleek white birds landed and loped towards them, forming an unbroken circle around the hapless pair. They scratched at the ground, they flapped their ragged wings, they stretched their necks forwards, opened their savage beaks and cawed menacingly. The smell of rotting meat filled the air.

'The ravens!' Twig muttered, drawing his sword. 'The white ravens!'

Cowlquape grasped his knife, and he and Twig stood back to back, weapons raised, in grim anticipation. Two against so many were impossible odds. Had they come so far only to fail here, almost within sight of Sanctaphrax?

'Listen to me,' he called out to them. 'You must listen to me.'

But the white ravens were in no mood to listen. They stabbed the air with their beaks and cawed all the louder. It could only be a matter of time before the bravest – or hungriest – of them broke ranks and attacked.

·CHAPTER TWENTY·

THE MOTHER STORM

The bright moon shone down impassively on the bleak scene in the Stone Gardens. Two individuals, the blades of their weapons glinting in the moonlight, stood together. In a circle around them, the flock of voracious white ravens scratched at the ground with their scythe-like talons.

'What do we do, Twig?' said Cowlquape.

'I . . . We . . .' Twig fell still. For the first time since he had set out on his quest to find his missing crew, he was at a loss to know what to do. Each one of the crew had been accounted for now, yet the quest was not over – or rather, it had changed. And if Sanctaphrax was not to be destroyed by the approaching Mother Storm, then Twig had to act – and act now.

All at once, the largest of the white ravens stepped forwards. It cocked its head to one side.

'Shooting star?' it croaked.

Twig's jaw dropped. Not only could the great bird speak, but it seemed to recognize him. 'Y . . . yes,' he said, nodding uncertainly.

'Friend of Professor of Darkness?'

'You know the Professor of Darkness?' Twig gasped.

'Kraan know,' the white raven acknowledged.

'Then you must help us . . .' Twig began, only to be drowned out by the raucous cawing of the restless flock.

Kraan turned and screeched at them to be silent, then looked back at Twig. 'Help you?' it said.

'I want you to deliver a message to the professor,' said Twig. 'An important message.'

'Important,' Kraan repeated.

'The Mother Storm will strike Sanctaphrax at midnight,' Twig said very slowly and clearly. 'The floating city must be evacuated at once. Tell him Twig is on his way.' He looked into Kraan's glassy yellow eyes, trying to guess what the bird might be thinking. 'Can you do that?'

Before the white raven could answer, the Stone Gardens were abruptly plunged into darkness. Everyone looked up. Curious dark clouds had swarmed in across the moon, where they squirmed and writhed; it was like looking into a barrel of woodmaggots.

The ravens croaked in unison – a raucous chorus of dismay.

At that moment, a bolt of jagged blue lightning hissed down through the sky and struck the ground nearby. Where it landed, the earth cracked and, as the smoke and dust cleared, the glinting surface of a newly emerging rock appeared from beneath the surface.

'This weather heralds the arrival of the Mother Storm,' said Twig grimly.

The white raven looked at him askance. 'You know what Professor of Darkness does not know,' he said suspiciously. 'How?'

'Because the secret was revealed to me,' said Twig, and pointed beyond the Edge. 'Out there, in open sky – where no professor has ever dared venture. Kraan, you must believe me. If you do not leave now, it will be *too late*. Too late for you, for me, for Sanctaphrax – *life on the Edge will end.*'

'Waaark!' cried the great bird. It beat its wings and rose up into the air. 'Waaark!' it shrieked again, and the circle of white ravens opened to let Twig and Cowlquape pass: they were not to be harmed. *'WAAARK!'*

'Find the Professor of Darkness,' Twig called. 'Give him my message.' Kraan wheeled round and flapped noisily off in the direction of Sanctaphrax. 'And Sky speed be with you,' Twig whispered.

The Stone Gardens receded behind them as Twig and Cowlquape hurried along the path that would take them to Undertown. All around them, the sky hissed and fizzed threateningly. Tendrils of flashing electric-blue light fanned out across the darkness. The Mother Storm was coming closer and the air was charged with her imminent arrival. Half an hour or more had already passed.

'Faster,' said Twig urgently, as he broke into a jog. 'Midnight is approaching. We must hurry.'

'I . . . I'm coming,' Cowlquape panted wearily.

Ahead of them, the spires and towers of Sanctaphrax glinted in the sparking air. And, as the wind grew stronger still, the entire floating city bobbed at the end of

the taut Anchor Chain like a bladder-balloon on a string.

Finally – and much later than Twig would have wished – the outskirts of Undertown came into view. Low wood-framed workshops with corrugated iron-wood roofs, a small tannery, a hull-rigging manufacturer's.

'Nearly there,' said Twig breathlessly.

Behind him, the sky had turned purple, while the electric-blue flashes grew more intense. They fizzed all round the magnificent buildings of Sanctaphrax and down the mighty chain which anchored it to the ground.

'This way,' said Twig, veering abruptly down a narrow alley lined with stalls of basketware and clay pots, still open for business despite the lateness of the hour. Cowlquape struggled after him, his legs rubbery and weak.

They turned left again. Then right. The whole of Undertown was buzzing, thronging. Goblins and trolls stood in anxious clusters looking up at the sky, pointing,

murmuring with disquiet. Something sinister was happening. Something that seemed worse than all the other recent storms put together.

Barging their way through the crowds, Twig and Cowlquape kept on. Right. Right again. Then left. And there it was – in the centre of an open paved area ahead of them – the mooring-platform for the great floating rock itself.

The place was already full of academics. They looked bewildered, frightened and, in their robes of office, out of place amidst the grime and chaos of Undertown. Twig glanced up at the floating rock, where overladen baskets were bringing still more of the citizens of Sanctaphrax down to earth. Kraan, the white raven, had obviously delivered his message and the professor had acted.

The air glistened and sparked, and a deafening clatter of thunder set the ground trembling. The gale-force wind howled down the narrow streets and round the square.

Head down, Twig strode directly towards the platform unimpeded; the gnokgoblins of the Anchor Chain guard had clearly abandoned their posts. He looked at the chain and sighed. No sword could ever sever its mighty links. He climbed up onto the plinth and crouched down to see how the end of the chain had been secured.

The mooring-block was an intricate contraption. An iron plate, with two raised arches in the middle, had been bolted through the platform and into the rock beneath. The end of the Anchor Chain was wound round a cogged-axle, with the final link fixed into place between the two arches by a massive levered cotter-pin. If Sanctaphrax was to be released, the cotter-pin would have to be removed. But how?

'A hammer, Cowlquape!' Twig shouted. 'I need a heavy hammer. For Sky's sake, find me one now.'

Cowlquape darted off into the crowd.

A cheer went up, and Twig looked round to see a stooped figure in black robes climbing from a basket which had just touched down near the dry fountain at the far side of the square.

It was the Professor of Darkness. Twig sighed with relief. If the Most High Academe of Sanctaphrax had left the floating city, then the evacuation must be almost complete.

And not before time, thought Twig, as a low, stomach-churning sound rumbled in the distance. It was the Mother Storm, and she was drawing near.

Where was Cowlquape with that hammer? Twig looked around for something – anything – that he might use to knock the cotter-pin free.

All at once, a brutal volley of hailstones – the size of ratbird eggs – hammered down on Undertown, smashing through windows, and turning fear to pandemonium as everyone ran screaming for cover. With his arm raised protectively, Twig looked up.

Boiling and bubbling, flashing and flickering, an immense ball of pitch-black cloud was tumbling in across the night sky towards them.

The Mother Storm was all but upon them!

Twig leapt down off the platform and levered one of

the slabs of paving from the ground with his sword. He dashed back to the chain-moorings again and slammed the rock into the end of the cotter-pin.

It moved!

Twig tried again. This time the cotter-pin jammed tight. He tried again. But it was no use. The pin wouldn't budge.

'Move, Sky curse you!' Twig roared in his fury and frustration. 'Move!'

'Twig!' shouted a familiar voice. 'What do you think you're doing?'

Twig looked up. The Professor of Darkness was hurrying across the square towards him.

'Please, Professor,' Twig grunted as he slammed the heavy rock into the mooring-block again and again. 'There's no time to explain.'

'Twig! No!' the professor cried. Pulling up his robes, he climbed onto the plinth and seized Twig's arm. 'Have you taken leave of your senses? What has happened to you – you of all people – that you should attack the Anchor Chain?'

Twig shook him off. 'All will be lost if I do not,' he said. 'The Mother Storm is almost upon us! She will strike at midnight.'

'But Twig, how can you say that?' said the professor.

'I have remembered what I

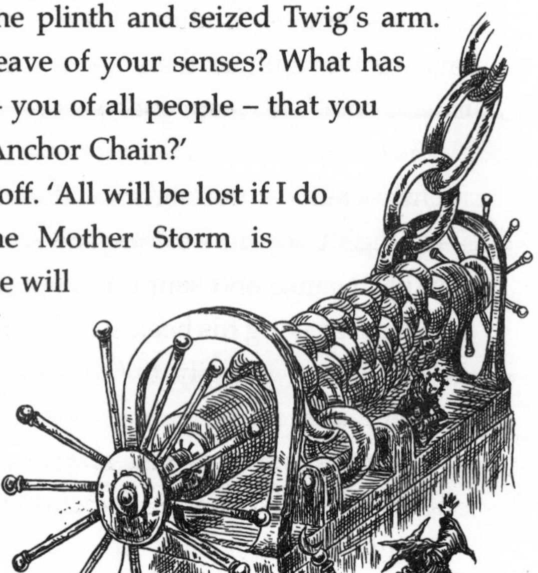

learned in open sky,' said Twig. 'What I had forgotten when you found me in the Stone Gardens. If life on the Edge is to survive, then Sanctaphrax must be unchained! The Mother Storm must be allowed to pass on to Riverrise unimpeded.'

'No!' the professor murmured, stunned. 'No.' His breathing quickened. 'I agreed to the evacuation . . . I feared structural damage might lead to injuries, or even fatalities. But to unchain Sanctaphrax! No, it cannot be. I should have remained up there with the rest.'

'The rest?' said Twig, and glanced up at the floating city to see a row of tiny figures peering down from a balustrade. 'Tarp? Bogwitt . . . ?'

'Oh, your crew are down, but several of the older academics refused to leave,' the professor said. 'The Professor of Fogprobing, the Professors of Windtouchers and Cloudwatchers – even that upstart, the Professor of Psycho-Climatic Studies . . . Professors evidently more loyal to Sanctaphrax than myself,' he added as, without any warning, he leapt forwards and shoved Twig with all his weight.

Distracted by the sight of the stubborn academics, Twig didn't see him coming. The heavy blow knocked him off balance and sent him keeling backwards off the platform, striking his head sharply on the edge as he fell. He looked up groggily, to see the Professor of Darkness standing above him.

At that moment, a bell rang out. It was the heavy, brass bell of the Great Hall, chiming the hour.

Bong! it tolled.

The professor looked up. 'You see,' he cried. 'Midnight, and all is well.'

The crowds milled about nervously, eyes to the sky, as colossal banks of clouds tumbled over and over one another. Despite the professor's hopeful words, all seemed very far from well.

Bong!

Far above their heads the massive ball of cloud pulsed in and out, like a great, beating black heart. The air crackled. The wind wailed. The Mother Storm was about to release – and squander – her rejuvenating power here at Sanctaphrax, far from Riverrise.

Bong!

Flushed and breathless, Cowlquape was suddenly at Twig's side. A hammer was clenched in his hand.

'Twig!' he cried. 'What's happened?'

Bong!

The sky rumbled and rolled. Purple and blue bolts of lightning plunged down to the earth, cracking paving-stones, razing buildings to the ground and sending the terrified inhabitants of Undertown and citizens of Sanctaphrax scurrying this way and that in search of safe shelter.

Twig clutched his throbbing head. 'Release the Anchor Chain, Cowlquape,' he croaked weakly. 'Before the bell tolls twelve.'

Bong!

Cowlquape leapt up onto the platform where the Professor of Darkness lay wrapped around the workings of the mooring block.

'Move!' he shouted.

'You'll have to kill me first!' the Professor said defiantly.

Bong!

Cowlquape stepped forwards and seized the old professor by the sleeve.

'No, no!' he cried out, tearing his arm free. 'If you think I'll allow centuries of knowledge to be lost, then . . .' The professor's voice was high and querulous. 'Then you're as mad as he is!'

Bong!

'Cowlquape, hurry!' Twig groaned, as he struggled groggily to his feet. 'Hurry!'

The storm roared. The earth shook. The sky shuddered.

'No, Cowlquape,' pleaded the professor. 'I . . . I'll give you anything you want!' he cried. 'Name your price. Your own department. A professorship. Tell me, and it is yours – only don't release the Anchor Chain!'

Bong!

'Here,' the professor babbled as he tore off his heavy chain of office. 'Take the great seal of Sanctaphrax. It's yours – only don't destroy our great city,' he begged as he reached out and slung it around Cowlquape's neck.

As he did so, Cowlquape grasped the professor by his bony wrist and tugged hard. With a cry of despair, the Professor of Darkness was wrenched from the winding-gear and propelled away from the mooring-platform. He landed heavily on the ground.

Bong!

Cowlquape turned, bent over and hammered furiously at the cotter-pin. Groaning and creaking, the toothed axle moved. Flakes of rust crumbled away as cogs and gears that hadn't been touched for hundreds of years juddered and turned.

Bong!

Above him, the approaching Mother Storm was drifting lower, filling up more and more of the sky as she descended. The heavy air was charged with electricity that set the hair on every head on end, and laced with the smell of sulphur and tar and toasted almonds. A great whirlwind spun round and round, causing Sanctaphrax itself to turn. Fearing for their lives, those beneath the great rock sped off in all directions.

Abruptly, the final link in the great chain sliced through the cotter-pin like a hot knife through butter. Sanctaphrax was free.

Bong!

'No!' wailed the Professor of Darkness, scrambling to his feet. He hitched up his gowns and dashed after the great chain trailing behind the floating rock. 'It cannot be!' he screamed. 'No!'

'Professor!' Twig called after him. 'Listen to me!'

But the Professor paid him no heed. Sanctaphrax was at the heart of his very soul. He would not – *could* not – live without it. He took a flying leap at the end of the chain, and clung on tightly.

'Professor!' Twig cried out.

Bong!

The bell tolled twelve. It was midnight over Sanctaphrax.

The Mother Storm bellowed like a mighty beast. Unchained, the Sanctaphrax rock soared ever higher and out of sight as the Mother Storm – pulsing with power and new life – rolled on across the sky to keep her dawn appointment with Riverrise.

Cowlquape jumped down from the plinth and ran over to Twig.

'Sky protect you, Professor,' Twig called, gazing upwards.

Cowlquape rested a hand on his shoulder.

'The Professor of Darkness was a good person, Cowlquape,' said Twig. 'Dedicated, loyal . . . like those other misguided academics who refused to leave.' He sighed. 'They couldn't let go of their beloved Sanctaphrax.'

'There they are!' came a loud, angry voice.

'They cut the Anchor Chain!' bellowed another.

Twig and Cowlquape found themselves confronted by a furious mob – academics, guards, basket-pullers – advancing towards them.

Cowlquape turned to Twig. 'What do we do?' he gasped.

Twig raised his arms. 'Friends! Fellow Academics! People of Undertown!' he called out. 'It is true, Cowlquape here released the Anchor Chain . . .'

The growing crowd hissed and booed.

'But had he not done so,' Twig shouted above the noise, 'the terrible storm you all witnessed overhead would have destroyed not only Sanctaphrax but also Undertown – and all life as we know it on the Edge!'

'Says who?' bellowed a tall robed figure.

'Why should we believe you?' demanded another. The cries grew louder, angrier.

'Because I speak for your new Most High Academe,' Twig bellowed back. The crowd hesitated. 'Yes, you heard me correctly; the Most High Academe!' He pointed to the heavy gold seal hanging from the chain round Cowlquape's neck. 'For that was the title conferred upon him by the

old Most High Academe, as is his right, according to the ancient customs of our beloved Sanctaphrax.'

Cowlquape shrunk with embarrassment. 'But . . . but . . .' he murmured.

'There *is* no beloved Sanctaphrax!' shouted an angry voice.

'Good thing, too!' shouted an Undertowner. 'Lazy academics!'

'Undertown scum!' came the furious response.

Scuffles broke out, punches were thrown. Then, the next instant, the crowd froze, each and every one, as their cries were drowned out by the frantic shrieking and cawing of the flock of white ravens circling the sky above them.

'The chorus of the dead,' the Undertowners groaned, scurrying away to safety.

'The white ravens,' whispered the academics, holding their ground.

In a great swirling blizzard of feathers the white ravens landed and stood in a protective ring around Twig and Cowlquape. The largest of them turned to Twig and thrust its great beak forwards.

'Kraan,' said Twig. 'Thank you for . . .'

'Lightning bolt hit Stone Gardens,' the bird interrupted. 'Blue lightning bolt. You remember?'

'Y . . . yes,' said Twig. 'I do.'

Kraan nodded vigorously. 'There, a rock grows. Biggest ever. Growing fast. Fast and fast. Must secure it. Secure it now. Before fly-away.'

Twig frowned. He recalled the sight of the glinting

new rock he'd glimpsed beneath the surface. 'You don't suppose . . .' he said, turning to Cowlquape.

'You mean,' said Cowlquape, 'you think this rock might grow big enough to be . . .'

'A *new* Sanctaphrax!' said Twig. 'That's exactly what I think!' He motioned to the academics before them. 'Quick! Go to the Stone Gardens, all of you! Take ropes, chains, netting, rigging, weights – anything you can lay your hands on. For the rock which is growing down at the Edge shall be your new floating city. Together you can build a new Sanctaphrax.'

The academics stared back mutely. Cowlquape stepped forward, hand on the chain of office round his neck. 'Do as he says!' he commanded.

For a moment, the academics remained still. Then a lone voice cried out. 'To the Stone Gardens!' and they turned and began to stream from the square.

Twig turned to Cowlquape. 'Ah, Cowlquape,' he said. 'How I envy you.'

'You envy me?' said Cowlquape.

'Surely,' said Twig. 'For you will be able to start afresh – to create the academic city the way it should always have been. Away with the pettiness, the backbiting, the whispered intrigue. For you are the bridge, Cowlquape, that will bring Undertown and the new Sanctaphrax together. No longer will merchants and academics look down on one another, for you have seen both sides, Cowlquape – and you have a good heart. Now you also have a new floating rock upon which to build your dreams.'

'And what about you, Twig?' said Cowlquape.

'Me?' said Twig. 'I must be reunited with my crew – both here and back at Riverrise.' He sighed. 'If only Spooler had not died . . .'

'Stay here!' said Cowlquape, gripping Twig by the arms. 'We'll build the new Sanctaphrax together. You and me . . .'

'My place is not here,' said Twig firmly. 'It never was. My place is at the helm of a sky ship with my loyal crew by my side.'

Cowlquape screwed up his face. 'But me?' he said. 'What about me? I can't do it all on my own.'

'Follow your heart, Cowlquape,' said Twig. 'Do that, and you won't go far wrong, believe me. Remember, just follow your heart.' He smiled. 'And I will follow mine.'

By the time the sky above the Edge began to lighten, the growing rock in the Stone Gardens had been encased in strong netting to which all kinds of heavy weights were being attached by the scurrying academics.

'Right,' said Cowlquape, satisfied that, for the time being at least, the rock was secure. 'I must hurry back to Undertown,' he said, 'to discuss the matter of a new Anchor Chain with Silex Makepiece of the League of Forging and Founding. In the meantime, I want you to supervise the rock. Ensure that enough weights are attached to keep it from soaring off.'

'Certainly, sir,' Vox, the tall apprentice from the College of Cloud, replied, his voice hushed, oily.

Cowlquape dashed off to the waiting barrow. Vox's eyes narrowed and an unpleasant smirk played on his lips. 'You little runt,' he muttered under his breath. 'I'll get you one day . . .'

When he reached the main square of Undertown, Cowlquape noticed a gathering around the dry central fountain. He leant forwards and tapped the barrow-driver on the shoulder.

'Thank you,' he said. 'If you could let me down for a moment.'

The barrow-driver lowered the shafts of the barrow and Cowlquape jumped out. He ran across to the fountain.

'What is it?' he said. 'What's happening?'

'*Sshhh,* your Most Highness!' said a gnokgoblin insistently. 'Listen.'

Cowlquape cocked his head to one side. From the depths of the fountain echoed a loud gurgling sound. 'What . . . ?' he began.

Then, all at once, as the first rays of the dawn sun fell across the square, there was an ear-splitting roar, and a powerful jet of water gushed up into the air – ten, twenty, thirty strides high – and poured down on everyone standing there.

Cowlquape gasped. 'It's happened!' he exclaimed. 'The Mother Storm has reached Riverrise. She has seeded it with new life. The waters of the Edgewater River are flowing once more. We are saved!'

Forgetting all about their former venerable status, the professors and apprentices leapt for joy with the Undertowners and frolicked in the torrent of water until they were all soaked to the skin. Their doubts were

washed away and, as they opened their mouths and drank the cold, clear water, their bodies were suffused with such energy and optimism, that they cried out in triumph.

'Long live the Edgewater River!'

'Long live Undertown!'

'Long live the new Sanctaphrax!'

And the air trembled with the tumultuous roar that followed. 'LONG LIVE THE NEW SANCTAPHRAX!'

Cowlquape smiled and stepped from the pouring water. The warm sun set his clothes steaming. 'Cowlquape!' came a voice. 'It is time!'

He looked round. There was no-one there, and for the briefest of moments, he wondered whether it wasn't Kobold the Wise speaking to him.

'Cowlquape! Up here!'

Cowlquape looked up, and shielded his hand against the sun. 'Twig!' he cried.

The young captain looked down from the helm of the sky ship, hovering in the sky above. Peering down next to him on one side were Bogwitt, Tarp Hammelherd and Wingnut Sleet. Although they were standing in the dark shadow thrown by the towering aftcastle, neither they nor Twig were glowing: the luminous light had been extinguished with the passing of the Mother Storm. On Twig's other

side were Teasel, Stile, Jervis and, bedecked in feathers and jewels, the brogtroll, Grimlock – most of Thunderbolt Vulpoon's crew. Cowlquape noticed the name of the sky ship, its gold letters gleaming. It was the *Skyraider*.

'I found them waiting for me at the boom-docks!' Twig shouted down. 'Now, I will return to Riverrise for the others – Sky willing! For Goom. For Woodfish. For Maugin . . .' He smiled. 'I came to say goodbye.'

Cowlquape's heart sank. Goodbye? 'So soon! You're going so soon, Twig?' he shouted.

'I must. But our paths will cross again,' Twig called back. 'For now though, Cowlquape, your place is here.'

The sails of the *Skyraider* billowed. The sky ship lurched forwards.

'Twig!' called Cowlquape.

'Fare you well, Cowlquape!' Twig cried out, as he turned his attention to the flight-levers.

The sky ship soared off into the sky. Cowlquape watched as it grew smaller and smaller, silhouetted against the lemon yellow of the rising sun. It had been wonderful accompanying Twig on his quest – and part of him yearned to be by his side now, on board the *Skyraider* and heading back for Riverrise. In his heart, however, Cowlquape knew that his place was not on board a sky pirate ship. It was indeed here that his duty lay.

Follow your heart, and I will follow mine, was what Twig had told him. It was all anyone could do. And as Cowlquape took one last, lingering look at the sky ship, he smiled.

Twig was following his heart; now it was time for him, Cowlquape, to follow his.

'Farewell, Twig, my friend,' he cried out. 'And may Sky be with you, wherever you may go!'

THE EDGE CHRONICLES

The Quint Trilogy
The Curse of the Gloamglozer
The Winter Knights
Clash of the Sky Galleons

The Twig Trilogy
Beyond the Deepwoods
Stormchaser
Midnight over Sanctaphrax

The Rook Trilogy
The Last of the Sky Pirates
Vox
Freeglader

The Lost Barkscrolls
The Edge Chronicles Maps

JOIN THE FREE ONLINE FAN CLUB AT
www.edgechronicles.co.uk

BARNABY GRIMES

Curse of the Night Wolf
Coming soon: Return of the Emerald Skull

www.barnabygrimes.co.uk

For younger readers:

FAR-FLUNG ADVENTURES

Fergus Crane
Corby Flood
Hugo Pepper

www.farflungadventures.co.uk

SANCTAPHRAX
UNDERTOWN
THE STONE GARDENS
THE